LAST CHANCE FOR THE CHARMING LADIES

SWEET HISTORICAL REGENCY ROMANCE

FANNY FINCH

STARFALL
PUBLICATIONS

GET FANNY'S EXCLUSIVE MATERIAL

Visit the author's website to get your free copy of Fanny Finch's bestselling books!

Just visit the link below:

www.Fannyfinch.com/free-gift/

LAST CHANCE FOR THE CHARMING LADIES

A FORTHRIGHT COURTSHIP

CHAPTER 1

MARIA STOOD on the porch of the plantation house, hand over her eyes.

Father should be back shortly. She knew that it was nothing more than a trip to check for letters at the post office. But she couldn't prevent herself from worrying.

He thought that she hadn't noticed or perhaps was merely tricking himself into thinking she hadn't. But Maria wasn't a fool. Or at least she didn't like to think that she was.

She knew that his health was getting worse.

He had been leaving the day-to-day running of the land to his men. She'd seen him in talks with some of the other landowners in the area. And letters to and from England had been going back and forth. But he would not tell her what was in those letters.

He grew tired more easily. Went to bed a little earlier. And she saw at dinner that his food was no longer being devoured with gusto but picked at.

Maria couldn't help but worry over him. The Caribbean climate rather agreed with her. But then, she had been born in it. Father and Mother had come from England to make their fortune here. Perhaps in his old age the climate was against him.

It could be that he had also stopped by to see Dr. Lawrence. She hoped that was the reason for his lateness. It terrified her to think that he had collapsed in his carriage.

Her father was a stubborn man, Maria knew. She herself was stubborn. Mother had always said that was where Maria got it from.

He would insist on riding even when he was not well enough for it. He would continue to pretend that he was fine up until the very last moment. How was she supposed to know when he wasn't doing well if he insisted on pretending?

It could be merely old age catching up with him. Her father had been older when he had married Mother. He was a good five to ten years older than most of the other landowners.

But Maria couldn't help but worry that it was something more.

And didn't that fill her with all kinds of dread.

Perhaps if she were a boy it would not matter. But she was a woman. If Father was ill...

She had no idea what Father had arranged for her should he pass on while she was still unmarried. It wasn't that she hadn't tried to get married. She knew her duty.

But there were so few people still out here in the colonies. Most men came out here either with families already, or with only an interest in building their fortunes and then leaving for England again. It was nearly impossible to find someone who would be a potential suitor.

Maria took a steadying breath. She was just doing that thing where she worried herself into a pit. It would start with one worry and then it would spiral into a complete and total mess. She was better than that. She was an adult.

Besides, where was the logic in worrying if she could do nothing about it? Father was very good at planning. Surely if he was truly ill he would have made plans. Even if he did not want to admit to Maria that he was ill. He was the sort of man who had something in place for every eventuality.

Still, she stood on the porch, waiting.

Another few agonizing minutes passed as she tried not to let her fear overtake her. It would be ridiculous for Father to come home safe and sound and learn his daughter had been fretting over him like a five-year-old instead of a proper young lady of nineteen.

Then she saw it: dust kicking up in the distance.

The roads of the town were cobbled but it was far too much work and too little reward to do so out here on the estate.

Maria waved happily. Father probably couldn't see her from this distance, but she wanted to wave anyway.

The carriage pulled up and Father descended. Maria hurried over to him. The evening breeze caught in her hair and made it even worse of a tangle than before.

"Hello, my dear," Father said jovially.

He always had this way of making himself sound cheerful. Even when Maria knew he wasn't truly, he sounded so much like it that he easily fooled everyone. People always said there was no one with a better temper than her father.

"Father." Maria took his arm to help him up the porch steps into the house. "How was your trip into town?"

"Very good, my dear." Father sighed. "Maria. Your hair, child. Honestly."

"What?" Maria patted at her admittedly messy dark locks. "There is no one about to see. I was helping the servants shuck the peas."

"Of course you were," Father said wearily. "You are quite tan, dear, it's going to give you freckles."

"I already have plenty of freckles," Maria noted. Mother had said, when Maria was a baby, that each freckle was the mark left from an angel kissing her. The more angel kisses you had the luckier you were.

"That you do. And your feet!"

"Well it was too hot to go out in proper shoes!" Maria protested.

She helped Father inside and got him seated in the sitting room. It would be different if they had visitors all the time. But nobody was ever coming to visit. The plantations were all so spread out.

If people wanted to socialize then they went to a ball or met in town at the port. It was simply easier that way. It wasn't as if a surprise visitor was going to be making morning calls.

"I really do wish that you would make more of a habit of lady-like behavior," Father told her.

Maria poured him a glass of water from the pitcher and handed it to him. "I shall have Betsy fetch you something to eat. Dinner is not yet ready but I think you could do with some tea."

"You take very good care of me," Father acknowledged.

She didn't like the sad tone in his voice when he said that. It made her worried.

"Any interesting news at the harbor?" she asked. "How is the war faring?"

"War is not a subject that a lady should be concerning herself with," Father said.

"Is there any other interesting news you could regale me with instead?" Maria asked.

Father sighed. "My dear. Someday you are going to need to learn the principles of discretion and holding your tongue."

Maria laughed. "Today is not that day, Father."

"No, but it will be soon."

Maria paused. There was something serious in his tone. A sense of...finality.

She sat down across from him. "Father? Is everything all right?"

Father looked down at his hands. Old, weather-beaten hands. Maria had often seen Father, when he was younger, helping out in the fields. All the gentlemen had to at some point.

She suspected that it surprised them. How hands-on they might sometimes have to get. She wondered if in England it was different.

She'd never been, of course. Both her parents were from there, but she'd been born on the plantation, on this island.

But she did want to go someday. The Caribbean was lovely. She loved the heat and the flowers and the wildlife. She loved the native songs and the relaxed atmosphere. But there was nothing to really do.

With Mother gone, Maria was left alone most of the day. She did a lot of reading and a lot of exploring around the land. She'd climbed trees until Father had put a stop to that.

Maria wanted to be around other people. She wanted to have proper friends for once. She wanted to be where there were people, where it was busy and exciting.

Her father spoke again, interrupting her reverie.

"I hate to uproot you like this, my dear. I know that this will not be easy for you." He cleared his throat. "But the time has come."

"The time has come for what?" Maria asked.

"For you to go to England. For me to return."

"What?" Maria fairly gaped at him. "But—not that I am objecting Father but—why? This is all so sudden."

"Perhaps," Father acknowledged. "Or at least, sudden to you. But I'm afraid the time has come. I have just received a letter as to that effect. It sets aside many doubts I was having."

"I think you had better explain," Maria said.

She was his daughter, yes. And she did not know much of the finer things in life, it was also true. But she had been running this household for the past three years since Mother's death. She was far from stupid and she did not appreciate being kept in the dark about something that so affected her future.

Father sighed. "I have worried for some time about your future.

"Dr. Perquon has made it clear that despite all attempts, this climate is not doing me any favors. That was part of why your mother and I came out here. It was hoped that the warmer climate would benefit my ailing health.

"And for a time, it did. I grew better. But now it seems nothing can prevent my health from fading. My body is determined to betray me."

Maria reached out and took his hand in hers, squeezing gently. She could hear a trace of frustration in his voice despite his casual tone and warm *c'est la vie* smile.

Father continued. "Since there is nothing to be done about my health, I turned to thoughts of you.

"I miss England. It is my home. I wanted to return to it, of course. Even more so, I wanted to introduce you to London society. I should have done so much sooner, in fact."

"I've been happy here," Maria protested. "I see no reason to take me away too soon. And you needed someone to stay behind at the house and take care of things there now that Mother is gone."

"That is all true," Father said. "Those were the excuses that I gave myself for keeping you here instead of sending you to London.

"But most girls your age were already presented to society a year or two ago. To be a young lady of nineteen who has not even been introduced..." Her father shook his head. "It is not unheard of, certainly. But it puts you at a disadvantage to be married.

"I should have sent you away to England. But you were all that I had. And I have been worried for you. The upbringing that you are used to is nothing like what you will encounter in London.

"Furthermore, I'm afraid that we are in a precarious position. I have been writing with the solicitors in charge of my family's legal matters in London. I have striven for years but unfortunately this plantation and all my holdings are tied up in a legacy.

"They will be passed down to the nearest male relative upon my death. In this case it is my cousin's son, a perfectly affable young man. I have heard nothing but good things of him.

"But he is not you. I have managed to leave you some money for when I die. It will help to inspire any man to wish to marry you. But you cannot live on it forever.

"You must find a husband and unfortunately you must do so quickly. Your age is against you and I am not much longer for this world."

"Father, don't speak like that." Maria's fears concerning marriage paled in comparison to her concern over her father's fatalism. "You are in better health than you think you are, I am sure. There is no reason to think such things."

"I must return to England and see about my affairs," Father went on. "I am sure that my relative will want an income a year rather than having to sail across the ocean to a plantation in the colonies.

"Therefore, I must sell this place and see about wise investments instead. To provide an annual income. And of course I must see to providing you with a bit of inheritance."

"But—" Maria stuttered. This was her home. This was all that she had known. The idea of visiting England was, had been, lovely but she also loved her home here. She didn't necessarily want to go to England forever.

Father smiled sadly at her. "I am sorry, my dear. I know this must be a lot for you to take in. But I have contacted the son of my closest friend from boyhood. He and his sister will be happy to receive you and escort you."

"And what of yourself?" Maria asked.

"I am too old and will be too busy to be a proper escort for you," Father replied. "I shall stay in town and focus on business while you stay with them. They are younger and will be better able to help you in finding a husband."

Maria shook her head. "I don't want this. Father. Please. I want to stay with you. At least give me that."

"This is for the best, Maria." Father's tone was firm and brooked no argument. "I will see you married and settled before my end if I am able. This is the way that it will be done."

"But—"

"No arguing. My decision on this has been coming for a long time and it is final. I was only waiting until everything was confirmed before speaking to you."

Maria felt frustration bubbling up inside of her and closed her mouth, nodding once before exiting the room. She didn't want to say anything that she would regret.

How could Father spring this on her so suddenly? When she had no idea of what was coming? Surely he could have spoken to her about this sooner. About his illness, about his ideas, about going to London, about inheritance and the importance of marriage.

She had thought that she would inherit the plantation and all the rest upon her father's death. She had thought that marriage was not something she need worry about as much because of that.

Now it turned out that she did need to worry about marriage, and fast.

Even worse than that sudden change was the fact that she had to leave home. A trip to a new place was one thing. But to leave all that she had ever known?

She was useful here. She ran the household. She was friendly with all of the servants and the workers. When she went into town everyone knew her name and she theirs.

Now she would know no one. She would be utterly alone.

How was she supposed to go into the house of strangers and trust them with escorting her? The son of her father's closest friend was all well and good in theory but had Father met him in person? He couldn't have unless it was when the son was quite young. Maria hadn't even been born when Father and Mother had come to the Caribbean.

All Father had was letters of correspondence. It was easy to

affect a certain manner in a letter. And even if the man was trustworthy, Maria wouldn't know him or his sister.

She was to be placed with strangers.

How was she to manage that? She knew hardly anyone even on
the island. Of course she knew them by name and such. But there
were hardly any balls or anything of that sort. It was quite impossible to call upon someone given the terrain.

Only the few who lived in town could have a social life and
those were usually of the lower class and therefore couldn't be associated with anyway.

Now she would be expected to live with strangers for months?
To...to associate with people?

A part of her was elated. Excited. She would love to attend the
balls that her mother had always spoken about.

Mother had missed those balls terribly. She'd been a very social
creature. It must have been for Father's health that she had jour-
neyed to such a remote and lonely place. She had never complained
and had found much to love.

But Maria knew that her mother always longed for London society. And she wanted to experience what had made her mother love
it so. It was a possible way to feel closer to her.

Not to mention that Mother had made them sound so
terribly exciting and wonderful. Full of glamorous gowns and
flirtatious gentlemen, the finest foods and beautiful music. It
was like a sort of fairytale in Maria's head when she pictured
it.

But the rest of her was terrified. How was she supposed to fit in
there? People in England must be quite different from people in the
Caribbean.

Her father had said as much many a time. Telling her "not in
England" was practically his hobby.

"They would not permit that in England," he would tell her
when she came in with three inches of her hem soaked in mud.

"In England you will not be allowed such behavior," he would
say when Maria was hungry and devouring dinner.

"When you are in England you shall have to watch your
tongue," he would declare when she had offered up her frank
opinion on a shipping charter.

"Well we aren't in England right now, are we?" she would always counter.

It wasn't that Mother hadn't done her best. Maria knew how to dance and could play the pianoforte and the harp. She knew needlework and was very good at drawing. In fact, the latter, along with watercolor, was her favorite hobby. She loved sketching or painting the plants and wildlife.

She was accomplished enough, in other words. It was just the idea of talking to people, of introducing herself to so many strangers for their scrutiny...well, it was intimidating. She dared any other woman not to feel the same.

But there was no way out of her predicament. Not that she could find.

Maria went back outside and sat on the edge of the porch. She had always felt best when outside.

She would have to go to England. If Father was being so firm about this then it was because he saw no other way. Father was not a man who made hasty decisions. Nor was he the sort of man who clung to a decision simply because it was his. He was almost always willing to listen to the advice of others.

The only times he refused to hear the opinion of someone else was when he had already gone through every option. When he knew that whatever this person was going to offer up, he had already thought of, tested, and discarded.

It had meant that he had sometimes missed the opportunity on investments because he would not act with haste. But it had also saved them many a time from getting involved in something that would have led to their loss of fortune and ruin.

No, if Father was being stubborn about this it was not out of ridiculous pride. It was not simply for the sake of feeling his power as the head of their tiny household. It was not so that he could look at himself in the mirror and say, *I am right.*

It was because there was no other way.

Maria wrapped her arms around her legs, tucking her chin over her knees.

She would have to be good for Father. She would have to be sure to do him proud. He must be stressed in such a trying time as this.

If only she were a man. She could help him out. Father wouldn't have to leave this lovely climate if he didn't want to. She could inherit the plantation.

Or, if Father insisted on selling it and giving her an annual income, she could at least assist him in dealing with the lawyers and such.

But she was a woman. And so there was nothing she could offer him but comfort and soft words.

And, of course, getting married so that he would not have to worry about her.

She was determined to make sure that he wouldn't worry about her. That would be unfair to him. She had acted like a child just now, Maria chastised herself. She ought to be supporting Father. She needed to trust that this was the right thing to do.

Father was a man of very sound judgment, after all. She could trust him. If he said this was what they needed to do then she would do it. She could listen to him.

Her job now was to support him. That was what Mother had her promise when she was lying on her sickbed.

She had asked Maria to remember to be the rock in Father's life. She had begged Maria to behave with the dignity and grace that Father would need as he grew older.

Maria intended to hold to that promise. She would go to England, then, if that was what Father wanted. She would make him proud.

She stood up, dusted off her dress, and went back into the sitting room.

Father was still sitting in the chair. He looked so frail. Maria wanted to throw herself onto her knees and put her head in his lap and cry. Her tall, strong father, reduced to a shell of himself.

But no, she must be the strong one. Just as she had promised Mother.

He looked up when she entered, his gaze inquisitive but not angry. Of course not. Father rarely got angry. He had such a good temper. Probably a better temper than Maria deserved. She knew that she was strong-willed and could be a trial.

"I must apologize," she said. "That was childish of me, to run out on you like that. Of course, we must do whatever you think is best, Father."

Father smiled up at her. "I must apologize as well. I should have informed you of this possibility much sooner. It was an oversight on my part to think that I need not include you in my planning.

"What's done is done now, of course. And I do hope that you will see what a good opportunity this is."

"Why of course," Maria said. She knelt down and took her father's hand. "I know that you are not as rich as some but you have always taken good care of us. Of me. I know you would have left it all to me if you could have.

"Never you fear for me. I shall go to London as you request. I'm sure that I shall get along with these people you mention. If they are at all like their father, with whom you were so close, and I am like you, we shall become the closest of friends.

"And I will find a husband. You know that must be my goal in any case."

"I had wished that you might have time for love to blossom," Father sighed. "And to be selective about who you share your life with. Now I'm afraid you no longer have that choice."

"A season is a matter of months, Father, not days," Maria reminded him. "I am sure that in that time I shall find a man we both deem suitable. I will make certain that he is someone of whom you may be proud to call your son-in-law."

Father smiled down at her and squeezed her hand. "My dear. You really are far too well-tempered for what I put you through. Thank you."

Maria smiled and squeezed his hand back. "It is my duty and my joy, Father."

She stood up. "Now, let us see about a proper dinner."

She shoved her fears into the back of her mind. Whatever her continued worries were about the future, they could wait until she was in London. For now, she would remain calm and collected for Father's sake.

It would all work out, she was sure. That was what Mother always said. It would all work out.

It had to.

CHAPTER 2

EDWARD REGINALD, the newly made Duke of Foreshire, was silently cursing both his family name and the title he had just inherited.

Father had been in perfectly good health. Strong as an ox, or so everyone—including the late duke—had believed.

It was perfectly unjust that something as banal and out of the blue as a horse riding accident should take his father from him.

Selfishly, though, Edward did not so much miss his father as he missed not being the duke.

He would never have admitted it to anyone except for his younger sister, but he and Father's regard for one another had been...cool.

They had respected one another. Or at least, Edward respected his father and he liked to think that his father had respected him.

It was impossible not to have some measure of respect for the late duke, frankly. He had been a powerful man with a lot of connections. He was a man of strong character and fortitude. A man who expressed his opinion well and often.

Edward had no idea how he was supposed to fill such large shoes.

His father had been a stern man. He'd made it clear what his expectations were for Edward. And Edward had thought that he'd at least been prepared for his role now that he was the duke, even if he knew he'd never been up to his father's expectations of him.

But now that he was the duke, he was finding himself more... overwhelmed than he had expected.

It wasn't so much the business side of things. The estate and the tenants were well in hand. He'd followed Father as he went on his rounds and had been walked through all the books and accounts.

No, it was the social side of things.

Edward had been kept a bit away from the social gatherings the last year or so in his training with Father. But it wasn't as though he'd been a hermit.

He knew how the whole thing went. Being the son of a rich man was bad enough. A rich man who was also titled? It meant mothers were all but throwing their daughters at him.

But if it had been bad enough before it was ten times worse now. A man who stood to inherit could still somehow fail to inherit. There could be things that got in the way.

It didn't happen often, of course. But it was better to be certain. And the stern hand of the late duke was well known. Edward wouldn't have been surprised if he'd woken up one day to find the servants packing his things up on his father's orders to kick him out of the house.

Now that he was duke he knew that his duty was to marry. The sooner he had heirs, the better. In fact, according to his father he should have already had heirs. Should already be married.

How Father had expected his son to find a woman to marry when he was constantly bringing him back to the estate to shadow him, Edward didn't know.

But now that Father was dead, things were even more urgent. If Edward died without an heir, then the dukedom would go to a far-off relative. He didn't even know who. His poor sister Georgiana would be destitute.

Marriage, however, did not appeal to him.

It did in the abstract, certainly. He wanted someone to share the rest of his life with. And he did want children. He'd always been good with children and enjoyed them, wanting some of his own.

But actually going through the process of finding a woman to marry was daunting and exhausting. Just thinking about it made him want to flee to the Continent.

The ladies that he met were not truly interested in him as a person. They only wanted his money and title.

He could appreciate a lady's predicament. It was the predicament of his sister, after all. He knew that they must find a husband.

But surely a woman should be looking for a man possessing a disposition that was complementary to hers? Surely she ought to be learning whether a man was honorable and responsible and a good conversationalist?

He could have been a boorish drunkard for all that the ladies of London society cared. He had the title and the money and that was what mattered to them.

It made him sick to think of it.

He wanted a companion with whom he could spend the rest of his life. Someone who could make him laugh. Someone to whom he could come home and relax with at the end of a difficult day. Someone in whom he could confide.

If he married one of these woman, who knew what their true nature would be? It would not be revealed until after the wedding.

When he spoke to them, they seemed to have no personality of their own. They agreed with everything he said. They changed personalities at the drop of a hat. They did nothing but compliment him.

It seemed to him, and to any man with half an eye, that these women were simply acting in whatever way they best thought would get him to marry them.

He wanted a woman who was true to herself. Not one who lied and indulged in those games of manners that played out at the balls.

That felt like an impossibility now that he was duke. He should have tried to insist upon finding a bride while Father was still alive. That way he would have known that the woman truly cared about Edward for his own sake. Not for the money he might inherit.

Now he was stuck.

Edward gathered up the invitations on his desk—the reason why he had been cursing his position in life.

The London season would be starting soon. Invitations were being sent out to everyone so that people might plan their schedules accordingly. There would be balls, intimate dinners, theatre, the art showings...

A whirlwind few months, to be sure. And on top of all of that, there would be this young lady to mentor: Maria Worthing, the only child of Mr. Alexander Worthing, Father's best friend who had moved to the Caribbean to make his fortune some years ago.

Edward had been quite a small boy at the time, only five when the Worthings had moved out of England. It was for Mr. Worthing's health, Father had said. He had always been a sickly boy but had a 'fantastical mind for business,' or so Father had praised.

From Father's accounts and from his reaction to the letters he and Mr. Worthing exchanged, Mr. Worthing appeared to be the only person besides Mother who had been capable of getting Father to smile.

When Father died, Edward had written to Mr. Worthing personally to inform him of the news.

Mr. Worthing had seemed to take it rather hard. However, he had also taken the opportunity to divulge his own situation.

It appeared that age and ill health were finally taking their final toll on Father's dear friend. Mr. Worthing was most anxious for his daughter, Maria.

She had been born in the Caribbean about a year after the Worthings had moved there. She had spent her entire life there, in fact. But her marriage prospects were not good there. And while Mr. Worthing was in the process of setting up an inheritance for her, she could not by law inherit his full estate.

The poor girl needed a husband, and quickly.

Mr. Worthing needed to travel to London anyway to handle his affairs in person. Edward thought it a bit fatalistic that this man should assume his death was so certain. However, it was probably wise to be prepared rather than to be caught off-guard. Make hay while the sun shines, and all that.

Mr. Worthing had asked if Edward could please be the formal escort for Miss Worthing for the London season. She had no one else and Mr. Worthing himself was far too frail to handle the amount of balls and social gatherings.

Edward had accepted, of course. How could he not? It was, he was certain, something Father would have insisted upon if he was still alive. And Georgiana would have a companion for the season.

Poor Georgiana, she was far too withdrawn and quiet. Father's stern hand had made her rather meek.

Hopefully a girl born and raised in a colony would bring a bit of spirit with her and it would rub off on Georgiana.

In any case, Edward had written saying that it would be his pleasure to serve as Miss Worthing's escort. His sister would be more than happy with a companion.

Mr. Worthing had warned Edward that his daughter was a "wild thing" and that she would need quite a lot of instruction regarding societal norms.

Edward was not worried about that. Parents tended to either think too much or too little of their children. Miss Worthing could not be so bad as all that. And any faults, Georgiana would surely help to straighten out with a kind suggestion. His sister was good at those sorts of things.

Unfortunately, agreeing to be the escort for Miss Worthing meant he had more of a societal obligation than before. Mr. Worthing had not come right out and said so—it would not be polite—but Edward could tell this was the girl's one and only season. Her one chance.

She could not, therefore, afford to miss a single engagement. That meant that Edward had to be at every single engagement.

It was a rather taxing prospect.

He would be assaulted on all sides by the unmarried women and their mothers. They did not even do him the courtesy of being subtle about it! It attacked a man's patience, that was for certain.

But he would have to suffer through it for Miss Worthing's sake. And for his sister's.

With Father gone, Georgiana could select a man of her choice. She had already had to lose one suitor because of Father's exacting standards. Edward did not wish for her to have her heart broken a second time.

As though summoned by his thoughts, there came a knock at the door and his sister poked her head in.

"May I come in?" she asked.

Edward smiled at her. "Of course you may."

Miss Georgiana Reginald was a lady of quiet, dignified beauty. She had remarkably pale hair, and thoughtful gray eyes set in a fine-boned face. She looked almost like a statue when she stood still. There was a sort of slow grace to her movements, like a ballerina caught in slow motion.

She was not the sort to light up a ballroom. But there was art to the curve of her neck, the droop of her eyelids. If a man thought to look a second time, she never failed to entrance.

All their lives, the two siblings had been mistaken for twins. They had the same defined cheekbones, the same wide, gray eyes. The same long nose. Even the same snow-colored hair.

Edward, however, was five and twenty, while Georgiana was two and twenty.

He did worry for her. Two and twenty was approaching the time of danger. The time when a woman could hear others begin to claim that she was past her prime.

It was a dangerous thing. Georgiana was quite all right for now with a rich brother. Edward would have sooner cut off his own arm than refuse to take care of her. Georgiana had been his sweet companion, and the only source of calm in the house all his life.

But there would come a time when Edward might not be around anymore. He feared for that time. His first act as the duke was to set up an account for Georgiana so that she might have an annual income should anything happen to him.

One never knew, though, did one? Father had been in the prime of health. And then a ridiculous riding accident had taken that all away.

After all, Edward thought, no matter how strong a man is, he cannot be strong enough to recover from a broken neck.

He must respond to all these invitations in the positive, for Georgiana's sake if nothing else. She must find a husband.

"Is something the matter?" Edward asked. He sat down and began to sort out the invitations. He had to have a thorough understanding of their social calendar, after all. And make sure that there were no two parties on the same day.

"Must something be the matter for me to wish to see my brother?" Georgiana teased him.

"No, of course not." Edward smiled at her. "But there is something you wish to discuss."

"Only that the rooms are all ready for Miss Worthing's arrival," Georgiana replied. She eyed the invitations in his hand. "I can take care of those for you, Edward."

"I know. And I wish that you would. But I ought to at least know what I am getting myself into."

"That is a fair enough approach, I suppose." Georgiana sat down and held out her hand. "May I?"

Edward handed over the invitations. Georgiana began to leaf through them. "There are quite a lot. I should think we will drop dead by the time the season is over."

"There are dinners, and balls after the dinners, and invitations to join various members in their theatre boxes for performances. And none of this includes morning calls," Edward said.

"Well, if we cannot find the girl a husband after all of this, then I shall eat my hat," Georgiana said. "The benefits of having a title, dear brother. No one dares not invite you."

"There are many on there that we might refuse," Edward said quickly. "Quite a few people are enough beneath our station that we are most likely expected to refuse, even."

Georgiana nodded absently, still looking at the invitations. "Yes, but Miss Worthing is beneath our station as well, Edward. She has no title and her father's income although good is not to the amount that one would expect of an acquaintance of ours."

"Yes, true, our fathers were friends due to having estates next to one another in their youth, or so Father told me."

"For her sake, we must accept these other invitations, so that she might also find someone who is not so intimidatingly above her," Georgiana said.

"Who is to say that she might not marry a baron or an earl?"

"Well, no one is to say that, of course, Edward. But if she can marry a man of five thousand a year as well as an earl then why not introduce her to the former in addition to the latter?

"She knows no one. She ought to make the acquaintance of as many men as possible. It increases her chances of being proposed to by the time the season is up."

"At this rate she will have little chance to make an impression on anyone. As soon as she meets a man she will be whisked off to meet another."

"Careful, brother, your bitterness is showing." Georgiana organized the invitations into a neat pile and set them on the side table. "Which reminds me that Miss Worthing is not the only person in need of a spouse."

"Yes, I am well aware of your predicament—"

"I meant yourself, brother. Not me."

Edward sighed. "Must we discuss this?"

"It is your duty."

"I am well aware of my duty, Georgiana. Do not think that I am neglecting it."

"But you do dread it," Georgiana noted. "I have seen it in how you avoid the subject. The way you look at those invitations as if they are bearers of the plague. Admit it, Edward. You do not wish to marry."

"Of course I wish to marry," Edward replied. "It is only that I do not wish to marry any of the girls of my acquaintance."

"Then we shall have to find some young ladies who are not of your previous acquaintance," Georgiana said. "There has to be at least one woman in the whole of England who does not put you off your breakfast."

"Find me a woman who is not simpering and who doesn't say only the things she thinks I want to hear," Edward replied. "Find me a woman who does not give into society's habits of malicious gossip and throws herself at a man not because she cares for his character but because she cares for his money.

"Find me a woman who is honest about who she is and how she feels. Find me a woman who doesn't care that I have a title. A woman who would love me if I was one of those men who only had a couple thousand a year."

His sister arched one eyebrow at him. "You make it sound as if these are Herculean tasks."

"They are, apparently, for I have yet to find a woman who embodies them." Edward knew that he sounded bitter but he couldn't help himself.

"Careful, Edward. It will not help you to let anger claim your heart. Women can sense such things and they are repelled by them.

All the ladies will inevitably fear that you will turn that wrath on them someday if they are to marry you."

"Perhaps I should cultivate it, then. It might scare them off."

Georgiana sighed. She reached out and took his hand. "Edward. You will not find love unless you open yourself up to the possibility of it. Nothing can find its way through a closed door. And I think you judge many women too harshly.

"If you recall, Father wanted me to behave as they do. And these are women who depend upon a husband for their livelihood. They cannot enter into business or the clergy or the military.

"Is it not understandable that they should throw themselves at you a little? That they should try to win you over? This is their entire life we are talking about. This is not merely a matter of the heart. Sometimes I wish that it were.

"These women treat marriage as a business and in a way for them it is. It is what saves them from poverty."

Edward squeezed his sister's hand, seeing how he had upset her. "I am so sorry, my dear."

Georgiana was not one prone to crying. When she was upset, however, her cheeks went pink. They were quite pink now, two small spots of color high up on her pale cheeks.

"It is nothing," she said, trying to wave it off.

"No, it is far from nothing. I should have been more considerate."

Georgiana had loved, once. Edward had approved of the man. He had been possessed of a steady temper and a soft wit. What was more he had loved Georgiana to distraction in a quiet, unassuming way that Edward had admired.

Edward was personally too given over to expressing his passions. Or so Father had been fond of saying. Indeed, Father had approved of the man's character.

The man's lack of fortune, however, was another matter entirely.

Georgiana had been instructed to not even see the man once her suitor's intentions were known. Father had said that the man was nothing more than a social climber. He was obviously after Georgiana for her money and status, he claimed.

Edward knew that was not so. As did Georgiana. Her suitor had been an honorable one. But there was no arguing with Father when he made up his mind about something.

The man had gone into the Navy, the last that Edward had heard of him. That had been four years ago.

Since then, Georgiana had not even come close to love. He thought that her suitors could sense it in her. She was polite and sweet enough. She had always possessed a marvelous temper, if a little on the quiet side.

But it was as though the potential suitors could read it written on her forehead. She did not and would not love them. And whether men wished to admit it or not, they wanted to be loved just as much as women did.

And so there had been no other suitors since that gentleman.

"Love is a luxury that women can scarce afford," Georgiana admitted. "Do not begrudge these women for doing what they must."

"But there is a way to do it with grace and thoughtfulness," Edward replied. "These women are making themselves into fools. I can see right through them. Surely there is a way to set about getting a husband without compromising who one is.

"And I will not stand for a wife who plays these flirtatious little games with everyone. Who discredits other women and thinks of nothing but the shallow.

"I want a woman of strong character. One who is true to herself. So far I have yet to find that either in the daughters of dukes or the daughters of simpler men."

"That is a fair assessment," Georgiana acknowledged. "But there must be at least a few who have not compromised their character in such a manner. We will find them for you."

"It concerns me that you are more thoughtful of my finding a wife than you are of finding yourself a husband."

"I am not the one with a title to protect," Georgiana pointed out.

"Ah, but you are the one swiftly approaching an age that is no longer considered marriageable."

"I have heard of ladies who were married as late as seven and twenty," Georgiana replied. She pressed her lips together for a moment, a sure sign that she was trying to hold back what she was thinking. But then she spoke, apparently deciding it was worth saying.

"Father is dead and I am sorry for it. I loved him in spite of the injuries he did to both of us. He did not mean to be harsh. And if he did it was because he thought it would give us the backbone we needed.

"I know that he loved us in his own way and cared for us. He wanted the best for us. I am not saying I am glad that he is dead. But now that he is gone I have the freedom to choose someone for whom I hold the highest esteem."

"You certainly do," Edward assured her. "I will of course wish to judge his character. Only the best of men will do for my sweet sister."

Georgiana smiled at him. "Thank you."

"But as to their wealth or status—so long as they are respectable and can support you, I have no objections. You need not have your suitors run a gauntlet of criteria with me as they would have with Father."

Georgiana nodded. "I am not a fool. I know that my time is fast approaching and that I must be wary of it. There are always younger ladies coming up behind who know how to entice.

"But now that Father is dead I have the luxury of finding a man who suits my temper. Not his. And I will hold to that."

"I think that is admirable of you," Edward told her.

After all, he could hardly complain about the way women were treating him and then go and tell his sister to do the same to other men.

"I wonder what Miss Worthing will think of all this," Georgiana said. "Life out on an island in the colonies cannot be at all similar to London. Although I'm sure the people there do try their best."

"No doubt she will be overwhelmed," Edward acknowledged. The poor girl would probably be quite reticent at first. He knew that he would be, if he was in her position.

He was actually rather curious about this Miss Worthing. He wondered what she would be like. He had grown up with women who were raised in London society.

To meet one who was just now being introduced to it sounded to him like a fascinating prospect. He was curious, and perhaps too much so, as to how Miss Worthing would react to the society around her.

Perhaps it was just that he himself was so jaded. It would be a change to see someone who had not yet gotten a chance to get used to everything that he had come to take for granted.

But then, Miss Worthing could be a spoiled or boring person. They knew a bit about her from Mr. Worthing's letters to Father over the years.

For example, they knew that she was an only child and that she had taken over running the household after her mother's death. They knew that she had a great deal of energy, or so her father said. But to a sickly man like Mr. Worthing, a normal amount of energy probably seemed like a great deal.

And they did have a general description of her so that they might pick up the right girl from the station in the carriage.

But as to the details of her disposition, neither Edward nor Georgiana knew. Children lacking siblings could sometimes be spoiled. Especially when in an isolated environment, such as an island plantation.

She could be withdrawn and shy. Or she might be demanding and rude. Edward sincerely hoped that she was of a cheerful and good-natured manner. But in any case, they had promised to look after her, and they would.

Georgiana had read the part addressed to her in the letters— about Miss Worthing's elocution.

"Do you expect you will have your work cut out for you?" Edward asked.

Georgiana pressed her lips together and thought for a moment. "I cannot say. Her father seems despairing of her manners although he praises her intelligence. He could be too hard on her as our father was. Or she could be a veritable native."

"Let us hope it is the former," Edward said gravely. "I have no wish to see our house and reputation destroyed by an uncouth lady."

"Her father is a well-spoken man," Georgiana said. "And seems both thoughtful and sensible in his letters. I am sure that his daughter holds at least some of his disposition."

"You and I have both met children who are nothing like their parents. You are hardly at all like Father."

"Yet our parents influence us," Georgiana replied, "whether we wish it or not. I do not think that someone who managed to endear themselves to Father so, and who has spoken so sensibly and kindly in their letters to us, could have such an awful child."

"I hope that you are right," Edward said. "But you are more forgiving and hopeful towards humanity than I am."

"I do wish that you would not let bitterness cloud your judgment so," Georgiana said. "You are far too good of a gentleman for that."

"When I can find myself true friends instead of false and a lady with a sense of honor, then my bitterness shall fade," Edward told her. "Until then, let us look at these invitations together. We must plan our calendar for the season."

His mind continued to dwell, at least in part, on the subject of Miss Worthing.

Hopefully, she would be a lovely girl. And he could grow to think of her as a sister of some sort.

Either way they would find out soon enough. She arrived in three days' time.

CHAPTER 3

MARIA STARED at the people and the city around her.

Ever since arriving in England it felt like she could do nothing but stare. The ocean voyage she had gotten used to within a day or so. There was precious little to look at on a ship.

But England! She had seen pictures of course. She had read about it in books and heard about it in descriptions from Mother. But seeing it firsthand was something else entirely.

It was so unlike the world that she was used to. Even the green of the plants was different. The colors were muted here. Not as bright and popping. The ground was different, the very air around her felt different. It was all so much she could hardly even begin to take it in.

She was frightfully cold all the time. Her father had tried to warn her when they were on their sea voyage, but she hadn't truly believed him about how cold it was. No wonder Father had to travel so far to get better.

Maria had to wrap herself up in layers all the time. Father assured her that over time she would grow used to it, but she wasn't so certain.

"I was born and raised in England," Father told her. "And I grew accustomed to the warmer climates of the Caribbean. You shall be able to do the reverse here."

But for now, it felt as though she would never be properly warm again. If there was a fireplace she would sit down directly in front of it. She noticed that she wore far more shawls and layers than the other ladies about her.

She only hoped that she would be permitted to dress warmly for the balls. She could not imagine how she would make it through the evening shivering like a sheet in the wind.

Father had taken up lodgings in London but in a different area of the city from where Maria would be staying with Lord Reginald and his sister. At the time she had gotten the news, Maria had not thought much of it.

Then she had gotten to London itself.

She had never seen a town so large. The port town from her home was much smaller than this. It was mostly the fort that took up room, and the ships in the harbor.

But this was something else altogether.

The journey from the harbor to London had not taken long and she had gaped the entire time like a bumpkin. And now she was surrounded by the hustle and bustle of so many people. Her eyes couldn't keep up with it all.

She felt exhilarated and terrified at the same moment. There was so much to see and to do. She wanted to take it all in. But she also wanted to run for the hills.

How could she possibly adjust from her relatively sleepy and slow island to this fast-paced insanity? What if she got lost? What if she couldn't make her way around? What if—

The carriage turned down a quieter lane, a broad one with lovely trees and luxurious townhouses.

Maria peered out the window. This was nicer. She liked the quiet. Hopefully this would stay quiet and she could have a place to retreat to when the city became too much.

The carriage pulled to a stop in front of what was obviously one of the larger, nicer houses.

Maria had never seen such nice buildings in a city setting before. She felt as though her own home paled in comparison.

She was helped from the carriage and walked up the steps to knock on the front door.

Her heart was in her throat. What if she did not like these people? What if they did not like her? What if she made a total fool of herself?

She reminded herself that her father was counting on her. He needed her to do this. Her future and her father's peace of mind depended upon it.

Maria seized the knocker and rapped sharply.

A moment later the door was opened by a servant. He looked at her calmly but quizzically, obviously interested to know who she was.

Maria curtsied. "I'm Miss Worthing, here to see Miss Reginald and Lord Reginald? I am to be their houseguest."

"One moment, Miss."

She was shown into a lovely parlor. It was far richer than hers back home.

No, not home anymore, she reminded herself. She had to stop thinking of it that way. The plantation was being packed up as she stood there. It had probably already been packed up in fact.

Some few pieces were being shipped to her for her own home so that she might bring her personal touch in when she married, and for the sake of remembrance. But the rest of it was being sold.

The only home she had ever known was being sold. She wouldn't ever be able to go back to it. The moment she had stepped onto the ship, that island was gone to her forever.

This new, cold island was to be her home now. And it wasn't as though she didn't want it to be. Part of her wanted to embrace it. She wanted to explore it and get to know it just as well as her former home.

But it still made her sad. To know that she could not return. She couldn't go back. Even if she did, the plantation would belong to someone else. None of the furniture would be there. It would all be gone.

Maria shook herself out of such maudlin thoughts. She had to present herself at her best to the Reginalds. It was imperative that she put her best foot forward.

There were the sounds of footsteps and she turned to see a lovely lady, a few years older than Maria, stepping into the parlor. She was pale, with light hair and gray eyes, while Maria herself had skin tanned from the sun, with dark eyes and dark hair.

Maria thought that they would make quite a contrast when they went walking or made morning calls. They were quite on the opposite ends of the spectrum.

The other woman smiled softly, kindly. "You must be Miss Worthing. I'm Miss Reginald."

Maria curtsied. "It's a great pleasure to meet you."

"I'll have them take your bags up." Miss Reginald signaled to her servant and he disappeared, presumably to take care of Maria's things. "I hope that you will like the room that we have chosen for you. I confess to not knowing your personal tastes."

"Anywhere you wish to put me is more than suitable," Maria assured her. "I'm looking forward to a soft bed and nothing more. You would not believe the frustration of sea travel."

"I can well imagine it, but I'm certain that whatever my mind conjures up pales in comparison to the reality." Miss Reginald indicated for Maria to sit. "I will have some tea brought up for us. You must be famished."

"Thank you," Maria replied. She was terrified of saying or doing the wrong thing. "You have a lovely home."

"You are kind to say so. I like it well enough. I confess I prefer our country estate. And your father is well put up?"

"Yes, Miss, he is," Maria answered. "I confess he seems much more prepared for this than I am. He is used to England in a way, although I know he has not been back since before my birth."

"Yes, this all must be very new to you." Miss Reginald looked down at her. "My dear, you are shivering most horribly, do you need a fire?"

"I apologize, I'm not yet used to the weather." Maria felt awful. "You really needn't go to any trouble."

"Nonsense, I shall not have my guest uncomfortable." Miss Reginald rang and instructed that tea be brought in with some sandwiches, and a fire done up.

"Now, do you have frocks?" Miss Reginald asked.

"A few, but not many. Father has given me an allowance so that I might purchase some new ones."

"You will certainly need them. It was wise of him to have you arrive a month before the season begins. We should have plenty of time to get you done up." Miss Reginald eyed Maria. "Would you mind standing up for a moment?"

Maria did so, and Miss Reginald looked her over, pacing around her. "Yes, I have several ideas. We must get you something in fashion of course. You are rather dark in your coloring. Some lighter colors will do nicely. And you can never go wrong with green when you have dark eyes."

Maria had never given much thought to her wardrobe. She had her few frocks that she wore until they were exhausted and then she got some new ones. She chose her favorite colors to wear, usually blue or lilac.

Now she had to think about fashion? She couldn't even begin to wrap her mind around it.

Miss Reginald must have seen something of Maria's trepidation on her face, for she smiled at her. "Don't you trouble yourself, my dear. I'll guide you through picking out fabrics."

Maria breathed a sigh of relief.

"You can sit down now," Miss Reginald let her know, sitting down herself.

The tea was brought in. Maria quickly poured herself a cup and ate the sandwiches quickly.

She paused when she saw Miss Reginald eyeing her. It wasn't a judgmental look. More of an assessing one.

"Yes," she said, "I see what your father meant. Sit up straight, please. And smaller bites."

Maria felt a rush of shame and did so. "I apologize," she murmured. "My mother taught me elocution. I had a governess when I was young but not for many years. I've not had much reason to use my manners the past few years. I've been quite alone on the plantation save for Father."

"You needn't explain yourself to me," Miss Reginald replied, her voice gentle and her eyes warm. "Your father wrote to us ahead of time and explained that there might be some difficulties in your integration into society.

"I am perfectly prepared to help you brush up on your skills. Whether that be dancing or table manners."

"I do have many skills," Maria hastened to add. She didn't want this elegant lady to think that Maria was a total bumpkin. "I can play the pianoforte and the harp. I'm an avid reader. And I can do needlepoint, and sketch quite well. And I know how to run a household, I've done so for my father for years."

"I'm sure you have many accomplishments," Miss Reginald assured her. "And I am glad to hear of them. You may avail yourself of our library and our pianoforte whenever you please. Although I am sorry to say that we do not have a harp."

Miss Reginald smiled at her, as though they were sharing a private joke. Maria smiled back. She had never had a close friend before. She was warmed by the kindness being shown to her.

"But we shall have to work hard," Miss Reginald added. "If we are to have you ready in time for the season to start."

There was the sound of heavier footsteps, and Maria turned in time to see a handsome man walk into the room.

He looked as though he could almost be Miss Reginald's twin. There were many similarities in their features. He had pale blond hair and piercing gray eyes. But while there was softness in Miss Reginald, a gentle sort of warmth, this man had a fire to his bearing.

Maria's breath caught in her throat. She had of course known many young men, although not enough to make them more than a passing acquaintance. Most of them had been officers stationed with the regiment at the fort.

But never had she been so struck by a man. The only word that she could think to describe him was 'handsome'. She was entranced by the firmness of his jaw and the command with which he entered the room. It was just herself and Miss Reginald, yet if the room had been filled with people she was certain all eyes would have turned to him.

This must be Lord Reginald, the Duke of Foreshire. He had only recently become duke, or so Father had said. In the last year or so when his father had died. This was to be his first season with the title.

Maria curtsied to him. "My lord."

Lord Reginald bowed. "You must be Miss Worthing." His voice was deep and sharp but not unkind. She liked it. "It is a pleasure to make your official acquaintance. Although we have heard from your father about you."

"Whatever he has said, it is a gross exaggeration," Maria assured him. Father could talk her up one side and down the other with pride. But he could also, at least in her mind, exaggerate the extent of her stubbornness and wild ways.

Lord Reginald laughed. "That is always the way with parents, whether it is singing our praises or damning our faults. They seem to make a habit of going too far in either direction."

Maria smiled, relieved that he seemed to like her. She was not sure what she would have done had he taken a dislike to her.

"I'll do my best to make you both proud," she said. "Not that—I know I'm not—but it will reflect poorly upon you if I do not do well, I am sure. I will do my best to prevent that."

"You are very sweet," Miss Reginald said. "I'm certain that you will give us no cause for embarrassment."

Maria was not so sure about that. Even just sitting in this luxurious parlor, she felt out of place. "Are all homes as expensive as yours?" she asked.

Then she clapped her hands over her mouth. "Oh my goodness, I am so sorry, forgive me, I didn't—I just meant—I'm not used to, uh..." Words failed her.

Lord Reginald made a sound like he was trying to hold in a laugh. "You can be honest," he told her. "I know that we have a rather...higher standard of living than many, including those out in the colonies."

"I'm sorry," Maria said again. She could feel her face burning with embarrassment and shame. She felt mortified.

"It's all right," Miss Reginald said.

"Perhaps next time you might say...luxurious," Lord Reginald suggested. "Or elegant."

Maria nodded. She wanted the floor to simply swallow her up and make her disappear.

"I think you're just upsetting her more," Miss Reginald noted softly.

"Oh, no, he's being quite lovely," Maria hastened to reassure the both of them.

Lord Reginald sat down in one of the chairs across from them. "So tell me, Miss Worthing, what was life like out there in the colonies? Is the Caribbean as wild and untamed as they say?"

He smiled at her and sounded as though he was genuinely interested rather than simply pulling her leg or being cruel, as his words might otherwise have suggested.

Miss Reginald gave her brother a slightly chastising look, raising an eyebrow in loving exasperation. "I'm sure that you needn't interrogate the poor girl, Edward."

"It's all right," Maria said. It was nice to have someone so honestly curious in her life. She hadn't anyone to talk to besides the servants back at home. "I like talking about it.

"I loved home," she told them. "I was sorry to leave it. And sorry that I shall not be able to return. It didn't really hit me, I think, until just now.

"But this is such a new world for me and I am excited to explore it. I hope that I won't give the impression that I'm not. I just think I always believed I would see England for a visit rather than coming to make a permanent home here."

"Go on," Lord Reginald said as she paused. He smiled at her encouragingly. "What were your favorite things about living there?"

Maria could feel herself relaxing the more that she talked. Miss Reginald smiled at her as well, silent but welcoming.

"Well, I...I liked the nature that's there. The plants and the animals. I was quite fond of sketching and painting them. I had a lot to do with running the household of course but not so much as you might expect. I'm sure that you have quite a lot more to do, Miss Reginald.

"As will I," Maria added, realizing. "But of course, it was just Father and myself out there and neither of us cared too much for propriety. As I'm sure that you've noticed." She could feel herself still blushing a little.

"But we didn't need much. It was quite simple. We didn't go to balls—there weren't any really—and I didn't need new dresses all the time or anything...oh! Not that I..." she fumbled again, looking at Miss Reginald in horror. "I didn't mean, Miss..."

"It's all right," Miss Reginald assured her. "Things are different out in the colonies. Here there are expectations that we must be prepared for. But if those expectations are not there then it is not a sin to be economical."

Maria nodded. "I was often out in the fields to take a look at things. To make sure everything was being handled properly. Especially with Father's failing health. He couldn't get out there anymore.

"He tried to hide it of course, he's a stubborn man and Mother always said I got that from him, but..."

Maria shook her head. "I'm sorry. You want to hear about the positive things, and here I am telling you my worries."

"They are legitimate worries," Lord Reginald pointed out. "Our father's death was..." he glanced at his sister. "It was sudden. I'm not sure if the lingering...issues your father has are worse than what we experienced but I'm certain that I do not wish either what we have or what you have to be thrust upon anyone.

"But it is unfortunately the way of the world." He gave her a kind, compassionate look. As if he really did want to take her pain away. "All that we can hope for is that the world will give us back as much as it takes.

"And this is fortuitous in its own way. Now we know one another. We shall be friends as our fathers were. And we are happy to introduce you to society in the proper way. The way that a young lady such as yourself deserves.

"We've learned that in times such as these it's important to look at the things that bring us joy. To focus on those instead of the things that are being taken from us. Sinking into despair never helped anyone."

Maria nodded.

"This season can be fun for you as well," Miss Reginald said. "I know that there is a bit of a cloud over it. It is only natural that your thoughts should turn this way.

"But this is your chance to shine! Your chance to show the world the beautiful, accomplished young lady that you are. I'm sure we can arrange for some of your sketches to be shown. And you shall be quite admired at parties for your playing."

"You would have had to go through this no matter what the circumstances surrounding it were," Lord Reginald reminded her. "And as insufferable as society can be at times..."

His sister gave him a stern look. Maria was curious but tried to stamp it down. She knew that it was not her business.

But there was an edge of bitterness and frustration to his tone that took her by surprise. She wanted to know more. Why was he so frustrated with society? What did he mean about it being insufferable?

Society seemed like such a wonderous thing to her. A place of fun and excitement. A chance to finally meet people and have friends and be properly introduced to men. Why should it be insufferable?

Lord Reginald cleared his throat and bowed his head towards her briefly. "I apologize. Of course this will be a marvelous opportunity for you. Think not of the particular circumstances that brought you here. You are blessed with this opportunity."

"I am surprised that your father had not sent you earlier," Miss Reginald said. "I presumed, erroneously it seems, that you had a society of sorts where you grew up. But you are nearly twenty or so I am told."

"Yes, Miss. Father couldn't bear to have me leave. Who else would run the household for him? And go out into the fields now that his legs hurt him? I was needed. But now that he is coming back to England as well, he can have me with him and there is no need for someone at the plantation."

Lord Reginald nodded. "You are none the worse for it. My sister here is two and twenty. I am certain that if she can bear it well then so can you."

He winked at her, and Maria realized that he was teasing her. He was teasing both of them.

She felt something warm and joyous bloom in her chest and smiled, ducking her head down to try and hide it. She had never been teased, lightly and warmly, by a man before.

It made her feel special. Wanted.

"Do you really...think that I'll enjoy it?" she asked. She felt like a child asking such a thing. She ought to be excited for this.

"I know that I probably sound ungrateful and I'm terribly sorry for it," she said. "I don't mean to be that way at all. You've opened up your house to me and you barely know me."

Miss Reginald sighed. "It's quite clear to me that you have had a taxing journey, Miss Worthing. Our job is to distract you from your troubles and make sure that you are fit to be a part of the society to which you belong.

"Why don't we dispense with such distressing talk and you can play a little pianoforte for us? Dinner will be ready soon enough and that will help you to recover. But I think some music might distract you until then. What do you think?"

She hadn't had a chance to play in all that time on the ship. And she did miss her pianoforte from back home. Mother had taught her to play on it since she was a little girl.

It wouldn't be the same but...it would be nice.

"I'll be terribly out of practice," Maria warned. "I couldn't play on the ship, after all."

"We understand," Miss Reginald said.

"It will do us some good to see someone who is not quite so practiced," Lord Reginald added. "Some of these women play and you know that they have practiced that one piece and nothing else."

"Edward, be thoughtful with your words," Miss Reginald warned him.

Miss Reginald stood and led them into the sitting room, where the pianoforte stood.

"I never play it as much as I should," she confessed. "I am much more inclined towards reading poetry. To my father's eternal despair."

Lord Reginald chuckled, helping to lift the lid. "Please, sit. I would love to hear you play. You must ignore my more...harsh comments towards those aspects of society of which I am not quite so fond."

Maria sat down, stretching out her fingers. "I hope you will not mind if I do a few scales first?"

"Be my guest," Miss Reginald replied.

Maria did her scales. At first her fingers were stiff and she despaired of how they ached when she tried to stretch them. She felt clumsy, slow, her fingers feeling heavy. Usually her hands were so light, and they flew over the keys.

But as time went on and she went over her scales her fingers began to remember. They caught up with her mind. They began to stretch—and it wasn't as easy, but they did it. And they moved faster, lighter, her wrists dropping the way they should, no stiffness in her.

She shifted from scales to playing a proper piece. She chose something light and simple to start out with, some childhood nursery rhymes and lullabies that she knew. There was no need to hurt her fingers or make a fool of herself trying to impress the Reginalds with her playing.

There would be plenty of time to show off her talents at balls later on. That was when she needed to impress people, in any case. She had to show off her talents for the men who were at the social gatherings.

Right now, she just wanted to play what she liked, for these two people who were being so kind to her and so open with her.

Miss Reginald had only a faint smile on her face. Maria suspected that she was not a woman prone to showing great fits of passion. But her eyes were warm and she seemed happy to sit there and listen.

Lord Reginald seemed outright delighted. He declared that he recognized some of the songs and would sing along. He sang along quite badly but Maria suspected that was on purpose. It made her laugh, at any rate, which she was certain was his design.

By the time that dinner came she was feeling much better, as Miss Reginald had said. Indeed her spirits felt infinitely lifted.

The Reginalds were right. How she had come to be in London for the season did not matter. It was not something that she ought to dwell on. She would see Father and they would deal with that but when it came to the season she was to have fun.

Father's sickness could not take away from her the joy of the balls and the importance of them. She needed to find a husband either way, whether Father was in perfect health or standing with one foot in his grave.

And with such people as the Reginalds guiding her, she was certain that she would have a wonderful time.

She could not have hoped for a more welcoming pair of people. Lord Reginald seemed delighted with her and Miss Reginald was as warm and kind as Mother had been. Maria was certain that she would come to consider them both family.

If only Lord Reginald was not quite so dashing. He could not help it, of course. And to him she must seem quite the backwards, wild thing. But his gentle teasing and his efforts at making her laugh always sent her into fits of blushing and stammering.

She wished that he would perhaps be less handsome or a bit

less inclined to smile at her. Then she might have a better hold of herself when she was around him.

It was only because he was the first man she had properly met and gotten to know. Or at least that was what she told herself. As soon as she was presented and introduced to society she would get to know many other wonderful men and this would pass.

After all, what could a girl like her possibly do to tempt a man of such stature and sophistication as Lord Reginald?

CHAPTER 4

THE FIRST THING that struck Edward was how completely unlike any other girl this Miss Worthing was.

He had found other women to be enjoyable in their company, yes. He did not despise women as a whole. But the women he enjoyed spending time with were usually women who were already married, but too young to have daughters to foist upon him.

The women who were old enough to have such daughters would spend all their time trying to get him to fall in love with said daughters. And the unmarried women were trying to do the same, flirting shamelessly.

It was only the ones who were newly married or with young children that he could converse with happily and peacefully.

But Miss Worthing was completely unlike all of them.

She looked a bit wild, for one thing. She was far more tan than any other woman he had ever seen. Her dark hair was thick and curling about her head and had obviously never seen a proper hairdresser.

Luckily Georgiana's own hairdresser would soon see to that. But he rather liked the freckles that dotted all over Miss Worthing's face, and how thick and untamed her hair was, and her bright eyes that sparkled despite how dark they were.

Her frock was a simple one and she was wrapped up in layers. Of course, she had been born and raised all her life in the

Caribbean. England must seem frightfully cold even in the summer.

She looked nothing like the fashionable ladies of his class that he had seen. Even the ladies whose families received five hundred a year were dressed more nicely than Miss Worthing was.

In fact, she looked not like a lady at all but like a servant who had been gifted the out-of-fashion clothes of her mistress. It was a custom to gift such things to servants if the fabric could not be reused in some other way.

Edward found himself pleased with the overall result. She looked like the sort of woman who did not care for her appearance. Of course there was nothing inherently wrong with wanting to look nice. But the way that these women often dressed up...

He knew they were dressing up just to catch a man. Not for their own pleasure. And this was the type of girl who looked and sounded as though she looked the way that she did because she liked it. Not because it was what society dictated or because it was what a man might prefer.

And then she spoke, and Edward had to try to hold in his laughter.

Oh, this poor girl was going to get eaten by wolves, metaphorically speaking, if he and Georgiana did not teach her to better hold her tongue.

But she meant kindly in everything that she said. There was no malice in Miss Worthing, he could see that much. And the way she had lit up as she talked about her island and running a household and her sketches.

This was a woman, he suspected, who liked to feel useful. Who liked to know that she could contribute to her household rather than simply spend all day preparing for the next social event.

They would have to find her a good husband. Edward had already promised her father that but now he meant the promise. A sweet girl such as Miss Worthing would need a man who understood her. A man who saw the pure heart shining underneath the initial display of ignorance.

She was clearly a talented girl. Her piano playing was sweet and simple. She clearly got joy out of it. Not at all like the women who had clearly learned only so that they might show off how accomplished they were while secretly hating the exercise all the while.

No, there had been this lovely look of rapture on Miss Worthing's face as she played. They would have to make sure she played at the balls they attended. The joy that she clearly had while she played shone out on her face and made her look quite beautiful. It would show her to her best advantage to suitors.

There were, however, going to be some setbacks.

She was a lovely girl and Edward took quite a shine to her. He teased her and got a blush and a smile out of her quite readily. It had been ages since he'd been able to do that to Georgiana. Ever since abandoning her suitor at Father's orders, his sister had been serious and withdrawn.

Teasing Miss Worthing was like having a proper sister all over again. He quite enjoyed it and suspected he would happily partake of her company over the next month.

However, her manners...

They had sat down to dinner and that had been when he and Georgiana had seen just how much work was ahead of them.

Maria seemed to know where all the silverware was and how to sit, fortunately. It was clearly not as though she were a heathen. But she was lax about her manners and tended to do things such as speak over someone or laugh until she snorted.

Georgiana was patient with the other girl and would gently point out better behavior. "And be careful about your elbows, Miss Worthing. Remember to ask instead of reaching."

"I feel like I'm a child of ten all over again," Miss Worthing admitted. "I must be embarrassing you both horribly, I'm sorry."

"There is no need for embarrassment," Georgiana replied. "It's only the two of us and this is why you were brought here early. So that we might have time to get rid of your bad habits."

She was not an uncouth girl and she seemed well aware of her own shortcomings. Edward could easily see how her manners had become lax. All alone with only a sickly father whom she had to care for...of course Miss Worthing would have bigger things to worry about.

She had to run a household, and take care of her father, and there was no one around except for the servants. It made perfect sense to him.

Personally he was finding he enjoyed her honest and forthright, albeit rustic, company over the company of poised but simpering ladies.

Once he got Maria talking on the subject of the local wildlife, for example, it was difficult to get her to stop. Edward didn't mind in the slightest. Normally it felt like pulling teeth to get someone to talk to him.

As a duke, he was generally the most important person in the room. And the result in people's minds seemed to be that they thought he ought to command most of the conversation in the room.

It was probably how his father had behaved but Edward was not the sort of person who liked to talk just to hear the sound of his own voice.

And when people did talk to him it was usually about something incredibly boring and insipid. But Maria was telling them all what she had studied about the local plants and wildlife.

"I wanted to know what I was sketching," she explained. "And so Father ordered me some lovely books on plant and animal species. I have sketchbooks just full of them."

She explained the different animals and how she would go for long walks by herself. "Father would despair of me," she said. "I would often come back all covered in mud."

The idea of a lady going on such a walk by herself was practically unheard of for Edward. He thought that it showed great independence on Maria's part and he applauded her for it, at least in his own mind.

This was the sort of thing he needed to think about when looking for a wife, he thought. He needed to look for a sense of independence.

Of course, Maria could not go on such walks now that she was in London. Georgiana made that quite clear to her. Maria needed to have a companion or escort at all times.

"There are periods when a lady may travel alone," Georgiana said. "To make a morning call, for example. Or if one has been invited to dinner by one's self. And countryside walks are most enjoyable and cannot always be done with a companion if one is alone at the house.

"But to go tramping about often and letting yourself turn into such a state would only bring about malicious talk. You must always carry yourself with care and pride. Especially in London."

Maria nodded, soaking up every word.

Edward hastened to reassure her that she could still do her sketches. "There are some lovely parks in the area. Perhaps tomorrow we can visit one of them and you might do some sketching there. You can even set up your paints if you'd like."

"I'm horrible at artwork when I'm the one doing it," Georgiana added. "But I would not at all mind bringing a book and sitting with you."

"You ought to sketch Georgiana," Edward said, an idea alighting in his head. That would be lovely.

Georgiana shot him an embarrassed look. "There is no need for that, surely?"

"I don't draw people often," Maria admitted. "Although I would do them for the servants as a present for birthdays or Christmas. They never get any portraits done of themselves so it's a lovely gift for them."

Edward could hardly imagine how Maria would handle a proper English Christmas. The cold would probably be unbearable to her, but perhaps the snow would delight her.

"I think that's rather kind of you," he said. He didn't know of anyone in society here who would think to do such a kind thing for their servants.

"Well, there was no one else to sketch besides Father, and he hates being sketched," Maria said with a smile. "But as I said I didn't do it often. I'm most likely horribly out of practice."

"Then you must use Georgiana to get some practice again," Edward insisted.

"Honestly," Georgiana said to him before turning to Maria. "Pay him no attention. He is a horrible tease and will do whatever he can to get a reaction. He is tired of what he considers to be the boring mores of society and will do whatever it takes to rattle something new out of anyone."

Maria laughed. "I do not mind, if you do not. I would be happy to sketch you or your brother. I only wish that you not place your expectations too high in regards to my talent."

"We shall prepare ourselves for a horrible mess and then be pleasantly surprised," Edward assured her.

It became clear that Maria's trip had exhausted her. She had become more and more tired as dinner went on. The poor girl was obviously trying her best to maintain her energy but by the time dinner was over her eyelids were drooping and her shoulders were horribly slumped.

Edward felt oddly protective of her. She was clearly so unused to this lifestyle. Her father's wealth would have normally given her a standard of living that was not too far off from this. Not quite to the same level of course but enough that she would not be quite so overwhelmed by everything around her. And she would have presumably been in houses such as this once or twice before.

But living out on a plantation with little to no social interaction? No wonder she was so bumbling and intimidated. It made him worry for her.

After Maria had been guided up to bed by Georgiana, Edward sat in the library. It was generally his retreat from the world. Georgiana loved the library as well for her reading and was indeed a greater reader than he was. But generally, guests tended to congregate in the parlor or sitting room. In the library, he could effectively hide from them.

Georgiana came in a short while later while he was going over some letters.

"I worry about her," he told her.

Georgiana sighed. "I know. I confess that I worry as well. She has no idea of when to hold her tongue."

"At least she is not saying anything that is malicious," Edward pointed out. "She is constantly apologizing for herself."

"She is a sweet girl," Georgiana agreed, sitting down next to him.

"They will tear her to pieces," Edward warned.

"I think that you are far too cynical," Georgiana said. "You need to be kinder in thought to those around you."

"And you are far too kind," Edward replied. "How many times have people insinuated that you are unmarriageable? How many times have they listed all the reasons why you have not yet been proposed to? Or stated that there must be a horrible reason why you are not married, when your father has left you such a great inheritance?"

Georgiana pressed her lips together and looked down at her hands. "That is unkind of you, Edward."

"I am not trying to be unkind. You know that I am not. But I am being honest. You know that I value honesty and I think it is important that I share my true thoughts with you. Just as I would expect you to be honest with me.

"People are cruel. Many people see this world as a competition. Who hosts the best balls. Who is more fashionable. Who can get a better husband and do it faster than the other ladies. Who can find the best wife or has the best horses.

"It's all about beating out one another and they will see her as an easy opportunity to gain a point by hurting her. Because they will see her as just another piece of competition in whatever game they are playing."

"And I think that you are being unfair to the many lovely people there are in society," Georgiana replied. "Edward, honestly. I know that the past few months have been trying for you. It cannot be easy and I'm certain that you feel under attack.

"But that is no reason to put everyone in such an unflattering light. I think that you need to be more generous in your estimation of people."

Edward scoffed. "I will be more generous when they give me reason to be."

Georgiana gave him one of those gently chastising looks that always told him, far more than words ever could, how disappointed she was in him.

Edward sighed. He hated when Georgiana was disappointed in him. Since Mother's death, Georgiana's opinion was the only one that mattered to him. Father's opinion had to matter to him. But he didn't honestly care about it, in his heart.

"I'm sorry," he said. "I wish that I could have a manner more in line with your own. I wish that I could give you the answers that you wish to hear. And that I could find peace within myself.

"But I find that day will not come until people are kinder to you.

And until I can dance through a ball without feeling as though I am in a river surrounded by piranhas."

Georgiana smiled softly. "I think that you are reading too many of those fantastical publications on world explorers."

"You must at least admit that you find the gossip draining," Edward said.

"I admit that...yes, there are times when it does drain me," Georgiana acknowledged. "But I also find myself having lively discussions on art. I enjoy theatre best when I am seeing a play or opera with others. It would be quite a lonely life if I was to isolate myself as you seem to want to do."

Edward didn't say anything. He didn't know what else there was to say. He couldn't think about it right now. He had so much to deal with still as the new duke and he could already feel exhaustion slipping in.

Where had his *joi de vivre* gone? Had it all vanished never to be recovered now that he had so many estates and assets to run?

Georgiana gave a little sigh. "Edward. I know that things have been hard for you. But it will get easier. You will learn how to balance it."

"I fear that I am going to be the same as Father," he admitted. "That I shall be nothing but stern and demanding for the rest of my days. That I shall become someone that everyone secretly loathes, or of whom they live in fear."

"You are nothing like Father," Georgiana assured him. "And the rest of society is not like him, either. There are wonderful people out there."

"Georgiana, the only honest, genuine person I have known in months is that young lady. And it will all be beaten out of her as soon as she attends her first ball. If she is not so traumatized by the unkind things said that she ever deigns to come out of her room."

"It will not nearly be so bad as all that," Georgiana replied. "You are being overly dramatic."

"We shall see who is right in a month's time," Edward said grimly. If a month could be enough to help make up for years without proper tutelage, he would be greatly surprised. But one could always hope.

"If you will not have faith in society," Georgiana said, "Then at least have faith in Miss Worthing. She seems to me to be a lovely and vivacious girl. She had great spirit."

"She is also facing a total upheaval of everything that she knows," Edward pointed out. "Her father is dying. Or at least he believes that he is, and the doctors seem to think so as well. He is putting his affairs in order and no longer hiding his condition.

"She has no friends, no one to turn to. She will be eager to make new acquaintances and she will be easily hurt when she is rebuffed."

"I think that she is of sterner stuff than you make her out to be," Georgiana said. "I appreciate how protective you are of her, Edward. But you cannot keep her from society. Nor can you keep yourself. Or me, for that matter."

Edward wanted to throw his hands up in despair but knew that would not lead to anything. Instead he nodded stiffly. "Well, time will tell soon enough."

Personally, he thought that Georgiana was overestimating all three of them. Georgiana was the stoic sort. But she tended to endure and endure, in silence, until she simply dropped in exhaustion from it.

Edward did not wish for her to keep suffering in silence. Nor did he wish for Miss Worthing's light to be snuffed out, so to speak. And his own patience was running thin. He was almost considering running to the highlands and becoming a hermit or barbarian or something of the kind.

But it seemed that he would make no headway that evening. So he said nothing, and merely announced that he would retire to bed.

They would find out in a month or so which one of them was right. And while he did so hate to be in a position where the other person got the chance to say *I told you so*...

Well, he almost wished that his sister was right. If only so that all three of them might not suffer more than they already had.

CHAPTER 5

MARIA DESPAIRED of ever getting anything right.

It felt as though every day was filled with nothing but Miss Reginald's tutelage. Maria often felt as though she ought to be placed under the care of a governess or a tutor.

Miss Reginald would have none of that. She was a very quiet woman, as Maria was learning. But that quietness hid a very strong character.

"I will not parcel you off to a governess or a tutor as though you were a child," Miss Reginald said on one occasion when Maria tried to bring it up again. "You are an adult. And a highly intelligent one as well. I will not have you treated in such a manner as though you were a dunce."

Maria often felt like a dunce, however.

For one thing, who knew that there was so much about fashion and dresses of which she had been previously unaware?

She knew the basic rules of propriety when it came to dressing, of course. And she knew what colors she liked to wear.

But now there was so much else that came into it. There were the colors that went well with her complexion, which she must take care to wear. But that wasn't all, for she must also think of what colors were in season.

And beyond what season it was—winter, spring, summer, fall—there was the 'season' of society, the London season, and the colors that were most popular that year. But she must of course not wear the same colors as everyone else or they would all be embarrassed.

"It is a thin line," Miss Reginald told her, "between going well with the fashions and imitating them too greatly."

Maria had no idea how to do that. She ended up letting Miss Reginald pick out her fabrics and cuts for her. She simply despaired of getting it right herself.

"Why can I not simply wear what I like to wear?" she asked.

"You may wear what you like," Miss Robinson replied, "in the context of the rest."

Maria thought that very frustrating. Why could people not simply wear what they wanted to wear?

"You are fortunate," the dressmaker told her at one point, "very fortunate indeed, my lady. Miss Reginald, she is a duke's daughter, now a duke's sister. And in London. She sets the fashions, my lady, that she does."

Maria had no idea what that meant. She had asked Miss Reginald about it, and she had sighed.

"It means that since I occupy such a high place in society and I am directly in London where all the fashions begin, what I wear shall be copied by everyone. That means, as my friend, you can find out what I am wearing and copy me before the others. Or perhaps your taste might even influence mine."

None of that seemed to make sense to Maria. Of course she wanted to look her best, who didn't? And of course she cared about what she looked like. But she wanted to wear the things she wanted to wear without worrying about what others thought. Or what others were wearing.

Table manners were another source of frustration. She had not realized how much hers had slipped until now. She felt quite like a barbarian.

When she said so, the duke had laughed. "You are not nearly as bad as all that," he had assured her.

The duke overall seemed rather amused by her. Almost like an older brother. He was very kind to her as well.

Maria only wished that she should not be so tongue-tied about him or around him.

It was only that he was so handsome and charming. He always

seemed to have the perfect, witty thing to say no matter what the situation.

Maria knew that Miss Reginald did not always appreciate her brother's comments. Maria wanted to ask her about them but thought that might be rude. And she was being terribly rude all the time without trying.

She honestly hadn't realized how much her skills had slipped during her time alone with her father. She doubted that Father himself knew. Business and his health had occupied much of his time the last few years.

Now she was learning just how much she had forgotten or had never learned in the first place. Many things that her mother had taught her were now out of date. It made sense, for Mother had been teaching her things that were respectful when she was a lady in London and that had been nineteen years ago.

Still, Maria was surprised at how much some things had changed. For example, the dances she knew were all horribly out of date.

"Not really anyone dances the way you do anymore," Miss Reginald said. She sounded apologetic. But she always did. Maria wanted to tell her that there was nothing to apologize for. It wasn't Miss Reginald's fault that Maria was so horribly unprepared to enter London society.

That meant that dance lessons had to be added on top of everything else. Miss Reginald agreed to a tutor on that at least.

Lord Reginald would often stop by to help be Maria's partner. Part of her loved that he did so. Part of her wished that he wouldn't.

Miss Reginald would sometimes scold him in her very gentle way.

"Do you not have business to be attending to?" she would ask.

Lord Reginald would always reply that business could wait but a lady's skills in dance were always of the utmost importance. Maria could not be sure how much he was teasing when he said that. Sometimes he would say something that was ostensibly a lighthearted comment. But there would be a weight underneath that cut through his tone and made her wonder if he was being serious or if bitterness had claimed him.

She worried about him. He seemed to be easily frustrated when it came to discussions about society. He seemed to take little joy in the prospect of balls or even going to the theatre since it involved seeing other people.

Maria disliked the prospect of someone being unable to find joy in other people and in life. But she dared not ask about it.

Perhaps, her fanciful mind conjured up, he had been abandoned by a woman that he loved. Or his best friend had thrown him over in order to win the favor of another lord.

These were childish little fantasies that did little to explain his manner. But sometimes she could not help but indulge in them.

Logic would inevitably prevail in the end. What lady would dare to refuse the engagement proposal of a duke? Even if she did not love him—well, Miss Reginald had taken time to warn her about that.

"Many marriages are not about love and that should not be at the forefront of your mind when you are getting to know a gentleman," she said. "The passionate love of Romeo and Juliet, of Guinevere and Lancelot, is not one that a young lady should hope for.

"Should it come to you, then by all means seize it. But sense, not sensibility, should prevail. You are looking for a man who can take care of you.

"That man should be of a disposition that appeals to you. You do not want to make yourself miserable if you can help it. And if one party in the marriage is miserable then usually both are.

"But do not sit about and wait for a prince charming to sweep you off your feet, my dear. You must think with your head and not with your heart. Find yourself a man with a good income, who is sensible and kind, and then you shall have met your husband."

If the fiery love of fairy tales was not to be hoped for, then what lady dared to refuse a man such as Lord Reginald? Unless another duke proposed to her, and such an idea seemed unlikely.

And then the idea of a best friend throwing Lord Reginald off to gain favor with another—again, preposterous. Who would abandon a close friendship with a duke?

Sometimes, Maria would jokingly curse Lord Reginald's status as a duke—in her mind. Her little curious fantasies would make so much more sense were he not in such a powerful social position.

Whatever the reason for Lord Reginald's dislike of society, however, he was nothing but kind to her.

He would accompany her and Miss Reginald on walks to the parks. Maria loved to sketch there and was permitted to spend a few hours there if she liked so long as she also had time to work on her social skills.

The plants and animals were not so varied in England as they were in the Caribbean. The differences in the flowers were subtler. And the shades were paler, pastel. But she was coming to enjoy them.

The machinations of the local squirrels were very interesting for her to record. They seemed to have their own loves, their own births and deaths, their own little dramas. It could just be her own flights of fancy again, true. But it gave her something lighthearted to focus on while she continued to sink into despair about her own situation.

She kept expecting Miss Reginald to give up on her. To hire a governess or to simply tell her that it was no use. Maria knew that the Reginalds had much better things to do than to spend their time helping her.

Except that whenever she tried to bring it up, neither of them would hear of it.

"Better things to do?" Miss Reginald said, quoting Maria's words back at her. "My dear, do not trouble yourself. I have nothing I would rather be doing. This is a most interesting exercise for me as well in terms of remembering what the rules are. I would not like to be rusty myself.

"And of course I can call upon my friends and sometimes do. But there is little else to do when the season is about to begin. There are things to do outside of the season but when it is so close to starting everyone is far too busy with preparations to bother with morning calls.

"I should be quite bored without you here to keep me company, I can assure you. You are not imposing upon me in the slightest."

Lord Reginald did not say anything directly to her. But she noticed that he took pains to be even more interested in her goings-on than before. It was as if he was trying to silently say that if she was going to think he had little interest, he was going to be stubborn by showing her even more interest.

He was quite a contradictory man overall. Maria said as much to Miss Reginald one night, close to the beginning of the season.

It had been nearly a month. Maria had picked up the dancing quickly but that felt like the only thing with which she could call herself accomplished. Her dresses were all made but that had been thanks to Miss Reginald's taste, not Maria's.

She was still dreading the first ball, which was to be in a few days' time. What if she said the wrong thing? What if she was impolite? What if she forgot which fork to use? What if...

Those fears swirled around her head constantly. That night they were sitting in front of the fire and reading. Miss Reginald was fond of her poetry. She had been educating Maria on it so that Maria might converse on the topic easily with others.

"There are also games that are played," Miss Reginald explained. "Word games and riddles, and often they involve poetry. You ought to be prepared. And besides, there is no harm in expanding one's mind and gaining a new accomplishment and topic of conversation."

They were reading, then, and Maria could not help but bring it up. Lord Reginald had just exited, after making one of his little aside remarks. This time it had been about the amount of time ladies took looking at themselves in the mirrors.

Maria had pointed out that men often did the same. "I have seen many an officer at the fort doing as much back home."

"Men are just as guilty of it, that is true," Lord Reginald replied. "I suppose I shall have to despise both equally, then."

He had then exited, saying something about letters.

Maria looked over at Miss Reginald. "Has your brother had a great wrong done to him?" she asked.

"Whatever do you mean?" Miss Reginald asked.

"I mean only that—and of course it is not my business—he seems to hold some kind of grudge against society." Maria smiled tentatively. "I keep expecting him to announce a duel against society at large."

Miss Reginald smiled. Maria had never seen Miss Reginald laugh in all the time that she had known her.

While she had her doubts about Lord Reginald and his motives, she had little doubt about Miss Reginald. There was a kind of mourning about her. Something very deep and quiet but very sad. Like the ocean, almost.

Maria wondered if it was her father's death, or her mother's, that had led Miss Reginald to be so solemn. But she could not deny that whatever it was, there was something inside Miss Reginald that was sad and broken and would not be easily repaired.

Still, it was pleasing to know that she could get Miss Reginald to smile. Maria would happily settle for that.

"My brother has had no specific injury done to him," Miss Reginald said. "It is only that he occupies a certain position in life. One that many women are eager to seize."

Maria frowned. "What do you mean?"

"You are a sweet girl," Miss Reginald told her. "I am glad that you are. You do not think as others do and I am not certain if it is a benefit to you or a weakness.

"In any case, my dear, I mean that he ought to marry. A titled man without an heir is in a position of danger. We know better than most how life can be so cruelly changed in an instant. Should my brother die without an heir, there would be an uproar. A most distant cousin should inherit. It would throw everyone into great confusion.

"But of course to have an heir, he must marry. And soon. His position is rather the same as yours, in fact. You both are pressed for time.

"The ladies of society know this. As do their mothers. We have so many invitations not only because of our wealth and title but because my brother is unmarried. The mothers are inviting us in the hopes that he will take a liking to one of their daughters."

"That is rather...mercenary of them, is it not?" Maria asked.

"You might see it that way, my dear, but are you not going to be doing the same thing with the other men?" Miss Reginald pointed out. "You have to secure a proposal by the end of the season. These young ladies are often in a similar predicament.

"Is it not fair for their mothers to wish for the best husband for their daughters? And for the young ladies to wish for the best husband for themselves?

"If a man enters the clergy and eventually climbs his way up to become the head of the church, we applaud him. If a lawyer wins many cases, we applaud him as well. Officers in the navy are expected to eventually become admirals.

"If we applaud ambition in a man then why not in a woman? A woman cannot pass the bar, or enter the clergy, or join the navy. Her profession is to marry. And so why should she not be ambitious in the same way as her male counterparts?"

"But when it comes to a man's profession, hearts are not on the line," Maria pointed out. "It seems to me that your brother has a right to feel agitation if he is being assaulted by these ladies.

"When they seek to catch him, they are toying with his affections as well. I can speak only for myself, but I should like to know that my spouse esteems me for who I am. Not for my money or because he has no other choice in whom he is to marry.

"I would like to know that I am truly valued by my husband. And if I wish that, then surely the man has a right to wish for the same from his wife.

"I am certain that despite the professional side of marriage for women, most of them marry with a certain degree of personal esteem for their husband."

"This is very true," Miss Reginald said. "And I agree with you. But many women feel a great deal of pressure from their families. Especially from their mothers. Many of them, I am sure, feel that the esteem will come after the marriage.

"Or it could very well be that they have a different sort of esteem in mind when they are thinking of marriage. For some women a husband who will provide for them and who is good-looking is all that they need.

"Many marriages are, after all, held rather separately. I can name several where the husband and wife rarely see one another or converse. Except in a public setting where they have been invited together such as a ball.

"Even then, there might be little in the way of leading one to think that they are married to one another."

Maria considered that. "I think that is quite distressing," she said at last. "My mother and father greatly cared for one another. Of course there was nothing that I could see outside the realm of propriety. In front of me, in any case.

"But I could always tell that however proper they were in front of others, there was much more tenderness that was done behind closed doors.

"They had this way of looking at one another...I have rarely seen it replicated. It was as though they were...astonished, almost, that the other person should be so wonderful, and should exist, and should have chosen to be married to them."

"That sounds beautiful," Miss Reginald said. "If only we could all strive for such a union."

"I wish that I could strive for it," Maria replied.

"But your parents might not have begun that way," Miss Reginald pointed out. "They were married a year before you were born. And I doubt you remember the first couple of years of your life with too much clarity.

"It could be that they grew into this tenderness for one another. And that you were simply too young to properly witness it."

"That could very well be true," Maria acknowledged. "But I hope that I might feel at least the beginnings of such views towards my husband when he proposes."

"We all hope for such things," Miss Reginald replied. "I am only telling you so that your hopes might not be dashed too roughly. And so that you might understand the position of these ladies.

"I do not appreciate how they fling themselves at my brother, either. I think that there is a way to do it with much more subtlety and propriety than the methods that they employ. But nor do I appreciate my brother's method of condemning everyone.

"We are all just looking to be loved, Miss Worthing. Remember that. We all wish to be safe and secure. To be taken care of. And to be made to feel wanted in someone's life.

"That is all that there is to it. Remember that and you will find that compassion never leaves your heart."

Maria thought that Miss Reginald might be the kindest person she had ever met. "I shall strive to remember that, Miss."

Miss Reginald smiled at her. "Good. Now, the hour is late and we have much to do in the next few days."

She did not say, 'to try to prepare you' but Maria knew what

Miss Reginald meant. Maria was not at all feeling prepared for this first ball. They had even been invited to dinner beforehand.

How on earth was she going to survive?

"Oh my dear, you look as if you are going to be led to the guillotine," Miss Reginald said. The words might have been teasing coming from anyone else. From Miss Reginald, they were sympathetic. "Do not worry. It will not be nearly so bad as you fear."

Maria could only hope that Miss Reginald was right and that this would all be easier than she had anticipated.

CHAPTER 6

IT WAS WORSE than Edward had feared.

If his sister had been a man then he would have put a wager down upon their little disagreement as to how society would welcome Miss Worthing.

Then he would now be collecting a tidy sum.

It wasn't that he was happy to be winning their little bet. Far from it. He had been hoping a little that his sister would be right and the society he had come to see as a pack of wolves would actually be kind to Miss Worthing.

But it looked as though their more gossip-ridden natures were winning out.

Edward was personally compiling a list of all the women who spoke ill of or towards Miss Worthing. He should not be marrying any of them. A woman who made fun of a poor girl doing her best was not the sort of woman he wanted for his spouse and life partner.

For a wife was a partner, truly, in every sense of the word. Especially when a man ran as large of an estate as Edward did, being a duke.

A wife had to be depended upon to run the household and sometimes the estate itself, the outer lands, while Edward was traveling or in town on business. His wife would have to help him with keeping the accounts and would of course be in charge of finding a proper governess and tutor to raise the children in any ways she was not raising them herself.

She would have to plan meals and dinners and balls. She would have to be allied with her husband in whom they considered friends and whose invitations they would accept or ignore.

Edward needed a proper partner. Someone to whom he could entrust his estate. Especially if something were to happen to him and his son—for there must be a son—was too young to take charge himself. His wife would need to be in charge of things until then.

How could he possibly trust any woman with what she said to his face, when these women were smiling to Miss Worthing's face and then turning around and gossiping behind her back?

He could never be certain that his wife was doing things as she should. He would have to double-check everything. He could not leave her alone.

No, none of these women were for him. Even more so because he personally could not be around someone who had such a callous nature.

Things had started out inconspicuously enough. Miss Worthing looked very fetching in her new dress. Edward took care to say so. The poor girl looked terrified in the carriage ride over and needed all the confidence that she could get.

When he told her that she looked lovely, Miss Worthing got the slightest blush in her upper cheeks. It was quite becoming. It would perhaps have been too much on a paler woman but with her tan from the tropics, it looked quite nice.

It had not escaped Edward's notice that his sister had instructed the seamstress to make Miss Worthing's dress similar to her own in coloring and style.

It was a clever move, if he did say so himself. Georgiana's dress was of a darker blue, the style a bit daring, as befitted a woman of high ranking who was fashion-forward and of an older age.

Miss Worthing's dress was in a lighter blue but cut from the same fabric style with the same light embroidery pattern on it. The cut of it was a little less daring but clearly in the same style.

It was a statement of intent to any other lady in attendance. Such a similarity in dresses, and arriving together, was not a coincidence. It told all the ladies present that Miss Worthing and Georgiana were friends. Why else would the sister of a duke let a woman lower in station than she was wear such a similar dress?

Miss Worthing would never be allowed to get away with it if she and Georgiana were not close and on good terms. Right away, Edward had hoped that would protect Miss Worthing a little.

All it had done was ensure that the gossip about her was said out of earshot of Georgiana.

They were high enough in society that all three of them had been invited to dinner. Miss Worthing had been asked because Georgiana had sent word round to all the households that Miss Worthing was to be treated as a sister to her and all invitations to Georgiana must also be extended to Miss Worthing.

Edward had held his breath a little as they had entered. Miss Worthing had walked presentably, but she had not truly glided as a lady should. And one could plainly see the awe in her face as she cast furtive looks around at the table and the furnishings.

Act as though this is the least impressive dining room you have ever seen, he wanted to hiss at her. Pretend that it is a hovel if you must!

Miss Worthing had once asked what was so wrong about being impressed with the furnishings and décor of a host's house.

"Of course, one may do so politely," Georgiana had answered. "But to do so in excess is to showcase one's lack of acquaintance with the finer things in life. And to showcase that is to declare yourself meaner than they are in annual income, and lower in station.

"If you act as though you are lower in station, they will treat you as such. And we do not want to give them the opportunity."

Miss Worthing was giving them plenty of opportunity now, however. She kept her mouth shut but her wide eyes said it all as she took in the food and the table arrangements.

Things only got worse when the conversation started.

"Where did you say that you were from again, Miss Worthing?" asked Miss Hennings.

Edward already disliked Miss Hennings. She was a catty woman who thought of nothing and nobody except herself. She had tried to insinuate herself into his affections long ago. He had shot her down, as graciously as he could. She seemed to take it as a personal quest to make him and his associates miserable ever since.

"The Caribbean," Miss Worthing said, smiling. She suspected not a thing, the innocent girl. "It was quite lovely there—"

She tried to explain about her home. Edward knew how much she loved it there and how she missed it. The weather especially was hard on her. She was constantly cold.

But when she tried to talk about how lovely the plants were, someone would make a comment about how wild and awful it was. People would offer up gossip they'd heard about 'running with the natives'. They would make snide remarks about how it took 'so very long' for things like fashion and deportment and dancing styles to reach those foreign ports.

Poor Miss Worthing was not so ignorant that she did not know when people were making fun of her. She was a fish out of water, but she wasn't a stupid one.

Edward could see her trying to hide her distress as she gamely answered questions about herself and her upbringing.

"Well yes," she said in response to a question. "I often had to go out into the field to help. Father was ill, you see."

"You would never catch me doing such a thing," Miss Hennings said, sounding both horrified and amused.

"What a state your poor skin must be in!" said another lady.

"Oh, no, I think it is rather fetching," said yet another. "It helps her to stand out from the other ladies, you know. I'm sure you will get many questions about it."

Edward knew that physical violence was not the answer but he did sometimes wish that he was allowed to slap women.

At least, however, this had an odd silver lining to it. He was so busy worrying about Miss Worthing that he had no time to fret over his own circumstances.

Unfortunately, as the dinner went on, the more nervous Miss Worthing got the more she forgot the lessons Georgiana had taught her.

At one point she even picked up the wrong fork. Edward had to stop himself from reaching over and fixing it for her. Miss Worthing was not a child and would not appreciate his interfering as though she were one.

But every mistake, every slip up, only made it worse for her. The others could see that they were rattling her, and it gave them nothing but delight.

It seemed that he was not the only person who was upset by this behavior. He saw some of the other men and women appearing uncomfortable. A few of them would try and change the subject.

But it wasn't enough, he feared, to make up for Miss Worthing's growing lack of confidence.

He could see her bad habits growing stronger as dinner wore on. She would make a comment about a lady's dress or accidentally interrupt a lord as he was talking. It was as though her nervousness made her restless and impatient, like a bird beating its wings against a cage.

Edward didn't know who he was more frustrated with.

Why did they have to poke and prod at her? Why did they have to treat her like a wild animal brought for their amusement?

But at the same time—had Miss Worthing learned nothing? Could she not remember that staying calm was the best of her options? That she must maintain her composure and not show them that they affected her?

It was unbearably frustrating. Edward was forced to sit there and do nothing. Except of course for trying to direct the conversation elsewhere.

"I have heard that a most entertaining play is being put on in the Haymarket Theatre," he said.

That got everyone discussing the theatre for a short bit. That is until Miss Hennings commented to Miss Worthing on what sort of theatre they had in the Caribbean.

"Is it all just natives running about and dancing?" she asked. "I should think that by the time you get a proper play it is a few years behind the times."

That seemed to be the final straw for Miss Worthing. She got two bright spots of pink high up on her cheeks but looked Miss Hennings directly in the eye.

"You seem to be under the impression that we live in the midst of an untamed jungle," Miss Worthing said. "I can assure you that the natives, as you call them, are surprisingly possessed of manners. For instance, they know how to properly treat a new acquaintance."

Edward almost choked on his wine as a laugh threatened to

bubble up inside of him. Well played, Miss Worthing, he thought. Well played.

Miss Hennings looked as though she were fuming over that. Edward shot a look over to Georgiana, who looked as grave as he felt.

Miss Hennings had been only amusing herself before. Now she was truly upset and would come after Miss Worthing with a vengeance.

Not directly, of course. Miss Hennings could see the stern look that Edward was giving her. She had to know that a direct attack against Miss Worthing would go nowhere. Not when Miss Worthing was so clearly the friend of a duke and a duke's sister.

But there would be other ways that Miss Hennings could sabotage Miss Worthing.

Edward was worried to find out what those ways were.

CHAPTER 7

MARIA THOUGHT she might crawl into a hole and die.

She had been nervous the entire way to the ball, but this was even worse than she had thought.

How could people be so rude and thoughtless? How could they say all of those things just to make sport of her?

And to make sport of her beloved island. Honestly. She would love to take them all there and let the "natives", as Miss Hennings seemed so eager to call them, have at them. It was not nearly so uncivilized out in the colonies as they all seemed to think.

If one were to ask the assembled guests, one would think that Maria and her father had been living in mud huts. That their servants had run around naked. That she hadn't even learned English or knew what a corset was until arriving in London.

Perhaps they might genuinely believe such things. Perhaps it was only that they were so ignorant. But Maria wasn't stupid. She knew when people were making fun of her.

And that gleam in Miss Hennings' eyes as she led the others in making their little comments...that was malicious. It was not out of ignorance and genuine curiosity. It was awful sport, plain and simple.

Maria felt like letting the earth swallow her up.

For the first time since coming to London, she genuinely wanted to find a husband as quickly as possible. As soon as she did she could stop going to these dinners and balls. Then she'd be free.

It certainly didn't help that the more nervous she got, the more things about her behavior she forgot. She and Father would interrupt and talk over one another all the time at home. And so she ended up interrupting someone that she was pretty sure was an earl.

As if that weren't awful enough, she grabbed the wrong fork at one juncture. She saw Miss Reginald shake her head minutely and so Maria quickly grabbed the correct fork. But the damage was done. She saw the looks that everyone was sneaking at her.

How on earth was she supposed to find a husband if everyone thought she was some wild creature who didn't even know how to eat properly at dinner?

She tried to shoot Miss Reginald a look pleading with her to have them retire early for the evening. But Miss Reginald didn't see it, and Maria knew that wasn't the answer.

If they were to duck out of the ball so early it would be seen as unforgivably rude. And Maria knew that she didn't need to give anyone another excuse to make a comment about her.

Besides, how was she to find a husband if she fled? She had to at least make an attempt to get to know the men assembled.

When dinner was finished, the other guests started arriving. That had been something else that Maria had learned from Miss Reginald. Apparently only the most intimate and honored of guests were invited for dinner beforehand.

It was a long and exhausting process, Miss Reginald said. Picking out who could come, who would get along with whom. How not to insult any guests by inviting others that they did not get along with or were too below their station.

And then actually figuring out the seating arrangements! That was a whole other headache, according to Miss Reginald.

Maria knew that she had only been invited to the dinner part because of Lord Reginald and his sister. And now she had messed it all up by falling all over herself throughout the entire meal.

If only those ladies hadn't had to poke at her so. They had asked such questions—and Maria knew they were not thoughtful questions. Lord Reginald's face had told her so even if she'd been unable to decipher it for herself.

Perhaps it was only that they were spending so much time

together through living in the same house. But she could tell from the way his jaw ticked and the distinct look in his eyes that he was upset. No, angry. He was angry with those ladies.

Maria could not help but remember all that he had said about society. Could it be that he was right? That there was nothing but cattiness and thoughtlessness to be found in London society?

She felt miserable. All those stories that her mother had told her. All the fun that her mother had. The friendships. The dances. It felt like a fairy tale now. A ridiculous one.

Perhaps Mother had just made up all the nice parts. Or exaggerated them. Made London seem like a place of wonders for the sake of the storytelling and the sake of her young daughter.

As they went to make their way to the ballroom and the other guests began to arrive, Maria found herself taken by the arm and moved to the side.

It was Lord Reginald.

"Pretend as though it does not affect you," he whispered quickly. "Or that what they say amuses you. When they see that you are hurt it only increases their appetite for hurting you."

"I cannot hide what I feel," Maria protested.

Lord Reginald looked saddened when she said that. "Nor do I wish that you had to. But you must. You will have to deal with their like far more often than you would wish to.

"If you show them that you are unaffected they will lose their taste for it. There will be no more sport in it for them."

"You make them sound like animals," Maria could not help but reply. "Perhaps I ought to kill them with kindness."

Lord Reginald looked as though the very thought made him want to roll his eyes with disdain. "Miss Worthing, please. Do as I suggest. It will make your life that much easier for you."

"I will do my best." It was all that she could promise. She was not trained in how to hide what she was feeling.

Lord Reginald nodded, guiding her back in line with the others and entering the ballroom. Hopefully nobody had noticed their quick little detour. "Good."

Everyone had moved into the ballroom and the music was being struck up. Wine was being served and the guests were drinking it. It was a much livelier affair than Maria had expected.

She could not help but gaze around her at the wide room. The wallpaper. The gilded chandelier that shone and sparkled high above them.

It was quite lovely, if she did say so herself. She knew that she was no expert in design or fashion. But she knew that this looked nice, at least to her.

Perhaps it wouldn't be too bad if she complimented the hostess on her lovely ballroom. It would be an excuse to get away from anyone she'd been forced to endure at the dinner table, anyhow. And it might make up for her lapses in manners then.

Their hostess was a lovely lady, with dark eyes and soft brown hair starting to go gray.

Maria remembered to curtsy. "Mrs. Dale, may I just say what an exquisite room this is. I love the choice in coloring."

To her surprise, Mrs. Dale did not insinuate that Maria was backward for being so enthusiastic. In fact she smiled, as if taken by surprise. "That is very sweet of you to say so. It took me forever to think of just the right wallpaper."

"How did you come upon it?" Maria asked.

To her surprise, again, Mrs. Dale happily told her. It was as though the poor lady had been waiting for someone to notice the hard work she had put into redecorating.

She led Maria through the room, describing the furnishings and explaining how she had handled the workers.

"It's not easy at all," she confided. "When you are mistress of your own house, you will learn."

"Oh, but I do know," Maria said. Then she realized that sounded impertinent. "Oh, I do beg your pardon. I only meant that—I helped to run my father's household, since my mother passed."

"You poor dear, when was that? And who was your mother, pray tell?"

That led to a surprisingly delightful discussion. Mrs. Dale knew her mother!

"Such a delightful creature she was," Mrs. Dale said. "Now that you tell me, of course I can see her in your face. Oh, the stories I could tell you!"

"Please do," Maria said. She was starved for more information about her mother, and even her father, and their lives when they were young the way she was now.

Mrs. Dale was the hostess and so couldn't spend all of her time on one person. But she did introduce Maria to a group of lovely older ladies that were of the same age. They had all known Maria's parents as well.

"Come, come, sit with us," said the Countess of Wistershire.

"Oh, she does look just like her," exclaimed Mrs. Rutlage.

Soon Maria found herself the center of attention from these older ladies. They asked her about life in the colonies the same as the younger ladies at dinner had. Except that these women spoke with gentle curiosity and listened eagerly to all that she said.

"I wish my son had found a lady as capable as you," said one woman. "He married this girl last year. She's pretty enough but not a thought in her head."

Maria blushed. "I'm certain that I'm not as much of a catch as all that."

Mrs. Dale was stopping by again and frowned. "What, because of what those young ladies were saying at dinner? Do not trouble your pretty head over them, Miss Worthing."

"It is because you have arrived to dinner with Lord Reginald," the Countess said wisely.

The other ladies all nodded.

Maria looked from one to the other. "What does that have to do with anything?"

"Why, it shows that you are intimately acquainted with him."

Maria flushed at the use of the word 'intimately'. "His father and my father were best friends in boyhood. I hope that I am speaking in truth when I call Miss Reginald my dear friend.

"But I have hardly spoken a word to the duke! He is always so busy. The fact that he makes time to become acquainted with me at all is quite thoughtful of him. I would not in any way call us greatly acquainted. We are not friends."

"Those ladies do not see that," Mrs. Dale replied. "They see only that you are staying in the home of the man that they wish to marry. And you are a pretty young thing."

"You are competition," Mrs. Rutlage said. "Dangerous competition. Whether you know it or not."

Maria was feeling quite overwhelmed. She could hardly dare to think that she was worth catching the eye of a baron, never mind a duke.

"One can hardly blame them," said another lady. "He is a most charming and educated gentleman. His wealth and breeding are more than enough to commend him, of course.

"But he is nothing short of a true gentleman. Anyone can see it. He is quite charming. And very well educated. He can converse with anyone it seems, and on any subject."

Maria wanted to laugh. Yes, it was true, Lord Reginald could be charming. But he was also stubborn and cranky. He preferred reading over socializing.

He was a marvelous person. And sometimes she wished he was less charming and handsome by half. But he was just a man. He wasn't some fairytale prince to fawn over.

Except that apparently according to these ladies at least, he was.

"I think it's quite unfair of them to judge me so. If I may be so bold," she said.

"Do not worry, dear, we think so as well," the Countess assured her, patting her hand. "But young ladies can be rather too caught up in the competition for a husband."

"They see other women only as threats," Mrs. Rutlage intoned.

"That seems rather self-centered of them," Maria noted.

It was probably naïve of her to say such a thing, but the other women just looked delighted with her.

"Just like her mother," said one. "Such a compassionate person she was."

Maria blushed. "Thank you." She hated that she was blushing but at least now she was doing it because she was being praised. At dinner she was doing it because she was being mocked and ridiculed.

"You know it is a shame that it took your father so long to get you to London," said another lady. "I would have loved to introduce you to my sons had you been here a year or two sooner. Alas, they are already married."

"I fear your sons would not wish to marry me anyhow," Maria confided to them. "I made a most horrible fool of myself at dinner.

Lord and Miss Reginald must be regretting their association with me even now."

"A ridiculous notion," the Countess said. "This is your first ball, is it not? Jitters are to be expected. It is only that most ladies have their first ball at fourteen or so.

"But even though you are older it is not through any fault of yours. It is only natural that you would be somewhat distressed. You needn't apologize for it."

Maria felt relief flooding her veins like cool, refreshing water. "That is wonderful to hear."

"But come, why are you speaking to us?" Mrs. Rutlage asked. "You ought to be dancing!"

"Oh, I'm quite sure nobody will wish to dance with me," Maria said.

It was not as though she was hiding in a corner. Although she was surrounded by the other ladies she could be quite clearly seen. If a man had wished to dance with her she would have been approached by now.

And she did not wish for one of the ladies to call over their son. If only because she did not wish for the embarrassment of knowing that she was a pity dance, a lady that they asked only because their mothers insisted.

"Are you so certain of that?" Mrs. Rutlage replied. Her gaze danced up over Maria's shoulder playfully.

Maria turned around to see Lord Reginald standing there. He cleared his throat.

"Pardon my interruption, ladies. I know firsthand what a gifted conversationalist Miss Worthing is. But I had hoped that I might trouble her for the next dance."

Maria stood up, probably too abruptly. She hadn't imagined that Lord Reginald would dance with her. But he probably had been pressed to do it by his sister. That way Maria would get in at least once dance that evening.

"Oh," she said, rather inelegantly. "I—yes. It would be my pleasure."

She curtsied to the ladies and allowed Lord Reginald to lead her onto the dance floor.

"I hope that I was not interrupting anything," he said. The last dance had just ended and so the other dancers were all getting into position.

"Not at all. Those ladies were being most thoughtful."

"They seemed to genuinely enjoy your company. I have rarely seen them look so delighted."

"Many of them knew my parents when they were young. It was wonderful to hear them speak more on my mother."

"You must miss her," Lord Reginald smiled at her as Maria took her position.

This, she knew. She had quickly picked up the new dances that the siblings had taught her. Maria relaxed a little, squaring her shoulders easily.

"I do," she admitted, as the music struck up. "Do you not miss yours?"

"I am much more used to it," the duke replied as they began the first steps. "My mother died when my sister and I were quite young. Yours is more recent. And I suspect that you were closer with your mother than we were with ours. Despite how much we loved her."

There was a pause as they separated and wove between some other dancers and were then back together again.

"But I fear that is a more depressing topic than dancing calls for," Lord Reginald said with a smile. "Tell me, are you feeling better since dinner?"

"Oh, yes, those ladies were quite kind. They said the most flattering things. Although I am sure that they were only trying to be kind to the daughter of a woman for whom they clearly had a fondness."

"Nonsense. Those women can be catty if they wish to be."

"I do wish you would be kinder in your disposition," Maria admitted, before she could think of what an impertinent thing it was to say. "I apologize, I—"

The duke shook his head as they countered around one another. "Never apologize for speaking your mind around me, Miss Worthing. I value your forthrightness."

He sounded quite earnest, as he always did. Maria had not valued, until this evening, how honest and plain Lord Reginald was in his manner. After dealing with that awful dinner, she had a new appreciation for someone who was direct in their manner.

"I am glad to hear it," Maria admitted. She hoped that she wasn't blushing. She wanted so badly to retain at least a little sophistication around Lord Reginald.

"In that case," she added, "I do wish that you would give more people the benefit of the doubt. Those ladies were nothing short of lovely to me. They treated me as if I were a long-lost niece."

"Most of their sons and daughters are already married," Lord Reginald replied. "Therefore, they do not need to size you up. They can treat you as an individual, rather than competition for their daughters, or a catch for their sons."

"And I think that is unnecessarily harsh of you in your judgment," Maria said.

"I shall believe it when I see it," Lord Reginald said, and left it at that. "In other news, perhaps you might twirl a little more when you turn."

"What for?"

"Why do you think that I asked you to dance?" Lord Reginald asked. "So that the other men might see you dancing."

Disappointment and elation warred equally in her chest.

On the one hand, it was sweet of the duke to dance with her so that he might get other men to dance with her. Dancing with a duke immediately upped her status in the room. And after seeing how well she danced, the other men would want to have a turn with such an able partner.

But on the other hand, it hurt to know that he was not asking her to dance simply because he wanted to. He was doing it as a favor to her. As a way to help her out. Perhaps even Miss Reginald had encouraged him to. It wasn't because he had a particular fondness for her and wanted to spend time with her.

She knew that she was nothing special to him. They had a bond through their fathers and because he was so generously letting her live with him. But sometimes a girl liked to hope...

In any case, it didn't matter. She wasn't—didn't—couldn't, entertain anything for Lord Reginald. It was only that he was charming and the first man of real acquaintance that she had in London.

The first man of real acquaintance she'd had at all, in fact.

So that was all that there was to it. It was just a passing, imagined fancy. Based solely on his proximity and familiarity. It would fade.

She had to find herself a proper husband. Not that Lord Reginald would not be. But a man that she actually had a chance at marrying.

And so she twirled a little more, and laughed appropriately as Lord Reginald told her amusing little anecdotes and added "be sure to laugh" at the end in a whisper. She truly did find it amusing, or at least, the conspiracy of it felt amusing to her, so the laughs were genuine.

"Very good," he instructed her. "I suspect that you shall have a full dance card after this."

Maria was filled with half terror, half hope. "But what on earth shall I say to them?" she asked. "I can hardly discuss my late mother with them."

"Just pretend that they are me. You seem quite comfortable and at ease in my presence."

"You I have known for a month. Of course I should be more at ease. But I shall have never spoken to these men in my life!"

"Then pretend that they are those lovely older ladies you were speaking to just now. You did not know them from Eve when you sat down with them. And yet you seemed to be well at ease with them by the time I walked over."

"But what if I forget the man's name or say the wrong one? What if I say something unforgivably rude?"

"You will not," Lord Reginald said firmly. As if he could will it into a universal law like gravity, just by saying so. "You must only have some confidence in yourself."

Maria wanted to laugh, but that would have been rude. Confidence? She was certain that her confidence was shot to pieces. If she'd ever had any to begin with.

Not even those kind ladies could truly bring it back. It was the younger men and women that she needed to impress. Her peers—at least in age.

The dance was ending, though. There was no more time to find or regain her confidence.

Lord Reginald escorted her off the dance floor. This would be the moment of truth now. The moment where another young man would approach her to dance...or not.

"I'll leave you," the duke murmured. "Otherwise the other men might think I have claimed you for the next dance as well."

He bowed to her, and Maria curtsied automatically.

Once he had left though, she felt terribly alone.

Lord Reginald was familiar to her. She felt safe with him. She felt adrift now. She couldn't go back to those ladies from before. Could she?

Nor could she see Miss Reginald anywhere.

"Pardon me, Miss Worthing?"

She turned. Mrs. Dale was standing there, a young man by her side. "Allow me to introduce you, my dear, if I may. This young gentleman was just inquiring about you. Mr. Upton, Miss Maria Worthing. Miss Worthing, Mr. John Upton. He is a fine friend of the family."

Maria curtsied. Mr. Upton looked to be a nice man. He had fine features, with dark hair and dark blue eyes.

"I was hoping that you might do me the honor of accompanying me for the next dance?" he asked.

Ah, so that was why Mrs. Dale had introduced him. Two people could not speak to each other unless they were introduced by a mutual acquaintance, and as the hostess, Mrs. Dale would of course know and could introduce everybody.

Although Maria could not help but wonder if Mrs. Dale had impressed upon Mr. Upton the need for a partner for Maria. She hoped that this was not a pity dance.

The job of a hostess was to ensure that all of her guests were enjoying themselves. If a young lady was not dancing, then the hostess could find and ask one of the extra gentlemen, if there were any, to step in for her.

At times, Miss Reginald had told Maria, that meant a married man had to step in and help.

This could very well be an example of that.

But Mr. Upton seemed genuinely pleased to take her arm and lead her to the dance floor, where they set up for the dance.

Maria could now see Miss Reginald, down a few couples and preparing to dance with someone else. Lord Reginald was on her other side, down a few couples, with a young lady in pink. Not, Maria noticed, one of the ladies from dinner.

The dance music started up, and she focused in on her partner.

Thankfully, Mr. Upton took up the thread of conversation almost at once. He asked from where she hailed, if she had any siblings, who her father was.

He seemed genuinely interested in her background, if a little intimidated by the thought of living in the colonies.

"I think I should die of heatstroke before the month were out," he admitted.

They managed to keep up the thread of conversation all through the dance, and more than once Maria got him to laugh. She wasn't even trying.

She was only saying things that came to her mind. She tried not to be rude, not to speak out of turn or to say anything that was too forward.

She should probably have been flirtatious or coquettish like Miss Reginald had tried to teach her. But those lessons in wit had quickly fallen to the wayside in favor of teaching her the new dance steps and reminding her of her table manners.

And so she just spoke as plainly as she could, and tried to compliment him. People always liked compliments. And she tried to listen as well. People liked to know that they were being listened to and that the person cared.

It seemed to be working. Mr. Upton secured the promise of another dance from her later in the evening. After that another young man came up, and Mr. Upton was pressed to introduce them.

That dance went quite well if she did say so herself. She hoped she wasn't bragging. It was just that the young gentleman seemed quite pleased with her.

Then after that Miss Reginald came up to introduce her to a few different men, acquaintances of hers. They quickly filled up her dance card and soon Maria found that she was dancing all night.

It was wonderful. It quite made up for the dinner before. She could almost forget how scared and hurt she had been earlier. Dancing was lovely. She had never realized how much fun it could be.

She whirled around the dance floor. She did her best to keep track of all of the men. They all seemed to be quite nice. Some were wittier than others. A few were a bit dull. Others were a bit too boisterous for her.

But they all got the same listening ear. She knew it would be rude if they thought themselves to not be valued by her. She could well imagine how difficult it could be for them to get up the courage to be introduced to her and then ask her to dance. She was a stranger to them—and she knew firsthand how terrifying it was to be introduced to a stranger and told to converse.

And so she did her best to listen and ask questions prompting them to tell her more. Besides, if she learned as much about them as possible she would sooner know if they would be well suited as her husband.

That was important to her. She knew that she only had the season. But she was not going to set either herself or a poor man up for misery by not being prudent. The man she agreed to marry must in some way complement her, even if hoping for genuine romantic love was too much.

All of the men were nice enough, though. They were all pleasant to look at. Although Maria tried not to focus on that too much, for she did not want to be vain. Not everyone was fortunate to be graced with handsomeness. A personality, she thought, could endear her to someone and make their face lovelier with time.

None of the men quite stood out to her, though. It was not that she was hoping for the feeling of being struck by lightning. But she was at least hoping for something akin to what she had felt when she first saw Lord Reginald.

It was silly of her, she knew. It was nothing more than a girlhood crush that she had on him. But it was all that she had to go on. All that she could pinpoint as something akin to the rush of affection she hoped to have for a husband.

Was it so wrong that it was her waypoint, her north star, when she had nothing else?

She did not even realize how tired she was until Miss Reginald found her after a dance. "I hope that was your last dance, my dear," she said.

"It was," Maria confirmed.

"Then I think it is time we went home."

"Oh, but I'm still enjoying myself!"

Miss Reginald shook her head. "Just you wait, my dear."

They bid goodbye to their host and hostess. Mrs. Dane especially impressed upon them the necessity of seeing them again. "You must call upon me sometime soon, Miss Worthing," she said.

Maria could only blush and stammer out her thanks and her assurances that she would stop by at the earliest opportunity.

They climbed into the carriage, the three of them. Miss Reginald looked content but Lord Reginald looked nothing short of relieved to be escaping.

"How did you enjoy it?" Miss Reginald asked as the carriage pulled away.

Perhaps it was good that they had left the ball. Maria's limbs were beginning to feel quite heavy. "I enjoyed it..." she had to stifle a yawn. "A great deal. More than I expected."

"Once that dreadful dinner was got through," Lord Reginald grumbled.

His sister shot him a warning look. "I think that you handled yourself quite well out there on the dance floor. You did not have to sit down once tonight."

"Yes, it was very kind of those gentlemen to dance with me. I am certain that it is only because I am so new. And because of my upbringing in the colonies. It must be so rare of them to meet someone from there."

Lord Reginald looked as though he might say something, but then checked himself, as if he had thought better of it.

"And did you like any of them in particular?" Miss Reginald asked.

Maria thought about lying for a moment, but then shook her head. She did not want to disappoint Miss Reginald but she couldn't lie to her. And it was only the beginning of the season. Surely she was not expected to fall head over heels at the first ball.

"I'm afraid not. They were all quite pleasant, though. I did not dislike any of them. It is only that I cannot bring myself to say that any of them is head and shoulders above the others in my preference."

"Of course not," Lord Reginald said. "They are all dullards."

"I thought they were quite interesting," Maria said. It was rude of her perhaps, but Lord Reginald had told her that he wanted her to speak her mind. And so she would.

"I think that they only need someone to really listen to them. They talked about all sorts of things. Did you know that Mr. Parhen collects butterflies? And that Mr. Upton was present at the birth of a foal as a child?

"And they were very polite in behaving interested in what I was saying about the Caribbean and the plantation. That is more than I can say for the people, men and women, who were at the dinner table.

"I think that they were admirable in their behavior. I know that we cannot all be as witty and possessed as you are, my lord. But I do wish that you would concede that point and be more generous of spirit."

Miss Reginald gave one of her tiny smiles. "Oh, Edward, you have found quite the match in this one."

"After the way that you were treated at the dinner table, you have the presence of mind to defend people so?" Lord Reginald asked.

"But of course," Maria replied. "That was only a few of them. It was quite awful and it did wound my pride. I cannot deny that.

"After that, however, I was treated to nothing but the utmost kindness. Those older ladies were so lovely. And the gentlemen were all lovely.

"I am certain that many other young ladies my age would also have been lovely, had I had a chance to meet them. I am not going to condemn everyone simply because of a few.

"Especially," she added, "When some of their remarks were probably justified. I must do better in my deportment."

She was determined in that now. If only because she was a coward and did not wish to be humiliated in such a manner ever again.

She turned to Miss Reginald. "Do you think that I could impose upon you to continue to assist me in this?"

"Of course, sweet girl," Miss Reginald said. She laid her hand gently over Maria's. "This was a good debut, Miss Worthing. I know it might not feel like it. But you are starting a good few years after most girls do. That's all. We shall get you up to snuff in no time."

"I hope so," Lord Reginald said. "I could barely hold in my temper this time."

"I will thank you not to ruin your own reputation by running to my defense," Maria said. It warmed her chest to hear him speak of having a temper when others mistreated her. But it would do neither of them any good if he did so.

"Let Miss Worthing fight her own battles," Miss Reginald replied.

Lord Reginald sighed, sounding very put upon by the idea.

Maria wondered if this was what having an older brother felt like. Of course it did not feel that way on her part. She was quite certain that one should not feel such a thrill in one's stomach around one's brother.

But in Lord Reginald's behavior—surely that was all that it was. He was used to caring for one sister. Why not tack on another while he was at it? That must be what was fueling his protectiveness of her.

Maria could feel her eyes sliding closed despite the jostling of the carriage.

"I told you it was a good time to leave," Miss Reginald said. She sounded amused.

"You were...quite right..." Maria said, stifling another yawn.

She barely remembered getting home and getting into bed. She suspected that Miss Reginald must have helped her.

"It is always so taxing?" she remembered murmuring at one point.

"You will get used to it," Miss Reginald replied. Maria could not see her but she could hear her. Her eyes must have fallen closed again. "Just give yourself time to adjust. You spent quite a lot more energy and stayed up quite a bit later than you are used to."

That was the last thing Maria remembered hearing before falling asleep. But the last thing she thought was that so long as she didn't have to deal with Miss Hennings and her ilk, she might succeed in this season after all.

CHAPTER 8

EDWARD PACED while he waited for Georgiana to come down after tucking Miss Worthing into bed.

"Poor thing," Georgiana said as she entered the room. "She is rather unused to the schedule that a ball demands."

"We must be better prepared next time," Edward told her. "She cannot be allowed to endure what Miss Hennings and the others put her through at dinner."

"I doubt that she shall," Georgiana replied. "She made many allies tonight. Our hostess and the older mothers were smitten with her.

"And the gentlemen were all rather taken with her," Georgiana added. She cast Edward an odd look as she said it, one that he could not decipher.

"Are you certain?" he asked. "They were not merely indulging her out of politeness?"

"Edward, I think that I can safely say that they were genuine in their fondness for her," Georgiana told him. "It was Miss Worthing this and Miss Worthing that while I danced with them afterwards."

"What on earth did she manage to do right during the dancing that she failed during dinner?" Edward wondered aloud.

"I think that it was she was one on one during the dance," Georgiana replied. "And it afforded her a better opportunity to simply listen. You know that she is good at that. She made each man feel special and she truly paid attention to them."

"Still," Edward said. He could not stop pacing. "I want it seen to, I want it known, that Miss Hennings especially is not thought of fondly by our household. And perhaps you can get the list of dinner guests in full from Mrs. Dane. We can identify the others who were so thoughtless and let the same be known."

"Do you not think that is a bit of an overreaction?" Georgiana replied. "Edward, you cannot prevent her from ever being slandered again. She has to learn how to take care of herself. Whether we like it or not.

"I wish that we could simply avoid dealing with such people. And I am not saying that it's fair that she must endure them. But she is going to have to learn how to handle it, either now or later. You cannot always be there to protect her."

Edward knew that she was right, but it still irked him. It was like an itch, deep down inside of his muscle, in his chest where he couldn't scratch at it.

"That may be so. But next time I shall say something."

"Then I hope that it will be something witty and distracting that will change the subject," Georgiana said. "As is appropriate. Rather than perhaps starting a miniature war."

"You say that as if it is a bad thing."

"But it is, Edward. You cannot be so reckless. Think of what will happen if we begin to draw battle lines. People will pick sides. It will become a massive scandal. And for what? Everyone must endure insults, Edward. It is unfortunate but it is the way of the world."

"So you would have me be like Father, then? Play the game of politics and manners? Lie to everyone, pretend to be everyone's friend?"

"That is not what I mean. And you know it." Georgiana's voice and face grew stern. "You can be pleasant without falling into Father's ways of overzealous politics.

"I am not asking you to lie or to betray your nature. I am only asking you to be courteous and to give people the benefit of the doubt.

"You like Miss Worthing's nature quite a lot. I think that most people are like her, underneath all of our posh ways and manners. They just want to be listened to and shown that we care."

Edward thought that perhaps she might have a point, but he could not shake the protective feeling he had for Miss Worthing.

He was worried that the rest of this night had been nothing more than a fluke. There were plenty of mothers who would see Miss Worthing as another bit of competition for their daughters. They would not be so kind to her then.

And there were many men who would behave as Miss Hennings did. Or even, if Miss Hennings and her ilk got to the men before Miss Worthing did, they could turn the men against her.

"I do not believe that our charge is out of the woods yet," he said aloud. "There are many ways in which she might still be hurt. And she must learn to manage herself at dinner."

"I agree," Georgiana replied. "But there is no need to tell her that. Her confidence is fragile enough as it is.

"The dancing at the ball and the kindness of those older women has elated her. But it will not last forever. Especially if you insist upon your little comments and upon forecasting gloom and doom.

"I will prepare her as best I can. But the only way she can truly survive people like Miss Hennings, whether they be a man or a woman, is if she gets practical experience. Only time will foretell how she'll manage."

Edward did not like that prospect.

He was not at all sure where this protectiveness was coming from. He was protective of his sister, of course. What man would not be protective of their sister, especially such a quiet one as his own?

Perhaps it was only that. Miss Worthing was a worried young girl. She tried to hide her worry, of course. She did a good job of acting cheerful. But her father's health and her own mission of marriage by the end of the season both weighed heavily on her mind. He could see it quite plainly.

It was natural that someone would see this young girl and feel for her. Who could not?

Well, he very much knew who could not, but they were people not worth thinking about any longer.

It only made sense that he would feel protective towards her. He dared any man in his position not to feel the same brotherly affection towards such a guileless and honest girl.

Especially one who was not afraid of him.

He had been genuinely impressed with Miss Worthing's ability to speak her mind around him.

Most women would have been far too impressed with his status. But Miss Worthing was not. She tried to be polite, he could see that. She often got this most amusing look on her face after she said something, as if she had only just realized how impertinent her words sounded.

But she never lied to him and she never apologized for having her opinion. She spoke to him as she would speak to probably any man no matter what his ranking in society.

Her worry over her impertinence, he suspected, was one that she would have no matter what his station was. It was not that he was a duke, it was that she strove to be polite.

And he appreciated that deeply.

Of course he should feel protective of her as a result. This was the first woman besides his sister who had spoken to him plainly in years. Especially since he had officially inherited the title.

He knew that it would only be a matter of time until someone or several people persuaded her to keep those opinions bottled up. He just hoped that they would not tramp on her spirit too much. He hoped that she would find a man who would value those opinions and her lack of guile.

"I see that I have lost you in thought again," Georgiana said. She sat down. "But tell me, how was the ball for you? I confess I was too busy helping our Miss Worthing to pay too much attention to how you fared."

Edward sighed, sitting down as well. He wanted to keep pacing but he knew the movement would only continue to stir his frustration and would irritate his sister.

"It was as usual," he said. He tried to keep the bitterness out of his tone, he really did. But he could see by his sister's face that he had not entirely succeeded.

"You must marry," Georgiana said. "Surely there is a lady among them who is thoughtful enough for you. Who is sweet enough of temper."

"I wish that I knew," Edward replied. "I feel as though I cannot truly judge their characters. Everything that I say is agreed with.

Half of them are too shy to even speak to me or look me directly in the eye.

"They spend half of their time simpering and blushing. How am I to judge a woman's character by that?"

"You could always choose a wife based upon her breeding and her looks," Georgiana replied. "Her family name will speak for much."

"I cannot have a wife that is unknown to me," Edward replied. "How am I to entrust my household to her? I am responsible for scores of lands and tenants and servants. I could never leave them in the hands of a woman who has no experience or whom I do not trust."

"I could help."

"You will not always be here, my dear. You will be married yourself someday, God willing."

Georgiana looked sadly down at her hands in her lap. "I do not know about that, Edward."

Edward scoffed, even as a lump formed in his throat that he had to swallow down. "Nonsense. You have good breeding, you're lovely as a flower, you—"

"I have tasted love once, Edward." Georgiana looked up at him, her eyes bright and shining but not with happiness. "I do not know if I can marry someone for whom I do not feel that deep and abiding affection."

"What was it like?" he asked.

He had never talked in detail with Georgiana about her feelings for her former suitor. Such feelings were not spoken of—it was such a delicate matter. All he had known were the facts. And of course Father's opinion of the matter.

But he had never felt such an emotion as was described in books and by poets and playwrights. How did one know? How was one certain?

Georgiana thought for a moment. "People say that you will simply...know, instinctively, when it happens. But that is I think a falsehood.

"I think that it is something that can creep up on you and dump you in the middle before you realize that you had even started on the journey. But other times it is something of which you are aware.

"You meet this person and you think, oh, I could possibly develop an attraction to them. And from there you are aware of every step that you take. Even if you cannot truly prevent those steps from happening.

"Do you know how you feel when you come home at the end of a long day? And you know that there is nothing else waiting for you? There is only tea and the fire and a good book?

"That is what it feels like. Only you get that feeling when you are seeing the person. It's just like coming home. Only you get an extra thrill because you know that they are happy to see you as well.

"It's that feeling of being the most popular person in the room almost? But it's more than that. It's the feeling of...of truly being seen and loved for who you are.

"You simply can't help smiling around that person. You feel rather ridiculous for it. As though all of your feelings are written on your face. It's almost like being a child again in that respect, where you can't control your emotions.

"It's kind of terrifying. And it's exhilarating. I often wonder if it's what being truly drunk is like. But when you know that the other person loves you back...it's the most wonderful feeling in the world."

Georgiana smiled at him, a smile of joy and sadness both.

"It feels like coming home," Edward repeated.

Georgiana nodded. "Yes."

It seemed like a terribly nice feeling to have. "Do you suppose that most people feel that way or grow to feel that way for their partners?"

Georgiana shook her head. "I expect most couples feel a sort of amicable mutual tolerance."

Edward could not hide his grimace. He wanted far more than that.

But how on earth was he supposed to get it?

"I do not understand how I am to find a suitable wife when all they do is show off to me their ribbons and dresses," he admitted. "I find nothing wrong with loving fashion but I need someone who can run an estate. Someone who will be honest with me."

Georgiana sighed. "I wish that I had an answer for you. And I wish that I could assure you that you will find that love. But I can do neither."

"I understand," Edward said, gently taking her hand. "And I wish that I could find someone to make you feel that way again. But you know that—if you choose not to marry, I shall support you."

He could never resent his sister. He had money enough, he could find a way to make sure she was always provided for.

Georgiana squeezed his hand, then released it. "I know my duty. I hope that I shall find someone that I can consider more than tolerable.

"But who knows? Perhaps my purpose in life is to be the old maid who runs your estate for you since you cannot trust your wife."

Edward scowled at her. "Do not predict such things."

Georgiana gave him a small smile. "Whatever you choose—or whomever you choose—I have faith that things will work out."

"I am glad that one of us does," Edward replied.

"Come, perhaps there is at least one that you would think of as a wife. At least in looks?"

Edward sighed. "No, no I do not think so."

"Well, I am on the hunt for a husband for Miss Worthing in any case. Tell me what you look for in a wife, and I can double my efforts."

Edward gave her a fond and playful glare. "I do not need my sister to play matchmaker."

"Ah, but your sister is a woman, and can discuss things with women in such a way that men cannot. I could figure out for you which women you would be most suited to.

"You say that many of these women are too shy to speak with you. Or you suspect that they are only agreeing with you and placating you. Perhaps then they will be less intimidated by me and I can see more of their true natures.

"I am certain that over time as your wife grows used to you that she will grow bolder with you. She will be more comfortable with being her true self around you. And when that time comes you want to be certain that the true character of your wife is one that is compatible with yours. Allow me to help with that."

Edward thought about it. He did not like the idea of using his sister. Goodness knew that she had plenty to worry about already. And she was taking on Miss Worthing as her personal project.

But he had to admit that her logic was sound. She could speak to these women more honestly and receive plain responses. He could not.

And if his wife started out shy or simpering or whatnot, he could trust in his sister's judgment that as time went on she would become more comfortable and her true—and hopefully virtuous—nature would show itself.

"I suppose I could allow you to lend yourself to my aid in such a manner," Edward decided. "But do not tax yourself. You might potentially find a husband. And you must find one for Miss Worthing as well. I do not want you stretching yourself too thin."

Georgiana shook her head. "In helping you, Edward, I could never tax myself. All I want is to see you happy. If I can help with that, then it is my pleasure."

Edward hoped that she was right then, and women would be themselves around her. He hoped that if any of them pretended to be better or different than they were that she would see through them.

After all, he was making little headway. And he had to marry soon. He had to produce an heir.

He went up to bed, and as he did so he passed the landing that led to Miss Worthing's set of rooms.

He sighed. It appeared that the both of them had an uneasy task ahead of them.

With a bit of luck, perhaps they would both come out the other side the happier for it.

CHAPTER 9

MARIA WORKED HARD over the next few days to try and elevate herself to the level of the other people she would see at the balls.

She wasn't entirely sure how well she succeeded.

For example, Lord Reginald and Miss Reginald kindly took her to the theatre one evening. What Maria hadn't realized was that going to the theatre was just as social as going to a ball.

They had their own box, which was lovely. She greatly enjoyed the play itself.

But before the show, and during the intermissions, and after the show, they had to speak to people.

Maria was consistently asked things like, "How do you not know this actress? She is quite famous." Or she was laughed at for mistranslating a French phrase in the play and therefore misunderstanding one of the jokes.

She was trying her best but she simply could not seem to win no matter what she did.

When she expressed her enthusiasm for the play, she was treated as though she was a child for being so energetic about it.

"Yes, I suppose that the lead actor was rather good," replied one gentleman when she gushed about the performance. "But this was one of his better nights. You ought to follow him in the papers, my dear. He's known for disappointing audiences. I wonder at them keeping him around."

Maria didn't know what to say to something like that. The man was insulting the actor but who was she to say if he was right or wrong? She didn't know. It was his condescending tone towards her that hurt the most. As if it was somehow her fault for not knowing everything about what was going on in the theatre company.

When she expressed admiration for the costumes, she got laughs. And not kind laughs, either.

What on earth was she supposed to do?

Lord Reginald, she could tell, still disliked how she was being treated. There were a few moments where she could see his jaw clenching so hard, she thought he might crack his teeth.

But he respected both her wishes and the wishes of his sister and did not cause a scene by leaping to Maria's defense.

She did wish that his actions would not warm her heart so much. How was she to find a husband if her thoughts kept turning to him?

Perhaps she should have realized it sooner. But she had never felt such a sensation before. She had not even had a true, girlish crush on any man. Beyond the passing fancy of thinking *oh, that one is handsome*, there had been no securing of her affections by anyone.

And so it hit her with quite a great deal of surprise and pain when she realized that she was in love with Lord Reginald.

It was at another ball. They had not gone to the dinner beforehand for they were attending a musical concert and therefore would arrive too late to partake. But they had come while the dancing was still in full swing.

Lord Reginald was escorting her into the room along with his sister as was proper. She knew that she shouldn't read into his escorting her and she didn't. She knew that it was his duty since her father was unable to.

But she was unable to banish the pleasure of entering the room with him. Of knowing that everyone could see them enter together.

Not in the manner of being pleased to be seen with a duke. She did not care for his title. She cared that he was a good and honest man. A charming and handsome one as well. The kind of man any woman would want to be seen entering a room with.

Then he had moved on to speak to some old acquaintances of his. Maria had looked around for someone that she knew. Mrs. Dale or Mrs. Rutlage, perhaps.

As she had done so she had necessarily turned around to look at all corners of the room. She had seen, therefore, how the women had flocked to Lord Reginald like a magnet.

She saw him bow to them and smile—that charming smile that made her breath catch in her throat. She felt childish for thinking so but in her mind that was how charming princes in fairy tales ought to smile.

He was clearly telling some entertaining anecdote or other. She could see how easily he commanded everyone's attention.

And he thought that women were only after him for his title and money? Did he not see what he was to them? How he fulfilled the secret romantic fantasies that all women had of a charming, handsome, honorable man who would take care of them and worship them like they deserved?

He even looked the part with his lovely suit. Maria could only stand and watch as if rooted to the spot.

And then she had thought—or realized, rather—that she would never be one of those women.

She never could be. For she already owed him so much. He and his sister had taken her in and treated her as family. Who was she to then steal more of his time? To go up to him and hang about him like those ladies did?

He was to marry one of them, anyway. A sophisticated woman with better family and heritage than Maria had.

It felt the way that she imagined being struck by lightning felt— in the worst possible sense of the metaphor.

She wanted to be back at his side. She wanted all those other women to stay away or engage him in conversation only as a friend. She wanted everyone to know that they belonged together. That she was his and he was hers.

She wanted to be the one that he married.

Oh, she would be such a good wife, or she would at least try. She knew how to run an estate. It was not so different from a plantation. Miss Reginald had been going over it with her, using the duchy as an example.

"You will not find an estate nearly so complicated as ours," Miss Reginald had told her. "And I know these accounts. So we will use those as your instruction so that you might be fully prepared when you are married."

She knew how to run it all. She'd make sure he never had reason to take it all in hand or to panic. She would read books to him or let him read books to her. She could soothe his aches after a long day of riding or tramping around his lands to check on the tenants.

She would do everything in her power to make him happy. She knew that she would. And in making him happy, she would be happy.

But he did not want a drab girl such as her. She was too tan. Too plain. Too honest and boorish in her manner. She hardly knew how to survive a ball. How could she be the gracious hostess and society woman that he would need?

No, he could never want a girl such as herself. He looked at her as a little sister. His protectiveness and thoughtfulness were lovely, but she was the one making them something romantic. That was all on her.

Maria could only hope fervently that he never found out about her feelings. That would surely embarrass him. And then he would seek to speak with her about it. To turn her down properly. Because he was honest and considerate that way.

Oh, the thought made her throat seize up as if she were about to cry.

She was hopelessly stuck. She was in love with a man who could never love her back.

The balls were less enjoyable after that. She couldn't help but keep Lord Reginald in the corner of her vision. It was as though she were attached to him somehow by a string or a magnet. She always seemed to be aware of where he was.

And wherever Lord Reginald was, his admirers were not far behind.

She was certain that she was the only person other than his sister who could see how weary the women around him made him.

He was charming, of course. He laughed at their jokes. He would make jokes of his own. But Maria could see the way his jaw would get more clenched as the evening went on. The way that his arms would grow gradually stiffer at his sides. How he would initiate conversations or share his own jokes less and less.

They wore him out. And Maria wanted nothing more than to shoo them all away. To tell them that he was done for the night and to take him home to rest.

But of course she had no right to that. And he had to stay. Both because of his position in society and in his mission to find a wife. But it felt so terribly unfair to him.

And unfair to her, to have to watch him go through this. But she knew that was all on her. He had not asked her to fall in love with him.

She had to suffer in silence. She could not impose her feelings upon him. And what could she possibly offer him as a wife?

Maria liked to think that she would emotionally support him. That she would be a good wife to him. But what about her family? Her wealth? There were other women who had far more to commend them in that aspect. And that was what Lord Reginald had to think about.

She tried to find interest in other men. Truly she did. But she found that she kept searching in them for qualities that Lord Reginald possessed. She was straining to hear his laugh in theirs. To see his eyes, his smile, in their faces.

At least it was good to have a yardstick, she supposed. Something by which she could measure how well a man would do for her.

She thought of what she liked in Lord Reginald. There was his charm and wit, of course. But she also liked his honesty and his forthrightness. She appreciated that he cared so much about his estate and his tenants. She liked that he preferred a quiet evening with books and conversation to balls.

Although she did enjoy the balls, she also found them no less exhausting. Miss Reginald assured her that she would not have to attend so many once she was married.

"It is only when you are seeking to find a husband that you will need to go to as many as you can," she had explained.

But Maria thought that a quiet evening of cards and reading was preferable to balls. Lord Reginald seemed to think so as well.

She needed to find a man who possessed those qualities, she

thought, if she had even a hope of being happy with him as her future husband.

But until then—until she could replace Lord Reginald in her heart with someone else—the balls just made her unhappy. She could see how unfit she was to be a potential bride. But she couldn't stop her heart from wanting him.

That particular night, it felt like too much. Lord Reginald was laughing at something that one young lady had said. Maria knew that it was probably exaggerated. He was always exaggerating how amused he was by a lady so as not to insult them.

But she couldn't stop the pang in her heart all the same.

As the dance ended, she asked her partner to please escort her to the ladies' room so that she might freshen up.

She hoped for a moment of privacy, a place to acknowledge her sorrow and then move on from it.

A bit of water to her face and neck helped to cool her down and make it look less like she was upset. A glance in the mirror reminded her of what she was: as good as nobody.

Her dress was nice. It was a lovely pale pink color, almost white. White dresses in this cut were quite in fashion at the moment. But Miss Reginald had told her never to copy the fashion exactly. And so she had dressed herself in the palest peach and Maria in the palest pink, but had both dresses follow the popular cut.

She thought she looked nice in it. At least until she saw how all the other ladies were dressed.

Then she was reminded that she was nothing more than a drab sparrow trying to dress up in the peacock's feathers.

"Get a hold of yourself," Maria told her reflection. "Nobody likes a girl who mopes."

She must be the life of the party if she was to convince a man to marry her.

As she exited the room, she nearly ran smack into Miss Hennings.

She had a distinct suspicion that this was not a coincidence.

Over the past few balls the young lady had made every effort to cause Maria to feel miserable and out of place. She would have thought that such behavior was above a lady of her own and Miss Hennings' age. Perhaps a girl of fifteen could get away with being callous and small-minded but a lady of eighteen or so ought to be more mature and compassionate than that.

Miss Hennings clearly did not care. Maria suspected that it was as the older ladies had told her: that she was envious of how much time Maria got to spend with Lord Reginald.

The Countess of Wistershire had confided in Maria at a previous ball that Miss Hennings was set upon marrying Lord Reginald.

"Her family are all ambitious like that," the Countess had said. "They must be encouraging her. She will settle for nothing less than the richest and most titled man she can lay her hands on. And right now, that is your lord."

Maria did not know how to tell the Countess, or anyone, that Lord Reginald was the farthest thing from 'her' lord. But the older ladies all insisted upon calling him that when referencing him to her.

It was rather embarrassing. She wasn't at all sure what they meant by that. Or by the significant looks they would give when Lord Reginald would come find her to dance with her.

He always gave her one dance a night. It was only expected of him, given their acquaintance and that she was in a way his unofficial ward, living under his roof.

But he did not have to dance with her. It was a great kindness, and certainly helped to keep her social status up.

He would always check in with her while they danced. He would ask if she had eaten and drunk enough. Made sure she was not too cold, offered to fetch her shawl if she was—"for I know this climate does not agree with your Caribbean sensibilities"—asked her if everyone was being kind to her.

In short, he would make sure that she was all right. He seemed genuinely concerned for her. As if she would have been eaten by wolves the moment that his back was turned.

But while it was kind and she treasured each moment spent with him, it was nothing more than his duty. He had promised her father that he would take care of her. And that was precisely what he was doing.

She couldn't see it as anything more than that. That way lay madness.

But now as she exited the ladies' room she was staring into the pale, smooth face of Miss Hennings.

That Miss Hennings was beautiful, Maria had no doubts. She had lovely dark blonde hair and wide blue eyes. Her skin was pale and smooth and rather like china in that it gave the impression of being glazed and fragile. It was a look that suited her. She had a fine figure, and a lovely smile when she was being flirtatious.

Right now, however, that smile was sharp and ugly. Like a rat.

"What a coincidence that we should run into each other at this moment!" she said. "I was just talking about you with some other young ladies."

Maria forced herself to smile. "Oh?"

Miss Hennings looked her up and down, then shook her head and clucked her tongue. "My dear, you really must learn to control your facial expressions better."

The term of endearment, which she so loved to hear from her father and Miss Reginald, sounded condescending and insulting when said by Miss Hennings.

Maria didn't respond to that. "Don't give them any ammunition," Lord Reginald and the various older ladies of her acquaintance had told her.

"Pretend that it doesn't matter," Lord Reginald had said. "That it does not affect you."

Maria forced herself to keep smiling. "Would you be so kind as to move out of the way?"

"Are you not curious to know why we were talking about you?" Miss Hennings asked, her voice falsely innocent. "I should be dying to know if it were me."

"We are two very different people then," Maria replied.

Miss Hennings' smile grew. "Yes, we are. You see, we were just discussing how dignified Lord Reginald is. How well he handles himself. Living with a young lady who has such an embarrassing crush on him, well. He bears it with a grace and dignity that not many men could achieve."

It felt as though all the air had gone out of the room, as if her corset had tightened by ten inches.

Was she really so obvious? Did everyone know? Did everyone see?

Miss Hennings' eyes blazed with triumph and Maria knew that she had not managed to keep her dismay from showing on her face.

"As I said, you really must learn to hide your emotions better. The poor man must feel quite uncomfortable. But he is bearing up rather well, we all think. It cannot be the first time that a young lady has fallen for him so obscenely. Even if said young lady is from such a...wild and unsuitable background."

Maria wanted to draw herself up and protest that her background was perfectly suitable. She was a gentleman's daughter. What more could possibly be asked for? She had been raised to the best of her parents' abilities. How could a word be said against either of them?

"But in any case, I hope that you know better than to do anything about your feelings," Miss Hennings went on. "It would only bring about humiliation for you."

She tilted her head and her expression grew soft. If Maria didn't know any better, she'd say that Miss Hennings looked genuinely concerned for her.

"He is never going to want you, my dear. He wants and needs someone sophisticated. Someone who knows the art of a witty conversation. Someone who was brought up in this world and understands it. Someone who will be able to help him navigate these balls. Someone who has a grasp on the politics."

She smirked. "Someone, Miss Worthing, who is in short the antithesis of you."

Maria almost wanted to applaud the woman for her audacity, for being so bold as to openly insult her.

Miss Hennings swept past her into the ladies' room, evidently deciding that the conversation was over and that Maria was not worth taking the time for an official farewell.

Maria all but stumbled back out to the ball. She felt quite in a daze.

Miss Hennings had just been unforgivably rude to her. And how! She had to know that she couldn't get away with such behavior.

Except that she had. Maria had just let the woman walk all over her. Perhaps such rudeness would not be acceptable in general but

Miss Hennings must have realized that Maria would be too shocked and hurt to fight back.

Maria excused herself, pleading exhaustion, and found a quiet corner in which to sit down.

She just wanted to burst into tears. Surely if these ladies had all noticed it then Lord Reginald had noticed it too. She felt heartbroken. Oh, he must be so embarrassed. Everyone must be laughing at her—and at him by extension.

But how could she even be all that angry with Miss Hennings? While her delivery was cruel, her opinion was correct.

Maria could never be what Lord Reginald wanted or needed. He needed someone closer to Miss Hennings.

Well, not someone with such a cruel temperament.

But someone with her knowledge of London society. Someone who could deftly compliment or insult with subtlety in order to take control of a conversation. Someone who could truly handle, with grace, the social responsibilities of a duke's wife.

Maria could not be that person. She'd been barely getting by at the balls as it was.

It only solidified for her as well the fact that everyone was laughing at her behind her back. She had thought as much. She was not stupid.

She knew that while she was getting better at dinner—mostly by not saying anything—and the men seemed to enjoy talking to her while she danced, she was far from ideal in her manner.

But to have it confirmed. To know that she was being laughed at. That everyone was talking of her with such pity...

Perhaps Lord Reginald was right all along. Perhaps society was nothing more than a bunch of selfish people making sport out of one another.

Maria wanted to bury her face in her hands. But she had to get back out there. Somebody would notice she was missing soon. She had to...

Her dark corner was infiltrated. For a wild moment she thought it was Miss Hennings, come to gloat some more.

Then she saw that it was not a woman, but a man. And of course the one man she most empathetically could not handle seeing at that moment.

Lord Reginald walked over to her. "Miss Worthing? Are you quite all right?"

She didn't dare test her voice, so she simply nodded.

Lord Reginald shook his head. "I can tell when you're lying, you know. You're quite dreadful at it."

"I shall try and do better then," she replied. If her heart was being worn so violently on her sleeve then perhaps she might benefit from some lessons in lying.

"I hope not," Lord Reginald replied. "Your honesty is possibly the thing that I admire most about you."

She gave him a small smile, unable to help herself at the praise.

"There it is," Lord Reginald said, smiling. "That's much better."

Maria immediately felt herself blushing and looked away. "You ought to be dancing," she said. "I'm sure that there are many ladies in need of a partner."

"Including yourself," Lord Reginald said. "Why are you hiding yourself away? Are you out of partners?"

"No," Maria replied. True, there was no one listed as next on her dance card, but she had not had it properly filled out anyway. She was fairly sure she would have been asked to do this next dance had she not hidden herself. Most of the other women had dispensed with their dance cards that evening as well.

"Then what is the matter?"

"Nothing is the matter."

"Yes, because lively girls who love dancing such as yourself take to hiding in dark corners for no reason."

She glared at him, only to find him smiling playfully at her. "You make jest of me."

"Of course, when you make yourself such an easy target for it. Come now, Miss Worthing." He offered her his arm. "Why don't we take the next dance. It will help to liven up your spirits."

Usually it would, but now dancing with Lord Reginald only promised to remind her of her humiliation and why she was so distressed in the first place.

Lord Reginald sensed her hesitance, for he took a small step closer. "Why not just a turn about the room then?"

"I suppose."

He sighed. "Miss Worthing, I am your escort. It is my duty—and one that I take great joy in—to look after you. Has anyone distressed you? Has any man taken liberties?"

Maria shook her head. "Nothing like that, I assure you. I should be in a much worse state, I think, if it were something as bad as all that."

"Well there is something."

Seeing that there was no way to get rid of him, she took his arm and allowed him to guide her in a turn about the room.

"There we are. We'll have a small chat about what is troubling you, and then it will be time for the next dance and you can be as lively as you please."

She wished that he were not so kind to her. His kindness only made it all worse. And did he know? He must know, if Miss Hennings and those other girls did.

But just in case, to preserve what remained of her dignity, she did not tell him the full story.

"It is only that I ran into a lady on my way out of the ladies' room," she explained. "And she said some rather distressing things."

She saw his jaw clench for a moment, and felt his arm tighten in hers. "What sort of things?"

"That I would never fit in. That I could not understand London society."

"I think that is a commendable thing," the duke replied.

"Is it? When I am making a fool of myself, or near enough to one, every night that I am out?"

"You will get better at that with time," he replied.

"It certainly does not feel like it."

"You have had a late start, that is all. You ought to have seen my sister when she was fifteen. I thought she would die of embarrassment at all the mistakes she made. She once stepped on the foot of another duke, did you know?"

"I did not know," Maria confessed.

"She is very dignified now. And well she deserves that dignity. But before she worked on all of that she was as jittery and nervous as you are. I suspect that all women start out that way."

Maria wasn't sure what to make of that. If nothing else it told her that Lord Reginald certainly thought of her as a younger sister. He equated her to a woman many years her junior in her behavior.

He would never love her as she loved him.

"May I ask who this lady was?" Lord Reginald asked.

"I would not wish to disclose her name. That is too close to gossip for me."

"I suspect that I already know who it is," the duke replied grimly. "But I appreciate your wish to protect their identity."

"If only because I know that you would go out of your way to be rude to her."

"You know me too well at this point, Miss Worthing."

He smiled at her fondly. Maria tried to be content with that. Even if he only looked at her as one would a sister, it was still fondness, was it not? Was that not something to be happy about?

She would just have to change her behavior so that he didn't find out her true feelings, and content herself with that.

CHAPTER 10

EDWARD WAS GOING TO—WELL, not kill Miss Hennings, of course not. But he was going to do something.

If only he could figure out what that something was.

Miss Worthing obviously could not see herself. She thought that she could fool him into thinking she was all right.

But if only she had seen her own face, she would have known how impossible that was to lie about.

She had looked devastated. As though someone had kicked a puppy in front of her.

Miss Worthing wouldn't say the name of the woman who had said such cruel things to her. But he knew. Who else would have the audacity?

He walked with her around the room, making witty observations about the men and women they saw. He told a few embarrassing stories about some of the men that he considered friends and would go out riding or shooting with.

It was a larger ballroom, and by the time they had circled it, Miss Worthing was in much better spirits.

She wasn't quite up to her usual standards. She was not laughing so easily and her gaze darted about the ballroom as though she was paranoid. She was probably trying to see where Miss Hennings was, Edward thought.

But she was no longer looking as though she might burst into tears. That was good.

He wished that they were of a relationship that he might hug her and hold her for a moment. She could cry on his shoulder and let it all out.

But propriety had to be remembered. He supposed that the poor girl would have to cry into her pillow that night. Or perhaps to his sister—he would tell Georgiana of what had happened. She could comfort Miss Worthing in a way that he could not.

When they had finished circling the room the dance ended. Almost at once another young man was at their side, asking if he might have the pleasure of Miss Worthing's company for the next dance.

Edward let her go with a surprising amount of reluctance on his part. Miss Worthing seemed resigned to dance again, if not up to her usual eagerness.

How could someone be so small-minded and selfish as to take another person's joy away for the evening?

He immediately sought out his sister.

Georgiana was sitting with some older ladies and chatting. His sister was far too selfless by half. She ought to be making sure that her dance card was full for the evening. Instead, she was letting the younger women dance when there was a shortage of men. As if her need to marry was not more dire than theirs with her older age.

"Might I steal my sister away for a brief moment, good ladies?" he asked, bowing and giving his most charming smile.

The other ladies all smiled back at him, especially the ones with eligible daughters.

"Excuse me," Georgiana said. "I won't be but a moment."

She allowed Edward to lead her away so that they might stand where they could observe the dancing.

"I suspect that Miss Worthing will be in need of some tea and womanly comfort tonight," Edward told her. "She was greatly distressed a short bit ago."

"I noticed that she had vanished from the hall. Was something wrong?"

"Nothing too dire. That is, her virtue was not impressed upon. Nor was it news of her father." That had been the other thing Edward had worried about when he'd seen Miss Worthing hiding away in a dark corner. "A young lady, whom she will not name, came up to her in the powder room. The lady told her that she would never fit in here and to give up trying."

"I suspect that you know who this lady is even if Miss Worthing would not name her."

"Who else could it be besides Miss Hennings? Who else do we know who is so tactless and thoughtless in her manner? Who else is so envious of anyone else who might spend time with me when there is no reason? I would not have her, with or without Miss Worthing's presence."

"She does not see it that way."

Edward made a scathing noise. "Well she will be made to see it that way. I aim to present her with a piece of my mind."

"Edward, please don't. She will only take her anger out on Miss Worthing since she cannot risk taking it out on you."

His sister was right, but it didn't mean that the anger inside of him abated.

"I only wish that there was some way to protect her."

"I know. I shall take her aside when we get home after the ball. A nice cup of tea and a good cry will be exactly what she needs.

"But she must find a way to toughen up. She is not the only girl who has had to go through such a situation. Nor is Miss Hennings the only lady who will ever treat her in that manner.

"It is not so important what they do. For there will always be people, men and women, like Miss Hennings. What is important is how we react to them."

Edward sighed. Georgiana gave him a shrewd look. "That is not just a lesson for Miss Worthing. You would do well to listen to my words as well. You allow yourself to get far too worked up. You only see the negative.

"People will notice that. And they will notice that they can easily get your ire up. You must learn to see the positive in others and remain calm."

Edward sighed. He watched as Miss Worthing danced with her partner. She seemed to be listening to what he said but with less attentiveness than usual.

Perhaps she was still upset. He ought to get her a glass of wine. That would help to calm her nerves.

"Are you even listening to me, Edward?" Georgiana asked.

He drew his thoughts away from Miss Worthing. "Yes, my dear sister, as always."

"Good, then perhaps you will actually implement my advice this time."

"Only if you implement my advice and actually attempt to dance. I am happy to keep you on in my house as a spinster but I have hope for you yet in marriage."

"You are far too hopeful when it comes to me and far too despairing when it comes to yourself. Perhaps you ought to switch those around."

Edward made a face at her. In some ways they were still like children together. Teasing one another and dropping propriety in order to be playful.

The dance was ending. "I shall go and dance with Miss Worthing and make certain that she is all right. Find yourself a partner."

"I wasn't aware I had joined the army and was under orders," Georgiana replied.

Edward did not bother to send her a response but instead made his way through the crowd in order to secure Miss Worthing for the dance before someone else did.

How could she not see that she was becoming popular? It was like watching the transformation of the swan into the princess in *Swan Lake*, only in extremely slow motion.

Every ball that they went to there were more people from the previous balls who were happy to see her. The older ladies that she had befriended had spoken to all of their children who were now befriending her. The men that she had danced with before had told their friends about her.

Word was spreading about her. Which was a good thing, Edward told himself. She ought to be popular. She ought to feel appreciated.

That was part of why Miss Hennings had said something, he was sure. Not only because she wanted to convince Edward to propose to her and saw Miss Worthing as a threat in that regard.

It was also because she was seeing Miss Worthing's popularity with everyone climbing. She was finding Miss Worthing a threat not just in regards to one man but in regards to her entire social circle.

It showed, at least in Edward's mind, the true cowardice of the young lady. To tear another person down in order to build someone else up showed just how little faith that person had in their own natural abilities to be liked and counted on based upon their own merits.

He stopped in front of Miss Worthing, who seemed surprised to see him.

"We haven't had our dance yet for the evening," he told her. "And I thought you might need a little respite. We need not talk at all during this dance if you prefer."

Miss Worthing took his arm and let him lead her to the dance floor. "You don't have to pretend to be cheerful for me, Miss Worthing, if you are still in distress. I know how hard it is to feign happiness when one is in distress."

He had had to do that twice. Once when his mother had died, and again when his father had passed. Everyone had given their condolences. They had not expected him to be too cheerful.

But then when he tried to turn down ball and dinner invitations people acted surprised. They would tease him or chastise him when he was quiet or not engaging.

In short, he had been told that they respected his mourning. But then they had not truly done so in their actions. Nobody wanted to be around someone who was melancholy of spirit.

When people would behave in such a manner when it came to a person in mourning, then he was certain that people would have little patience for the hurt feelings of a woman bullied at a party.

Miss Worthing looked at him gratefully—but also, he imagined, a little guiltily.

She was probably upset that she was taking him away from the other women. And thinking that she would be bullied more because of it.

"Don't worry," he told her, leading her out onto the dance floor. "Our little dance is practically a tradition at this point, don't you think?"

Miss Worthing's lips quirked upwards at that and Edward felt a rush of warmth and triumph at having made her smile, even for the barest moment.

"Now," he told her, "you don't have to say anything. You can just dance."

Some people might have thought that conversation would help someone get over such an awful event as being talked to as Miss Worthing had been. But Edward suspected that would be too much to ask of her in that moment. Asking her to listen and pay attention to something was more than she could handle.

So instead, they danced in silence.

It wasn't an unpleasant silence. It was quite comfortable, actually. Dancing was a chance to converse. Nearly every moment that a man got with a lady was a chance for them to converse in order to get to know one another better.

The aim, of course, being to figure out if the person was someone you wanted to marry, of course.

But there was value, Edward thought, in being able to quietly share space with someone and have it not be awkward.

They moved through the dance, and as promised, he didn't say anything. Occasionally one of the men or women from the other partners would include him in their conversation and he would speak to them briefly. But that was all.

It was as alone as Miss Worthing could get without disappearing into a corner again.

As the dance went on, she kept herself quiet. She seemed very lost in her own thoughts except for when her gaze darted around as if to see who was watching. Edward wished that there was something he could say to allay her fears and concerns.

The time of silence that the dance lasted for was actually quite nice. He appreciated it. He could enjoy the dance and focus on the movement of it without conversation distracting him.

Miss Worthing actually danced very well, he realized. He had known it objectively, of course. He had been the one with whom she had practiced and learned the new steps from his sister.

But now he got to witness how truly graceful she had become at it. She was energetic, but the energy was contained. Lovely. Every movement was planned and executed with perfection.

The previous times he had danced with her he had been

engrossed in conversing with her. He had been trying to make her laugh or had been laughing at her in turn. This was entirely new to realize and pay attention to.

She did look rather lovely in her dress tonight as well. The pale pink of it brought out the natural color in her cheeks and contrasted well with her dark eyes and thick dark hair.

Edward dared to say, at least in his own mind, that she was beautiful. She had been pretty enough when she had first come to stay with them. But now with help from his sister in learning how to do up her hair and wear dresses that flattered her in color and fit, it brought out all that had originally been hidden.

It was no wonder that she never needed to sit down at these dances. What man in his right mind would let the evening pass without asking for a dance with her?

Edward felt an irrational pang of jealousy at the thought of someone else dancing with Miss Worthing. That someone else thought of her as beautiful and sought to do something about that thought.

But why should he be jealous?

It was nothing more than concern over the girl. That was all. There were many rakes out there and in some ways Miss Worthing was still naïve about how low some people would stoop.

He was in charge of her. He had promised her father that he would take care of her. That he would guide her and keep her safe. That was all. He was merely upholding that promise.

After spending so much time with the girl, was it not natural that he develop a strong affection for her?

He should be counting his blessings that she was such a pleasant girl and he had not instead found himself with a great dislike for her.

Miss Worthing did seem to raise herself up in spirit as the dance went on. He performed a few steps with an extra flourish, which earned him a wider smile. Color returned to her cheeks and warmth returned to her eyes.

By the time the dance ended, he thought that he could see new resolution in her eyes.

"There you are," he told her, as they bowed and curtsied to

signal the end of the dance. "It is good to have you back in your natural spirits, Miss Worthing."

Miss Worthing smiled at him, blushing a little. She did blush rather easily, he had noticed. It felt as though everything he said was bringing color to her cheeks. The poor girl was not at all used to people paying her attention.

"I am glad to see you think so, my lord," she replied.

"Off you go then," he told her, ignoring the stab of odd jealousy in his gut. "I suspect that far more enticing suitors than myself await you."

Miss Worthing curtsied again, smiling at his jest, and allowed another young man to come up and ask her for the next dance.

Edward wished that he could continue to dance with her. He had been so entranced by her movements and by watching her face that the dance had seemed to last scarcely ten minutes.

But asking a woman to dance a second time was a huge sign of favoritism. Especially at a ball such as this when there were plenty of women sitting down who deserved a turn on the dance floor.

To play favorites in such a way was to play with fire. Many people would take it as a sign of a proposal coming soon. Of course, the idea of proposing to Miss Worthing was absurd. It was only that he wanted to spend more time with her.

He paused. That...that thought did not sound quite right in his head.

Before he could examine it further, another young gentleman of his acquaintance was approaching him with three young ladies in tow.

Edward sighed. No doubt one of the ladies or all three wanted to dance with him and had impressed upon his acquaintance to make them known to one another.

As he gave himself over to the attentions of the three ladies, he could not help but keep an eye out for Miss Worthing.

She seemed to be enjoying herself more after that dance with him. She was moving with more energy and conversing easily with her partner as she usually did.

Why then did his stomach feel so oddly hollow?

"My lord," said one of the ladies, and he turned back to show her he was listening to her ramble about place settings and some not-so-subtle hints about what a lovely hostess she would make when she was married.

He would pursue the odd thought that had been in his head later. When he was safely back at home and away from all of this...rabble.

CHAPTER 11

MARIA HAD NEVER BEEN SO grateful for Miss Reginald to tell her it was time for them to depart.

They bid goodbye to everyone and climbed into the carriage.

"Thank the Lord," Lord Reginald muttered. "I feel as though I cannot even breathe."

Other than his one remark it was an oddly silent carriage ride. Maria was wrapped up in her own thoughts, but so it seemed were Lord Reginald and his sister as well.

They pulled up to the house and Lord Reginald hurried out. It was as if he wanted to put as much space between himself and the ladies as possible.

Be honest with yourself, Maria thought. He wants to put space between himself and you.

He must know, then. He had to know, after that dance.

That kind, lovely dance he had given her. No talking, no obligations. She could give herself over to the movement and the music. It was just what she needed. She'd been struggling still even after their little walk and talk.

And it had been surprisingly comfortable. She had not felt at all awkward despite not speaking a word the entire time. It was as if they were simply able to exist in one another's space and that was enough.

He had made her smile a few times. She had known that he was doing it on purpose. Making himself look a bit of a fool in order to get her to laugh. It was sweet of him and only made her love him more.

All of her emotions must have been laid out in her face and her eyes for him to see. How could he not know after so much time? How could he possibly be unaware?

No, he had realized when he saw her during the dance. When he looked into her eyes and saw her breathless gratitude. He had to have realized then.

Now he was desperately trying to put space between them.

She could not blame him.

Miss Reginald guided her out of the carriage. What surprised her was that she then accompanied Maria to her bedroom and rang for tea to be brought up there with some biscuits.

"My brother told me that you have had a difficult night," she said, sitting down on the bed. "Go on, change into your nightshift. Then we shall have some tea and talk about it."

Miss Reginald changed as well while Maria did. It felt odd to see the other woman in just her nightgown. Miss Reginald always seemed so poised and put together. For her to be wearing such casual clothing with her hair done only in a braid...it was odd, but not unpleasantly so.

It was how one might be with a sister, Maria thought. Casual and intimate.

"Now," Miss Reginald said. "We have our tea. We have our sweets. We are comfortable. Tell me what happened."

Maria looked at her. "Do you promise me that you shall not tell your brother?"

"I certainly shall not tell him. It is an easy promise. What is said between two close friends is sacred."

Maria was still nervous. What if Miss Reginald thought her ungrateful and thought she had designs upon her brother? What if she was upset with her?

But she couldn't keep the whole story to herself.

And so she told her everything. Including that it was Miss Hennings.

"Please, do not do anything to her. I hate that I am sharing her name, only it is that I must tell someone or I shall burst."

"It is perfectly all right," Miss Reginald soothed her.

She drew Maria in and laid Maria's head on her shoulder, stroking her hair.

It was so similar to how Mother had treated her that Maria couldn't help it. She began to cry.

"Oh, my dear girl!" Miss Reginald got the food and drink out of the way. "It's all right, darling. You just cry it out."

"I promise I make no presumptions," Maria said through her tears. "I did not mean to have feelings for him. And I know that it is not my place to have them. It is only my embarrassment at people knowing."

"It is rather humiliating," Miss Reginald agreed, "when everyone knows how you feel and can say what they like about it. Even though their opinions ultimately do not matter, it still stings.

"But you must remember that, Miss Worthing. The only opinion that matters in this is my brother's, if he is aware of your feelings. Nobody else's opinion does. People will always gossip and say what they like. It is only up to you what you can do about it."

She stroked Maria's hair for another few moments, then pressed the tea back into Maria's hands. "Drink up."

"You would make a very good mother," Maria confessed.

"I hope that I shall have the chance one day," Miss Reginald replied.

There was another pause, and then she added, "Whether you and my brother ever come to an understanding or not, I hope that you will call me Georgiana from now on."

Maria nearly spilled her tea. "Do you mean that? You are not saying it simply because I am upset?"

"No, dear girl. I'm saying it because I want you to know that you have someone always in your corner."

"I would like it very much then if you would call me Maria."

"It is a lovely name, I shall be happy to call you by it."

They drank and ate in silence for a little while. As with Lord Reginald, it was a comfortable silence.

"He does not know," Georgiana said at last. "My brother is an intelligent and educated man. But he can sometimes be dreadfully unobservant.

"Furthermore, I suspect that your feelings are not so transparent as you fear. I believe that Miss Hennings made a guess, and found in speaking to you that her guess was correct."

"I am sorry to have proven her right then," Maria said.

Georgiana smiled at her. "That is what it is important to learn. You must act as though it does not affect you."

"It would be easier if I had more wit."

"That will come with time."

But Maria knew that Lord Reginald was a witty man. A clever one as well.

If he truly did not know of her feelings, and Georgiana really did not mind...and he was a man of honor and family name and wealth. She could not do better than him.

And it would please her father greatly to be married to the son of his childhood best friend, would it not?

Perhaps if she made an effort to be clever and witty like everyone else. If she showed that she could navigate the world of society as well as any other lady who'd been born to it. Perhaps then she might have a chance at winning over Lord Reginald.

She looked at Georgiana. "You would not object," she said slowly, "if we were to become sisters?"

Georgiana smiled at her. It was one of the warmest smiles that Maria had ever seen from her, despite how small it still was. "I feel as though you are my sister already.

"It is not my place to take sides or judge whom my brother chooses to marry. But if I were to pick someone...if I am plain, then yes. I should like it to be you.

"But that is up to him. I will not sway him one way or another on the subject."

"I would not ask you to," Maria assured her. "I only wished to know that you would approve if it did come to pass. I would not want to do anything that would make you unhappy. I value your opinion above nearly all others."

"And you value my brother's the most, I presume," Georgiana said shrewdly.

Maria found herself blushing again. "Yes. I must confess to that."

Georgiana sighed. "He is a good man. And I do think that you two would balance one another out. He would teach you to be more aware and wary in social situations. You would teach him how to relax and see the best in people.

"But he is a stubborn man, my dear. He does not always see what is right in front of his face. If you are to make a grab for him, truly and earnestly, you must be prepared for that.

"And you must especially be prepared for the other ladies. They will see you doing it. As will their mothers. They all already watch you as a hawk watches a mouse. They will not stand for it.

"If you think that Miss Hennings is being difficult now, she will become even worse if she sees that you have gone from merely being in his company to actively pursuing him. And she is not the only one.

"Are you prepared for such a thing? Are you truly prepared for the fight that you will find yourself in?

"I ask you not to deter you. I only want you to make sure that you are ready. I would not wish for you to jump into the fray and be hurt because you did not expect what was coming.

"You might find it preferable to go after another man after all. One who is not so titled or rich or handsome. He will be easier for you to obtain and there will be less competition for his affections."

Maria shook her head. "No. I shall, of course, if your brother chooses another or sets me aside. But until I have such confirmation from him to cease, or until he has chosen another woman for his wife, I think I shall pursue this."

She had never backed down from a challenge before. When Mother had challenged her to practice the pianoforte for an hour every day, she had done it. When Father had challenged her to take a hold of the accounts, she had done it.

She could paint and draw and run a plantation. She was not going to turn into a coward, not over something so important to her.

And she had Georgiana's blessing. That was the sweetest gift to her.

"I can see the determination in your face," Georgiana said. "I cannot tell you if it frightens or amuses me. Probably a little of both."

"Both is good," Maria replied, laughing a little.

They finished up the tea and biscuits and set them aside. "Allow me to play the mother just this once and tuck you in," Georgiana said.

Maria obliged her. It had been so long since she'd been treated in such a fashion. It made her miss her own mother terribly, and she felt her eyes growing a little wet as Georgiana tucked her in and smoothed back her hair.

"It is nothing," she said when she saw Georgiana's look of concern. "It is only that I miss my mother."

"I miss mine," Georgiana replied.

"You said that you hoped you would become a mother," Maria said. "Why has that not yet happened? Surely many a man would wish to marry you."

Georgiana sighed, and Maria saw a great gulf of sadness open up in her eyes.

This is why she never laughs, Maria thought.

"I fear that you and I are a bit too much alike," Georgiana said. "I fell in love with a man and would have no other.

"He proposed, but my father disapproved of the match. He felt that my suitor was too low for me. He was not noble, you see, and was simply a naval officer, although he was a gentleman.

"Father forced me to break off the engagement. My suitor went away, and I have not seen him since. And I know it is foolish of me, but as of yet I have been unable to convince myself to turn my affections to any other man, or to receive theirs."

Maria reached out and took her hand. "I am sorry."

Georgiana smiled sadly at her. "Do not be. It is not any fault of yours, and so why should you apologize for it? I am the one who has condemned myself by refusing to marry someone whom I do not truly esteem. And I fear that there is only one person who holds that position in my heart.

"I say all this not to concern you with my woes. I say it to warn you. You must marry by the end of the season. Your father's health fails, and he might not make it until next year's season.

"Therefore, you must marry. If you make yourself available only to my brother and he does not realize...I fear that you will have missed your chance with other men and therefore your chance to be saved.

"And so I caution you. Make yourself available to my brother if that is where your heart lies. But do not make the mistake that I did and continue to do. Do not shun the idea of another man being your husband. Welcome into your heart the idea that you might not love the man that you marry.

"For who knows? You might come to love the man in time. And there are other ways in which you might find happiness in your marriage. Running a household, for instance. Raising children. Calling upon friends. Hosting social events. Attending theatre. Your artwork.

"I don't wish for you to become stuck, or to entrap yourself in a situation from which you cannot escape. That is all. I care about you, my dear. The last thing I want is for you to end up like me. Especially since you do not have a rich brother who is willing to put up with your stubborn heart and lack of convention."

Maria nodded. "I understand."

She could not guarantee that she would follow Georgiana's advice. After all, if she could control her heart she would have. But she would try. She did not wish to disappoint her father. And she did not wish to end up destitute.

She lay in bed for a short while after Georgiana had left, contemplating the evening and all that had been said to her.

Miss Hennings was right. Lord Reginald needed someone who could navigate the social scene. Someone who could keep up with the witty banter.

If she could do that, she could show him that she was capable of being a match for him. She was not merely the naïve backwater girl that he must protect. She would be a woman of wit who could stand on her own two feet in a social setting.

It would show him that she was not a girl. She was a woman. She was an adult who could handle herself when someone threw a barb at her. She'd toss one right back.

Maria nodded to herself. Yes. She would show Lord Reginald that she could be like the other women. That she could hold her own. And then he would be certain to look at her in a new light.

Plan decided upon and mind made up, she finally allowed herself to sleep.

CHAPTER 12

Miss Worthing seemed to be in better spirits the next day.

Edward was grateful for it. When he asked Georgiana what they had spoken about, she would not tell him.

"It is a matter between ladies," she said. "But rest assured that it seemed to do her some good. Emotions cannot be bottled up for too long."

Edward saw that there was no use in trying to pry and so he left it at that. "I noticed that Miss Worthing's spirits seemed rather down. I thought that we might take her to the park before we retired to prepare for the ball tonight?"

Georgiana smiled brightly at him. "I think that is a marvelous idea. I shall fetch her."

"Tell her to bring her art supplies," Edward added. Sketching and painting always served to raise Miss Worthing's spirits. And he did enjoy watching her work.

He got himself ready and then waited at the bottom of the stairs. The ladies joined him just a moment or two later. Miss Worthing seemed to be in high spirits once again.

That pleased him. She ought to always be in such good spirits. It pained him when she was not.

Sure enough, Miss Worthing was also carrying with her the art supplies.

"Here, allow me," Edward said, taking them from her. He could carry them much more easily.

Miss Worthing thanked him with a grateful look and he felt that pleased warmth in his chest once again.

They set off for the park, which was only down the street. It was a lovely day, although a bit gray. But then, that was to be expected most of the time in England.

They walked through the heart of the park, where they could see nurses walking children and babies, other artists sketching, and some ladies enjoying a picnic.

There was even a game of cricket going on at one end of a field. Edward smiled, remembering his own games as a boy.

Not that Father had generally encouraged a lot of play. Father had believed in rigorous studying and a high education. But he had acquiesced to a certain extent since he had also wanted Edward to be strong and athletic.

They searched for a while until they found the right place for Miss Worthing to sit and set up her paints and art. Georgiana had brought a book with her and settled down on a bench to read.

Miss Worthing set herself up at a discreet angle where she might also observe and sketch Georgiana, without Georgiana noticing.

Edward gave her a wink and a smile to show his approval. There was a proper portrait of Georgiana in the manor, as was tradition. But these more casual sketches, these more intimate moments where Georgiana wasn't even aware she was being drawn...

He rather liked the idea of that. It would show the future generations of the Reginald family how their ancestors really behaved, what they truly looked like, instead of those stiff formal portraits.

Miss Worthing blushed and returned his smile, beginning to work.

Edward sat down next to her. "What made you take up drawing?"

"It was something that helped me to focus and calm down," Miss Worthing admitted, a smile lurking at the corners of her mouth. "And so Mother had me do more of it. Apparently, I was a rather...untamable child.

"And there were so many plants and animals and people to sketch. It was never boring for me."

"I can easily imagine it," Edward said.

The picture in his head of a smaller, younger, and infinitely wilder Miss Worthing was an adorable one.

"You must have been quite good at convincing people to sit for you," he noted.

"I've always been good with people," Miss Worthing said idly. "At least, until now," she added, ruefully.

"You're better with them than I am," Edward remarked.

Miss Worthing gave a small laugh. "Oh, yes. Getting teased and gossiped about constantly is a true sign of the affections of others."

Edward immediately felt awkward and cursed himself. It was not often that he found himself wrong-footed. Especially with Miss Worthing. They had spent so much time together that it almost felt as though he had known her their entire lives.

At least, in the level of comfort that he felt around her. He trusted her and accepted her presence in his life as much as he did Georgiana's.

"Forgive me," he told her. "I only meant that you seem to be able to handle people better than I do. You have such patience with them."

"I have had to be patient, I am afraid," Miss Worthing replied. "I often had to settle issues among the servants and the workers.

"And at the plantation...I am certain that you have seen how I first behaved with your servants. I think that I startled them quite out of their minds!"

Edward smiled. He had indeed noticed how unusually friendly Miss Worthing was towards the servants. It had, in fact, alarmed said servants. Edward's valet had spoken to him about it, stammering the entire time.

A lady, the daughter of a gentleman, speaking to servants as though they were longtime friends? It was confusing for everyone.

"I know now that it is not proper and that I must respect them but also respect the divides between us," Miss Worthing said. "But you must understand that there are quite a lot of rules here that simply did not exist growing up.

"There was no one out there except for Father and myself. If I was to converse with anyone, it must be a servant. For there was nobody else.

"And of course I was running the place and I did not wish to seem cruel. And so it naturally developed from there."

Miss Worthing paused in her drawing, staring contemplatively out into nothing for a moment before resuming. "I learned while I was running things that people are well-intentioned.

"Even if they do something wrong, oftentimes they believe that they are doing what is right. People can indeed be selfish or small-minded. But oftentimes they are operating from their highest sense of right. It is only that they were not taught a better way.

"It strikes me that this is the same case for Miss Hennings and the others. Nobody has taught them any better and so how should they know any better?"

"I think that perhaps you are being too generous with them," Edward replied.

He could not personally believe that this young woman who had been so cruelly treated was finding a way to excuse the actions of those who had treated her that way.

Something of his thoughts must have shown on his face, for Miss Worthing laughed, a twinkle dancing in her eye. "I see that you do not agree with me, my lord."

"I think that you are generous of spirit, that is all," Edward replied tactfully.

"No, no, do not dance around the subject," Miss Worthing said. "We know each other too well for that now. Do not ever be afraid to speak your thoughts to me."

Edward smiled at her. As always, he found himself incredibly grateful for her forthrightness and plain manner of speaking. He wished that all people were as such.

"It is only that there is only so far that an upbringing can excuse a person. There are numerous examples around them of how to better behave. And surely they must be aware that they are hurting people when they say such things.

"And so while I can appreciate your opinion, I do not think that I can so easily excuse them."

"That is fair enough," Miss Worthing replied. "But where does that get you? If you take the stance that all people are going to be small-minded and will disappoint you, then others can sense it in your manner.

"People, I have noticed, are rather attuned to one another. They can sense things about one another even if they do not realize that they sense it. And so they end up behaving accordingly. Even if they could not articulate to you exactly why they behaved as they did. They were only playing off of what was given to them.

"That is why I take such care to truly listen to people. So many people only pretend to care and pretend to listen. And while stamp collecting or something might seem boring to you, to that person it is a subject of great interest and importance.

"And they can tell when someone is only pretending to listen to them. And so it hurts them. They become unhappy and withdrawn or irritable and aggressive or mocking.

"But when you take the time to truly listen to them and show that you care about what they care about, simply because everyone has the right to an opinion and a personality...it really is marvelous, my lord, the sort of blossoming that happens.

"Why, there are many young men I have danced with so far whom I have heard many other ladies write off. But if you only give them a genuine ear, it is wonderful how much wit and entertainment you can get out of them."

Edward was not so sure. He had seen too much false fawning and even bald-faced lying from people to believe in their innate goodness.

But he did believe in Miss Worthing. And he thought it admirable that she took such a stance.

When he told her so, Miss Worthing only blushed.

"I fear that you give me too much credit and other people too little. You know, I could have become the prickliest of people upon arriving in England."

"Whatever do you mean?"

"Well, I was taken from my only home. I endured a most uncomfortable journey by sea. My father is ill. And I have no one, yet somehow, I am to find a husband and marry him whether I like his company or not.

"That is enough to make any woman prickly, I should think. But you have not seen me sour in manner. Not that I have not been tempted at times."

"I can certainly imagine that you would be." Edward had felt the transition to duke was trying enough. Having to do such a thing while moving to an entirely new country where he knew no one sounded like a disaster waiting to happen.

"But would it have done me any good?" Miss Worthing asked.

"Not in the slightest."

"Yet some people cannot help themselves. You never know what another person is going through. There are things, you know, that are not spoken of in polite society.

"A husband might drink too much. A family may be desperately in debt. The mother might be dying. There could be any number of things that would force a person out of their good humor.

"Therefore, I always try to give the person the benefit of the doubt. I try to be kind to them. To show them that I am truly paying attention to them. Sometimes all that people need is a little good honest attention."

Edward smiled at her, feeling incredibly fond of her. "You are too kind of a creature. I shall have to make certain that nobody takes advantage of it."

Miss Worthing blushed and turned back to her drawing.

Edward realized, suddenly, that all that Miss Worthing had said could also apply to him.

He had lost his father. And while he did not get on with the man, he had loved him.

Part and parcel with his father's death came the duchy. And then that meant he also had to get married. Suddenly, he was the most eligible bachelor in all of England.

And he had allowed it to make him, as Miss Worthing had put it, 'prickly'.

He had fallen into the very trap that Miss Worthing had described. And he expected everyone to understand and put up with his issues while he had no sympathy for their own.

"Miss Worthing," he said, "I do believe that you have shown me the error of my ways."

"As you know, my lord," Miss Worthing replied, intent upon her sketch, "that is my greatest joy in life."

Edward laughed.

They spent an hour or two at the park and then packed it all up to return home.

Georgiana was full of praise for the novel she was reading. Apparently, she felt quite a kinship to one of the main characters, the sensible elder sister.

Miss Worthing was more than happy to listen to Georgiana talk on. Edward, however, was still dwelling upon his conversation with Miss Worthing regarding human nature.

He did not see Miss Worthing or his sister for the rest of the day. He had to hole himself up in his office in order to take care of some estate business.

He did wish that the women trying to earn his affections would understand that. Their profession, so to speak, was earning a husband. The balls and dinner parties and house calls were their offices.

However, he had to maintain his social obligations as well as go to the banks and the gentlemen's clubs, attend meetings, and send letters and go over accounts.

He had to do both things and so he could not always have his mind completely on the social aspects of his life. When he sometimes wanted to talk business with the other gentlemen at the ball, the women acted as though he were committing a great crime against humanity.

When he could not join on the morning calls, however, both his sister and Miss Worthing nodded in understanding.

"I hope that your business goes well," Miss Worthing said quietly. She looked almost shy.

Edward could feel a smile tugging at the corners of his mouth. It felt like a natural reaction to her. Miss Worthing was present, and therefore that was reason to smile.

"Thank you. I hope that your morning calls are pleasant." He suspected that she needed all the luck and well-wishing that she could get on that front.

Since he did not see her until they were ready to depart for the ball, he had not truly spoken to her either since their brief exchange that morning.

Miss Worthing was quiet on her way to the ball. But then, they all usually were. Except for his sister when she was giving Miss Worthing last-minute instructions and reminders.

"Keep your head up," she would say. Or, "remember to keep your hands light, as though they are floating."

This time, Georgiana was silent. She seemed to think that now was the time for Miss Worthing to sink or swim on her own. No reminders would be able to replace the actual training in Miss Worthing's mind.

Edward hoped that the ball tonight would go better than the one last night. He would have to seriously intercede if Miss Worthing was treated in such a manner again. No matter what Miss Worthing and Georgiana thought of the matter.

He wouldn't stand by while an innocent girl was treated like dirt. Especially when it was inadvertently his fault.

They were invited to the dinner before the main ball once again. Edward held his breath as they entered the dining room. Would Miss Worthing be able to handle herself?

They all sat down. Georgiana was across the table from them but Miss Worthing was just diagonal to him, on his left side.

Hopefully he could at least then have a chance to head off any insults at the pass.

Miss Hennings, he noticed, was unfortunately in attendance. She looked at Miss Worthing the way that Edward had seen falcons look at a mouse.

Everyone settled down, and conversation began. Miss Worthing, he noticed, seemed unusually nervous but also determined.

The conversation started, and it was not long before Miss Hennings saw fit to try and take it over.

"But of course," she said, "not all of us can be so fortunate as to our upbringing. Why, there are those who did not even have the benefit of a governess!"

It was a dig at Miss Worthing, of course. Her mother had brought her up, and after her mother's death there had been no further education for her in the department of manners.

"And yet," Miss Worthing replied, "there are some who manage to behave in such a manner despite having the best governess afforded."

Edward nearly dropped his spoon. He stared at Miss Worthing. There were two spots of color high up on her cheeks, not her usual blush.

He was torn. On the one hand, he wanted to congratulate her on the comment. On the other hand, it was so unlike her. It was unkind, and he had never known Miss Worthing to be unkind in all the time that he had known her.

Then he saw the gleam in Miss Hennings' eye, and silently groaned.

Now, it seemed it was an actual war.

CHAPTER 13

MARIA COULD SEE that her comment had only angered Miss Hennings further.

Well, that was no matter. She would find a way to best her. She had to show that she could hold her own among these people. That she could dish out just as well as they could. Otherwise, how else was she to prove that she had the social ability worthy of a duke's wife?

In response to the remark about the governess, Miss Hennings insulted Maria's mother.

"What is the saying, that the apple does not fall far from the tree?"

Maria winced, as if in sympathy. "Well, at least I am certain that I did come from that particular tree."

Miss Hennings' face went quite pink. Maria had heard from the older ladies that there had once been a rumor that Mr. Hennings was not, in fact, Miss Hennings' true father.

It was owing to the fact that Miss Hennings looked nothing like her father, while her two brothers very much did. Personally, Maria did not care one way or another. But it was most certainly a sore spot for Miss Hennings.

Lord Reginald looked quite odd. He did not seem to be proud, or impressed, as Maria had hoped.

She did not quite understand that. Why should he not be

pleased at her wit? Surely he would be happy that she was finally scoring a hit against the woman who had treated her so cruelly?

Perhaps he was merely in shock. Maria pressed on, determined.

It felt as though she were in a sporting match of some kind. Only their equipment, their weapons, were made of words.

Maria saw quite a few guests looking as though they were trying not to laugh when she would say something particularly clever. She had to stifle her own smile of triumph.

You see? she wanted to say to Miss Hennings. Two can play your little game.

She tried not to look at Lord Reginald too much. After all, she had just been accused of having feelings for him. If she paid him too much attention now Miss Hennings was sure to seize upon it.

As it was, Miss Hennings seemed to feel that Lord Reginald was too dangerous a subject to approach. It could have been that she worried that if she brought him up to insult Maria, that Maria could then throw Miss Hennings' own pursuit of him back in her face.

So long as Lord Reginald was not addressed, Maria did not care so much for the reason why.

She was feeling quite triumphant by the time that dinner ended. For the first time, she was one of the witty ones at the table. She was no longer the subject of the jokes—she was the one making the jokes.

It was intoxicating, in a way. No wonder people strove to be the most entertaining person in the room. The attention and praise she could feel on her went to her head faster than wine ever had.

But then dinner ended. And she stood up, and turned.

And saw Lord Reginald's face.

He was not happy with her. He was not proud, or impressed, or pleased.

He looked thunderous.

Maria could feel her stomach knotting terribly. She had never seen the duke look like this before. He was staring at Maria as though he did not even know her. As though she were a stranger, and an unpleasant one at that.

She swallowed. It struck her, suddenly and horribly, that she had taken a misstep. At some point, she had done something wrong.

As they all started to file out into the ballroom, she saw Georgiana try to give her brother a warning look.

Lord Reginald did not seem to see it. Instead he walked up to Maria and took her arm.

"We," he said, "are having a small talk, Miss Worthing."

Maria looked over at Georgiana, who just looked upset.

Seeing no other option, she allowed the duke to lead her into a private corner. Knowing the entire time that she had, somehow, just messed everything up.

CHAPTER 14

EDWARD COULD HARDLY SEE, he was so full of fury.

What sort of behavior was that? What kind of—who had kidnapped Miss Worthing and taken her place as an imposter? It was the only possibility that he could think of as to why she had suddenly become as awful as the women who had tormented her.

To bring up that old rumor about Miss Hennings' parentage! And then to keep going, as if that was not already crossing the line.

He had no tender feelings for Miss Hennings. If he never had to endure another evening with that woman, it would be too soon. But that was most decidedly crossing the line.

Of course, Miss Hennings had and would cross the line. Goodness knew all the things she had insinuated about Miss Worthing as well as any woman who had dared to speak to Edward.

But he had not expected the same from Miss Worthing. He had expected better from her. No matter who was saying it or who it was directed at, such things went too far. They were too unkind.

Miss Worthing seemed confused and frightened. As though she were unaware of how she had so badly messed up.

Well, Edward would be sure to educate her.

He turned her to face him once he was certain that nobody was paying them attention. Georgiana had looked worried but had the good sense not to follow them.

He was far too upset and would not stand for anyone's interruptions or interference. Not even from his sister. And he did not wish to sour the evening more by snapping at Georgiana.

"Care to explain your behavior?" Edward asked. He did not care to make his tone gentle. He was angry, and Miss Worthing ought to know it.

Miss Worthing stared at him, eyes wide, face pale. "I—I am not certain as to what you mean, my lord."

"Your behavior," he said. "At dinner, just now. What on earth was that about? What were you thinking? Are you at all the girl that I have come to know?"

Miss Worthing seemed to be at a complete loss. She stared at him, uncomprehending.

Did she really have no idea how badly she had just behaved? How frustrated with her he was? How ashamed of her?

If she did not understand, then he would make her understand. She had to know that what she had done was completely outside of the bounds of propriety.

"The way that you behaved and the things that you said were so outside of the realm of what is considered proper that I cannot even find the right words," Edward told her.

He knew that his tone was harsh, but he could not find it within himself to care. He was almost shaking with the force of his disappointment.

Yes, that was what he felt—disappointment. He had faith in Miss Worthing. He had loved how unlike everyone else she was. How kind and thoughtful. How honest and plain.

Now she was behaving exactly like the rest of them.

"I had put my trust in your character," he told her. "I had faith in your honesty and your forthright manner. I appreciated how genuine you were.

"And now I see that you are as bad as the rest when you feel the occasion calls for it. Tell me, which is the real Miss Worthing? The one who claims to believe the best in people? Or the one who airs a sordid rumor in front of everyone at dinner in order to humiliate a woman?"

Miss Worthing's eyes shone bright with unshed tears. She opened her mouth as if to speak, but Edward did not want to hear her excuses.

"If you are ever to behave in such a manner again, I shall not be escorting you," Edward told her. "I shall either stay at home and you can make do with another man or on your own. Or, you are welcome to stay at home while I go out with my sister.

"I will not tolerate such behavior, not now and not ever. I do not know what has come over you but I never wish to be privy to it again."

"I have said nothing that has not been said in some manner towards me!" Miss Worthing burst out, sounding terribly upset.

"And that makes it all right for you to dish it back to them?" Edward replied. "Where do you have the right to be on the moral high ground? Why is it all right for you to say such things but not for them?"

"I only—"

"You were not thinking, that is what you were doing," Edward replied. "You let your baser emotions get away from you. Your anger and your pettiness.

"Before today I had not even thought that you were capable of such feelings. I rejoiced in it. I wished that all the world could be as you are. Or as you were, rather.

"I hope that I shall never see such behavior exhibited from you again. I cannot help but associate with the people at these gatherings. I must, and so I do. But I can choose who I escort and who I let under my roof.

"I will not allow myself to be so closely associated with someone who behaves as you have just now. I cannot even begin to express the depth of my disappointment."

Miss Worthing really did look as though she were holding back tears. Edward had to give her points for maintaining her composure as best she could when she was so clearly upset. Miss Worthing was not the sort of person who was good at hiding how she felt. Normally he would have been proud of her for holding herself together so well.

Not so this evening.

Edward knew that he had to leave or he would only continue to rant at her. He did not see how that would help her any. His message had been delivered, loud and clear.

"I shall be going into the ballroom now. You may enter as well or you may not. I do not care. But the next time I see you, I shall expect the conduct to which I have become accustomed.

"That is, I shall expect the compassionate and thoughtful person that I have come to admire. Not whatever mean-spirited shallow girl that I have been presented with tonight."

He took a deep breath, steadying himself. "I bid you good evening, Miss Worthing."

He left her standing there and went on into the ballroom.

CHAPTER 15

MARIA ALMOST COULDN'T BREATHE.

And not in the usual way. Not in the breath-stolen-by-charm sort of way. That was for when Lord Reginald was smiling at her or winking or making her laugh. Or simply, well, being himself.

No, this was in the awful stomach sinking sort of way.

She wanted to crawl into a corner and be forgotten there for all eternity.

Oh, she had been such a fool. Such an awful wretch. She had only been trying to show that she could handle herself around Miss Hennings and the others.

And now she had alienated the one person that she was trying to impress. The one person whose opinion mattered above all others.

She wanted to burst into tears.

But she could not. She still had the ball to endure. Oh, how could she be expected to handle the dancing and conversation when all she wanted to do was disappear from existence?

He had been right in all of the things that he had said, as well. The duke was not the sort of man to get angry lightly, but once he had, she had understood why.

Bringing up the rumor that she had heard about Miss Hennings was cruel. Of course she knew that. But Miss Hennings had been cruel to her and so she had thought that it would be seen as a clever hit. Quid pro quo, so to speak.

Instead, Lord Reginald saw it as her descending to their level.

And he was right, of course. In striving to impress him she had lost her way and dashed herself upon the rocks. She wasn't sure that she would ever forgive herself for this.

Almost more important that her self-assessment was the duke's opinion of her. Would he ever forgive her?

He didn't seem likely to. The fire in his eyes and the stony sternness in his voice—it had made him look almost more than human. It had been a bit terrifying. This was a man, she realized, with a temper. All of his grumblings were nothing compared to this.

Her pain and that sick, awful feeling in her stomach were accompanied by a fair bit of shock as well.

She'd had no idea that he thought of her so highly. Well, up until now, at any rate. He had praised her quite highly and didn't even seem to realize it.

To see that she had once been someone that he respected, someone in whom he had faith...once it would have given her the greatest joy. Why, even that morning she would have been walking on air to hear him say all the things that he did.

But now it was nothing more than salt in the wound. He had once thought of her that way. He had once held her in high esteem.

Now, it was the opposite. He must despise her.

Oh, he had not said as much, not outright. But it was plain in his manner. His anger at her was like a touch that she could feel against her skin. It burned inside of her stomach and pricked at her eyes.

Perhaps she should move in with Father? Remove herself from the duke's house?

Surely he would not wish to see her again. Not after that. Not after what she had done.

She had not thought that there could be anything worse in the world than loving a man and knowing he did not love her in return.

Now she knew that there was indeed something worse, and that was when the man that you loved did not even want to be in the same room as you.

Maria realized that she was still standing in the dining area. Only now she was quite alone.

Nobody was looking for her. Most likely nobody noticed that she was missing. All of that barbed wit at dinner and for what?

For the duke to hate her and for the people who had been so entertained by her to forget her the moment she was out of their sight.

She could hear people laughing and conversing. She could hear the music starting up for the first dance. There was the sound of carriage wheels rolling over the cobblestones and horses neighing as more guests arrived.

Maria swallowed down the lump in her throat. She would not let herself cry. Not here. But it hurt to know that she would never belong.

She was stuck. Either she was herself, and nobody cared for her and they made fun of her. Or she tried to be like them, and she alienated the man she loved and respected, and was forgotten easily by everyone else.

Perhaps this was a sign. Perhaps she would never find a husband or make friends. It could be that she was doomed to a life of misery once Father was gone.

For the first time since leaving her home and coming to England, she felt truly and utterly alone.

"Oh, my poor dear."

The moment she heard Georgiana's voice, Maria lost all composure. To her horror and shame, she began to cry.

Georgiana pulled her into a hug. "There, there, just cry it all out. Nobody shall be in here. You can cry to your heart's content."

"I do not deserve to be so upset," Maria protested, even as she continued to stain the shoulder of Georgiana's dress with tears. "I have no right. I deserved to be spoken to like that. I was awful."

"You made a mistake, my dear. Such a good heart as yours does not deserve to be spoken to like that. Especially when it is your first offense."

"You are being too generous with me."

"No, my brother is being too harsh. I shall speak to him about that."

"Oh, please do not!" Maria said, pulling back so that she might look into Georgiana's face. "Georgiana, you mustn't. I was truly awful at dinner."

"I did wonder about that." Georgiana raised an eyebrow. "Why did you behave as you did, Maria? It is not at all like you."

Maria sniffled. She felt like she was five years old again and had been caught by Mother trying to sneak cookies from the kitchen.

"I realized that I was expected to be witty if I was to be a duke's wife," Maria admitted.

Off of Georgiana's amused look, she added, "I know, I know. It was foolish of me.

"But I thought that I might stand a chance if I could prove to Lord Reginald—and to everyone—that I could hold my own. That if someone were to attack me that I could respond.

"After all, as a duke's wife, I must be sociable. There are certain expectations that must be met. And of course there will be those who are envious or who seek to improve themselves by taking me down.

"I had to be prepared for that. And I would have to handle it all with wit and ease. If I continued to simply endure it as I did, what sort of socialite would I be? Everyone could see how I was being hurt by it. They saw that I was an easy target.

"The wife of someone such as Lord Reginald could never be like that. And so I sought to prove that I was capable."

Georgiana, thankfully, did not laugh in her face. Instead she took Maria's hands and guided her to sit down back at the table. Georgiana took the chair next to her, facing her.

"I am going to tell you something, dear girl," she said, "and I want you to listen to me very carefully."

"You are right in that the wife of a duke must be prepared for such things. And you are right in that she must handle it with grace.

"But that does not mean that you have to lower yourself to their level. It doesn't mean that you have to be mean-spirited or thoughtless.

"The reason that Miss Hennings and others would attack you is because they could see how much it affected you. They could see how much it hurt.

"Half of a person's entertainment in tearing someone down is seeing that person falter. But if the person does not even seem to register it, then where is the fun in that? Where is the game in going after someone if that someone simply refuses to play in return?

"If you were to lob a ball at someone and they would not hit it with their bat, you have no game. They have been the ones throwing the balls, yes. But you have been the one who has hit them with the bat. You have responded and shown your hurt and it only encourages them.

"I wish that I could say that it discourages them because they see that you are hurt and mend their ways. But alas, life is not always so kind.

"You will only shake them off your back if you refuse to play. Show them that you do not care. Do not respond. When they send you unkind words, return them with kindness.

"It might be better than they deserve, it is true. But it will utterly baffle them. It will take all of the wind out of their sails. And while it is better than they might deserve, it is exactly what you deserve.

"For you, my dear, do not deserve to have your reputation damaged by behaving as they do. You do not deserve to feel the odd lack of satisfaction, the empty feeling, that comes with acting like that. And you certainly don't deserve to be lectured so harshly."

Maria was of the opinion that she very much did deserve to be lectured for her behavior. But she understood what Georgiana was saying.

"I am sorry," she said. "I am associated with you. This must reflect badly upon you as well."

"Never you mind about me," Georgiana replied. "This will all be forgotten about in the morning. There is always another scandal to talk about. And there is always something that happens halfway through a ball that puts everyone on the edge of their seats."

She smiled teasingly, squeezing Maria's hands. "Do not let this bring you down," she said. "Remember it for the future. Do not repeat your mistake. But do not make the further mistake of thinking that you are now unworthy.

"You are a lovely girl and it is my every wish to see you happy. But that happiness starts with you. No outside person can give it to you if you feel that you do not deserve it.

"Am I making sense? Or do I just sound like one of those ridiculous great-aunts who mumble nonsense and claim to talk to spirits."

Maria laughed.

"Ah, there she is," Georgiana said. "There is the Maria Worthing I know. Cheer up, my dear. The storm will pass."

"I am not so certain that it will pass for me in the eyes of the duke," Maria admitted, sobering again.

"You leave the duke to me," Georgiana replied. "Perhaps you ought to endeavor to spend some time alone tomorrow. I think that some time to yourself and away from us will do you some good. After all, a person needs time to center one's self and there is such a thing as too much time around other people."

Maria nodded. "Thank you, Georgiana. I don't know what I've done to deserve all the kindness that you've shown me."

"You've simply been yourself," Georgiana replied. "And that is what you should continue to be. Do not compromise who you are for anyone, not even my brother. Do you promise?"

Maria nodded. "I promise."

CHAPTER 16

THE NEXT MORNING, Edward found that Miss Worthing was not coming down to breakfast.

"She has gone out?" he said in surprise when he asked the butler where she had gotten to.

"She is going on a short trip," Georgiana said, entering the dining room and taking her seat at the breakfast table.

"Where to?" Miss Worthing had to be back in time for the ball that evening and they had planned to go on another walk to the park that day.

Georgiana managed to spread butter on toast with all the foreboding and aggression of a general arranging his troops on a battlefield.

It was rare to see his sister truly angry. That did not happen often. Georgiana was a woman given neither to the ecstatic heights of joy nor the deep valleys of despair.

It meant, however, that when she did give herself over to a strong emotion, it was like the fury of a summer storm out on the high seas. Georgiana was an ocean, calm on the surface but with depth underneath. When she was angry...it was a sight to behold.

And Edward was realizing that at that moment, Georgiana was furious.

"I hardly think it should matter to you where she does and does not go," Georgiana said. She set down her toast and looked at him with a gaze that, if looks could kill, would have pierced his heart with all the strength of a dagger.

Edward had a feeling that she knew about his argument with Miss Worthing last night.

Furthermore, he had the feeling that she was not on his side about the matter.

"Of course I care where she is," he told her. "I worry about the girl."

"And I suppose that it was worry that led you to argue with her so furiously last night."

"She was behaving in a manner that was both unbecoming and most unlike her."

"She was trying to fit in, Edward. You can hardly blame the poor girl for that."

"When it is at the sacrifice of her character, yes, I can."

Georgiana raised an eyebrow at him. "Not everyone is out to make sport of everyone else. Much of our acquaintance with one another is built upon the exchange of wit and wordplay.

"You disdain these social gatherings and yet you engage in them. Miss Worthing enjoys them but cannot engage with them. She was only trying to bridge that gap.

"You need to be more generous in your manner. How can you not see the world as she sees it? How can you not see the good in the people around you instead of forever focusing on the bad? You praised her for her manner yet refused to adopt it yourself.

"That is nothing short of laziness and I will not stand for it in my brother. Not when I know that you are capable of better.

"She was miserable, knowing that she could not measure up to everyone else's standards. She was emulating others. Is that not what we do? Is that not how we learn to be wittier, kinder, and so on? By following the example of those around us?

"She did not mean to be unkind. You of all people ought to know that. What with how closely you have been observing her this entire time."

"Whether she meant to be or not, she was. She turned into one of those simpering ladies who think of nothing but gossip and fashion—"

"As if they have anything else to talk about! As if you do not admire their fashionable clothes and listen in to the gossip yourself!

"You are not allowed to chastise them as a hypocrite. You would enjoy these balls far more if you would simply get over yourself and stop acting like such a child."

"She—"

"Went too far, yes. As we all do at times when we are desperate for affection and recognition. When we have nothing but ill-suited role models to guide us.

"But that was no reason for you to put her in her place in such a harsh manner. You have put her in such a state of distress I am surprised that she was able to get out of bed at all today."

Edward was certain that a physical blow would hurt less than the cold and furious tone his sister was leveling at him in that moment.

Georgiana seemed to sense his distress. Attuned as she was to the feelings of others. She sighed, setting down her cutlery. Her voice and face gentled a bit. They were still firm, but no longer enraged.

"I understand how you felt. You wanted her to be herself, because you value who she is and you hated the thought of her giving up her sense of who she is in order to do what is popular.

"You wanted to protect her from herself. And you were frustrated by what you thought was someone giving in so easily to the shallow behavior of those around her.

"I understand that. But you were too harsh in your manner, Edward. You are always too harsh on the people around you. You must learn to be forgiving and to assume the best in others instead of the worst.

"After all, you know that I always act from my highest sense of right. As do you. But even in doing that we can make mistakes. We can be thoughtless.

"You were thoughtless last night. I would even go so far as to say that you were cruel. You did not have to be so harsh with her. I know that you probably were upset at yourself as well. For letting her behavior be this way. If I had to guess I would surmise that you thought you had not provided her with a good enough example yourself. Or that you had failed to protect her from such awful influences."

Edward could only nod his head, acknowledging at how his sister was once again able to somehow read his every thought.

Georgiana tipped her head to the side, giving him a look of fond exasperation. "You cannot take such responsibility upon yourself. You have to give Miss Worthing credit for her own actions, both good and bad. Neither are your fault or responsibility."

"How can you say such a thing?" Edward asked. "How can you be so nonchalant about it? You must feel a sense of responsibility for her as well. You must care that she is patterning herself after people not worth giving the time of day to."

"Of course I care," Georgiana replied. "But it is not my choice. I cannot control her. And you must recognize that. You cannot control the people around you. The sooner you realize that and the sooner you realize that people have good intentions, even if it does not come across that way, the better off you will be."

"But was I not right to point out that her behavior was thoughtless and callous? That she was possibly hurting people?"

"If you had done it with kindness and love, then yes. But to rage at her only made her condemn herself. It made her feel as though she was worth nothing. No lesson in propriety is worth tearing down a person's self-esteem in such a manner."

Edward could feel shame begin to creep into his stomach, an unpleasantly hot and sinking feeling that made his entire body feel heavier.

"You acted out of concern," Georgiana said gently. "I understand that. But you must apologize for being so stern with her. It was an overreaction to her behavior and an overcompensation for the personal responsibility you felt.

"She only wants to be seen as someone whose company is enjoyed, the same as everyone else. She only wants to fit it. It is natural that she will stumble a little in finding her way. Who does not wish, at least in part, to be at the center of the room? To have everyone gaze upon them and think, what a woman of wit? What a charming young lady?"

"I would prefer a kind lady," Edward said. "One who is known for her graciousness and compassion and honesty."

"Then perhaps you ought to tell her that," Georgiana said.

Silence fell for a moment as they both contemplated their own thoughts.

Georgiana was the one to break it.

"Edward, you know that it is never my place to lecture you."

"I know. But I sorely needed a lecture this morning after such behavior. You are right in that I am too harsh with others. I was only...I did not wish her to become someone she was not. I did not want her to lose the spark that I saw in her, that flame of honesty and sweetness that I so valued.

"I know that others will value it as well, given time. I can see that, even if she cannot."

"My dear brother. Sometimes I wonder at how you can be so blind."

Edward looked at her in confusion. Blindness at his own harsh nature? Blindness at how his words had so affected Miss Worthing? Blindness at his hypocrisy?

Georgiana sighed. "Just as I would never presume to lecture you, I would never presume to know your heart. Or to counsel you one way or another regarding your future.

"You have always done the same with me. You have respected my feelings and I appreciate that. I know that you had thoughts about my engagement but you never said anything one way or another."

"Well it was—"

"You do not need to provide me with an explanation. That is not why I am bringing up the subject."

Edward nodded and let her proceed.

He had personally approved of her choice in fiancé. While her suitor did not have a noble title or a large income, he was a man of honor. He was a good man. And he had loved Georgiana. That much had been clear. He would have taken care of Georgiana and given her the gentle love that her nature deserved.

But it was not his right to choose or reject someone for her. And when Father had been so firm about it...well, he had known that it was not his battle.

But perhaps he should have stuck up for her and her suitor more.

"I should have spoken up in your defense," he said. "I let Father bully you."

"It was ultimately my choice to make," Georgiana told him. "You could not have made the decision for me."

"But I could have helped to persuade Father to back off or to even give his blessing."

"I could have married him with or without Father's blessing. It was my own cowardice and lack of faith in our relationship that doomed us. I chose to break off the engagement. Not you, and not Father."

"I could have given you the strength—"

Georgiana held up her hand in a stop motion. "I did not mention it so that we might begin to debate over what should and should not have been done by either of us.

"I only brought up the subject so that I might thank you for the respect that you have always had for me. Not so that we might reminisce or lose ourselves in the conversation. There is no point in talking about the past.

"You did not meddle in my affairs. You let me figure things out for myself. And I appreciate you for that.

"And so I have tried not to meddle too much in yours. I have tried to give you advice when I have seen you unhappy or struggling. But I have never tried to direct your steps too much in one way or another.

"But it seems to me that you are not able to see what is right in front of you. You're not able to distinguish your own emotions or understand what you're feeling."

Edward frowned. "What do you mean? What are you aiming at?"

Georgiana sighed. "Have you not found it odd how protective you are of Miss Worthing? That you are so concerned for her?"

Edward stared at her. "She has no experience and no friends. Of course I am concerned for her."

"But the extremity of it. That does not strike you as odd? You have never shown such a predisposition towards any other woman before."

Edward thought about that. It took him a little aback. "I... suppose that I have simply never had the chance to get to know a lady as well as I have gotten to know Miss Worthing. I have spent quite a lot of time in her company, as you know."

"Yes. And that does further prove my point that you must be gentler about your assessment of others. Had you only run into Miss Worthing at a ball, you might think her as silly as the other girls."

Edward shook his head. "No. I should not think that. Her disposition is so unlike theirs. She is too much herself for me to think that."

Georgiana hummed her agreement. "And yet I almost wish that you had simply met her at a ball as another young lady. I think that you might have realized all of this much sooner."

"You are talking in circles to try and get me to realize something but I am still in the dark. What is it? Speak plain."

Georgiana sighed. "Have you not noticed that your feelings for her are like one of a suitor?"

That brought Edward up short.

That was not—but could it—he wasn't thinking of Miss Worthing in that manner, was he?

He thought back over his actions. The way that he always sought her out in the ballroom to make sure that she was all right. The way he wanted to protect her and defend her against those who were rude to her.

How he enjoyed spending time with her. He took her to the theatre, the park, the art galleries. He always sought her out for a dance and would find himself wishing that he could ask her for a second one.

He enjoyed walking with her around the ballroom the other night. And when she was upset he wanted nothing more than to make sure that she was all right, to cheer her up and help her to feel better.

But was that truly love of a romantic sort? Or was it simply because of their spending so much time in close quarters? Was it only because he knew her better than he knew any woman besides his own sister?

Edward felt conflicted. Something about what Georgiana was saying felt so terribly right to him. But he couldn't quite accept it. Not fully.

"I see that this is a surprise to you," Georgiana said. "You have not even once considered her as a potential match for yourself?"

"Her father's instructions were that I help her to find a husband. That I be her escort."

"You say that as if her father would object to his daughter marrying a wealthy and educated member of the nobility. Or that he would be upset at his daughter marrying the son of his best friend."

"I still do not understand how Father ever showed enough camaraderie and emotion to make anyone wish to be his best friend."

"Father was different when he was younger, I am sure," Georgiana replied. "We can all allow bitterness to change us. I think Father's bitterness at the world, his materialism—I do not know what sparked it or where it came from. But I do fear that you could become the same way if you are not careful."

Edward acknowledged that.

"In any case," Georgiana said, "am I to understand that for some reason or other, you had fixed her in your mind as off-limits?"

Edward nodded. "Yes, I suppose that one could put it that way. I had promised her father that I would treat her as a sister and so I did. That was the only way that I allowed myself to think of her."

"But that is not how you treat her," Georgiana said. "You treat her as though you were her suitor.

"Did you not wonder why Miss Hennings and the others continued to treat her as they did?"

"They would treat her that way no matter what. It is not merely a question of her association with me."

"She does not merely associate with you, Edward. Have you not noticed how those older ladies who love Miss Worthing so will titter when you come up to ask her for a dance?"

"They will titter at anything. You know that they live for gossip now that their own brushes with romance are finished."

"Have you noticed, then, how none of the other young men have dared to ask Miss Worthing for a second dance? And how none of them have called upon the house?"

"I had been concerned about that, I admit. I thought that it was only her nature. They wanted a woman who was more worldly. More like the other young ladies in her manner."

"Perhaps. But they all scatter when you approach her. None of them ask her to dance before you do. They know that it's your right to dance with her first."

"What are you talking about?" The other young men that he knew didn't behave that way.

"I see that you haven't even noticed it happening." Georgiana's mouth twisted oddly, and Edward realized that she was amused. "Edward, no man has made a move to court Miss Worthing, never mind go so far as to propose to her, because you have been acting as though you are her suitor."

Edward stared at her. He probably looked like a fool, with his mouth open and everything. "Are you—are you serious? This is not in jest?"

"Why on earth would I jest about something as serious as this?" Georgiana asked. "This is a matter of the heart of which we are speaking, not to mention the future of both yourself and Miss Worthing. I would not jest over something like that."

Edward knew that, objectively. But it still felt so impossible to him that he could not quite believe that Georgiana was serious.

"Everyone has truly thought this whole time that I am courting her?"

"Your behavior has certainly suggested as much to them," Georgiana replied. "Even if there has been no formal declaration. And you haven't done anything so terribly bold as ask her for a second dance or anything of that sort. But I suppose that everyone just assumed that you were taking things slowly or trying to be polite. It would be rude of you to show too much favoritism when you're in such a social gathering, after all."

Edward stared down at his plate of food. He was no longer hungry, although not from upset but rather from sheer shock.

Could he have been so terribly unaware of his own feelings?

He had always prided himself on his intelligence, on his ability to observe. Yet here he was being told that he did not know himself at all. That his own motivations and his own heart were so unknown to him and so different from what he thought.

Did he have romantic feelings for Miss Worthing? It was not

something he could accept at the drop of a hat. He was not a hero from one of those novels where he stared into the sunset and suddenly knew beyond a shadow of a doubt.

It did, however, make an awful lot of sense. In fact, it made a horrible amount of sense.

His irrational jealousy. The way he couldn't even consider other women and thought only of Miss Worthing. How he kept thinking of how best to take care of her and worrying about her safety.

He was always trying to stick close to her. He always knew where she was. He wanted her to be happy and enjoyed spending time with her.

All of that could just be brotherly affection, of course.

But then if he imagined holding her in his arms—treating her as a husband would a wife—

That felt right. More than that, it felt comfortable.

He remembered what Georgiana had said before about what it felt like to be in love. About how it had made her feel safe. Like coming home, only home was a person.

When he thought of Miss Worthing, that was what he thought about. That was the sensation. In fact, he could not picture coming home after meetings to a house that did not have her in it.

Georgiana gave him a small smile, her eyes softening. "I see that you are beginning to understand."

"I am not sure that I do, still," Edward replied, feeling dazed. Almost as if someone had clocked him upside the head.

"What do you not understand?" she asked gently.

"How I could have been so blind as to my own feelings. How I could have treated her in such a way that everyone else could see how I felt but I myself could not.

"I have been unfair to Miss Worthing. My behavior was preventing her from finding a suitor since all of the other young men thought that I had set my sights on her. And as a duke, they would not dare usurp me.

"I have made her more of a target for the ladies, and without knowing why. At least if I had been aware of my behavior I would have been able to counter it in other ways. I could have made it clear that anyone who disrespected Miss Worthing would face my wrath, since I was her suitor.

"I would have actually had a right to protect her in the way that I wanted. But instead, I have been placing her in an awkward position where she could not defend herself and I was not defending her as I should be.

"I took away her ability to gain a husband without truly providing for her as if I were her suitor. I gave her all the disadvantages and none of the benefits or privileges.

"In short, I feel that I have behaved...as a cad would."

"You are not a cad," Georgiana replied immediately. "A cad knows what he is doing and whom he is hurting and he does not care. You care. You were merely mistaken and unaware. It happens to the best of us."

"You are more forgiving of me than I am of myself."

"That is generally how it goes in life, I have found. We are our own harshest critics."

Edward gently pushed his plate of food away. He knew that he would not be finding his appetite again for some time.

The more that he thought about having romantic feelings for Miss Worthing, the more it made sense.

All of those feelings that he had been shoving aside. The feelings that he hadn't been letting himself properly examine. The feelings of confusion and frustration that he hadn't been able to place...

And of course the extreme disappointment that he had felt last night. The sadness and anger. The way that he had felt almost betrayed.

It was because he was in love with her.

He had a wild, awful thought: he was glad that Father was dead. He would never have approved of the match. The daughter of his old best friend she might be, yes. But she was also not a noble and not nearly an equal to the Reginald family in wealth.

When he voiced this, Georgiana shook her head. "I think that Father would have been more sentimental than you give him credit for."

"Well we shall never know either way."

"No. But we are still waiting with bated breath, if I may say so out loud, to see what you will do about this now that you are aware of it."

"Do?"

What could he do? He had ruined his chances with Miss Worthing. His behavior last night was far too harsh. It was deplorable.

What he should have done was say that he liked her exactly the way that she was. That she didn't have to change herself in order to get people to accept her. That her lack of guile, her belief in the best in people and her enthusiasm for the world around her had all endeared her to him better than witty remarks and clever asides ever could.

He should have told her that he didn't understand the need for acceptance. But that was because he was born a man and born to wealth and privilege as well. He never needed to struggle to be accepted. He already was. Even when he was sullen and scolding.

And so while he didn't understand it, he should have told her he could appreciate it. But that she wouldn't ever have to struggle for it ever again because he would elevate her to such a level that people would never dare to reject her.

He should have told her how he felt.

But he hadn't even realized how he felt. He'd had no idea. And so he had retreated into anger. He scolded her. He had behaved abominably.

She must hate him now. Must be resolved to reject his very presence. Had she not fled the house before he was even awake? Edward was an early riser. He was generally the first person awake in the household.

To have taken breakfast, dressed, and left the house already before he was even up...Miss Worthing must have been greatly determined.

It could not have been clearer that she greatly disliked him now. That she felt he was her enemy.

"There is nothing that I could do now," he told Georgiana.

Georgiana raised an eyebrow. "Not even tell her the truth?"

"I am not one of those heroes in plays," Edward replied. "This is not an opera. Performing a massive monologue or aria is not going to win her favor."

"Again, I think that you judge too harshly. Perhaps a grand declaration is not needed. But the idea of being honest and saying what is in your heart, that I think is important.

"All those fancy, flowery speeches? All those romantic tropes that you ridicule? They did not come from thin air. They were rooted in truth. All such works of fiction are.

"I think that if you apologize sincerely and explain how you feel then all will be forgiven. Miss Worthing is a generous soul, as we've both acknowledged. She's kindhearted. She will not bear a grudge against you."

"I think you know as well as I do that I am not the best when it comes to truly saying how I feel," Edward replied. "When I must be clever and feign things, then yes. But when I am speaking my true opinions...you know how harsh I can become."

"This is true. But if you truly make an effort, I think you shall pull through. Write things down beforehand, perhaps."

The idea of taking the time to write things out properly did appeal to him. He could double-check everything to make certain that he was not giving offense or digging himself into a deeper hole than he had already.

"Perhaps you might look over whatever I write?" he asked. "In order to be certain that it is...that it will be received properly?"

"I could do that, if you so insist," Georgiana replied.

Edward nodded. "I will not," he said, "tell her of my feelings just yet. I need...more time to get properly acquainted with them."

This realization was still so new to him. He could not share it with Miss Worthing. Not until he was more secure in it. Not until he could step forward with confidence and say, *yes, I choose this woman. I love her.*

If he could not do that in his own mind, then how could he do it with her? He would not grace her or any woman with anything less than total certainty. Especially when Miss Worthing was already doubting herself so much. He would not give her reason to doubt him.

But he could apologize for his deplorable behavior. He owed her that, if nothing else.

Edward stood up, pushing himself back from the table. "I should go and...begin work on that. Do you know when she will return?"

Georgiana graced him with a small, proud smile. "It is my

understanding that she will return this afternoon in order to get ready for the ball."

He put his hand on her shoulder, squeezing gently. "I really do not deserve you as a sister. I am not certain if I have ever expressed such a sentiment before, but it is true."

Georgiana patted his hand. "Apologize to Miss Worthing properly and you shall be well on your way to deserving both of us."

Edward left the dining room and headed for his office.

He had a letter to write.

CHAPTER 17

MARIA DRESSED and left quite early that morning. She did not even bother with breakfast.

Instead, she went across town to one of London's best hotels.

She went to see her father.

Maria already felt terrible for having not seen him in all of this time. He had told her not to worry about him and to focus upon finding a husband and enjoying the London season.

But he was her father. He was all the family that she had. She should have taken more time for him.

Lord Reginald's words still rang heavy in her ears. How could she have been such a disgrace?

He must hate her now. She had destroyed any care and esteem that he had held for her.

She had only been trying to be more like the other women in order to make him happy. It had backfired horribly. Now he liked her even less than before.

Having Lord Reginald think of her as a younger sister or a friend was better than the cold dislike he must now hold for her.

It was childish, but now she wanted nothing more than to go back to who she was before. To when and where she knew who she was. When she hadn't even had to think about who she was because it was that instinctive for her.

But she could not go back to the plantation, which was being sold. The Caribbean held nothing for her now. Although she did have the next best thing—not the place, but the person, who most felt like home to her.

Father.

She wanted to see him and curl up and be his little girl again. She had never disappointed Father. He would always love her no matter what. She felt safe with him. Herself. Without judgment or reservations.

When she was led up to his hotel room, she nearly collapsed into his arms.

"Oh, Father. How I have missed you." Such an emotional outburst was not unusual for her. Or, well, it was now. Since Miss Reginald had trained that out of her. But with her father, she could be herself again and be as emotional as she liked.

Father hugged her back, happy and surprised to see her. "I shall have room service called up for us, my dear. It is too early for you to have eaten yet."

Maria nodded. She was suddenly famished.

They ordered up food and Maria ate quickly, not caring if she was following her manners. She eagerly asked Father how things were going on the business front and inquired after his health.

"I am managing quite well," he told her. Although he could not quite disguise his cough as he spoke with her.

Maria tried not to fret. It was easy to see that the climate did not agree with him. He looked paler and more wane. Thinner, as well.

"Have you been getting enough sleep?" she inquired. "Have you been following your diet? Have you gotten enough water?"

"My dear, please do not trouble yourself with me," her father replied with fond exasperation. "I want to hear all about your lovely time. Not trouble you with my woes."

"They are your woes and therefore they are mine," Maria reminded him. "You are family and you know how deeply I care for you. Never hesitate to share your news or chastise me for inquiring after you. It is nothing short of my duty as your daughter."

Her father took her hand, patting it gently. "You are always too good to me, my dear. You have been since you were a child. I know that sometimes I am too hard on you, but I do value you. You have been nothing but an angel to me all these years."

Maria felt a swell of guilt rise in her like an ocean wave. "I fear that you should have been even harder on me than you were," she whispered, pulling her hand away.

Father's eyebrows rose. "Oh?" he asked, sounding mildly surprised but not upset. "And what brought on such an opinion, might I ask?"

Maria took in a deep breath, and suddenly the entire story was spilling out of her.

She told of how she had struggled with the training that Miss Reginald had given her. How backwards she had felt. As if she had been walking on her feet her whole life and was now being told to walk on her hands.

She talked about how she had been shamelessly teased. Considered to be prey or beneath everyone else's notice. How she had struggled and managed to get on friendly terms with some people but not others.

"The men will all dance with me and are quite pleasant," she admitted. "But none of them show me any particular favoritism. They seem to enjoy my company but not one of them seems inclined to call upon me or to take it any further than a dance."

The one point of pleasure was speaking on the older women.

"They knew you and Mother," she gushed. "They are most kind to me. They treat me as if I were their own child."

But, she admitted, none of them had recommended her to any of their sons as a potential wife.

"I did not understand it," she mourned. "I believe that they are earnest in their regard for me. The same with the men. And not all of the young ladies are awful. I have conversed with some of them and they are quite pleasant.

"I was unsure as to why they would not recommend me to their sons. But then..."

She relayed the rest of the story to her father. She even included her deplorable behavior from the night before. And how Lord Reginald had chastised her.

"I deserved every word that he said to me," she admitted. "I did not like it. I said many horrible and rude things back at him. Things that might be true but did not deserve to be said in that manner. I was unkind. I was angry and so I lashed out.

"But he is a good man. The best man that I know. For all he is cranky and dislikes going out and about at parties.

He has been most generous, you know. He has danced with me so that I might learn the new steps. He has never teased me or been unkind. He escorts me everywhere and takes me to the park and loves my sketches, and…"

Maria trailed off, for she feared that she had revealed too much of her heart in her words.

Her father smiled kindly—but knowingly. "It seems to me that you esteem him beyond what one normally would a friend."

Maria could feel herself blushing. It was more prominent now that she was in England and her tan skin was growing paler. "I did not mean to," she confessed. "It just sort of…happened."

"As these things do." Her father took a sip of tea, contemplating. "And now you fear that you have lost his friendship and his respect."

"Oh, but I deserve it. I was only trying to be what I thought that he would want. A woman who is sophisticated and witty."

"And so you tried to be like the other women and ended up going too far."

Maria nodded.

Her father sighed, setting down his teacup. "My dear, there is nothing wrong with emulating those around you. I do not think that was the issue. Whether your young man acknowledges it or not."

Maria felt her face heating up again. "He is not my anything, Father."

"But he is young," Father replied. "I think that you young people get so swept up in one another that you forget that the person you are experiencing such feelings for is young as well."

"He is several years older than I am."

"But he is not yet at my age, and indeed there is a great span of years between the two of us. Therefore, I have every right to call him young." Father smiled, and she knew that while he was being forthright, he was also teasing a little.

"Now, my dear, it seems to me that this young man did not have an appreciation for what you were trying to do. It is natural that we would try to act like those around us. That is how we learn the right ways to behave, after all.

"And there is nothing wrong with wanting to be witty or sophisticated. Your mistake came in going so far that you behaved without compassion and that you betrayed your true nature.

"You must never go so far that you are no longer acting like yourself. Do you understand? There must be balance. You can mimic the traits of those around you whom you admire but not at the expense of your own character."

Maria looked down at her empty plate, feeling ashamed. "I fear that I have failed you," she admitted. "That I have not been the daughter that you raised. The daughter that you should be proud of."

Father shook his head. "It would be impossible for you to go through life without making mistakes. That is not how life works. To err is human, after all, as Mr. Pope stated so eloquently.

"I think it is important to remember that you made a mistake with good intentions. You wanted to be accepted. I do not see how there is anything wrong with that."

"I would argue to the contrary, Father, and say that they were selfish intentions. I wanted people to embrace me. And most importantly I...I wanted Lord Reginald to see that I would make a good wife. That I would be able to hold my own in society.

"That he would not have to babysit me, so to speak. Or waste his valuable networking time at a ball protecting me. That he would not have to endure people making fun of his wife. He would be sure to hear any rumors or gossip about me. Even if nobody dared to say such a thing to his face.

"I was thinking...how could I possibly be a proper wife to him if I was a source of embarrassment? I would bring him nothing but shame. And of course he would only continue to see me as nothing but a child, a ward in a manner of speaking, if I did not show him how adult and sophisticated I could be.

"And so it was for my own selfish feelings that I acted. It was not out of compassion or with the wellbeing of others in mind."

"I think that you are right," her father said. "But I also think that you are too hard on yourself. You saw where your weaknesses were and how you could not be the best wife for Lord Reginald. And so you sought to remedy that. That is, at least, a bit unselfish in that you were thinking about what he needed."

He reached out and gently tucked a lock of errant hair behind her ear. "We are going to make mistakes in life. All of us. I made a dreadful mistake in not sending you to London sooner. It was selfish of me to keep you at home. Now you are ill prepared, and it is because of me.

"I could have even had you moved into town to stay with a family there and learn from a governess. But I wanted you with me. You were my pillar of strength, my dear. You were running the plantation these last few years. Not me."

Maria opened her mouth to protest. She would not have her father putting himself down in such a fashion. She would not have wanted to be sent away. She would have protested mightily. And what father wanted to give away his only child?

"Ah," Father said, cutting her off before she could begin. "You see what I mean? We all have moments where we behave selfishly and make mistakes. It is how we are. The mistake itself is not important. What is important is that we acknowledge it, and do what we can to make amends.

"There is a saying: no use crying over spilt milk. I think that is very wise. Why would you sit there mourning your mistake when it is so much easier for everyone if you simply clean it up? So long as you sit there and dwell on it, the mess continues."

Maria nodded. It made sense.

Part of her, she could admit to herself, had wanted her father to tell her that she had done nothing wrong. She had wanted to be absolved of her sins, so to speak.

But she had known that she had made a dreadful mistake. Wishing would not change that. And so she was grateful that Father was being so kind and understanding about it.

"Do you think that I have lost all chance with him?" she asked. "Lord Reginald, I mean?

"I know that it is probably wrong of me to wish to marry him. I feel as if it is taking advantage of his hospitality. He has been so good to me...could it be only that I feel for him because he is the man I am close to? Because I feel as though I owe him?"

Father considered that. "It could be possible, yes. If you were a different woman. But I know your heart, Maria. You are a sensible girl. Given to flights of fancy I think but not when it comes to serious matters.

"You always dealt with the plantation well, and the workers. You settled disputes and handled the accounts. That is not the work of someone who is unable to see things how they are.

"Had I glimpsed in you some sign of too quick an attachment towards others...or had seen that you were given to misinterpreting the intentions and behavior of others...then perhaps I would caution you.

"But you have always behaved with a level head. You see the best in others and I am grateful for that, truly. But you are not one to see a spade and call it a pickaxe."

Maria giggled a little at that. That seemed to have been her Father's intention, for he smiled, pleased.

"I think that if you feel romantically towards the young man then that is a true feeling. It is not out of gratitude or a misunderstanding of your own heart.

"And you have danced with many other men, you say. You have not shut yourself off from the world. If another man were capable of catching your fancy then I think that he would have by now."

"Then what do I do?" Maria asked. She could feel tears pricking at the corners of her eyes. "How do I fix this?"

"I am certain that the duke will forgive you," Father said kindly.

"You did not hear him, Father," Maria replied, trying to keep her voice from wavering. "He was livid. It was as though I had betrayed him. And perhaps I did.

"I know that he is not fond of how most of society behaves. I know that he is often bitter about it. Especially after how his father was. And how the ladies such as Miss Hennings use their desire to marry him as an excuse to be cruel to other women.

"He must feel hurt to think that I was becoming like them. Perhaps he even felt that it was a kind of violation of his trust."

"You will not know for certain if it's too late unless you talk to him," Father pointed out.

The very thought of speaking with Lord Reginald again was terrifying. How could she even begin to look him in the eye after all that she had done? And how upset he had been with her?

But Father was right. She would never get an answer about anything if she was to run away from the situation like a coward.

And she really had no other option. What was she supposed to do? Manage to hide somehow from Lord Reginald in his own house? Move in with Father in his hotel?

Stop going to balls or only go to balls that he was not going to be attending?

It was ludicrous. It would be so much easier for the both of them if she would simply swallow her pride and her fear and apologize.

She had handled the running of a household for the past few years. She had crossed an ocean. She had said the final farewell to her mother. Surely simply apologizing to someone when she made a mistake was not so hard as all of that?

Still, it terrified her.

Father gave her a sympathetic smile. "It will not be easy, I know," he told her. "But it's important for you to do. No relationship is perfect all the time. There will be moments where you have doubts or disagreements and you make mistakes.

"It's inevitable, and one shouldn't become too despairing at the prospect. It is simply how life works. It is important how you handle it, however. If you cannot handle a disagreement or making a mistake at this early juncture then you should not enter into the relationship at all.

"And all relationships are going to be like this, my dear. It is only that, for reasons unknown, we seem to be more scared of it when it comes to romance.

"If you had a friend and you argued with them—Miss Reginald, for example—would you not seek to amend things?"

"Well of course."

"But you would not fear for the end of your friendship?"

"Not necessarily. I should be ashamed, of course. I should wish to apologize for my behavior and for upsetting her so. But I would not believe it to be the end.

"I know how much she cares for me, after all. And I know that she knows how deeply I care for her. I would seek to make amends before any real damage could be done by her assuming that I was walking away from our friendship. But that would be all."

"Then why would you approach a potentially romantic relationship any differently?" Father pointed out. "You and the duke have a friendship. That much I think we can acknowledge. Why would you allow the possibility of romance to paralyze you with a fear you would not otherwise feel? Should you not give the relationship the same respect and treatment that you would any other?"

Maria nodded. It didn't replace her fear, not exactly, but it helped the situation to make more sense. It made it all seem more logical, and less...less dramatic than she had been picturing it in her head.

"This will not be the last time that you make a mistake, Maria," her father said. "And there will be times when the duke, or whomever you decide to marry, will make mistakes as well.

"If you allow this to make you afraid and cause you to run away then you have lost the relationship before it has truly begun. Apologize, accept the consequences, and ask what you might do to earn his trust back and to repair your friendship.

"From there, you will see how it unfolds."

Maria nodded, leaning around the table to hug him. "I have missed you, Father. And I have been terribly remiss in not visiting you more."

Father shook his head. "You were doing as I had instructed. You cannot be remiss in that."

"That does not mean that I cannot make time for you," Maria replied.

Father sighed. "Very well, then. I must admit that I have missed you. Tell me all about what you have been up to. And do not think to spare my feelings by omitting anything unpleasant. You are a most horrible liar, Maria, and always have been."

Maria smiled. This felt more normal, more the way things had been.

"If you insist," she said, teasing him.

The next few hours were quiet ones, but good ones. Father was in no condition to do anything strenuous. They went for a short walk through the hotel gardens, but mostly they stayed sitting and talking.

Or, rather, Maria did most of the talking and let her father listen. He told her there was not much for him to tell her. He had been wrapped up in business and had nothing so entertaining as balls and plays to speak to her about.

She was happy to oblige him, if that was what he wanted. She told him of their walks in the park and the art galleries and showings. She relayed to him the well-wishes of the older people she had met at the balls who remembered him and her mother with such fondness.

It seemed to do Father good to hear about all that she had been up to. Maria resolved to spend more time with him and tell him about her adventures. Not that she considered them much in the way of an adventure. But to her father, stuck in offices all day and then with the doctor...it certainly seemed like it.

She hardly even noticed the time passing until she looked at the clock and noticed that it was already well into the late morning. She had been with her father for hours.

She had told Georgiana where she would be going by giving her maid a note to give to her upon awakening. But Maria still had an obligation to the ball tonight. She had to return and get ready. And she didn't want to make Georgiana too worried.

"I really should go," she told Father reluctantly. "But I'll be sure to visit you more often."

"And you will have to tell me how it goes with your young man."

"For the last time, Father, he is not 'my' anything," Maria sighed. "But yes, I shall be sure to tell you how my apology to him goes."

"I am glad to see you in better spirits," Father told her. There was an edge of melancholy to his voice that made Maria sad.

She took his hands. "I am glad to see that you are holding up so well. But I want to take advantage of every moment that we have left together. I'll return soon."

Father nodded, and Maria had to hold in her own melancholy as she left the hotel and headed back to the Reginald household.

She knew that she only had so much time left with her father. She had noticed the coughs he had tried to hide. The circles under his eyes. He was holding up remarkably well given the arduous journey across the sea and then the change to a damp, cold environment.

In the face of that...in the face of her father's impending illness and even his...well.

It made her own romantic woes seem so much smaller and less important in comparison. She had been wringing her hands over something as simple as a mistake, something that an apology could fix, while her father was setting up his finances for his impending death.

If her father could deal with his own mortality with such dignity and grace, how could she not deal with something as simple as telling the duke that she was sorry? Her father was giving everything up. Selling the plantation. Rearranging his finances.

Surely she could manage a few earnest words.

Maria squared her shoulders and entered the Reginald household. She could handle this. She would handle this.

And whatever the outcome would be, she would accept it with dignity and maturity. In a way that would make her father proud.

She looked around the foyer. Should she go to Lord Reginald now? Wait for him later? She didn't want to disturb him but she also didn't want too much time to pass. The longer they went on without a reconciliation, the more awkward it would become. Especially with their attending social events together.

"Miss Worthing?"

Maria nearly jumped out of her skin, turning.

There he was. Standing there, looking oddly contrite and unsure.

She took a deep breath. Now, or never.

CHAPTER 18

EDWARD HEARD her the moment that she entered the house.

He felt rather like a stalker, sitting there in the parlor and waiting for her to come home. But he had finished writing his speech and had it approved by Georgiana. There was really nothing else that he could do except wait for Miss Worthing to return.

He had struggled for quite a long time over the writing of his speech. He did not want to seem too harsh, as he was wont. Nor did he wish to sound flowery or pompous.

Georgiana had gotten an amused gleam in her eye when she'd read the first few drafts of his letter.

"Edward, really. You must learn how to appeal to the softer feelings of a woman. God help you if you ever attempted to write any form of love poetry.

"I have also failed to notice any sort of declaration of your more romantic feelings for Miss Worthing."

"I thought it best to leave them out." He had felt like a schoolboy, shuffling foot to foot and struggling to meet her eyes instead of looking down at his feet. "I have only just realized them. How can I express my feelings to her when I am still getting properly acquainted with them?"

"That is fair enough, I cannot fault you for that reasoning. But if you are to hold yourself back in your words, you ought to hold yourself back in your actions as well. Give the other poor men a chance at the ball tonight. And I mean a proper chance. No hovering over Miss Worthing or swooping in to ask her for a dance first thing."

He had wanted to clench his jaw and grind his teeth at the thought, but he had nodded curtly. "I shall do my best."

Then he had gone to rewrite the draft of his speech.

Now he could hear Miss Worthing pausing in the foyer. Was she hesitant? Was she nervous?

Was she scared of him?

He would not blame her if she were, after how harshly he had spoken to her the night before. He must have intimidated her. He knew how nervous Miss Worthing got when interacting with other people.

He and his sister were the only two people around whom she felt truly comfortable. And what did he do with that trust? With that feeling of safety? He had shot it to bits as if he were going shooting for clay pigeons. And he had been just as merciless about it as well.

He would never forgive himself if she were truly scared of him. If she flinched when he went to speak with her, refused to meet his eyes, stepped away when he came near.

But there was nothing for him to do except approach her. If he let it go for too long then the silence would become more awkward than it already was.

Besides, the longer he waited, the more that she would think that he didn't regret anything that he had said. That he truly thought her to be shallow and all of the other horrible things that he had said to her, about her.

No, he must do this now.

He stood up, reading over the paper in his hand one last time, even though he already had it memorized. Then he folded it up and placed it inside his pocket and walked out into the foyer.

Miss Worthing gave a little jump when she heard him approaching and turned. Her eyes met his.

She looked tired. More than that, she looked nervous. He had made her that way, had he not? He had made her nervous to be around him.

It used to be—just yesterday—that she smiled at him when he

drew near. That she was eager to spend time in his company. That she welcomed his time and his presence.

Now it was the opposite. And it was all his doing.

He tried to stand tall and not shuffle about. He was a duke, for goodness' sake. He handled the affairs of dozens of tenants. He attended meetings all over London. He charmed his way through the networks and careful social and political maneuverings of the various clubs in the city.

And here he was, getting nervous over a simple apology.

Miss Worthing looked at him with a mixture of concern and apology in her eyes. Why was she feeling apologetic? He was the one who had made a horrible mess of things.

He cleared his throat. "Miss Worthing, I—"

"You must allow me to apologize," Miss Worthing blurted out.

He blinked, startled. "You—I beg your pardon?"

Miss Worthing twisted her fingers around one another. "I know that you are most likely still angry with me. And I cannot blame you for being cross.

"I was a most awful person last night. I was scared of being teased and made a fool of yet again. I was worried about dragging you and your sister down by association if I continued to be seen as a backwards bumpkin.

"I wanted to be treated as the others in the ball are. I wanted to be seen as an equal. As someone who was sophisticated and mature.

"I wanted to be like the other women. Not that I approve of cattiness or thoughtless behavior. But I let myself indulge in it because I wanted to be included. I wanted to feel as though I were welcomed by everyone. That I was the same as everyone else.

"And that was wrong of me. I should have stayed true to myself. Or at least stayed firm in my ability to think kindly of others. And to put them before myself.

"I was thinking selfishly and that allowed me to behave selfishly. It was wrong of me. And I let you down. I know how much you value honesty and forthrightness and compassion. I had none of those things last night.

"You were right to chastise me. All of the things that you said were true. I only hope that you will now give me a chance to make it up to you. To show you that I am earnest in my contriteness.

"Please, tell me that there is some way that I can show you how apologetic I am. How much I regret my actions. You and your sister have been so terribly kind to me while I have been here. You have treated me with so much kindness and respect.

"And you owed me nothing. You could have so easily found an excuse to turn me away. Or you could have simply housed me and then ignored me for the rest of the time.

"You didn't have to dedicate as much time and care to me as you have. As you did. You welcomed me as if I were family. And I can never repay you enough for that or properly show you the depth of my gratitude.

"And I paid you back for your kind treatment by disappointing you and acting in the way that I know you deplore. I only wanted to fit in and to show you that I could fit in. That I was not helpless in society. That I could mingle and handle whatever was thrown at me at a ball.

"But it was misguided of me and I apologize. I do not know how often or how many ways I can say it in order for you to believe me but...it is true."

Miss Worthing's breath left her in a final, shaky gasp. She stood there, wringing her hands a bit, but determinedly meeting Edward's eyes.

Edward was astounded. He had never considered the fact that Miss Worthing might think that she had to apologize.

He supposed that she might think that, from her perspective. After all, what he had said was overly harsh, but it was also true. She had become unlike herself.

But surely his reaction had been too much. She had not deserved the extreme reaction that he had given her. She should be coming to him expecting an apology. No, demanding one. She should not be standing there nervous and worried in front of him.

It was supposed to be the other way around.

Still, he understood where she was coming from if he thought about it. Were he in her shoes, he would be apologizing as well. She knew that she had done wrong, behaved badly, and she was trying to fix it.

He could not fault her for that.

Miss Worthing, however, seemed to be taking his continued silence for disapproval and anger rather than astonishment.

"Please do not be angry with me," she blurted out. "Or, if you are —I cannot tell you how to feel. I would never presume... I only..."

All of the things he had been thinking of saying flew out of his head.

"Miss Worthing, please," he said, interrupting her before she could work herself up any further. "You do not need to continue to press for my forgiveness. It is given. Given, in fact, before you even sought it."

Miss Worthing, it appeared, was now taking her turn to be astonished. Her words died away and she stared at him. Her mouth was open a little and she was starting to blush again.

It was easier to see her blushing now that her tan was fading. The English weather was not conducive to obtaining dark skin. In a way, he missed the tan. But he liked that he was able to see her blush better.

"I do not understand," she said at last. Her voice was very small. Like that of a mouse. "I behaved horribly. How can you forgive me so easily?"

"Especially when I was so angry?" he asked, adding on the part of her thoughts that he knew she would not say aloud.

Miss Worthing looked horribly embarrassed and gave a small cough. "Yes. I mean—that is—you had a right to be angry. I did not think that it would fade so fast, that is all. After a transgression such as mine."

He shook his head. "No. My anger was quick to rise but it was wrong of it to do so. I allowed it to control me and to hurt you. I should have been more sympathetic. I should have realized how frustrated and scared you were feeling at those parties."

"You had a right to feel that way," Miss Worthing replied. "I am not saying that you should be quite as bitter as you are about it. But I appreciate how you long for more compassion from others. You expect better from people because you see the potential for much more in them than they are choosing to give out."

Edward was once again taken aback. Flattered, even. He did not realize that she held him in such high esteem. He knew that she did esteem him, of course. But he had not thought she had such a high opinion of him as all this.

How could she read his heart better than he did? How could she look past the bitterness and frustration to see the real reason behind his disillusionment with the people around him?

He shook off the odd feeling of being...settled. Of warmth and happiness that bloomed in his chest. Was this what Georgiana had spoken of? That feeling of coming home?

But he couldn't focus on that right now. This was not about him. This was about apologizing to Miss Worthing.

"I cannot even begin to express to you how much I appreciate your words," he started. "Your apology and the esteem in which you hold me are both more than I deserve.

"I appreciate that you feel the need to apologize for your actions. If I am being honest, I feel that there was a need for a correction in your actions and I am glad to hear that you've acknowledged it."

Edward winced. That sounded condescending.

"That is not what I mean. I only wish to say...thank you for your apology."

Miss Worthing gave him a tentative smile. "I did need correcting. You do not have to worry about speaking the truth to me."

"No, but there is a mighty difference between a truth kindly told and a truth told without thought or consideration for the other person's feelings," Edward said.

"I was unnecessarily cruel to you in my assessment of your behavior. I should have had a thought to how you were feeling and the position that you felt you were in.

"I find that I am...I am realizing that I am too harsh in my behavior. My father was as well. I had vowed that I would never become like him. But my father would be harsh in his callous treatment of others. In how he lied to everyone and was charming on the surface but would stab anyone in the back if it got him further in a deal.

"We had plenty of money. We had one of the highest titles in the land. But nothing was good enough for him. He was always climbing the ladder. Always trying to be the most powerful person in the room.

"When your father wrote to us and we learned that our father had once gotten close enough to anyone to call them a friend...it astounded us. We couldn't quite believe it.

"Not that we thought that your father was lying, of course. Father had mentioned him once or twice. And he knew far too many details about our father for him to be lying. But it surprised us, you see.

"My father ruled us with an iron fist. And I promised myself that I wouldn't be like that. That my manner would be entirely different from his.

"But in striving to be unlike him I fear that I fixated on the wrong thing. That I was seeing only how he would lie to everyone and be a social climber. And so I grew to resent anyone else who did that, who behaved the way that he did. The people who would simper and lie and do whatever it took to get in the good graces of the people in power. The way they would make snide remarks and hurt others just to feel some kind of superiority and sense of control.

"And in hating that...as much as it was right for me to dislike it, it made me just as bitter and angry as my father was. For different reasons, of course. And for reasons that I like to think are better. But still."

"You are only trying to hold people up to a higher sense of right," Miss Worthing protested. "How on earth is it wrong of you to hold high standards?"

"When you allow it to make you unpleasant and refuse to give people the benefit of the doubt," Edward replied. "The way that you always do."

"I could hardly—"

"You had such passion in your voice when we spoke in the park," Edward told her. "When you protested at how humanity was truly good, and I just had to give it a chance. That if I reached out with kindness that was what I would get in return."

Miss Worthing's blush, which had faded, returned with full force. "I apologize. I was only speaking my thoughts."

"As you should have. And you were right." Edward sighed. "You can well imagine my surprise when you then seemed to have changed your tune at the next ball. When you seemed to have become that which you had said you disliked. And that which you knew I loathed."

"It was foolish of me, I know," Miss Worthing replied. "I hardly know what I was thinking."

"That you wanted to be accepted and treated as one of them," Edward said. "You wanted to be given the respect that you deserved, and you thought that this was the only way that you could obtain it. It is hardly unreasonable that you tried it out."

"It might have been reasonable, but it was not right," Miss Worthing said firmly.

Her stubbornness was endearing, but he did not know how to say that out loud. Not without sounding like a fool.

He waved her protests away. "Then we shall agree on that and let it fall by the wayside. That does not excuse how harshly I treated you. I was out of line. No matter how you had behaved, it would not be an excuse for my behavior.

"I can only promise you that I will endeavor to do better in the future. I know that it is not much. I know that you deserve better from me. But it is all that I can think of. Other than a gift of some kind, and I suspected that you would not appreciate the idea."

"No, I should not have appreciated it. I would have felt as though you were trying to...buy my affection. Even though I know that was not the case, it would have felt that way."

Edward nodded. He had suspected as much. "I hope that you will accept my apology as it is."

"Of course I shall. As if I could do anything else."

He did not understand how her forgiveness could be given so easily and completely. She looked at him happily, eyes wide, as though she could not even believe that he was no longer angry with her. As though the chance to accept his apology was the greatest opportunity that had ever been placed in front of her.

Edward knew that he had not truly earned her forgiveness. But he was going to take it, and happily, nonetheless.

"In that case, then, let us call ourselves friends again," he said.

"Is that what we are?" Miss Worthing sounded tentative once more. "Friends?"

"I should like to think so," he replied.

Perhaps they could be more than that. If he played his cards right. If he could only find a way to express himself.

Right now he still felt adrift. Lost. A bit confused. He couldn't even begin to open up his heart to her. Not when he was still parceling out his own feelings.

But looking at Miss Worthing...seeing how she was smiling again. How she was happy again. That was a good step forward. That was a start.

"Friends, then," Miss Worthing said, her smile widening into something more like what her smiles usually looked like: shining and confident.

He could not help but smile at her in return.

CHAPTER 19

MARIA DREW in a shaky breath as she looked at herself in the mirror.

Georgiana seemed to be taking extra care with Maria's appearance today. Although Maria could not fathom why.

"Is this ball particularly important?" Maria asked. They were only a month into the season, so she was not sure that it could be. But one never knew. Certainly she did not.

Georgiana hummed, surveying the work that the maid had done on Maria's hair. "Not necessarily. The earl and his wife always put on a splendid affair, of course. The lady is an expert at being a hostess. But I would not call this a particularly important ball, no."

"All right." Maria was at a loss, then. But Georgiana was fussing over her as if this was her first ball all over again.

Perhaps there would be some eligible men there that Maria had not yet met? Georgiana would be anxious that Maria make a good first impression. That was probably what it was.

Or it could simply be that Georgiana was trying to boost Maria's spirits. She must know that Maria still felt a bit down in her manner and was trying to cheer her up by helping her to feel beautiful.

After apologizing to Lord Reginald and receiving his apology in return, Maria felt a bit better. Her apology had been well received. Indeed, it had been received with a grace and eagerness that she had not expected.

In fact, Lord Reginald had behaved as though he had not

expected her to apologize at all. He had seemed most surprised at her words. But it was not as though he thought that she would not apologize out of a lack of manners. Rather, it was as though in his mind she had nothing to apologize for.

That puzzled Maria. He had at last agreed with her that her behavior was not that of a proper young lady and that she ought to feel badly for it and do better. But he had seemed far more concerned with his own reaction and how it had hurt her.

It was far more generous than Maria thought that she deserved. And while she doubted that he harbored any romantic feelings for her, it warmed her heart to know that they could at least continue their friendship.

In fact, he had insisted upon calling her a friend. That was far more than she could have expected. Last night, even this morning, she had been certain that she had lost his esteem forever.

She could not deny that confirming that he only cared for her as a friend did sting a bit. She had not consciously been hoping for more from him, of course. She knew now that all hope of that was gone.

But apparently a part of her, one that she had not even acknowledged, still held out hope that he might feel something for her other than friendship. A fondness of a different sort.

But it was no matter. She would not let herself dwell on it. She had earned back his friendship and that was more than enough for her. It ought to be more than enough.

Perhaps now that she knew her hopes were entirely dashed, she ought to truly focus on finding another man to be her husband.

She had not really been trying this past month. Not when her heart was caught up with Lord Reginald. But now was the time for that. She would run out of balls in the season before she knew it.

There were plenty of gentlemen who had been perfectly nice to her over the past month. She should turn her attentions towards them in earnest and see what came of it.

After all, if she'd had any chance with Lord Reginald, it had been ruined by her last night. Friendship was almost more than she deserved to ask for.

How ironic, she thought, that in trying to prove to him that she deserved to be his wife, she had proven just the opposite. She had chased him away. Now she would never have him.

It made her feel a little silly. Like she was one of those tragic heroines in opera, doomed to marry a man she did not love while pining for another who would not even give her the time of day.

Maria did not see herself as a tragic figure. She did not embrace such a fate. But it did sting of that, just a little.

You will get over it in time, she told herself. Her feelings for Lord Reginald would fade. She would make them fade.

And she would grow to love her husband. She could manage that. If he was a good man, an honorable man, then of course she could grow to care for him.

A part of her mind whispered that she would never care for him as she did Lord Reginald. She ignored that whisper. She had to believe that she would come to esteem her husband the way that she esteemed Lord Reginald or else she would collapse into a puddle of despair.

Many women did not love their husbands when they were first married, she told herself. Surely respecting one's husband and receiving moderate pleasure from his company was enough.

Her father was dying and yet he was managing to uphold his end of things. He was settling accounts and doing what he had to in order to make sure that her future and the future of his holdings was secure.

How could she do anything less? He was counting on her. Trusting her to be an adult and to navigate the treacherous waters of finding a husband without him.

She could not then betray that trust because she was childish and could not set aside her feelings. A woman must be pragmatic when it came to these things.

If she did not have a proposal in place by the end of the season she would be destitute. Her father would have sent off all of his holdings to that distant cousin, whatever his name was. There would be nothing for Maria.

She could live with Father in his hotel until he passed on. He would have made sure that, at least, was provided for. But she would not be able to afford all the new gowns and the theatre tickets and all the rest that being a part of the London Season required.

This was her only chance.

She could not blow it over something like a broken heart. As immense and as powerful as that broken heart felt to her in that moment.

It was nothing so glamorous as going off to war, forsaking home and love and comforts to die for one's country. It wasn't nearly anything so dramatic as all that. But it was something similar, she told herself, in that it was setting aside what one wanted in order to do what one knew to be the right thing.

Well, if all of those soldiers could manage it on such a heavy scale, surely she could manage it in this.

She would earnestly get to know the men at the ball tonight. Reacquaint herself with the ones that she had already met a few times before.

Then she would make herself a short list that night after the ball. After all, if she was marrying for pragmatic reasons then why not be pragmatic in her choosing?

She would make a short list and then slowly eliminate the names off the list as she got to know the men on it better. Then... she gave herself a month. Yes. Then she would have only one or two and could grow closer to them and they to her and she would have a higher chance of one of them proposing to her by the end of the season.

Maria caught Georgiana's eyes in the mirror. "You seem lost in thought," Georgiana said. "Did the reconciliation with my brother not go as well as you had hoped?"

"Oh no, it went quite well," Maria said. "Or, I think that it did. He was very grateful for my apology and accepted it readily. He even seemed surprised that I had apologized."

"I believe he felt that his transgression was the greater one," Georgiana replied.

"I did not feel as though he had done anything wrong, at least not at first," Maria acknowledged. "But I understand now what he was truly apologizing for, which is that he allows himself to become too harsh in his judgement. He seemed earnest in his desire to do better and I hope that he will. For his own sake."

"Yes, he will be happier once he does," Georgiana replied.

"All finished, Miss," the maid said, stepping back out of the way.

Maria turned to look at Georgiana head-on. "What do you think?"

"I think that you look like a vision," Georgiana assured her. "You will be the belle of the ball."

"I would not go so far as to say all of that," Maria said, blushing.

Georgiana smiled at her and helped her up to standing. "I hope that you will enjoy yourself tonight, my dear. You deserve it, truly."

Maria tried to remember her father's words. She had to find a balance between fitting in and staying true to herself. That was what life was about: balance.

She would find a way.

Lord Reginald said nothing when they descended the stairs to meet him in order to get into the carriage. It only cemented for Maria how she had missed out on her chance.

Normally, Lord Reginald would compliment Maria on her looks when they met up in order to leave for the ball.

This time, however, he said nothing. He did seem to be rather at a loss for words in general, however. Georgiana murmured something to him that Maria could not catch, and he quickly led them to the carriage.

He must be lost in his thoughts, Maria decided. Perhaps it was a business matter?

But no, she must not spend all of her time thinking about Lord Reginald. She was moving on. She had tried, and she had failed. No sense in crying over spilled milk, as her father had said.

They arrived at their destination and Maria descended, trying to remember how to breathe.

She hoped that she had not burned any bridges with her behavior the night before. She did not think that she would have, given how Miss Hennings seemed to still be invited to all manner of balls. But one never knew.

They entered the ballroom and Maria had to try to remember all of the things that Georgiana had taught her. Head up, glide, small steps...

It was maddeningly difficult to ignore Lord Reginald, but she must. She spied Mrs. Rutlage and moved over towards her immediately, engaging her in conversation.

"You look quite the picture tonight, Miss Worthing," Mrs.

Rutlage told her. "I should not have believed it was you had you not addressed me. You do not look at all like the same girl that I first met a month ago."

"I hope that I should take that as a compliment," Maria replied.

"Very much so," Mrs. Rutlage said. "Not that you were in distasteful outfits or anything by any means. But there is much more confidence in your bearing now and you wear the clothes as though they truly belong to you.

"When we first met it was as though you had borrowed your mother's dress and were terrified that she should find out about it at any moment. And now look at you.

"I dare say that your posture is improved as well. But then I am a stickler for such things."

"As is Miss Reginald. She had me balancing books on my head for weeks."

Mrs. Rutlage laughed. "And how goes it, living with the Reginalds? Do they continue to treat you well?"

"I should expect nothing less from them. They are both saints."

"Yes, they are quite fond of you." Mrs. Rutlage's tone of voice carried an odd significance to it. One that Maria could not quite place.

"In any case I must fill my dance card," Maria said. "I hope that you will not mind. I expect to be rather busy tonight."

"That is how it should be, my dear," Mrs. Rutlage said. "A bright young thing such as yourself should not be expected to sit with us gossiping old birds all night."

"You are far from that," Maria replied. "You are all still quite lovely in my opinion."

"You are too kind. Now off you go, my dear. Enjoy yourself."

Maria was not so certain of the 'enjoying herself' part of things. But she was on a mission, and she was doing it properly now. She wasn't going to allow herself to be distracted.

She half-wondered if Lord Reginald could tell that she was avoiding him. It was not that she was avoiding him for his own sake. She believed him when he said that he had forgiven her.

But she had to stay away from him or she would fall into her old habits. She would try to impress him. She would focus only on him. She had to remain strong and keep herself focused.

She filled up her dance card rather quickly. She was more active than she usually was about it. Before she had always waited for a gentleman to approach her.

This time, she would find a way to enter into conversations that included the gentlemen, and then find a means to mention she was looking for partners to fill up her card. At least one of the gentlemen was sure to offer.

Mr. Upton was one such person whom she recognized from previous balls and who was happy to ask her for a dance. He was practically falling over himself for the opportunity, hardly letting her begin the conversation before asking her.

Maria made sure that her dance card was full before letting herself be led out onto the dance floor for her first turn. If Lord Reginald stayed true to his habit of coming up and asking her for a dance while she was engaged talking with someone else, she knew she would be weak and say yes.

She couldn't do that. She couldn't allow herself to hope.

Instead she made sure that she was out on the dance floor as much as possible.

Find a balance, she kept reminding herself. Emulate the others without losing yourself.

She did her best, making witty remarks but making sure that they were not cruel or thoughtless. She didn't gossip but she shared humorous stories from her time back home growing up. She tried to be outgoing and engaging in a way that she hadn't let herself be before.

Fear had always paralyzed her. She had listened instead of talked. And she knew that the people she spent time with appreciated her listening. The way that she genuinely cared about what they were saying. She didn't let go of that.

But ever since that first dinner she had been scared to death of saying the wrong thing. Or of saying too much. Now she let it all out again. She could be herself and she could be witty. She could be both.

The surface might change or alter, adapt depending upon the company she was keeping, but that didn't mean she had to give up the core of who she was.

Her partners seemed taken aback by her newly confident behavior, although not in a negative way.

"I must say," Mr. Upton said as she danced with him, "you appear to have undergone a most positive change of heart, Miss Worthing."

"What do you mean, sir?" she asked.

"There is a pleasant determination to your manner that I had not noticed previously. Have you had an uplift in spirits?"

"I recently paid a visit to my father," Maria said, being as truthful as she dared. "He is feeling poorly but it always does the both of us good to see one another."

From there the conversation moved on to other subjects. Mr. Upton seemed delighted at her newfound energy. And he was not the only person to comment upon it.

Almost all of the men that she spoke to spoke of how much more confident and at peace she seemed. Many asked if she had received unusually good news lately.

Maria only laughed and told them that she was especially happy with her new dress and that she had gotten to visit her father.

Everyone seemed to accept this without too much curiosity and certainly not any doubt. The lie came easily. More easily than she had expected.

Perhaps, despite her disaster the night before, she had gotten better at this whole conversing thing. Better than she had expected. Perhaps all that she needed was to give herself the confidence to go with it.

She tried to remember what Edward and Georgiana had told her, for while Edward had said it in anger that didn't make it any less true. And Georgiana had said it to her previously, although she had not listened as she should have, apparently:

Maria could not control others. They would be kind or cruel as they saw fit. But she could control her reaction to them. She could refuse to give them any power over her.

Miss Hennings could say and think whatever she wanted. But Maria was the one who decided if those words and thoughts hurt her or not.

What was it to her if Miss Hennings thought she understood

Maria? The important people knew better. They knew who she truly was.

She would not allow herself to become someone that she wasn't and she wouldn't allow herself to disappoint the people that she loved in order to please or defeat someone who was so clearly beneath her notice. Someone who did not deserve her time.

And so when she spied Miss Hennings approaching her—or rather the group of people she was speaking with—she squared her shoulders and refused to give Miss Hennings that power over her ever again.

"Miss Hennings!" she said brightly, turning to greet her. Maria pictured playing with kittens and puppies and eating chocolate truffles. That way when she smiled at Miss Hennings, it was a genuine smile.

"I hope that you are enjoying the ball," Maria went on, before Miss Hennings could say anything. "That is quite a lovely frock that you have on. Is it new?"

"As always," Miss Hennings replied. She seemed taken aback but quickly recovered. "I wish that I could ask the same of yours."

Maria ignored the comment. "I think that the cut rather suits you. Is the wine tonight not divine?"

Miss Hennings again seemed taken aback. Maria hadn't just ignored what Miss Hennings had said. She had acted as though it hadn't even been said. "I...yes."

Maria looked over at the other people she was talking with. "Miss Hennings was at the first ball I ever attended. I was still quite the bumpkin, I fumbled horribly throughout the entire meal." She then smiled at Miss Hennings, as if the entire thing were an inside joke between friends.

Miss Hennings looked as though she were choking a little. By acknowledging her own mistakes and owning up to her faux pas, Maria had essentially taken away all of Miss Hennings' ammunition.

Maira could not deny that it was a marvelous thing to watch Miss Hennings struggle in such a manner. It was not particularly kind of her to think that way, but she could not help but relish the revenge just a bit.

"I had just come to London for the first time, you see," Maria went on. She then launched into an amusing story about landing in England and the weather change and how it affected her.

It was an exaggeration of her actual experiences, and a humorous exaggeration at that. But the party need not know that. All they knew was that it was an amusing story, and charmingly told.

Miss Hennings looked to be completely at a loss.

"Shall I be your partner for the next dance, Miss Worthing?" asked one of the men in the group.

Maria curtsied. "I would be delighted, sir."

As she moved to take his arm, she heard Miss Hennings whisper, "Well played, Miss Worthing."

She didn't outwardly acknowledge it, but inwardly, she smiled.

It was well played, if she did say so herself. She had done nothing cruel or thoughtless. Indeed, her kindness seemed to have bowled Miss Hennings over as surely as if Maria had chucked a massive croquet ball at her.

In fact, she did not see Miss Hennings much after that. And it was always from afar. Miss Hennings seemed to have noticed that Maria was staying away from Lord Reginald. That, on top of Maria's new attitude, seemed to have created a kind of ceasefire.

She could see Miss Hennings approaching Lord Reginald at one point and Maria could not help but bite down on her lip to hide her smile.

Simply because Maria was no longer taking up Lord Reginald's attention did not mean that he was going to be open to Miss Hennings.

Is that what Miss Hennings thought? Had she been operating under the mistaken notion that Maria was somehow stealing Lord Reginald from her? That Miss Hennings had him in the bag until Maria had come along?

If that was the case, then Maria almost pitied the other woman. To be operating under such a mistaken notion was only going to end in Miss Hennings' disappointment.

That was a small consolation to her. Lord Reginald would never marry a woman as cruel or as petty-minded as Miss Hennings. Maria knew that he would choose wisely.

Perhaps, in time, she would even come to like the woman that he chose. She would have to be a woman of remarkable character.

She hoped that Lord Reginald would approve of Maria's choice of husband. Whoever that man ended up being. She was compiling a list in her head already and was surprised at how many men were on it.

Everyone was being so engaging tonight. Seeking her out. Who knew that such a little change in her own attitude and behavior would create such a large change in how others perceived her.

It meant the ball was the most fun she had ever had. This was what Mother had spoken of when she had told Maria stories about her time in London before the Caribbean. This was the glamor and entertainment that Maria had envisioned as a child.

She merely had to behave with confidence. Take the bull by the horns, so to speak. And everyone followed her lead.

Could it be that she had been such prey to them before because she had known that she was prey? Because she had been nervous, and they had picked up on it? Sensing what an easy target she would be?

Now, with her confident behavior and her determination to truly engage with everyone...everybody else was sensing it. They were treating her as an equal. As if they had known her their entire lives.

She had to admit that this feeling was a bit intoxicating. It went to her head in a way that wine never did. But she resolved not to let it knock her off balance. She would not overextend herself.

But it was a revelation, to realize that this whole time being herself really was enough. It was simply a matter of having the confidence and gregariousness to go with it.

It was not only the men who were remarking on the difference, although they certainly did. Some of the younger ladies with whom Maria had yet to truly make friends made some remarks as well.

"You must call upon me," seemed to become the phrase of the evening.

Maria found that she was actually getting invitations to things. That the ladies her own age were finally accepting her.

"I am attending a theatre performance tomorrow, you must join me at my box."

"I hear you are attending my ball with the Reginalds? Come early for dinner, I shall add you to the list."

"Be sure to remember my address, and please bring the darling Miss Reginald with you. I shall expect you both."

I belong here, Maria told herself, and for the first time she actually felt it. She did belong here. She was just as good as any of them.

She was finally feeling like one of them.

Oh, she could hardly wait to tell Father! And Georgiana. She would be most pleased to know that all of her hard work with Maria was finally paying off.

She was tempted to tell Lord Reginald as well, but...she could hardly bother him with such a thing. Not when she was trying to keep away from him and not fall into the trap of trailing after him.

No, she would keep it to herself unless he asked after her. She would not wish to be rude, after all. It was not his fault that she was in love with him and he did not return her affections. How could she possibly blame a man for that?

Emotions could not be controlled, after all. If they could then she would be able to get rid of her own.

But for her own sake, she must not seek him out. She must not dance with him. She must not let herself fall into the trap of being around him overmuch, else she would forget to think of anything else and be caught up all over again in how wonderful she thought he was.

If only he could read her thoughts. He would think her the most ridiculous of women.

Luckily, whenever her thoughts turned towards him, there was another dance to distract her, another partner. It was even better than her first ball, before she had become too downhearted with the feeling of being an outsider.

Her feet fairly ached by the end of it. Mrs. Dale remarked at one point that she had never seen Maria dance so much before.

"I have hardly had time to talk to you all," she said to the older ladies. "I deeply apologize."

"That is what morning calls are for," Mrs. Dale informed her. "You are young and unmarried! That is what balls are for. Dance to your heart's content, my dear, and never you worry about us."

She hardly even noticed the time passing. It seemed to all be a whirl to her. The moment she stopped to catch her breath there was another person there to claim her attention, either for a conversation or a dance.

When Georgiana finally caught a hold of her, Maria thought she might faint. Usually she didn't feel the exhaustion until they were already in the carriage but now she could feel it seeping into her bones while she was still at the ball.

It was an odd combination of exhaustion and elation. She was full of energy, fairly bursting with it, giddy with it, but she also thought she might burst into tears from how tired she felt. Even her eyes ached.

"You have had quite a time of it," Georgiana told her. "I think that it is time we set off home."

"If you think it is best," Maria replied.

She kept a hold of her dance card so that in the morning she might go over the men that she had danced with and form a proper list.

Lord Reginald helped her with her coat. He seemed oddly quiet. Maria had not danced with him that night—for the first time since this whole affair had started.

It made her ache inside. It made her feel bereft.

But of course, it was likely that he had hardly noticed. She was the one aching with unrequited feelings, not him. Lord Reginald was being quiet for other reasons, she was sure.

A man such as him had plenty to occupy his mind, after all. He might have heard some distressing or frustrating business news. Or it could be that he was simply tired after dealing with people such as Miss Hennings all evening. She would not put it past the lady to have pushed Lord Reginald beyond the limits of his endurance.

Maria settled into the carriage. She was unsure how to handle the carriage ride home. Would Lord Reginald ask how her evening went? Would Miss Hennings have said something to him about Maria's changed behavior?

Would he be proud of how she handled herself this evening? She liked to think that he would be. Not that she would ask him. She wanted to ask him of course and even a few days ago, perhaps even yesterday, she would have.

But she had to remain strong. She had to...

Maria woke again when she felt Georgiana gently shaking her.

"Oh my dear, you really have exerted yourself this evening."

She could hear the amusement in Georgiana's voice and blinked her eyes open slowly.

Lord Reginald was already out of the carriage and arranging things for the evening, unlocking the front door and such. Georgiana helped Maria out of the carriage.

She couldn't believe that she had fallen asleep. She felt terrible. But Georgiana simply seemed amused by the entire thing.

Under such circumstances, she hoped that Lord Reginald would understand why she didn't bid him a proper goodnight. She could hardly remember getting up to bed.

"You wore yourself out," Georgiana said, helping her get tucked into bed.

Maria nodded, so tired she could hardly speak. "It seemed to be...a success."

"Oh my dear," Georgiana replied, an oddly knowing tone in her voice. "You have no idea how much of a success it was."

That was the last thing she knew before falling asleep.

CHAPTER 20

EDWARD SAT down in front of the fire, in a daze.

It felt as though he were almost outside of his own body. Floating. Lightheaded except all over.

He loved her. He loved *her*. He *loved* her.

Not that he had doubted what Georgiana had said before. Not that he hadn't already had his suspicions, had been trying to decipher the workings of his heart.

But it hadn't hit him, truly, until tonight. And it had felt like a ton of bricks had been dropped onto his head.

First, there had been when Miss Worthing descended the stairs.

Edward suspected Georgiana had purposefully ensured that all the stops were pulled out for Miss Worthing's outfit that night. She had looked like a vision.

Of course, Edward had already been aware that Miss Worthing was pretty. How could he not be? He had spent quite a lot of time around the woman and he was not blind.

Besides, she was possessed of a different kind of beauty than most. Perhaps it was her upbringing but there was a wildness to her, a striking sort of look to her, that made her stand out from the crowd.

So, yes, he was aware that Miss Worthing was possessed of a lovely face and form. But never before had he been dumbstruck by her.

As she had descended the stairs in her white dress, her hair done up to expose her face and elegant neck...he had found himself without breath.

Small crystals or other sparkling stones had been set in her dark hair so that it looked like a nest of stars in the night sky. And while her skin had gotten paler since coming to England, it was still dark enough to create a lovely contrast against the white muslin of her dress.

His breath had caught in his throat and he had suddenly found it quite hard to even imagine getting any words out.

Miss Worthing must have noticed something odd in his manner, for she had taken care not to address him too much as they made their way to the ball.

Edward could hardly blame her. Thinking back on how he had behaved he must have looked like quite the fool. He had forced himself to look out the window in order to prevent himself from simply staring at her.

It was as though he had been trying for ages to solve a complex math problem, and he finally understood the logic of it. He did care for her, he did, and not as a brother or as a friend, but as a lover. As a husband should.

He could have put off the subsequent ball as merely his own bias, but he was certain that something in Miss Worthing's manner had changed that night.

It could not merely be his own revelation. It must color his perception of her behavior, to be sure. He was not denying that. But he could not be so imaginative as to conjure up everyone else's behavior.

He was not necessarily a jealous man. He was not prone to envy. And so he did not think that he imagined the looks that the men were giving Miss Worthing as they danced with her.

Nor could he say that he was the sort of man who gave a person more credit than they were due. Indeed, if his sister was to be believed—and he did believe her—he was more inclined to give someone less credit than they were due.

And so he could not be imagining how Miss Worthing was more confident. More outgoing. How she managed to be more cheerful and confident, without becoming thoughtless and catty the way that she had last night.

No, he could not be imagining that. But what, then, had caused such a change in her?

Perhaps it was her father. She had gone to see him that day, after all. That was where Georgiana had finally told him that Miss Worthing had gone to after Edward had nearly torn his hair to pieces worrying about her.

That should have been another clue. Of course it would be natural for him to worry about a woman he had promised to take care of. But if his sister knew where Miss Worthing was going, that should be reason enough for him to relax.

Georgiana was, after all, an eminently sensible woman. She would never have allowed Miss Worthing to go anywhere or do anything that was unsafe or untoward. There was, therefore, no reason for him to have been so worried.

But he had been. And that should have been a sign.

In any case, it must have been Miss Worthing's visit to her father that had put her in such a wonderful mood at the ball that night. His condition must have been better than she had feared. Perhaps his illness was not so severe as the doctors had predicted.

It was wonderful news, of course, but Edward dared not presume. It was all that he could guess at, however, when it came to Miss Worthing's renewed spirits.

He dared not consider it his own apology to her. While he did not doubt her when she said that she took it in good grace, he had noticed that she avoided him all night.

He had not even been able to find her for their customary dance together.

That had troubled and upset him more than he could admit out loud. He had grown used to their dance. He had come to see it as a touchstone of his evening. A way to genuinely enjoy himself and to relax after dealing with people he disliked, and a way to bolster himself for the next half of the evening.

But he certainly couldn't march across the ballroom and demand that she fit him in for a dance. As much as he might want to do just that, he had to respect her wishes. If she, for some reason, did not want to dance with him then he had to accept it.

It could be that while she had accepted his apology, she needed a bit of space. He could not blame her for that. If she needed some time to acquaint herself with the fact that he was no longer angry with her—that indeed he had no right to be quite as angry as he had been—then that was her choice.

But it had been like a blow to the chest to realize just how much he had come to rely upon that dance to anchor him at these occasions.

Of course, if they were married, he could not necessarily dance with her. But he could have her by his side for much of the ball so that would balance it out. And he wouldn't have the likes of Miss Hennings after him anymore either.

It had struck him, then—and struck him again now, thinking back on the evening, staring into the fire as though it could hold the answers—how easy it was to imagine.

How easy, how simple it would be. How already similar to their current situation it would be. Miss Worthing already lived with them, after all.

She already spent almost all day, every day with him and with Georgiana. He had to be called away to work on things from time to time but such was the life of a landowner and nobleman. His wife would have to contend with the same thing.

And he knew that he would be comfortable around her. That she would respect the fact that he was not truly inclined towards social gatherings. That he wanted honesty in a partner.

He could trust her to run the household. Miss Worthing had run her father's household and indeed the plantation itself back in the Caribbean. As her father's health had failed she had taken on more and more of it.

After all of that, and an ailing father on top of it, Miss Worthing would certainly be able to run the household. Edward could trust her far more than he trusted any other young lady that he knew.

But even with all those sensible reasons...they were not why he was now sitting in front of the fire, recalling every moment of the evening, trying to sear into his memory the vision of her dancing.

It had nothing to do with sense. He liked to think that sense was part of why he cared for her. After all, no matter how deep an infatuation, he had his land and his family's future to consider when choosing a wife.

But sense was not involved when he had looked at her on the

dance floor and missed doing that with her. Sense was not there when he had felt a pang of sorrow and frustration as she had laughed at something her dance partner had said.

He had wanted to make her laugh like that. To be the one bringing that smile to her face. To be moving about the ballroom with her.

He wanted people to see Miss Worthing in the middle of the dance floor, shining like a star, and say, "That is the Duke of Foreshire's wife."

For she was a star. A lovely one. He wondered if she had been able to see it. Had she noticed? Had she realized how something about her energy drew every eye in the room to her that night?

Miss Worthing had always been lovely. He would never deny that. It was not as though she had been this...ugly duckling that became a swan.

But she had been awkward. Afraid. Unsure. And those traits had rendered her either invisible or a target.

That night, it had been different. She had possessed a confidence and ease of manner that made her transformation complete. For the first time, he overheard people speaking of her looks, how lovely she was. How fine her dress was.

Suddenly, everyone could see what Edward had been seeing and taking for granted all along.

For he had taken it for granted. And now he feared there was no chance of him earning a special place in Miss Worthing's heart the same way that she occupied a special place in his.

Her newfound confidence had extended even to Miss Hennings. The lady had come up to Edward at one point during the ball. She had, apparently, just come from speaking to Miss Worthing.

"I see that your shadow has at least abandoned you," Miss Hennings had noted. "You must be quite relieved to no longer shoulder such a burden."

"If you are referring to Miss Worthing," Edward had said, as coldly as he could manage while still being polite, "I can assure you the care of her was never a burden."

"Oh but of course," Miss Hennigns had said. "You are too generous in spirit to ever see it that way. But you must admit that you are freer now to think of your...other impending responsibilities."

Oh, how he had longed to turn to her. To say coldly and with finality, if you are speaking of marriage, Miss Hennings, I fear you will forever be barred from that conversation in my thoughts.

It would have given him such satisfaction. To call helping out a young lady a burden. To insinuate constantly about his needing to marry, as if it were not gauche to do so.

It fairly made his blood boil.

"She is quite a strange creature," Miss Hennings had gone on. "She was very polite to me. Almost as if someone had put her up to it. Did you finally install some manners in her?"

"I can assure you, Miss Hennings, that if Miss Worthing was polite to you it was certainly not because of my influence."

Miss Hennings had stared at him, her mouth agape.

Edward smirked in recollection. He had not been able to smirk in the moment. That would have been taking it too far. That would have been cruel.

But he had certainly felt like doing so. It had taken quite a lot to maintain a stoic face.

"We have been distant as of late," Miss Hennings had said, trying again. "I ought to call upon your lovely sister. I suppose that you will also be at home—"

"I'm afraid I will not be. I have much business to attend to in town in the mornings."

Miss Hennings had looked rather as though she had swallowed a lemon. She had looked back through the crowd to the dancers.

"I suppose that I ought to congratulate you."

"Upon what, Miss Hennings?"

"Oh, do not make me say it aloud," she had said. Or spat, rather. She had been in quite a state. "Everyone has been speculating on it. Of course I refused to believe it. I knew that you could do so much better for yourself.

"But it seems that I was mistaken, and so I must offer you my congratulations. I am sure that your choice will provide you with what you deserve."

Edward had sighed then. He did not take pleasure in this. He might be harsh but it was also almost sad how Miss Hennings behaved. She must have had a very empty and lonely existence if she clung to him, and to her meanness, in such a fashion.

"I am not engaged to anyone, if that is what you are hinting at," he had told her firmly. "I do wish that you would speak more plainly in your manner, Miss Hennings.

"But if you did, perhaps we would have struck up a better friendship than the one that we have. As it is, while I am not currently engaged to Miss Worthing, I would rather be engaged to her than to any other woman in this room."

There were many other things that he could have said in that moment. Things that he honestly wished that he could say then. But that would have been straying from honesty into needless cruelty.

He did not need to be cruel to make his point. And if he was, then he would have to take back everything he had said in chastising Miss Worthing the other night. For he would have become a hypocrite.

Miss Hennings had looked...appalled was probably the best word for it.

Edward had bowed to her as politely as he could. "I must bid you good evening, Miss Hennings. I believe I see my sister."

And so he had left her.

Oddly enough, it had not left him with the feeling of triumph that he would have expected.

Instead it left him feeling sad. Pitying, even.

For Miss Hennings must have been living such a terribly empty life, he thought. For her to be so focused upon marrying him that she would be heartless and cruel to others. For her to make such despairing remarks about other women. To be so blind as to her own behavior and how it looked to others.

He could not help but wonder what sort of empty life she led. He pitied her for it. His own life was rich and wonderful. Even more so now that Miss Worthing was a part of it.

As he had walked away, Edward had found himself genuinely hoping that Miss Hennings would learn her lesson from this. That she would become better.

Perhaps she would find someone who would see through the anger and pettiness that she projected. Someone who would give her the love and understanding that she seemed to need. Someone who would validate her and find the softness lurking inside of her and bring it out into the light.

Maybe, he had realized in that moment, Miss Worthing had changed him.

A few weeks ago, he would never have had such a thought about Miss Hennings. He would have been pleased at taking her down a peg. He would not have mustered such sympathy for her.

But Miss Worthing believed that people were inherently good. That everyone had good motivations.

Certainly, if someone as good as Miss Worthing could be tempted to behave poorly, as she had the other night...could there not be good in the other people that he felt were such a torment to him?

It was something odd to think about but not in an unpleasant way. It had gotten him to think that perhaps he really ought to be less harsh on people. Perhaps he ought to be kinder.

A little confidence had clearly gotten Miss Worthing a long way that evening. But as he had watched her, he had seen that the foundations for her popularity were already laid down. Her kindness had done that.

The people around her must already remember how well she listened. How anxious she was to make friends. How much she cared.

Without those, Edward doubted that the rest of the night would have gone as well. He was sure it was her previous actions that lent her such an easy time of it tonight. All that she had needed was that final boost of determined confidence.

Whatever her mission was that night, she had succeeded in it. She had truly been the belle of the ball.

Edward did not think that she had sat down once that night. He had seen her constantly being pulled from group to group and from dance to dance. Everyone had wanted to get a piece of Miss Worthing.

He could not help but feel proud, his heart swelling just at the memory of it.

But of course, with all of that came a sense of melancholy.

He would have to let her go now. One of the other men, Mr.

Upton perhaps, or another, would be sure to snap her up now. It was as though she had been a flower that finally bloomed after much anticipation. She was an orchid, a tropical flower, rare and wild and all the more beautiful for it.

Edward stared into the fire. Oh, how he had longed for her that night. What irony, to realize what he wanted only when it was too late for it.

He was determined not to sink into despair. He was not that sort of man. But surely he could be allowed a bit of brooding in front of the fire before turning into bed.

"I had a suspicion that you would still be awake."

Edward jumped, startled. He turned to see Georgiana in the doorway.

"And I had not thought that you would be."

He had thought he was quite alone in the house now. He felt embarrassed to have been caught like this. Although of course Georgiana could not read his mind and therefore could not know precisely what he was thinking.

His sister moved up to him and sat down, warming her hands in front of the fire. He saw that she was still in her finery from the ball. Or, well, most of it. Her jewelry had been taken off, as well as her gloves, and her hair was now in a simple braid. But she was still in the dress.

"You ought to get ready for bed," he told her.

"I ought to say the same thing to you," Georgiana replied. "Tell me, what keeps you up at such an hour? It was an exhausting evening and I know how much you hate to waste the morning sleeping in."

Her eyes shone, as if she knew a great secret that he did not. That was something else for which he had Miss Worthing to thank. Since becoming friends with her, his sister had greatly improved in her spirits. She even had a bit of a teasing atmosphere about her at times.

Edward made a mental note that he must properly thank Miss Worthing for all that she had done. Both for him and for his sister. His feelings for her aside, the poor girl seemed to be under the impression that she owed them everything. When the reality of it was that they owed her just as much.

"There is something on your mind," Georgiana said. "I can tell. Is it one of your lady friends? The ones who still think they can win your heart?"

Edward debated not telling her anything at all. It would spare him some humiliation, certainly. But this was his sister. She had always been wise in her counsel. And if he could not confide in her, who could he confide in?

And he felt that he must confide in someone before he lost what little sanity he still possessed.

"I am about to say something to you," he said, "and you are not to hold it against me for the rest of my life."

Georgiana frowned. "Have you done something regrettable? Have you made a bad business deal?"

Edward was alarmed that her mind had jumped to such awful conclusions. "Good heavens, no. And I apologize if I phrased this in a manner too dire. I only meant that I am about to say that you were right, and I was wrong."

"Well, I am right about a great deal. What was it that I was right about in particular this time?"

That teasing, right there. Miss Worthing had brought that out in her. Edward had to reign in his smile. This was a serious matter.

"You were right in that I had somehow managed to give my heart away without realizing it. Tonight I saw Miss Worthing and I..." He shook his head.

Georgiana tilted her head, giving him a sympathetic smile. "I did wonder at your manner. You hardly said a word to her all night. I think the poor dear thought you were still holding back on her after the night before."

"I certainly hope not. Nothing could be farther from the truth. It is only that I saw her at the top of the stairs and...I sound rather like one of those tenors at the opera, do I not?"

Georgiana narrowed her eyes. "I always thought of you as more of a baritone."

"Sister. Dearest companion. I am trying to be serious."

"And I am trying to show you that letting yourself fall down into a well of despair is not going to help you any."

Says the woman still in mourning over a lover from years ago, he thought but did not say. That would have been unkind. And besides, Georgiana had born it all remarkably well. She had not retreated to her room or spent days crying.

There had been a heavy weight that settled about her shoulders. But he doubted that most people who knew her noticed. She was so quiet and solemn already.

"The point is," Edward said, "I did not realize just how strong my feelings for Miss Worthing were until tonight."

Georgiana looked down at the fire. "I confess that I might have had something to do with her ensemble."

"You are a devilish creature."

"I wanted you to realize what everyone else already knew: that you are in love with her."

"And quite a lot of good it does me when she does not return my feelings. She practically hid from me all evening."

"I can assure you that Miss Worthing holds you in the highest esteem."

"Well, I am sure that she does, but she—to think that after all of the things I said..."

Edward had to stand up and pace. The energy inside of him could not be contained. "If I were to propose to her she would accept out of a feeling of gratefulness and obligation.

"You should have seen her tonight, Georgiana. She was the center of attention. I cannot stifle her now. Not when she could have any man that she wanted. I could not deprive her of choosing someone who would truly suit her."

Georgiana shook her head gently. "But you would suit her. You do suit her."

"Do not flatter me." Edward put his hands behind his back, pacing, trying to keep his steps measured and not too hasty. "I understand now. What you said. About that feeling of home. That was how it was, precisely.

"I was in that crowded ballroom and feeling lost and all I had to do was turn and find her. It was as though I always knew where she was in the room. I wanted nothing more than to go to her."

"Then why did you not? I did not see either of you two near each other all night."

"She did not want me."

"You did not ask."

"Her manner was plain enough."

Georgiana sighed. "I think that you have spent so much time with ladies coming after you that you have forgotten that traditionally it is the man who goes after the lady."

"We only just returned to solid ground after our mistakes of the previous night." He still felt that he was more in the wrong than Miss Worthing was, but she insisted upon recognizing her own culpability and he respected that. They had both misstepped.

"I think that you underestimate your charm, brother."

"I would not dare to presume." Edward at last sank down into a chair again. "You saw her tonight, Georgiana. You saw how she was. It was magnificent."

"She finally had the confidence. Yes. I saw. I was quite proud."

"You ought to be. You coached her into this."

Georgiana nodded but seemed lost in thought.

"She even played Miss Hennings. She was so kind to her that the woman was at a complete loss. But do you know—I believe that Miss Worthing is finally rubbing off on me. I felt bad for the poor woman. She really is a sad creature if you think about it."

Georgiana hummed quietly.

"It was a terrible thing, though. To realize how I felt. It was as though a dam had been broken open." Edward scoffed at himself. "Now I truly sound like a horrible poet."

Georgiana took a deep breath. "Edward, if I am to tell you something, will you keep it in the strictest confidence?"

"Of course."

She nodded, as if to herself. "I would not normally say anything. Indeed I am chastising myself even as I speak. I think that it is a violation of privacy and the gentle unspoken promise between ladies, that we will keep one another's confidence."

Edward frowned. "Are you certain that you should be saying anything then?"

Georgiana nodded, this time with more determination. "I must. If there is no other way to convince you, and I do not think that there is, then I must. In order for you and that dear girl to both obtain the happiness that you deserve."

Edward's breath caught in his throat and he stood up before he even realized that he was thinking of moving. "Georgiana. Are you suggesting..."

"Miss Worthing confessed to me only last night that she loved you," Georgiana blurted out.

"I know that it is wrong of me to tell you so. Indeed, I have struggled all night over it. I tried to present her at her best to you. I tried to boost her confidence. I had hoped that you would at least accept what you were beginning to realize after our talk.

"And you did accept it. I was glad of it. But now you are insisting that she does not feel the same way. And right now, that poor girl is probably thinking that she has no chance with you whatsoever and I will not allow it. I simply will not. She has already cried too many times over this matter and you and I both know that she deserves better than that.

"She has been in love with you for quite some time. I believe that is part of why she was so devastated after you chastised her. And part of why none of the other men have made a move to court her properly. They could sense it from her even if she never gave any definitive sign.

"Her love for you is what Miss Hennings was so cruel to her about that other night. And it was with the aim of impressing you that she tried to behave as she did last night. It backfired horribly but you can understand her sentiment.

"She saw that she was not the socialite that you, a duke, would need in a wife. And so she tried to become that. Of course that is not what you want—I know that, Edward, and I did not encourage her, please do not look at me so sternly.

"But she wanted so badly to fit in and so badly to show you that she could handle society and could be that partner at balls for the networking that you will need to do."

Edward felt as though he was reeling. This put everything into a new light. It made him feel twice as awful as he had before for how harshly he had treated Miss Worthing during the ball last night.

"Surely I would have noticed," he managed to get out. It seemed fantastical to him that such a thing could have happened without him realizing it.

Georgiana gave him a fond but pitying look. "You hardly noticed your own feelings, Edward. How on earth were you going to notice hers?"

"A fair point," he admitted.

"She would die of shame if she knew that I was telling this to you. She is utterly convinced that you will never return her affections. And I am breaking her confidence in sharing this with you so please, do not tell her that I told you.

"I tell you this not so that you might laud it over her or act in haste. I am telling you so that you might know that if you wish to move forward with her, the way is clear. You will meet no resistance."

Georgiana paused. "Well, you might meet some resistance, only in that the sweet girl thinks that she is unworthy of you. But that is an issue easily cleared up by yourself I am sure. If you wish to pursue it."

"If I wish to—" Edward hardly knew what to think.

He was half in elation. It was as though his heart had taken flight. To know that the powerful emotions he felt for Miss Worthing were returned. To know that if he offered her his hand she would take it. That he might get to have her by his side, as he so longed for...

But he was still half afraid. And filled with a great deal of confusion and concern as to how he had failed to notice such a thing.

He turned to his sister. "Have I behaved...badly towards her? Have I been cruel? Have I tormented her and led her on without realizing it?"

"Not at all," Georgiana assured him. "You were merely kind to her. Loving. You danced together while she was taking lessons. You have escorted her everywhere. I am not surprised that love has blossomed between the two of you."

"Then you are saying that she loves me only because I am the man to whom she has grown accustomed." His heart sank.

Georgiana shook her head. "It has been a month, Edward. She has met many men, frequently, at these balls and other gatherings. If she were capable of developing feelings for one of them then she would have. It is not as though she were a hermit or shut away.

"She had the chance to form an attachment to other men. To

charming, well-off, handsome men. And she chose you. She loves you. She's quite adorable about it, really."

Edward considered that. Did he dare to hope? Was it possible that he could allow himself to celebrate?

"If you do not believe me," Georgiana went on, "then you might ask her directly."

"But is it not too soon?" he asked. "Ought I not to court her properly?"

"What do you think that you have been doing this entire time?" Georgiana inquired. "Again, I ask, why do you think that the ladies were so envious and none of the gentlemen have made a proper move towards her?

"You have been her escort, yes. But whether you realized it or not, you have already been courting her. Indeed, a proposal at this junction is probably what everyone is expecting."

He thought of what Miss Hennings had said. How she had assumed that he and Miss Worthing were already engaged. He had thought that she was jumping the gun out of spite but perhaps she was not the only one doing so.

But it did not matter what others thought if Miss Worthing was not comfortable with it.

"Are you certain that I would not be overstepping my bounds?" he asked. He felt, for the first time in his life, hesitant. Unsure of his course.

Georgiana pursed her lips, looking amused. "I do not think it would be possible for you to overstep your bounds in this matter. Within the lines of propriety of course. But Miss Worthing will return whatever affection you wish to give her."

"I do not even know what to think," Edward confessed.

"Perhaps you should try not thinking and focus instead on what you are feeling."

There was a bit of fond exasperation to her tone, as if she were thinking that if only Edward had stopped using his head and had used his heart long ago, this whole matter would have been settled already.

Edward gave her a stern look. "You cannot blame me for being cautious in this."

"I can certainly blame you for not taking enough time to learn yourself," Georgiana replied. "Everyone could see how you two felt about one another. It was only out of concern for you that Miss Worthing did not say anything."

Edward felt an odd sense of pride and pleasure at that. Unlike all of the other ladies who threw themselves at him, Miss Worthing had not done anything to indicate her interest.

And she was not after him for his title or money. At least not according to Georgiana, and besides, Edward trusted Miss Worthing's character. He knew she was not the sort to marry a man only for that.

If she was after title or money, in any case, there were plenty of easier men to go after and to charm.

But she wanted Edward for who he was. She truly cared for him. And yet she had done nothing about it because she had thought that Edward did not want her.

His heart went out to her.

"What if I did not love her?" he asked.

Georgiana's face darkened, and her eyes grew sad. "Then I imagine that she would have found someone else to marry out of esteem, if not love. I believe that was why she behaved as she did tonight. She was determined to try and move on."

Edward could well imagine the empathy that his sister felt for Miss Worthing. Edward suddenly realized just how lucky Miss Worthing was.

For he did love her back. Indeed, if it was not such a late hour, he would have gone to her at once in order to tell her so. He wanted to reassure her that he would give her everything that he had to take care of her. That he wanted to see her smiling at him every morning over the breakfast table.

He wanted to tell her all of this, and more, although he knew that he should probably prepare himself first. He would not want to end with her feeling insulted or as though he only offered out of altruism or because he knew how she felt.

But what if he had not returned her affections? She would have been like Georgiana. Except that Miss Worthing did not have the luxury of a brother who would so willingly care for her and did not care that she didn't marry.

Miss Worthing would have had to marry one man while loving

another. And while he could hope that she would have come to love her husband, it still struck him as rather cruel. Or at the very least, unfair.

But fortunately, that was not how things were going to go. Because Miss Worthing's affections were returned.

He should have known from the start. He had taken a liking to Miss Worthing at once. Had been lauding her, both in his mind and to Georgiana, for her behavior and manner.

He had constantly compared other women unfavorably to her. He had enjoyed spending time with her and had sought her out.

How could he have been so blind? He should have seized upon it at once and courted her while fully aware of it. He could have proposed to her a week ago, even.

Georgiana must have sensed his thoughts, for she shook her head. "Do not dwell upon what you should or should not have done. I can read it well in your face that you are chastising yourself. You must not be too harsh on yourself.

"What is important is not what you might or could have done in the past but what you do here and now in the present. Which, I would recommend, is first and foremost going to bed."

"One would be forgiven for mistaking you as the elder sibling," Edward replied, with affected crankiness.

Georgiana rose, elegant as ever. "In any case, I am going to bed. I suggest you do the same. Your thoughts and your love will, I should hope, keep until the morning."

"Perhaps...you could arrange to be out of the house for a time?" Edward asked, hesitantly. He did not wish to impose too much upon his sister, but he also did not see how he could catch Miss Worthing alone if Georgiana was in the house. The two ladies were inseparable.

Georgiana inclined her head. "I think that I can certainly manage such a thing. I shall call upon some friends. Miss Worthing is expecting some calls, I believe, and so will have to stay home."

Edward felt a possessive, fiery feeling rise up in his chest. "Those calls are, I hope, from women only."

"I can assure you that if they are not, you will easily be able to set it all to rights." Georgiana sounded amused.

Edward supposed that having to dispel any illusions of

courtship that various men might now possess was his just punishment for taking so long to realize how he felt.

"Very well. I shall not expect to see you tomorrow then."

"Not in the morning, at least," Georgiana replied.

Then she went up to bed.

Edward stared into the fire for another moment before putting it out and going to bed himself. His thoughts were still in a bit of a whirlwind. He hastily scribbled down some notes to himself. He could fashion them into a proper speech in the morning.

His sister was right: he needed sleep.

He wanted to be at his best tomorrow.

CHAPTER 21

MARIA SLEPT in that morning and awoke only when she heard the front door closing.

It was a rather heavy door, and no matter how much they all tried to close it quietly, it inevitably sounded throughout the house.

She opened her eyes. That must be Lord Reginald, going out to handle his business for the day.

It was probably a sign of her cowardice, but she was glad. She did not know if she could face him quite yet.

Maria sat up, looking at the clock on the wall. Oh dear. It was much later than she usually got up. Georgiana must be waiting for her.

Fortunately Georgiana was the sort of person who could easily entertain herself. Especially if there was a book of poetry present.

Maria dressed quickly and simply. She was not going out that day, not until the dinner party and the opera that night. Several people last night had let her know that they should be calling upon her and she would not wish to miss them.

As she got ready, she glanced at her dance card from the night before. She had kept it so that she might mark it down for her list of potential husbands.

She paused, her hand suspended in the air, halfway to the pen she kept nearby.

...surely she could work on the list later. It wouldn't do to keep Georgiana waiting any longer than she already had been.

Maria finished getting ready and went downstairs. She had probably missed breakfast at this point. She hadn't realized quite how much she had exhausted herself last night. If she was going to be this busy at balls from now on she would have to get used to that.

As she got to the bottom of the stairs she headed straight for the library. That would most likely be where Georgiana was.

But as she started to cross into the sitting room to reach the library, she froze.

Lord Reginald was sitting there, reading the paper.

Maria could hardly breathe. She had not prepared herself. She had not expected to see him that morning.

She could hear her heart pounding and heat spreading over her face. He looked unbearably handsome in the late morning light. She wanted to run her hands through his pale hair, erase the worry lines from the corners of his eyes.

Another part of her wanted to back out of the room, quickly, before he noticed her.

Lord Reginald looked up. Maria's breath caught in her throat. Too late, he had seen her.

He gave her a small, almost tentative smile. "Good morning, Miss Worthing."

"Good morning, my lord." She glanced around. "Is your sister not around?"

"She left to make some morning calls. She told me that you had to stay at home and to let you know that she hopes you enjoy your visitors. She'll be back in time to help you prepare for the dinner tonight."

He was still looking at her with this oddly anxious smile. Maria wasn't sure how to interpret it. What did he have to be anxious about?

Unless he had disapproved of her behavior again last night and was trying to think of a compassionate way to tell her so. Or he had noticed how she felt about him and was now unsure how to behave around her. She would not blame him either way.

She had thought that she had behaved perfectly acceptably last night but what if she had gotten it wrong again? And of course he would be uncomfortable if he knew her feelings. He must be wondering how to act in a way that would still be kind without leading her on or helping her to draw hope where there was none.

Maria wondered if she might beat a hasty retreat without it seeming too awkward when Lord Reginald spoke again.

"I am glad to see that you are awake." He stood, folding up the paper and setting it aside. "I was hoping that I might compel you to join me on a short walk through the park."

"I'm afraid that I am expecting visitors," Maria said apologetically.

"It will only be a short walk, I hope," Lord Reginald replied. "I can instruct the servants to have any visitors wait until we return. It will not take but a moment."

Maria nodded. What else could she do? She did not see how she could refuse without being rude. And it wouldn't take very long at all.

And, God help her, she wanted to spend time with him. She was still a lovestruck fool and she wanted whatever amount of time and affection he was willing to give her.

Perhaps, however, this was his way of taking her somewhere he could let her down gently. Maria's heart sank and her stomach twisted painfully.

It would make sense. A park was a public, neutral space. She could walk a little ways on her own if she needed some time to herself afterwards. Or he could remain at the park while she returned to the house to receive visitors.

They would not be interrupted at the park, and so there was no chance of someone walking up to them while she happened to be restraining tears. And the park was a happy place for her, a calming place.

It was very thoughtful of him, really, to put such care into selecting a place to reject her. Even the word 'reject' felt too strong. It was as though he was setting her down gently to the side, out of reach.

But of course she should have known that this was coming. Miss Hennings, of all people, had noticed Maria's feelings. How could Lord Reginald have failed to do so?

He must have seen her at the ball last night and thought she was moving on. She had done her best to showcase that by her actions, after all. He must be thinking that it was now safe to officially tell her there was no hope, now that she seemed to be showing an interest in other men.

It explained Georgiana's absence as well. She had told Maria that she did support the idea of Maria and her brother united in marriage. But she had also told Maria that she was not going to interfere either way.

Whatever Georgiana's thoughts on the matter, she was going to stay out of it. Maria was certain of that. Georgiana was not the type to sway one person in a particular direction without being asked first. And Maria could not see Lord Reginald asking for his sister's opinion on this.

Except, perhaps, in how to break the news gently to her. As gruff as he could be, Lord Reginald was not a cruel man. Especially after their little disagreement and subsequent apology. Maria was certain that he would be as kind and gentle as possible about the entire situation.

Indeed, the only thing Maria could feel, other than sadness, was shame. She should have done a better job of hiding her feelings.

How awful must Lord Reginald feel now? How embarrassed? How uncomfortable?

She must apologize to him once he had said his piece. She would have to let him know that she bore him no ill will. That she could not blame him for anything he did or did not feel. Emotions could not be controlled, after all.

And, of course, she must ask him to forgive her for behaving so indiscreetly enough that he knew of her feelings. She would assure him that she had never intended for him to know how she felt. That she felt nothing but kindness towards him no matter how he felt towards her.

Maria scrambled to think of the right words, to sort them into her head, as Lord Reginald approached her. "Will you not need a coat?" he asked.

She looked down at herself. "I'm afraid that I am not in any shape for walking. I did not think that I would be leaving the house."

Lord Reginald's eyes were soft as they gazed upon her. She

strove not to misinterpret that as true affection. He loved her as a sister, she must remember that. They were friends. Nothing else.

"I think that you look perfectly well," he told her. "Of course if you prefer it you may change. But if you are worried about your appearance you need not be. You look quite well to me."

Maria could feel herself blushing and did her best to ignore it. "If you think so, then I am perfectly ready to go out."

Lord Reginald helped her to get her coat, and then they walked in silence to the park.

Maria was certain that she could not be imagining the odd quality of the silence between them. The household was a quiet one. Usually she and Georgiana would read when they were not out making calls. And Lord Reginald would be out doing business, or else quietly writing in his office. Even when they were all engaging one another in conversation, it was quiet.

It was what Maria had been used to at the plantation, honestly. She would chat with the servants in a way that she simply couldn't here in England. She'd had no idea until coming here how strict the rules for interacting with servants were.

But otherwise, it was just herself and Father in the house. It wasn't much in the way of being raucous and social. And so she was glad that the Reginald household was rather similar.

But during those times, the silence had always been comfortable. Something that she could relax into. Something she didn't have to think about. It simply was three people who enjoyed one another's company spending time with one another.

Now...now it was something entirely different.

She could feel the tension coming off of Lord Reginald in waves. Maria wondered if she should simply tell him that she knew. That she understood. Perhaps that would ease the way for him?

A broken heart was not an easy thing to deal with and she was not going to pretend that it was. But she was an adult. She could handle this with some level of maturity, surely. Lord Reginald need not worry about her crying or pleading with him or doing anything else to make him uncomfortable.

She would respect his decision. She could not guarantee that she would not cry to herself when she was alone in her room later on. But that was just between her and the four walls of her bedroom.

As they entered the park, Maria could not help but recall how they had done this just the other day. Only it had been under much different, and happier, circumstances.

Oh, how happy she had been that day! How much she had enjoyed their talk and sitting quietly sketching while Lord Reginald had watched.

That had been such a perfect day in her eyes. And then she had gone and ruined it that evening with her behavior.

But up until then, it had been lovely. At the time she had looked forward with eagerness to when they might return to the park. She had longed for a repeat of those precious hours.

Now...now, she was dreading it.

The sky was no grayer than it had been on that day. The flowers still bloomed. There were children running about the green. And yet everything felt more subdued. Sadder. More... muffled, almost.

It was as though there was a happy layer to the world from which she was now separated.

Lord Reginald directed them into a path that would lead them around the circumference of the entire park. It afforded a lovely view while simultaneously keeping them separated from the main groups of people who were more towards the middle.

Maria couldn't help but think it was clever. It allowed them a good view but gave them privacy for their discussion.

She wanted to scream at Lord Reginald to spit it out already. She knew what he was going to say. The continued silence only tortured her further and delayed the inevitable.

At last, after what felt like hours, Lord Reginald cleared his throat. Maria might have been imagining it, but it looked as though he drew a small folded piece of paper out of his pocket, glanced at it, and then put it back into his pocket.

Had he prepared a speech? Had he truly worried that much over how to let her down? He was too kind to her.

"Miss Worthing," he began. "I hope that what I am about to say will not seem presumptuous. I have struggled as to how to properly address the issue at hand. But I fear that, in the end, there is no way to be completely delicate in such a matter. Not when there are such strong...emotions, involved."

Maria's eyes were already beginning to burn. She blinked quickly and forced herself to keep breathing normally, taking slow, deep breaths.

She very carefully did not look at Lord Reginald. She did not dare, for surely if she did, she would burst into tears and that would be awful for the both of them.

"It has come to my attention that I have been remiss in my presentations to you. I was a fool who did not know my own heart. In doing so, I fear I have put you in a most cruel position."

He was being awfully kind about it, and unnecessarily so. There was no reason for him to put it on himself like this. The fault of her feelings was hers alone. He did not compel her.

"Believe me, had I been aware of things, I would not have kept you hanging in such painful suspense for so long a time."

Was she imagining it, or was he speaking to her with an added layer of tenderness? He almost always spoke to her with kindness and attentiveness. But this was something else. Something more.

"I must confess, however, that I have learned something about myself over the last few days of knowing you. I have learned that I am not so astute when it comes to my own motivations, and my own behavior, as I once thought.

"Indeed, you have assisted me in providing me with some of those insights. I found myself relying upon your observations of human character at least once during the course of the previous evening."

Maria turned and looked at him instinctively, despite her initial decision not to. She had to see if he was jesting with her. But when she looked at him, Lord Reginald merely gave her a small, fond smile.

He seemed to be in earnest.

It was affirming to know that he listened to her and respected her so much, even after her mistakes. But what was it leading up to? Was he trying to reassure her that despite his lack of romantic feelings he still valued her?

Maria looked away again. Because she was a coward.

Lord Reginald continued on. "I...I am not good at this sort of thing. Just as I suppose anyone who has never done a thing before cannot expect to be all that good at it on his first attempt. But I shall try. I want to try.

"You make me want to try a lot of things. You make me want to try to be kinder. To be more understanding of others. You make me want to forgive the transgressions of those around me.

"You make me want to recite poetry. You make me want to dance for hours. You make me want to try to be gentler with my words.

"In short, I think that you make me want to try to be a better person. And I could not ask for more in a companion. Someone who challenges me to be better and yet loves me for who I am... it is such a rare and pleasing combination that I hardly know what to do with myself.

"I can only ask your forgiveness in being such a fool for so long. But now that I have come to realize how I feel, nothing could be plainer to me.

"I wish to always have you by my side. Not being with you all last night at the ball, not even getting to dance with you once, was torture to me. I missed you as one might miss a limb."

Maria could hardly believe her ears. What was he saying? This did not at all sound like a man who was about to reject her. But could she allow herself to hope? Could she be that daring?

Lord Reginald continued onward. It was as though he was a man pushing through a snowstorm in order to reach home. No matter how difficult it became, he must endure. He must finish and reach his goal.

"I can only hope that you will forgive me for my behavior and my lack of awareness—indeed, my lack of sense. And I can only hope that you will now believe me when I say that despite my utter idiocy, I do... I am..."

Lord Reginald paused. He stared out ahead of him for a moment, then, as if gathering up his courage, squared his shoulders and turned to face her.

Maria was caught, held in place, by his expression. He looked terribly vulnerable. It was a look that she had never beheld on his face before. His eyes, although gentle, bored into hers. He took each breath as though it might be his last.

"You must believe me, Miss Worthing," he said, his voice soft and low, "when I tell you that you are the dearest creature in the world to me. I love you. So deeply, indeed, that I did not even notice it and now it has become intertwined with the very core of my being."

Maria felt as though a strong enough breeze might blow her over. She was in shock. It was everything that she had wanted to hear and yet it was so unexpected that she did not know what to do.

"I love you," Lord Reginald repeated, this time in an even softer voice. "And I wish—above all other things—to make you my wife. If you will have me."

Maria's heart was thudding in her ears. She wasn't sure if she was going to start laughing hysterically or burst into tears. He loved her? He loved her. He *loved* her.

Out of all the people that he could have chosen, he chose her. Lord Reginald, a duke, a man with education and money and wit and a title to boot. A man handsome enough that he most likely could still have gotten any woman he wanted even if he didn't have all the rest.

And he had chosen her. Not any of the far more eligible ladies of his acquaintance.

She knew that he would never jest about a thing like this. Otherwise she would have suspected this of being some kind of awful prank. Because how could it be true?

Yet, it must be.

He was saying that he loved her, and now he was...proposing to her.

Lord Reginald made a face of frustration, although it seemed to be frustration at himself. "I fear I have not said it as I should. I must make it official." He smiled at her. "You must forgive me—this is my first proposal."

Maria laughed at that, quickly clapping a hand over her mouth. But it seemed that laughter was what he had wanted from her, for he smiled.

"Miss Worthing," he started, and then corrected himself. "Miss Maria Worthing. Would you do me the honor of becoming my wife?"

CHAPTER 22

EDWARD FELT as though he could hardly breathe. It was as if someone had put his lungs into a vice.

Miss Worthing stared at him for a moment, her dark eyes wide and soft. She seemed to be torn between joy and shock and, perhaps, something else, for it looked almost as though she might cry.

"I...I do not understand," she said quietly, almost as though she were speaking to herself and hadn't realized the words had been said out loud.

That was an understandable statement for her to make. "How can I help you to understand?" he asked.

"It is only that..." Maria scrunched up her face, as if thinking, before meeting his eyes again. "You could have anyone that you wanted."

"Perhaps." He did not wish to float his own boat too much. There were sure to be other ladies out there who for one reason or another were not inclined towards him.

"But I'm..." Maria gestured at herself.

Edward shook his head. "Exactly. You are you."

He gently took her hands in his, as he had so often wanted to, and now knew why. "You are as honest and forthright a person as I have ever met. Even when you make a mistake, your intentions are pure and you own up to your mistakes and vow to do better.

"You see kindness around you. You believe the best in people.

You listen to them and care about their interests and their accomplishments.

"You are a highly capable young woman. You ran an estate for years in order to help your father. And I know you worry about him constantly.

"I could not picture a better woman, one more suited to be my wife. You have all of the traits that I have said I wished for in a life partner. And here you were, right in front of me this entire time. I was merely too blind to notice it until last night."

A lovely blush, deeper than any of her previous ones, worked its way into Miss Worthing's cheeks. "You flatter me, sir."

"Do you not believe me, then?"

"I am afraid that my belief in my own worthiness might take some time," Miss Worthing acknowledged. "But I cannot bring myself to disbelieve your declarations. Most likely because I do not wish to disbelieve them.

"Surely you must know how I feel. How I have felt, for some time. I know that I have most likely been the most obvious of fools.

"My esteem for you could hardly be hidden. Many people have commented upon it. Even your dear sister knows. In fact I was certain that you had figured it out and were taking me on this walk in order to let me down gently."

"Let you down?" Edward stared at her, agog. "No, the farthest thing from that. And I can assure you that I did not notice a thing. I was completely unaware of your attachment."

"But I was such a fool over you!" Miss Worthing said. She sounded confused, amused, and dismayed all at once. "Why, even Miss Hennings commented on it!"

"Miss Hennings, I fear, has been let off too easily," he grumbled. He should have given her the verbal thrashing she deserved.

Miss Worthing squeezed his hands. "Please do not attack her for my sake. You know she really is a sad creature. I hope that she will find happiness someday. For she must be quite unhappy herself to continually try to inflict it upon other people."

He could not help but smile just a little. "I was thinking along quite similar lines last night, in fact. When she came up to congratulate me upon my engagement to you."

"She truly said that?" Miss Worthing was clearly amused now, although also astonished. "And with no official announcement. The nerve of her. But I confess I am more entertained by it than anything else."

"As am I." And then Edward realized—Miss Worthing had not officially responded to his question. "Am I to assume that I ought to put a formal announcement into the papers?"

Miss Worthing gave him a sly look, one of hesitant joy. "Yes, I do believe that you ought to. But you must forgive me, this is my first acceptance of a proposal."

He smiled helplessly.

Miss Worthing cleared her throat, squaring her shoulders and speaking in a most official voice. "Yes, my lord, I accept your proposal."

He laughed and offered her his arm. "Then this walk has become infinitely more pleasant."

She took his arm, leaning into his side. "How on earth did you discover that you had feelings for me? How could you not have been aware?"

"I mistook it all for protectiveness, since I was your escort," he replied, feeling somewhat sheepish. "I never took the time to properly examine any of my feelings. I merely... brushed them off.

"It wasn't until you were no longer at my side that I realized how you were usually by it. It was your absence that convinced me. I had not realized until then how much I had grown used to your presence."

He shook his head. "No, that is not right. I had not merely grown used to it. I relied upon it.

"And then I saw you dancing with all of those other men, and could not claim you for myself. And it stirred up a jealousy within me that I had never before known.

"I realized that in looking at you, I felt the same pull towards you that I feel towards my home in the country. The same pull that I get when I am returning to my bedroom after a long day. That warm sensation of safety and being settled. Yet you were not a place, you were a person.

"When I spoke to my sister about it, she had quite a lot to say to me about my behavior."

"Oh dear," Miss Worthing said, smiling. "I am certain that she did."

"She told me my behavior had, this whole time, been as one who is courting a lady. That already many people assumed a proposal was forthcoming if it had not happened already.

"That was why, or so I was told, none of the other men had made a move to call upon you or do anything besides enjoy your company during a dance."

Miss Worthing gaped at him. "Is that why? And—oh, that must be why there were all those significant looks between the older ladies. Oh, what fools we have both been! I had not the faintest idea either."

"At least you knew your own heart. I did not. Not until last night. And by then I feared that I had lost you. I worried that my temper and the charms of other men had already done too much damage."

Miss Worthing put her hand on his arm, her eyes very dark and very serious. "You will never lose me," she promised.

It felt as solemn as a marriage promise. And Edward knew that she did not say such a thing lightly. "And you will always have me," he replied.

Now he was anxious to get home, despite the loveliness of the park. He wanted to be in private with her, wanted to discuss things now that they were on the same page and their hearts were open to one another.

But he could not rush her by cutting through the park. It would elicit stares, if nothing else. So he kept them at their leisurely pace.

He answered her questions as best he could, about how and when and where. And she did the same with him. The more that they talked, the more certain he grew. He wanted to spend the rest of his life with this woman.

"Your sister must have been quite firm with you," Miss Worthing laughed at one point.

"She was, quite so," he replied, smiling. "She was astounded that I had no idea of how I had been behaving. She would, I think, have been more amused at the whole affair if she had not been so worried about you as well."

"She is too kind to me," Miss Worthing replied.

"I fear that she is too kind to me as well. I probably deserved a good smack with a newspaper for my sheer stupidity."

Miss Worthing laughed again. He loved that he could make her laugh. "My father will be dreadfully pleased. He so longs to meet the both of you."

"And I long to meet him. I really ought to get his permission before anything else moves forward."

"He will not hesitate to give it," Miss Worthing assured him.

They continued to talk until they exited the park, at which point they both fell silent. It was so different from the silence they had shared on the way to the park.

Edward now understood why it had been such an odd silence. He had, of course, been plenty nervous himself about it. But he had not realized at the time that poor Miss Worthing thought that he was orchestrating this in order to tell her that he knew of her feelings for him and did not return them.

How ironic, that the truth was actually the opposite.

They reached the house and entered the foyer, and Edward could hold himself back no longer.

"I know that propriety must be observed and that I must obtain your father's permission and all the rest," he told her. "But I must profess a most profound and overwhelming desire to kiss you."

Miss Worthing blushed quite prettily once again, and then grasped his hands in hers. "I suppose that I can let my fiancé kiss me, at least the once."

And so he did, just the once, softly, feeling his chest fill with warmth.

When he pulled back, Miss Worthing was smiling at him, her eyes bright with happiness.

He resolved to make it so that her face would always hold such joy.

EPILOGUE

MARIA LOOKED over the papers once again.

It was not that she wasn't looking forward to her wedding. Not at all. She was excited for it—more excited than she had ever been in her entire life.

She and Edward were finally going to be together. She would get to arrive with him at the theatre and at the balls. And she got to leave with him as well. She would get to go on long walks with him. She would become the support and trusted partner that he needed and deserved in running his properties.

Nobody could doubt their connection to one another, their relationship. People would continue to offer up their opinions. People always would. But what did it matter? Who cared what anyone thought anymore?

Now that she knew that Edward loved her in return...now that they were going to be joined as one...nobody else mattered. No one else's opinions counted. Only Edward's.

And Father's, of course.

Maria had struggled not to rush the wedding preparations or try to schedule a date too soon in advance. The wedding of a duke was a very important affair, after all.

They had to take the time to compose the guest list, and for the guests to receive the invitation and take the trip to be there to attend. They had to make sure that everything was in order and perfect for the high-ranking members of society who would be attending.

But oh, how she had worried and fretted over Father's health. While her own future was now secure, Father still had to tie up his own finances.

Edward had been most helpful in that regard. Maria had been nervous when Edward and her father had first met. Not that she thought they would truly dislike one another, but...there was so much riding upon it.

Her father was such a gentle soul and Edward could be so blunt. And Edward was not his father's son. Would Father be disappointed, she had wondered. Would he be looking for his childhood friend and be sad when he saw a stranger?

But it had all worked out beautifully. Her father had loved Edward almost immediately.

Maria knew that she was not second best for being a woman. Not in her father's eyes. But she did know that it warmed his heart to be able to have a son as well as a daughter.

Edward was able to work harder and longer than her father could. He helped to smooth things over, to move around the money and ensure that all loose ends were tied up.

It allowed her father to relax and rest the way that he should be at his age and with his illness. Even if Maria had not already been in love with him, she would have fallen in love with Edward instantly for taking care of her father that way.

And so her father was well enough to walk her down the aisle at her wedding.

It was a moment that every girl dreamed of. Maria had certainly dreamt of it. And she had continued to fret internally that something might happen. That her father might take a turn for the worst. That he might not get to see his daughter on the happiest day of her life.

It was one thing to know that one's child was engaged. Her father knew that Maria would be well taken care of by Edward. And that she would be happy. But to know it wasn't enough. To see it was so much better.

That was what Maria wanted for her father. To actually see it happen. To not only know beyond a shadow of a doubt but to see it unfolding before his very eyes.

And now he would.

But that hadn't stopped the fear, of course. And on top of all of that, she had needed to plan.

She hadn't realized just how much work was going to go into this. She knew, objectively, sort of. And Georgiana had tried to warn her. But just like with her father knowing his daughter was happy and settled and seeing it being two different things, so was knowing that she would have much work to do and actually doing that work two very different things.

Still, Edward and Georgiana had done their best to assist her. Edward insisted that it was the least that he could do, seeing as Maria was not the only one getting married.

"We are each one half of a larger whole," he would tell her when she tried to shoulder the responsibility herself. "You cannot take care of all of this on your own. You must allow me to help you. It is my duty and my pleasure."

She had not been all that certain. Surely Edward had far too much to deal with already? Surely he did not wish to handle such details as what sort of flowers they were choosing?

But he had patiently helped her through all of the decision-making and through contacting the necessary people. He had been the one to request the vicar to put up the banns. It had been as much his wedding planning and his taste as it was hers. She was immeasurably grateful for that.

Georgiana had been the one to make up the guest list.

Edward had, understandably and rather true to his nature, wanted nobody to come.

"Surely it can only be family," he had tried.

"And insult a good two thirds of society," Georgiana replied. "That is certainly the best way to start your marriage. An auspicious beginning, indeed."

Now that her beloved brother was going to be married, and was very much in love with his fiancée, Georgiana was growing in confidence. One of the signs of this was her growing sense of dry humor.

Maria appreciated it. It must have been the knowledge that her brother's future and happiness were now secure. Perhaps it was that Georgiana had needed a close friend just as much as Maria did.

But whatever it was, Maria was glad to see the woman that she already considered a sister coming out of her shell.

Or at least, doing so in little ways around Maria and Edward. Maria wasn't sure that Georgiana would ever become a social butterfly. But that was all right. Georgiana's quiet meant that she balanced out Maria and Edward. Edward might have preferred quiet evenings at home to balls, but quiet he was not.

Maria didn't know anyone really in England, still. Mrs. Dale and the Countess and Mrs. Rutlage and all those other older ladies were of course invited. They had been so kind to her.

None of them were surprised to hear of the engagement. In fact, they seemed to think that Edward had proposed weeks before he actually had.

"We thought he was your suitor all along," Mrs. Dale said at one point.

Maria wondered if she and Edward were the two blindest people in England. It seemed that everyone had known how Edward felt long before he had. Certainly, Maria had not seen it.

But aside from those ladies, who was she to invite? She had no close friends. And so Georgiana had taken it upon herself to assemble the guest list.

"There are people that we must invite whether we enjoy their company or not," Georgiana had explained as she started the list.

Inviting people for political reasons was not something that Maria was familiar with. She was not all that fond of the concept, either. But it must be done since she was the wife of a duke. And she accepted that, if it meant she got to spend the rest of her life with Edward.

Then there were the many people who had known the Reginald family over the years. Georgiana explained that she and her brother were not necessarily close friends with these people but they must be invited anyhow.

"We carry on an association with them," Georgiana said. "Our families know one another. It is a sort of...long-standing, polite acquaintance. It would cause us more problems to not invite them than it would to simply extend the invitation and then pretend that we care when they show up."

Maria was happy to go along with whatever Georgiana suggested for the guest list. She was happy to go along with Georgiana's opinion on practically everything. She had felt terribly in over her head this entire process.

The one immediate benefit, however, was that Miss Hennings and her ilk could no longer say a word against her.

She sometimes wondered if one of those women would not have better served Edward as a wife. They would have highly enjoyed creating a guest list. They would have been excited to parade themselves in front of all of the nobility and the who's who.

Whenever she so much as began to suggest such a thing to Edward, he would shut her down immediately.

"I love you," he would tell her. "That is reason enough to make you my wife. Even if you were not already trustworthy, akin to me in character, and more than capable of handling the matters of a large estate such as mine."

Whether Miss Hennings thought that she would make a better wife to Edward than Maria did, Maria would never know. The lady could not dare say anything. Not even behind Maria's back.

Now that she was officially engaged to Edward, everyone was eager to earn her favor. The ladies dared not say that she was an unworthy pick. There was a risk of it getting back to Edward, after all. And nobody wanted to risk his wrath.

Everyone was unceasingly polite. Maria could tell that some of them didn't really mean it. Miss Hennings, for one, avoided her. So did a few other women.

But it didn't matter to her what they thought. She couldn't control what they thought of her. She couldn't change them. The only opinions she cared about were Edward's, Georgiana's, and her father's, and she knew where she stood with them.

"I wish that I had realized my feelings for you sooner," Edward would tell her when he would see yet another person going out of their way to be nice to Maria. "That way this whole mess of how you were treated could have been avoided."

"You mustn't blame yourself," she would remind him. "I was just as blind as you were. I thought that you would never notice me."

"Of course I noticed you," Edward would say with a smile. "I noticed you from the first moment I met you. How could I not?"

Now that he had admitted his feelings...Edward was a blunt man. An honest man. And now that honesty and bluntness were translated into his expressions of his feelings for her.

He would tell her how lovely she looked. How amusing he found her. How much she made him laugh. How he loved spending time with her. There was never a moment of the day where she could not feel his love, wrapping around her like a warm blanket.

She doubted that most people would recognize Edward in those moments. When at parties he projected such a charming, man-about-town personality. When doing business, he was hard-hitting, firm, and forthright.

But when he was with her, it was like all of those layers got peeled away. He could be soft and gentle. It was as though he was saving all of his gentleness throughout the day so that he might give it to her.

She still treasured every moment spent with him. Although it felt better now that she did not feel as though she were stealing those moments, either from his business or from someone worthier of his time.

And now...now they were only a few days from the wedding, and she had to deal with these papers in front of her.

Maria glanced out the window. They were back in London again, and she was finding that although she loved the city and their home there, she was missing Foreshire.

Edward had taken her there just a few weeks ago. She was to be the mistress of the place, after all. He could have waited until he and Maria were properly married but he had said that he wanted her to take some time to get to know the place before she was officially its mistress.

"You will have to hit the ground running, so to speak, when you are my wife," he had said. "I would rather you already have a familiarity with the place that you must run."

It had made perfect sense to Maria. But all practical thoughts had flown out of her head when she had first set eyes upon the estate.

She had never seen a proper English estate before. Nor had she

truly gotten a chance to indulge in the English countryside. At Foreshire, she had both.

It was lovely. Her happiness at the place could hardly be
contained. She walked through the woods and the fields and dales,
exploring as much as she wished.

Edward would often go on those walks with her. He introduced
her to the head gardener and some of the undergardeners, who had
shown her the grounds. There were rose beds, a hedge maze, an
orchard, and more.

"I would very much like to be involved in this," she admitted. "Is
that all right?"

The idea of working with the gardeners to help plan out the
gardens sounded like a lovely thing to her. It reminded her of the
plantation where she had to help look after the fields, only more
fun because this was about planting what was beautiful rather than
food to sell.

Edward had seemed quietly delighted with how much she took
to the house and the grounds. He took her on a tour of the galleries
on the first floor, showing her the art that his family had collected.

"I hope to add to the collection," he told her. They were walking
arm in arm. It was one of her favorite indulgences now that they
were engaged. She could take his arm and let him guide her
anywhere, feel the warmth and strength of him beside her.

There was a portrait hall, where the likenesses of Edward's
ancestors were preserved for all time. There was one of Edward
himself, much younger, with Georgiana and their parents.

"I should get my portrait done again, now that I am an adult."
He had given her a sly look. "And you must have one as well, now
that you are to be a duchess."

Maria had blushed, and Edward had laughed. He loved it when
she blushed. Loved that he could fluster her.

Not that she didn't have her own revenge. She loved it when she
could catch him off guard and make him laugh in that wonderfully
startled way of his. And she loved when she could come down the
stairs in the morning and see his eyes widen as he took her in, as
though in the night he had forgotten what she looked like.

Still, it was a new idea to her. Being a duchess. Having a title.
Marrying Edward seemed separate to that. Her painting up in the

portrait gallery of a massive and beautiful estate? That felt like something entirely different from walking down the altar to speak her vows to the man that she loved.

But it was a part of him. For all that he did not speak or act like someone who was higher in rank than anyone else, he was. He was almost next to royalty in power and position.

To her, though, he was simply Edward. He always had been.

"What are you thinking on?" came Edward's voice from the doorway.

Maria drew herself out of her thoughts and turned to smile at him. "Only that I do not think of you as a duke."

"Oh? In what manner of speaking?"

"Well, I know that you are a duke. I know that you have a title. But I have never truly thought of you that way. The way that one thinks of nobility, I mean.

"I knew that you were of a higher rank than I was because of how Miss Hennings and the others would treat me. And how eager they were to obtain your favor.

"But for some reason, I confess that I cannot quite reconcile the idea of you with someone who is only a rung or two down the ladder from our king."

She thought a moment. "Or perhaps it is better to say that I think of those things only as an afterthought. The first thoughts I have of you are not connected to any of that, though. Not to your land or your titles or anything of that nature. You are simply... Edward."

Edward smiled at her, crossing the room so that he might take her hand in his. "And that is part of why I love you so. Everyone else sees the title first. You are the opposite.

"On a practical note, I think that is how it must be between a wife and a husband. How else are they to handle matters and converse as equals? I must have some measure of respect and trust for you. And if you were to spend your entire marriage bowing to me and being intimidated by me then we should get nothing accomplished.

"But on a more personal note...I have never wanted a wife who will be as butter, soft and easily molded and melting at every suggestion I make as if it were a command.

"I wanted a woman that I could trust and who would tell me the truth of things. Someone who could balance me out. Someone who would stand up to me when I was wrong and was not afraid to have an opinion which differed from mine.

"And I found that in you."

Maria felt herself blushing again, as she always did when he praised her. She supposed that in time she would grow used enough to his compliments and praise that she would not grow so horribly embarrassed when he said them. But a part of her wished that she might never grow used to it. That she might never take any of her husband's love for granted.

"Tell me," Edward said, squeezing her hand and then releasing it, "what matter are you puzzling over now?"

"Nothing much. I am only double-checking the accounts for the wedding."

She had to make sure that they had paid everyone properly, for the cake and flowers and the dress and such.

Maria was terribly excited for Edward to see her in her dress. She knew that many people simply wore their best dress for the occasion, but Georgiana had insisted upon Maria getting a new one. She hadn't let Edward see it yet. Not until the day of the wedding.

But she must make sure that all accounts were squared away before the wedding. She would hate to go off on her honeymoon and then find out that Georgiana had to handle some outstanding accounts while they were away.

They were going on a small trip to the Continent. Edward had been a few times before and was terribly excited to show her all of the art galleries. Maria was most looking forward to the Italian countryside and the ruins of Greece and Rome. Her fingers already itched to sketch them.

Edward hummed quietly, peering over her shoulder and bracing one hand on the desk to take a look.

"It looks quite in order to me," he said, his gaze scanning the figures.

"I am simply used to triple-checking everything," Maria confessed. It was the way of things, a holdover from her time on the plantation. Every penny must be accounted for and she hated the idea of failing Father in any way.

Now she was engaged to a man to whom money was of no consequence, but she could not so easily let go of the habit of frugality.

Edward smiled at her as if he were proud. "It is an admirable habit," he told her. "I understand your desire to be careful. And while I might be able to afford any number of sums you throw at me I appreciate your dedication to accuracy. Many a family has lost their fortune by too-casual bookkeeping."

Maria smiled up at him. It was such a joy to not have to hide herself around him anymore. She could let the adoration she felt seep out of her instead of holding it back.

Now that she could express exactly how she felt, she wondered at how she'd been able to hold it all in for so long. If she had been obvious to everyone before then she could hardly imagine what she looked like to them now.

Like a lovesick, besotted fool, no doubt. But that didn't matter. Not when she was a lovesick, besotted fool who was loved in return. Not when she knew that Edward felt as strongly about her as she felt about him.

"I did come in here with a purpose," Edward said. He reached into his pocket and pulled out a small, rectangular box. He presented it to her with a teasing flourish.

"I know that you are not a fan of being spoiled," he told her. "But I hope that you will appreciate that I want to spoil you and am holding myself back as much as I can. This is a... concession to a little tradition that I hope you will accept."

Maria took the small box and opened it, trying not to gasp too loudly or look too astonished at what was inside.

It was a beautiful blue necklace, sparkling up at her. The design was delicate, curving, like tangling vines with blue flowers that peeped out.

"Sapphires," Edward explained. "For the tradition... something old, something new, something borrowed, and something blue. I heard you've gotten a new dress for the occasion and I'm sure that the other two are taken care of. But I thought that I might indulge myself in giving you this gift to fulfill the last one."

Maria gently took the necklace out of the box, holding it up to the light.

It was far too much for an unmarried woman to wear. Young ladies were expected to wear only very simple adornments. To do otherwise would be to act vain or as though one needed baubles and flashy outfits to attract a husband.

But a married woman could get as dressed up as she pleased. It showed that her husband took good care of her and bestowed upon her gifts, the way that he should.

Now that Maria was going to be married, this was the perfect sort of gift that she could accept and wear.

"If it does not go with your wedding ensemble then I suppose you could wear it to a ball," Edward said, sounding hesitant at Maria's lack of response. "You are under no obligation to wear it at all, in fact, if you do not wish to."

She looked up at him, smiling. "No, it is perfection. I really could not have thought of a more beautiful piece of jewelry."

Maria stood up, handing him the necklace. "Here. Put it on me and we shall try it out. Just to see."

Edward took the necklace from her, his eyes shining. Maria turned around, making sure that her hair was out of the way. She felt the cool metal slip over her skin and could only imagine how regal she looked in it.

She turned around. "What do you think?"

Edward was staring at her with that expression on his face—the one that she had grown to recognize was love. "You look beautiful," he told her.

"You always say I look beautiful."

"And it is always true."

Maria felt her cheeks heating up and gently touched her fingertips to the necklace. It sat perfectly against her skin. "It will go wonderfully with my dress. You really are too generous with me."

"You are my future wife. There is no such thing as too generous."

Maria ducked her head, still unused at times to how her emotions played across her face so plainly in front of him. But then she forced herself to raise her head and meet Edward's eyes once again.

"Well then, I will look forward to showing off how generous my husband is at our wedding."

Edward took that as his cue and took the necklace off of her again, placing it carefully back in the box. "Do you think that you could take a break? Go to the park with me for a time?"

No matter how busy he got with his business affairs—of which Maria knew there were plenty—Edward always made time for her. She hoped to continue to be worthy of that, that he would always set aside time for her.

She took the arm that he offered her. "I don't think there will ever be a day where I say no to an offer like that from you."

Edward's eyes were shining at her, his smile easy, his face relaxed and open. "And there will never be a day when I do not offer."

Maria could feel her heart swelling up inside of her chest like a bird spreading its wings. They had the rest of their lives together for walks in the park, for gifts, for soft moments exchanged in private.

She could hardly wait.

THE EXTENDED EPILOGUE

I am humbled you read my novel *"A Forthright Courtship"* till the end!

Are you aching to know what happens to our lovebirds?

Visit a search engine and enter the link you see below the picture to connect to a more personal level and as a BONUS, I will send you the Extended Epilogue of this Book!

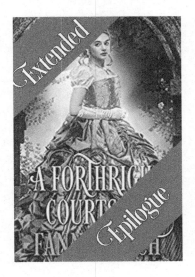

https://fannyfinch.com/ff-001-exep/

A LOVE WORTH SAVING

CHAPTER 23

GEORGIANA TUCKED a lock of wayward blonde hair behind her head as she surveyed the guest list.

Poor Maria was looking forward to the wedding, as all girls in love do, but she still had next to no idea how to plan one.

She was doing her best, of course. But when it came to the guest list she was at an utter loss as to who all should be invited.

It didn't help that Maria's fiancé and Georgiana's brother, Edward, was the Duke of Foreshire. Occupying one of the most prestigious positions in the land, his wedding was not merely a gathering of family and friends.

It was a social and political gathering as well.

Georgiana had taken on the task of helping to figure out who all to invite. Her future sister-in-law, meanwhile, was focusing on things like flower decorations and her dress.

She didn't mind helping out. She never had. On the contrary, it made her feel quite useful. Without a husband, helping out her brother with the running of things was all she had to make her feel needed.

Of course, soon Maria would be taking over things. Already Edward had been taking her down to the estate and instructing her on how things were run. Getting her familiar with the servants, all that sort of thing.

Georgiana knew that Maria would do a marvelous job as the mistress of the Foreshire estate. Already Maria had run her father's plantation in the Caribbean. She had a firm head on her shoulders.

What was more, Georgiana suspected that Maria would like living in the country better than living in London. There was more nature for Maria to sketch and paint. Fewer social gatherings for Maria to worry about. Plenty of heath to take walks upon.

But as much as she looked forward to her brother's happiness, Georgiana felt a pang of loss.

She did love Maria. Maria was a sweet girl. A lovely girl. And she would make Edward dreadfully happy. In fact, she already did.

But soon, Edward would officially no longer need Georgiana.

It meant she would officially be a spinster.

She could already feel it creeping upon her when out at balls and dinners. Nobody dared say too much, of course. She was only the sister of a duke. But everyone knew that if Edward caught wind of any unkind word against his sister...

Well. It wouldn't be pretty.

And so Georgiana knew she was spared some of the more unkind remarks that other older, unmarried women faced.

But it didn't prevent people from saying anything at all. And she did hear them.

Just the other night she had overheard two ladies gossiping as to how someone such as the sister of a duke could remain unwed.

Was there something wrong with her? they asked one another.

Could it be that she was in disgrace, and that part had simply been covered up?

Had her father arranged things so that she had no inheritance?

Was her personality so abhorrent that even the enticement of riches was not enough to sway any man?

Perhaps she was ill, and would soon die, or could not bear children?

On and on it went. Georgiana was glad that she had never cried easily. Unlike poor Maria, whose emotions you could see as plain as day on her face.

But then, Maria had not been brought up the way that Georgiana had. Maria's father and mother had allowed her to express her emotions however she pleased.

It was a wild sort of upbringing and it had not exactly served her well when she first came to England. But sometimes, Georgiana envied Maria.

Her own mother had died when Georgiana was still young. She'd been a quiet, gentle soul.

Father had been another matter entirely.

He had taught his children that emotions were a thing to be avoided at all costs. Certainly not something to be expressed. If he had caught Georgiana crying, ever, he certainly would have given her something new and painful to cry about.

Last night, however, she had been glad to have such a tight rein on her emotions. Otherwise, she might have burst into tears on the spot. Overhearing those unkind remarks, those speculations...

It was partially her own fault. She had never been outgoing or gregarious. Men liked women who were flirtatious and charming. It took Georgiana forever to get comfortable with someone.

And after Robert...

But of course she could not call him that, even in her head. Captain Trentworth. It helped, a little, to maintain that distance.

After her engagement to Captain Trentworth had been called off, she had found herself hesitant to draw close to any other man.

What if she were to fall in love yet again and Father forbade it once more? How many times could her heart be broken before she gave up completely?

And as much as her father tried, he could not succeed in getting all the titled young men to look at Georgiana as an option. She was quiet. Her beauty was not one that was easily noticed.

And while men respected her father, few wanted him to be a part of their family. Or to be a part of his. He was feared rather than loved.

But by the time Father had died, it had become too late. She was older. There were plenty of other women far more suitable for the unmarried men of high society.

Perhaps she had doomed herself. She ought to have simply thrown herself at the nearest, richest man and been done with it.

There were plenty of other women who had done such a thing. They seemed rather happy. Marriage did not necessarily mean spending all of one's time together.

Now, she doubted that any man would have her.

She supposed that she could bear it well enough if it were not for the unkind remarks from everyone else. And for the burden she would be upon her brother.

They were lucky that Edward was so rich. And that he had a title. If Edward were struggling financially, to place upon him the burden of taking care of his sister as well would have been the most selfish of actions. Georgiana would rather have married the next man who looked at her than burden Edward so.

But although she was not burdening him financially, she knew that their reputations were linked.

It was always that way in society. If one girl in a family eloped and got married at Gretna Green, then all of her siblings were now under suspicion.

Edward might be an upstanding man. He was rich and of strong moral character and business sense.

But with his sister unmarried, people were invariably going to ask how that came about. They would wonder if Edward had scared off any suitors with outrageous demands or awful behavior.

And then, of course, there was simply having to live with him. She was always welcome in her brother's home, she knew that. And Maria especially would value her friendship and opinions.

But to live on with them. When she could be of no real service. When she was like a perpetual guest who never moved on.

It sounded like a burden to her.

Her brother and Maria would never think of it that way. They were far too kind. But Georgiana knew how it would look to everyone else. And she knew that her own guilt would not allow it to stand.

What on earth could she do about it? There was no solution except to get a husband. And that time, she suspected, had passed.

Perhaps she ought to ask her brother about setting her up in a small apartment in Bath. Nothing fancy, of course. Just a modest little place.

It would be imposing upon him financially, but only the same amount that she would if she lived with him.

This way, she would not have to burden their new family with her constant presence. It would give her a nice feeling of independence.

Bath was a lovely vacation spot. But it was also the place for people to go when they had nowhere else. The elderly with their ailments. The spinsters. They all went to Bath.

At least if she moved there, she'd be among her own kind. She wouldn't stand out. She would simply be one of many.

As long as she remained here, however, she would be a painful point of gossip for her family. People would say what they liked about her.

They could even use gossiping about her in order to get at her brother. Nobody dared criticize Edward to his face. Especially since his reputation was so clean. But if anyone felt like attacking him, they could attack Georgiana instead.

It was an awful situation. And she did not wish to leave her family or her home. But what else was she to do?

Going to Bath was an elegant solution to the problem.

She would wait and speak to Edward about it when he and Maria came back from their honeymoon. There was no reason to bother them with such a thing until then. Planning a move to Bath would require some thought. They were already so busy with planning the wedding.

Besides, Georgiana would be needed to run the household until the couple returned from their honeymoon. No reason to bother about moving when she couldn't even move until then.

Edward would not like it. He was a stubborn man. But he would come around eventually, for he was also sensible.

There came a soft knock at the door.

"Enter," Georgiana called.

Her maidservant entered, with a letter in her hand. "This came for you, miss. In the mail."

Georgiana thanked her and took the letter. Why, it was from Julia!

Julia Weston was Georgiana's dearest friend. Georgiana hadn't gotten to see much of her this season, what with educating Maria and then helping to plan the wedding.

Oh, how she had missed her. She and Julia used to do everything together.

Eagerly, Georgiana opened the letter. She skimmed it quickly, then read it again in more detail. She grew quite astonished.

It seemed that Julia was inviting Georgiana to join her—at Bath, of all the coincidences.

My dearest Georgiana,

How I have missed you so! I know that you are quite well but I do miss our girlish fun patrolling the balls together.

Mama is feeling much better. The air at Bath does her good, as the doctor said. Papa is itching to get back to London but you know how he can get.

I have quite enjoyed my stay in Bath. Indeed, I was hoping now that the season was over that you might journey to meet me here. I am gathering some acquaintances together for a proper few weeks of enjoyment and visitation.

I know that I am rather more social than you are, my dear. But I hope that you shall come, if only to see me again. I promise you that you shall be my favorite if you do. I shall never allow you to leave my side.

What do you say, my dear? Shall you come and enjoy the special waters of Bath with me? See if they are as good as everyone claims? Meet some charming new people?

Perhaps we shall finally cast the gloom of the single life off of your shoulders and fashion you a new cloak of love.

Thinking of you always my dear,

Julia

Georgiana sat, contemplating the letter.

Julia was a rather fanciful girl, although harmless. She was prone to poetic language and flights of fancy. She was also, as she had pointed out herself, rather more social than Georgiana was.

This little gathering of acquaintances sounded a bit daunting. Georgiana doubted that she should know anybody among the set.

Julia was younger than she was, and still had many prospects for marriage. If only looking after her mother's health and mediating between her parents didn't take up all of her time. If it weren't for that, Georgiana was certain that Julia would be married by now.

Surely this was a sign that she ought to speak to Edward about an apartment in Bath. Going to visit Julia would be the perfect excuse to discreetly look into living there.

And, of course, she would get to see her best friend again. She mightily looked forward to that. She had missed Julia. The girl always knew how to brighten a dark day. There was no one better for cheering Georgiana up when she was down in the mouth.

All in all, it sounded like a rather fortunate turn of events.

Georgiana composed her reply. Yes, she would love to join Julia in Bath. Would Julia be so kind as to help her make some discreet enquiries about living situations while she was there?

She also reminded Julia that she ought to be receiving her invitation to Edward and Maria's wedding shortly, if she had not got it already.

Perhaps, indeed, the two of them could now journey up from Bath to the wedding together.

The letter written, Georgiana found her brother downstairs in his office.

"Edward, I have received the most lovely letter from Miss Weston."

"Have you? I had wondered at not seeing you two arm in arm as usual. I suppose that helping Miss Worthing kept you rather busy."

"Yes, that was indeed the case. But, Edward, I hope that I am not imposing. Should you decide that you are against it, I will of course bow to your will.

"But it occurs to me that my part in the wedding preparations is rather finished. I have finalized the guest list and put down explicit instructions on the seating arrangements. Even the greatest of dunces could not mess it up.

"Miss Worthing is handling her end of things quite well. Better than I think she believes she is.

"Now, if you feel that my presence is still required here, then of course I shall stay. But I was hoping that..."

"Georgiana, please," Edward said, raising a tired eyebrow at her. "You only babble when you are nervous. And you should never have cause to be nervous with me. Speak your mind."

She took a deep, slow breath. "I was hoping that I might be allowed to travel to Bath for a few weeks to spend time with Julia. Before the wedding.

"We would then journey up to you together. I would be there the week of to help you two prepare. And I should still look after the house while you are on your honeymoon.

"Julia has extended the kindest invitation. And I have never been to Bath before. I hope that you will not mind. I must confess that I do miss her so."

Edward thought for a moment, then nodded. "If Miss Worthing can spare you. I am worried for her state of mind."

"You are always worried for her in one way or another. I think you forget what stern stuff she is made of."

"Is it not the job of a fiancé or husband to worry about his bride?" Edward countered, smiling.

Georgiana smiled back. "And a more conscientious fiancé or husband there never has been, I am sure. I shall check in on Miss Worthing and see what she thinks."

Edward nodded. "Who knows? Perhaps you will find yourself a husband there at last."

She knew that he did not mean it in a thoughtless or mean-spirited way. But it still hurt her to hear her brother say such a thing.

Edward had made it clear that she was not a burden to him. That he was happy to take care of his sister. That he did not view her inability to get married as something to look down upon her for.

And yet, Georgiana knew that it was her social duty. She was failing, no matter what her brother said. And she knew that in the back of his mind, Edward still thought she would eventually get married. That she would at last find the right person.

She appreciated that her brother still had such faith in her ability to get a husband. But it made her feel as though she was leading him on with false hope.

While she didn't like to admit it or think about it, she feared that her chance at marriage had actually passed.

It felt quite unfair. The universe, God, fate, had given her an amazing man. She had fallen in love with him, because how could she not have?

And then she had lost him. And now she was afraid—and had been for some time—that he was her one and only chance at love.

She supposed that at least one of them ought to have faith, though. If she could not have faith in herself, it was nice to know that her brother still had faith in her. Or at least faith in her ability to draw a man in.

Georgiana left her brother trying not to let the melancholy get to her. She found Miss Worthing—Maria—in the drawing room.

"How is your morning going, my dear?"

Maria looked up from her papers, smiling. "It's going rather well, all things considered. I'm only feeling halfway to panic today instead of all the way."

"I am glad to hear it," Georgiana said with a laugh.

Maria was rather nervous about this whole wedding business. She would never admit it, but Georgiana knew that part of the reason was that she feared her father's health would not last him until the wedding day.

It would be a damper, to say the least, if they had to interrupt planning a wedding in order to plan a funeral. Maria desperately wanted her father to be well enough to attend the wedding and walk her down the aisle. And who could blame her?

Perhaps Georgiana shouldn't leave. How could she abandon Maria at such a stressful and worrisome time? She ought to simply throw her letter in the fire and write another one to tell Julia that she couldn't make it.

"Do you need anything?" Maria asked. "I confess that I'm eager to be distracted from this mess of letters."

"I've finished with the guest list and the seating arrangements," Georgiana told her, handing her the necessary papers.

Then she showed her the letter. "My dearest friend, Miss Julia Weston, has invited me to stay with her in Bath.

"I was hoping that I might take her up on her offer and visit her for a few weeks. I would, of course, be back in time for the wedding.

"And if you need me, then of course I shall stay here. This is your wedding and it is more important than my visit. I can go to see Miss Weston at any time but a wedding only happens once."

Maria shook her head. "Georgiana, please. Never hesitate to ask for anything from me.

"After so long of my nervousness with you, after how much I owe you for your guidance and patience with me... you never need work yourself into knots over me.

"I shall always be happy to accommodate you. And you are quite right, all that I've needed you for is rather finished.

"Besides, I must learn to stand on my own at some point, mustn't

I? When I am mistress in my own right I can't possibly impose upon you whenever I have a question. I must learn to stand on my own two feet."

Georgiana smiled at her. She was impressed at how much Maria had grown.

When Maria had first come to England she had been horribly nervous about everything. She had been lacking in sophistication and had let everyone intimidate her. She'd been like Georgiana's shadow, following her everywhere.

Now, she was more confident. She could handle herself at balls without faltering. She no longer needed Georgiana or Edward for everything.

Luckily, she had done it without letting go of her sweet, guileless nature or her forthright behavior.

"If you're absolutely certain," Georgiana said, hesitating still. The last thing she wanted was to leave and then have a crisis occur.

Maria stood up and crossed over to her, taking Georgiana's hands in hers. "I promise you, Georgiana. You ought to go and have your fun.

"You deserve it, truly. You've been doing so much work for the both of us. It's not your wedding and yet you've been doing half the planning.

"I think that a little vacation is the least that you deserve. And after you've had to escort me and train me, practically all season long. It's the least that we can do to allow you to enjoy this time with your friend.

"And I look forward to meeting her at the wedding, as well." Maria squeezed her hands and let go.

Georgiana let out her breath slowly. "Thank you. I appreciate it. I know that you've been terribly nervous throughout this entire thing.

"And I want you to know that if you ever do need me, that you are to write me at once and send it by the fastest means possible.

"I do not wish for you to feel as though you are alone. There might be unexpected bumps in the road. And you are a sister to me. So never hesitate to call me back if you need. Do I have your word on that?"

Maria nodded, smiling still. "Yes, I promise. But I expect that everything will be all right. And this will be a much-needed break for you. You have been working yourself into knots over me and now over the wedding."

Georgiana didn't think of it that way. She was family, and the only close friend that Maria had. It was natural that she should help with such things.

Normally the mothers of the bride and groom would help to handle such matters. But with both Maria's mother and Edward's long gone, Georgiana had been happy to step up and lend her expertise.

But she was rather used to being the one who helped everybody else out. Perhaps Maria was right and it was time to do something for herself for a change.

"I shall send a letter to Julia telling her that I shall be heading out at once," Georgiana said, finally allowing a smile to turn up the corners of her mouth.

She departed and officially sent the letter. Anticipation began to fill her lungs like sweet country air.

She was going to get to go to Bath. And she was going to get to see her dearest friend. This was perhaps the most excited that she had been in years.

Yes, a vacation would be just what she needed. And then she could gather information and make plans for moving to Bath. She could present them all to Edward when he got back from his honeymoon.

It wasn't exactly the sort of life that women dreamed of when they were young. Maria had gotten that sort of life: marrying the love of her life who happened to also be a rich duke.

But it was a life that would allow her some measure of dignity. And that was all that she could ask for at this rate.

Georgiana went upstairs, already going through the list of clothes and supplies in her mind.

She had some packing to do.

CHAPTER 24

ROBERT TRENTWORTH READ over Miss Weston's letter again.

He had been dear friends with Miss Weston, once upon a time. That had been the last time that he was back in England, many years ago now.

But of course, he had been so close with her because he had been in love with her best friend, Miss Reginald.

Georgiana.

He had only just started to call her by her first name, at least in his mind, when it had all been taken away from him.

Robert did not like to think of himself as a man who was unreasonable. Being unreasonable didn't help you last long in His Majesty's Royal Navy.

But he was a man of principle. A man who stuck to his convictions and did not allow himself to be easily swayed by others. A man who stayed strong in his decisions and in what he believed.

And unfortunately, the woman he had fallen in love with was not the same way.

It still frustrated him, all of these years later. He knew that he should let it go. Men and women had their hearts broken all the time. What made his so special?

And yet, he could not quite forget Georgiana Reginald.

She would probably be married to someone else by now. Someone of whom her father had approved.

The duke was a hard man. A man with his own principles, principles that did not align with Trentworth's own. In fact, he was certain the duke's principles did not align with most people's.

Of course most people wanted their daughter to wed a man of wealth. But a man of honor who was moving up in the world, who came from a good family, was that not also good enough for most?

The Duke of Foreshire had disagreed. Nothing short of a titled man of wealth would do for his daughter. Just as nothing short of the daughter of a titled, rich man would do for his son.

It made Trentworth all the more furious when he thought of how he was now a rich man. He had no title, it was true. But he had made his way up. He was now a man with ten thousand pounds to his name and more to come.

And yet, that wouldn't have been good enough for the Duke of Foreshire.

Robert weighed the possibility of Miss Reginald, or whatever her new last name was, being there.

Most likely not, he should think. The London season was on the tail end and he was sure that as a fashionable lady she would still be a part of it. There was no reason for her to go to Bath.

Besides, Miss Weston had hinted in her letter that all the ladies in her party would be unmarried.

Robert knew what she was about, of course. Miss Weston was a lively girl who delighted in matchmaking. And while normally he would object, he couldn't deny that she had a fair point.

It was high time that he found himself a wife. His career in the navy was finishing up. He could soon become a proper gentleman among the rest of upper society. And he would need someone to share his life with.

Of course, he also wanted someone to share his life with. He did not intend to die alone. And he wanted children, as well, if possible.

So while he would normally remind Miss Weston that he did not appreciate other people meddling in his life, he was grateful for it this one time. Perhaps he could find his future wife among these ladies.

Miss Weston herself, of course, was not an option. Although they had the highest regard for one another, there was not a spark of romance between them.

She honestly reminded him of his sister, who unfortunately had died as a child. Indeed, he was the only one of his siblings to survive to adulthood. A tragedy for his poor parents. He was only glad that he had been able to make them proud before they passed on.

But Miss Weston aside, surely there had to be another lady or two among the party that he could consider as a bride.

He could only hope that his own manners had not become too dreadful in his time away. Being in the navy and at war did not necessarily keep one up to date on proper dining room etiquette.

It was going to be interesting to finally be back in England again. He loved the sea and always would but he did so long for the rolling green hills of his homeland. To be on solid land for so long a time would be a nice change.

He supposed that he ought to respond and let Miss Weston know that he would be attending.

Seeing her again would be interesting. He hadn't seen Miss Weston since Miss Reginald had broken off their engagement. He was surprised that she remembered him.

Although he supposed that he should not be. Miss Weston remembered everybody and was a good-natured person, and they had got on well.

This would be good for him, he told himself. He would finally be able to get over Miss Reginald and find someone with whom he could spend the rest of his life.

He composed a polite reply to Miss Weston to inform her that he would be happy to re-open his acquaintance with her and would be glad to join her party in Bath.

Then he began to think about what he would need. He would actually have to worry about what he was wearing to dinner for once, no longer able to simply throw on one of his uniforms.

This was going to be interesting, he told himself. If nothing else, it would be interesting.

CHAPTER 25

GEORGIANA WATCHED through the window of the carriage as it rolled along.

Her stomach was knotted in anticipation. She did not like to think of herself as someone who was easily excitable. But this was the first time that she would be meeting so many new people in so long of a time.

She was even nervous about seeing Julia again. What if she had become boring? What if she and Julia were no longer as close as they had been?

What if these new people did not like her? What if she was only setting herself up for more ridicule? She was certain that she would be one of the oldest members of the party.

Was she only setting herself up to be hurt? Would she spend the whole time feeling like an outsider, as usual? Only it would be worse than usual, because it wouldn't be random women that she was feeling rejected by. It would be her dearest friend.

Georgiana forced herself to breathe slowly and carefully. She had never been the sort of person to give into panic. She would not do so now. Especially when she didn't even know if there was a reason to be upset.

She needed to give Julia more credit. Julia had always been a lovely and loving person. It was only Georgiana's own insecurities making her think this way. Why on earth would Julia give up a decade of friendship in such a manner?

No, it would all be fine. She just had to remember to keep her head firm on her shoulders.

The journey into Bath was pleasant. It was nice to travel alone, but also lonely. She was so used to travelling everywhere with her brother, and now with her brother and Maria.

But she must get used to it now that spinsterhood would soon be upon her. She was six and twenty. Some people would be generous and say that she still had a chance. But Georgiana knew the truth.

Now, she made certain to look out the window as the carriage rolled through the streets.

There were plenty of lovely-looking places that she could see herself living in. She couldn't get something too expensive, of course. She would never ask such a thing of her brother.

But something modest, not too near the town center...

The carriage rolled to a stop in front of a lovely townhouse.

Georgiana had hardly gotten out of the carriage before the front door was flying open and Julia was hurrying out of it.

"My darling!" she cried, seizing Georgiana's hands and spinning her about.

Georgiana was not one for making a spectacle, but she could not begrudge Julia a little enthusiasm after so long apart.

Julia hugged her quickly and then directed the servants to bring in Georgiana's things. "Oh, I have so much to discuss with you! I want to hear all about how your brother came to meet this young lady of his!"

Georgiana smiled. "Well, it is quite a story."

"I was beginning to fear that your brother should never choose anyone. He is quite picky, is he not?"

"That is certainly one way to put it."

"But how did you come to meet this creature? She sounds delightful from what you have told me of her in your letters."

"She knows nothing of London society and was raised quite wildly on a plantation in the Caribbean," Georgiana said. "Which of course, would make her perfect for him."

Julia laughed. "Only your brother. That is quite like him. We ought to have tried such a thing sooner."

Georgiana nodded. She was just glad that her brother was now happy. She had seen how bitter and frustrated Edward was becoming with society, especially with the women.

She had not had the slightest idea how to help him. She had feared that he would become like their father. Father had been bitter and hard-hearted. Edward did not deserve to become like that.

Maria did not understand, and perhaps never would fully understand, what a great service she had done for Edward. Georgiana would be forever grateful to her.

But of course, Maria would not see it as a service. She was in love with Edward. Making him happy was simply a part of what made her happy. And vice versa. Making Maria happy was Edward's greatest joy.

Georgiana sometimes got a little pang of sadness when she watched them. It was not envy. Envy suggested that she wanted to take away from them what they had. And she could never want that. She could never begrudge either Edward or Maria anything.

But she could not help but wonder why she could not also have that happiness. Why only some people were allowed to have that wonderful, uplifting kind of love and others were not.

"They are wonderfully suited for one another," Georgiana said. "You shall see it when you attend the wedding. I have never seen two people who were more complementary in their manner."

"I have," Julia said quietly.

Georgiana knew to what she was referring but said nothing. She was not going to rise to the bait.

"You and Captain Trentworth were remarkably well suited," Julia went on. Her voice was still quiet, and more serious than usual. "With all due respect to your brother, I have never seen two people who fell more amicably and smoothly into the deepest of affections."

"That was many years ago," Georgiana replied. "We were but children then. Or at least you and I were. And the past always tends to be viewed through rose-colored glasses."

Julia made a noncommittal humming noise.

Georgiana had known Julia for a decade, however. No, for longer than that. Since they were but young girls, children. She knew every tone of voice and every facial expression that Julia had.

"I'm getting the most suspicious feeling," she said, trying to keep her tone lighthearted.

Indeed, she felt a creeping cold suspicion curling up her spine and settling over her shoulders.

"That is odd," Julia replied. "I can assure you that you have no reason to fret. You know how I have always supported your acquaintance with Captain Trentworth, that is all."

It was true. Julia had advocated hard for Georgiana to go against her father and marry Captain Trentworth.

But Julia had two loving parents. They could be trying at times and there were arguments between the three of them once in a while. But Mr. and Mrs. Weston would never disown Julia. They would never kick her out.

Georgiana's father certainly would have.

She would have had to go to Captain Trentworth with nothing. No inheritance, no blessing. And if her father had snubbed her, the rest of society would have followed.

Of course, Father was now dead. And rather unexpectedly, from a riding accident. But how was she to know that at the time?

Father had been in the best of health. He was expected to live another decade. How could she have known that there would have only been a few years of being an outcast? As far as she had been aware, it would have been at least a decade.

But there was no use in crying over spilled milk and thinking about it all now. She did, however, wonder what Julia was up to.

Julia was up to something. Her protestation could not soothe Georgiana's worry. She knew when her friend was scheming, and Julia most certainly had some sort of card up her sleeve.

"We have not been acquainted for many years," Georgiana reminded her. "In fact, I see no reason why you should even bring him up at all."

Julia opened her mouth, then seemed to think better of whatever thought she had. "I shall show you to your room. Then we can get some tea and you can catch me up on everything that's been going on."

Georgiana's room was lovely, with a good view of the street. As they took tea, however, Georgiana admitted that there wasn't much news to share.

She told Julia all about how they took in Maria and how Maria and Edward came to fall in love and had become engaged.

"But aside from that whole story," she said, "I'm afraid that not much has been going on in my life."

"You were in London, though! During the season!" Julia protested. "Surely you have some good gossip to share."

"Julia, my dear, you ought to know by now that nobody talks about that sort of thing with me. I'm quite the wallflower."

"You are simply a woman of elegance and taste. They know you will not approve of gossip."

"And yet you still ask me to find out if I have any!"

"Well, perhaps you had overheard something. You strike me as the sort of person who overhears a great deal. You know that people seem to make the mistake of forgetting that you are around and then they shall say anything."

Georgiana had to smile at that. "I am not certain if I should find that to be an insult or not."

"You have a remarkable ability to vanish into the wall," Julia said. "I think that you should take it as a compliment. It means that you can hear things that other people do not."

"It makes me sound rather like a ghost or something out of those gothic novels," Georgiana admitted.

"You may think of it however you like," Julia replied. "I would prefer it if sometimes people would forget that I was there."

"No, you do not," Georgiana replied. "You like to be the center of attention."

"But it does get rather exhausting. Everyone's always trying to talk to you and you have to be constantly pleasant to everybody. And you have to please everybody at once. It's rather more trouble than it's worth at times."

"But you get bored out of your mind if you do not have some party or other to go to in the evening."

"That is true, you have caught me in a corner." Julia laughed. "Now, are you not a little curious as to who else I have invited?"

"As you are about to tell me, I see no reason to be curious. You will inform me as to who you have invited. Even if I did not wish to know."

"But you do wish to know, do you not?"

Georgiana sighed. Julia really was a stubborn creature. "Yes, I do wish to know. Are you happy to hear it said aloud?"

"Oh, quite." Julia smiled like quicksilver, fast and slippery and gone in an instant. "There are two young ladies besides you and myself that will be there."

"I think you ought to be careful in classifying me as a young lady. I am six and twenty."

"I say that you are still young. And I shall be quite stern with anyone who says otherwise."

"Very well. There are two other ladies who will be joining us? Are they close with you?"

"Of a sort. One of them, Miss Perry, is from our country home. I have known her family off and on our entire lives. But I would not call us close, in a manner.

"I have invited her so that I might get to know her better. She is the only one of her family who is not married. She has three brothers, can you imagine! And a sister."

"Quite a family," Georgiana agreed.

Of course, having a lot of children was the norm. To be an only child as Julia was or to have only one sibling as Georgiana did was unusual.

Georgiana could hardly imagine what it would be like to have a large number of siblings. She had wanted a lot of children once upon a time.

Now it seemed that dream was going to be beyond her. It was not something she spoke about often. But she had dreamed...

"Do you remember when we were children?" Julia asked. "And we listed all the boys and girls we would have, and named them?"

Georgiana nodded. "I was determined that my first boy would be named Edward. I looked up to my brother so. I still do."

"I remember searching through the history books and novels to find the most fanciful names. Do you remember, I wanted to name one son Tybalt? After Romeo and Juliet?"

"You always did have a rather active imagination."

"I expect that I shall not have twelve boys as I originally envisioned," Julia mused.

"I expect that I shall not have any," Georgiana said. She couldn't help it. Things just slipped out around Julia. They were so close that she could not help but tell the truth of how she was feeling.

Julia made a soothing noise and reached over to pat Georgiana's hand. "You mustn't give up hope, my dear. I know that you will get to grow old surrounded by children and grandchildren."

"You are far more optimistic than I am." Georgiana looked away so that she would not reveal all of her emotions.

Sometimes it felt as though that was all that she thought about, all that she and everyone else talked about. Her inability to get married.

When she was younger, the prospect of marriage was something fun. And once you were married, it simply became one of many things to talk about.

But when it was something she needed and couldn't seem to get, all everybody could talk about was whether or not she would get married.

After a time, the reassurances almost hurt more than the insults. At least the people insulting her were being honest. She could never tell if the person offering her hope was being genuine or if they didn't truly believe in it and were only saying it because they felt they had to.

And when it was someone like her brother or her dear friend offering up the hope... well, then Georgiana felt as though she was only letting the person down by continuing to remain single.

She knew, of course, that the ones she cared about didn't see it that way. But she couldn't shake the feeling that she wasn't only failing herself. She was failing them. She wasn't living up to their expectations for her. And that she was somehow being less than her best. That she was making a mess of things, somehow.

"Oh dear," Julia said softly. "I've upset you. I'm terribly sorry, my dear. You know that I only wish for you to be happy."

"Let us move on," Georgiana said, forcing herself to look Julia in the eye once more. "Tell me more about this Miss Perry."

"She is a dear girl from what I know of her," Julia said. "I am rather hoping to get to know her better during this visit. She's rather lively. I can imagine she's had to be what with three brothers to compete with.

"And her family is good. Her father runs the rectory back in my home county and one of her brothers has gone into the navy. She's one and twenty and a bit sillier than I think you'll be used to. But she has a good heart. Rather playful."

"One would hope," Georgiana said, "that at the age of one and twenty, all the silliness will have gone out of a girl."

"The silliness has yet to go out of me," Julia replied. "At this point I expect I shall always have some."

"You are also rather too saucy for your own good, my dear. And the other young lady?"

"Miss Everett. She's a quick wit and a bit bossy. I got to know her here in Bath. She's gone away, back to London for the season, but she will be back in time for the visit. I expect you might have run into her at some ball or other?"

"Again, my dear, you overestimate me. I haven't even heard of the girl."

"She's nineteen and can be rather sharp in her manner. I think that she's put a few people off with her wit if I am to be honest. But she's really a good-natured person. I think that she simply doesn't always understand how her words can be interpreted."

"Can she take it as well as dish it out? People often are too harsh with others and then tear up the moment anyone suggests the slightest thing about them."

Julia shook her head. "She's got quite a tough skin. She's had to have one. You see, her mother married a bit below her station but her aunt married quite well—a baron.

"Her aunt was rather kind and took the girl in to raise her alongside her cousins. But I'm afraid that she hasn't always been well-treated by their acquaintances because of her parentage."

"That is a pity," Georgiana said.

She hadn't seen such treatment up close until she and her brother had taken in Maria. Then she had gotten to see just how cruel people could be to someone simply because they were a little different than everyone else.

Georgiana could not help but wonder how long it would be before people started to say such cruel things about her.

"It sounds to me," she said, "as though Miss Everett developed her quick wit in order to get back at those who attacked her."

"That is rather my theory," Julia replied. "My hope is that once she is among friends she will truly blossom."

"And are those the only two that you have invited?"

"Of the ladies, yes. I have invited three gentlemen as well."

"You are scheming, Julia Weston. Do not think that I don't know how you work. Your every thought is known to me."

"Rather ominous, except that I don't mind if you know my every thought. Besides, I know all of yours." Julia smiled cheekily.

"The first gentleman is a Mr. Tomlinson. He's recently come into an inheritance after his uncle left him everything, having no children of his own.

"It's quite lucky for him, as he is the third son and had no real prospects other than the clergy or perhaps as a lawyer.

"He's visited Bath from time to time and I've become curious to get to know him better. He is of a most patient temper. I think that you will quite like him."

Georgiana fixed her friend with a stern look. "By which you mean, you hope that I will quite like him and that he will quite like me. I know what you are thinking."

"Honestly, my dear, I do not care if you like him or if you like the other gentleman I have arranged to bring here," Julia replied. "One will do just as well as the other."

"And who is this second gentleman?"

"His name is Mr. Norwich, and he'll be a count when his father dies and he inherits. He used to study under my father when Father was taking in boys for tutoring.

"We've been rather nice acquaintances during this whole time and I thought that he would round out the party well. He's a cheerful man. The sort that's never had to want for anything and so is rather lighthearted about life as a result.

"But not in an insufferable way, fortunately. He just lightens up a party, brings life into it. I think that you two will get on as well."

"I am starting to suspect that you have set me up," Georgiana said. "But you're going to fail. You've had two lovely young ladies come and join us. They will be certain to draw the eye of the gentlemen far more than I will."

"You might have given up on yourself," Julia said, "but I have not. It is the job of a friend, I should think, to retain hope for you when you have lost it for yourself."

"And I think that you are beating on a dead horse."

"Well, we each are entitled to our opinions," Julia replied. "Soon, we shall see which of us has the right of it."

They would see, Georgiana thought, a bit grimly. She did not have much faith in her own prospects.

But, Julia had faith.

Perhaps that would suffice for now.

CHAPTER 26

ROBERT STOOD IN THE STREET, watching the carriages as they rolled by, taking in the people as they strolled.

England had not changed as much as he would have thought that it would in his time away. But he was sure that while the outside looked the same, the details were probably quite different.

He was planning on learning a great deal when he got to the Weston residence. There would be births, deaths, marriages, and scandals to get caught up on.

Miss Weston would, of course, be an excellent source for such things. She was always at the center of everyone's attention. If Robert was remembering her correctly, she was the kind of person who drew energy from being around other people. People could sense it, and so she drew people towards her.

Of course, she might have changed in the time since Robert had last seen her.

He knew that he was only setting himself up for heartache, but he hoped that in all of his questions, he might be able to find out about Miss Reginald.

She and Miss Weston were the best of friends, after all. Miss Weston would be sure to tell him what was going on with Miss Reginald.

Of course, the answer would be that she was married to some rich, titled man and had been for some time. Perhaps she even had children.

He knew that she had wanted children. A few, if possible.

He told himself that if he ran into her, he would be cordial. That he would greet her as he would any other long-lost acquaintance.

But it would be hard. Once upon a time he had known her thoughts better than he had known his own. There was nothing of him that was unknown to her. He had bared his soul in letters to her, speaking of his hopes and dreams.

And she had done the same, telling him of her fears and concerns. Of her desires, both the silly girlhood ones and the more serious ones. They had talked about everything from what flowers they would like to plant in a garden to their favorite novels and the state of the Empire.

Now, of course, her husband would know all of those things.

How would it be? he wondered. Would Miss Reginald think that she still knew him? He could not presume to still know her, he must keep reminding himself of that.

It had been years. She had a right to change, just as he did. He would be insulted if she acted as though she still understood him completely. He must not insult her in the same manner.

Of course, this was all assuming that he actually ran into her on this trip. Miss Weston had not breathed so much as a word about Miss Reginald in her letters. He could be working himself into knots for no reason at all.

It would be best, he thought, if he asked Miss Weston about Miss Reginald as soon as possible and got the lay of the land.

That way, when he did eventually run into her, he would be prepared. He could at least put on a good face and pretend to be happy for her.

Was he bitter? Possibly. He could not pretend to be perfect. He was the sort of man who did not forget, although he tried to forgive.

He hoped that he would be able to forgive Miss Reginald.

Another one of the men who was invited was Mr. Edmund Norwich. Robert actually had served a bit with Edmund's younger brother, Fitzwilliam, and through him had written to ask if he might impose upon the Norwich residence for his time in Bath.

Mr. Norwich had been more than happy to offer his home to Robert.

It has been some time since I got to make a new acquaintance, he wrote in his letter. And any friend of my brother's is a friend of mine.

Robert rapped upon the appropriate door and waited to be shown in.

Mr. Norwich was an amiable-looking man. He was not handsome exactly but had the sort of jovial air about him that immediately endeared him to others. It gave him the kind of face that you just wanted to keep looking at.

"Captain Trentworth." They shook hands. "It is a pleasure to meet you. My brother has mentioned you in letters with the highest of praise. And he is not an easy man to impress."

"No, he is not, and I am glad to know that I have earned his respect."

"I hear that you have come up in the world recently," Mr. Norwich said, offering him a drink. "Are congratulations in order, then? Or condolences?"

Robert sighed. "A bit of both, I'm afraid. I had a rather... eccentric aunt. She died recently and it turns out that she was secretly this very popular novelist.

"I'll hide the titles from you, for she wished to remain anonymous and I would like to keep her secret out of respect for that. But suffice to say they have made quite a bit of money.

"None of us knew this, of course. She had a small legacy left to her by her father and she lived off of that, as far as any of us were aware.

"But she died, about six months ago... and I knew that I was always her favorite, but it turns out she had left me everything. And there was quite a bit of everything."

"I think I can say that a secretly rich family member leaving us money is what many a man hopes for," Mr. Norwich pointed out with a small laugh.

Robert smiled. "True, true. And I've made quite a bit as a navy man."

"That was why my brother joined," Mr. Norwich said. "He's the second son, of course. So I'll be getting the title and the estate when our father has passed on. But he's made quite a name for himself as well as some income while serving."

"That's why I went into it as well," Robert agreed. "I've got a size-able income coming from that as well."

"We'll have to talk about how to handle all of it," Mr. Norwich counseled him. "See about getting you a proper family estate now that you're a gentleman of leisure like the rest of us."

Robert chuckled, trying to mask the pain that shot through him like a bullet.

When he had imagined being able to buy an estate, one that he could entail and pass down onto his children, and their children, and their children...

Well, that had been years ago. When he was talking about the future with Miss Reginald.

He hadn't really allowed himself to think about it since then. Not when he was still out at sea and worrying about if he would even get back home alive.

And if he had no wife, then what was he doing worrying about an estate?

Oh, how they had talked about it. He wanted to buy something modest, something that Miss Reginald would enjoy. He had put great thought into her opinion and her wishes.

Now, of course, he would have to buy an estate. He was going to be changing his lifestyle. The ship and cannons that had filled his life were being replaced with hunting trips and balls. And part of that was having a home base.

It had not failed to strike him, the irony of the situation. He was now going to have nearly all of the things that had caused Lord Reginald, and therefore his daughter, to reject him all those years ago.

But he shoved that bitterness down for now. Mr. Norwich was only trying to be friendly and helpful. It was rather kind of him to offer to lend a hand.

As the son of a titled man, Mr. Norwich would be well versed in how to navigate getting an estate and handling it. How to be a member of higher society. How to handle one's accounts and one's income.

It was a great kindness for him to help Robert out like this. Robert would not forget it. And he must be sure to show that gratitude. This was not the time to be sharing his woes over a long-over heartbreak.

"I appreciate it," he told him. "Truly. Tell me, have you met the other people that Miss Weston has invited for this whole party of hers?"

"I'm aware of them," Mr. Norwich said. "But I cannot say that I know any of them. One hears about people, of course. But I fear that I know nothing of their characters and I daresay they shan't really know anything of mine.

"Miss Weston did that on purpose, actually, or so I believe. I've known her for quite a few years and she's always been a lively thing.

"I think that she is trying to help people to meet one another. To get acquainted in a way that they would not have otherwise."

"I hope that she is not thinking of muddling the status quo," Robert said. "She's a troublemaker at times, you know, although there is always some altruistic reason behind it."

Mr. Norwich nodded. "It is that way with her, I've found. But we shall see what all is going on soon enough. She's sent us an invitation to dinner this evening."

"Of course she has learned that I am staying with you. I swear that lady finds a way of finding out everything. She probably knew about my aunt before I did."

Mr. Norwich laughed. "Well, you shall get an opportunity to chastise her for it at once."

"That is true."

Robert wasn't sure if he was looking forward to the dinner or not. "I'm afraid I'm rather rusty on my manners. You might have to coach me."

"If there was ever a group of people who wouldn't mind if you have to double-check which fork to use, then it would be the group of whichever people Miss Weston has invited."

Mr. Norwich showed Robert to his room, and then left him to get ready for dinner.

Robert stared at himself in the mirror once he was ready to go. The last time that he had been out in society, he had fallen in love. He had been a man in love, a man engaged. He had gone from being an insecure boy to a man who thought he had the world in the palm of his hand... and then had become a man crushed.

Now he was older. Hopefully wiser. And trying to do it all over again.

He was not stupid. Miss Weston had hinted in her letters that there would be some lovely young ladies in attendance. Mr. Norwich was a highly eligible bachelor.

And he himself might be considered a highly eligible bachelor nowadays.

An only child, Miss Weston had always been strong-willed and perhaps had been given a little too much head by her parents. It would not surprise him if his hunch was right and she was trying to take the opportunity to matchmake.

He wasn't sure how he felt about that idea.

On the one hand, Miss Weston obviously knew what kind of woman he liked. She had been one of the few people who had known about his engagement to Miss Reginald.

Indeed, the young lady had actively encouraged the engagement. She had been open in her support of the match and had stated several times how well-suited she thought the two were for one another.

And so if she was trying to matchmake him with someone, there could be little doubt that she would know the sort of woman that would catch his eye.

But would that only hurt him more? To be faced with a woman who was so like Miss Reginald and yet, not her at all? But would a woman who was entirely different not be at all to his taste?

He did not know.

Robert tried to be a man who knew his own heart. But in this, right now, he was entirely lost.

Did he want to be set up?

He knew that he needed to marry. What was more, he wanted to marry. He wanted someone to share the rest of his life with. Someone to go on long walks with. An ally at dinner parties.

But to find someone in the house of the woman who had been the best friend of the woman to whom he had once been engaged...

It was all a bit frustrating and confusing, that was all. Dare he even say awkward?

Looking at himself in the mirror, Robert knew that he looked like a proper gentleman. But he didn't quite feel like one.

He still felt like he was that terrified young man underneath it all. And a soldier on top of that. How was he supposed to fit in with all of these men and women who had never known the sea? Who had spent their entire lives going to balls and social gatherings?

It was, frankly, rather scary. He didn't like to admit it. After all, it wasn't as though his life was in danger. He'd faced down real danger before and come back out the other side.

And yet now, the idea that a mutual acquaintance was trying to matchmake him was making him more nervous than going into a sea battle against the French.

There was a knock at the door and Robert knew that it was Mr. Norwich checking up on him.

"Out in a moment," he called.

Well, whether he felt ready or not, it was time to go over and see what was going on. Get the lay of the land.

He supposed that after all, he could always simply keep a polite distance if he didn't feel an affinity for the ladies.

It could be worse, of course.

He could be seeing Miss Reginald again.

CHAPTER 27

THE LADIES ARRIVED FIRST.

Georgiana knew that she would like Miss Everett right away. She was similar enough in character to Georgiana but had a sharp wit that had Georgiana smiling a great deal more than she usually did.

Miss Perry, she was less sure about. The girl was rather silly, as Julia had warned. It wasn't that she was a stupid girl. But she was still rather behaving like a girl rather than an adult.

It could be charming, Georgiana supposed. But there was a way to go about it without coming across as quite so... ridiculous.

Maria was rather guileless in her manner. It was true. And some people thought of her as more girlish than womanly. But she was thoughtful and intelligent and a good listener. Those things, in Georgiana's opinion, gave her a sense of maturity.

Miss Perry didn't seem to have that. At least not from what Georgiana could tell from the half hour of getting to know her before the dinner started.

Miss Everett, on the other hand, had a definite sense of maturity to her. Georgiana could see how people might be put off by her wit. But Georgiana had grown up with Edward for a brother. And of course their sour father. After that, she doubted that anything Miss Everett said could faze her.

And at least none of it was malicious. That would have drawn the line for her. But instead it was all simply blunt. Rather like Maria, in some ways. Certainly like Edward.

Julia was flitting between the three of them, being her marvelous, energetic self.

And then the men arrived.

The first one through the door was Mr. Tomlinson. He was a very handsome man, with strawberry blond hair and an easy smile. He was very affable when he and Georgiana were introduced to one another.

"I've been hearing wonderful things about you, Miss Reginald," Mr. Tomlinson said. "Your friend Miss Weston here was simply full of your praises."

"Miss Weston, I'm afraid, can be a little overenthusiastic in things," Georgiana replied. "I'm quite a boring person, truly, once you get to know me."

"You'll have to excuse me if I don't quite believe you," Mr. Tomlinson said. "Anyone who is a friend to Miss Weston must be at least somewhat capable of holding attention in a crowd. I think I shall have to withhold my judgment until I get to see more of you."

Georgiana thought it a very pretty speech of him. It made her unsure. Men who were good with their words, who had silver tongues, tended to put her on her guard. It tended to suggest a lack of sincerity in their words, a lack of true feeling.

In her experience, the sort of people who could so easily make up honeyed speeches didn't really mean them. It was when the person was searching for words and struggling through that it showed how much emotion was behind it. The greater the emotion, the harder it was to get the words out.

But of course, there was no reason for Mr. Tomlinson to have any particular emotions towards her or anyone else in the party. He could just be a man of wit, the way that Miss Everett was a woman of some wit. She didn't need to judge him too hastily.

Then the next man arrived.

Or rather, the next two men.

Georgiana's back was to the door, for she was looking at the sheets of music at the pianoforte. She played, and she and Maria liked to duet, taking turns playing the instrument and turning the pages.

She heard someone enter, and then the introductions Julia was making. That must be Mr. Norwich.

Then she heard someone else enter—and her heartrate picked up.

It had been so long, but she had not forgotten the distinctive sound of his boots on the floor. The way that he walked, the length of his stride.

Even before Julia said anything, Georgiana could sense him. Her heart already knew.

"And this is Captain Trentworth," Julia was saying. "He is staying on with Mr. Norwich for a time and I have added him to even out our number."

Even out? While there would now be three men and three women, there was still Julia to consider.

Although Georgiana supposed that Julia could now sit at the head of the table...

She shook herself. How could she be wondering about dinner seating at a moment such as this?

Julia had to know that Captain Trentworth was coming. She knew everything that was going on around her. This couldn't possibly be a last-minute addition.

She had known that Captain Trentworth would be in town. She had invited him to join her party. And she had done all of this, knowing how Georgiana felt. Knowing how their last meeting had gone.

And she had said not a word of warning to Georgiana about it!

Georgiana took a deep breath. She would be having a firm talk with Julia later, once everyone else had gone.

For now, she had to figure out what she was going to do about Captain Trentworth.

Dragging Julia off to the side to lecture her would not accomplish anything. She had to find a way to control her emotions, and quickly.

Captain Trentworth must have known that she would be here. What did he think of her? Why had he come? Did he despise her?

He had certainly seemed to, when she had broken off their engagement all those years ago. He had spoken quite frankly to her. It had been clear just what he thought of her choices and her principles—or rather lack of them.

He couldn't possibly have forgiven her, could he? Did he want to take this chance to start anew? Or was he here simply to rub it in her face that she was not his wife?

Georgiana had no idea. But she would be damned if she would let herself be made a fool of by herself, of all people. She was not going to show a bit of emotion that was not cordial and appropriate for such a setting.

She took a few deep breaths and steeled herself. In all likelihood, Captain Trentworth was perfectly fine with seeing her. He had probably gotten over her ages ago. After all, they had parted with him despising her.

When you despised someone, surely that quickly turned to indifference. He probably hadn't thought of her at all in the intervening years and if he had it would have been only with pity or anger.

No, she was the one who was still clinging to an emotion, a kinship, that was no longer there.

It was up to her to remain calm.

Georgiana turned and walked across the room to him. The years had been good to him. When she had first met Captain Trentworth, he had been younger and, of course, good-looking.

But now he had gone from good-looking to full-on handsome. He had dark, deep blue eyes and rich brown hair as he had before. But now the eyes were darker, and he had grown into his face. The jawline had strengthened and the lines that had appeared gave him an air of dignity.

He was more handsome now than he had been when she had first fallen in love with him.

Oh, she was in so much trouble.

She felt a fool for doing so, but she quickly looked to see if there was a wedding ring. There was nothing there. But of course men did not always wear wedding rings. He might simply not have chosen to.

But Captain Trentworth was a loyal man. A man who clearly and firmly stated where he stood. If he was married she had the feeling that he would wear a ring simply to proclaim his partnership with his wife.

The woman that he picked, after all, would be a lucky one. One of high character and principle. One to whom Captain Trentworth had given his whole heart.

She had been that lucky once. She had held his heart in her hand.

And she had crushed it.

She knew the moment that he saw her, for he froze. It was quite a physical reaction.

And then she knew—Julia had not told him about her, either.

How terribly unfair of Julia to do such a thing to them. And now their first meeting in years was to be in front of other people. In a place where they could not speak plain and work out their emotions.

They would have to be cordial to one another and pretend as though nothing intimate had happened between them years ago.

How on earth were they to manage?

"Miss Reginald," Captain Trentworth said. His voice had grown deeper and richer in the intervening years. It made her feel warm all over. "I had not expected to see you here."

"Nor I," Georgiana admitted. "I had not realized that you were back in England. Are you on leave?"

"In fact I have retired," Captain Trentworth said. "I have come into money during my service and recently come into some inheritance as well. I felt that it was high time that I settled into a life in society at last."

"You two know each other?" said another man.

Georgiana curtsied to him. He was tall and thin, with a solid presence and warm brown eyes. This must be Mr. Norwich, unless there was yet another man that Julia had failed to warn Georgiana about.

"This is Miss Reginald," Captain Trentworth said. "Unless I am mistaken and you have married in my time away."

"No, sir, I have not."

"And this is Mr. Norwich," Captain Trentworth added, almost as an afterthought.

"You surprise me," Mr. Norwich said. "You did not give me the impression that you were acquainted with such a lovely lady as this."

Georgiana smiled politely. He was only flattering her. She was not nearly the lively beauty that the other three ladies in the party were. Already she could see Miss Everett making everyone laugh while Miss Perry was flattering Mr. Tomlinson and making him smile.

No, Mr. Norwich was only flattering her. It was the way of these educated men. She only had to not make the mistake of believing them.

Julia came up then and started inquiring after Mr. Norwich's family. Georgiana suspected that it was a sly way of getting herself and Captain Trentworth alone.

Oh, she was most certainly going to talk to Julia about this later on.

"I am surprised," Captain Trentworth said quietly. "I thought that you would have been long married by now."

"It was not to be, it seems," Georgiana said carefully.

Captain Trentworth wasn't even looking directly at her. He was instead staring at one of the paintings on the wall.

Was she truly so abhorrent to him? Was he so very angry with her still?

"And you?" she asked. "I would have thought that you would be married as well by now."

"I have been out on the high seas," Captain Trentworth replied. "There are those who bring their wives with them but I am not one such man. I wanted to wait until I retired and then spend time with my wife."

"And yet you would have married me," Georgiana could not help but point out.

"You were a... special case," Captain Trentworth replied. "But I have since learned that logic is to win the day. As you so wisely taught me."

That had, indeed, been one of the things that Georgiana had said to him when she had broken off their engagement.

To have him flinging her own words back at her felt like a slap in the face. So he was still angry with her. He probably even hated her.

Well, at least now she knew.

"And how is your father?" he asked. Whether it was to get in another dig at her or to change the subject, she did not know.

"I'm afraid that he passed last year," she admitted.

Captain Trentworth stared at her. "But he was in the prime of health, last I heard." His surprise seemed genuine.

Georgiana nodded. "Yes. It was a riding accident. Rather sudden."

"Oh." Captain Trentworth seemed wrong-footed. "I—my sincere condolences."

"Thank you."

"I know that I... said some rather unkind things about his character the last time that we were together. And while I will not pretend that I did agree with him on, well, anything... I know that he was still your father. I'm sure that it was quite a sad time for you, and I am sorry."

Captain Trentworth had hated her father, and vice versa. She thought it rather kind of him to say such condolences to her. He sounded genuinely contrite.

"I appreciate it. I know that you two did not see eye to eye and I would never expect you to fall to your knees in mourning. But to have you acknowledge my grief means... quite a bit."

Captain Trentworth nodded once, jerkily. "And I suppose then that your brother is now the duke."

"Yes. He has stepped up to the task admirably. There was a learning period but he has handled it with grace."

"I recall that he was a rather stoic man. I am not surprised that he handled the whole thing well. I wish him the best of luck in his continued work in the position."

"He is engaged, in fact," Georgiana could not help but add. "To a most wonderful young lady. She is as a sister to me."

"I am glad to hear it. It is a sad thing, if a family member marries someone of whom one is not fond. And your brother has an excellent judgment of character, if I remember correctly."

"Yes, he does." She decided it was best to simply gloss over how horribly Edward had nearly botched the entire courtship.

If only she and Captain Trentworth were how they used to be. Then she could tell him of how Edward had not even realized that he was in love with Maria until Georgiana pointed it out to him.

She would tell him all about how Maria had not understood why no man would call upon her, when it was because Edward was acting as her suitor without either of them realizing it.

She would tell him of how Edward had gone too far in chastising Maria for her behavior one night, and how it had nearly ruined the entire thing.

But they were not that close. Not now. And if she were to tell the story to anyone other than someone as close to her as Julia, or as a fiancé, then Edward would be horribly disappointed in her. Her brother was a private man, just as Georgiana was a private woman.

But oh, how she longed to tell Captain Trentworth the whole story.

Georgiana could have slapped herself. Only a few moments in his presence and she was already wishing to confide in him and share everything with him as she once had.

She was still a silly girl underneath it all. As silly as Miss Perry. Perhaps even more so. She was six and twenty. She ought to be more sensible than this. Captain Trentworth was not hers to confide in. He had not been for some time.

It was only that they were seeing each other in person and communicating after so long apart. Old habits died hard, after all. It was nothing she could not easily get over after a short while.

She need only hold herself in until she got used to the new status quo.

"When is the wedding?" Captain Trentworth asked.

Making small talk like this was painful. Georgiana almost wished that the floor would open up beneath her and swallow her up.

"In only a couple of months," she said. "We have just sent out the official invitations. I would have sent one to you, except that I did not know that you would be in England..."

"No, of course. Very sensible of you to assume that I would be out on the sea. And I would not expect you to try and get an invitation to reach me there.

"You will pass on my congratulations and best wishes to the happy couple, I hope. I have always had a great deal of respect for your brother. And I'm certain that whomever he has chosen as his wife is a lovely woman worthy of good wishes."

"She is, and I appreciate your kind thoughts. I shall convey them. I know my brother will be happy to know that you think so well of him."

Edward had held his peace on the matter of Georgiana's relationship with Captain Trentworth. He had liked the man, that much she knew. He had always had the greatest of respect for him and had conveyed it in every meeting between the two of them.

But Edward had said nothing, either for or against, her engagement to Captain Trentworth. It had been a matter strictly between Georgiana and their father.

He had recently told Georgiana that he felt it was not his battle to say anything one way or another in regards to her choices. He regretted it, in fact, and had confessed as much to her quite recently.

It had been his feelings for Maria that had spurred the apology. He had told Georgiana, with great feeling, that he ought to have stood up for her choice in husband. That he should have supported her and Captain Trentworth's engagement. Defied their father.

Georgiana did not blame Edward. It had not been his battle to fight. As much as he wanted to protect her and help her, he had been right to stay out of it. At least, if you asked her.

She had been the one challenged to stand her ground. And she had allowed her love to slip away. It was nobody's fault except for hers.

She wondered if Captain Trentworth would agree with her on that. Most likely, given the things that he had said to her when they had last spoken.

But that was all living in the past. She ought to pay attention to the present. And Captain Trentworth clearly bore her no good will. He was, however, making an effort to be polite. She ought to do her best to do the same. Rise to the occasion and all that.

"And how is your family?" she asked. "Your parents?"

"Both gone by now, I'm afraid."

"I'm terribly sorry. It is a shame that I never got the chance to meet them."

She was going to meet them once their engagement was officially set. Captain Trentworth had gone to ask her father's permission to marry her. Then they would go and tell his parents. And then they would put it in the papers.

Now she would never get to meet the surely lovely people who had produced and raised such a wonderful man.

What was more, he had been their only child. Captain Trentworth had cousins but no siblings. That might make him terribly lonely nowadays. No intimate family to whom he could go home.

"They would have liked you," Captain Trentworth admitted. "And you would have liked them. But I'm afraid that is not saying much. Everyone liked them. I had yet to find a person who was not won over to them by the time a morning's call was finished."

"Were they sociable then?" Georgiana asked.

He nodded. "Very."

"And yet they produced you," she said. It was so easy to slip into teasing with him. It had been her habit with him for so long, it was difficult to shake off. "Where on earth did they go wrong?"

Captain Trentworth looked as though he was trying to suppress a smile. "There is only so much that one can do when one's child is determined to be antisocial, I suppose. I was a stubborn one."

"And remained so."

He nodded once, curtly.

Georgiana decided that she'd had quite as much awkward small talk as she could stand at that point. "Have you met Miss Everett?" she asked, quickly turning to the girl as she walked by.

Miss Everett was happy to be introduced to Captain Trentworth and engage him in conversation.

Georgiana faded into the background, as usual.

She was used to it, of course. There was no reason why she should be so upset. And yet, she was.

It was because of her stupid girlish feelings, that was all.

This was clearly a lively group of people. She wasn't lively. Not in the slightest. She could appreciate it, but as an observer. Not as a participant.

To her surprise, however, after a short moment Mr. Tomlinson joined her at the fireplace.

She had taken up a post there from which to observe everyone without being too far away. She could smile or nod if someone looked in her direction but need not participate fully.

"Any particular reason why you are imitating the artwork?" Mr. Tomlinson asked.

He clearly had a knack for teasing and being charming. "I'm afraid if you're looking for someone with whom you can banter, I am not the best of choices," she told him. "I am much better if you are in need of a listening ear or a sympathetic face."

"I have heard quite the opposite from Miss Weston," Mr. Tomlinson replied. "She informs me that you are a gifted conversationalist."

"That may be true in her eyes. But Miss Weston has always had a rather higher opinion of me than I think is warranted. It comes with having known one another since childhood.

"And if I am any sort of wit, I'm afraid it is only with those I am deeply acquainted with. I fear otherwise my tongue shall fail me."

"Then I shall have to become deeply acquainted with you," Mr. Tomlinson said with a smile.

Georgiana was not sure what to make of that.

On the one hand, she was certain that many a woman would see it as a flirtation. She was tempted to see it that way.

But she suspected that it was a flirtation which did not mean anything. She was not going to fall into the trap that so many other girls had become victim to. That is, the trap of thinking a man such as Mr. Tomlinson was serious when he flirted.

Men such as Mr. Tomlinson flirted for sport. It was fun for them. It was nothing serious.

She feared for the day that the poor man actually fell for a woman. She suspected the woman would not know that he was truly serious in his intentions until the actual moment of proposal. And perhaps not even then.

"I am sure that we shall become better acquainted over the next few weeks," Georgiana replied. It was a neutral enough answer that she would not offend him with. But she was also not promising anything to him or showing too much interest.

She had hurt her heart once. She wasn't going to get it hurt again over something as ridiculous as thinking a man of charm was serious in his pretty words.

Julia clapped her hands. "I have been informed that dinner is ready," she announced. "Shall we retire, then, to the dining room?"

Everyone was in agreement, and flowed out into the dining room.

Georgiana gave a sigh of relief when she saw that she was not sitting next to Captain Trentworth.

She was next to Julia, and then across from her was Mr. Norwich. Mr. Tomlinson was next to her, and then diagonal to her was Miss Perry. Miss Everett was on Mr. Tomlinson's other side, and across from her was Captain Trentworth.

Hopefully this would go well.

Conversation was lively, and again, Georgiana found herself staying quiet. It was not that she felt that she was ignored. It was simply that she preferred listening to speaking. Everyone had quite a lot to say.

Miss Perry was rather silly, and seemed determined to get the attention of all three men as often as possible.

Georgiana supposed that she could be sympathetic. To be young and pretty and looking for a husband, of course there was a feeling that one must keep one's options open.

It was almost like a competition, or a game. How many men could one have on a string all at once? How many suitors could one win over?

Georgiana had never been that way. But then, she was not the sort of person that shared herself with others easily or liked to flirt.

It had felt like a miracle when Captain Trentworth had been interested in her despite her quiet nature. And an even bigger miracle that he was a man whom she had genuinely been attracted to.

Now, she tried her best to balance out Miss Perry's enthusiastic nature. Julia was keeping up with it and doing a lovely job as hostess. Her mother sent word that she would be well enough to join them for a quiet game of bridge or two after dinner.

"You are all lucky that Father has gone back to London," Julia assured them all. "He hates card playing and would be regaling you all with his hunting stories.

"They're rather entertaining the first time around, but after the tenth time, they're far less amusing."

Georgiana had heard Mr. Weston's stories many a time, having grown up with him. She could agree with Julia's assessment.

"I feel as though the moment a man becomes a father, he is

obligated to be as boring as possible," Miss Perry said. "My father is quite a bore. He does nothing but read his law books."

Georgiana felt a bit uncomfortable.

"I hope that you will not say your husband is boring once you have had your first child," Mr. Tomlinson said with a laugh.

"I shall of course do nothing but compliment him when he is in the room," Miss Perry replied with a mischievous glint in her eye.

Georgiana felt it was just skirting the edge of disrespectfulness. She could see that Captain Trentworth looked uncomfortable as well, as though he were thinking the same thing.

She remembered how they used to be at parties together. They had been allies, often thinking along the same lines on things. Such as when a guest was getting rude or scandalous.

Now, she struggled not to instinctively look over at him to catch his eye. They were not secret allies anymore. Once, she could read the very look in his eye as though he had spoken aloud. Now, she did not know him at all.

It had been years. He had changed. He no longer cared for her. She must remember that.

Miss Everett and Captain Trentworth seemed to be holding up a lively conversation throughout dinner. She asked him often about his time in the navy.

Georgiana tried to listen in spite of herself, but found that Mr. Tomlinson kept trying to speak to her as well and it was distracting her.

He inquired about her family, and about the wedding once she told him about it.

"I am surprised that it took Edward so long to marry," Julia said. "But then, he has always been a very particular person."

"That he is," Mr. Norwich said. "He is like his father in that way, if I may say so."

"You are welcome to say so," Georgiana replied.

Edward was not like their father in many ways. Edward was actually compassionate and full of passion and able to forgive.

But they were alike in their stubbornness and their determination. They were both hard men and inclined towards bitterness if they were not careful. Edward fought against it, fortunately, while Father had given into it.

But she was certain that Mr. Norwich meant it as a compliment and so she did not say anything to contradict him.

"It is rather sad, isn't it, to have one's sibling getting married?" Miss Perry asked. "I know that I have felt terribly envious when my siblings got married before me. Even if I am the youngest.

"My condolences to you, Miss Reginald, that you must put up with your brother's nuptials and all that it entails while you are still single."

Georgiana knew that she did not mean it unkindly. But it still hurt.

If she were younger, then perhaps it would be easier to deal with. But with her age and her lack of suitors...

Well. It only served to remind her that she would never be a bride. Never have her own wedding. And while she was not at all envious of her brother, it hurt to have the whole thing brought up.

"Indeed, I could not be happier for him," Georgiana replied. "I love my brother dearly. We have always been quite close. It warms my heart to see that he is going to be happy."

"Oh of course you are happy for him," Miss Perry replied with a conspiratorial smile. "But it is a different thing, to be happy for someone and to be happy in general, is it not?"

Georgiana saw that there would be no persuading her otherwise and said nothing, letting the subject change.

Was she happy?

She wasn't sure. She was content. Was that not enough? Was that not all that most people could hope for? Especially women who were quickly ageing out of the opportunity for marriage?

The rest of dinner passed pleasantly enough. Mr. Tomlinson still chatted with her a great deal more than Georgiana thought was necessary.

Not that she disliked his conversation. It was only that it confused her. Surely he would rather be talking with the witty Miss Everett on his other side or the radiant, energetic Julia?

When dinner was finished, Julia summoned her mother and they split up into four for bridge.

Georgiana did not speak to Captain Trentworth for the rest of the night. It was all very nice, overall. A lovely evening. She liked everyone well enough.

Miss Everett and Mr. Norwich were her favorites of the new people. Mr. Tomlinson she could not figure out and Miss Perry was rather too childish and unthinking in her behavior and comments for Georgiana to completely fall for her.

But Captain Trentworth...

He was the same as ever. Or so it seemed to her. He was older but his personality retained all the things that she had loved about it.

He was quiet but offered up an insightful or witty comment or two when the occasion called for it. He spoke the least out of everyone that evening, but it was clear that he put great thought into the things that he did say.

That was one of the things that Georgiana had loved about him. Indeed, it was one of the first things that had drawn her to him and caught her attention about him.

There was not a word wasted with him. Unlike many who spoke merely for the sake of saying something or did not think their comments through fully before they spoke.

What wisdom, she had thought all those years ago. To know that it is better to wait and think it all through and miss one's chance, than to say too much or to say the wrong thing.

She still thought it was wise. But now she wondered what all it was that he was not saying.

Was he thinking about her? Or had he dismissed her from his thoughts? Was his silence when the conversation turned her way simply because he had nothing to say? Or did he have things to say, but things that were far from appropriate in polite company?

She did not know, and that terrified her.

When the time came for everyone to depart, the ladies were enthusiastic in their goodbyes. "We shall call upon you tomorrow," Miss Everett assured them.

Mr. Tomlinson was also enthusiastic in his farewell. "I greatly look forward to seeing you at our next get-together," he told her.

Mr. Norwich was reserved but warm in his farewell.

And then there was Captain Trentworth.

He said a verbal farewell to Julia. But to Georgiana, he simply bowed, and then left.

Georgiana felt as though she might be sick.

"I think that went rather well, don't you?" Julia asked as the door closed behind their guests.

Georgiana simply stared at her.

They were most certainly going to have a talk.

CHAPTER 28

ROBERT SAGGED against the door of his bedroom the moment that it was closed.

Miss Georgiana Reginald.

She had been there.

He ought to have known. He ought to have not trusted Miss Weston on this whole thing. Of course she would have some kind of scheme cooked up.

What was she thinking? Miss Reginald obviously had no idea that he was going to be there. And he was just as flabbergasted.

To spring such a surprise upon both of them in such a manner was most frustrating. He would counsel her on it, if it were his place. But he was not her brother, her father, or her counsellor. He had no right.

He only hoped that Miss Reginald would say something to Miss Weston about it. She was a sensible woman, or he remembered her as one at least. And they were close friends.

If anyone could say something to Miss Weston about not meddling in such a manner, it would be her.

But oh. Age had not disgraced her. It had only made her lovelier.

Miss Reginald was possessed of the kind of elegant beauty that only came into its own as she matured. It was quiet, a sort of graceful, ethereal beauty. Not the lively kind that was vibrant when one was young and then gone so quickly and easily.

When he had seen her, his breath had caught in his throat.

She reminded him of a lily flower. The pale, almost white blonde hair. The icy blue eyes. The pale skin and swanlike neck. The smooth, flowing manner in which she moved.

In that moment he had realized that he was certainly not over her. He had suspected, of course. But seeing her had confirmed it.

His feelings for her were just as strong as they had been when he had left her all those years ago.

Robert scoffed. He had left her? She had left him first.

He might have left the country, but it was his duty. His career. She had broken off their engagement. She had ended it. Not him.

What was he supposed to do? He could not simply leave. That would be incredibly rude not only to Miss Weston but to all the other people that would be expecting him.

He also suspected that the two men would need some help in handling Miss Perry. She was a rather enthusiastic young woman. The kind who wanted nothing more than to have all attention on her—especially the attention of the gentlemen around her.

It was not something that he could exactly blame her for. It was her career, almost, to find a husband and secure her future. But there was a way to go about it with grace and dignity.

Miss Perry had not yet managed that.

Still, there was no harm in her. It was only that she had to be handled evenly among the three men.

Miss Everett was a lovely and witty young woman. She had a tough skin, something that he appreciated.

She was the kind of woman that he could depend upon to behave the way that she said that she would. She was blunt without being malicious. The sort of woman, honestly, that he theoretically would consider as a potential wife.

If only Miss Reginald were not there. Why was she not yet married? Surely someone else had seen her grace, her beauty, her thoughtfulness.

He could see how much it cost her. Those comments that Miss Perry had made were not meant unkindly. But he had seen how they had hurt Miss Reginald.

He had wanted to leap to her defense. And he would have, had things not been as they were. He would not allow her to think that he still cared for her.

After all, it was clear that she did not still care for him.

She had been polite enough to him all throughout the evening. But of course she would be. She was raised well and was an elegant woman. She would never let her frustration or anger show in such a manner.

But he had noticed that she had never once looked at him during dinner. She had not even addressed him.

It was easy to miss if one did not know her well and was not looking for such a thing. Miss Reginald did not speak often. Usually it was in response to a direct question or comment aimed at her.

But he had noticed. He knew her.

Once, they would look at one another periodically at dinner or in a ballroom when they were thinking the same thing. It had felt as though they were synchronized. They would look at one another and be having a private conversation all of their own.

Comments, reactions to the things said around them... it was all said silently between them, just with their eyes.

Now she would not even look at him.

It was a sign, to him, of how firmly she had placed him out of her thoughts.

When she had broken off their engagement she had clearly set him aside in her heart as well as socially. He should have known that, of course.

But he had been hoping, without even realizing that he had been doing so. And now he had to swallow his disappointment and move on.

It would not be easy to do. Not with her right in front of him so intimately for the next few weeks. But he would manage. He had to manage.

He had been in the war, for goodness' sake. Surely he could nurse a broken heart. One that had been broken for quite some time. This was nothing new to him. He would be just fine.

If only he could truly believe that.

CHAPTER 29

GEORGIANA TURNED and leveled a stern look at Julia. "What exactly did you think that you would accomplish by this?"

Julia smiled at her. "Are you not surprised?"

"Surprised? Yes. Pleased? Not in the slightest."

Julia sighed. "Georgiana. You must see that this is a second chance!"

"A second chance to live through my heartbreak? A second chance to be humiliated?" Georgiana felt near tears.

It was so rare for her to cry. She would not be doing so over something that should not even be making her so upset.

"You misled me, Julia. You deliberately held back information from me. Information that you knew would greatly affect me. I felt like such a fool when I saw him.

"I was unprepared. I was scrambling to cover my emotions. I had no idea what to do or to say. I must have looked like a proper fool to him."

"So you do still have feelings for him?" Julia asked eagerly.

Georgiana narrowed her eyes at her. "No. You are not allowed to matchmake. That is not happening here. I don't know what stories you've heard or fanciful novels you've been reading lately but that is not how this works.

"I will not allow you to use me or the good captain for your own amusement. We are not characters. We are not in your imagination.

We are flesh and blood people and we will not be toyed with or manipulated.

"He does not love me. His behavior made that quite clear. And why should he? I rejected him. I hurt him and told him that he was not good enough for me."

"That is not what you said. You had to obey your father. How on earth could you possibly go against him? You did what you thought was best.

"It was not because you did not love him. Surely he has to know that. Surely he must see that—"

"He does not have to see anything, Julia. I turned him away. In his mind, that says that I did not, and do not, love him.

"He believed that if I truly cared for him I would have defied my father. Whether it is right or it is wrong, that is what he believed."

"And I think that is unfair to you. And besides, your father is dead now! And Edward would never go against such a match. He is a good man and would take good care of you. You would be provided for. And what is more, you love him. Edward would surely give his blessing."

"He is not going to ask me again, Julia. And your meddling is not going to go unnoticed by him. He will be cross with you and he will have a right to be."

Julia finally seemed to be starting to understand how upset this had made Georgiana. And how unfair it was to both her and to Captain Trentworth.

"I'm sorry," Julia said softly. "I did not mean to be cruel. You know that I wouldn't mean that.

"I only thought that I ought to get you two back together. That if I did, there would be that spark once again. That you two only needed to be together in a room.

"But I knew that if I told one of you that the other would be there, then you wouldn't have come. You would avoid it. And how else was I supposed to give you the second chance that you both deserve?"

Georgiana sighed. "I understand that you had good intentions, Julia. You always do. But did you not think of how awkward it would be for us to see one another for the first time with no preparation?

"The last time that we saw one another, I was rejecting his

proposal. Breaking off our engagement. Telling him that he wasn't good enough in the eyes of my father and that I had to go with my father's wishes.

"It was years ago, I know. But that doesn't change how awful it was for both of us. It was the hardest thing that I ever had to do.

"I can only imagine how much it hurt him. And now to have to see me again..." Her voice failed her and she had to stop.

Julia gently placed her hands on either side of Georgiana's upper arms. "Oh, my dear. You are still quite in love with him, aren't you? All of this time?"

Georgiana nodded. She did not trust herself to speak. She stared at a spot on the wall over Julia's shoulder. If she looked her friend in the eye, she knew that she would burst into tears.

"Is that why you truly have not married?" Julia asked. "You could not give your heart to anyone else?"

"That is part of it, yes," Georgiana admitted. "I could not give my heart and I think that men have noticed it. It does not help that I am quiet by nature, I think."

"I ought to have been throwing these things for you much sooner," Julia said sadly. "You really are not the type of woman who stands out at her best during a ball, I'm afraid."

Georgiana shook her head. No, she truly was not.

"I know that it is foolish of me to hold myself back all of this time," she said. "I ought to have been working hard to get a husband. I have been horribly lazy about it.

"But how could I trust that my father would not reject yet another man that I fell for? And I was so selfish. I could not bring myself to marry a man for whom I held no affection."

"Do not beat yourself up about it, my dear. It is understandable."

"Understandable, perhaps. Stupid, certainly."

Julia sighed, dropping her hands. "You are as always too hard on yourself. We all hope for love."

"But hope is not the same thing as reality. I ought to have done more to avoid this. Now I am headed for spinsterhood."

"Do not say such a thing."

"Do not speak the truth? You heard Miss Perry tonight. She did not mean to be cruel but we all know to what she was referring."

"She is a silly girl, Georgiana."

"From the mouth of babes, Julia."

"You are a stubborn creature, did you know that?" Julia smiled fondly. "You are quieter than your brother but you are his sibling. You are your father's daughter. You have that streak of iron in you."

"I did not have it when it mattered," Georgiana said with a sigh.

"How could you have gone against your father? No. You did what you knew that you had to do.

"Now, I will have no more of you thinking such awful things about yourself. I apologize for my misstep. My intentions were pure, I swear. I only wanted you and the good captain to be happy. I care for him and I love you dearly, as you know.

"But I see now that I was wrong to surprise you both in such a manner. I hope that you will handle my mishap with grace. But please do not take this as an opportunity to list all the reasons why you feel that you have failed.

"You have done the best that you could with the choices that were before you. And surely that is all that we can ask of ourselves in life."

Georgiana nodded. She would do her best. But it would not be easy. Not when the reason for her shame would be right in front of her all the time. Hating her.

"Let us go up to bed," Julia advised. She was still speaking in that soft, soothing tone. "A good night's rest and everything will seem better in the morning. You will see."

Georgiana doubted that. But then, she had said much the same thing to Maria after that horrid night where Edward had chastised her so awfully.

Everything had turned out better in the morning for Maria and Edward. Perhaps Georgiana needed to have a little faith that things would turn out all right for herself as well.

She nodded. "Very well. I will see you in the morning then."

"I look forward to it. We shall go looking at possible places for you to live, does that sound nice?"

Georgiana had the suspicion that she was being placated, but she was too exhausted to mind. "That would be lovely, dear. Thank you."

As she climbed up to bed, she was already dreading the next morning. Hopefully everything would seem better, as Julia had said.

Perhaps, if nothing else, she and Captain Trentworth could end this as friends. That would be the best that she could hope for at this stage. But she was determined to try.

Offering him up genuine friendship was the least that she could do after she had treated him so unfairly all those years ago.

Yes. That was the least that she could do. She would try and be a good friend to him. Since she had failed to be a good wife.

CHAPTER 30

Robert went to handle some business with Mr. Norwich in the morning.

He was grateful for the other man's help in all of this. He was not used to dealing with this sort of thing. Mr. Norwich was being most helpful.

After their business was concluded, Mr. Norwich went off to see some acquaintances while Robert took a walk through town. He wanted to get familiar with it, the feel of it, the streets and turns.

He was simply strolling down a lane when he paused.

There, at the end of the lane, looking at one of the houses, were Miss Reginald and Miss Weston.

They looked as though they were inspecting the house. But why would they be doing a thing like that?

He did not approach them and merely watched as they seemed to discuss for a moment, and then turned around the corner.

Once they were gone, he went up to the house to take a look at it himself. He might be mistaken. They could have simply been calling upon whoever lived inside and then having a small discussion on their way out.

Yet, this was in a neighborhood that was a bit below what the daughter of a rich gentleman and the sister of a duke might be found in.

Could there truly be anyone of their acquaintance who lived in this quarter?

When he got in front of the house, he got his answer.

There was a small 'to be let' sign in the window, along with a request to inquire within.

He could not think of any reason why Miss Weston would be looking for a place to let. Miss Reginald, on the other hand...

Bath was a fashionable place where those of the upper class who were a bit outside of the norm could escape to. The elderly, the spinsters, those with debilitating illness or other physical issues could settle down there.

Miss Weston was young enough that she did not quite need to worry about spinsterhood just yet.

But Miss Reginald, at the age of six and twenty...

She must be looking for a place to lodge.

He knew that Miss Reginald was a woman of pride. Her whole family was like that. She would never impose upon her brother by living with him.

But by taking a small, inexpensive place in Bath, she could retain her dignity and some measure of independence without having to burden her brother by being a constant presence in his home.

Not that he thought the current duke would mind. Edward Reginald, from what Robert remembered of him, was quite fond of his sister. He would never feel that it was an imposition to take care of her.

But Miss Reginald might not see it that way.

Robert felt a sharp ache in his chest. She was so certain that she was out of prospects that she was looking into an apartment. She had truly given up.

How could she?

How could a woman of her caliber have not had any offers? How could she have not found any other man to marry her?

Had her father turned down other men besides himself? Had he been a tyrant until the end and ruined all of her prospects?

It was the only thing that he could think of. He could see no other reason why an elegant and thoughtful woman would have never had another suitor since himself.

He knew that she was quiet. She was not the sort of person to draw attention to herself. But surely that soft, mature nature would draw in discerning men.

It had certainly drawn him in, at any rate.

But with one thing or another, whatever the reason, she was not yet married. And now she was giving up.

He wanted to run after her and grab her and tell her that she must not abandon hope. She was a wonderful woman. A frustrating woman who had broken his heart, true. He still had some issues with how she had handled their engagement.

But it did not change her overall character. She was a lovely woman. And she deserved to be married. She deserved to have a wonderful, loving husband who would provide for her. A man who would give her all that she deserved.

Of course, he could not tell her such a thing. It would be completely out of line and improper.

Not to mention that it would completely show his hand. It would reveal how much he still cared for her despite his best efforts. And despite her moving on quite fine on her end.

Still, it did not sit well with him. He did not like the idea that Miss Reginald was giving up.

She was a woman of strength. He had always known that. People often mistook her quiet nature and lack of energy for a weak spirit. But that had never been the case. She was firm in herself.

It was why he had been so surprised when she had refused to disobey her father and had broken off their engagement. She was someone who knew what was right and what was wrong. Someone who was firm in her beliefs. Someone who knew what she wanted.

He had been flabbergasted when she had ended things. How could this be the same woman that he had fallen in love with? This woman who so easily bent to the will of a bitter, tyrannical man who cared for nothing except status?

Now it seemed he was seeing that strange weakness once again.

It was none of his business, he told himself. Whatever he felt, he had no right to say or do anything about it. Miss Reginald would make her own choices in life and he could not meddle. As much as he might like to.

CHAPTER 31

GEORGIANA'S HUNT for a home had gone about as well as she expected.

She had a few prospects, none as grand as she had been secretly hoping, but nothing that left her feeling too disheartened. Certainly nothing that had her gasping in horror.

This was something that she could make work. She just needed a little time to get used to it.

Living alone, if she did not entertain anyone and instead went calling upon other people or went to the public balls... it would keep her expenses down. She would not need much. She only would have to employ a couple of servants. No more than three, certainly.

Edward would not be pleased when she laid it all out for him. He would try to insist upon her staying at Foreshire with him and Maria. But she would not impose upon him.

She had to retain some level of dignity.

Julia was not a fan of the idea either.

"Are you sure that you want to go ahead with this?" she asked for the tenth time as they returned to the Weston residence.

"My dear, do you really think that you will get a different answer if you ask me enough times?"

"Hope springs eternal," Julia replied cheekily.

Georgiana sighed as she entered the house. She had in her hand a list of the places that they had visited. She would shorten the list later on after they finished doing the morning calls.

Julia had promised to keep secret what Georgiana was planning. She did not want anyone to know about it. Otherwise everyone would begin to speculate, and it would be all over for her.

Everyone would say that she was officially a spinster. And while she was planning for it she would rather that nobody started gossiping about it any earlier than she could help it.

They changed quickly, and then Miss Perry and Miss Everett arrived.

Miss Perry, unfortunately, was no less talkative than she had been the night before. But she was a bit easier to handle when there were no men around. She was much more willing to listen and she appeared to be calmer in her manner.

It was almost sweet. Georgiana had seen it so often in young women. The eagerness to please men, to find a husband. It sparked a bit of nostalgia in her. Once, she had been that young and that hopeful. And possibly, at times, that silly.

Miss Everett she enjoyed speaking with.

"I think that we ought to attend one of the public balls that they host here," Miss Everett said. "I know that one's enjoyment of them can rather depend upon how many acquaintances one has.

"But between the four of us, we ought to know enough people to make it all pleasant enough. What do you say?"

Miss Perry was all for it, to nobody's surprise. Julia was also in support of such an idea.

Georgiana was less certain. She was never a fan of crowds. But how could she possibly say no?

"It sounds like a lovely time," she said instead.

Julia gave her a pleased yet sympathetic smile. "It will not be nearly so bad as you fear, I think," her friend said quietly.

Georgiana begged to differ. She had come to Bath to get away from the crowds of people who were more than happy to snub her. Now she was about to fling herself into that mess all over again.

Still, she got herself ready. Or as ready as she could possibly feel.

One of the benefits of being nearly a spinster but having a rather rich brother was that at least she was not trapped in her fashions.

Many poor unmarried older women could not afford to constantly update their wardrobe. Normally a husband or father would pay for such things.

But if a father was dead or trying to save money in his old age, and there was no husband...

Georgiana had seen many a woman wearing dresses from last year, or perhaps even two years ago.

It was a sad thing. The dresses themselves usually were quite pretty and fit well. But that did not matter to society. What mattered is that they were in a fashion that had been popular last year or two years ago.

That was enough for people to make comments.

Edward, of course, would never stand for his sister to be laughed at. He had stressed time and again that no expense should be spared for her and that Georgiana should never fear to spend money on herself.

Georgiana would never claim that she was comfortable with spending her brother's money. But it was nice to know that she could afford to keep up with the fashions. It spared her at least one more way to be laughed at by others.

She had no time to get a new dress today of course. But she had ordered some new dresses before she had left for Bath in order to have them ready when she arrived.

She put one of them on—a pale green. She had been told many a time that she looked very good in pink, and pastel colors were in this year.

But pink was the color of young women. And that, Georgiana told herself firmly, she was not any longer. She should keep up with the fashions. But she should not pretend to be someone that she was not.

"Are you all ready?" Julia asked as Georgiana finished inspecting herself in the mirror.

"Do you think that I look as though I am trying too hard to stay young?" Georgiana asked.

She thought she looked nice. She aged well—but so had her mother. It ran in the family. She appreciated that her beauty was the kind that made her look stately as she got older.

But it did not matter so much what she thought as it did what society thought. She had learned that long ago.

Julia smiled at her. "You look ageless, as always. I quite envy your looks, I shall be a wrinkled old potato before long."

"Never," Georgiana declared loyally.

Julia laughed and took her hand. "You look lovely. Now come, we must be sure to get there in time or all the men shall have been placed on people's dance cards already."

Georgiana allowed herself to be led down the stairs to where the other ladies, Mrs. Weston—who was their escort—and the carriage were waiting.

Miss Perry was fairly vibrating with excitement. They always were at that age. Georgiana had always felt that she was the only one who was not fairly jumping up and down on her way to every ball.

"I am excited to meet so many people," Miss Perry said. "I do hope that the gentlemen from last evening will be there as well. Such stimulating conversation, and such manners!"

Miss Everett sent Georgiana a conspiratorially annoyed look, as if to silently say, she will praise any man she thinks might marry her.

Georgiana gave an understanding smile in return. It was always hard not to see other women as competition, especially when one was younger. She could understand Miss Everett's frustration.

"I think my favorite so far," Miss Perry said once they were in the carriage, "is Captain Trentworth. A military man, he must be so brave. And I like the idea of a self-made man. You know he will be responsible.

"I've heard far too many stories of men who inherited wealth and simply wasted it because they did not appreciate it! Is that not sad? Not that I think Mr. Norwich or Mr. Tomlinson are that way, not at all.

"But it does give one some measure of comfort, does it not? To know that your husband understands the value of a dollar."

"I should think it would be a sad thing for your husband to know such a thing," Miss Everett replied. "After all, if he knows the value, then he knows how much you are spending on baubles at the high street."

Julia laughed, as did Miss Perry, since Miss Everett spoke with an amused air and not in a pointed manner. Wit, Georgiana thought, was often reliant on tone. Words that were friendly and indulging in one tone became harsh and criticizing in another.

It was true, she could not help but think. Captain Trentworth was a self-made man. He had inherited some fortune but made the rest.

It was why so many young men went into the navy during war. It was a chance for them to take the spoils of the ships they attacked and raise themselves up in society. Second and third sons could become as rich and influential as their elder brothers.

If only her father had seen that, Georgiana thought bitterly. She hated to think ill of her father. But she was also under no illusions about what kind of man he had been: a harsh one. Too harsh, if you asked her.

Georgiana tried to ignore the surge of sadness and envy that rushed up in her as Miss Perry praised Captain Trentworth.

Why should the girl not praise him? He was a fine man. A handsome one, well spoken, with a distinguished career and now a fortune to boot.

Georgiana had no right to him. None at all. She could not begrudge the younger girl her feelings. Especially when Miss Perry seemed inclined to have feelings for nearly any man put in front of her.

But oh, how she couldn't help hoping that Captain Trentworth's taste had not changed so much. That he still was inclined towards the quieter, more dignified women.

To lose him to a flighty young thing such as Miss Perry felt like it might be too much to bear.

Lose him? Georgiana chastised herself. She did not have him and therefore she could not lose him. She had given him away long ago and now had no right to him.

The carriage rolled to a stop in front of the dance hall. Georgiana took a deep, calming breath as the other ladies descended.

Miss Perry hurried directly in. Miss Everett cocked an eyebrow, like she was looking at the den of a lion and considering if it was worth it, before following suit.

Julia waited for Georgiana. She was always kind that way. Never letting Georgiana be forgotten. It was that kindness, at the heart of her, that Georgiana knew made Julia so popular. People could sense it in her.

"Mother is the laziest of escorts," Julia said as they walked into the ballroom. "She will find a place to sit and then go to sleep, you mark my words."

"I do not think you give your mother quite enough credit," Georgiana replied. "She would be on her feet in a second if there was a whiff of trouble directed towards us. You must remember, she stood up to my father and that was something no man in England was capable of doing."

Julia laughed. "Oh, I do remember! It was when you wanted to accompany me on a country tour. We were going up to the north. And your father put his foot down."

"And your mother marched right over to Foreshire and gave him a piece of her mind. I was terrified for her! I thought that he would not only kick her out but would get her ignored by society in general.

"But instead he agreed to let me go with you! I thought her quite the miracle worker then. I still do."

Julia smiled. "Well, she had spirit. Father says it's where I get mine. But now that she is so ill..."

Mr. Weston's illness had been more sudden and had necessitated the move to Bath. He had recovered, however, and was now back in London on business.

Mrs. Weston's illness was longer and slower. It was why the family had decided to stay in Bath. If it did her husband good then surely it would do her good as well, would it not?

That was the thinking behind it, in any case.

Georgiana knew that Julia was simply deflecting from her mother's illness and her fears about it by making fun of her mother's exhaustion.

She only hoped that Julia did not say such things where Mrs. Weston could hear them. She feared that if so, Julia would have cause to regret it.

They stepped into the ballroom, and Georgiana was immediately assaulted by the sounds and sights around her.

Men and women were already twirling around the dance floor,

moving like interlocking cogs and wheels in a clock as they stepped around and through one another.

The women were all wearing pastels, as was the current fashion. Many of them were also wearing white. It was the previous year's fashion and it had not quite yet faded from popularity.

They moved around the room like butterflies, gliding and flittering from conversation to conversation. Georgiana could hear their laughter like bells.

The men were all looking fine in darker suits, standing like pillars, the lot of them. Steady and impeccable and immoveable. When they moved, it was with grace and stateliness.

Georgiana hadn't seen most of the people in this room before. She recognized a few as people that she had seen in London during the season previously.

Most of the people in Bath, however, were not quite at her level. Although she hated to think in such terms.

Public ballrooms were for people of a slightly lower social status than those with titles. Most of the people here were not people that Georgiana would generally speak to out of deference for the class system.

But not tonight. She couldn't possibly snub ninety percent of the people in this room.

And she was of the higher status. That meant she could talk to whomever she pleased. Most of them could not approach her but if she wanted to start a friendly conversation then that was her right.

And she would have to. If she didn't, everyone would think her the most horrible snob. When the truth was she was simply not the best at conversing in crowds.

Georgiana stood in the doorway for a moment, observing. Wondering who she should approach first to converse with.

Perhaps she should get a glass of wine first? That would give her another moment to compose herself. She could not imagine that she would be asked to dance, so having the glass would be a good excuse for any man not to ask her.

Julia squeezed her arm. "I see Mr. Tomlinson."

"Perhaps you ought to go over and say hello, then."

Julia looked at her in astonishment. "Oh, no, I meant for you!"

"Oh, Julia, please, no matchmaking. It's terribly unfair to the poor man."

Julia fixed Georgiana with a frustrated look. "Do you honestly mean you did not note how he was looking at you last night? My dear Georgiana. The man thinks you are quite lovely."

"I'm certain that he thinks of me as no lovelier than any other lady of good breeding. Men and women can enjoy one another's company without it being a sign of romantic infatuation, you know."

"Of course it is possible. I am certainly managing to do it with Mr. Tomlinson, Mr. Norwich, and our dear captain." Julia's look was sly. "But I know the difference, Georgiana, between friendly affection and romantic intent."

"We have only met the once, Julia. I will not have you making up wild conjectures about myself or Mr. Tomlinson. Certainly not about the both of us together."

Julia pouted. "My dear, surely you must realize that my partial aim in asking you here was to help you to finally be wed?"

"Trust me, Julia, I have drawn that unfortunate conclusion already," Georgiana said dryly. "Are you going to persist in this endeavor? And am I going to have to retire for the evening before it has even properly begun?"

Julia sighed. "No, I will not, and therefore you shall not. If you insist on being such a stick in the mud about it."

"I hardly know the man."

"Many women hardly know their husbands."

Georgiana knew she could not afford to be picky. But surely it wasn't too much to ask that she spend several evenings with a man before any talk of marriage was made? Rather than just one?

"I am going to get myself some wine. Would you like any refreshments?"

Julia shook her head. "No, I think I see Mr. Norwich. I should like to bid him good evening. Miss Perry I see is already hard at work dancing and flirting."

"She does both very well, it seems."

"Go on, get your glass of wine, then," Julia said with a smirk. "But do not think I don't see your aim, Georgiana. You ought not to let a glass stop you if a man asks."

"A man will not ask. Therefore, I will have a glass handy. It gives him an excuse and spares me my dignity. What little of it there is left."

Georgiana went towards the refreshments table while Julia sought out Mr. Norwich, who was standing over by a staircase.

Julia, Georgiana noted, was the sort of woman who was good at conversing with men and being their friend without there being any misunderstanding about intentions. If she did not have feelings for a man, she was remarkable at somehow being able to show such a thing without offending anyone or leading anyone on.

Georgiana was just about to pick up a glass when Mr. Tomlinson appeared at her elbow.

"Good evening," he said, bowing to her.

"Good evening, sir." She curtsied.

Now that the idea was in her head, Georgiana could not help but notice how he had sought her out and was now smiling at her.

It was all just nonsense that Julia had filled her head with. She was not going to start either getting paranoid or getting her hopes up.

Besides, she did not know Mr. Tomlinson well enough to formulate an opinion on him. Whether that opinion was in favor of him or not.

"I had been hoping to see you here," Mr. Tomlinson went on. "I'm afraid there aren't many large homes here in Bath.

"People cannot really host balls in their homes here. Nothing of any proper size, anyway. And so we must avail ourselves of these public rooms."

"They are not nearly so bad," Georgiana said. "I think it is rather nice that everyone can get to know people that they would not otherwise have the opportunity to meet."

"I suppose that is a nice way of looking at it," Mr. Tomlinson said. "I am fortunate in occupying the position where I may speak and be spoken to by almost anybody.

"But I can imagine, as the sister and daughter of a duke, that you have more pressing societal obligations."

"It is true," Georgiana admitted. "It can be trying at times, having to always be the one to start the conversation."

If she were to marry, her status would switch over to that of her husband's rank.

It was a nice idea, to be a little less... important, so to speak. She had never wanted to be the person who made everyone stop and bow when she walked into a room.

Father had liked being that person. He'd reveled in it. And Edward was slowly learning how to handle it.

But Georgiana wanted a simpler life. She always had. If she married a man who was not titled but had a good income, she could achieve that.

Could Mr. Tomlinson be that man?

No, she told herself firmly. She was not going to leap to any foregone conclusions.

She could not completely blame herself for thinking in that way, though. It was how she had thought of nearly every man she had met her entire life since her first season.

None of them came close to Captain Trentworth, of course.

She shoved that thought aside as well.

"I think that it is admirable of you to handle your station with such grace," Mr. Tomlinson said.

"And what of you?" Georgiana replied. "You have recently come up in the world. I ought to be congratulating you. Along with giving you my condolences."

"Please, no need for that," Mr. Tomlinson said. "My uncle's time was long coming. We were happy to see him released of his pain."

"I am glad to hear that it was dealt with so well, then."

"I admit to some trepidation," Mr. Tomlinson said. "Before, I was the youngest of three brothers. Everyone was polite to me of course. I was the son of a gentleman after all.

"It was expected that I would go into the navy or the clergy. And now I'm an heir in my own right. It makes people treat you differently.

"To be honest, it can be confusing. I feel as though I almost no longer know who my friends are. If I may take a more pessimistic view of things.

"Yet I have the feeling that you would treat me the same had you known me before the inheritance as well."

He smiled at her.

Georgiana could feel her face warming slightly in return. "I think that a very high compliment given how little we still know of one another."

"But I could tell it almost immediately," Mr. Tomlinson replied.

"How is that so, Mr. Tomlinson?"

"Well, by virtue of your being friends with Miss Weston. And that she invited you to dinner last night.

"Had you been one of most people I know who are concerned only with status, you would not have become friends with her for despite her wealth she has no title in her family.

"And had you only made an exception for her and would have been embarrassed to be among such company as ours, she would not have invited you to dinner.

"We all have those people of our acquaintance who are of a higher level than we are. And we know that we are their friends, but we also know that we are an exception to their rules.

"Yet, Miss Weston invited you to dinner where there is only one person who is going to inherit a title and his father is not yet dead.

"Miss Everett and Captain Trentworth have both come from even lower backgrounds than myself and Miss Weston.

"But you treated all of us with grace and dignity. One would not have thought at all that there was any difference in our status."

"I am only carrying myself with the kindness and thoughtfulness that I should think all of us are brought up to show," Georgiana replied, unused to the praise. It made her uncomfortable.

"And yet, so few people employ it," Mr. Tomlinson replied. "And so I commend you for it. You have my utmost respect, Miss Reginald."

Georgiana thanked him, and turned to fill up her glass once more.

"Since I have you here, and I am not engaged for the next dance..." Mr. Tomlinson's voice rose hopefully. "Might I ask if you will accompany me and be my partner for it?"

Georgiana was unsure. On the one hand, he was a perfectly nice man. And she could not so easily refuse.

On the other hand, his high praise of her was very discomforting. She was not at all sure she was worthy of it. And his charm, as it had last night, made her question his sincerity.

But then she saw, over his shoulder, Captain Trentworth enter the room.

He looked around, as if searching for people that he would know and with whom he could converse. He looked marvelously fine in his suit. Dignified as always. And handsome.

Georgiana could feel her heart starting to beat faster.

She must not be tempted to converse with him. She must not stand around waiting, hoping that he would choose to come up and converse with her.

She had to remain strong.

And so she turned, and told Mr. Tomlinson, "I would be delighted to take the next dance with you."

He seemed to be genuinely happy to hear her say so, and offered her his arm. Georgiana took it and let him lead her out onto the floor as the music paused to allow everyone to shuffle around and change partners.

This part was always awkward at balls. Everyone had to move to their new partner if they had one set up. If not, they had to get out of the way quickly. New dancers came on. Everyone was moving about and it was chaos for about thirty seconds.

But then it all settled again, and the next dance began.

Georgiana took her place in the line, across from Mr. Tomlinson.

It felt like ages since she had danced.

Of course, she had done so plenty during the season. But there were always more women than men at those parties.

She had been asked to dance a few times only out of courtesy, she knew. So that she would not have to sit down the entire night.

Most of her dancing had, in fact, been when she was instructing Maria and helping her to practice.

But that did not mean that she had forgotten the steps. She knew them quite well. When one had been dancing since childhood as she had, it was not something easily forgotten.

Dancing with a man that seemed to be interested in her, however, was an entirely different matter.

She forced herself to give Mr. Tomlinson a small smile as the music struck up.

After all, how could he help it if he was the kind of man who

charmed easily? People could not always help it if they were naturally witty or had a way with words.

Miss Everett was also quite a wit. Why should Georgiana judge
Mr. Tomlinson but not Miss Everett?

She ought to give him a fair chance.

If nothing else, focusing on him would keep her from thinking
about Captain Trentworth.

A part of her wondered if he saw her, hoped that he did, also
hoped that he did not.

Then she realized that the dance was starting and she ought to
not only move her feet but pay attention to her partner.

That was the thing about dances: they were not simply for the
enjoyment of dancing itself, or music, or exercise.

Rather, they were a chance—one of the only chances—for men
and women to converse uninterrupted and to get to know one
another.

It wasn't exactly private. There were other couples all around
them. Anyone could overhear their conversation and oftentimes
couples would interact with one another, and conversations would
be shared between multiple couples.

But it was still one of the few places that a man and a woman
could get to know one another and spend a great deal of time
together.

And while conversations could be overheard or held by multiple
couples, most couples were too busy being focused on one another.
It was as close to private as one could get.

It made an excellent place for a man and a woman to get to
know one another and see if they were suited for each other.

Georgiana waited for Mr. Tomlinson to start the conversation.
Not that it was conventionally the job of the man to begin the
conversation. But Georgiana had always been better at listening.

And Mr. Tomlinson struck her as the sort of man who conversed
easily and was happy to start a conversation. It was probably best
that she let him. Without making a fool of herself.

"How is it that you have never been to Bath until now, Miss
Reginald?" Mr. Tomlinson asked.

As she suspected. He barely waited to take the first step before
asking her.

Not that it was a bad thing. Georgiana wasn't sure how to feel that he had conversation so readily at hand.

"I'm afraid I've been busy helping to run my family estate," she said. It was true. After Mother's death, it had fallen to Georgiana to help run the estate of Foreshire while Father handled his business and trained Edward in everything.

"Remarkable," Mr. Tomlinson said. "I find it is a true sign of an intelligent woman if she can run an estate. Of course, so many young ladies still have their mothers alive. But I do wish that mothers would take more care to help their daughters learn."

"It is unfortunate that my mother was taken from us at so young an age," Georgiana replied. It had happened long enough ago that it no longer pained her. She could discuss it. "But it did give me an advantage in that respect."

"I wish that someone had given me a bit more direction with my understanding of estates," Mr. Tomlinson said. "I ought to find a wife who knows what she is doing in that respect. Being the third son, my father never bothered with that.

"But he did give me an excellent education in the classics. Latin and Greek and all that. It fostered in me a great love of books."

"Well then, you will always find yourself with friends," Georgiana replied. "I have found the easiest way of making acquaintances is to ask if anyone has read the latest novel. Or, barring that, ask everyone's opinion on the Judgement of Paris."

Mr. Tomlinson smiled, delighted. "And am I to understand that you have your own opinion on the subject?"

"I think that it says quite a lot about the folly of man," Georgiana replied. "He gives up the things that would help him to live a long and happy life in favor of possessing a woman he does not even know, simply because she is beautiful."

"Many men fall into the trap of wanting a beautiful woman without looking for any other substance," Mr. Tomlinson pointed out.

"I certainly hope that you are not that type, then, sir," Georgiana said. "I should hope that you will have a happy marriage and not a frustrating one."

"Well, I think that hopefully I shall be lucky enough to find a woman who is possessed of both brains and beauty."

"My brother was so lucky, and so I think you can hold out hope that you will be as well."

"Ah, but we cannot all be dukes."

"I can assure you, sir, she did not marry him for his title."

"I did not mean to imply such a thing, I apologize."

"No, I did not take offense, I did not mean it that way. I only wanted to let you know. I know that most marriages especially at such high levels are not done for love."

"Indeed they are not. I am glad to hear that your brother's is based on mutual admiration."

"It is, the deepest of admiration. Although they were both quite slow on the uptake. They did not realize the other returned their feelings. But it is all happily sorted out now.

"Still, I understand that most women marry for security and men marry for beauty or security of their own."

"Or out of loneliness, there is such a thing as that for us men as well."

Georgiana inclined her head. "That is true."

Conversing with Mr. Tomlinson was not so bad as she had feared. He was charming, yes. But he was not so glib with his words as she had expected that he would be.

He seemed, instead, happy to discuss more serious subjects with her. That had been something she had appreciated in Captain Trentworth as well.

No, she told herself. Stop it. She must not think of him.

The dance ended, and she curtsied to Mr. Tomlinson. "Thank you for the dance, sir," she told him.

"The pleasure was all mine, Miss Reginald." He smiled at her, but it was a smile with intent. She had not seen such a smile directed towards her in quite some time. It was the sort of smile that a man gave when he planned on making sure he saw a lady again, and frequently.

Georgiana quickly set out to find Julia. Perhaps her friend had been right. Perhaps Mr. Tomlinson did intend to court her.

She did not know how to even begin thinking about that.

CHAPTER 32

ROBERT ENTERED the ballroom and his gaze was immediately drawn to her.

Miss Reginald.

She looked radiant in a lovely frock of pale green. All of the ladies were wearing pastels or else some shade of white. Many of them were also blonde, although none of them had hair as light as Miss Reginald's.

There was no reason that his eye should immediately go to her. As though it were being pulled on a string. After all of this time...

There was no reason for it. And yet. She was the first, and truly the only, lady that he noticed.

She looked stately. Compared to the other young ladies who fluttered about like butterflies. Not that they weren't pretty enough. But oh, she was quietly radiant. Like the moon.

Robert watched her as she spoke with Mr. Tomlinson. He felt a spike of heat inside of him, the angry kind of heat that he knew well: envy.

There was no reason for him to feel such a thing. He knew that he could not, should not, want Miss Reginald. Not when she no longer wanted him.

But he could not control his heart. And it seemed that it had remained faithful to her after all this time.

Let not one more poem or novel speak of the inconsistency of men. His heart had remained true even while it starved from a lack of affection from her, from a lack of words or looks from her or of her.

But she was as untouchable to him as if she were still across the vast ocean.

Robert watched as Mr. Tomlinson evidently asked her to dance, for a moment later they were going out to join the other couples as the music changed.

He realized then that he was standing in the doorway still, like an idiot, and stepped aside. He stood with his back to the wall, watching.

He knew that he should be making friends. Finding the people that he knew. Socializing. But he could not bring himself to look away.

Oh, she looked as beautiful as he had remembered. She moved about the dance floor with the same unconscious grace, as if she didn't even have to think about it.

She was doing that thing where she smiled politely, that small smile he'd seen her give so many times to so many people. Miss Reginald so rarely smiled good and proper. And only once or twice had he gotten her to laugh.

It had felt like the greatest victory in the world, getting Miss Reginald to laugh. She was not a woman given over to melancholy. At least, not that he could recall. She might have changed since then.

It was not that she did not feel amusement. More that it was quietly contained within her. She was a woman who was altogether composed, and it took quite a lot, either good or ill, to rattle that composure.

Robert found himself hoping, selfishly, that Mr. Tomlinson would not be able to make her laugh.

"Captain Trentworth!" It was Miss Perry. She was a sweet enough girl and she did look rather pretty in her muslin. She was a bit too flighty for him, generally.

But she complimented him and seemed to admire him. It was, he could admit, a balm on his bruised soul.

"I was beginning to fear that you would not come," Miss Perry went on. "I said as much to Miss Everett, she will back me up on this."

Miss Everett was trailing behind. She curtsied when she had finished approaching. "It is true, sir, she has mentioned you."

"I am flattered to have been so sought after," Robert replied.

He had to admit that he liked Miss Everett quite a bit better than Miss Perry. Of course he would never say such a thing aloud to either lady. It would be terribly unfair of him.

But both seemed eager for his attention. Although Miss Everett hid it better. It flattered him.

After the rejection by Miss Reginald and now watching her dance with another man... he could not help but feel the pull towards these younger ladies.

And they were ladies of good breeding and with lovely faces to gaze upon. Why should he not enjoy their company?

He only needed to get used to being around Miss Reginald again. Then his traitorous heart would remember why it should not feel for her any longer. He would grow immune.

As he spent more time with these other ladies—perhaps Miss Perry and Miss Everett, perhaps others—he would grow fonder for them as well.

It was as it should be, truly. He only had to get practiced at it. Work his way up to it.

"Nobody has such entertaining stories here as you do," Miss Perry said. "Your tales of the high seas were the most fantastical thing I've ever heard, I must swear to it. You ought to write a novel."

"Any sailor could tell you the same stories," Robert replied with an indulgent tone. "And I daresay they would tell them much better. I am no man of letters. You ought to see my correspondence, it is most dreadful."

He had not corresponded much with anyone. Not since Miss Reginald.

The letters he had written to her then. How he had poured over them, agonizing over what to say. He had rewritten many of them, realizing that some were too passionate. The letters of a man to his wife, which Miss Reginald had not yet been.

Now never would be.

Those letters had been such a lifeline. He could still recall what he had written, and what she had written in return. He could even recall what he had written to her originally that he had then thrown out before starting again.

Every letter he received from her he had held in his hand, imagining her own small hand folding the letter up carefully before handing it to the messenger. Her penmanship was remarkable and he could envision her sitting at her desk with the sunlight pouring through the windows, carefully crafting each word.

He had been a foolish boy then. Every man had his moment of foolish, young love. That had been his.

He had no intention of writing love letters again. Not even to his wife.

"I'm certain that you will improve with practice," Miss Perry said. There was no mistaking the flirtatious nature of her tone.

Robert held in a sigh. He had nothing against ladies who flirted. But he was not entranced by such things. He did not enjoy playing the flirting game.

First of all, it was a game for younger men. He was looking for a wife. He could not find time to dawdle. Younger men who had many years to find a wife could flirt and take their time. They could play those games and enjoy the chase without really needing to actually catch the woman they were pursuing.

Second of all, he was aware that he could not be the only man that Miss Perry spoke to in such a manner. She needed to marry. She was the only one left of her siblings still single.

There must be immense pressure on her to get out of her parents' house.

He could understand it. Truly, he could. And although he did not think he was the man for her nor she the woman for him, his heart went out to her. She really was still a child in many ways.

"I would have to find a reason to practice," he said. "Luckily, given my advance in status, I should have plenty of letters of business I will need to send shortly. A few of those and I should be back in the swing of things, I presume."

Miss Everett gave him a conspiratorial smile, as if to say that she saw how he had neatly dodged that bullet.

"Oh." Miss Perry looked a little disappointed.

He did feel bad for her. "Do you know many people here?" he asked.

The ladies looked around. "Not terribly many," Miss Perry admitted. "But I hope to get to know quite a few more. That is why they have public balls, isn't it? To meet new people?"

"I'm certain that's why Miss Weston arranged this," he assured her. "Perhaps you could let me have this next dance, then? And in the course of it, we might speak to some other people and make some new acquaintances."

Miss Everett gave him an amused look that clearly said it's your funeral.

But he did feel a bit protective of Miss Perry. In fact, as he led her out onto the dance floor he wondered...

Well, she was from a good family. She was a sweet girl. She had a pretty face, although not nearly so lovely as Miss Reginald's—although he shot that thought down immediately. It did him no good to compare other ladies to Miss Reginald.

Feeling protective of a young lady was a good start to a relation-ship, was it not? Giving her a stable home in which to live. That would be nice.

But would it be enough for him? Probably not. He needed someone that he was not merely protective of, or amused by. He needed someone that he could truly respect. Someone he consid-ered to be an equal.

As the dance began, however, he could feel himself warming in a brotherly way towards Miss Perry. All she truly wanted was a handsome man to pay attention to her.

He suspected, from some of the remarks that she made, that she had been rather looked over compared to her other siblings. That must have been hard on her.

Now it was her time to shine and she wanted to make the most of it, understandably so.

To that end, he laughed at her jokes and made her laugh in turn. When the time came for the dance to end, he found some men that he had met through Mr. Norwich and introduced her to them and vice versa.

Miss Perry seemed quite happy to be making the acquaintance of these new men. She was a likeable girl, really. A little too flirta-tious for Robert's taste but a sweet girl at heart. The other men quickly warmed to her and she was asked to dance by several of them.

"Congratulations," Miss Everett said, coming to stand next to him. She was watching Miss Perry be led out onto the dance floor for another turn. "You've managed to get her off your back."

"She is a sweet girl," he replied. "Only not the sort of girl that I am looking for."

"Are you looking, then?" Miss Everett asked. "I did wonder. Some men are. Some are not. Some only want the sport of it."

"I hope I did not strike you as the sporting sort."

"No sir, indeed not. In fact, you struck me as the opposite. I wondered if you had any intention of marrying at all. Or even engaging in a flirtation."

"I'm afraid that I am a serious man. I take such things seriously."

"That is all well and good if you ask me. I have seen my cousins break their hearts repeatedly over men who were not worth their time. Men who did not take courtship as seriously as they ought to.

"I do not think that men often realize how important such things are to women. How hard we take it when we learn that the man we have been dreaming about is not as devoted to us in his heart as we have been to him."

"If you were to ask for my honest opinion," Robert began.

"Oh, always," Miss Everett assured him. "An honest opinion is the only kind that is worth having. I am not the sort of woman who prefers blissful ignorance. I find that it is not nearly so blissful as one would hope."

He chuckled. "Well, I would tell you then that I believe the reason many men do not take it so seriously is that they are not dependent upon it for their future."

"That is fair," Miss Everett acknowledged. "But one would think that they would understand how it is for us ladies and show a little more courtesy."

"Careful, Miss Everett, that tone rings strongly of bitterness."

"I assure you, sir, there is no personal bitterness in it," Miss Everett told him. "I am merely a woman of strong convictions."

Robert wished that Miss Reginald had such strong convictions and that she had stuck to them. If so, he might have been happily married by now.

"I am glad to hear it," he said. "There is nothing more frustrating to me than a woman—or a man, any person at all—who cannot hold to their true beliefs. Principle is of the utmost importance to me."

"Then we are in agreement, Captain Trentworth," Miss Everett told him. "I grew up as the ward of my aunt and uncle. They had a great deal of money.

"But their children—my cousins—were and are quite undisciplined. There is no moral that they tout that they will not then give up in pursuit of whatever pleasure they fancy. What they extoll one moment they will renounce the next if it will suit their needs better.

"It was quite frustrating to deal with, growing up. That I can promise you. But it gave me the steely resolve that I fear makes me rather unlikeable to many that I meet. I simply must be myself. And I must hold true to what I believe and what I think. No matter what others may say about it."

"Then I believe we shall get on rather well, Miss Everett," Robert told her.

His eyes scanned the room almost unconsciously for Miss Reginald. When he did not see her, he forced himself to focus back in on Miss Everett. He would not waste time on Miss Reginald. Not anymore.

"I am glad to hear it, Captain Trentworth," Miss Everett replied, smiling. "Tell me, do you have any family?"

"None to speak of, I am afraid," Robert answered her. "My parents died a few years ago. I have no siblings. I do have some cousins but I am not close to them. My aunt was my only family and I had not seen her in years. It was quite a surprise to me that she left her fortune to me."

Robert gave a small laugh. "I suspect that it was because I am the only one of my cousins to have truly made something of myself. The others are quite lazy, you know.

"But then they come from families with money. As do your cousins. Why should they understand the meaning of work and principle?"

"Careful," Miss Everett replied with a smile. "That rings strongly of bitterness, Captain."

He had not meant to sound bitter and he knew that she was

only teasing him. But it was true. He was bitter. He was bitter against the late Lord Reginald, the duke, for his lack of understanding.

He was bitter against all of the people who had looked down upon him and who now treated him as an equal without realizing the irony of it, the falsity of it. The hypocrisy.

And most of all, he was bitter over Miss Reginald. The woman who, damn him, he still had feelings for.

But Miss Everett... she had to rely upon the kindness of her family. She must marry, of course. Her uncle would not support her forever.

However, she understood what it meant for him to raise himself up like this. She was a woman with wit, someone he could consider an equal. She was someone with whom he could talk about serious things.

She was lovely as well. Not... he must admit, not in the manner of Miss Reginald. But he did like her spirit. And she had her principles and convictions and she would hold to them. She was a woman with a strong spirit.

He could do worse, could he not? He could keep looking, he supposed. He could be picky. Weigh his options. Consider for longer.

But why do so when there was a woman right in front of him that seemed to fit all that he had told himself he wanted in a wife?

This must be the universe gifting him with something after taking his former intended from him so cruelly. He must not waste that opportunity.

Of course, he was not about to get down on one knee and propose marriage right that moment. It would not be proper. Nor did he want to.

He must go slowly. Grow to know her better. Miss Weston, he was sure, had plans for all of them to spend more time together. Activities, more dinners and so on.

When he was secure in his choice of Miss Everett, he could properly court her.

He was not going to let himself fall in love in an instant and then roll pell-mell head over teakettle into the heat of it without first getting his bearings. Not this time. He was going to be smart about this.

And if Miss Everett turned out not to be the woman that he wanted to marry then he would know long before he proposed to her.

But how were you supposed to know that Miss Reginald was not the person you were supposed to marry? His thoughts, as always, sought to betray him.

How was he supposed to know? She had been perfect right up until she had given into her father's demands. He could not have seen that, could he? Not until the moment that it happened. And it could not have happened until he proposed and asked for permission, could it?

But things were different now, he reminded himself. Things were better. He was rich now. He was distinguished for his service. Perhaps most important of all, he was older and wiser.

He was not going to let himself fall like that again.

He would be careful.

"The next dance is starting," he pointed out to Miss Everett. "I wonder, would I be able to request the pleasure of your company for the dance?"

"You certainly may," Miss Everett replied. "I would be delighted."

He led her out onto the dance floor. This would be a marvelous chance to see what kind of conversationalist Miss Everett was. That was what a dance was for, after all, was it not?

Well, that and seeing how well she moved and looked in her frock. Dancing was a chance for ladies to show themselves off in form as well as in wit and personality.

Chatting with Miss Everett throughout the dance was pleasant. Robert had to wonder if she knew that it was a sort of audition.

Of course she must—but that was what all courting began as, wasn't it? The man and the woman were both auditioning one another for the post of husband and wife respectively.

Miss Everett proved herself to be well educated in books and the classics. She was witty and had observations about the rest of the people in the room that left Robert chuckling for most of the dance.

Yet he could not help but compare her to Miss Reginald, try as he might to avoid thinking of his former intended.

Miss Reginald was also skilled in books and the classics. Her father had insisted upon an educated and intelligent woman. The late duke had hated stupid people, and no child of his was going to be so.

Robert could recall Miss Reginald telling him of the demands that her governess had made upon her at her father's request. How harsh her father had been.

"He only wanted the best," she had told him at one point. "He refused everything except for exceptionalism in everything that was done or said by myself and my brother."

Robert remembered feeling heartbroken for her. Miss Reginald had come to love reading, thankfully. Especially poetry.

But it had been cruel, he had always thought, that her father should push her to be so accomplished. Her childhood had been filled with lessons. Lessons in painting, musical instruments, embroidery, singing, reading, writing poetry and calligraphy for its own sake as an art form, dancing, and so on.

No wonder, Robert had always thought, Miss Reginald was so dignified. She'd had to be. How else was one to endure such endless demands? One must either break or develop the most stoic of countenances.

Miss Everett was far from stoic but her knowledge was just as good as Miss Reginald's, at least in the manner of reading. She was not so well versed in poetry.

Robert told himself that it was no matter.

Yes, he and Miss Reginald had often spoken of poetry to one another. They had exchanged lines from poems in their letters to one another. They had even tried to make up a few of their own with minimal success—neither of them was cut out to be the next Lord Byron.

But it had not mattered the real quality of the poems. Only that they were sharing them with one another. The spirit of conspiracy and creativity had been upon them.

It had been quite childish in some ways to tell the truth. But was that not what love did? Did it not make one see the world as a child would once again? Did it not fill life with a new kind of wonder and gaiety that had previously been forgotten?

Miss Everett, Robert could tell, was far too serious for that sort of thing.

But of course she would be. She had not grown up the daughter of a duke. Her entire life depended upon marrying someone and she had been surrounded by impetuous and spoiled cousins.

However, he reminded himself, Miss Reginald seemed serious to most of the people that she met. She was not a lively person. Miss Everett, in fact, was more lively in manner than Miss Reginald.

If Miss Reginald could be impressed upon to indulge in such silly nonsense as writing poems to her fiancé, then surely Miss Everett might be the same way.

Robert did think that perhaps Miss Everett's wit had something missing in it. It seemed to sometimes hold too much acid in its tone.

Not that she was truly malevolent in her words. Certainly she was better at reading the room and watching her words than Miss Perry was at times.

But there was lacking the genuine thoughtfulness and warmth that he had so appreciated in Miss Reginald...

For Heaven's sake, man, he wanted to yell at himself. How could he possibly get on like this? When he kept only comparing the ladies he was with to another woman? A woman with whom he had no chance and from whom he was supposed to be moving on, he might add.

He had seen her dancing with Mr. Tomlinson. He was rich enough now thanks to his uncle. No title, but that was now something that she did not have to worry about.

Unless her brother was following in his father's footsteps.

In that case, he might very well see Miss Reginald with Mr. Norwich. The man liked her. He had said as much on their way home last night from the dinner.

He was not actively pursuing the lady just yet the way that Mr. Tomlinson seemed to be. But who knew? It would not be long, Robert was sure, before Miss Reginald's charms prevailed upon him.

After all, Robert had been rejected flat-out by the woman many years ago. And her charm was still working perfectly fine on him, even from across the room.

It was rather frustrating, to say the least.

When the dance ended, Robert escorted Miss Everett back to her evening escort, Mrs. Weston.

Mrs. Weston was a woman of failing health but she had once possessed great spirit, as Robert recalled.

"Ah, Captain Trentworth!" she said as he approached with Miss Everett. "There you are. I hope you will indulge an old woman by giving her a few moments of your time. We hardly got to speak at dinner last night."

"It is not at all an indulgence," he replied. He allowed Miss Everett to be led off by another man who asked her to dance. He bowed to Mrs. Weston. "It was always a pleasure to speak to you previously, when I visited your house."

"Ah, yes, when you were courting Miss Reginald." Mrs. Weston's eyes gleamed. Miss Weston was truly her mother's daughter. "You know, it always saddened me when that bully of an old man would not allow her to marry you."

"She is the one who broke off the engagement."

Mrs. Weston gave a snort. "My dear boy. Allow me a moment to be indelicate. I am sick, you know, and we must make allowances for people in the throes of ill health such as myself.

"I can see your bitterness written all over your handsome face. And it is in your voice just now, when you spoke of her. And I tell you plain that if you blame that girl for the way that she behaved, well, you do not know women at all, do you?

"Would you ever go against the orders of your commanding officer in the navy? I should hope not, for disobeying orders will lose you the war.

"And if you would not go against him, why, then how can you expect a girl to go against her father? And such a powerful father as well. That man was a duke, you know, my boy. He could have shut her off from all of society.

"And what was she supposed to do then, hmm? Sit at home and do nothing but knit while you were away? No friends? No callers, no balls to distract her? And what if you were killed in the war? She would have been completely alone and left with nothing, and her father would not have taken her back.

"You know that he would not have. He was a stubborn old fool. I know, we must not speak ill of the dead. But we had an understanding, the former duke and I. I did not lie in my opinion of him while he was alive and I think he would thank me to not start lying about my opinion of him now that he is gone."

"I'm sure that he is looking down on you with appreciation," Robert managed. He bit down hard on the inside of his cheek to keep from laughing.

"My dear boy, if he is looking upon us and observing us now, he is not looking down," Mrs. Weston said sagely, with a wink. "He is looking up."

Robert had to turn his laughter into a snort. "No wonder your daughter is such a terror, Mrs. Weston. I can see quite plainly where she gets it from."

"Her father has often told her to look at what I do, and hear what I say, and then do the opposite," Mrs. Weston replied. "Captain, I am quite serious in what I am telling you.

"For all of my jokes, this is a very serious matter. You could go out and earn what you were not gifted. She could not. It was simply not a risk that she could take.

"And could you ask any person that you loved to undertake such a risk for you? What a selfish and thoughtless, I dare say, way to behave. You are a loving man, I think. You were treating poor Miss Perry with such kindness just now. She will learn, you know. Most girls do.

"Do not be bitter over it. Think of the position she was in. I certainly cannot blame her for it. We are not all heroines in great operas, you know. Those ladies who sing so shrilly and are always willing to throw themselves upon the knife for true love.

"I think it's the fact that most of them are Italian. But anyhow, my boy—and do not give me that look, I am old enough to be your mother and can therefore call you whatever I please. If only for your own sake, learn to look upon her with kindness again. Forgive her.

"For if you do not, it will eat at you. And where will you be then? Do you want to spend the rest of your life angry and wasting your energy on someone when you are not even getting anything good out of it in return?

"Nobody wants to deal with a man whose back is twisted from the bitter, gnarled nature of his thoughts. Do not become that sort of man."

"I appreciate the lecture," Robert replied with a smile in spite of himself. "You are full of wisdom, as always."

"She is still free, you know," Mrs. Weston said, undaunted. "I have rarely seen an affection between two people as I saw between the two of you when you would call upon the house.

"If I were you and I had a second chance at such a thing, I should not give it up. Not for the world."

"And I suppose that Mr. Weston's courtship of you was not filled with such passion?"

"It was filled with fondness," Mrs. Weston replied. "But the deep and abiding love that poets are so happy to spout out like water-falls... no. It was not that.

"Oh, don't give me that pitying look. I have been quite happy. He has become my greatest friend, I shall have you know. Scallywag."

Robert couldn't hold in his laughter this time. "Mrs. Weston, you are truly a terror."

"Oh, good. That is my main goal in life now, you know. Beauty has failed me. Age and health are rapidly fleeing from me. My wit is all I have left."

"And your wisdom."

"Oh dear, if you think that I actually have any of that, Captain, I do worry about you."

"You were only just now asking for me to take heed of your wisdom," Robert pointed out.

"As well you should, for compared to you and your foolishness I am a sage."

Robert laughed again. "I shall think on what you've said." He took her hand and pressed it warmly. "Shall I leave you to your observations of the ballroom, my lady?"

"If you could find my wayward daughter and send her to me, I would appreciate it, thank you, Captain."

Robert chuckled, bowing, and went off to find Miss Weston.

CHAPTER 33

GEORGIANA COULD HARDLY KEEP her heart from leaping into her throat as she left the dance floor and saw Captain Trentworth walking onto it... with Miss Perry.

Of course, why would he not? He knew her and it was practically the sacred duty of the men in the ballroom to make sure all the ladies got an opportunity to dance.

Captain Trentworth probably knew very little of the people about. He would have to ask Miss Perry or Miss Everett to dance. It was the way of things.

Still, Georgiana could not prevent herself from wanting desperately to flee the ballroom.

It was not the case and she knew it, yet she felt as though every eye in the room was upon her. Watching her watch Captain Trentworth with Miss Perry. Asking her silently how she felt, if she was going to fall apart, if she was going to remember to breathe.

She wasn't sure about that last part. Breathing felt rather difficult at the moment and it had nothing to do with her outfit.

Miss Perry seemed to be entertaining the captain very well. She was making him smile and even laugh a few times.

But that was nothing, truly, was it not? Captain Trentworth had always been easier to make laugh than Georgiana had been.

Indeed, the first time he had made her laugh, she had known that he was the man for her. She did not laugh easily and never had.

A side effect of being raised by a stern father and stern governesses who followed her father's example.

But Captain Trentworth had been able to do it.

She had not laughed since she had broken off their engagement. At least, not at any time that she could recall.

"You are distressed," Julia said, sidling up to her. "And after you had such a lovely dance with Mr. Tomlinson. Tell me, what ails you now? What brings that look to your face? And how was Mr. Tomlinson?"

"I fear that you might be right," Georgiana admitted. "He was quite frank about some things, such as what a lady ought to know about running an estate and all. And he seemed quite interested in me. Asking all sorts of questions, you know. None of the usual talk about the weather."

"You see?" Julia said with glee. "I told you so, did I not? But why do you say that you are afraid that I am right? Is there something wrong?"

"It is only that I barely know him," Georgiana replied. "And he seems to be moving along quite quickly."

"My dear, I'm being frank here if only because you have insisted that it is so—you do not have much time. Your words, you will recall, not mine. I think that you are still young and eligible enough.

"But if you are convinced that you do not have much time then what are you doing waiting like this? Surely it is a good thing that he likes you so well and so quickly?"

"If only I knew that he truly liked me so well. I am well connected, you know. I will have a large sum to give to my husband upon our marriage. I have good breeding. What if he is only after those? He is so well spoken and has leapt right into what seems to be a flirtation after only a single dinner with me."

"Most men are quick to act," Julia pointed out. "Especially with ladies they truly esteem. And he probably fears that you will be snapped up by someone else. Captain Trentworth, perhaps."

"You can see well enough that Captain Trentworth has not spared a thought for me at all." Georgiana could not keep the despair out of her voice.

Julia followed her line of sight and saw Captain Trentworth

dancing with Miss Perry. "Oh, my dear. I am sorry that it pains you. You are really still holding a torch for him, aren't you?"

"It is nothing to speak on."

"But you did not see him as you were dancing with Mr. Tomlinson. Captain Trentworth's gaze went straight to you. I saw it, for I was going to go over and speak with him myself. Until I saw how he was looking at you. His eyes were ablaze!"

"You are, as ever, prone to dramatics, Julia."

"And you are, as ever, prone to thinking too little of yourself, Georgiana. I tell you that the man still has feelings for you."

"Oh, yes, and you got that all in a look? This is England, Julia, or have you forgotten? Land of the stiff upper lip? Captain Trentworth is a man of discretion. He would never show his feelings in that way."

"He would if he did not realize how obvious he was being. You said that your brother and his bride did not realize how the other one felt. Even when they were being painfully obvious to everyone else around them.

"What if it is the same here with Captain Trentworth? What if he simply does not realize how he is behaving? How his heart is written on his sleeve?"

Georgiana sighed. "You are incorrigible. It is my lot in life to suffer this way, it seems. And now I sound as dramatic as you do.

"He has every opportunity to show me that he still holds affection for me. He has behaved towards me with nothing but the barest of civility. He is angry towards me for how I treated him but nothing more."

The dance ended, and she watched as Captain Trentworth led Miss Perry off the dance floor and stopped to converse with Miss Everett.

Of course. Miss Everett was far more suited to the captain than Miss Perry, as sweet and well-intended a girl as she might be.

"You do worry me so, Georgiana," Julia said. "It is nothing to converse with a woman, nothing at all!"

"And yet, as Mr. Tomlinson has just proven, a single conversation. A single dinner. Might be enough to persuade a man into thinking of marriage."

"With the right woman, perhaps."

"Well then who is to say that she is not the right woman? Who is to take that possibility away from her?"

"I think that there is no woman who is as right for him as you."

"That is your opinion, Julia. And a bold one at that. And your opinion is not the one that matters. His does and his alone. No amount of your wishful thinking and scheming can change his opinion if he does not wish for it to be changed."

Julia sighed, watching as Captain Trentworth and Miss Everett sank deep into conversation.

"Would it be so bad, my dear? If you married Mr. Tomlinson? If he turns out to be as good of a man as he seems to be and as I hope he is."

"I do not know," Georgiana admitted. "If the captain was not here... I would say yes. I have little choice in the matter at this point, do I not? I must do what I can to preserve my dignity and my place in society.

"But now... I find that I am as weak as I was all those other times that men seemed to be growing close to me. I would think of the captain and my heart would retreat and grow cold.

"And those men could sense it. I know that they could. And so they, too, retreated.

"My brother, I think, suspects some of it. That my own foolish heart and behavior was part of the reason why I was never proposed to or properly courted after the captain.

"And I know what I should do at this moment is welcome the courtship of Mr. Tomlinson with open arms. And a part of me wants to. Yet... I do not know."

"Well, you know my opinion on the matter," Julia said. "I have not been subtle about it. But whatever you decide, you must do it soon. Neither man will stand still in his course while you fret over what you will decide."

"That is true."

Georgiana watched as Captain Trentworth bowed, apparently asking Miss Everett to dance. He escorted her out onto the floor.

"They are well suited for one another," Georgiana admitted quietly. "She has the strength of character that he appreciates. The wit that he likes. She is lovely to gaze upon. I think she would make him a good wife."

"So would you," Julia replied. "And would she love him to the depth and breadth that you would, and do?"

Georgiana wanted to cry. Would she? Would the lovely, the young, the witty Miss Everett truly give the captain all that he needed and deserved?

Part of her wanted Miss Everett to be capable of it. If only so that the captain might be happy and find someone deserving of him.

But the other part of her, the selfish part, wanted it to not be so. She wanted there to be no other woman for the captain, no person for him but herself.

She could easily recall the days when they had exchanged letters. How they had talked then of the poets of love! They had written one another passages from poems they read and had even tried their hand at writing their own poems to each other.

They were quite pale imitations of the great poets, if Georgiana recalled correctly.

But what was important was how back then, she had seen love as a wonderous thing. It was new and exciting. It made everything better. Colors were brighter and food tasted better. She felt like dancing all the time, as if her body was moving to music that her ears could not quite catch.

Now she knew better. Love was painful. It sank its claws into a person and held on long after the person wanted it gone. She tried to banish it but it always came back like some kind of plague or great illness.

Love was a sickness.

She watched Captain Tretnworth and Miss Everett dancing and felt that sickness inside of her still. Oh, what she would do to banish it!

But she knew of no cure. If she did, she would have cast that hideous love from herself ages ago and married the first man who proposed to her. She would have been the excellent flirt that she was supposed to be.

She would have married a titled man, as her father had wanted. She could have had a child by now, perhaps even two children.

But love had taken a bite out of her like a lion and its teeth were embedded in her to this day.

Georgiana turned away. She would not torture herself further by continuing to watch this. What sort of self-hating person was she to watch as the man she loved flirted with another woman?

She ought to go and get some air. Yes. That would do. She would step outside and get some air.

"I will return," she told Julia. "I only need a moment."

"If you say so. Please do be careful."

Georgiana walked slowly and sedately, and told herself that in doing so, she wasn't actually fleeing the ballroom.

CHAPTER 34

ONCE SHE WAS OUTSIDE, she felt much better. She was away from everyone and from the stifling heat of the ballroom.

The cool night air was soothing. The rumble of the carriages was familiar and comforting. She would spend a few minutes composing herself. And then she would return, and all would be well.

"Are you quite all right, Miss Reginald?"

She turned to see Mr. Norwich standing there. "I beg your pardon," he said, "but I saw you leaving. I thought you might want an escort. Are you well?"

She nodded. "It is only a moment's distress, nothing more."

"Would you mind if I stood with you, then? I only fear for your safety."

"That is kind of you."

Had it been Mr. Tomlinson, she would have sent him away. But Mr. Norwich was of a calmer and more stoic disposition and he had not yet made any attempts to flirt with her. She felt quite safe in his care.

"You are welcome to stay," she told him.

"Do you wish to talk about what caused you your distress?" Mr. Norwich asked.

Georgiana sighed. "I'm afraid that it is not the sort of matter that one can really discuss with strangers."

"Ah, an affair of the heart then, I am guessing?" Mr. Norwich smiled in understanding. "I do not wish to belittle ladies in any way. But that is usually what is causing the distress.

"And I suspect that if it were simply a quarrel with a friend that you would tell me of it at once. But courtship is such a confusing and important game that we all play, is it not?"

"You speak wisely, sir."

"Then I am correct in my guess?"

"Yes, that you are."

"Then might I also guess that the exact reason for your distress is unrequited love?"

Georgiana nodded. "I made a grave error, many years ago. I hurt a dear man. And now he is back, and I find my heart is still his. But his is no longer mine. He seems to be looking to give it to someone else."

"Well, the night is still young," Mr. Norwich pointed out. "A man may feel passion on the dance floor that rapidly subsides once he is off it.

"I have danced with many a woman that I was convinced I should marry. And then once I had concluded the dance and took a few moments to compose myself I realized what a fool I was.

"I admit that sometimes it took me until the carriage ride home or even the next morning. But I did come to my senses.

"So if you see the man for whom you care with another woman and it seems to be going well, I would not worry too much. Worry a little, but you never know. It could only be the fancy of a moment."

"I fear that if it is not this woman, it will be another. I'm sure that he has quite forgotten me."

Mr. Norwich grew serious. "Madam, if I may say so—if you were the woman who once held my heart, I would not soon forget you. Not in a lifetime."

Georgiana gazed at him in astonishment. Mr. Norwich shook his head.

"I see that you do not see it. I am not surprised. Ladies such as yourself rarely realize their charms.

"You are a singular woman, Miss Reginald. Every man in the room can see it. My surprise in you having not yet married is genuine, I can assure you."

Perhaps it was as she had said to Julia, then. It was not that she was not undesirable. It was that the men had known that they could not truly win her.

And even in marriages of convenience, gentlemen did like to imagine that the lady to whom they proposed held some measure of affection for them. Even if it was not true.

But with Georgiana, there was no such thing as pretense. She could not hide how she felt about something or someone.

And so those men must have seen that she was untouchable, and so they did not try to touch.

Oh, was it really all her own fault? That she was now suffering as she did?

"I fear that I have put you in even more distress than you were previously," Mr. Norwich observed.

"It is nothing," Georgiana informed him, struggling to get her wildly beating heart under control. "I only feel so stupid. For not seeing what others see."

"We so rarely see ourselves in a true light," Mr. Norwich replied. "Now, I do not know this gentleman. I cannot make any certain claims. I know only that I esteem you and would allow myself to go further than that with you if I thought I had a chance of winning you.

"If this gentleman is at all like myself, then he will be the same way. How can you know that all is lost until you try? You lose all of the wars that you do not start. All of the battles that you do not fight.

"I would suggest that you do your utmost to win him back and see what happens. I think that you might be surprised at what your efforts yield."

There was a bit of poetic justice in that, Georgiana supposed. She had never pursued any man and had always let them come to her. She was no flirt.

But she had been pursued by Captain Trentworth and she had rejected him. Was it not fair, then, that for her redemption she now be the one to pursue him and fight for him?

"I sense some resolve returning to your cheeks," Mr. Norwich said proudly. "I am glad to see it. You are a lovely woman, Miss Reginald. Do not sell yourself short."

"I shall try not to," she replied.

Mr. Norwich handed her a handkerchief so that she might dab at her eyes. "I do my best to be of service to others. That is what my father has taught me.

"Having said that, allow me a moment of selfishness, if you please. Should this man reject you and set aside your heart. Do not hesitate to bring it to me. I should keep it and honor it as a man should."

Georgiana finished dabbing at her eyes and handed his handkerchief back to him. "You have brightened my evening with your kind words. Although I am not certain that I am worthy of them, they are appreciated nonetheless. If I am rejected, I shall think on your offer."

She was drawn towards Mr. Norwich more than she was drawn towards Mr. Tomlinson, at least in their general disposition. That was something to think on at least.

But could she really find the courage to pursue the captain? To make it clear to him that she was still his if he wanted her? Would he even pay attention to her? Would he even notice or care?

There were so many reasons to doubt. So many ways that it could all go horribly wrong.

But Mr. Norwich was right about one thing: she would lose every battle that she did not fight.

If the men simply stood on the banks and said that they would not fight the war, then the war was lost! And that was what she was doing, wasn't it?

She was saying that it was useless to try and fight and so she was not even going to try. But she did not really know, did she?

Until Captain Trentworth looked her in the eye and told her, "Miss Reginald, I have no interest in having you as a part of my life now or ever," how could she know what he thought?

It was all merely conjecture, wasn't it?

She was her father's daughter in some ways. And her father would never have stood for accepting mere conjecture and assumptions in closing a business deal.

No. He would demand facts. Confirmation. Proof.

That was what she ought to demand.

Georgiana turned, looking Mr. Norwich straight in the eye for the first time since he had stepped outside. "Mr. Norwich, if you would be so kind. I should like to be escorted back into the ballroom?"

He bowed to her. "Certainly, Miss Reginald. It would be my pleasure. Is that a determined gleam I catch in your eye?"

"It very well could be, sir. I could venture to say that your little talk has done wonders for my resolve."

"I am glad to hear it. I shall look forward to watching to see how this all plays out."

With that, he escorted her back into the ballroom.

Where Captain Trentworth, whether he knew it or not, waited.

CHAPTER 35

ROBERT LOCATED Miss Weston without much difficulty.

All he had to do was follow the sound of laughter. Miss Weston was most usually to be found in the middle of it, either laughing herself or causing it.

He found her talking with Miss Everett and Mr. Tomlinson. About what, he wasn't sure.

Robert had to stifle the flare of envy that ignited in his chest when he saw Mr. Tomlinson. It was certainly not the other man's fault if he had an interest in Miss Reginald. What man in his right mind would not have an interest in her?

Besides, it was only a dance, was it not? That was all that Robert had seen. A dance alone was not enough to seal a man's affections or his desire for courtship. Robert himself was proof of that as he considered whether or not to try courting Miss Everett.

"I do hate to interrupt this lovely conversation," he said, turning to Miss Weston. "But your mother is summoning you."

"I must go and see what she requires." Miss Weston curtsied to them all.

She hurried off and Robert turned to look at the two remaining people. "I hope that you are enjoying your time in Bath?" he asked Mr. Tomlinson.

"Immensely, sir," Mr. Tomlinson replied. "Much more than I had expected. And what of you? How are you finding England now that you have been back for a few days? Is it as you recall?"

Robert made to tell him that he was surprised at how little had changed, when none other than Miss Reginald joined their group. She was accompanied by Mr. Norwich.

She looked as though she had been in distress. Robert doubted that anyone else would notice. Miss Reginald was remarkably good at hiding her feelings.

But he knew. The years had passed and yet he could still tell when she had been upset.

Back in the day the reasons she had been upset were usually linked to her father. He had comforted her in person and in letters many a time as she had confided her distress to him.

Her father was a strong-willed and powerful man. Robert remembered that quite clearly.

Could he truly expect any woman to go against such a man? When that man was a duke who could destroy her if he wanted to? When that man was her father and all of society and good breeding expected her to follow her father's will?

The late duke had been an unreasonable man in many ways but Robert had to face the fact that some people would not consider him unreasonable at all in expecting his daughter to marry a man with a title. She was the daughter of a duke, after all.

Had he been too hasty and bitter in his judgment after all? As Mrs. Weston had suggested?

Robert's fingers ached from the urge to reach out and touch her. To comfort her as he once had been able to. Whatever had been hurting her? What had been worrying her?

Was it something to do with her family? Were things not as well as she said? Or was it the Weston family? He would not be surprised if Mrs. Weston's health was worse than people were letting on.

If only he could speak to her as he once had. If only he knew the things to say to make it better. He had once. Now... he was not so sure.

Mr. Tomlinson greeted Miss Reginald and began asking after her. He inquired if she had gotten around to trying the wine. He asked if she had enjoyed the night air. He asked about where she had gotten her dress.

All rather trivial matters to ask about and yet he had not cared at all to ask them of Miss Everett. Robert felt that angry envy clawing up inside of him again.

"Tell me," Mr. Tomlinson said, "are you engaged for the next dance?"

Miss Reginald was going to say no. Robert could see it in her eyes. She did not have a partner.

Before he could even begin to ask himself why he did it, he said, "Actually, she is engaged to dance with me. I hope that is all right, Mr. Tomlinson. I assure you that I shall pass her onto you next if the lady is of a mind to accept it."

"I see no problem with the arrangement," Miss Reginald said. She looked at Robert with wide eyes, her face a trifle paler than usual. She seemed to be quite frightened of dancing with him.

Perhaps she was afraid that he would scold her for her behavior all those years ago. Or that he would find something new to scold her about.

Had she been so upset by him then? Had he hurt her so much?

He had thought that she did not care but perhaps she had. He knew better than almost anyone how well Miss Reginald could smother her true emotions when she wanted to.

She never laughed or cried without giving herself permission to do so. She had hidden her great dislike for her father from nearly everyone in society, including her father himself. As far as he knew, she'd managed that until the day her father had unexpectedly died.

Why should she not then manage to hide her heartbreak from her fiancé? Of course, he had thought that he knew her well enough that he and he alone could tell what she was feeling at every moment.

That might have been his own arrogance. Why shouldn't she be able to hide herself from him in that moment?

She had been the one breaking off the engagement, after all. It was probably not right of her, at least in her mind, to show distress about it. She wouldn't have thought that she had the right to be upset while she did it.

Could she have been truly upset? Had he missed it and thought her cold-hearted?

Now Miss Reginald was looking up at him with parted lips and wide eyes, the slightest tremor in her fingertips as she took the arm he offered.

He worried that she might faint or burst into tears or do something equally uncontrollable. Not that she truly would. She would never allow herself. But she looked as though she wanted to.

"Shall we?" he asked her, keeping his voice low.

Miss Reginald nodded.

He drew her out onto the dance floor. They had used to dance with each other every ball if they could help it. It was one of the few times they could be together without being under the watchful eye of an escort.

Normally he would visit her at the Weston residence, as Mrs. Weston had been reminiscing. He had wondered at that and thought at the time that it was only that Miss Reginald did not want to be in her father's house any more than she could help it. She was usually at the Weston place as often as she could be anyway, courtship or no courtship.

But could it be that she knew the whole time that her father would not approve? And she had been struggling with her courage the entire courtship?

Robert had so many questions—questions that he was not sure he had a right to ask. Certainly not in the middle of a dance where many other couples might overhear them and start to gossip.

People talking about either himself or Miss Reginald was the last thing that either of them needed.

Robert was unsure how to start the conversation. Miss Reginald seemed to be waiting for him to do it. In fact, she seemed surprised that he had asked her to dance at all.

"I saw you earlier today," he blurted out. "You were out with Miss Weston and seemed to be studying the houses quite intently."

"Do not tell anyone," Miss Reginald asked, "but I am thinking of taking up a little residence here. Nothing much, you understand."

"Have you grown to like Bath so much in the short time that you have been here? I thought that you only arrived yesterday morning."

"That I did."

"And yet it has already worked its charms on you."

"It had its charms for me before I even arrived," Miss Reginald said.

Robert drew in a breath. "I do not like the idea of you finding a residence here. It suggests to me that you are planning for a future that you do not deserve."

"Do you expect that any other sort of future awaits me?" Miss Reginald replied. "A woman must be practical, you know."

"And you have always been practical." He could not completely keep the bitterness out of his voice.

Asking him to be practical was one of the things that Miss Reginald had said to him when she had broken off the engagement.

Miss Reginald appeared to be in great distress upon hearing him say such a thing. "I see that you continue to lick your wounds over what was said between us.

"Captain, I hope that you will believe me when I say that I have always regretted the words that I said to you, even as I said them. I never wanted to hurt you."

"How could you not expect to hurt me?" Robert asked. "I was—I possessed the deepest of feelings for you. Surely you were not unaware of that at the time. My behavior could not have been more obvious than if I had taken out an advertisement in the paper."

"And was my own behavior so mysterious to you? Were my feelings not also plain? Or did you expect that the letters I had so tenderly written were all for my own amusement?" Miss Reginald replied. "It was not to hurt you that I told you we must end things. Surely you know that."

"And yet, hurt me it did. You had to know that it must, no matter how kind your intentions or how well you tried to phrase the rejection. I had pinned my dearest hopes and dreams to you."

"And I had pinned mine to you. You were the brightest star in my life. You know how unhappy I was. My brother was often away. I had no one but you and Miss Weston. And I certainly never felt for her the way that I felt about you."

"I am glad to know that I do not have competition from Miss Weston then. I fear I should lose that one."

Miss Reginald bit her lip, trying to hide her smile. Robert could not prevent the thrill that shot through him at knowing that he had made her genuinely smile once more.

"You are exactly the same," she admitted. "Well, not exactly, of course. Time has changed us all. But you are in so many ways still the same man that I knew."

"You must find it quite dull," Robert said. "Everyone expects an educated man because of my new wealth, or a great war hero with marvelous stories because of my profession. Yet, I am the same, simple man as I always was."

"I think it is wonderful," Miss Reginald admitted. Her blue eyes were locked onto him. It was a testament to her skill as a dancer that she was able to continue to move without missing a step, despite clearly not paying attention to a single thing she was doing. Her eyes were fixed on him.

"This world is constantly changing around me. And it feels as though I am failing to change with it. And that it is not a good thing. But then I see you and your constant nature and I am encouraged by it. Refreshed by it. Dare I even say, comforted by it."

Robert stared at her as they circled around one another. "I find that you are unchanged as well. I had thought that you would be many different things, things that I did not know. Yet here you are. And here we are. The same as we were. Or mostly the same."

"The important things are the same," Miss Reginald said. She said it so quietly that Robert had to strain to hear her.

"Such as your feeling towards poetry?" he asked her.

He could hardly dare to think that she meant what he thought that she meant. Would she risk herself like that to tell him so? To let him know that her feelings towards him were also unchanged?

Was this all just a flight of fancy? Was he reading too much into perfectly innocent phrases and looks?

How he wished he could take her by the shoulders and shake her and simply ask her. Do you still love me? Have you always still loved me? I fear that I have always loved you and always will. Do you know what you still do to me? How you throw me into melancholy and despair?

The only way he could directly ask her would be, of course, to either write her a letter or to ask her in private. He could not risk asking her in a ballroom where anyone might hear.

But he could not write her or see her privately without people talking. Or without showing too much of his hand. If he was wrong...

It was a predicament, to be certain.

"Such as my feelings towards poetry," Miss Reginald acknowledged. "And my feelings towards my old acquaintances."

She looked up at him, her blue eyes full of earnestness. It was as if she was silently begging him to understand what she was saying.

He stared down at her. Could it be? She was saying, wasn't she, that her feelings towards him were unchanged? That she loved him now as she loved him then?

All thoughts of Miss Everett or of any other woman were flown completely out of his head. He could not recall the face or name of any other lady. Only Miss Reginald.

He was still in love with her. He had always been in love with her. He might continue to be in love with her until the day he died. Even if she rejected him another time.

He could see it now—being married to another woman but loving Miss Reginald. How unfair to every party involved!

"I wonder, though," Miss Reginald went on. She sounded a little as though she were stuck in a snowstorm and forcing herself to move forward despite the difficulty and the possible pain. "I wonder if my former acquaintances still think of me in the same manner.

"I have made mistakes with them, you know. Or rather, circumstances did not allow me to make the choices that I wanted to in regards to them.

"Rather sad, do you not think?"

"Very," he replied.

Miss Reginald's mouth turned up the slightest bit at the corner before she grew sober again. "Well, I had lost all hope of amending those mistakes. As I'm sure most of us would have.

"But I was reminded tonight that of course we are to lose all of the chances that we do not take. And I have nothing to lose at this juncture. You saw what my business was about this morning.

"When that is what is facing me, what have I to lose by being plain with someone? Someone who I still trust, someone who I know even if they no longer care for me, they will not humiliate me or speak anything of what I might have dared to make known to them during a dance."

Robert hardly dared to breathe. It felt as though his lungs had seized up.

"I have come to realize," Miss Reginald went on, "that it is my own fault that I am still not wed. For what man wishes to love a woman when he knows that she is in love with someone else?

"Of course he may not know with whom she is in love. But we can tell, can't we, when someone's affections are already taken and we are receiving merely the pale imitation of it?

"It seems that I have dug my own grave, so to speak. I think that is rather ironic, do you not agree?

"In any case. I find it helpful to laugh at myself over it. You might not. But you are still as you have always been to me. You have never left the occupation that you held previously, at least in my heart.

"I know you must be horrified at me. To be so bold. But when and where else am I to say it? And so there is only left for me to ask if you revile me as I have feared all this time that you would. That you would scorn me. You know I was almost trembling with fear of it last night?

"You would have every right to treat me in such a fashion, you know. But there it is. And unfortunately I suppose that you are going to inform me that men are quickly recovered from such passions. That it is the realm of the romantic and silly woman only to remain constant in the face of such abject despair and lack of reciprocation.

"We are silly at times, I know. But I hope in this I have not been so. It was not that I was holding out hope. At least, not consciously. I struggled, truly I did, to put such thoughts from my mind. To banish them thoroughly.

"But I suppose that I must resign myself to the ridiculous workings of my heart. As we all must in time. After all, if the heart was something logical then we would all be able to fix the many incidences of history that have led to ruin. Romeo and Juliet would still be alive, to name but one example."

Robert chuckled. "A fine example indeed. I hope that I am not to meet that sort of fate and that neither will you."

Miss Reginald looked at him with eyes that were filled with agony and hope in equal measure.

He could not help but respect her for her choice. She was right in that she had little to lose. What was the risk in putting herself out there to a man that she cared for? What was the worst that could happen?

She was already going to be gossiped about for not marrying yet. She was already looking into staying at Bath permanently as spinsters did. She had no other prospects who could be offended by her statement should they hear of it.

If there was ever a time to throw caution to the wind and exhibit some bravery, this was it.

Robert was unsure of how to respond. Part of him wanted to flee. How could he be certain that risking his heart for her yet again would be worth it?

But another part of him wanted to confirm all that she had said. He wanted to agree with her and admit that yes, he had always felt as she did. She had never truly left his heart. He would take her in his arms in a moment's notice.

There was so much to consider. So much to gain and so much to lose depending upon what he said next. Could he dare himself to trust in her this time after she had failed him so heartily the last time?

He was not sure that his own heart would survive yet another disappointment from her.

And yet, she was looking at him as though he alone held the key to her happiness. To even, indeed, her life.

He was unsure, still, of what to say.

He could tell her how he felt, perhaps, as though he was torn in two. He could admit that he was unsure of her and whether he could trust her. That he still cared for her and that he wanted to trust her. But he was not sure of her welcome and whether the heart he placed in her hands would stay there this time.

Perhaps he could tell her that there was at least some hope? That she would have to prove to him that she would remain true to him this time?

Before he could say anything, however, he dimly—as if from another room—heard the music drawing to a close. The dance was ending.

Almost as though he had materialized there, Mr. Tomlinson was at Miss Reginald's elbow.

"I believe that means it is my turn to take the lady?" he said, smiling jovially.

It was clear that the man had no idea what was passing between Robert and Miss Reginald, the pleading, raw look that she was giving him with her eyes alone.

He wanted to snarl at Mr. Tomlinson to go away and while he was at it to never come near Miss Reginald again. But Robert could not afford to be a possessive man with her. He did not have the right and it certainly would not become him. He had seen men be possessive of their women and it was not a pleasant sight to endure.

"Miss Reginald." He bowed. "I suppose that we will have to continue our discussion at some other point."

He told himself that he was not a coward for not answering her at once. Even if it was only to tell her that he needed time to think.

Could he truly risk it all again? She was asking him to, as surely as she was risking herself.

But he found himself admiring her bravery in speaking up and saying something. It was courageous of her. Despite having little to lose there was always the pain of rejection should she be wrong about him. That, he knew well, was a painful experience.

He had been angry with her for her lack of conviction. Surely this showed a bit of that, did it not? Was this not exhibiting the behavior that he told her she needed to showcase more of when they had their last meeting—and their last argument?

And there was no reason for her to say no to him now, was there? Her father was dead.

Ah, but there was her brother.

Robert watched as Mr. Tomlinson danced with Miss Reginald yet again. Twice in one night. It showed his favoritism to her.

It seemed that Robert had competition. Although not truly. Miss Reginald had said that her feelings for him were unchanged. That must mean that he was ahead of Mr. Tomlinson. A great deal ahead, in fact.

And Miss Reginald did not seem to be actively encouraging him in his idea of courtship. She was being nice enough to him. Of course she was.

But he saw no tender looks. No great smiles. Nothing that would encourage him unduly if he were in Mr. Tomlinson's place and trying to win a lady.

Then again, Miss Reginald was a withdrawn woman. The other man might not be noticing the difference between her simply quiet nature and her genuine lack of interest.

Robert had seen her in the throes of great emotion. He knew how she behaved when she was inclined to be in love with someone and when she was not. But Mr. Tomlinson did not know this and therefore might have some cause to hope and continue his pursuit.

Did Robert want to put a stop to that? Did he want to attempt this courtship again?

He thought, then, of her brother.

He remembered the now-duke of Foreshire, then merely Edward Reginald, as a good man. They had enjoyed one another's company when they ran into one another at dinners and balls.

But Robert still did not have a title. And he knew that Edward was, in more ways than he wanted to admit, his father's son.

Would Edward approve of the match? Or would he provide Miss Reginald with the same ultimatum that her father had?

Robert could quite easily see it. Edward had to be practical, after all. He had to think about alliances and how he might provide both for himself and for his sister.

Most members of the nobility still married strategically. Of course it was not so nearly as obvious as it was back in the days of, say, Richard the Lionheart. Nobles had constantly been jockeying for power then. Infighting between them was still common.

Now, of course, things were more civilized. But marriages among the nobility were not simply out of love. They were to secure fortunes. To protect land. To gain seats in Parliament or gain an ally in political matters.

Edward would want to use his sister for that, surely. Especially as a young duke still new at this game. His father's death was sudden. It had to have thrown things into upheaval not just for his family but for all the nobility.

Robert did not think that Miss Reginald was aware. How could she be? She would not be so bold with him if she knew that she was probably going to need to marry someone else.

Unless she did know and was throwing in her bid so boldly now so that they might marry before her brother could enact whatever plans he had for her.

But that would mean she would be going against her brother's wishes, which Robert could not see her doing. Miss Reginald had obeyed her father because she had no other choice.

But she obeyed her brother because she loved him.

Miss Reginald and her brother had always been close. They had been allies united quietly against their father. Supporting one another in whatever ways they could.

She had often spoken of her brother in her letters to Robert and always with great fondness.

Robert had admired Edward, and he had enjoyed their time spent together, little as it was. And he had loved him for the sake of his sister and her love for her brother. Miss Reginald loved her brother and so therefore Robert loved him.

But years could change a man, as could responsibility. Sudden responsibility at that. And could he really say that he knew Edward well enough to state with absolute certainty that the man would allow his sister to marry someone beneath her station?

He was not so beneath her station as he had once been. He had come up in the world. But for her to marry someone without a title who was also the man that her father had once forbidden her to marry...

There might even be something in the will of her father preventing her from marrying anyone who did not have a title. Robert would not have put it past the old tyrant.

Well, it was a sad fact, but it was a true one: Miss Reginald would need permission from her brother.

And Robert did not think that Edward would grant it.

CHAPTER 36

GEORGIANA HAD NEVER WISHED, so fervently, for a dance to end.

Captain Trentworth had been about to give her his answer. She could sense it. How she had bared her soul before him! How painfully obvious she had been!

There were ladies much younger and more ridiculous than she who had not behaved in such a way. Miss Perry had not even been so plain.

But how else was she to know? How else was she to end the torment in which she had been placed?

And he had seen it in her eyes. She could not disguise it. Not when she was struggling so hard not to simply tell him in plain speech that she loved him still. That when he had walked through the door last night she had nearly fainted with the power of all that she still felt for him.

Was she making a fool of herself? Was she setting herself up to be hurt yet again? Would he reject her? Laugh at her for continuing to have such feelings for him, for thinking that she ever had a chance?

She hung onto hope that she was not sure she deserved. He had not looked angrily or coldly at her. If anything he had looked surprised. Taken aback. Shocked, even. As though he was not sure what to think.

Well, she could not truly blame him for being so surprised. She had thought she was quite obvious in her continuing affections but did not every person? And after rejecting him summarily previously, how could she expect him to believe her so easily this time? How could he possibly have any hope?

But she had told him now. The secret was out.

He must at the very least let her down gently if that was the case. She knew that he would. He was not a vengeful man. At least, the Captain Trentworth that she had known once had not been vengeful.

Georgiana could hardly think through her dance with Mr. Tomlinson. When she did, it was with a sort of vague distress.

He had asked her to dance a second time. That was a firm statement of intent, a statement that he liked her.

When the ball was a small one and there were not many people to be had, then of course men and women ended up dancing together more than once. This was especially true if there were more women than men, as there usually were.

But in a crowded and public ballroom such as this, Mr. Tomlinson had no small number of options before him. He could select any number of ladies to be his partner. He didn't have to repeat a single one of them if he did not wish to.

And yet, with only a couple of dances in between, he had chosen to dance with her twice.

He was most certainly trying to let her know that he would begin courting her.

Georgiana could not tell him that her heart belonged to another. After all, if Captain Trentworth rejected her offer then she must marry someone to preserve herself. Mr. Tomlinson was as good of a man as any.

And he was continuing to ask after her rather nicely. He wasn't being the completely charming man that she had first been wary of. He seemed genuinely interested in her thoughts.

She could do worse, couldn't she?

But first she had to know what Captain Trentworth would say.

She could not turn away Mr. Tomlinson firmly. Of course, she could not turn him away firmly even if she already had her answer from Captain Trentworth. There was propriety and manners to be thought about. She could not embarrass Mr. Tomlinson.

But if she had her answer, she would then know whether to tell the servants tomorrow if they ought to say that she was out of the house when Mr. Tomlinson called. She would firmly tell Julia not to sit them next to or across one another at dinner.

Then again, if Captain Trentworth's answer was no, then she would have to do the opposite. She would be sure to stay at home so that Mr. Tomlinson might call. She would ask Julia to sit them together in some way at dinner.

It was the bargain that she made with herself. She was to blame for her impending spinsterhood, was she not? Therefore, she was going to give herself one last chance. Go all in and risk it and see if perhaps she might win it all.

But if Captain Trentworth turned her down, then that was it. She must somehow be wholehearted in accepting any man, Mr. Tomlinson or otherwise, who courted her.

As the dance ended, she took a deep breath and turned to find Captain Trentworth.

He was standing in the back, against the wall, and speaking with Miss Everett once again.

Jealousy stabbed at her. Oh, please, do not let her be too late. Do not let Miss Everett already be successful in taking the captain away from her.

Georgiana approached them politely, curtsying. "Miss Everett, I have scarcely seen you all night. How are you liking the ball?"

"It is enchanting, as all balls can be," Miss Everett replied. "And a wonderful opportunity for observing people, as well. I find people quite fascinating to watch, personally. And you, Miss Reginald? I see you have had a livelier time of it than I think you suspected."

"It has been a surprising evening in many ways," Georgiana replied.

"I will leave you two, now that I am finished keeping our captain company," Miss Everett said. "I promised a dance to Mr. Norwich and I must not delay any longer in paying my debt."

She curtsied to them both and went off.

"That girl is shrewder, I think, than we have previously given her credit for being," Captain Trentworth observed. "I do not think she has a dance with Mr. Norwich."

"I must thank her in some way, then," Georgiana confessed. "For if I had to go another moment without knowing your thoughts I would completely lose my composure."

Captain Trentworth sighed. "Miss Reginald. I have been made aware of the error of my ways in being so harsh with you all those years ago.

"But in learning that I was not right to ask you to go against your father, how can I ask you to go against your brother?"

"What?" Georgiana blinked rapidly, as if trying to reconcile what she saw with what she was hearing. "What on earth do you mean? I do not understand how I would be going against my brother."

"I still am without a title," Captain Trentworth replied. "And at this point I never shall have one. The daughter of a duke, the sister of one, has some expectations attached to her, does she not?

"I am certain that if I were to ask, your brother would much prefer that you marry Mr. Norwich, who is set to inherit a title. And a rather good title, at that.

"I would not ask you to betray your family once again. I understand now—or rather I have been made to understand—what a difficult and indeed impossible choice it is for a woman to make.

"You must forgive me, then, if I am hesitant to speak aloud the things that still dwell in my heart and that try to compel me to answer your words in kind."

Georgiana stared at him. Anger, hot and quick, bubbled up inside of her. "Are you suggesting, Captain, that my brother will be like my father? That he will be the same sort of hard and unyielding man that my father was?"

"I have no reason to believe otherwise."

"Were your times together hunting and at balls not enough for you?"

"Your brother is a duke now. That changes things. He will want to use you to set up an alliance or advantageous partnership of some kind."

"If you think that, then you do not know and never have known my brother. He would never use me in such a way. He is the kindest of men and has always respected me."

"Are you certain that you are not deluding yourself? We are apt to think more highly of the people we love than perhaps they deserve."

"Yes, that is true," Georgiana said. She knew there was fury in her tone, but she could not keep it out. She would never stand for anyone to think or say such things of her brother. Not even the man that she loved. "It seems that I have thought more highly of you than you have deserved."

"You cannot blame me for thinking that your brother would not approve." Captain Trentworth seemed almost astonished at her daring and her words.

To tell the truth, Georgiana was a little astonished at herself.

"I can, and I shall," Georgiana replied, drawing herself up. "When I had no friends, no suitors, and no one, I had my brother. Our mother and father are gone and it is only the two of us. We have been all that the other one has.

"And he has always loved and supported me. Even as the rumors started. When other men would grow impatient with their sisters and tell them to marry the next man who came along, demand that they throw themselves at someone, or even arrange it behind their sister's back... my brother has done nothing but speak to me with patience and understanding.

"Did you know that he has apologized to me? My brother, apologized! For something that was not even his fault!

"He blames himself, at least in part, as the reason why you and I did not marry."

Georgiana looked around the room to make sure that nobody was eavesdropping, but it seemed that everyone was occupied with other matters.

She kept her voice low and her posture as casual as she could so that observers might not realize that she was breaking all rules of propriety and starting a spat.

But her brother was worth starting a spat over.

"He believes that he ought to have stood up to our father and told him, demanded, that he let us marry. He felt that if he had said such a thing it would be all right.

"I had always appreciated how he kept out of that matter. It was my problem and not his. I appreciated that he respected my independence and that he let me fight my own battles.

"When he apologized to me I told him this. But he still, I think, carries some guilt for his lack of action. As though anyone, even his only son, could dissuade my father when he had made up his mind about something.

"Your words anger me and fill me with dread. For if this is how you so hastily judge my brother, how on earth would a partnership between us last?

"I am ashamed of you, to know that you have been so unkind in your judgments and so quick to jump to a conclusion. Without genuinely asking me or my brother. Without waiting to meet him and see if he would greet you with open arms as he once did.

"He would do so again. I know that he would. He cares not for who the man is. Only that the man can provide for me, and that he makes me happy.

"Do you think that I would even think of encouraging Mr. Tomlinson if my brother wanted me to marry a title? Do you not think that I would have found a way to let him know during our first dance that there was no hope?

"I do not believe in stringing on a man when there is no happy ending for him at the end of the road. It is cruel and unkind. And at my age I do not have the time for the games of flirtation or the thrill of the chase.

"I would have found a way to let him know during the first dance. He would never have asked me for a second.

"But I did not. I did not actively encourage him, no. I did not flirt with him, per se. But I did not actively discourage him either. And that ought to tell you what my brother thinks on the subject."

Captain Trentworth was staring at her in frustration and surprise. Georgiana could not even begin to understand what he was thinking.

After a moment of what appeared to be contemplation, he spoke.

"I think that you are giving yourself and your kind too much credit."

"My kind?"

"Those with titles," Captain Trentworth said. "The nobility. To some of you it matters terribly, of course. I think mainly to the men for they are the ones who hold most of the responsibility when it comes to them.

"For the men, the title is not just a title. It is land, business, tenants for whom they must care. But for the women, I do not think that you always consider how important and above everyone else you are considered.

"People who have food do not think about not having it. And people such as yourself who come from nobility do not think about what it is like to not be a member of that class.

"But I can assure you, Miss Reginald, that we without think of it a great deal. We must think of it. For you are always finding little ways to put us back into our places.

"How am I to think? Once I was rejected because of my lack of money and title. Now I have one, but not the other. And it is the latter that is infinitely more important to you all.

"How many nobles have been destitute and living off of charity only to be treated better by the rest of society than people with wealth and respectability, simply because one is called baron and the other is not?

"You cannot blame me for feeling some sort of hesitance and for assuming that the status quo would be maintained by your brother. I did know him once and he was a good man and an honorable one.

"But he was not the duke then. Having a title and responsibilities changes people. I have seen it time and again in the navy. A man is one way but once you give him a command he is a completely different person.

"I was not as respectful of our differences as I should have been, once. I was foolish in thinking that love would simply conquer all. I am wiser now. I understand the power of family and society.

"And I will not allow my heart to become wounded once more. I will not be foolish and step too quickly and without looking into a pit."

"You make it sound as though I am willfully leading you to your doom," Georgiana replied. "Is the idea of entering into a courtship or even a friendship with me again so very abhorrent to you? I had not known that such bitterness lurked in your heart."

"You call it bitterness if you like. I call it common sense."

"Well, I too possess some common sense," Georgiana replied.

"And it is telling me now what a fool I was for waiting for you, whether I did it consciously or not.

"I felt for you all of this time. Clearly, I was a silly girl who had read far too many love poems. Lord Byron would be proud of me, I can presume, but I am not proud of myself.

"You must forgive me for troubling you in such a manner, Captain Trentworth. You will have to accept my excuse that it was merely the nostalgia for my youth that led me to behave in such a bold manner.

"I hope that you will not judge me too harshly for speaking to you as I did during our dance. You must dismiss all of it. It was clearly folly."

Captain Trentworth looked, again, as though someone had come out of nowhere and struck him across the face. He looked as though he had no idea what to say in the slightest.

Well, good. At least she had that victory to warm her when she was feeling cold and alone and helpless tonight.

"If you will excuse me," she said, curtsying. "I must take my leave."

He didn't even try to stop her. She didn't quite think that he would. A part of her hoped, just a little, that he would do so. That he would tell her to stay and apologize for the things that he had said.

But there was no apology. No word to halt her. Not even a look.

Georgiana made her way quickly through the ballroom, circling around the other side so that as the dance ended, she was on the side of the men.

Miss Everett and Mr. Norwich finished their dance. Apparently she must have prevailed upon him to ask her.

Georgiana did not want to encourage Mr. Tomlinson in his flirtations. Not yet, anyway. Not tonight. Not while her heart was breaking to pieces inside of her that very moment.

Tomorrow, yes. Tomorrow she would be strong. Tomorrow she would do what she must.

Tonight she just had to get home and cry.

"Mr. Norwich," she said, feeling breathless. "I apologize greatly for how I am about to prevail upon you. But I cannot ask the three

ladies that I am with to retire while they are still enjoying themselves. Their escort is the same as mine.

"Therefore I must beg you, please, if my escort will allow it—
Mrs. Weston—would you please escort me home? I cannot stay a
moment longer, I am not at all well."

Mr. Norwich looked at her with grave concern, his gaze
wandering over her face as if looking for signs of a fever. "Of course,
Miss Reginald. You need only ask. I will find Mrs. Weston and ask if
such a thing is permissible."

"Thank you, sir." She curtsied. "It means more than I can
possibly say."

Mr. Norwich went off to find Mrs. Weston.

Georgiana went to find Julia.

She found her, thankfully, alone. Julia was refilling her wine
cup. She looked up when she heard Georgiana approach, a smile on
her face. It widened momentarily upon seeing that it was Georgiana, then fell completely as she saw her friend's expression.

"Why, my dear girl, whatever is the matter?"

Georgiana did her best to get her breathing under control.
Around her closest and dearest friend, her composure threatened to
crack completely and shatter. She must not allow it.

"I'm afraid that I am retiring for the evening," she said. "I am not
at all well. Mr. Norwich has agreed to escort me home. That way
you, Miss Perry, and Miss Everett might continue to dance as you
please.

"He is asking your mother right now if he might have permission to take me. I am certain that she will grant it. You will find me
asleep when you return and I hope that you will keep me that way.
Do not ask me why I am ill. I cannot speak of it."

Julia stared at her. "Georgiana. I have never seen you in such
distress, not since... well, not since you had to reject the captain."

"Then I am certain that you can guess the reason for my distress
now and you need not ask any more about it."

"You—but you said—"

"It was the other way around this time. It seems that our differences are, to him, impossible to reconcile. Now if you will excuse
me. I find myself quite at odds with the atmosphere of this room."

Mr. Norwich walked up to them at that moment, in a fortuitous coincidence. "Mrs. Weston has graciously given her permission for me to escort you home in my carriage. Miss Weston, good evening."

"Good evening." Julia curtsied. "Please do take care of her. She is my dearest friend in the world."

"I can promise you that I shall."

Georgiana wondered if Captain Trentworth could see that she was being escorted from the ballroom. Surely he could be under no illusions as to how much he had upset her. Surely there was no doubt in his mind as to how distressed she was.

She wondered if he would think anything of her being escorted by Mr. Norwich. Then she reminded herself that she did not care anymore.

Well, that was a lie. She did care. But she shouldn't care. Captain Trentworth had made it clear how much he truly disdained her family lineage. To think such things of her brother, and to judge Edward, without even getting to meet him even once!

He had not seen Edward in years! Yes, that might mean that Edward had changed. But that did not mean that he got to judge the man before even seeing him in person once again.

If anything, surely realizing that Edward could have changed meant that Captain Trentworth had no right to judge him and should meet him as soon as possible to understand Edward's character anew.

Mr. Norwich silently passed Georgiana his handkerchief again as they exited the ballroom. "You might as well keep it, Miss Reginald," he said, with a trace of humor. "You are getting more use out of it than I am."

"This has been a night of despair and elation and back to despair again," Georgiana admitted. "I thank you for being so selfless and kind in all of this mess."

"I think that you have gone after what you wanted and failed and are now seeking to avoid making a scene. Such dignity and courage ought to be supported, in my opinion."

They went down the steps and Mr. Norwich ordered his carriage to be summoned. Most people were still at the ball. It was the height of things. Only a couple of hours had passed since it had begun. This meant it did not take long for the carriage to be fetched and brought over.

Mr. Norwich helped her in, climbing in after. Georgiana dabbed at her eyes with the handkerchief. Oh, her father was turning over in his grave. She was starting to cry, and in front of a relative stranger. A stranger who was also a man.

All of her decorum had flown completely out the window. She could not even recall the last time that she had cried like this. Or cried at all. Father's funeral, she thought. That had been the last time.

"I take it that things did not go as you had hoped?" Mr. Norwich asked gently.

Georgiana shook her head. "Not at all how I had hoped. But perhaps how I ought to have expected them to go. I fear that I was too optimistic about my chances."

Mr. Norwich sat there gravely for a moment, then said, "Is the gentleman to whom we have been referring Captain Trentworth?"

Georgiana nearly groaned in despair. "Am I so very obvious?" If Mr. Norwich had observed it then perhaps others had as well. She could be a laughingstock tomorrow.

"It is only that after our conversation, you danced with him, and then after Mr. Tomlinson took his turn you went up to the captain again. I only noticed because I was keeping an eye on you. I thought that you might need someone to come in and provide assistance. And so it was, but I'm afraid I was engaged in dancing at the time."

"I feel awful for poor Miss Everett. First I interrupt her conversation with Captain Trentworth, and then the whole time you are dancing with her you were keeping an eye on me."

"Do not worry about Miss Everett," Mr. Norwich replied kindly. "She is young with plenty of men that she can enchant. I'm sure that she will forget about it all in a half an hour's time."

Georgiana nodded. That was true enough, she supposed. "I hope that you will not be harsh with him. I know that he is a guest at your house while he is in Bath. Do not trouble yourself over it."

"It is not my matter to trouble myself over," Mr. Norwich replied. "Unless he has impugned your honor in which case I would happily take him to task on it."

"He has angered me," Georgiana admitted. "And I think that he has thought of my family in an unfair manner. Judged us too harshly. But my honor is intact. He would never cross that line. He is a good man at heart. Just, I fear, an angry one."

"Men often fall into that trap," Mr. Norwich acknowledged. "He must be struggling to adjust to civilian life again. And he seems like the sort that would hold a grudge."

"Rest assured, I will not say anything to him one way or another about the subject. Unless, of course, he asks for my opinion. In that case I will not be able to stay silent. I think it is important that one is honest when one is asked to be."

"I could not prevail upon you to lie, nor would I ask you to. It is unfair to ask someone else to compromise their integrity to preserve my dignity. I fear that I do not have any dignity left, in any case."

Mr. Norwich appeared troubled at that. "Miss Reginald, I think that you are too harsh on yourself. I have seen many women behave with ten times the lack of decorum that you did. And we all, despite our best efforts, have our moments of extreme emotion."

Georgiana twisted the handkerchief in her hands, staring down at the fine white linen. All she could hope for was that this night would be quickly put behind her.

"I know that it probably seems awful right now," Mr. Norwich added, his voice soft. "I have experienced many such nights. Perhaps not of this exact nature, no. But we all have our moments where we are in the pits of despair.

"A good night's rest and a satisfactory breakfast usually help me to see things better. I might suggest a walk in the morning. The fresh air and sunshine will do you a world of good.

"Nothing is so bad as we first think it is. I do not think that all is lost."

"With this gentleman, it is," Georgiana replied.

Mr. Norwich looked contemplative. After a moment of silence, he said, "I suppose it might be. But you have at least one gentleman who is willing and able to step up in his stead. Mr. Tomlinson danced with you twice tonight."

"That he did."

Mr. Norwich glanced at her. "Are you not fond of him?"

"I have only known him for two evenings."

"That is fair. But it proves that you still have a chance to make a happy marriage of things with someone other than the captain."

"I appreciate your optimism, Mr. Norwich. No doubt in the morning I shall think of things that way as well. But right now I must... I must let this storm inside of me pass."

"I understand that. You are a woman of good sense."

"How so?" Georgiana felt like the opposite of sensible.

"You understand the importance of letting our emotions pass through us," Mr. Norwich replied. "Bottling them up will not help. Indeed I have found that it only makes things worse."

"I am glad to hear that you think so."

The carriage rolled to a stop in front of the Weston residence. Mr. Norwich helped her down and walked her to the door. "I hope that tomorrow things look less bleak for you, Miss Reginald."

"I hope so as well. Thank you, sir, again. Your kindness will not be forgotten."

Mr. Norwich bowed to her, she curtsied in return, and then he departed.

Georgiana let herself into the house.

After reassuring the servants that she only needed her bed turned down for the evening and perhaps a cup of tea, Georgiana went up to her room. She got into her nightclothes and got assistance with her hair.

Tea was kindly brought, and she forced herself to drink it. The taste was sour in her mouth and it was hard to swallow but she knew that she would feel better once she had something to settle her stomach.

After she made herself finish the tea, she crawled into bed.

She was tempted to write to Maria, honestly. She wanted to ask her if she had thought of things the way that Captain Trentworth did. Had Maria felt as though she would never belong because she didn't have a title?

Georgiana didn't think that Maria had felt that way. But then, she hadn't thought that Captain Trentworth had thought that way either.

She hugged her pillow tightly and let herself cry. She had thought that it was bad enough before when she had to reject him. Now she knew that this was worse.

At least then, she had known that he had wanted her. That he would have married her in a heartbeat if she—or rather her father —had allowed it.

But now she was giving him her whole heart and he did not want it. He was thinking up excuses as to why it could not happen. He was telling her that she was no longer worth the risk to him.

And from the man who had once told her to risk it all and marry him despite her father's wishes!

It struck her as a great hypocrisy.

Not that she would tell him that. She had already strayed far enough over the border of propriety. She must not go any further.

And besides, what good would chastising him further do? Would it help her cause? Would it change his mind? Would it really bring her any peace?

No, she did not think that it would accomplish any of those things. And so what would be the point?

Instead she simply cried until she fell asleep from it.

CHAPTER 37

ROBERT COULD NOT FAIL to notice Miss Reginald leaving almost as soon as their conversation had ended.

Not, he corrected himself, their conversation. Their argument, rather.

He had been blunt with her. And she, to his surprise, had been blunt in return.

He wanted to shake her and ask her how dare she think that she could ask him to risk so much? After he had already risked it all for her once and been struck down?

Surely it was fair of him to expect a bit more reassurance this time around? Surely he had a right to be angry with the way the class system had denied him, and most likely would deny him again, the woman that he loved?

He had a right to be angry. And for her to be just as angry back at him! Where was that fighting spirit all those years ago with her father? Where had it been then?

He was aware that he was stewing but he did not know how to stop himself.

He could barely remember the rest of the night. The first moment his mind became clear again was when he and Mr. Norwich departed for home.

Robert had noticed that Miss Reginald had gone home with Mr. Norwich rather than with Mr. Tomlinson. He felt an odd sort of vindication at that. Even after they had parted ways in anger, she still did not give Mr. Tomlinson any indication that he was the favored one.

"Did Miss Reginald get home safely?" Robert asked as they got into the carriage.

"She did." Mr. Norwich looked as though he wanted to say something, but ultimately decided to keep silent.

Robert wanted to ask if she had said anything about him. He did not think that she had. That would be gossiping. And while she had been upset—he had seen that clearly—Miss Reginald was not one to sob and fuss and spill her feelings out to someone she barely knew.

Her last words to him, delivered in that cold tone, still hurt. It felt like a slap in the face.

He had never heard Miss Reginald dismiss anyone in such a manner. He had honestly not thought her capable of such anger or such coldness.

A part of him was impressed with her but mostly he was angry. Angry that she would be so lacking in understanding. Angry that she thought she could just speak to him once and it would be enough. Angry that she did not appreciate why he was so frustrated.

He hated himself for still wanting her, even now.

But he would not pursue her. He was not going to risk himself like that again. And after the way that she had spoken to him? No. No, he would not do it.

"You seem rather out of sorts," Mr. Norwich noted.

"I have had an unusually trying evening," Robert replied. He did not know how to say anything more than that without turning it into a tirade.

Besides, Mr. Norwich would inherit a title himself when his father died. He could not possibly understand Robert's predicament either. In fact, he might even be offended.

Mr. Norwich said nothing more, evidently deciding that if Robert was not going to talk about it, then he was not going to press the matter. Robert was grateful for it. He did not appreciate it when people were nosy and got into his business.

When they reached Mr. Norwich's residence, Robert excused himself at once and went to bed.

He could not get to sleep easily, however. He tossed and he turned. He played Miss Reginald's words over and over in his head.

She had seemed so earnest out on the dance floor. Laying it all bare before him. For anyone to be so bold was admirable. But for a woman to do so to a man when traditionally it was supposed to be the other way around...

It was brave of her. He had to give her points for that.

But how could she think that just telling him that she still cared for him would make him run back into her arms? That it undid all of the damage?

He would simply have to refuse Miss Weston's dinner invitations for the next few weeks. He couldn't bear to cause anyone else discomfort while he and Miss Reginald were so clearly at odds.

And, selfishly, he didn't want to have to make small talk nearly every evening with someone with whom he was upset. He needed some space away from Miss Reginald.

Of course, that was what he had done last time, the traitorous part of his mind whispered. He had fled back to the navy and across the ocean.

He'd had no choice, really, he'd been signed onto the navy long before he met Miss Reginald. He could not abandon that. Even if they had gotten married he still would have gone.

That reminded him of what Mrs. Weston had said.

What if he had died out there? And Miss Reginald had been ostracized by society thanks to her father? She would have had other widows and navy wives, perhaps. But she wouldn't have had much, not truly.

He could concede that was a fair point. Nobody should ask the person that they loved to condemn themselves to be an outcast from the world that they knew. And then to risk poverty and starvation should their husband not return.

That was fair, and he should have appreciated that more at the time.

But for her to refuse to acknowledge that he had every right to be worried over her brother! That he couldn't place his faith in the estimation of a man that he had known years ago.

And she had to admit that he was right. Those of the higher class did look down upon the rest of the gentry. Oh, yes, there was much mingling among them. But to mingle and to marry were two very different things in their minds.

He would not apologize for telling her the truth about the snobbery of her class. Snobbery into which her brother might very well have bought over the last few years.

He was being cautious, as he had not once been. He was learning from his mistakes. She could not be angry with him for wanting to pull away.

How could he be asked to risk himself yet again? To put himself in front of yet another duke and ask and be rejected? It was better for both of them that he not even get his hopes up. Or her hopes, for that matter.

Robert would send a message to Miss Weston first thing in the morning to let her know that he would be unfortunately unavailable for future dinner parties. He could claim it was business or something that was running him ragged.

He did have to attend to his new estate, after all.

Miss Weston was a clever woman. She would undoubtedly see right through his excuses. But she could not call him out on them. He would be fine.

And she could find someone else to fill in the empty chair at the table. Of that, Robert had no doubt. Perhaps she could even make it a gentleman who would actually be interested in her.

If you asked Robert, Miss Weston was far too worried about the romances of other people and spent far more time on them than she should. And not nearly enough time or worry was spent on her own romances.

If she was not careful, she could end up in the same predicament that Miss Reginald was currently in.

And he was back to Miss Reginald again.

She had said that it was her own fault that she was still unwed. Could she have really meant that? Had she been loyal to him in her heart all of this time?

But if so why not tell him? Why not ask him to wait until her father died?

It was unpleasant, but he had seen other couples do so. They got engaged in secret and then waited until the objecting relative was dead. Then they had the mourning period, and the moment that was over the banns were put up in the local parish.

Had Miss Reginald proposed such an idea, he would have been all for it. He had to go out to sea in any case. Why not give her the freedom to continue to dance at balls and throw her father off the scent while Robert had to be off fulfilling his navy contract anyhow?

Yet she had led him to believe that she didn't really care about him. Or, at least, she didn't care about him as much as she cared about her father's opinion. She had told him that they could not be together.

There. Simple as that.

"I'm afraid that I must return to you the affections that you have so kindly and freely given to me."

He could remember it like it was yesterday. He had protested, demanded to know why. He had thought that he had hurt her! That he had somehow offended her. As if any of it was actually his fault.

It was nothing that he had done, she had assured him. Nothing at all.

"You have been my greatest comfort and my dearest friend," she had told him.

But if so, then why was she breaking it off? He had begged for her to tell him what he might do to keep her by his side. Begged, as though he were a dog and not a man.

He had thought it romantic at the time, of course. Why should he not think that? Books and operas and plays and poems were all full of men throwing themselves at the feet of their lovers to beg for absolution.

Not that he had gone so far as to throw himself at her feet. He had not been quite that far out of his dignity.

"My father does not give his blessing," Miss Reginald had told him. "And I cannot go against his wishes. And so we must part. Please, do not think that it is anything against your character.

"My father is a particular man, as you know. He cannot stand the thought of my marrying someone who has no fortune and no title to recommend him.

"I hate to say such a callous thing but I must be honest. I know you will appreciate that. Or, at least, you have always said that you appreciate honesty.

"I swear I did not lead you on. All that I said was true and from my heart. I hope that you will be happy with someone else. But you must understand now that we are to part ways."

That had been when he had argued with her. His pleas had turned into declarations. Disbelief had turned into anger. They had argued, and most fiercely.

He had told her that she should defy her father. She had said that she couldn't. He had asked her why not? Was her love for him not enough? Would he not provide for her as a husband should?

She had replied that it was her duty to obey her father and that Robert, as a good man, could not ask her to go against such a cardinal rule of family and society.

It had just gone round in endless circles from there.

At no point did she let on that she cared for him enough to still carry a torch for him. Indeed he had thought that he felt her affection dim for him even as they spoke. She had become calm in manner, no longer impassioned. He was losing her, he had thought.

Yet that whole time she had been missing him and wanting him? To the point where other men could pick up on her longing for someone else and would not court her?

It was ludicrous.

And yet... he had not suggested a solution either. He had not, for example, suggested a secret engagement.

Perhaps she had been waiting for him to present the idea? Perhaps she had felt that she could not outright propose such a thought, given that she was supposed to obey her father?

Perhaps she had simply wanted him to be the man, be her guardian and safe place, and provide her with a solution.

He wanted to get up and go to her house... Miss Weston's house, rather... and wake her up and demand that she explain exactly what she was thinking all of that time long ago.

If only he could know what her mind had been like, a part of him felt, he would be able to lay it all to rest.

It was all a moot point now of course. He was not going to get any answers. And he was not going to waste any more time on it. He should have laid it all to rest years ago.

Robert turned over and told himself sternly that he was going to go to sleep. No more thinking about Miss Reginald. No more imagining her eyes, wide and simultaneously sad and hopeful. No more seeking her own or holding onto his heart for her.

No matter how tempting it might be.

He was going to move on now, finally. She'd said her piece and he'd said his and what else was there to think about or talk about after that?

It took a while, but eventually he slipped into a fitful slumber.

CHAPTER 38

GEORGIANA AWOKE to find Julia sitting at her bedside.

"I brought you breakfast," she said. "Well, I brought it up the stairs, anyway. I carried it myself."

"You ought to have let the maid do that," Georgiana said, rolling over to look at the neatly piled food on the tray.

"Oh, no, I wanted to be the first person that you saw when you woke up this morning. Besides, I just asked for a tray and then piled on all that was there from breakfast. I didn't want you to have to come down if you didn't want to.

"Mother sends her regards, by the way. She wants to know if that stupid captain made a mess of things again and if you need her to put him in his place more thoroughly. As if she has the strength for it."

Georgiana sat up in bed and let Julia place the tray over her lap. "Your mother continues to be a terror even as she sleeps for half the day."

"It gives me hope that she'll get better," Julia replied honestly. "If her tongue can manage such strong words then surely her body can manage a bit of strength as well."

"The mind and the body are two very different things, you know, Julia. I've known men in great health who suffer from going soft in the head as they get older. And then there are men who have the most painful gout and all manner of ailments but could debate with Socrates."

"I know." Julia sighed and sat back against the pillows next to Georgiana. "But one can hope. I certainly haven't given it up. If I do then what else is there? It's no fun to sit around waiting for one's mother to die, is it?"

"I suppose not."

Georgiana's own mother had died quickly. It was not so unexpected. She had been in ill health off and on over the years. But it was not the slow, drawn-out, will-she-or-won't-she business that Mrs. Weston seemed to be suffering through.

It was odd, almost, the difference between the deaths of her mother and father. In a sad way. It had taken years for Georgiana to be able to properly and casually talk about her mother's death.

Her father, meanwhile, had died only a little over a year ago and already she could speak of it freely.

It made her feel like a callous person. But it was a testament to the sort of person that her mother had been compared to the sort of person that her father had been.

"I know you asked me not to ask about it," Julia said. "But I want to simply know if you're all right."

Georgiana started eating. Not because she wanted to, but because she knew that she must. As with the tea last night, the food stuck in her throat and her stomach twisted.

If she did not eat, however, Julia would notice at once and commence with nursing her. And that was the last thing that Georgiana wanted. She hated to be fussed over.

"I will be all right eventually," she said after a moment. It was all that she could promise.

But she knew that it would be true. Not that she would be all right in the sense that she would stop being in love with Captain Trentworth and she would be happy again.

But all right in the sense that she would learn how to manage it. Just as she had learned how to manage her sadness over her mother's death.

Time was all that she needed. It was remarkable, what the passage of time could do to a person. How it could help someone to adjust.

"Will you be accepting Mr. Tomlinson's courtship then?" Julia asked. "I've invited him and Mr. Norwich to dinner. I won't invite Captain Trentworth, if you don't want me to."

"You must invite him. It will raise such awkward questions if you do not."

"Your comfort, Georgiana, means more to me than any potential awkwardness."

Georgiana leaned her head on Julia's shoulder. "You are quite a wonderful friend, did you know that? I hope that you do. I really do not know what I would do without you."

Julia leaned her head on top of Georgiana's. Georgiana could feel her smile. "I suspect that you would do just fine, somehow. You are more than you give yourself credit for being."

Georgiana sat up straight again. "Mr. Norwich said something similar last night. Did you put him up to it?"

"Oh, goodness, no," Julia replied, laughing. "But I am glad to know that he thinks so highly of you. And that you are finally being told by people other than myself what a lovely lady you are."

Georgiana shook her head. "Incorrigible, as always. You know, someday, we are going to have to find you a gentleman to put you in your place."

"The right gentleman for me will know better than to do that," Julia replied. "In fact, he will delight in my schemes and incorrigibility."

"Well, goodness help us all in that case."

Julia laughed again. Georgiana continued to eat in silence for another few minutes. Julia watched her.

"You know," Georgiana said, suddenly wanting to talk about it, "I've been thinking. Was I wrong?"

"Wrong in what?"

"Wrong to turn down Captain Trentworth's proposal that I marry him despite the lack of a blessing from my father."

Julia gaped at her. "Georgiana. I know that I make light of many things and could be said to break many rules but that is a large one."

"I know."

"Your father was one of the most powerful men in England."

"I know."

"He would have barred you from society. Perhaps even from

seeing your brother. Your childhood home, certainly. You would have had to live on the salary that the navy provided."

"I know."

Julia looked at her, scrutinizing her. "Yet you are still wondering if you were wrong. To preserve yourself and to save you both."

"Both?"

"A man who persuades his wife to marry him against her father's wishes is not the sort of man that other gentlemen trust. Oh, yes, it's all very nice and romantic. Very Romeo and Juliet of them.

"But it makes other men concerned. If he would try to get a blessing, and then not receive it, and then do the thing anyway... despite the lack of a blessing... what else might he do? Who else might he double-cross?

"It makes it so they cannot trust him. Perhaps he bullies his wife, they think. Perhaps he forced her to marry him. Perhaps the father had good reasons for not approving of the match."

"I had not thought about that," Georgiana admitted. "That is why I am wondering if I did the right thing. I was thinking only of myself. I was being terribly selfish."

"It is not selfish to put one's needs before another person's wants," Julia said. "Captain Trentworth wanted to marry you. But you needed to be taken care of. You needed a steady income upon which you could rely. You needed to be a part of the society in which you had grown up. You needed your friends and family.

"He would have taken that all away from you if you had married him against your father's wishes. Whether that is what he meant to do or not, that is what would have happened.

"You would have lived a life of uncertainty. A life of frustration and loneliness. And that is not how a marriage should start. That is not what a relationship should bring you.

"Was it difficult? Yes. Was it unkind? Possibly, to him and to you. But was it necessary? Also, yes."

Georgiana sipped her tea. Julia eyed her. "Were you two going over that night? Presenting your arguments once again? Is that why you were so distressed?"

Georgiana shook her head. She had come this far. She might as well tell Julia everything.

And if she could not tell it to Julia, well, who could she tell it to then? Julia was her best friend. Her dearest friend. And she was the only one who had been there when it had all happened originally. She had witnessed nearly all of it.

Georgiana therefore told her everything about last night.

It was hard to talk about. It was still difficult for her to even think about. But she must tell someone. And she should do it before she inevitably lost her courage and kept it bottled up for years.

"I think that Mr. Norwich is a better man than I first expected," Julia admitted. "I think his advice to you was sound."

"Except that look at what it got me: a broken heart."

"Yes, but you would have gotten that had you not said anything so plainly either. Only in that case it would have been a long and drawn-out process.

"You would have been trapped there wondering about his relationship with Miss Perry, or Miss Everett, or any other woman with whom he danced and conversed.

"You would have done your best to convince yourself that it was all in your imagination. That you were being paranoid. But then you would have convinced yourself in the other direction: that you were right and all hope was lost.

"It would have been terribly drawn-out and awful for you. Not to mention quite dramatic. You would have been stuck in the middle and it wouldn't have been fair. Not to you.

"And not to Captain Trentworth either, come to think of it. He deserved to know how you felt and to have a chance to respond to it properly."

"He responded to it, all right," Georgiana said sadly. "He made his feelings on the matter quite clear."

Julia sighed and wrapped her arm around Georgiana's shoulders, giving her a squeeze. "This isn't the end of the world, my dear. Although I'm sure that it feels like it."

"If I were younger that might be one thing," Georgiana admitted. "And I do not even mean in the sense of being too old for marriage.

"I mean that, I have been in love with the same man for years. Even when there was no hope. Not a letter, not a word about him or from him.

"Surely if I was capable of loving someone else it would have happened by now? If I was younger and this was happening I might have hope of that. But it seems to me now to be an impossible hope.

"I feel rather stupid for asking this, but it really does not strike me as fair. Why should God grant me these feelings for Captain Trentworth if I should gain nothing from them? What is it supposed to all mean?"

"My dear, you know that when you start to get philosophical you are out of my depth." Julia's tone was teasing but loving. "I'm afraid that I do not have an answer for you."

"What do you think that I should do?"

"Well, I think that you ought to think on a smaller scale, for one. No more raving at God. Instead, have your breakfast. Finish your breakfast. Then go on a walk.

"Perhaps you might take Mother to one of the bathing pools? She would love the company and she will cheer you up immensely with her observations about everyone around her."

"I can sense a scandal already." Georgiana smiled at her.

"Just keep everything in perspective. Think about the little things. The big things will work themselves out in time. But I think that what you need right now is a bit of relaxation, perhaps some pampering."

"And what about dinner?"

"Do not worry about any of that," Julia assured her. "I promise you, I shall take care of everything. What else are your dearest friends for, if not to help you when you are feeling down?"

"I hope that if our predicaments are ever reversed, you will come straight to me and allow me to help you in return," Georgiana said.

She doubted that bright, vivacious Julia would ever have reason to be in such a state. But if she were, Georgiana would do whatever was in her power to set things right and to help Julia feel better. She wanted Julia to know that.

Julia hugged her. "Of course. I know that I can always count on you. If I am ever in such a state as you are in, you know that you will be the first person I shall go to.

"Although I must say, and I mean no offense by it, I hope that I am not ever in your state."

"Perhaps if you actually did something about the business of getting married, you might be," Georgiana replied.

"Ah, her wit has returned! She is beginning to make a full recovery. This doctor prescribes fresh air, bathing, and the stimulating conversation of my mother."

Julia pecked Georgiana on the cheek and then left the room. "I shall leave you to it! See you later, my dear, and focus only on the little things!"

Georgiana looked down at her plate. She was not sure if she would be able to keep Captain Trentworth entirely out of her thoughts. But it was something, to focus on the small things.

Only thinking about the present moment and focusing on the things that she could control. That sounded like good advice.

Her questions about what to do regarding Captain Trentworth and Mr. Tomlinson could all wait until later. Those problems weren't going to go away the moment she stopped thinking about them.

But coming back to them later with a fresh mind was a good idea.

Georgiana settled back against the pillows. She could manage this. She would have to.

CHAPTER 39

ROBERT WAS JUST FINISHING READING the paper when the servant entered.

"There is a Miss Weston to see you, sir," he said. "Shall I show her in or tell her that you are not at home?"

If he told the man to inform Miss Weston that he was not at home, she would know that he was and that he was only lying to avoid seeing her.

Robert did not want to have to deal with the sort of storm that would kick up. Besides, he saw no reason why he shouldn't see her. It would mean that he could decline all future dinner invitations in person rather than by post.

"Show her in."

Miss Weston entered in such a state that Robert jumped up at once in concern. "Whatever is the matter?"

"Oh, you are quite lucky, Captain, that there are some bounds of propriety to which I must adhere!" Miss Weston hissed. "I cannot believe you. And to think that I had placed my hat in your ring!"

"What on earth are you on about? Do you need some water or tea?"

Miss Weston looked like the personification of a summer storm. Her eyes were blazing and her cheeks had spots of color on them from her rage.

Robert could suddenly and quite clearly understand why the Furies and Valkyries and so on of legend were all women.

"What I need, Captain Trentworth," Miss Weston snapped, "is a proper apology from you to Miss Reginald. Preferably in writing. And with a great deal of poetic groveling. But I'm not terribly picky."

"I see that you have probably heard some of what transpired last night."

Robert was under no illusions that Miss Reginald had sent Miss Weston here. That was not Miss Reginald's way. She must have been upset and told Miss Weston the whole thing.

And now Miss Weston had taken it upon herself to start upon the war path.

He was not surprised.

"Some?" Miss Weston's voice rose slightly in pitch. "You, sir, treated her with the most bitter and unfair judgment! You are a thoughtless man, yes, a cruel and thoughtless man.

"You with your talk of principle. I remember the things that you said to her that day. You were in my house for that final conversation if you will recall.

"I am not prone to listening at doors but it was difficult not to hear! And Georgiana told me of the entire thing afterwards—begging me not to be angry with you all the while.

"She is far too forgiving. I understood your manner once but I cannot understand it now, nor will I allow it!"

Robert's blood boiled. "You dare speak to me in such a way? You, a flighty young girl—"

"Young I may be, and a woman I may be," Miss Weston shot back. "But flighty I am not. Nor am I a fool. Not in this. In this you are the fool, the greatest of fools, to let that woman slip through your fingers when she gave herself to you.

"No, more than that! You did not merely let her slip away. You rejected her! After she took such a risk and poured her heart out to you!"

"Miss Weston. You are in a state. And you are disturbing the household. Will you please—"

"Be quiet? Go away? No. No I shall not." Miss Weston took a few steps towards him. "Is this not what you have always said that you value, Captain Trentworth? A woman of principle who stands up for her beliefs?

"Well, it is my belief that you are a proper idiot and an unkind man. To judge her brother and Miss Reginald in such a manner, while in the same breath condemning their class for judging people like you sight unseen simply because you do not have a title!

"You are a hypocrite, sir. A hypocrite. And you are so blind that you cannot even see how much of one that you are!

"The last time you and Miss Reginald exchanged words was when she ended your engagement. You told her that you objected to her lack of principles.

"You told her that you hated how she bowed to her father instead of standing up for what she wanted and what would make her happy. That she agreed with her father instead of defending you.

"Is that not what she did last night? You attacked her brother. And you knew that she loved you and wanted your approval. But did she give in to you? Did she bow her head and say you are right to judge my brother for the sins of his father?

"No. She stood up for the man that she cares for. The man who has been the best of brothers to her. She defended him, even though she knew that it would cost her the man with whom she was in love.

"You ought to applaud her! You ought to thank her for exhibiting that which you so proclaim you care about! And instead you all but spat on her for it!

"And to think that you would let a small thing as her brother possibly, maybe, perhaps, objecting to your union—that you would let that alone stop you!

"Oh, sir, no. Where is the daring man with whom my best friend fell in love? The man that wanted her to risk it all for love? Were you willing to risk it all last night? Were you going to risk Lord Reginald's disapproval? Were you going to take the chance that he might actually, shockingly, approve?"

Robert was agog. Literally. His jaw had dropped open. Never in his life had any woman dared to speak to him in such a manner. Nor, indeed, had many men even dared.

But here was Miss Weston, standing like a pillar of righteous justice. And speaking to him quite outside the bounds of propriety.

Speaking to him as if she were his mother, in fact, and he had just broken a prize vase.

Miss Weston was not quite finished yet, however.

"Did you know anything about the story of how Lord Reginald met and came to propose to his intended bride?" she asked.

"I know only that they both took quite a long time to realize that their affections were returned," Robert managed.

"She has no title," Miss Weston informed him. "She was raised in the Caribbean, in fact. On a plantation. Her mother died while she was young. She grew up quite wild, in fact.

"Her father and the late Lord Reginald were close friends growing up, and so when the time came, Miss Worthing—for that is her name. Miss Worthing. Her father sent her to the new Lord Reginald and Miss Reginald so that they might educate her and be her escorts for the London season.

"She was horribly bullied, the poor thing. She was the target of several women. I think out of envy over Lord Reginald. A single duke, you know. But in any case, she was always saying or doing the wrong thing.

"She had no title. She was not particularly rich. In fact, she had to marry or at least obtain a proposal by the end of the season or she should get nothing. Her father was dying and could leave her with very little.

"And did this wild girl get rejected by the duke? No. He fell in love with her. He proposed to her. He is going to marry her.

"You decided that he was going to be like his father. I suppose that is a sound assumption to make when merely hearing about someone. But you did not even take the chance to meet him again. You did not say, I will run the risk of him being like his father, because I want to be with you no matter what the circumstances or troubles that might come our way.

"Is that not what is promised when one gets married? Or have I been hearing it wrong in churches all of these years? The words are in sickness and in health, and for better or for worse.

"You assumed that it would be for worse, and you ran. Like the coward that you are."

Robert looked over Miss Weston's shoulder to see Mr. Norwich standing there, eyebrows raised in surprise and—it looked like he was actually impressed. As though he might even be struggling to smother a smile.

Of course Mr. Norwich would be the one to find this all amusing. He was not the one who was being yelled at.

"Well?" Miss Weston demanded. "Have you nothing to say in your own defense?"

"I might, if you would allow me to get in a word edgewise," Robert replied, a tad sardonically.

Miss Weston was unimpressed with his tone and merely arched an eyebrow. "There is nothing that you can say in your defense. What you can say is, 'I am terribly sorry, Miss Reginald' and 'You must try and forgive me for my horrible and inconceivable behavior, Miss Reginald'."

Robert gestured at her, looking over her shoulder at Mr. Norwich. "Are you not going to kick this woman out of your house for her improper behavior?"

"I might, if I did not find it so amusing," Mr. Norwich replied.

Miss Weston bestowed a grateful smile upon Mr. Norwich, and then turned back to Robert. "That woman has been in love with you all of these years.

"She has never spoken of it. I think that she has felt ashamed that she could not be sensible and move on like so many other girls. Or that she could not simply marry for security.

"But she has been faithful to you in her heart. As constant and true as if you were actually engaged or married to one another.

"And when she takes the greatest of risks and tells you about this... When she tells you how she feels and is the exact sort of courageous woman that you claim to want—you tell her that she is not worth it? You insult her brother? You tell her that she and all people like her are pretentious?

"I know that you have suffered. I understand that. I am sure that you have languished in your love for her just as she has languished in her love for you.

"But you do not get a monopoly on suffering! You are not the only one who has had to make sacrifices in your life. You are not the only one who feels the pains of a broken heart.

"I will not stand for your hypocrisy and your selfishness. I let it go by before but now I see I should have stopped you from getting on your boat and given you a piece of my mind long ago.

"Now, you will apologize to Miss Reginald. I do not care how or when but you shall do it and you shall do it soon. If you do not, I will make certain that you are barred from every party and every ball and every dinner.

"I may not be a duchess or have a title to my name. But I am good with people. I am popular. People listen to me. You might call it flighty but I will use it and I will get you back to where you were all those years ago, money or no money!"

Miss Weston was fairly shaking with rage. Robert had no doubt in his mind that she would do it, too. He knew her mother and he knew her father. Miss Weston was born from them both.

If anyone had the ability and the spirit to do such a thing for the sake of her friend, it was Miss Julia Weston.

Mr. Norwich cleared his throat. "Miss Weston, I think some tea might be in order for you. You must have worked yourself up to quite a thirst. Would you mind accompanying me to the drawing room? I think you will appreciate the... calming color of the wallpaper."

Miss Weston looked for a moment as though she might argue. But then she allowed herself to be led out of the room.

Robert was left alone.

Alone... to think.

He did not appreciate Miss Weston's behavior. Not in the slightest. But he also did not dare risk invoking her wrath.

He was now in a position of respectability, with his career and his money. Miss Weston vowed to take that all away from him. Leave him barred from society as he had been when he'd been just a poor sailor.

No. He could not allow that to happen. He would not let one vengeful woman destroy all that he had built.

That meant he would have to apologize.

A letter. That ought to do it. He could not bear to see Miss Reginald in person. Who knew what he might say or how he might feel.

He would write to her and apologize while Miss Weston was

being given tea with Mr. Norwich. He would hand it over to Miss Weston as she left, and then he too would leave. He would quit Bath altogether.

Not that he was under any illusions that even if he apologized, Miss Weston would let him come to her dinners anymore. But there was too great a chance that he would run into Miss Reginald elsewhere.

He could not stand that. He had to get her out of his mind. He had to get away from her. Then he would meet some other charming girl and marry her.

That way if he did run across Miss Reginald again and he was tempted, his marriage would stop him. He would be forced to stay away from her and to remain true to his wife.

There. That would solve everything, would it not? He would not trouble or harm Miss Reginald again. At least, according to Miss Weston's standards. And she would not be able to trouble him again. Or if she did, it would be only in his heart and they would never have to speak of it. He could pretend that it did not exist.

A satisfactory solution, if you asked him, all around.

Robert quickly procured a pen and paper and began to write.

He was not going to apologize for all of it. He was not so hypocritical or cowardly as Miss Weston claimed. How dare she even suggest such a thing?

He did, however, apologize for not taking Miss Reginald's risk into consideration and for treating her revelation of her feelings with less decorum and gentility than they deserved.

He also apologized for making assumptions about her brother.

Not that he truly thought that he was in the wrong about that. But he knew that if he did not include it, neither Miss Weston nor Miss Reginald would truly forgive him, and he would be right back at square one.

He wrote quickly, only stopping to check that he was not saying anything that would land him in even more hot water with Miss Weston.

He had no idea what was being said over tea but he could imagine that if anyone was capable of calming down someone as worked up as Miss Weston had gotten, it was going to be Mr. Norwich.

When he finished he quickly folded up the letter, wrote Miss Reginald on the front, and then retired to the drawing room.

Miss Weston was just finishing up her tea, it seemed, and she was rising to go.

"Thank you for being such a gracious host," she told Mr. Norwich. "I apologize that you had to hear such a personal conversation."

"No need to apologize, Miss Weston," Mr. Norwich replied. "It was the most entertainment I have gotten in weeks. I admire your spirit."

Robert sent him a look of betrayal that Mr. Norwich ignored.

Miss Weston turned, saw Robert standing there, and immediately adopted a rather impressive look of disdain. "Please, don't bother groveling, I'm not the one that you should be doing it to."

"I was only hoping that you might give this to Miss Reginald upon your return to the house," Robert told her, handing the letter over.

Miss Weston took it and curtsied, then exited, saying nothing more to him.

Once the front door had closed, Mr. Norwich said, "I should hate to be the one in her crossfire. You made quite the enemy, Captain."

"I wasn't even aware that was what I was apparently doing last night," Robert replied. "I was only speaking my mind. I don't think that a man can be faulted for that."

Mr. Norwich rang for the tea service to be cleaned up. "I think you ought to dwell on the whole thing a little longer," he said. "You seem like the sort of man who takes time to contemplate things."

Robert frowned. "Why do I sense some scheme in how you say that?"

"There is no scheme," Mr. Norwich replied. "I think only that you are more emotionally invested in this matter than I am. Therefore, I am able to be detached and see things in a calmer way than you are at the moment. If you take your time, eventually the emotions will go away. And when they do, you will be able to see the entire situation in a much clearer light."

Robert wasn't certain how much more clearly the situation

could be seen. But he didn't want to get into an argument again, although he suspected that wasn't what Mr. Norwich was after.

"I'm afraid that I will have to take my leave of you," he said, changing the subject. "I have loitered in Bath for too long. I really ought to get to London and start organizing my assets properly and speaking to someone about purchasing an estate."

"I am not entirely surprised to hear that you are going," Mr. Norwich replied. "After what I have just witnessed, I can imagine that Bath feels a little too uncomfortable for you at the moment."

"That is certainly one way to put it," Robert admitted. "Thank you for all of your generosity and hospitality. I appreciate your guidance."

"Never hesitate to write if you have any more questions," Mr. Norwich assured him. "I will be going up to London myself eventually. You will have to keep in touch so that I might look you up when I am there."

"I should like that, thank you, sir."

Robert packed quickly, for he had only brought a few things. There was not much that he really owned. There was nothing much that he could keep on a ship and he had to be able to move it around quickly.

He would have much more soon once he finished handling his aunt's estate. It would take a lot of work but that was clearly what he needed right now.

Something to distract him. Something to focus on besides the ridiculous affairs of the heart. He would get himself settled with an estate and handle all of his inheritance and whatnot.

Then he could go back into this whole finding a wife business. Far, far away from wherever Miss Reginald happened to be.

When he finished packing and saying his goodbyes and got his carriage to London, Bath fading behind him... he told himself that it was good to cling to his anger.

His anger would be what preserved him. It had been what had gotten him through the last few years, wasn't it?

He just had to remember it. It would be what he could cling to when his heart tried to betray him and remind him of all of Miss Reginald's charms. As it inevitably would try to do.

Robert turned away from Bath and faced front, toward London. He had other things to think about.

He told himself that the twisting in his gut was just a heavy breakfast.

CHAPTER 40

GEORGIANA WAS SITTING and reading poetry to Mrs. Weston when Julia returned from her walk.

"How are you doing, Mother?" Julia asked, coming over and giving her mother a kiss on the cheek.

"Quite well, thank you. We ought to keep Georgiana around all the time. I forgot what an attentive companion she is. I would say she's like a daughter to me but she behaves far better than any daughter of mine."

"Oh, hush, you cat," Julia replied, refilling her mother's cup of tea.

The Weston women bantered back and forth like this. There was no real heat in it. When Georgiana had been a child and first introduced to the family she had been surprised by this behavior. She had worried that the members of the family all hated each other.

Coming from a stern household such as the one her father cultivated, she did not understand that people could be so lighthearted with one another—that it was possible to tease.

Now she knew much better, and only smiled indulgently as the younger and older Weston women went at it with one another.

"Oh!" Julia turned, presenting Georgiana with a letter. "And this is for you. You must allow me to read it, though, when you are through. I have to make certain that it is properly done."

Georgiana recognized the handwriting at once. Her heart

seemed to stop for a moment, then proceeded to hammer in her throat.

It was Captain Trentworth's handwriting.

She opened the letter slowly. Before, when they had been corresponding, she had opened them slowly in order to savor it.

Now, she did it because she was afraid. What could he possibly have to say to her? Was he going to somehow find a way to hurt her even more?

The letter inside was brief, done up in his spidery handwriting, the one that she had once known—still did know—as well as her own.

Dear Miss Reginald,

It has been brought to my attention rather forcefully that I did you an ill service yesterday.

I do not know if seeing you in person to either speak with you or deliver this letter is the best thing. It is clear that we are a source of great emotion and pain for one another and I do not wish to stir up any great feelings of sadness within you.

Please forgive me for not appreciating how much courage you used last night. You gave your heart to me and spoke plainly and that took great effort. I should have been more considerate.

I also must apologize for the things I said about your brother. I cannot say that I understand the bonds between siblings as I do not have any. But I understand one's loyalty to family. Had my parents been insulted in such a manner I would have been as upset as you were.

I hope that this letter finds you well and that you will not think too harshly of me.

Sincerely,

Captain Robert Trentworth

Georgiana sat there, staring at the letter.

It did not sound like a true apology. He was still angry, she could tell. Oh, the words were all right enough, for the most part. But the opening line. And the use of 'I must' for his apologies.

She had heard and read Captain Trentworth's apologies before. They sounded nothing like this.

And there was nothing in the letter about his feelings, if he still had any.

No, she had run him off for good. She had tried, and she had failed. There was nothing left but to give him up properly, in her heart.

"What does it say?" Julia asked.

"Nothing good, if we are to judge by her face," Mrs. Weston said.

Georgiana wordlessly handed the letter to Julia, who read it over.

"Why, that is hardly an apology!" Julia protested. "I ought to—"

"You ought to do nothing," Georgiana replied gently. "Am I right in suspecting that you are the reason this matter was 'forcefully brought to his attention', Julia?"

"I might have stopped by Mr. Norwich's residence during my morning calls and... informed the captain of a few facts." Julia looked innocently out the window, but Georgiana was far from fooled.

"You are a horrible liar, Julia Weston, and you always have been. How badly did you behave? I hope that you did not insult Mr. Norwich."

"Mr. Norwich was quite amused by the whole exchange, actually. He gave me tea while the captain wrote this apology note. I believe that was the most exciting thing that Mr. Norwich has experienced in quite some time."

"Of course it is," Georgiana sighed. "How you manage to make what is normally considered completely unacceptable something that is amusing and applauded is beyond me."

"It is my special talent," Julia replied. She set the letter down. "Well, I am certainly not inviting him to dinner any longer. But I shall hold back on completely destroying him. How do you feel about it all, my dear?"

Georgiana sighed and allowed herself to slump back in her chair. "I do not know how I ought to feel. It does not feel like a proper apology. But perhaps I should accept the fact that no matter what I do, I will never, in his mind, make up for what I did."

"You did what you thought was best," Julia pointed out.

"But I took no risks," Georgiana replied. "I had no courage. If I had married him... my father would have died much sooner than we expected. Edward would reinstall me in society. He never agreed with Father on the decision to refuse to give his blessing."

"But you didn't know that at the time," Mrs. Weston added. "You were weighing love against survival. Now is the time to be brave. Now you can afford it. But not everyone can afford to be brave. Your father looked like he was going to live for years."

"At least you know that now you did all that you could," Julia said softly, encouragingly.

Georgiana was not sure that she did. But she could not think of anything else she could have said that would make it all better.

"Perhaps I should have been slower," she said. "Perhaps I should not have tried to dump it all on him so quickly. I should have taken my time to allow him to grow used to the idea that I might have feelings for him again..."

"You put yourself out there and you did exactly what he had said that you were incapable of doing," Julia pointed out. "I think that is something that you ought to be proud of yourself for."

Georgiana straightened up. "Well. There is nothing for it now."

She could remember well how she had counseled Maria during her time when she was fighting with Edward.

She had told the girl to go to bed and that it would all be better in the morning. She had told her not to worry, that it would all work out.

Well, she must tell herself those things now. She was going to be fine. She would get through this.

A servant entered. "A Mr. Tomlinson wishes to call," he said.

It was later in the day, which was clever of him. The later in the day that one called, the better friends one had to be with someone. Because if one called late enough, one could receive an invitation to stay and have dinner with the family.

Since Mr. Tomlinson was already invited to dinner that evening, he must have seen the opportunity to call later and simply stay on through until the food was served.

"I do not know if I can receive any callers today," Georgiana admitted.

Julia stood. "Tell him that my mother and Miss Reginald are out of the house, but I would be happy to receive him in the other drawing room."

The servant bowed and exited.

Julia placed her hand on Georgiana's shoulder. "You may have your day, my dear."

One day. She could relax until dinner and by then she would be composed enough to handle everyone.

Tomorrow, though... and at dinner tonight as well, most likely... she would need to start receiving Mr. Tomlinson's flirtations with more open acceptance and grace.

There was no use in hiding herself away anymore. She had to get married and he was quite clearly offering.

It would, if nothing else, force her to take her mind off of Captain Trentworth. It wasn't proper for her to hold a candle for one man while being married to another.

Yes... if nothing else, it would save her in that way. Save her from herself.

She could hear Mr. Tomlinson speak with Julia in the foyer, although she could not hear what was being said. She then heard him leave again. Evidently, since Georgiana was not there—at least not to his knowledge—Mr. Tomlinson was not interested.

Well, if Georgiana had needed any more confirmation, that was it. He was clearly interested in courting her.

Georgiana sighed and picked up her book of poetry to continue reading. One day, just as she had told Maria, and then all would be better.

It would have to be.

CHAPTER 41

ROBERT WAS CONDUCTING business in London and had only thought to himself—well, it was one of those rare days with sun.

He didn't have an appointment for a little while. Why not enjoy one of the parks?

He was walking along the perimeter of one when he heard someone calling out his name. He turned in surprise and saw—

Well, of all the luck. The universe had to be laughing at him.

Sitting just a short ways off from him was a lovely young lady with dark hair, sketching something. Approaching him was a man about his age. The man had been sitting with the lady but was now quite near.

And it was Lord Reginald, Duke of Foreshire. Miss Reginald's brother, Edward.

"Captain Trentworth, I thought that it might be you." The duke smiled. "It has been ages. I had no idea that you were back in England. Is... is my sister aware of your arrival?"

"We met one another in Bath," Robert replied, unsure how else to respond. "She looked quite well."

"Wonderful." The duke looked as though he were hoping for something else to be said, but when Robert was silent he added, "Would you like to meet my intended?"

He brought Robert over to meet the lady sketching. "This is Miss Maria Worthing. Soon to be Lady Reginald."

The duke sounded immensely proud when he said it. As though

he could not think of anything in the world more wonderful than making this woman in front of him a duchess.

Miss Worthing curtsied to Robert. "It is a pleasure to meet you. You know my lord and Miss Reginald?"

"I was friends with them, a few years ago," Robert said. "Before I was called off into the navy. I've been away serving my post for some time. I only just returned."

"That is marvelous. We are glad you've come back safely," Miss Worthing said. She smiled up at the duke. "Perhaps we could invite you to dinner sometime. I am still getting used to the idea of playing hostess. I shall need practice. And there is no better practice than among friends, is there not?"

Robert was completely taken aback by the charming, guileless nature of this girl. It was as Miss Weston had said. He could sense a bit of wildness to her. Rather like when a man had a pet lion. The lion was tamed but it was still a lion.

And the duke was looking at her as if she were the center of the universe. Robert would not quite say he looked besotted. The duke had too much of a dignified bearing for that. But it was something quite near it.

"Tell me, what brings you to London?" the duke asked.

"I have some business to take care of," Robert explained. "I recently came into an unexpected inheritance. On top of what I earned during my career—I'm looking into buying an estate. Establishing myself as a member of the gentry."

"Marvelous," Miss Worthing said. "I think that's quite good of you. I do admire you men, I had to marry into it."

The duke looked as though he was biting down laughter. Robert could see why they got on, if Miss Worthing entertained the duke so easily. And how could anyone not be charmed by her sweet nature?

"You should return to your art before the light changes, my darling," the duke pointed out.

Miss Worthing cried out. "Oh, you are quite right. It's such a fickle thing. A pleasure to meet you, Captain Trentworth."

She curtsied, and then went back to her sketch.

The duke looked at Robert, and his eyes were much graver now. "Have you spoken with my sister?" he asked quietly.

"Upon what matters?"

"You know what matters I speak of," the duke replied. "I am surprised that you have not called upon us to ask for my blessing."

Robert stared at him in amazement. The duke... expected Robert to come and ask for his blessing? He could hardly expect such a thing if he did not want it to come to pass, could he?

The duke was speaking to him softly, conspiratorially, as though he were eager to hear Robert say that yes, he was there to ask for the blessing to marry his sister.

"Forgive me," the duke said, still speaking quietly. In deference to Robert's privacy and Miss Reginald's, no doubt. "Perhaps things have changed. I have not asked if you are married or engaged with another lady. I should not have assumed."

"But you did assume," Robert said. "Why did you?"

"I cannot betray the confidences of my sister," the duke said.

Robert swallowed hard. "You think that she still holds me in her affections."

The duke looked away, out over the horizon. "As she was to you then, she is now. That is all I will say on the matter. I cannot elaborate. She would curse me if I betrayed her thoughts to you or to anyone. Our privacy is our greatest privilege. Our father was not fond of providing us with any."

"I recall his preferences well." Robert could not keep the bitterness out of his voice.

The duke gave him a wry smile. "You have little reason to love him, alive or dead, I should think."

Robert could feel his face heating up in embarrassment. "He is your father. I should learn to be more respectful."

He should also apparently learn to hold his judgement. The duke was smiling at him and seemed to have been waiting expectantly for Robert to propose marriage to his sister.

How could he have gotten it so wrong?

The duke shook his head. "Neither of us were fond of him. One must not speak ill of the dead and all of that. I doubt that he would approve of my union with Miss Worthing, despite her being the daughter of his best friend."

The duke glanced over at Miss Worthing, and the love that Robert saw in the man's gaze took his breath away.

"Are you engaged with someone else, then?" the duke asked, turning back to him. "Are congratulations in order?"

"I am afraid not," Robert replied. "I was... under a misapprehension. There is another man attempting to court your sister. I thought that he might make her a better suitor."

It was a lie, but he could hardly delve into the entire story.

The duke shook his head. "If I may give you some encouragement, there is no man better suited for her than you. That has always been my opinion.

"I ought to have said so to my father. But I tried to keep out of what I felt was my sister's battle, out of respect for her. She appreciates it, or at least says that she does. But I wonder if I should not have said something.

"In any case, if that is all that is keeping you from pursuing her, I would say Godspeed. The wind is in your sails and not his. And if the two of you were to come to me asking for a blessing, I know which man I would bestow it upon."

Robert could only stare in surprise and amazement. He had not expected this in the slightest.

He truly had some apologizing to do.

"I will seriously consider what you have said," he told the duke.

"Good. And do please come and dine with us tonight if you do not have a previous engagement. Miss Worthing is serious in her need to practice her hosting skills. She is quite nervous about it and we must do all that we can to ease that."

He spoke with such open affection for her. It was clear to Robert that this man was not at all like his father. The former duke had never shown such affection for anyone. Yet the current Lord Reginald looked like he worshipped the ground that Miss Worthing walked on.

"I am not engaged tonight," he told them. "It would be my pleasure to come to your house for dinner."

"We look forward to it," the duke told him.

Robert walked away feeling as though he were in a daze. He had been welcomed in with open arms. The duke had apologized for not helping to plead his case with their father all those years ago. He had expected that Robert would be asking him for his blessing to marry Miss Reginald.

He had sorely misjudged the new duke. He would have to send a proper apology to Miss Reginald.

No wonder she had defended her brother. And with such fire and spirit as well. Miss Weston had pointed out that Miss Reginald had risked losing someone that she loved in order to defend her brother.

It was precisely what he had wanted her to do all those years ago, only it was to defend him to her father and risk losing her father instead.

They had both been so much younger then, however. Miss Reginald had grown in maturity. Perhaps it was now, then, that she possessed more strength of character and fire and could stand up to people in a way that she could not before.

Perhaps it was that now she did not have anything left to lose.

And did it really matter either way?

She had risked herself for him as he had asked her to all those years ago and he had all but spat in her face for it. He had allowed his bitterness to cloud his judgment and make him assume the worst in people.

If he got back to Bath and she was already married to someone else, he would have no one to blame but himself.

But did he deserve, even, to go back to Bath? To make a claim for her?

After the way that he had behaved, he would not be surprised if he had lost all chance with her. Miss Weston seemed inclined to slam the door in his face, at any rate. Goodness knew if she'd even let him get through her to speak to Miss Reginald.

It had been weeks since he had left Bath. So much might have happened in that time. She could be planning on putting up the banns right at that very moment.

No, she would not, he told himself. Not without writing to her brother. If there was truly a proposal afoot, then the duke would know about it and therefore he would have said as much to Robert.

This must have been what Mr. Norwich was talking about when he said that Robert would need some time to go and get a clear head and see things better.

Mr. Norwich of course could not have known about running into the duke. But he must have realized that time would help to get rid of the pesky cloud of emotions—namely anger—that were in Robert's way. He had realized that something, anything, would come along and help Robert to see things in their true perspective.

Could Miss Reginald ever forgive him for his deplorable behavior?

He had wrapped himself in his righteous anger and his judgment and had not allowed himself to see things as they really were. The shoe was on the other foot now and he was the one who had indeed wronged the other.

Miss Weston had been right in all that she said. As rudely as it was delivered.

No wonder Mr. Norwich had been so amused by the entire thing. He had realized that in a few weeks, Robert would come to his senses and agree with everything that Miss Weston had said.

Everything that Miss Weston had called him, he now called himself. He was a coward and a hypocrite. He had truly behaved like the worst of men.

What could he possibly do to make it up to Miss Reginald?

Perhaps... he could take the duke into his confidences somewhat.

At dinner, or rather after dinner when Miss Worthing had retired, he could ask the duke what he ought to do. He would say that he had been unkind in his manner and wished to make amends. No need to go into details.

He would ask Lord Reginald what could be done. Did his sister fancy a particular kind of sweet that could only be gotten in London? Was there a book that she had her eye upon?

He would then purchase the gift or say whatever the duke thought it best that he say. He would write it down so that he would be sure to remember it.

And then, he would return to Bath at once and apologize using whatever gifts and words that the duke had suggested to him.

Robert paused. But could he ask for anything more than forgiveness?

She might no longer love him. After the way that he had treated her, what sensible woman would? But sense did not always come into love. Perhaps there might be hope for him.

Did he dare to ask for anything? Perhaps he ought only to ask for forgiveness and then go from there. He could return to her life slowly. Get her used to the idea of him in her life once more. Prove to her that he was serious in his apologies.

And then... then he could propose to her. Not right away. Doing it slowly and giving her time so that it was not a shock to her. After all, an apology and then a proposal all in one fell swoop, it would be a great shock to her.

She would have known, of course, that his last apology was a shallow one at best. Miss Reginald had read plenty of his letters back in the day. His style had not changed that much.

In reading it she would have realized that he was still angry with her. But now he had a chance to make a proper apology to her, to mend things the right way. Instead of simply casting off whatever half-hearted apology-cum-farewell that he had given her previously.

He might have to do it when Miss Weston was out of the house, however. He did not trust that young lady to not try and claw his eyes out or something else unseemly.

But he could wait until Miss Weston was gone, at any rate. He had a feeling that Miss Reginald, if she did forgive him, would do so much sooner than Miss Weston did.

Right. He would go to dinner and enjoy himself. And then he would ask for help in making amends with Miss Reginald. He would return to Bath and apologize.

And somehow, someway, he would make it so that he could propose to her. Life had given him two chances with her. She had ruined the first, or perhaps they both had. He had certainly ruined the second.

They said that the third time was the charm, and besides, if he messed this one up, he wasn't all that certain that the universe would grant him a forth chance.

He had to get this one right.

CHAPTER 42

Georgiana told herself the next day that she was ready. She was prepared.

She could do this.

Dinner last night had been fine. Julia had seated her across from Mr. Tomlinson but not next to him, thank goodness. Georgiana had needed a moment more to get her bearings.

Mr. Norwich had been seated next to her, which had been wonderful. He was gracious and thoughtful and she was ever so grateful for his attentiveness.

Miss Everett and Miss Perry expressed their dismay that Captain Trentworth would not be joining them any longer. Julia made up the excuse that he was called into London for urgent business concerning his new inheritance and that he sent his condolences.

It was a truly believable excuse and delivered with all the aplomb and grace of a true hostess. Nobody, Georgiana was sure, suspected a thing.

There was another young man at dinner by the name of Mr. Lawson. Trust Julia to find another man to round out the party at the last minute.

Everything had gone fine. Georgiana had not spoken much. Mr. Tomlinson had been eager to engage her in conversation and so she had simply asked him about topics that he had studied well. Then she listened to him while he spoke at length about them.

"Cleverly done," Mr. Norwich murmured to her at one point.

Having Mr. Norwich at her side was almost as good as having Edward there.

Edward.

She would have to tell her brother at some point what had transpired. She was not yet sure how. How did she even go about telling her brother that she had found her love, and lost him again, and that this time it was even uglier than before?

Edward would be so disappointed. He had always held out hope for her and for Captain Trentworth as well. He had liked the man and respected him greatly.

Perhaps other sisters would not tell the full story to their siblings. But she and Edward had no secrets from one another. They had only one another to rely upon growing up. They certainly couldn't ever confide anything in their father.

She would feel awful if she did not explain all that had happened to her to Edward. But he would be furious, of course. Ready to track down Captain Trentworth and defend her honor.

Maria would hopefully help with that. She was wonderfully good at helping Edward to let go of his bad tempers.

It would still be an awkward letter to send, however. Georgiana could not deny that.

She would have to send the letter soon, of course... but if things continued as they seemed to be with Mr. Tomlinson...

Perhaps she should save her letter until later? When she could balance out the bad news with the good?

Mr. Tomlinson did not seem to be wasting a moment of his time, after all.

Hopefully if she was to tell her brother all the unfortunate business that had transpired, she could end it with some good news as well. He would be happy for her, he would have to be.

Even if she knew in her heart that Edward would not be as happy for her as he would have been if she had married Captain Trentworth.

But that was only Edward's brotherly concern for her coming out. He wanted her to be happy and he had seen that the captain had made her happy. If she could convince him that Mr. Tomlinson made her just as happy—even if it was a bit of an exaggeration—then all would be well.

So she left the letter writing aside for the time being.

After dinner she went straight to bed, trying to rest herself up. And if she cried into her pillow again, just a little, nobody had to know about that.

Now it was the next day, and she knew what was coming.

She stayed home with Mrs. Weston while Julia went out on morning calls. Georgiana could have joined her. But she knew that Mr. Tomlinson would try to call and she saw no reason to delay the inevitable.

Besides, she was not quite up to going out and seeing everyone and being quite that sociable.

Miss Everett stopped by. "Miss Weston called upon me but not you," she said. "She said that you were not feeling quite well enough to go walking around town. So I thought that I might stop by and see you instead."

"You are very kind," Georgiana told her as she rang for tea. "You were a delight at dinner last night. I am sorry that I could not be a bit livelier."

"Well, if you are feeling a bit under the weather, that completely explains it," Miss Everett replied. "And here I thought that it was mere distress over the captain leaving."

Georgiana nearly started in her seat but caught herself in time. "What do you mean?" she asked. "If anyone had reason to feel distress at his departure it was you. I saw how you two were interacting and it appeared to be quite lively. Your wits were well matched."

"Yes, I thought so," Miss Everett replied. "But then I realized that he had eyes only for you."

Georgiana could feel her heart thumping wildly. "I'm sure that you must be mistaken."

"Oh, no, not at all," Miss Everett replied. "I admit, it was unfortunate. I think that we should have made an excellent pair. But he was always following you around the room. Surely you noticed?"

"I'm afraid that I did not."

It felt as though someone had slipped a dagger between her ribs. Captain Trentworth had been watching her? His gaze following her around the room? So much so that another woman had not only noticed but decided that she had no hope of winning him for herself?

Georgiana wanted to scream with frustration. She had nearly had it all. She had nearly had it and then she had lost it.

But she was not even sure that it was her fault that she had lost it. Was it not his as well? If he truly gazed upon her like that and loved her with such obvious tenderness, then why did he not feel she was worth fighting for?

If he thought that her brother would not approve of the match, then why not make the same argument that he had made all those years ago?

The only answer was that at some point along the way, the captain had decided that Georgiana was not worth fighting for. That whatever she felt for him or even whatever he felt for her was not enough.

It was beyond frustrating. It made her want to behave like Julia, to scream and rant. But there was nothing that she could do to change someone's mind if that someone did not want their mind changed. She could not control anybody.

There was nothing for it but to move on.

"I think that perhaps you were mistaken," she told Miss Everett. "I can assure you that there is no love lost between the captain and myself."

Miss Everett looked doubtful. "We talked much of principle and determination when we were dancing together," she said. "I would have thought that he was the sort of man who went after what he wanted.

"I know what it is that I saw. But if he was not possessed of the courage to pursue you and make it known to you, then he does not deserve you."

Georgiana was pleasantly taken aback by the younger lady's assertion. Of course, younger people were always so certain in their convictions. But it was pleasant, nonetheless.

"I am flattered by your assessment," she told Miss Everett. "Now, you were mentioning something about a letter from your cousin?"

The subject effectively changed, Miss Everett talked at length about the mistakes and dramatics and woes of her cousins.

It was certainly a distraction, and by the time that she left, Georgiana was feeling as though she might even be able to properly handle Mr. Tomlinson when he inevitably arrived.

Mr. Tomlinson was a nice enough man. He could handle his income. He came from a good family. There were certainly worse situations in which she could find herself. Worse men she could marry.

And then, just as Miss Everett was about to step out the door, she said,

"Mark my words, I think that the captain shall be returning. When he does, you better get a proper explanation out of him before you let him go a step further."

Georgiana did not understand why everyone was so certain that Captain Trentworth would be back or that he was so head over teakettle for her. But she simply smiled, and thanked Miss Everett, and closed the door.

Now. Hopefully that would be the absolute last she heard of Captain Trentworth.

It was only a short while later that Mr. Tomlinson called. Georgiana asked for him to be shown in and rang for some more tea. She also got some biscuits for Mrs. Weston, who had long ago fallen asleep in her chair and needed to be woken up.

"Mr. Tomlinson." Georgiana stood, curtsying, and he bowed. "Please, do have a seat. To what do we owe the pleasure?"

"Merely that I enjoy your company and am always eager to have more of it," he replied. "Tell me, what book is that by your elbow?"

She told him about the poetry she had been reading to Mrs. Weston. Mr. Tomlinson was not well acquainted with it, and she answered some of his questions on it.

It quickly became apparent, however, that he was not truly interested in the poetry. He was truly making an effort on her behalf and for that she could thank him.

Unfortunately, she couldn't ignore the sinking feeling in her chest when Mr. Tomlinson, clearly relieved, changed the subject to fashion.

Georgiana followed fashion, of course. How could she not? But she was not an enthusiast for it the way that Julia was. The most that she had ever paid attention to fashion was when she was teaching Maria about it.

She would have much rather had someone with whom she could discuss books and poetry. It saddened her to remember, and she could not help but dwell on, the fact that she and Captain Trentworth had been so enthusiastic together about those subjects.

Of course, she reminded herself, as Mr. Tomlinson's wife, or as any man's wife, she would not be with him constantly. He would have his business. She would have calls to make and the household to run.

Even when they both went to balls and dinners they would not be together constantly throughout. They could not necessarily sit together, for example. That would depend upon their hostess. And the aim of being at parties and dinners was to get to converse with people that one did not usually. So why would one sit with one's spouse, whom one saw all the time?

It wasn't the end of the world if her interests did not precisely match up with Mr. Tomlinson's. He was trying, that was more than she could say for most men.

He stopped to listen when she spoke. He asked her opinion on things. He found witty ways to compliment her. He dominated the conversation a little more than she would have liked but it was clear that he did not realize that he was.

He was not her ideal man. But he was a good man and he was making a true effort. For that she ought to be grateful.

After their visit concluded and she showed him out, Georgiana returned to find Mrs. Weston looking at her with gleaming eyes.

"Whatever you are going to say," she told the older woman, sitting down again, "you had better say it."

"He is a nice enough man," Mrs. Weston said. "A gifted charmer. He was consistently finding ways to compliment you on your eyes."

"I noticed."

"They are very fine eyes, in his defense. You are far from plain in your features."

"Thank you. However, you cannot blame me for sensing that there is something else that you are thinking on."

"I cannot help but notice that he does not stir in you any sign of mirth."

"You know that I am not one inclined towards laughter."

"Ah, but the captain could get you to laugh."

"Let us not talk about the captain any longer."

"Surely you should wait for a man who can make you laugh? One who shares your interests?"

"If I were still eighteen then perhaps I could. But I am six and twenty. I cannot afford to wait. Not any longer."

Mrs. Weston peered at her for a moment, then nodded. "You blame yourself for your lack of marriage thus far, do you not, my dear?"

Georgiana felt her stomach twist and she looked up at Mrs. Weston, startled. "What do you mean?"

"I mean that you feel it is your continued feelings for the captain that prevented you from being courted by any other men," Mrs. Weston said. "If only, you tell yourself. If only you had moved on from him, you could have been emotionally available to those other men and they would have courted you.

"But I think you forget, my dear, that marriage is not all about emotion for men. Of course they want a wife who is devoted to them. Just as we want a husband who is devoted to us.

"However, men must marry as well as women. They must have an heir to continue on the estate and the family line. There is pressure with them as well.

"Had any of them really wanted to, they would have courted you anyway. They would have seen your lack of true affection as a challenge. You know how men like a challenge. They like to feel powerful.

"To know that they changed your mind and convinced you to love them would have, I think, been a triumph to them. Who knows why they chose not to pursue you? But you mustn't blame yourself. You will not gain anything by it."

Georgiana nodded. "Perhaps that is true. But whether it is my fault or not, one cannot deny the march of time. I have to wed. Or else I have to begin making preparations to spend the rest of my life as a spinster. You understand how it works."

"I understand," Mrs. Weston replied. "That does not mean that I have to like it. And you know that you will always be invited into our home and to our social gatherings. Whether you are married or not."

"Thank you." Georgiana sighed. "Well. I suppose that I ought to arrange for Mr. Tomlinson to sit next to me at tonight's dinner."

Mrs. Weston pursed her lips together. "You do whatever you think is best, Georgiana."

Over the next couple of weeks, Georgiana allowed Mr. Tomlinson to court her.

She did not think that anyone who did not know her as well as, say, Julia did, would be able to see that she felt no real passion for the courtship.

Georgiana knew that she was a quiet person by nature. A little withdrawn. Not prone to showing great emotion, generally. It did not surprise her that Mr. Tomlinson and everyone else seemed blissfully unaware of how little passion he stirred in her.

But passion did not matter now. What mattered was that he was a kind person who was interested in taking care of her. She would no longer be a burden to her brother.

Was that not all that she was allowed to ask for?

Mr. Tomlinson accompanied herself, the Westons, Miss Perry, Miss Everett and Mr. Norwich on a trip to the seaside and on a picnic weekend.

Georgiana could tell that Julia was doing it for her benefit. Trying to help Georgiana get the proper courtship that she deserved. And putting them in various situations so that Georgiana might see every side of Mr. Tomlinson's character.

She appreciated her friend's thoughtfulness. She knew that Julia was as unsure about Mr. Tomlinson as Georgiana was. Part of Julia, Georgiana thought, still rooted for Captain Trentworth. As angry at him as Julia might be.

But Julia said nothing one way or another. And neither did Mrs. Weston.

It was appreciated. Georgiana had received enough of people's opinions on her love life for one lifetime, thank you.

Mr. Tomlinson continued to be charming in every aspect. He seemed to always have the right words to suit the occasion, whatever that occasion might be.

Georgiana could see why he had been aiming to become a

lawyer or a clergyman before his uncle had gifted him with inheritance. Mr. Tomlinson had a way with words that would have served him well either in the pulpit or in the courtroom.

She did her best to appreciate his attentions. She could not bring herself to force laughter out when she did not feel it. But she smiled and listened and thanked him when he complimented her —which was a lot.

Honestly, sometimes she felt as though he complimented her a little too much.

It made her wonder, sometimes. Not that she thought he was going to turn into a monster upon their marrying. But someone who was always so complimentary like that. It did worry her a little that he might be putting on a bit of a front for her.

On the other hand, even if he wasn't putting on a front, she wasn't sure that she wanted to be constantly complimented. It made her feel less like a wife than a pet cat that needed daily stroking or treat feeding.

She wanted someone who respected her and would debate with her. She wanted someone who treated her as a partner. The way that Edward and Maria treated one another.

Oh, of course, Edward was devoted to Maria and gazed at her like she was the brightest star in the night sky. And he was protective of her, true.

But he didn't treat her like a child or as though she was nothing more than a pretty face. He loved Maria's wide knowledge of books and supported her hobby of art. It was Maria's intelligence and willingness to discuss such subjects that had helped to draw Edward to her.

There were, however, far worse ways to be treated by a husband. Complimenting one's wife too much was hardly the greatest sin that a man could commit in a marriage.

She did not get to be picky. And perhaps, when they were married, she could help to influence him. Let him know in gentle ways how she did and did not wish to be treated.

If life gave you lemons, she reminded herself, then you used them to make lemonade.

This was far from being handed lemons, but the point still

stood. She would find a way to look at everything optimistically and change any little quirks for the better.

Georgiana could tell that the rest of society in Bath thought a proposal was forthcoming. Mr. Tomlinson made sure to dance with her twice at every ball that she went to.

He attentively asked if he could refill her drink when it drew near to empty. He generally stood by her while she conversed during the balls—unless he was dancing with another woman. He did have a societal obligation to dance with as many ladies as he could during a ball, after all.

Miss Perry was forever making remarks about it. Remarks that the poor girl plainly thought were subtle but everyone else knew were about as subtle as a bag of flour dropped on one's head.

Miss Everett didn't say anything on the matter, the same as Julia. She probably had plenty of thoughts about it. Georgiana could not imagine that a woman of her wit did not. But she kept her thoughts to herself. And for that, Georgiana was grateful.

Mr. Norwich did not make any remarks to everyone the way that Miss Perry did. However, one night as he was bidding Georgiana farewell, he told her,

"I would not resign yourself to a loveless marriage of convenience quite yet, Miss Reginald."

Georgiana had no idea what that was supposed to mean. Mr. Norwich merely bowed and left for the evening. While she stood there, bewildered and at a loss.

Mr. Tomlinson could hardly have been unaware of everyone's speculation, but he took it in stride. He seemed pleased that people were talking about his courtship.

Georgiana hoped that he did not mind some of the things that she was overhearing. Comments such as,

"Did you know that Miss Reginald is possibly getting married at last? I thought it should never happen."

And,

"Well, I wish him the best of luck with her. You know there must be a reason that no other man has wanted her all this time."

And,

"I think he will come to regret it. Quiet thing like her? And so mature? He's just so lively. I can't imagine they'll be happy."

And,

"Well of course you know she's getting a large inheritance once she marries. And the daughter of a duke. I'm not saying they don't also truly care for one another of course but, still... one has to consider things like that..."

It was enough to make Georgiana ill. She had hoped that once she finally had a suitor that the nasty things people said would die down.

Apparently, she had been greatly mistaken.

People finally had something new about her to discuss and oh, were they ever discussing it. Everybody had an opinion about her being courted by Mr. Tomlinson.

Many people seemed happy for her, and for that she was grateful. But for every person who was genuinely happy for her, there seemed to be another two who had some absurd theory as to why she was really being courted. Or why it had taken her so long to be courted.

Theories ranged from being touched in the head to having some kind of terminal illness to being unable to conceive a child. Georgiana did not even know how someone was to find out if they were barren before even attempting to create a child, but it seemed no logic could stop the determined gossipers.

And of course, there were all of the people who said that she was only being courted for her money and status. Mr. Tomlinson had a sizeable inheritance from his uncle but there were those who said it wasn't going to be enough for him.

And those who said that now that he had money, of course he was going to want a title.

Georgiana was almost grateful that she was not in love with the man. She felt bad for him, of course. And she wanted the rumors to stop. But she could only imagine how upset she would be if it was someone she loved about whom they were speaking.

She could only imagine how much it would hurt if it was the captain about whom they were speaking. Captain Trentworth had never cared for titles. In fact, it seemed based on their last conversation that he despised them.

And he would never marry anyone for their money. That had

been one of the things that Father had accused him of when she had begged Father to give his blessing.

If someone from a good family such as Mr. Tomlinson, who had been a part of society all his life, who had come into his inheritance fair and square... if he could be subject to such ridicule then she could only imagine the horrid things that everyone would say about Captain Trentworth.

It was a terrifying thought. And it made her grateful that while she did respect Mr. Tomlinson, she did not love him.

Georgiana did her best to ignore those things. She focused instead on the positives. On the fact that if things went well she could hold her head up high at parties again. That she would have her own household to run, which she did greatly enjoy doing.

She would get to have a proper estate in the country. She did love the country. And she would hopefully not be too old to have children. She did want a few.

A boy, yes, of course. And a girl. She had loved coaching Maria. It had reminded her of how much she wanted to be a mother.

She had long ago given up hope for that. Instead she had hoped only to possibly find a husband. And then to disappear from society with dignity.

Now she might very well get her dearest wish of a child or two. If she was to only have one, she hoped it would be a boy so that he might inherit. But she really did not care too much what kind of child it was—so long as it was one that she could love and raise and to whom she could be a proper mother.

No longer would she have to feel embarrassed at balls. She would be married and therefore did not have to dance. Maria missed dancing, Georgiana knew. She greatly enjoyed it.

In fact, if one came down at night, one could often find Maria and Edward dancing quietly, even without music, gazing into one another's eyes like all those sappy couples from love stories.

But while she had nothing against dancing, Georgiana had never felt it was her favorite pastime. She was glad that she would no longer have to sit out a dance and feel as though it was a snub. Nor would she ever feel as though she had to dance or else risk looking more like a spinster than she already did.

Now, she could sit and chat with everyone and not feel a single obligation.

There were many pleasant things to look forward to, she told herself. So what if it did not come with love? There was security and happiness to be found. Romantic love was not everything.

It was a great deal, yes. But it was not everything.

Of course, when lying in bed at night, her heart told a different story. She could remember so well the way things had been with Captain Trentworth.

She still had his letters, although she refused to hurt herself further by taking them out and reading them. But it did not matter. She had them all memorized. She remembered everything.

How he had challenged her on her opinions. How he had rewritten sentences again and again because he was struggling with how to express his emotions. How he had made her laugh.

She longed for that once again. She longed for him, specifically. But if Mr. Tomlinson had been more like that, she might, perhaps, have made room for him in her heart.

But Mr. Tomlinson did not engage her in discussions on stories and word use in poetry, or the symbolism of a passage in a play. He did not challenge her views but instead simply complimented her for having them.

He could not make her laugh. And his words flowed so easily from his lips that she could quite clearly imagine him saying them to any woman. They sounded too practiced.

But the captain was not there. He had left her. He had made it clear where he stood. And Mr. Tomlinson was there. He was making an effort. He was actually there, in front of her. Showing his affection.

He was fighting for her.

And that was more than she could say for Captain Trentworth.

Her heart would follow her head in time. She just needed to give herself some patience. Until then, she'd let logic rule the day as it ought to have been doing for years now. Mr. Tomlinson was the one courting her. And so Mr. Tomlinson was the one that she needed to be thinking about.

CHAPTER 43

GEORGIANA WENT DOWNSTAIRS to breakfast a few weeks after the whole debacle with Captain Trentworth to find that there was a letter already waiting for her.

"It was dropped off first thing this morning," the servant informed her. "By a messenger from Mr. Tomlinson."

Georgiana opened the letter and read that it was an invitation for herself, Mrs. Weston, and Julia to accompany Mr. Tomlinson on an outing for the day.

She showed it to Julia and her mother, who both accepted. Mrs. Weston had a knowing look in her eye. "I suggest you dress your best, my dear," she told Georgiana.

Georgiana felt nerves start to turn her stomach upside-down. She responded to the invitation letting Mr. Tomlinson know that they would be delighted to accompany him. She then went upstairs to change into her best.

Julia helped her out. "You're shaking," she noted as she helped Georgiana pick out a frock.

"Your mother said that I ought to wear my best for a reason," Georgiana replied. "I can think of only one reason why she should say that. And I do not know if I am prepared."

Julia frowned, turning Georgiana so that she might lace her up. "Why would you not be prepared? If you and my mother are right and he is proposing, then is it not what you were planning on this entire time?

"I admit that only a few weeks is a little short. But it is under-standable when one is your age. Mr. Tomlinson is probably eager to help you end your status and also, possibly, to help with getting you pregnant as soon as possible. The older a lady gets the more dangerous the pregnancy, you know."

"Yes, it is quite logical given my age," Georgiana replied. "It is not that it is too soon. I knew that this would be coming. And yet now that it is here I find myself wanting to be sick."

"Please don't, or if you do, warn me so that I might get you a basin."

"This is not a laughing matter, Julia."

"Well one of us must make it so. Or else you will work your nerves into such a state that you will not even be able to leave the house."

Georgiana smiled at her. "You are always making things light-hearted and I do not think you get nearly enough credit for why."

"There is enough seriousness in the world already," Julia replied. "I must do what I can to provide the sunshine."

She then took Georgiana's hands in hers. "But, my dear. Wanting to be sick in a basin is not the proper reaction that one should have when realizing that one's suitor might be proposing today."

Georgiana looked off to the side. "I apologize. I feel as though I am still failing in some way."

"You are not failing," Julia said firmly. "You cannot control what your heart feels. And you are bearing yourself with dignity.

"Many a girl in your predicament would be allowing Mr. Tomlinson to court them out of spite. Or to make Captain Trent-worth jealous.

"But you did not even encourage him until you knew there was no hope with the captain. And you are allowing him to court you out of logic and necessity. I see nothing to apologize for in that.

"You are bearing up with grace, when many other ladies would be weeping and wailing still. You did not kick up a fuss. You did not make a scandal of anything. I think that you are to be commended for how well you are handling this."

"And yet, it still does not sit right with me."

Julia sighed, and drew Georgiana to the bed so that she might sit down.

"My mother has spoken to me often about how she came to marry my father. She was not in love with him at the time, you see, although they did get on.

"They grew to love one another in time. And I thought, growing up, that what she was trying to tell me was that it was all right if a marriage did not start out in love. That love would come.

"And she was saying that, at least in part. But that was not all of what she was saying. She was also telling me that when she married him, although she did not love him, she felt happy with her decision.

"She was all right with not being in love with him. She was glad to be getting married. She looked forward to it. There was no doubt in her mind about it.

"And so, if I am to wed, she told me, it is all right if I do not love my husband. But I must not go into it if I am anything other than happy with my decision.

"I think that is what you ought to think about now. It is all right that you do not love Mr. Tomlinson. But you should be going into this with pride and happiness.

"You should be glad that you are going to be proposed to. You should not be feeling ill about it. I know that men often like to laugh at the idea of a woman's intuition.

"But I believe that intuition exists. I think that your body when it is making you feel ill in such a manner is trying to tell you something. I think that you know, whether you like it or not, that Mr. Tomlinson is not the right man for you.

"And one must think not just of one's self but of the other party as well. Is it truly fair to Mr. Tomlinson to marry a woman who does not love him?"

"But in the case of your parents was it not so?"

"Yes, but my father did not love my mother either. He found her rather pretty and he appreciated her wit. And he knew that he wanted to marry and have children. That was what he truly wanted —a child. And since he found my mother tolerable enough and he needed to secure a marriage, he proposed.

"But Mr. Tomlinson cares for you. He has been impressed by you since the moment of your meeting. I think that, for one person to give a lot and not to receive as much in return...

"I think that it would be uncomfortable for you both. That he would feel unfulfilled and not understand why for some time. That when it did come time and he understood, that it would hurt him.

"And that you all the while would feel shame, for not loving him as he loved you. That you would feel guilty and be doing what you could to make up for it. And that is not a fair situation to put you in.

"It would breed unhappiness in you both. Because neither of you would be getting from the other what you truly needed.

"If Mr. Tomlinson simply needed a wife then I think it would all be more balanced and you would be able to respect one another. But when there is a lack of balance... that worries me.

"And I do not want you to be unhappy. That is the last thing that I want for you. You are like a sister to me. If the idea of him proposing makes you unhappy then I don't think that you should do it."

Georgiana looked at herself in the mirror. She thought that she looked rather nice. But she no longer looked like she was eighteen. She was six and twenty and she looked it.

Maybe it would make her unhappy. But would it make her any unhappier than being a spinster would? Was it not the fair price that she had to pay for retaining her place in society?

There was a soft knock at the door. One of the maidservants stuck her head in. "My apologies, Miss, but your mother sent me to inform you that Mr. Tomlinson's carriage has arrived."

"Thank you," Julia replied automatically.

She looked back at Georgiana. "We have to go on this outing now. And it will be quite lovely I am sure. You don't have to follow my advice, of course. But I hope that you will think on it. I only want what is best for you."

"And you think that a life alone as a spinster is what is best for me?"

"Compared to a life where your husband grows to resent you for not loving him and you are unhappy and feeling guilty and ashamed all your life? Yes. I think that is what is best for you."

Georgiana sighed. "You never were one to mince your words, Julia."

"I like to think that people appreciate me for it," Julia replied.

"But the carriage is here, so I'm afraid we don't have much time to ruminate on it.

"Whatever you decide, I will support you. You will hear no complaints from me or chastisements once you have made your choice."

"Thank you." Georgiana took one last look at herself in the mirror, making sure that her hair and all were in place. "Let us depart, then."

Mr. Tomlinson and Mrs. Weston were waiting for them when they descended the stairs into the foyer.

"You look delightful," Mr. Tomlinson told her. He seemed to truly think so, smiling at her with a happy gleam in his eyes.

Georgiana felt her stomach twist in guilt. This was a man who seemed to think she was a delight. Who smiled dazedly at her, as though he wanted nothing more in the world than to stare at her.

She would have thought that marrying him would be a kindness to him. She would be giving him what he wanted, after all.

But was Julia right? Would it, in actuality, be unfair to him?

They got into the carriage, Georgiana's thoughts swirling about her head like a summer storm. She had to do the smart thing and say yes should he propose. But she also had to do the right thing. Could it be that the smart thing and the right thing were, in fact, two different things in this case?

"I hope that you will enjoy this," Mr. Tomlinson said as the carriage went into motion. "It is the most charming little spot, you can see for miles. I was walking there the other day and thought that it would be the most perfect spot for a picnic. And I know that you ladies do not get nearly so much fresh air as you would like."

Mrs. Weston thanked him for his thoughtfulness. "I've been continuously told that the air will do me good. Let us hope that my doctors are to be believed, then."

"But madam, surely you believe your doctors?"

"I believe that they think they know better than anyone else," Mrs. Weston sniffed.

Georgiana glanced at Julia, who had to stifle a smile. Mrs. Weston had her opinions, and they were strong ones. When the doctors came to visit there was usually quite a row.

As they rode the carriage up, it was mostly Mr. Tomlinson and

Julia who kept the conversation going. Georgiana found she could not bring herself to speak.

Fortunately, that was not so unusual. She generally kept quiet while Julia took over the conversation. And Mr. Tomlinson was always happy to talk.

At least this way, Mr. Tomlinson did not need to know that her silence was from her frayed nerves.

The spot that he had chosen for them was rather lovely. The grass was soft and inviting, the sun was bright but not unbearable, and the air was clear and sweet.

"I declare that there is nothing so marvelous as the English countryside!" Julia announced as they set themselves up. "No wonder people are always waxing poetic about it in books."

"If you start waxing poetic about dead leaves," Georgiana said, "I shall have to draw the line."

Julia only laughed.

They took their luncheon, which was lovely, and Mrs. Weston inquired after Mr. Tomlinson's cook who had prepared the meal, and all in all, it was a pleasant enough afternoon.

If only Georgiana didn't feel quite so much like having her lunch all come back up the same way that it had gone down.

She honestly didn't know which answer was the right one to choose. If she said yes, would she be setting up the both of them for a life of misery?

Or would she only be condemning herself by saying no? Would saying yes be all right, would it be not so bad as Julia had feared?

But then, what if he was not proposing today? It was a perfect set-up for it, that was true. The picnic, the weather, the spot that was chosen. Julia and Mrs. Weston were there, of course. But that could not be avoided. It would have been improper for Georgiana to spend so much time with a man without being married to him.

In short, it was a perfectly planned and executed moment for someone to propose marriage.

Yet, she could be overreacting. He could not do it today. It had only been a few weeks. Surely Mr. Tomlinson must want to take more time and be certain, wouldn't he?

They ate and chatted—or rather the other three chatted and Georgiana listened.

Perhaps he wasn't going to propose. Perhaps she was getting all worked up over nothing. Perhaps...

And then, as they finished their luncheon, Mr. Tomlinson stood up and asked, "Miss Reginald, I don't suppose that I could prevail upon you to accompany me on a short walk?"

Georgiana almost wanted to ask Julia to come with her. She knew that such a thing would prevent Mr. Tomlinson from being able to propose. Proposals were supposed to be done in private, as with most romantic things.

But she could not do that. Why delay the inevitable? Why put it off when it was only going to happen at some point anyway?

Georgiana stood up and forced herself to put on a smile. "Of course. It would do me some good to stretch my legs."

When Captain Trentworth had proposed to her it had been at the estate owned by the Westons.

That had been where she and the captain had met so as to avoid her father.

Captain Trentworth had shown up with a determined look on his face that day. And he had politely asked if everyone save for Miss Reginald could leave the room.

Georgiana could remember how she had trembled. How nervous she had been, but excited, more than nervous. She had wanted to burst out laughing and burst into tears all at the same time.

She had hardly breathed until everyone had left the room and he had begun to speak.

He had told her of how she knew his heart better than anyone, and so what he was going to say would probably not come as a surprise, but he must say it all the same.

He had told her of how his greatest joy in life was her. That he had joined the navy to serve his country and because it was the best option available to him, but now he was happy to protect her.

He had spoken of how her letters were what kept him going. How she gave him hope, at last, that he might have a future. That he had a purpose beyond simply following orders.

Georgiana had burst into tears for one of the few times in her life, overwhelmed by the joy welling up in her at the things he was saying.

He had stuttered a bit, clearly nervous. He had told her that if only he were better with words, he could give her some poetic speech. But perhaps it was better this way because his love for her rendered him speechless, and therefore she could see how much she affected him.

Georgiana had quite agreed. His being overcome with emotion had only endeared him to her more.

When he finally got around to asking if she would marry him, he had laughed apologetically.

"I see that I have spent all of my time rambling and stuttering about how I feel and I have not even got to the question," he had said.

She had said yes, enthusiastically, thinking there was nothing else in the world that would make her so happy. And nothing in the world that could take her happiness away from her.

And then her father had refused to give his blessing. He had told her that if she married the captain, he would cut her off from everything.

And so happiness had become despair.

But the anticipation she had felt then was nothing like the vague sick feeling that she was feeling now. Back then, she had been full of happy nervousness, wanting it so badly. She had dreamed of that moment.

Now, she was dreading it. She wanted it to happen only so that she might get it over with and be done. But she did not actually want it to happen.

But she felt so awful for feeling that way. Mr. Tomlinson had been nothing but kindness to her. He had every right to propose to her after all that she had let him court her.

And he was saving her. She should be grateful to him. He was rescuing her from a life of humiliation. It was awful of her to be handed her redemption and to dislike it so much.

Was this what Julia had been talking about earlier? When she had said that Georgiana would live her life ashamed of herself, feeling guilty?

She did not want to spend the rest of her life feeling this way.

But surely it would change with time? It must change with time?

She could grow to love him, possibly? Or at the very least grow to care for him more than she did now.

There were those that said familiarity bred contempt, but there was also the idea that the more time you spent with someone, they grew on you. You grew accustomed to them. And in time, that feeling grew into fondness. And hopefully from fondness into something more.

Georgiana could hope and plan for that, could she not? Surely unhappiness while married and then unhappiness while single were not the only two choices before her.

But Julia had pointed out that it might be unfair to Mr. Tomlinson to place him in a position where he gave love and got none back in return.

She could not guarantee that she would grow to love him. As much as she wanted to guarantee that, for his own sake—she did not know the future. It would be unfair of her, wouldn't it, to ask him to take care of her and support her and do all of those things for her, and then not be able to give him the one thing that he asked for in return.

Georgiana honestly did not know which option she should choose. And that was causing her more stress than almost anything else. If only she knew her answer, she could give it, whether yes or no, and it would all be settled.

But she didn't know her answer. And she was going to have to make up her mind, and quickly.

Mr. Tomlinson led them through the shade of the trees along a little path. "I saw this," he said, "and as soon as I did, I knew that it was the place where I must take you."

Once again, honeyed words. Romantic ones. Miss Perry would undoubtedly be swooning. As would nearly any other girl that Georgiana could think of.

But it wasn't right for her. He wasn't right for her.

Did it matter, though? Did it really matter at this point if he was the right man for her or not? Surely the security and status that he brought her were more important than the man himself?

It was a selfish way to think. But perhaps it was time that she was a bit selfish.

"You cannot be unaware how I feel for you," Mr. Tomlinson said as they strolled through the shade. "From the moment that I met you I felt that there was something special about you. I thought that here was a woman whose company was worth getting to know.

"You have not led me wrong since. You are an elegant woman, and as thoughtful as a man could hope for. I have savored every moment together and am humbled that you would allow me to spend so much time with you."

Georgiana's heart felt like someone had wrapped a fist around it and was squeezing tightly. She was worried she wouldn't be able to breathe. And not out of excitement but out of sheer panic.

"It has allowed me to hope that perhaps you might return the affections that I hold so dear." Mr. Tomlinson turned and smiled at her. "And so it cannot be any surprise to you when I ask you if you will do me the honor of becoming my wife."

Georgiana could not say yes.

But neither could she say no.

Perhaps... perhaps she could stall? Give herself more time.

Edward and Maria's wedding was coming up. She was to leave Bath in just a day or two in order to get back to Foreshire in time to help with the final preparations.

What if she told him that it must wait until after the wedding? That would give her at least a week.

And if she did decide to answer yes to his proposal, then she could do so while Edward and Maria were on their honeymoon and Mr. Tomlinson could ask Edward for his blessing when they returned.

It would be positive news to greet them with, should she say yes. Edward would be pleased. Maria... Maria believed in true love and all that, so she might see through it. But she would not contradict Georgiana's decision if Georgiana was firm in it.

Yes. Asking Mr. Tomlinson to give her some time. That would be a clear middle ground. A compromise with herself.

She smiled at him. It didn't feel right on her face. You can do this, she told herself.

"I am beyond flattered by your proposal," she told Mr. Tomlinson. He was watching her hopefully, and she did so hate to disappoint him. "It was not something I had dared even hope for. That a man of your charm and stature should feel so strongly for me is a dream I had long ago given up on.

"But as you know, my brother's wedding is fast approaching. I must depart Bath in just the next day or so. I cannot in good conscience get engaged to anyone while my mind is so elsewhere.

"Would you do me the kindness of allowing me to give you my answer once the wedding has concluded? I feel it would be doing my brother a disservice to announce an engagement during a special time that is supposed to be for him and his bride."

Mr. Tomlinson looked terribly disappointed, his eyes darkening sadly, but then as she spoke they lit up again. "Oh, but of course. You are, as always, considerate of others. I would not wish to intrude upon your brother's happiness.

"I will await your answer once the wedding is concluded. And please do convey my warmest wishes to your brother and his bride on the day."

"Of course I shall, and Mr. Tomlinson, I do appreciate you understanding my predicament."

For once in her life, Georgiana felt no qualm about lying. She was too busy being filled with relief that it had worked. Mr. Tomlinson was not suspicious, nor was he downtrodden.

Again, she could not help but wonder if his consistently cheerful perspective meant that he really did not care quite as much. She wasn't sure if she was glad at the suggestion or not.

If he did not truly care, then that was a good thing. It meant that she would not be breaking his heart one way or another.

Yet, on the other hand, she did wish to see a bit of disappointment that he could not have an answer at once. If she was asking a lady for her hand in marriage, she would want an answer at the first available opportunity.

She did not tell him this, of course. What sort of person told a man that his accommodating reaction to her delaying of an answer to his proposal was unsatisfactory?

Georgiana did want to take the opportunity to ask him, did he truly understand love? Did he genuinely love her? Or was he merely experiencing a bit of infatuation and taking it as the deep and lasting affection of honest love?

But she could not ask him without insulting him somehow, and she could not have that. Not when she still might have need of him.

What a horrible way to phrase it! When she still might 'have need of him'? It made him sound like a bauble or an object rather than an actual person.

Her thoughts were a jumbled clutter in her head. It was as though she were falling and no longer knew which end was up.

But he had given her a week or so to ponder.

That would have to be enough.

"Shall we walk back to join the others?" Mr. Tomlinson suggested.

"I would like that, thank you, sir," she replied. She needed Julia's energetic presence to lighten everything up before Georgiana became properly melancholic.

Julia and Mrs. Weston were chatting amicably in the manner of two people who are talking merely to cover up the fact that they are waiting for some important news.

Julia stood up as Georgiana and Mr. Tomlinson emerged from the path and walked back to them. "Did you enjoy your walk?" she asked, looking straight at Georgiana.

"It was lovely in the shade," Georgiana replied.

"We had a splendid time," Mr. Tomlinson added, sitting down again and helping himself to a tart.

Julia gave Georgiana a look that clearly stated she expected Georgiana to tell her everything once they were alone.

Thank goodness that Mr. Tomlinson had not been awkward about the whole thing. Indeed, he was in just as high spirits afterwards as he had been previous to his proposal.

The rest of the afternoon was spent pleasantly and amicably, and the carriage ride home saw no sort of resentment from the gentleman.

The only sign that he had proposed to Georgiana was as he dropped them off at the Weston residence, where he reminded Georgiana in a low voice,

"I shall eagerly await your answer once the wedding has concluded."

Then he ordered the carriage to drive on.

Watching the carriage pull away, Georgiana felt her stomach twist again. She had to figure out her answer. Soon.

"Well?" Julia said, all but dragging Georgiana into the house so that they might talk properly. "What happened? He must have proposed, he must have, but neither of you said anything when the two of you returned.

"But he did not seem at all upset, so you cannot have said no to him." Julia searched her face. "What happened? You must tell me everything."

Georgiana could see Mrs. Weston watching her with just as much interest. She sighed.

"Horrid gossipmongers, both of you," she teased. "Very well. He did propose to me, in fact. He was very pretty about it."

"A little too pretty, if I am reading your tone correctly?" Mrs. Weston said. "Oh, do not give me that expression, dear. It has been clear to me for some time that his suave phrases are not appealing to you."

"I hope that he has not noticed that," Georgiana replied. She would hate for him to think her rude.

"I wish that he would, so that he might see how unsuitable in the long run you two are for one another."

"Mother," Julia chastised. She looked back at Georgiana. "Go on, then."

"Well, he proposed, and I honestly did not know whether to say yes or no. And so I told him that I could not give him an answer until after my brother's wedding. He was most jovial about it. Said he had not the slightest issue with it."

Mrs. Weston frowned. "If I were a man and I proposed to the lady with whom I was in love, I do not know if I could be so patient."

"That was my thought as well," Georgiana admitted.

"In this I am actually on Mr. Tomlinson's side," Julia said. "If I loved someone, I would put their needs above my own. You obviously need some time, although you were not entirely honest as to why.

"I should have acted as he did. Put on a brave face for you and told you that it was no matter. I would trust that you would be true to your word and tell me your thoughts as soon as the wedding was over as you had promised."

"That is a wise way of looking at it," Georgiana admitted. And now she was back to square one with Mr. Tomlinson caring far more about her than she cared about him.

He cared about her enough to set his own feelings aside and let her take whatever time that she needed. He was being respectful of her family.

Was it not terribly unfair of her to put him through this?

"Focus on the wedding," Mrs. Weston advised.

"Are you going to tell Edward about it?" Julia asked. "He might have some good advice for you."

That... that was actually a good idea. Edward was a practical man. He would know how best to advise her. And other than Julia, there was no one in the world who knew her better.

Edward had always regretted not taking her side against Father when Captain Trentworth had proposed to her. This would be a chance to include him in her decision-making. Hopefully he would then feel that he had redeemed himself.

"I think that is a wise suggestion," Georgiana told Julia.

"Two wise things said in the span of five minutes," Mrs. Weston quipped. "One would almost think that she had a head on her shoulders."

"I shall write to him at once," Georgiana said. "So that the letter might get to him before I do. I will never be able to tell him in person. I shall be too embarrassed. The last post of the day has not yet gone out, has it?"

"Not to my knowledge," said Mrs. Weston.

"Excellent, I shall write to him at once."

Georgiana hurried up to her room and pulled some papers out from the desk.

She kept it shorter than she might like, since time was of the essence. And she did not want to detail the entire mess with Captain Trentworth. She did not think that should factor into her decision-making with this.

In fact, Captain Trentworth should probably not figure into her thoughts at all.

Dear Edward,

I hope that you will not find a letter so shortly before my arrival alarming. My best wishes to you and to Maria. I look forward with breathless anticipation to seeing you both soon.

I am writing to inform you that I have been proposed to by a worthy gentleman by the name of Mr. Tomlinson. He is the third son of a gentleman but was brought up in the world by a large inheritance from his childless uncle.

He is a charming man possessed of a sociable nature and an amiable disposition. He would certainly provide me with stability and a lovely home. However, I am unsure as to whether or not I should accept his proposal.

I do not feel the passions for him that he seems to feel for me. It has been pointed out to me that this would be most unfair to him if I were to marry him, for people deserve to receive back the love that they give out.

However, it might also behoove me, as you know, to enter into a marriage. Especially with a gentleman of his standing in society and with his income. I do not wish to be a spinster, for all that you say I still have some time before I become one.

Your advice has always been sound, dear brother. There is nobody whom I trust more. What is your advice in this matter?

You need not write me back. I shall be with you in person shortly. But I hope that the day or two that you have before I arrive will help you to think the matter over satisfactorily.

I remain as ever,

Georgiana

She sent it off with the last post and hoped that her brother would have enough time to formulate a proper answer before she arrived.

Of course, he might want more information, some details. She could provide those for him. But that was the heart of the matter. Should she marry a man who loved her but whom she did not love in order to secure herself? Or should she say no and possibly spare them both misery? Misery that she was not even fully certain they would experience. But it was a possibility, nonetheless.

Edward was a sensible man. The only time that she had seen him be anything other than completely possessed was when he had fallen in love with Maria. He had then failed to realize it and had wondered why he was so protective of her, why he cared for her so much, why all other men knew to avoid courting her.

But in this, he must be sensible. This was not his own heart of which they spoke. It was hers. And he would want to be sensible and pragmatic as needs must so that his sister could have the best future possible.

Edward would help her to figure it out. He was her older brother and had always looked after her.

She had faith in him.

CHAPTER 44

ROBERT MADE sure to dress his best for his dinner with Lord Reginald and his fiancée.

Not that he generally tried to dress up too much for those who were of a slightly higher station than he was. First of all because he did not usually feel that they were worth it.

Second of all because if one dressed up too much for the higher classes, they could sense that one was trying to show off and imitate them. They tended to find it hilarious and not in a complimentary way. Like the sparrow trying on the peacock feathers in that fable. Aesop, Robert thought it was.

But no matter. The point was that he did not usually try to dress up for those who were a little higher up than he was. This was not just anyone, however. This was a person that he actually wanted to impress.

He wanted Lord Reginald to know that Robert had put time and care into his appearance and that this dinner meant something to Robert.

The duke might never know—Robert hoped he would never know—what Robert had said of him to his sister. But Robert still felt, nonetheless, that he ought to do what he could to make amends and showing the care that he put into his appearance for this dinner was one such way.

When he arrived at dinner, he was surprised to find that he was the only guest.

"We did not want to distract ourselves from our catching up by having too many other guests," Lord Reginald explained. "I wanted to be sure to give you my full attention."

He then leaned in and whispered, conspiratorially, "And I did not want to give Miss Worthing too much stress in organizing things last-minute."

Robert was charmed in spite of himself by the duke's consideration for his intended. Miss Worthing did seem to be in a state of nervousness.

"Not yet used to playing hostess?" he asked.

"I was in charge of running the household at my father's plantation," she explained as she led them into the dining room. "So I am used to planning simple menus and the running of the accounts and the day-to-day.

"But we never had any reason for guests. We were so out of the way. And fancy dinners were quite beyond our needs. So all of this is new to me in that respect!"

She indicated where Robert should sit, and allowed her fiancé to pull out her chair for her before sitting.

"You are doing a marvelous job," Robert assured her.

Miss Worthing beamed at him. "I only hope that I will do so marvelous a job at the wedding dinner."

"Have you received an invitation?" the duke asked. "I confess that I left the making up of the guest list to my sister."

"She has been a most marvelous help," Miss Worthing said. "Helping me with everything. I was at such a loss. I never could have done any of it without her."

"She did not invite me, but she told me so when we met in Bath," Robert said. "And she apologized profusely. She explained that she thought I was still going to be overseas and she had no idea how to reach me to send an invitation.

"I agreed with her and told her that it would have been nearly impossible for her to reach me. I am still in the dark as to how Miss Weston, whom I'm sure you will recall, managed to get a letter to me."

"Since it is Miss Weston, I am not surprised that she managed it," Lord Reginald replied. "She is the sort of determined girl who always manages to get what she needs."

"Quite so. In any case, your sister apologized and I told her there was no need for such things."

"Perhaps we could squeeze in an extra guest?" Lord Reginald looked over at Miss Worthing. "We would have to consult with my sister, I should think. As she is the one who knows all of the place settings and such."

"I could manage," Miss Worthing said staunchly before Robert could begin to panic properly. "It is only one person. And I believe you did tell me to have an extra place in case your sister was in need of a partner?"

"Yes, it is always easier to take away a spot than to add one," the duke acknowledged.

"I shall go over it all tonight after dinner," Miss Worthing said with a determined note in her voice. "It will all work out and Miss Reginald need not trouble herself about it. She has gone to enough trouble already, goodness knows."

"Are you certain that you wish for me to attend?" Robert asked.

What he really wanted to ask was if they were certain that Miss Reginald would want him to attend the wedding. Especially if he was to be placed near her during the ceremony and at dinner.

He did not wish to cause her any more pain than he already had. He had undoubtedly burned every bridge that he had with her.

"Of course we wish for you to attend," Lord Reginald said. He sounded astounded that Robert would even ask the question. "I know that you may consider yourself to be more a companion to my sister than to me.

"But if you will recall, we attended some marvelous hunts together. And you were a breath of fresh air at some otherwise dreadful balls. I may not have supported you as I ought to have in certain... endeavors of yours. But I always considered you to be a friend."

"Tell me, was he as cranky and sour at balls then as he is today?" Miss Worthing asked. "I much prefer them now that I can converse without causing a scandal, but I have always loved to dance. My lord here, however, much prefers to stay in."

"She says that," the duke said with a teasing smile, "but she enjoys a quiet night with a book as much as anyone."

Robert could not help the tightness in his chest. It was so easy to see that they were in love with one another. The tender looks with which they regarded one another.

The gentle teasing. The blushes and smiles. The easy atmosphere they had around one another. As though they had already been married for some time.

Robert wanted that. He wanted it so badly. And he had not ever felt that way with anyone except for Miss Reginald.

But soon, soon he would be able to ask Lord Reginald about an apology and he would be able to make amends and possibly...

Possibly...

Dinner was entertaining and the conversation lively. Miss Worthing did have a touch of wild in her but she played the part of the hostess well. She was educated and well-read, and Robert could easily see her becoming popular in her role in society.

"You have found quite the lady there," he dared to tell the duke when dinner was finished.

Miss Worthing bid them both goodnight, and Robert politely turned away as the duke pressed a soft kiss to her cheek before she went upstairs.

"I shall fix it all up in the plans before I go to sleep, so that you will be able to attend," she told Robert. "I am very glad to have met you, sir. I am certain that we shall be good friends. My lord has good taste in the people he chooses to keep company with."

"She is the greatest lady in all the world, if you ask me," Lord Reginald said as they watched her go up the stairs to her room. "But then, I am biased."

"I would not be so inclined to agree on the greatest in all the world part. But then, I am also biased."

Lord Reginald turned to him, a question in his eyes. "You still care for her then? Truly?"

Robert looked away. "I do not know if I can have her."

"She has always been yours, Captain. You need not fear that."

A servant entered, some letters on a silver tray. "Your mail for the day, my lord. As you requested."

"Ah, of course. Thank you." Lord Reginald took the letters from the tray and the servant exited.

"These are mostly business," he said apologetically. "I prefer to read them before bed. Then I can dwell on them and wake up refreshed and with a plan in mind.

"I had not thought to tell the servant not to bring them because of you coming to dinner. I apologize."

"It is no matter."

Lord Reginald was just idly shuffling through the letters and about to put them in his pocket when he paused. "There is one from my sister."

"Is there?"

Robert had little doubt that it did not concern him. But his heart beat faster nonetheless. Was this about to detail all the awful things that he had said to Miss Reginald? Was he about to be kicked out of the house?

The duke opened the letter and read it out loud.

"Dear Edward." The duke smiled. "You know how she is not one for flowery language."

He continued to read, interrupting once or twice to provide his own commentary.

"I hope that you will not find a letter so shortly before my arrival alarming... she is to arrive here either tomorrow morning or the day after to help with the final preparations... My best wishes to you and to Maria. That is Miss Worthing. I look forward with breathless anticipation to seeing you both soon."

The duke was obviously cheered by the letter. But Robert dreaded what might be read next.

"I am writing to inform you that I..." Suddenly, Lord Reginald's face fell. It registered shock, and perhaps, a bit of disappointment.

"Perhaps I ought to bid you goodnight and allow you to read the rest in solitude," Robert suggested. After all, he would rather show himself out of the house than be kicked out.

"No, stay, you must... you must hear this." The duke sounded shocked. He cleared his throat and read,

"I am writing to inform you that I have been proposed to by a worthy gentleman by the name of Mr. Tomlinson."

Robert's heart plummeted.

So he was too late.

"I know the man," he said. "He is a gentleman."

"Yes," the duke said, still silently reading. "It says here that he is the third son but was brought up in the world by a large inheritance from his uncle."

"That is quite right. He has quite the income now." Robert was finding it difficult to talk. He wanted to find some dark corner to hide in so that he might sink into his pain and guilt for a while before facing the world again.

He had brought this on himself, of course.

Miss Reginald had given him her heart. She had laid it all out for him. And he had rejected it. It was his own fault that he had lost her.

Of course she would go to the charming Mr. Tomlinson. Why would she not? He was offering her a home and security. He was charming and complimented her. He was doing everything that Robert had been too foolish and angry to do.

"It says that he is a charming man," the duke continued on, sounding rather dubious, "possessed of a sociable nature and an amiable disposition. 'He would certainly provide me with stability and a lovely home'..."

Robert cleared his throat. "If you will excuse me, I must retire for the evening."

The duke looked up. "No, stay, it is not fair that you would have to endure this trial alone."

"I fear I am not one fit for company, all of a sudden."

The duke looked genuinely upset. "Captain, you must not give up hope. This is most unexpected. She has written to me and not once has she even mentioned this man before."

"It is my own fault," Robert admitted. "I drove her off with some unjust and unkind things that I said. I am not surprised that another man saw his chance with her and took it."

"I said some rather unjust and unkind things myself," the duke replied. "To Miss Worthing. The argument that we had—" The duke sighed, chuckling a little as he shook his head. "I thought that she would never forgive me. I did not think that I deserved to be forgiven.

"And yet she not only forgave me—she apologized. She thought that she was the one who had been in the wrong! And while I am inclined to believe that you were the one who was in the wrong, that is because we are talking about my sister and I am far too inclined to think that she is beyond reproach."

The duke smiled at the memory, his gaze far away. "I think that you might be surprised if you would apologize to her, what might happen."

"But she has already been proposed to by another man," Robert pointed out. "I cannot compel her to break that engagement off.

"Once before I tried to compel her to go against a promise that was made. I asked her to abandon her duty as a daughter to her father. I asked her to possibly ruin herself, to turn away from all that she had known.

"I cannot possibly ask her to open herself up to ridicule a second time. That would be unfair of me. You know how grave it is for a woman to break off an engagement. There must be extreme circumstances."

The duke shook his head. "Let me finish reading the letter—"

"I will see myself out." Robert bowed. "I have made a mistake, and this is the consequence of it. I must accept that.

"I wish you all the best, my lord, and I look forward to seeing you and your bride on your wedding day. I am grateful and pleased that you would wish to invite me. Thank you for your hospitality this evening."

The duke gave a small sigh, then bowed as well. "Have a good evening, Captain."

Robert left with the duke reading the rest of the letter. As he allowed a servant to see him out, he thought he heard the duke call for him again, but he must have misheard.

He went out into the street, knowing he ought to retire to the hotel he was staying at but not wanting to find himself inside again.

Walls felt too confining at the moment. He needed fresh air and darkness and to be alone.

He had thought that he knew pain before when he lost Miss Reginald the first time. But he had not truly known. It was bad enough when he lost someone that he loved because of circumstances beyond his control.

But when it was because of his own folly? His own anger and frustrations? When it was because he had been callous and unthinking?

He could not bear it.

Robert had no idea how he was going to make it through the wedding. Miss Reginald probably would not bring her new intended to the wedding. Unless the letter was sent in order to ask that he be added to the guest list.

But Robert did not think that Miss Reginald would impose upon her brother in such a last-minute fashion. At least he would not have to suffer the punishment of seeing her with Mr. Tomlinson.

Seeing her at all, however, would be bad enough.

He must still apologize, he resolved. He must apologize and gift her something so that at least she would understand that he realized how poorly he had behaved.

He had treated her unfairly and in a most ungentlemanlike manner and for that he ought to apologize.

It was only that now there would be no declaration of love to go along with it.

He wandered the streets for goodness knew how long. He would certainly not recommend it to any other man walking alone. But he had been in the navy and he knew how to take care of himself should danger arise. Besides, he took care to keep to the nicer sections and parks. No sense in being reckless.

For far too long, he tried to think of another angle, another way that he could come at this which would allow him to be with the woman that he loved. But he could think of nothing.

After what felt like hours but could have been mere minutes—he lost all sense of time—his thoughts turned to how he might apologize.

He had not gotten the chance to ask the duke about his thoughts on how Robert might best make up for his transgressions. Now, he did not know how to ask.

It was clear to him that the duke wanted Robert to be with his sister. Indeed, the duke had seemed not only surprised but disappointed to read that she had chosen another.

Robert was sure that the duke would warm to Mr. Tomlinson in time. Mr. Tomlinson was an amiable man with a charming and easy air. Exactly as Miss Reginald's letter had described.

The duke might be disappointed now, but he would come

around and learn to enjoy Mr. Tomlinson's company. Certainly, the man was a better conversationalist than Robert was. And he wasn't the sort of man who would lose his temper and give himself over to bitterness and ruin all chances with someone.

But for now, Lord Reginald seemed to be firmly in Robert's corner. Robert was grateful, although still a little surprised at it.

It meant that he could not go to Lord Reginald for advice on how to apologize. For surely the duke would take it as an opportunity to try and get Robert to try and win over his sister again, and Robert could not have that.

Lord Reginald was a duke. There was little that could be done to destroy his reputation. Someone would have to be very powerful themselves, and work hard, in order to unseat him from society.

But the sister or daughter of a duke was not the same as being a duke oneself. Miss Reginald would receive quite a lot of gossip for breaking off an engagement.

Even if it was not yet publicly announced. It could not be, for the duke had not given his blessing. But there would be talk. Miss Weston, for one, would probably be eager to sound the trumpets about it.

There would be talk, and then if she broke it off, there would be even more talk. Goodness knew that tongues were already wagging about Miss Reginald's age already. Discussing her impending spinsterhood. Asking what was wrong with her, the daughter of a duke, that men still did not wish to marry her.

He could not risk subjecting her to such ridicule. Of course her brother probably thought that she would be safe or that he could protect her. Robert, however, was not willing to take the risk.

Once before, he had not understood what he was asking of her in requesting that she marry him against her father's wishes. Now, he was older and wiser. He knew better than to play so lightly with or ignore the rules of society.

He would not ask her to punish herself like that, not again.

And, he thought as he rounded the street that would take him back to his hotel, was this not what love was? Was it not doing what the other person needed and not what you wanted from them?

He wanted her. He was, indeed, quite convinced that he needed her. That she was integral to his happiness.

After all, if she was not, why would he have dwelled on her for so many years? Why would he have been unable to let go of her in his heart?

But that was not what Miss Reginald needed. He was not, evidently, what she needed. Therefore, he had to let her go.

She needed someone who was charming, who knew how to compliment her. Someone who would not hurt her or allow their anger and resentment to turn them into a horrid, well, beast for lack of a better term.

It was possible that he was getting a little dramatic from sleep deprivation.

Mr. Tomlinson would provide her with respectability, compliments, children, a home, stability, and charm. He would be a life companion. Surely, that was all and more that she asked for? That any woman asked for?

And he would love her. How could he not? The man had been smitten from the first, Robert had seen that. He was surprised that more men were not smitten with Miss Reginald. A grave oversight by the male sex, if you asked him.

She would be loved and cared for. And that was what Robert wanted her to be.

He also wanted to be the person loving and caring for her but that was his own selfish desires. He had to think of her, and she would be getting all that she needed. That was what mattered.

CHAPTER 45

GEORGIANA WAS AFLUTTER with nerves as the carriage deposited her at her brother's house.

What would he say about her letter? Would he urge her to accept the proposal at the quickest opportunity? Or would he want her to reject it and wait in case there was another offer? Would he tell her that spinsterhood was preferable to a loveless marriage?

The moment that she stepped in the door, someone came flying at her, enveloping her in a hug.

Ah, Maria. Not yet used to putting her natural exuberance and urge for physical touch in check. Georgiana privately did not mind if Maria was tactile around her. The younger woman was like a sister to her.

"Hello, my dear, and how have you been?" she asked, hugging Maria in return and then stepping back to examine her.

Maria's cheeks were pleasantly flushed and her eyes were sparkling. "Oh, I am quite well! My stomach is having difficulty with food lately but I am simply so excited, it feels as though I've been dancing all night at a ball and could keep doing it."

"You must remember to take deep breaths, darling. And where is that wayward brother of mine?"

"He is going over things in his office, but I shall fetch him for you."

Maria hurried out of the room and Georgiana took the time to direct the servants in taking her bags up to her room. Already she was ticking through the list of things that had to be done.

She had to meet with the vicar and make sure that everything was in order. She had to double-check the confirmed guests who would be there. She had to...

Edward appeared, smiling, with Maria on his arm. "Georgiana." He released Maria and went over to Georgiana, taking her hands. "We've missed you."

He sounded as though he genuinely meant it—and she knew that he genuinely meant it. Her brother was far from the kind of person who would lie to spare someone's feelings.

Tears nearly welled up in her eyes. It had been such a difficult few weeks, filled with such trials and emotions and confusions.

To be back with her brother, to have him saying that he missed her, to be back in her home feeling safe... it was almost too much.

"Oh, my dear sister," Edward said. His face grew grave. "You seem upset."

"Come and sit down," Maria said, still fairly bounding with energy. "I shall fetch us some tea."

Edward led Georgiana into the drawing room, where he had her sit down. "Now, tell me—your letter was very brief. Explain to me all that has happened while you were away."

"It is a long story," Georgiana replied. "I do not wish to burden you with it."

"Would it have something to do with Captain Trentworth?" Edward asked.

Georgiana nearly jumped up out of her chair. "How—"

"Miss Worthing and I ran into him in London, and invited him to dinner. He confided in me that he had treated you most unfortunately and that he had to make amends.

"I believe that he was intending to ask me how he might best go about making those amends... but then your letter arrived." Edward looked terribly guilty. Georgiana had not seen him look so down on himself since he had been ten and broken Mother's favorite teacup.

"I read your letter out loud, not realizing what it contained," Edward admitted.

Georgiana inhaled sharply.

"The worst part of it is," Edward went on, "he left before I could finish reading it. He was in great distress. I let him go, only reading further as he was already heading out the door and it was too late for me to stop him.

"I tried to leave word at his hotel, but I learned that he has gone to look at an estate and will not be back until the wedding. Which we have invited him to. Of course now it must be quite awkward but at the time I thought that I was helping you to be reunited with him."

Georgiana was trying not to look too horrified for her brother's sake. She could tell by his heavy tone that Edward already felt badly and she certainly didn't want to make him feel any worse.

But oh. Oh no. Robert now thought that she was engaged to Mr. Tomlinson.

"Did he seem... very upset?"

"He did," Edward confirmed. "He cares for you still, Georgiana. Deeply. He was hesitant to speak plainly, of course, as a man of discretion. Especially to the brother of the woman of whom he was speaking.

"But I could see it all over his face. I could hear it in his voice. He feels for you now as he did then when you had to reject him."

"I... he said such horrid things, Edward," Georgiana admitted. "Unfair things. And so I said horrid things in return."

"It occurs to me," Edward mused, "that another young man and another young woman did the same thing. The young woman made a mistake and the young man overreacted terribly. He acted like the worst cad, if you were to ask my opinion.

"Both were of the opinion, after the whole argument was had, that the other one would never forgive them. That it was all over and that there was no chance of them making amends and returning to one another's favor.

"And yet, when the time came..."

Georgiana sighed. "Edward, please. This is nothing at all like you and..."

"Shh, let me finish," Edward chastised gently. "When the time came, they were able to patch it up. They both felt horribly for how they had behaved and wanted nothing more than to apologize and be amicable again.

"If Miss Worthing and I could work out our issues and survive our tribulations, then why should you not be able to work out yours? I have every faith in this positive outcome."

"You have always had too much faith in me," Georgiana replied with frustration. "I cannot even begin to chronicle how frustrating it is when you do not see the world and my life for what it truly is, Edward.

"You continue to believe that I will get the happy ending that you feel that I deserve. And perhaps I do deserve it. But that does not mean that I will actually get it.

"I must make a decision, and soon. And Captain Trentworth does not factor into it."

"He wishes to factor into it," Edward replied. "Forgive my plain speech, my darling sister, but he loves you. He is in love with you. I could see it—if only you had seen his eyes that night when I read your letter aloud. I curse myself for it.

"He all but fled the scene because he could not bear to hear another word. He looked like a man who had been delivered a killing blow. It was distressing simply to watch."

"And why are you telling me all of this? To cause me distress as well?"

"To help you see that you can have marriage and security, and have happiness as well," Edward replied. "Georgiana. He will be at the wedding. You can tell him then that you are not engaged. That you were proposed to but asked for some time to consider.

"You can tell him that you forgive him for his transgression— after he apologizes for it properly as I am certain that he will. And then he will propose to you on the spot. I would stake my entire fortune on it. I would stake Foreshire on it."

"I hope you will not stake my love on it," Maria said, appearing again with the servants bringing in tea behind her.

Edward's entire face lit up as she approached them. He reached out his hand and took hers, squeezing it gently before releasing it so that Maria could sit down.

"My darling, I do not think anything in the world would compel me to stake that on it."

Maria smiled and blushed, immensely pleased. Georgiana ignored the pang of envy that shot through her like hot poison.

She did not at all resent their love. Far from it. She was overjoyed to see her brother and Maria so happy. But she did so want to have that as well.

And she did have it, at one point. With Captain Trentworth.

Could it be? Was she allowed to hope that he wanted to apologize and fight for her? That he would, indeed, propose to her once she let him know that she was still available?

She did not have to give Mr. Tomlinson a response until after the wedding. If she saw Captain Trentworth during the wedding, where he was a guest, then perhaps... she could settle this whole thing once and for all?

The third time was the charm and all that, or so the saying went.

But no, that would be too much to hope for, would it not?

Then again, Edward was not a man given to exaggeration. To strong beliefs, yes. Very much so. Sometimes too strong. But if he believed in Captain Trentworth then there had to be good reason behind it. He would not go around making things up.

Maria glanced over at Edward, as though wondering if she should say anything. Then she sucked in a breath and looked back at Georgiana.

"I think that you have nothing to lose at this point," she said quietly. "At least, not by trying. You have until after the wedding to give your answer.

"Captain Trentworth is going to be at the wedding now. It provides you with the opportunity that I think you need. You can hear from him directly what his thoughts are, and tell him that you are not yet promised to anyone.

"I am not saying to be overly optimistic. I know that is not your way. You do not wish to believe in yourself, I think, because you want to be prepared for disappointment."

Georgiana looked over at her future sister-in-law. Maria was a girl who was prone to too much honesty. She sometimes said things without thinking, but only in the sense that she was not always proper—she was never malicious or thoughtless.

But that lack of tact did not mean that Maria was lacking in intelligence. Some people would mistakenly think so upon meeting her and noting her age and exuberant personality. Those people quickly found themselves put in their place.

Maria was well-read, intelligent, and quick-witted. And it

seemed that she had done just as much observing of Georgiana in her time living with them as Georgiana had done of Maria.

Maria smiled gently. "You need not be so hard on yourself. I think, Georgiana, that this is one time where you may allow yourself to hope.

"And as I said—what have you got to lose? You will either be embraced or rejected by Captain Trentworth at the wedding. And then afterwards you can give Mr. Tomlinson your answer either way."

"Have courage," Edward told her. "That is what Mother always said. She encouraged us to have compassion, but also to have courage.

"I fear that I thought only of the courage, while you thought only of the compassion. You have it in spades, Georgiana. But I think it is time that you remembered the courage as well, just as I have, through Miss Worthing, remembered the compassion."

"I cannot accept the proposal of another man or even bring myself to discuss it with another man, while the first one waits for my answer. It makes him so clearly the second choice, the safety net. That is unfair to him."

"That is a fair point," Maria said to Edward.

Edward sighed. "I think that you do not need marriage, Georgiana. I will provide for you all of my life. I will set up a stipend so that if I am to die before you do, you will still have an income and will be taken care of properly."

"You can live with us as long as you like," Maria added. "Truly. I will miss you when you are gone, if you do choose to go."

"Society will not be so kind to me as you are," Georgiana pointed out.

"There are plenty of women and men who have managed to make it while not fully complying with the expectations of society," Edward said.

"I think," Maria added, quietly, "that in the end, you will be happier alone and enduring the occasional gossip, than you will be married to a man whom you do not love.

"Some women can pull it off, yes. And I have nothing but respect for them. But you have proven yourself to not be one of those women.

"You warned me not to follow in your footsteps and not to be imprudent, back when I was unsure if my lord would return my affections. You knew then that you could not marry someone for whom you did not hold the deepest of affections.

"Remember that now. And do not do either yourself or this Mr. Tomlinson a disservice by marrying him. It would make you both unhappy, I promise you. It is in your nature to only truly be yourself with the people that you love. And if you do not love him, how can you truly be yourself?

"That, I think, is the greatest sadness of all. To not be able to be one's self. And Mr. Tomlinson would note it. He would know that you were holding your true self back from him. And that would, I should think, wound him deeply.

"And you deserve to be all that you can be and all of who you are. And you can be that on your own more than you can be that when entwined so intimately with someone you do not love. Or at least, it is so in your case."

"I will ensure that nobody dares to breathe a word of disregard in your presence," Edward added, his voice a low rumbling growl like impending thunder.

Georgiana had no doubt of that. Edward had inherited their father's stubbornness and his inclination towards being too condemning. If anyone could halt an entire tide—or ninety percent of the tide—of gossip, then it would be Edward.

"You are too sweet," she told her brother. His grumpiness really did come from the compassion that he felt for others, and from his frustration at humanity not living up to the high standards of which he knew they were capable.

"You will think on what we have said?" Maria asked. "We do not want you to be unhappy, Georgiana. Whether Captain Trentworth proposes to you or not—and I am in agreement with my lord in thinking that he shall—you will not be happy with Mr. Tomlinson.

"It is that simple. And when you are in a position such as the one that my lord is offering you... why not take it? Why force yourself to be unhappy simply because it is what society wants?

"You are not doing anything scandalous by remaining single. Your brother will provide for you. Truly, Georgiana, it will not be so bad. It will be worse to share the house of a man who slowly grows to resent you for your inability to return his love."

"My friend Miss Weston said rather the same thing."

"Miss Weston strays too close to the manner of a troublemaker for my liking," Edward said. "But she is an intelligent and observant woman. And I am inclined to agree with her and with Miss Worthing on their assessment."

"It is three against one," Maria said triumphantly.

Georgiana let out her breath slowly.

Edward said that Captain Trentworth wanted to apologize to her. That he had behaved as a man in love would.

Could she take that risk?

Could she be brave, as she had not been all those years ago when the choice was first presented to her?

Of course, back then she had not had her brother able to support her. She had her father threatening to destroy her. But now... now she had a support system.

She had Julia and her family, who would always keep her in society by inviting her to parties. She had her brother, who would support her and defend her. She had Maria, who would make sure that Georgiana was always necessary and would have Georgiana help to plan all her events.

It seemed that she did have a safety net after all: the people who loved her. They would help her to be brave.

"It appears," she said quietly, "that I have to write a letter to Mr. Tomlinson. I must arrange for us to meet. I will not reject him through writing. That would be unkind."

Maria and Edward looked at one another, beaming happily.

"This does not mean that I agree with you and think that the captain is going to propose," Georgiana warned them. "It is only that I have decided that you are right, and I should not marry a man whom I do not love."

Mr. Tomlinson would get over it in time. She hated, whether she intended it or not, to have led him on. But she had faith that a man of his disposition would move on with a little patience.

Maria jumped up from her chair and hugged Georgiana again. "I am so happy for you!" she declared. "I am certain that soon you will be announcing your wedding and going through all that I have gone through. Or rather what you have already gone through in helping me, but you will be doing it as the bride this time."

Georgiana smiled. She really had done half of the work in organizing and planning this wedding.

"Perhaps you can help me," she said as Maria pulled back and sat back down again.

"I know that you are in jest so that you might ease your heart," Edward said quietly. "But we have faith. Even if you do not. Even if you are unsure of yourself—be sure in us. Trust in us and what we see in you.

"After all, we did not see that we loved each other. You figured it out long before I did, and certainly the rest of society did as well. I was completely in the dark.

"If that can happen to me, then I think you can possibly try to accept that there might be things happening of which you are not yet aware, either. And that I just might be right about the captain.

"I am your older brother, you know," Edward added, a teasing note in his voice.

Georgiana smiled at him, finally reaching for her tea. She felt as though she could eat properly for the first time in weeks. "That you are," she told him. "That you most certainly are."

It was time to be brave.

CHAPTER 46

GEORGIANA WAS glad to hear that Mr. Tomlinon would be going to London on business anyhow. She would hate to ask him to come up to the city on a special trip, only for her, and then only so that she might reject him.

She felt terribly, but she no longer felt sick to her stomach. She felt only so awful for Mr. Tomlinson's sake. She hoped that he would soon find someone else upon whom to bestow his affections.

But as for herself, she no longer felt that horrible, sickly, twisting feeling in her stomach. She felt overall much calmer than she had previously.

That told her that she had made the right decision. It was a risk, yes. And she would have to be prepared for possible ridicule and comments behind her back the rest of her life should Captain Trentworth not propose as her brother believed.

But she would rather endure those comments than trap herself and Mr. Tomlinson in a marriage that might make miserable monsters of them both.

Maria went with her to meet Mr. Tomlinson at the park. She would be painting and sketching, which was fortunate. Maria was an observant girl at all times, except for when she was deep in her art.

Edward liked to tease that an earthquake could happen, and if Maria was in the middle of a painting, she would not notice but would carry on as always.

While Maria did her art, Mr. Tomlinson and Georgiana could talk and she could give him her answer.

He met them at Maria's favorite bench, for it gave her an excellent vantage point over the lake with the swans. Mr. Tomlinson seemed to be in good spirits.

She hated to have to destroy those spirits momentarily. But it was important that she let him know as soon as possible. That way he could begin to heal and move on as soon as possible.

"Miss Reginald. And this must be Miss Worthing, your future sister-in-law."

"Only a few days now," Maria said, beaming. She practically vibrated with excitement whenever someone mentioned the wedding. She was especially joyful, Georgiana knew, because her father was still alive and well enough to walk her down the aisle.

Maria then went about getting her paints and all set up.

Georgiana took a deep breath and focused on Mr. Tomlinson.

"Sir, I hope that you will not mind my asking you here on such quick notice. I am glad to hear that you are already in London. For what I am about to say could not fairly be said through paper and pen.

"I know that I told you I must wait until after the wedding, but circumstances and my own heart have contrived to change that.

"You are a charming man. An educated man. And, most importantly, a good man. I know that any woman who marries you will be happy in your care."

Mr. Tomlinson's eyes lit with understanding, and he nodded. "Ah. But that woman is not to be you."

She shook her head. "No, it is not. I have received your attentions with great appreciation. And my first inclination, I must admit, was to say yes to your proposal.

"But while I respect you and find you most amiable, I do not love you. And I fear that your affections for me outweigh mine for you.

"I know that some would say that I am foolish for rejecting a man such as yourself. Especially at my age. However, despite the security of a marriage with you... I could not subject you to a union in which you loved someone who did not love you in return.

"That struck me as too unfair. Too unkind of me. And while one could say that I would grow to love you, I cannot make decisions based upon a distant, future hope, one that may not even come to pass.

"I can only make decisions based upon what I know and understand in the present moment. And in the present moment, I feel no such passions for you as you feel for me.

"Perhaps if you cared for me less I would be more inclined to accept. For we would then be on more even footing. But I would not for all the world join with you when I could not give back to you all the love that you gave to me."

Mr. Tomlinson listened to her carefully, and then nodded. "I think that your judgment is unexpectedly compassionate. I would not expect anything less from you, of course. But I know what straits you must be under.

"For you to set aside any fears and think of my wellbeing in the matter, and to be so honest with me... it is a rare woman who can do such a thing.

"I cannot pretend that this does not cause some ache in me. But you are correct in that I would not wish to give someone my heart without receiving theirs in return."

He bowed to her. "I wish you the best of luck, Miss Reginald. For you deserve a man who will cherish you. I hope that you find him and that you cherish him in return."

"Believe me, sir, I wish nothing but the best for you as well. You are a most amiable man and deserve a lady who will love you with all the joy and affection that you will undoubtedly bestow upon her."

Mr. Tomlinson gave her a wry smile. "Were there ever two people more amicable about the turning down of an engagement?"

Georgiana smiled in return. "I highly doubt so, but I am glad of it. I feared greatly how I should tell you, for I knew it would hurt you and that was the last thing that I wished for you."

"Well, there is plenty of time yet and plenty of women who are in the world," Mr. Tomlinson replied. "I will not let myself sink into despair. That is not in my nature."

"Nor indeed would I expect it to be."

Mr. Tomlinson said his goodbye to Maria, turned to go... and then paused.

He turned back to Georgiana.

"May I express my wish," he told her, "if I may be so bold—that Captain Trentworth might come to his senses and give you the marriage you so richly deserve."

He bowed once more, as Georgiana did her best not to gape at him in surprise, and then he walked off.

Maria looked up a moment or two later and looked around. "Oh, that was rather fast, was it not? I expected him to try and win you over with some charming rhetoric."

"I suspect that he knew what I was not telling him," Georgiana replied faintly. "Namely that my heart belonged to someone else."

"Rather astute of him," Maria said, turning back to her art. "I am glad that he took it so well. Edward would have flown into a temper, would he not?"

"If it was because of you, my dear, I have no doubt he would have called for a duel," Georgiana replied, only half joking.

Edward was not exactly known for his patient temper.

"Well, it is a happy thing then that I return his affections," Maria said, not concerned in the slightest.

Georgiana sat down on the bench, breathing heavily as her heart raced in her chest.

That had gone much better than she had hoped for. She had expected some resentment, some anger, perhaps an attempt to persuade her to change her mind.

There might very well be some discord in Mr. Tomlinson. Some anger or resentment. But if so, he had not shown it to her. He had respected her decision and taken it in good grace.

She greatly appreciated it.

And now there was nothing left but to focus on the wedding and on helping her brother and Maria. Then, the day of...

It was quite a coincidence, she could not help but think. The day that would seal the fate of her brother and Maria and bind them to one another was the day that would seal her fate as well.

That was the day that she would either know her greatest joy or get confirmation on her greatest sorrow. She would know whether she was to be a blushing bride herself soon enough, or if she was to fully enter and embrace her spinsterhood.

Georgiana took another deep breath. This was her chance to

show courage, she reminded herself. Her chance to do what she had not been able to do before and risk herself for what she wanted.

She only hoped that it would pay off.

CHAPTER 47

ROBERT WAS NOT AT ALL LOOKING FORWARD to the wedding.

He had been doing his best to distract himself in the days leading up to it. He had gone into the country to look at a few estates that he might possibly buy.

That hardly worked. The entire time he could not help but wonder what Miss Reginald would think of them.

Robert had never thought to buy an estate simply for himself. It was for when he had a wife, and the hope of children on the way.

Buying an estate only for himself felt like an extravagance, a waste. And a symbol of something that might never come to pass. An empty dream.

As he walked through the grounds, he could not help but remember what Miss Reginald had said in her letters about the sort of home she would love to live in.

She had wanted a garden. Nothing large or ornate. But something, just a little bit of earth, in which she might plant some flowers.

She had wanted to find a gardener and undergardener with whom she could converse. Someone she might even help physically with the planting and weeding.

"Having a little something to do with my hands," she had written. "Something that I have truly worked on and can call the fruits of my labor... it would be quite lovely."

They had spoken about her love of sunshine and his indulgence in wanting a hidden room. As a child he'd read stories about people in estates who used the old priest holes and such to commit dark deeds or to escape bandits or some such. It was a childish notion, but he had always wanted something like that in his house.

Miss Reginald, of course, had not laughed at him. She had said it sounded delightful and endearing.

When he had pictured walking through the houses, on the grounds, asking questions, he had pictured Miss Reginald by his side, on his arm. She would be asking her own questions and making her own observations.

Now he was all alone.

He found himself asking the sort of questions that he thought she would ask. Inquiring after things that Miss Reginald would care about were she to try and move in.

Every time, he would curse himself after the fact for his weakness and his folly.

And so it was that the day of the wedding came and he had completely failed to distract himself.

He dressed in his best, of course. He might be nursing his wounds but there was no reason for him to be anything but polite and courteous at Lord Reginald's wedding. Miss Worthing must have gone to some trouble to rearrange things on such short notice, no matter what she claimed to the contrary.

It was the least he could do to show up and be a proper guest.

When he arrived at the church, he found that there were swells of other wedding guests already there and still arriving.

The wedding of a duke, Robert supposed, could not be a small and intimate affair no matter how much one might hope for it.

Robert did not recognize a majority of the people that he saw. Some of them he supposed he must have known from when he was last in England. But he could not recall.

Doubtless they would recognize him and expect him to recognize them. And then they would be horribly offended when he did not.

Ah, well.

He made his way into the church, admiring the decorations and the flowers. He could be imagining it but he felt as though he could sense Miss Reginald's touch in the décor.

Of course, it would all be to Miss Worthing and Lord Reginald's taste. But the way the flowers were so delicately arranged. The draping of the silk. It spoke to him of Miss Reginald's careful and graceful touch.

He was obviously going off on flights of fancy now.

Robert navigated his way through the crowd and found himself a seat. He was not quite at the front where the family sat but he was near enough.

His breath caught in his throat—he could see her.

Miss Reginald was seated in the front row as was proper. There were some other people there as well. Most likely distant cousins and other nobility.

The Reginalds did not have much family, from what Robert could recall. And he vaguely remembered someone telling him that Miss Worthing did not have anyone other than her father.

It seemed that instead, the Reginalds had decided to flatter the various nobility that they had to invite for political reasons and put them towards the front instead.

It was a clever move. Robert suspected that they had Miss Reginald to thank for that as well. Miss Worthing and the duke had said that she was the one to handle the seating.

Robert could see her sitting up at the front. Her back was to him. He could not see much of her dress, but her hat and hair were wonderfully done.

He wished that he could go up and say hello. But no. He would not cause her distress.

He looked around but did not see Mr. Tomlinson anywhere. As he had suspected, Miss Reginald had not wanted to cause problems by asking her brother to invite another guest at the last minute.

Robert promised himself that he would approach her at the earliest convenience in order to congratulate her and apologize.

Normally he would not want to bother her until after the wedding had concluded, but he feared that she would notice he was there. How could she not? And once she had, she would worry about him and be upset that he was there.

It would be best if he simply let her know as early as possible that he bore her no ill will and that he was the one at fault. That way she could relax and enjoy the wedding instead of fretting over whether or not Robert was going to tear into her again.

Then he heard everyone in the church grow quiet as the minister stepped up with the duke at the front of the room. A hush fell over the room.

Lord Reginald looked quite handsome, but he also looked quite nervous. As if he was afraid that this was all a dream and he was going to wake up and find that Miss Worthing did not even truly exist.

Robert wanted to tell the man that there was no reason to fret. Miss Worthing was quite real, and quite obviously adored the duke.

But then the music started up and the doors to the church opened.

To tell the truth, Robert could hardly remember the wedding ceremony once it was all said and done. He kept being distracted by Miss Reginald.

She turned to look back at Miss Worthing as she entered with her father. As she did so, her eyes caught onto Robert's.

They stared at one another for a moment. Miss Reginald looked startled, like a deer in a forest. Her gray-blue eyes widened and her cheeks flushed.

Robert could not read the expression on her face. There was no fear there. No surprise. Could it be... anticipation?

He spent the rest of the ceremony staring at the back of her head and desperately wondering what she was thinking.

Was she angry with him? Was she looking forward to rubbing her engagement in his face?

That did not strike him as the sort of behavior that Miss Reginald would want to engage in.

But one never knew for certain, did they?

If she did want to bestow a little superiority on him, she would be well within her rights. He had behaved most disgracefully.

He supposed that he would just have to wait and find out. He would be getting his answer one way or another when he approached her.

The ceremony continued on, and Robert did his best to try and pay attention. But his thoughts just kept drifting to Miss Reginald.

What if he could persuade her to drop her engagement? What if she said yes? What if—surely there would not be too many people who would know of it. And she had only just gotten engaged.

She would not dare announce it until her brother returned from his honeymoon. Otherwise it would be stealing the attention from the duke and Miss Reginald would never do such a thing.

She could, theoretically, end the engagement. And then he could propose, say to her all the things that he wanted to say, give her all the praises that she deserved to hear...

No, Robert reminded himself sternly.

That was thinking of himself again. That was what he had done the first time. When he had demanded that she go against her father, he was not thinking of Miss Reginald and the trials that she must endure if she said yes.

No, he had been thinking only of how much he wanted her. Of how she ought to naturally make such sacrifices for him. He had not given the proper thought to what sacrifices he should be making for her.

Being in love with someone was about caring for them and doing what was best for them. Not what he wanted.

The ceremony ended.

Lord Reginald and the former Miss Worthing, now Lady Reginald, kissed happily in front of their friends, family, and assorted peers.

Robert clapped along with everyone else. The couple did look immensely happy. Lady Reginald had tears in her eyes.

The large assembly followed the couple out of the church, where it was announced that dinner would be held at the Foreshire estate. The couple got into a carriage and went on ahead so that they might change for dinner.

Especially Lady Reginald, who had quite the train to tackle.

Everyone was chatting about the ceremony as the other carriages pulled up. Most people seemed inclined to want to talk for a little while longer. Oh, did you see the flowers, and oh, did you see her dress, and oh, did you see the way that they looked at one another?

Robert immediately sought out Miss Reginald.

She was standing off to the side, apparently having tried to get some respite after talking to everyone. She would have to be a part of the receiving line at the dinner as she and the newlyweds welcomed all the guests into their home.

It was not a task that he envied her for.

But it was good luck for him that she was standing alone. There were other people around but so far they seemed content to gossip amongst themselves. He must move quickly, before someone else engaged her in conversation.

He walked up to her as the first people began to fill the carriages.

"Miss Reginald."

She jumped, startled, but then curtsied. "Captain Trentworth. My brother told me that he had invited you to the wedding. I hope that you enjoyed the ceremony."

"It was the first time that I have attended a wedding where the couple were so clearly in love," he told her truthfully.

Miss Reginald smiled softly. "They are devoted to one another. And to think it took them so long to realize it. They will be happy, and that makes me happy."

Robert glanced around. "I hope that you will not mind if I ask you to take a stroll with me through the church garden? I fear that I have... a great apology to make to you, and I fear it would embarrass both of us to do it in front of others."

"I see nothing scandalous in a small stroll," Miss Reginald replied evenly.

Robert took a deep breath. Here was his chance. "Let us walk, then."

He would do it properly this time.

CHAPTER 48

GEORGIANA HELD her breath as Captain Trentworth led her through the church garden.

The garden was small, accompanied by the cemetery. Not exactly the most romantic of strolls. But she cared not one bit. So long as she got to tell the captain the truth, that was all that mattered.

And it was a nice garden. There was honeysuckle and some pretty wildflowers and some roses. A proper English garden.

She hoped to have one of her own someday.

Once they were out of earshot, Captain Trentworth stopped walking and turned to face her. His hands were behind his back and he looked... troubled, almost.

"You must allow me to extend to you, first and foremost, my most sincere apologies.

"I was chastised by your friend Miss Weston and even partially by Mr. Norwich. And yet I was a stubborn fool who gave you an apology not even worthy of the name.

"I knew that you would be able to tell that my heart was not in those words that I wrote. But I cared not. At the time, all I thought of was my own wounded pride and my bitterness."

His gaze bore into hers, dark and earnest. Georgiana felt that she could not move from the spot if she tried.

"You were right to tell me off soundly in the way that you did. I was judgmental. Harsh. Unforgiving. I allowed my anger to control me.

"From the beginning, I have realized how selfish I have been. Asking you to risk your entire life and go against your father was selfish of me. Had I been acting as a lover truly should and thinking of what was best for you, I would not have urged you to undertake such a course.

"Then when I returned and met you once again, I selfishly tried to turn away from you. I did not want to hear your apologies. I tried to grow close to other women in front of you. Even though my heart had not forgotten you, I shoved you rudely out of my thoughts.

"And then, when you opened your heart to me and took a risk, the sort of risk that I had once abandoned you for not taking—I threw it back into your face.

"I made awful assumptions about a man who had never done me any harm. It was because I was still angry at your father and since he was dead, my anger was visited on the son instead.

"That is no excuse and I do not mean it to be. I only wished to explain my reasoning, as terrible as it was."

Georgiana wished that she could say something—let him know that she understood and that all had been forgiven. From the moment he started speaking, she had forgiven all of it.

But this was clearly something that he had to say. And she could hear the voices of Julia and Mrs. Weston in her ear, urging to keep silent. Reminding her that she deserved an apology.

Captain Trentworth took a shaking breath, as though he had been underwater and was just now breaking the surface.

"I did you a great wrong, Miss Reginald. My... my dear Miss Reginald. For that is what you still are to me."

Georgiana could have sworn for a moment that her heart stopped and the earth tilted slightly, sending her reeling inside.

Captain Trentworth's gaze upon her was unhappy, but soft.

"I understand that congratulations are in order. May I extend my most sincere ones. But I wish for you to understand the scope of my fault and my apology.

"To be unkind to someone about whom one does not care is bad enough. But to slander a woman—the woman—whom you value above all others...

"Truly, I have been shown how little I have deserved you, now or back then. I hope that you will not hold it too much against me should we meet in the future.

"You showed me your heart and you defended your family, as you were quite right to do. And I did not appreciate it as I should have. I should have laid myself at your feet. I would do so now, if I were allowed.

"But that is no matter. I hope that you will be happy. I hope that you will believe me when I say that I hope for nothing but your happiness. And I hope that you will find it in your heart to forgive me after I have twice treated you ill."

He bowed to her. "Good day, Miss Reginald."

"Stay." The words were out of her mouth before she could even register that she had thought them. "Do not turn away from me, Captain. Not when you have yet to give me leave to speak my heart."

Captain Trentworth turned back to her, waiting. He looked like a man who was expecting the noose.

Georgiana took a deep breath. She thought that she might cry from pure relief.

He was not only apologizing to her—he did still love her. He did! There was still hope that she might get to be with him, that her long wished for happiness was not entirely out of her reach.

"Captain, I accept your apology," she told him. "It was genuinely said. And I can well imagine that it took you much writing out to fix upon the precise words."

Captain Trentworth blushed slightly and looked down at his feet. "You still know me far too well, Miss Reginald."

She smiled at him and waited until he once again raised his eyes to her before speaking again. "I cannot pretend, nor do I wish to pretend, that your actions and words towards me did not wound me.

"They did, and they wounded me deeply. I was in a state that night such as I have never been since you last left me. However, I can understand your anger.

"I am grateful beyond what I can say to know that you have come to see my brother as I do. And I am humbled and appreciative that you have come to see how you hurt me so.

"But," she said, taking another deep breath, "there is one thing in which you are gravely mistaken."

"Oh?" Captain Trentworth sounded mildly concerned. As though there might be something else that he ought to apologize for, only he had forgotten what it was.

Georgiana allowed her smile to take over her face. "There is no need to congratulate me. I am not promised to anyone."

Captain Trentworth stared at her. He looked like a man who had been struck by lightning. "You—but your letter, to your brother, I—"

"You did not stay to hear all of it, did you?" she asked gently. "In it I detailed the positive attributes of Mr. Tomlinson. But then I told my brother that I had not yet accepted this proposal. That I had asked him to wait until after the wedding.

"I was writing to my brother so that he would be prepared. So that when I arrived in person he could give me his advice.

"I was so torn, Captain, on what to do. I thought that I had no other prospects. And that after you, a secure marriage was all that I could hope for. That a loving marriage was beyond my reach.

"And so I wrote to ask my brother if he would tell me his opinion on whether I should say yes or no.

"I took his advice, and just two days ago, I told Mr. Tomlinson that I would not be accepting his proposal. I am free in every respect."

She was not free in her heart, of course, for that belonged to Captain Trentworth. But there would be time for her to tell him that. She must first see what his reaction was.

Captain Trentworth stared at her for a moment. "You are—you are not engaged."

She shook her head, still smiling. His utter astonishment and confusion was rather endearing. "No."

"You are free of all promises."

"Yes."

"There is no one else? Mr. Tomlinson is a charming man, he has much to recommend him, he has a large income, he—"

Georgiana shook her head again and dared to take a small step towards him. "If I may be so bold, Captain. He has many things to recommend him, that is true. But he is missing the most funda-mental thing of all."

Captain Trentworth stared at her like a starving man, one who would live or die upon her next words.

"He is not you," Georgiana confessed.

Captain Trentworth took a small step forward, staring down into her eyes. "Then I am not too late?" he asked. "You would give me yet another chance?"

"I fear I would give you as many chances as you asked for," Georgiana admitted. "And then some."

Captain Trentworth glanced away, clearing his throat. "I... I confess, Miss Reginald, that a part of me that indulges in fancy had hoped... but common sense dictated..."

He shook his head and then looked back at her. "I find I do not quite have the words."

"You need only say four little ones," she advised him, laughing lightly.

Captain Trentworth took her hand. "There is that laughter. I have so longed to hear it."

"I have been saving it for you."

He brought her hand up to his lips and kissed her knuckles softly. "You know that I am not one who does well with his own words," he said. "But do you remember that poem from Byron?

"She walks in beauty, like the night

"Of cloudless climes and starry skies;

And all that's best of dark and bright

Meet in her aspect and her eyes;

Thus mellowed to that tender light

Which heaven to gaudy day denies."

Georgiana blushed and had to glance down at the ground lest her face give too much away. "She Walks in Beauty," she said, naming the poem.

Captain Trentworth had written it out to her in one of his letters. It had been 'their' poem. She was surprised that he still remembered it by heart, although she supposed that she ought not to be.

He nodded. "That is you, to me. How you have always been to me. And always will be.

"One shade the more, one ray the less,

"Had half impaired the nameless grace

"Which waves in every snow-white tress—"

Georgiana laughed, for she remembered that as well. The original words were 'in every raven tress', but Georgiana's hair was the opposite of dark. She was always the lightest-haired woman in the room.

And so Captain Trentworth, when he had written it out to her that first time, had changed it to 'snow-white'.

He squeezed her hand. "Or softly lightens o'er her face;

"Where thoughts serenely sweet express,

"How pure, how dear their dwelling-place."

Georgiana smiled at him and finished the poem for him:

"And on that cheek, and o'er that brow,

"So soft, so calm, yet eloquent,

"The smiles that win, the tints that glow,

"But tell of days in goodness spent,

"A mind at peace with all below,

"A heart whose love is innocent!"

Captain Trentworth nodded, tenderly tucking a lock of unruly hair behind her ear. "I have often thought of you and that poem. I think of it, and I think of you. I think of you, and I think of the poem.

"I am no poet myself. As our previous letters often showed."

Georgiana giggled in remembrance and he smiled at her.

"But I do have a good memory for the words of others. And his have stuck in my heart, as has every word that you have written or spoke to me.

"I will quote that poem, or any poem, at you if it will convince you to allow me to do what we should have done all those years ago: join us together as one.

"Tell me that I may finally call you mine. As you have always been in my heart."

His eyes were so terribly earnest gazing into hers. Georgiana's breath caught in her throat.

This was what she ought to feel when proposed to. This was how she ought to feel when she was about to give her answer. No doubts. No sick feeling in her stomach.

Just beautiful, wonderful, certainty.

EPILOGUE

ROBERT COULD NOT FIND it within himself to breathe.

He wanted to keep begging her, imploring her to say yes, but he was out of words. He did not know what else to say.

Miss Reginald was gazing up at him with wet, warm eyes, a smile dancing repeatedly across her face. Her soft laughter still rang in his ears.

She had recited the end of the poem for him. She had gazed at him in rapturous wonder as he recited it to her. Please, let this be the moment. Let all his dreams finally come true.

"You know, Captain," she said slowly, a teasing light entering her eyes, "you have not yet asked me directly."

He started. "Have I not?"

She shook her head, pressing her lips together in a vain attempt to hide her amused smile. "No."

"Well then." He was a proper idiot. "Allow me to rectify that. Miss Georgiana Reginald, would you allow me to make you my wife? Will you marry me?"

She squeezed his hand, where it was still caught with hers. "Yes," she whispered. "Yes, always."

He caught her around the waist and spun her, his sudden rush of elation too energetic to be ignored. She laughed, clinging to him, letting him spin her like children.

Robert set her down, smiling helplessly. Then he remembered —they were at a wedding for someone else.

"I must apologize—it was not my intention to take anything away from your brother's momentous day. I simply could not—I fear I allowed myself to get carried away."

Miss Reginald smiled at him, shaking her head. "There is no need. We shall tell them once the dinner is finished. But I certainly encouraged you to become carried away."

He chuckled. "Well, yes, when you tell a man that you are still in love with him, of course he is liable to get a little carried away in response."

"We will tell them after dinner," she repeated firmly. "They will be overjoyed for us."

"I do not want to interrupt this special day," Robert protested.

"Nonsense. They will be upset if we wait too long to tell them. They wanted us to get together. They encouraged me to definitively say no to Mr. Tomlinson and take the chance that you would still want me."

Robert released a breath. "It appears that I have to thank the both of them, then."

"You were right, in a way," she said. "I needed to be courageous. I needed to take the risk, and so that is what I resolved to do."

"You were also right," he told her. "I was selfish. And I will do my best to not be selfish with you from now on."

He took a deep breath. "May I take the liberty of kissing you, then?"

Georgiana blushed. "You most certainly may."

He pulled her in that final inch and kissed her softly, tenderly, as he had so longed to do for all those years.

Georgiana melted into him. He thought that he would never want to stop holding her.

She pulled back and he released her, squeezing her hand one last time before stepping away.

"You will have to be in the receiving line," he told her. "And I have no doubt that you have many other duties. Some of which you have deliberately volunteered for, I am certain, so that the bride will have as little to do as possible."

Georgiana laughed. He was terribly excited to keep making her laugh for the rest of their lives. "I have taken on more than I might normally would, it is true. But you must remember that there is only one parent in this entire matter and he is too sickly to really handle things.

"And why should the bride not relax on her wedding day? I shall expect her to do the same for me on my wedding day."

"Which will come as soon as we can be allowed," Robert assured her. They had already wasted so much time and he did not want to waste a moment more if he could help it.

Georgiana looked as though she might burst into tears out of happiness.

"Shall we?" he asked her, indicating for them to head out.

She nodded. "Yes, we must."

The rest of the evening passed by in a blur. He was almost vibrating with impatience. He could hardly wait to ask Lord Reginald for his blessing. He knew that the duke would not withhold it.

But he had to bow and exchange pleasantries with everyone. He had to pretend to care about all of the small talk that all of these people that he didn't even know were making.

The one bright moment was when he got to say hello to everyone in the receiving line and he could spend a moment with Miss Reginald again. She smiled at him, the smile of two people sharing a wonderful secret.

After dinner, after the dancing, after the celebration... it was finally, finally time for everyone to retire.

The lord and his new lady finished saying goodbye to everyone. The guests filtered out with their good wishes. And Robert waited in the drawing room while Miss Reginald finished instructing the servants on the clean-up.

When the duke and the duchess finally closed the door on their guests, they entered the drawing room with knowing smiles on their faces.

"My lord," Robert said. "I was hoping that I might have a moment of your time, privately?"

Lady Reginald curtsied to them both and exited the room—no doubt to run immediately to Miss Reginald and ask her for information on everything.

Lord Reginald smiled at him. "Captain."

"My lord." Robert took a deep breath. Even knowing what the answer would be this time, and that it would be a positive one, he still found himself anxious. "I would like to ask for your blessing in taking the hand of your sister in marriage."

The duke's smile widened. "I take it that you have proposed and she has said yes?"

Robert nodded. "She had more presence of mind about it than I did, my lord."

Lord Reginald chuckled. "That was how I felt when I proposed to my wife."

Robert could tell that the duke had said 'my wife' for the sheer enjoyment of it. He could not blame the man.

"You have my blessing," the duke informed him. "And when my wife and I return from our honeymoon I shall expect us all to begin preparations immediately. I am personally of the opinion that my sister has waited long enough."

"I quite agree, my lord. And frankly, I have no wish to wait any longer than necessary either."

"Edward," the duke told him. "We are to be brothers. You may call me by my Christian name."

"Robert," Robert replied. "And it is an honor to call you brother."

"The honor is all mine."

The two women entered, arm in arm. Miss Reginald looked rather nervous, while Lady Reginald was beaming.

The duke—Edward—smiled at his sister. "I have given my blessing, my dear."

She went to him and took his hands, kissing his cheek. "Thank you," she said, and Robert could hear how her voice wavered with emotion.

She turned and crossed the room, allowing Robert to take her by the arm and pull her in. She was his, at last.

Finally, all was as it should be.

THE EXTENDED EPILOGUE

I am humbled you read my novel *"A Love Worth Saving"* till the end!

Are you aching to know what happens to our lovebirds?

Visit a search engine and enter the link you see below the picture to connect to a more personal level and as a BONUS, I will send you the Extended Epilogue of this Book!

https://fannyfinch.com/ff-002-exep/

LOVE LETTERS TO A LADY

CHAPTER 49

Julia Weston looked forward to a great many things in life.

She looked forward to balls and dancing, to long walks and picnics, and of course shopping.

But most of all, she looked forward to nothing better than a lively dinner party.

Balls were all well and good and she enjoyed them immensely. There was something oddly intimate about balls, the way that one could carry on a conversation with a friend and it was busy enough that nobody could overhear you.

A proper dinner party, however, was the best for lively conversation. A group of witty people, discussing anything and everything over dinner. And then cards and games afterwards!

It was all quite fun.

Dinners also had the added benefit of being easier on Mother. She did her best to go to balls but Julia didn't want to overtax her. With a dinner party, Julia could play host and Mother could take dinner by herself. Then she could come down and engage in the card games.

Sometimes dinners could be awfully boring if there weren't the right sort of people at them. Stuffy people with no imagination and no literary bent and nothing to talk about but the weather.

She did so hate those dinners.

Fortunately, this was not going to be one of those such dinners.

She was hosting it and therefore she was in charge of who was invited.

Of course there were always courtesies to be upheld. And she had to invite a few people for Mother's sake. But overall it would be a lively affair.

Julia looked herself over in the mirror. Georgiana, her dearest friend, had always said that Julia was blessed for liking her appearance. Most women seemed to hate how they looked and wanted nothing more than to look like someone else.

But Julia had always liked her dark hair and dark eyes, her sharp eyebrows and thick eyelashes. She knew the thing nowadays was to be pale and fragile-looking. Georgiana fit that perfectly with her white-blonde hair and gray eyes.

Julia, however, thought she was quite content just the way that she was.

The light blue frock she was wearing, with its slightly darker blue ribbon around the middle, quite complemented her look. Or so she thought.

"I think it's ravishing, don't you, Mother?"

Mrs. Weston, Julia's mother, had once been a great beauty. Julia could remember being a child and watching her mother get ready for a ball in the evening.

It had been like watching a queen get ready. In fact, Julia had once thought her mother must be nobility of some kind. Why else would someone be so regal and so beautiful?

But illness had done away with all of that. It broke Julia's heart to see her mother in such a state.

Of course, Mother bore it all very well. Her mind had not gone and her wit, often spoken of in social circles, was as sharp as ever.

But she could rarely stand to go out for long periods of time. She spent most of her time at balls sitting. Friends went to her now instead of her calling upon them, for walking too much and in the sun tired her immensely.

Just a short two months ago, Julia and her mother—along with Georgiana and a young gentleman—had gone on a picnic. Mother had not complained once, but she had slept all the next day in order to recover.

Sometimes, Julia wished that there was something she could

do. That she could be like a heroine in a novel, and learn that there was a cure! A great, wonderful cure, if only she could compel an expedition to go to the heart of deepest Africa, or the highest mountains of Tibet, or the wilds of South American jungles to find it.

Julia had never seen anything wrong with indulging in a little flight of fancy now and again. In her mind's eye she could see herself, triumphantly grinding the rare tropical flower into a powder and putting it in a soup, presenting it to her mother.

Then Mother would be well again, and become the joyful, beautiful person that Julia remembered from her childhood.

But flights of fancy always ended. And she would have to face the truth once again.

Neither Mother nor Father were fans of pessimism. And Mother was a woman possessed of an unusual determination.

But Julia could not help but worry. This was her mother.

Mother raised an eyebrow. "I hardly see the point of wearing that frock, my dear."

Julia frowned at her dress in the mirror. "Why would you say that?"

"Because the point of looking lovely is to show yourself off to potential suitors. And since you are woefully picky about said suitors you might as well wear black for all your frocks are worth."

"Mother!"

"Well there is little point in setting out a bird feeder if the feeder is empty," Mother replied tartly.

"Mother—"

Father appeared in the doorway, knocking lightly upon the open door. "May I enter?"

Julia sat down in her chair in despair. Father always took Mother's side.

"You look lovely," Father announced. He always said that. Julia was convinced that she could put herself in a sackcloth and Father would say that she looked quite fashion-forward. "I am departing for London in the carriage. Do me a favor and don't cause too many scandals while I'm gone."

"Please impose upon your daughter the importance of finding a husband," Mother said.

"My daughter? Why is she always only my daughter when you are cross with her?" Father asked.

He then looked over at Julia. "But you really must give some thought to marriage, dear. Your mother is right.

"You will not be young forever. Look at how panicked dear Georgiana became after so many years. Your mother and I will not be around forever."

Julia sighed. She had heard this whole lecture before. But it was so hard to think about marriage when she had yet to meet a man who held her attention for any length of time.

She knew, objectively, that she must find a husband. Knowing objectively, however, and feeling the pressure of it were two different things entirely.

Father frowned at her. "Are you even listening to me, Julia? I know that I have recovered from my illness. But it will not be the last illness that I have. I am no longer in the prime of health.

"In fact, your mother and I are rather of the opinion that if you do not treat your suitors more seriously, you are to have your other freedoms restricted."

"What?" Julia stood up in shock and horror at that. She knew that her parents allowed her more freedoms and more headway than many other ladies. She was not at all anxious to give any of that up.

Father nodded solemnly. "Yes. It has become clear to us that we have allowed you to behave as if you were already mistress of a home—"

"Because Mother is ill!" Julia protested. "She shouldn't have to handle such things when I am around!"

"Your reasons are thoughtful," her mother said. "And it was born out of necessity. But it has allowed you to become far too certain of yourself."

Julia could hardly believe what she was hearing.

"And you think that springing this news upon me in such a fashion will help me to be more inclined to follow such advice?"

"It is not advice," Father said. "It is an order. We are your parents and when we tell you that you are to set about properly finding a husband then you are to agree and do as you are told."

Rarely did Father speak so firmly. Julia wanted to ask why he was being like this. Had she done something wrong? Had she embarrassed the family in some way?

Perhaps he was worried that his illness would come back. Both of her parents had been feeling poorly when they decided to move to Bath. Although Father now felt better, they elected to stay for Mother's sake.

Could it be that Father had news about his illness that he had not told Julia?

Fear stuck in her throat, closing it up. Of course, she could not know for certain. And Father would never tell her if that was the case.

It could simply be that he was seeing all the other young ladies getting married. Georgiana had just gotten engaged to be married and many had already started to call her a spinster.

Perhaps it grated on his pride. His daughter was the talk of the town and yet, not wed. It must be hard on him, to hear about all of these other women getting married and his own daughter was not. His daughter, said to be the star of many a ball.

Julia could appreciate that. But how could she be expected to marry a man when they were all so shallow? None of them truly appreciated her wit. Or seemed to think of her as anything other than an opportunity for her dowry or ability to bear children.

She loved her life with her parents far too much to be compelled to marry a man whom she did not love. They seemed to love her, but often without truly knowing her.

And she certainly did not love any of them.

Her parents, she knew, had not been in love when they had married. But surely they could understand that she wanted more?

Their marriage had worked out. They loved one another now. But not everyone was so lucky.

Her mother sighed. "You will not be young and sparkling forever, my dear. Women are not diamonds.

"It is important that you start to think about this seriously. Georgiana was fortunate in that her brother was rich and willing to care for her after her father passed.

"You have no one. No brother, and I highly doubt your cousin Fitzwilliam shall wish to care for you. That is not at all fair to force upon your relative.

"It is your duty to get married. It is not a privilege. It is time that you started to take that duty more seriously.

"At this dinner there will be several eligible young men. I shall expect you to pay close attention to them. Any one of them would make you an excellent husband."

Julia groaned inwardly. She should have known that something was afoot when Mother showed such care with the guest list.

Normally, Mother didn't care to see the guest list at all. "Whatever you think is best, dear," she would say. "So long as there are people with whom I might converse."

Not this time. This time, Mother had gone over everyone. Julia had thought it odd, but she had dismissed it from her mind.

Mother must have been ensuring that men of whom she approved as potential sons-in-law would be present.

Julia wanted to seethe. She wanted to put her foot down—literally—and declare that she would not marry until the greatest of love compelled her to.

That was not the proper thing to do. The mature thing to do. Marriage was not about love. Marriage was about duty.

She had been living on borrowed time, so to speak, and now that time was up.

Julia searched her parents' faces. Found the worry hidden in the lines around her mother's eyes and in her father's clenched jaw.

They only wanted what was best for her, she told herself. They wanted to make sure that she was well taken care of, so that if Father took a turn for the worst again they needn't worry for her.

Julia nodded, swallowing down the protests she wanted to give.

"I shall do my best," she said. "You have my word on that."

Her father nodded brusquely. "You are quite the young lady," he said. It was as close to open affection as her father got. In fact, it might have been the highest compliment he had ever paid her. "I am certain that any man would be grateful to have you."

Julia bowed her head, grateful for the compliment.

And just like that, the somber mood was broken. "Well then," her father said. "I am off. Write to me frequently, my dear," he added, directing his words at Julia's mother. "You will receive my letters shortly."

"I await them with bated breath," her mother said dryly.

Julia had to smother a smile, for she knew that her mother secretly kept, carefully preserved, each letter that her father sent her.

Her father exited, and her mother fixed Julia with a look.

She had many looks. All of them managed to convey, in a single moment, a myriad of cutting thoughts.

It was quite a talent. Julia wished that she herself had such a skill.

"You will do as your father said," her mother told her. "And it would please me if you would not trouble and tease the poor men too much."

Julia snorted. "Mother, if they cannot handle my teasing while we are at a single dinner, how ever will they handle me as a wife?"

Her mother sighed, as though Julia were the bane of her existence. "Show yourself in your best light, that is all I ask. Your father has not put a time limit upon you but remember, I should like to see you wed before I am too ill to go."

Julia held in her groan of frustration.

The clock, it seemed, was ticking.

CHAPTER 50

JAMES NORWICH WAS USUALLY the sort who looked forward to dinner parties.

He could freely admit that he was the sort of man who rarely found a reason to be serious. Not that he did not take things seriously when it was required.

Rather, he tended to see things in an optimistic light and to find reasons for good cheer.

Dinner parties were always an excellent opportunity to exercise the wit of which he was so fond. And the Weston dinners were his favorite of households.

Mr. Weston had been James's instructor when he was a boy. He had always been fond of the man, although James had learned he would not be there that night.

Mrs. Weston was a woman of exceptional backbone and wit. James had grown up admiring her greatly and wishing for a mother like her. His own mother had been a vain woman.

But it was Miss Weston for whom he held the greatest of admiration.

No, not even admiration. He would never breathe it to another soul but his fondness for the lady had taken even deeper roots nearly two years ago now.

He could admit, to himself at least, that he was in love with her.

Miss Julia Weston was a most singular woman. Well read, educated, lively, and witty. She brightened any room that she was in.

She was fond of meddling and a bit mischievous. Perhaps a bit too much for some men. But to James, she was everything.

He admired her strength and her strong moral determination. A few months ago he had the privilege of witnessing her, against all propriety, give the dressing-down of the century to her best friend's suitor when he had done her wrong.

The suitor had, of course, seen the error of his ways and wooed his lady properly. They were to be married shortly and Norwich had been invited to the wedding. He was quite looking forward to it.

But the point still stood that Miss Weston had put herself at quite a risk addressing a gentleman in such a manner. But that had not mattered to her. What had mattered was that justice was done and her friend was protected.

Norwich had hardly been able to contain his amusement and his pride in watching her.

He had known the lady since she was quite young. And while she had never lost that youthful exuberance, he had come to be proud of the strong, intelligent, and determined woman that she was today.

He would have proposed to her in a moment, if he had thought that he had half a chance.

Miss Weston, however, had often made it clear that she viewed him as a brother. She teased and exchanged witticisms with him. She confided in him and was comfortable with him.

Never had he observed her giving him the flirtatious looks he had seen her casting at others. Or that other women had cast at him.

He was aware that he was a catch. He would be a count once Father died. Although, hopefully, that would be a long time in coming.

It was coming, though, and women were aware of it. He was more of a catch than he would have been without the title, even if he'd had the same annual income.

Many ladies had made it clear that they would be happy to become Mrs. Norwich. But none of them, he feared, caught his fancy nearly so much as Miss Weston.

Sometimes he wanted to be rid of all pretense and simply

declare himself. But what good would that do anybody? It would only serve to make Miss Weston feel awkward.

They had known one another nearly all their lives. They were not always close, per se. But they understood one another better than most. Or so he liked to flatter himself.

To have someone upon whom she relied as a friend turn around and impose his feelings upon her—he would be loath to do that to her.

Perhaps, had he been a better man or a stronger one, he would have warned Miss Weston that it was high time to marry.

She was not yet approaching the age where people would call her a spinster. She still had a couple of years left before that.

However, her father had been in ill health recently. And to have gone through several London seasons without a marriage... or even a proposal to speak of...

She was a free spirit, Miss Weston. He respected that. In fact, it was one of the things that he appreciated about her.

But he feared for her.

Perhaps he could propose to her under the guise of helping her?

But she would be insulted by that. Miss Weston did not like to be pitied or treated as someone to be protected and coddled. She would see it as condescension.

James instead resigned himself to another evening of pining for her and getting nowhere with it.

There are other women in the world, he reminded himself. Why can you not content yourself with them?

Perhaps he was in his own way as particular as Miss Weston.

Seeing that it was time to go, and far past the time to disperse with his melancholy reveries, he hastened to summon the carriage.

The Weston house was already lively and filled with the majority of the guests when he arrived. No sooner had he stepped over the threshold than he was seized upon the arm by Miss Weston.

She greeted him enthusiastically, with her usual turn of phrase:

"Oh, Mr. Norwich, there you are! And thank goodness for it!"

It always seemed that the moment of his arrival was the moment that Miss Weston was about to go completely off of her mind about something. And that his presence was a godsend and a saving grace.

He had never quite thought of it that way himself. He had always known it was one of Miss Weston's flights of fancy. She could be dramatic when she wanted to be—which was often.

"You will not believe the dire straits that I am in," she told him, hurrying him through the parlor to the fireplace. "Go ahead and guess. See if you can ascertain what is so distressing me."

"Your frock is not in the exact color of blue that you were dreaming of," he replied, deadpan.

Miss Weston looked quickly down at her frock. It was a most becoming shade of pale blue and went well with her dark hair and eyes. "Why, is there something the matter with it?"

Only that you look incredibly bewitching while wearing it. James shoved that thought aside. They were dangerous to think, for he never knew when he might lose himself and say one of them out loud.

And then he would really be in for it.

"Nothing at all," he replied. "It was only the first thing I could seize upon that might put you in such a state."

"Is that all you think that I think on?" Miss Weston replied in an arch tone.

"Oh, no, not at all. I think that you spend a great deal of time thinking how best to embarrass us poor men who deign to dance attendance on you. And some time, of course, for how you shall style your hair. It looks most fetching today. Did you think on it all yesterday afternoon?"

"You are the worst of men," Miss Weston declared. But she was giggling all through it. "Honestly. Why any of us put up with you, Mr. Norwich, I shall never know."

"I think that my incoming title and my great wealth have something to do with it."

"Oh, yes, there is that. I suppose that a title must make you half tolerable. When a man has a title, he goes from being plain to somewhat handsome. From boorish and brainless to simple of soul and ponderous. From arrogant to educated."

"Ah, but I know that I must be at least partially tolerable in truth and not simply because of my wealth. Otherwise, you would never bear to spend any time with me. I should never receive a dinner invitation."

"How do you know that my father is not uncommonly fond of you as his former student and forces me to always invite you?" Miss Weston replied. "Perhaps I am secretly filled with a seething hatred for you?"

"I highly doubt that you would wish to confide in me if that were the case."

Miss Weston's cheeks colored slightly. "How do you know that I have something to confide in you?"

James could not hide his pleased smile. "You are most fanciful when you have something serious that is at hand. You use humor to make light of it so that it will not seem so daunting a subject."

Miss Weston sighed, her face growing a bit more serious. "That is true. You know me far too well. I blame all the years of dinners.

"My parents have given me a stern lecture. I am to start looking in earnest for a husband and to welcome any suitors. They say that I am running out of time." Miss Weston bit her lip in agitation.

"I confess that I am... aggravated by this news. But I am even more worried by what it might mean. What it might indicate for my father's health."

James shook his head. "I am sure that your father is hale and hearty, Miss Weston. It is only a precaution."

"Mother wishes to see me married before she dies," Miss Weston added, her voice soft. "I had not thought her condition quite so bad. It is a malady that lingers, is it not? She has many years yet in which to snap at me and feel poorly."

"Parents are prone to worry," James replied, trying to soothe her. "And it is unusual that you are not yet wed. You must admit to that."

"I suppose that it is unusual, but you know I have a rather intense disposition. What man would be content to marry a woman who will be treated as nothing less than his equal? With her opinion heard and respected?"

"I think you would find, if you would only pause for a moment and look about you, that there are any number of men who would be happy to court you."

James, of course, was one of those young men, but Miss Weston did not need to know that.

Miss Weston gave a small laugh. "When they first meet me I am sure that they do wish to court me. I am not unaware of my physical charms. But you have seen my temper and my liveliness. What man upon knowing me better could possibly put up with that?"

"You underestimate yourself and your ability to stir affection in men."

Miss Weston sighed, looking around them. "Mother helped me to cultivate the guest list. Normally she does not care so much. I ought to have known that something was afoot when she put such thought into it."

"You mean she wishes for you to marry one of the young men assembled?"

James had no hope that he was one of those young men. He had always been invited to dinners at the Weston residence. He had to be invited as a matter of course.

Miss Weston nodded. "Or at least, they are a beginning. Some men that I may begin to consider. They are all from good families. Half of them have titles of some kind."

"Oh, you poor thing, with your mother offering up such rich, titled, handsome young men to you. Truly, you do suffer."

"Do no patronize me, Mr. Norwich, I pray, not tonight."

Miss Weston, to his surprise, looked quite upset. The color in her cheeks was not the light pink of pleased embarrassment. Rather it was the bright red of genuine dismay.

"I find that I feel rather lost," she admitted. "I do not know where I am to begin. You are the only person here in whom I can place my complete trust and comfort.

"I feel quite suddenly as though I am surrounded by wolves. And that I must decide which of them I am to allow to eat me. I know it is quite a dramatic way to think of things. But you know that I am a dramatic person and it is as near as I can get to how I feel.

"My temperament... is not one of pragmaticism. I wish to marry someone that I... well, for whom I feel those tender emotions that we English seem to be so allergic to speaking on save in the writing of clandestine letters and poems.

"And I will not accept any man who does not truly regard me. I hope that he will have those feelings of a deeper nature towards me. But some genuine regard would be a nice start.

"But you know as well as I do that most of these men are not looking for that. And so I must be faced with the choice of changing my disposition or disregarding my parents' wishes. I am, as I am sure you will understand, loath to do either."

James wished that he could draw her into his arms and offer up the proper comforts that a man might offer to a wife. That he might tell her that he regarded her as the best of women and that he would do everything in his power to make her happy if she would marry him.

All that he could do, however, was offer up his usual, sensible advice.

"I think that you are allowing your emotions to run away with you," he told her. "It is something that you have been in the habit of since you were a girl. Just as you have often told me that I am too inclined to be lighthearted about a situation given the privileges of my upbringing.

"I have always appreciated when you would put me in check about my own faults and so I shall do the same for you. Marriage is not such a daunting prospect as you seem to fear it is.

"And no man would even think of changing your disposition. You are quite popular for a reason, Miss Weston. I would trust in the invitations you receive and the fact that you never once have to sit down in a ballroom.

"If you show an interest, the men of society will heave a sigh of relief knowing they at last have a chance. And there are more of them than are assembled here tonight. Including ones that might at first seem boring or monotonous. There are many that will, I think, surprise you."

As he spoke, he could feel his own hopes slipping away. Not that he'd had many hopes in the first place. But he had entertained the quiet notion that he might, someday, pluck up the courage to tell Miss Weston how he felt.

If he could do that, then, well, it was but a little thing to go a step further and imagine that she said yes to his proposal. That she had secretly all this time held the same regard for him that he had been secretly holding for her.

Now, though, other men would see that the seemingly untouchable, marvelous Miss Weston would be at last open to their attentions.

It would not be long before they flocked to her in a way that none of them had dared to do before. James often wondered if women truly understood how intimidating they could be to men.

Every woman he spoke to made a great fuss about how nervous they were regarding courting. But did no woman think about how nerve-racking it was for the men as well?

Especially when the woman in question was as lively, as opinionated, and as educated as Miss Weston.

He did not at all wonder why no man had dared to propose to her yet. They had all feared the cutting wit she would employ. Why bother starting on what was sure to be a hopeless quest?

It was, after all, why he himself had not tried to woo her.

He drew himself up. This was not the time for him to sink into his own thoughts. He must be optimistic and cheerful, for Miss Weston's sake.

"You will find it much easier going than you expect," he told her. "You will see. And I shall be there every step of the way if you would like."

Miss Weston gave him a smile that could have lit up a pitch-black room. "You are as always my savior and an administer of good judgment. I shall be sure to return the favor when a young lady finally catches your eye."

If only she knew, James thought.

"I do marvel at your consistent lack of interest in the matter of romance," Miss Weston went on. "One would think that a man such as yourself would desire a companion. Goodness knows you talk my ear off enough."

"Well perhaps I save only my most witty banter for conversations with yourself," James offered up. He wasn't saying it in jest, but Miss Weston did not have to know that. "Perhaps I sit silent and melancholy at home all day."

Miss Weston laughed. "I have not seen you be melancholy once since I have known you! Serious when the matter calls for it. Thoughtful and even grave when someone is in distress. But sitting about and nursing imaginary wounds of the heart? Talking wearily about existence and the cycle of life? Never."

"You know me too well. Clearly I must endeavor to change up my behavior so that I might throw you off again. You know that keeping you on your toes has always been a particularly favorite pastime of mine."

"I most certainly do know it! And I despair of ever meeting your standards for wit. No wonder you have yet to find a lady to call your wife. They must all scatter at your approach, knowing you are such a fearsome monster of demands."

"Truly, it would take a lady of exceptional bravery to have to put up with me. If you hear of any lady lion tamers, do be sure to send them my way."

He would have crossed oceans for the soft light in Miss Weston's eyes and the carefree smile on her face. He would have crossed a mile barefoot on broken glass to ensure that she would always smile that way. That she would never have any worries, anything to make her cry.

"You must admit," he told her, "I do not have quite the same constraints that you do. My father has not even passed away. There is no pressure on me to marry quite yet."

"Ah, but you never know," Miss Weston replied. "Miss Reginald's father passed on quite suddenly and her brother had to ascend to the dukedom far earlier than expected.

"Not that I think such a thing will happen to your father. I certainly do not wish such a thing. But we can never be certain about life, can we, truly?"

"A wise observation. Perhaps I ought to think of marriage. But if so I will never tell you such a thing."

"And why ever not?"

"Because you are the most delightful meddler that any man has, I daresay, come across in his time on earth. You never see a situation that you cannot make better with your exuberant touch."

"I think you mean to say my light and gentle touch."

"Miss Weston, the only things light about you are your feet when you dance and the only thing gentle is your touch on the piano keys."

He knew that Miss Weston would not hesitate to try and play matchmaker with him if she thought that he was on the lookout for a wife. It would be troublesome enough if she was merely a meddling friend.

But when she was also the person with whom he was in love, it became a real danger.

Miss Weston laughed again. "You are too harsh with me, sir. If I was ever in danger of becoming too arrogant in my judgment of myself, I would hasten to your door at once.

"For I know that within five minutes of conversation with you, you would have introduced me again to the idea of humility. And put me surely in my place."

"Everyone needs a friend like that, do they not?" James countered. "You have people complimenting you all day long. You are hardly lacking for flattery from friends.

"I am providing you with a necessary service by reminding you of the ways in which you are still human. Still prone to weaknesses and flaws like the rest of us."

Miss Weston sniffed. "And I suppose that I ought to return the favor then by pointing out to you your own flaws."

"You already do, and quite nicely, I must admit. Or was it some other Miss Julia Weston who told me at last week's ball that I was off the beat of the music on the dance steps?"

"That must have been some other lady. I would never do anything but compliment your dancing."

This was an outrageous lie, and they both knew it. Miss Weston had never once complimented him on his dancing.

James was one of the best dancers at any ball he attended, and he was quite aware of it. Miss Weston was the same. Inevitably, she would try to use some complicated variation to trip him up and he would respond.

Insulting his dancing was, between the two of them, a further sign of their friendship.

There was the discreet announcement that dinner was ready, and Miss Weston curtsied to him. "I must lead the pack, as you know. I have put you at the far end by my mother. I hope that you will not mind being deprived of my sparkling conversation for an evening.

"It is only that she wishes for me to pay attention to these men, and I wish for her to have a dinner companion who will be properly attentive to her."

"It would be an honor. I do not mind in the slightest." He bowed to her.

He meant it as well. Miss Weston might complain about her parents but she was fiercely protective of them. Especially her mother with her ill health. To be chosen as Mrs. Weston's dinner companion was a high compliment from Miss Weston. It meant that James was trusted completely.

He had to take his small victories where he could get them.

As he moved to find Mrs. Weston and help her into the dining room, he reflected that it might be a blessing that he was at the far end.

If he had to sit there and listen to all those other young men throwing themselves at Miss Weston, he might do something drastic. Like punch one of them. Or propose on the spot.

CHAPTER 51

JULIA HAD RARELY HAD such a frustrating dinner.

She had picked out the guest list herself with Mother. And while Mother had her opinions, all of the people that had been chosen were people with whom Julia enjoyed conversing.

It was only that now she knew she was supposed to choose one of the men to wed... or at least try to choose one of them...

Now, all she could see were their flaws.

Mr. Harbinger was far too chatty and would talk forever. And not usually about anything particularly interesting. He would wax poetic for a full half hour about the weather, for goodness' sake.

Mr. Blithering, on her left, was far too full of himself. A man who thought too much of his own character could never think so much of his wife's. Julia refused to be married to a man who would not give her the respect that was due to her.

It was a little more difficult to converse with others, since they were seated far away from her.

But oh, what she wouldn't give for it to be an ordinary night.

On an ordinary night, Mr. Blithering's arrogance would be amusing. Something to tease and indulge. Mr. Harbinger's boring anecdotes would be something to quietly and inwardly snicker at.

Now, they spelled doom. She might be forced to be paired with such a man!

Julia would never have admitted it to passing acquaintances, and indeed had admitted it only to two people in her entire life, but she wanted a proper romance.

She wanted a man who respected her. A man who was crazy about her. A man who would do ridiculous things like send her love poetry.

Oh, she was well aware that it was ridiculous of her to think such things. But Georgiana and her suitor had exchanged copies of love poems. Surely Julia could wait for someone who would do the same for her?

Marriage, however, was mostly a pragmatic game. Mother had been overall pragmatic in her marriage. Although she had admitted to Julia that out of her potential suitors, she had chosen Father because she had most liked his personality.

Julia wanted more than just 'like'. She wanted to feel the madcap rush of love. The fathoms deep swells of it. The aching pain in the stomach. She wanted what novels and playwrights spoke of, what Shakespeare and numerous others had so exalted.

Unfortunately, that seemed to be beyond her reach at the moment.

It seemed to be beyond the reach of most ladies and gentlemen that she knew. For all that ladies and even gentlemen liked to wax poetic and giggle about courtship... there was something ruthless and businesslike about it.

For instance, she had seen many women cut down other women, humiliate them, in order to eliminate the competition for an eligible man.

It was worse in women than in men, but Julia understood that. Men married to continue the family line and to solidify their status in life. But they did not need a wife in order to survive.

Men could be financially independent. Women could not. A woman needed a husband or she would starve. She would be outcast from society.

It was the terrible fate that had awaited Georgiana Reginald, had she not been reunited with Captain Trentworth and everything worked out between them.

Julia did not wish to be one of those ladies. Nor did she wish to become catty and competitive. Or to be subject to such behavior from other women.

She simply wanted a sweet romance with a gentleman with whom she could converse. Was that too much to ask?

All right, so maybe more like a passionate romance than a sweet romance. And maybe she wanted more than simply being able to converse with the gentleman that she would marry.

But still. All that talk about love and romance, that must be because enough people experienced it. She didn't want it to be some fanciful thinking. Something to dream on. She wanted it to happen to her.

In any case, no dinner had dragged on the way this one had. She had found herself almost willing her mother to descend into a coughing fit so that she might end the whole affair.

Of course it was an awful thing to think. She quite hated herself after she'd had the thought. But she was feeling so utterly miserable.

She did not even have the pleasure of speaking with Mr. Norwich throughout dinner. Usually they sat close enough to each other that they might converse. Especially at dinners that she hosted, for she always made sure to put him by her side.

Mr. Norwich was always a lively commentator. No matter how dull or annoying any other dinner guests might turn out to be, she could always rely on him.

Unfortunately, she'd had to put him with Mother this time.

Now she did not even have the support of her friend to make up for this torture. And for all their banter, she knew that Mr. Norwich supported her.

They had known one another nearly all their lives. He had been one of her father's pupils back in the day.

Of course, he had been such a rambunctious boy then. Julia had thought him most distasteful. He had grown up in great wealth and stature and seemed incapable of understanding that not everyone was so blessed.

He had lived in a happy little bubble. Julia had been incredibly impatient with him over it.

At first, he had not respected her. He had looked down his nose at her for being a girl. He had declared that she could not possibly hold her own against him.

Well, there was nothing that Julia liked so much as a challenge.

She had taken to reading her father's books late at night by candlelight. She had doubled the time she spent practicing her dancing. She had memorized poems and passages from plays.

Whenever Mr. Norwich had come to banter with her, she had been ready for him.

If he spoke loftily about philosophy, she knew her Greeks as well. If he tried to stump her with religion, she knew that too.

In time, he had to concede that Julia was just as intelligent and capable as he was.

It was still a triumph that she thought on with great pride.

Father had later on confided to her that he was glad that she had been so competitive. It had spurred Mr. Norwich into furthering his studies and made him a more focused student than before.

As their rivalry had faded and their mutual respect for one another had grown, friendship had grown in its place.

She could now count Mr. Norwich as one of the few people whom she trusted completely. And whose company she truly enjoyed.

And for that she'd had to put him next to Mother. Who else out of those assembled could she trust to look after Mother with such care?

Julia put Mr. Norwich out of her mind. He was an entertaining and loyal friend, but not what she needed to think on at the moment.

After dinner finished they retired to the sitting room where Julia got out the cards for those who wished to play. Mother was a fan of bridge. Luckily, Mr. Norwich was quick to gather some people up to make them an even four so that Mother could play.

Julia resolved to speak to the men that she had not had the pleasure of sitting next to at dinner.

Although 'pleasure' might be a dubious concept in this respect.

It was as though now that she knew she might have to spend the rest of her life with one of them, these men were no longer interesting. All she could see were their flaws.

She was not impressed, not swept off her feet.

It was probably unfair of her to expect to be like a heroine in a play and simply fall smack in love with a man the moment she saw him across a room.

That seemed to happen to heroines all the time in plays.

But surely when she spoke to a man there ought to be a spark of some kind. The only time she had any sort of fun was when she spoke to Mr. Norwich about how the bridge game was going.

He was a tease, of course, as he always was. He could be grave when the situation called for it. But Julia had not seen him be serious about anything other than the whole affair with Georgiana.

He had been most kind and thoughtful to her. It was why she still considered him a dear friend even though he often drove her quite out of her mind. When the cards were on the table, he came through.

Mother took her sweet time in saying goodbye to all of the men. She talked with Mr. Norwich for some time but that was not unusual. Mother had always been fond of him. Julia dared to even think that he was perhaps like a son to her.

She knew that Mother had always wanted more children. She could only hope that she managed to somewhat make up for being the only one.

Mother always said that Julia had enough energy for five children, at any rate.

But talking with all the other young men—that was unusual. It was probably Mother's way of subtly reminding Julia what her new focus was supposed to be.

As if Julia was capable of forgetting something as big and life-changing as that.

When all the men and women had left, Julia all but collapsed onto a chair.

"How was it?" her mother asked, pouncing at once. "What did you think of them?"

"Mother, honestly?" Julia sighed. "When I made this guest list I was not thinking of men that I should potentially like to marry. I was thinking only of people that should entertain me in the moment."

"Well, that was your first mistake, my dear." Her mother sat down in her favorite armchair. "You ought to have been thinking about marriage. You have gone without thinking on it for far too long.

"You need to invite men not because they will provide a moment's diversion. Rather, you must invite men that you can potentially see yourself marrying. If I was able to properly play the hostess, you would give your requests to me.

"There are of course social obligations to consider. People that we must invite to other dinners or mix in with the gentlemen and young ladies.

"But in any case, there is no reason why you should not be disposed towards the men who were here tonight. They are all fine, upstanding gentlemen of good income and from distinguished families."

"As if that is all there is to entice a woman to marriage," Julia replied.

"That is all that should be needed to entice you," Mrs. Weston shot back without missing a beat. "Ladies cannot afford to be picky."

"But they are all so terribly dull, or so awfully full of themselves. I should hate them before the year was up."

"I have the slightest suspicion that you would hate starving even more."

Julia sat up straight. She wished to glare at her mother, but that wouldn't do. Mother was feeling poorly. What if this was their last conversation and Julia was horrid to her?

"Please, Mother. Try not to inject every sentence with your usual acid. I am well aware of my position."

"Clearly you are not aware of it enough or you would have taken pains to try and find a husband before now."

"It is only that I have been so focused on you. You and Father are so wonderful and I worry about you both."

"You do not have to butter me up."

"I am not buttering you up. It is the truth. I worry about you. I worry about Father as well. Do not mock me when I am genuine. I should think you would know by now when I am being so."

"And can you not see that we are worried for you? A parent's chief concern is not their own health but the wellbeing of their child.

"If you wanted to set us at ease you had best do so by finding a husband. Not by fretting over my hot water bottles and what the doctor tells us, which is of course always different from what he told us on his previous visit.

"That is always the way with doctors. We cannot do much about my health. But I suspect I can manage well enough.

"You will have a much harder time of managing if you are still unwed by the time your father passes."

"Is Father gravely ill?" Julia blurted out before she could stop herself. "Should I be worried for him? More so than usual, I mean? Is he all right?"

"Your father is fine, so far as I know. And it is not like him to keep important things from me. If he were ill I think I should know it."

"Then why impress this upon me all of a sudden?" Julia knew she was close to being petulant but if her fate was to be unleashed upon her like an anvil then she felt she had a right to know why.

"It would not be sudden if you had given it the proper thought all of this time."

"Have people been speaking about me? Saying unkind things?"

"Is it not possible that a sickly mother and a tired father simply come to realize that their daughter has been of marrying age for quite some time? And that they wish for her to be safe rather than sorry? To be prudent? Is it not possible that we simply long for grandchildren and to see you settled? That we worry for we know that life is short and unexpected?"

Julia crossed over to her mother, sinking down to her knees and placing her hands in her mother's lap. "Do not work yourself up so. Breathe carefully. Would you like some water?"

Mrs. Weston sighed. "That is what I am talking about, my dear. You are quite worried for us. We appreciate it, for we love you. It is not everyone who can say they have such a conscientious daughter.

"But you cannot waste your youth on our old age. It is not right. I fear that someday you will look up and find that in tending to us, you have condemned yourself."

Mother placed her hand gently on Julia's head. "And that is not something that any parent should wish, is it? Being a parent is ultimately a selfless act. You give of yourself to your children. It should not be the other way around. That is not how it is meant to be."

Julia bit her lip. "But... Mother, what if I cannot be satisfied only with respect between myself and my suitor? What if I wish for something deeper? For a proper romantic courting?"

Mother stroked her hair. "Romance is not all about fine letters and poetry and flowers, my dear. Romance is found most often in the little things.

"Someone who makes you laugh. Someone who knows when you are truly upset. Someone who is loyal and steadfast. That moment when they pass you the sugar without looking because they know how you like it in your tea. When they have bought you a book they saw because they thought you would enjoy it.

"That is where true romance is found. Flowers fade and so do kisses. Jewelry is empty when you realize it is a way of buying your affections. Or buying your forgiveness when your husband treats you ill.

"But in those little moments. Where you are shown how well they know you, how much they pay attention. That is romance.

"And if you were to pay a little more attention and think of things in that manner, I think you would find that romance is truly right in front of you. More of it than you would expect."

Julia was not so sure. Mother was an intelligent woman. But she was also a pragmatic one. She had declared Romeo and Juliet to be nothing close to the sort of romance one should emulate.

"It is about the folly of grudges," she had said. "I should never use Juliet as an example of how one must behave in love."

And so really, what did Mother know? Mother did not have a truly romantic bone in her body.

"But at least, Mother, you can understand why I should wish for romance?"

Mother sighed. "I am not one for such things, but I suppose that I can see the appeal. I fear that if that is what you are waiting for, though, you will not find it.

"Look instead for the small shows of affection. They are more numerous and with the passage of time they are what will sustain your heart."

Her mother took her hand off of Julia's head. "It is high time that I went to bed. I am quite exhausted."

"Did Mr. Norwich look after you? Were you well taken care of?"

"He was most attentive. You know how well he knows me by now. He is a sweet boy."

"He has not been a 'boy' for some time, Mother," Julia replied, smiling as she stood up. "I am glad that he looked after you."

"I can look after myself, you know. I am not quite so much an invalid yet that I am incapable of sitting around and talking. But I do appreciate the care you have for me, Julia. I know that I do not always show it. But I truly do.

"I hope that you will do me the favor of caring for yourself as I wish to care for you. That you will see yourself through your mother's eyes. I cannot find the strength to attend balls with you and assist you in finding a husband. That is a failure on my part."

"No it is not!" Julia was filled with indignation on her mother's behalf. "You cannot help your illness."

"Nevertheless, it is my duty as your mother to help you in such things. I cannot. Therefore, I am not providing for you as I should be. You have to take it wholly upon yourself.

"Treat yourself as I wish to treat you. Find yourself someone. And do think on my advice. If you look for romance in the smaller things and the more mundane I think you will surprise yourself with how contented you are with it."

Mother went up to bed then. She moved with a quiet dignity, despite her illness. She did move more slowly than she had in previous years. But she did not allow her back to be bent or her head to fall.

Julia hoped that if she were ever in the same situation that she would bear it so well.

She hoped that she could bear this present situation well.

If only she could be pragmatic. But that had never been in her temperament.

She supposed that she would have to simply focus in on the men and see what she could turn hopeful.

Hopefully it would be something more exciting than what she had dealt with tonight.

CHAPTER 52

JAMES HAD OVERALL TOLERATED the dinner. It would have been nothing less than enjoyable had he not felt the specter of Miss Weston's news hanging over him.

Could he even dare to throw his hat in the ring?

The fact that Miss Weston had confided this information to him suggested against it. She would not have told him such a thing if she was intending to think of him as a potential suitor. She had told him this as a friend, as a confidant. Not as someone that she was hoping would propose.

No, he dared not let his fancy run away with him. Miss Weston had seen him as an ally. A support. Perhaps someone who could help her in avoiding rakes. Not as a suitor himself.

He had done his best not to focus upon Miss Weston all through dinner. Instead he had turned his attentions to the other young ladies and gentlemen, and to Mrs. Weston especially.

Despite her ill health, she had been the true authority at the table. She had sat at the head while Miss Weston had sat at the foot.

Her demeanor would have done royalty proud. She had smiled indulgently whenever James had checked up on her. As though she did not truly need his help but appreciated it all the same.

"You needn't be so concerned for me," she had told him at one point. "I am not so sickly as my daughter fears."

He had genuinely enjoyed her company. Her wit was such that not everyone could stand to be around her. One had to have a thick skin to tolerate Mrs. Weston's company. It was no wonder that her daughter was so lively herself.

But despite Mrs. Weston's wit, he could not completely relax. He had kept looking over at Miss Weston. Watching her interact with the other gentlemen.

None of the men, in James's opinion, were good enough for Miss Weston.

He knew that he was biased in the matter, horribly so. But if he was to watch the woman that he loved fall for another—or at least marry another—then that man must be one that she deserved.

And Miss Weston deserved nothing but the best.

He had dismissed each man in his mind as he had seen Miss Weston converse with them. Too boring and never knew when to fall silent. Too full of himself. Not nearly enough of an interest in literature. Unable to keep up with her wit.

And so on.

When it was time to go, he was relieved. It had been a fine dinner. A fine game of cards. But everything had been tinged with sourness because of his newfound knowledge.

He almost wished that he had not heard. That Miss Weston had not told him. At least then he could have gone on as he had before. In blissful ignorance.

No, he told himself. James was not the sort of man who preferred to go on like that. He appreciated knowledge. He liked to know the lay of the land in any situation.

His younger brother had always teased him that James ought to be the one pursuing a military career. For James was the one who cared about foreknowledge and strategy. Planning battles, his brother had said, would well suit him.

Of course, James had to stay alive and safe at home in order to learn how to run the estate. But it was a fair point.

Now he knew, and although he hated it, he could now prepare.

Perhaps it would help to find some suitable men? Some men who truly were worthy of Miss Weston? He could then send those men her way along with a subtle endorsement.

He lingered behind, hoping that he might suggest such a thing to Miss Weston. He would not presume to help her in her quest without her permission. If he did so and she found out she would find some way to make her displeasure painfully known to him.

To his surprise, however, Mrs. Weston came up to escort him to the door.

"Mr. Norwich," she said quietly, "I hope that you will forgive a sick old woman for requesting a moment."

"You are nothing close to old," he assured her. "And I always have time for you, dear lady."

"You flatter me," Mrs. Weston replied. "That is probably why I like you so."

"You are fond of me, I should hope, because you know that my flattery is sincere and not made up in order to get on your good side."

"True enough. My husband beat such false pretenses out of you at an early age." Mrs. Weston sighed. "Mr. Norwich, I must speak plainly. The time has come for Miss Weston to marry. In fact, that time came quite a while ago and we have all ignored it.

"There are quite a few men that she could marry and who would be proper husbands to her. I would not object to her marrying any of them."

She grabbed his arm then, her grip surprisingly tight. "But Mr. Norwich. You must know how Mr. Weston and I both think of you. You have been the pupil of whom he is the fondest. You have been more to us than any other boy we tutored.

"We think of you as a son and love you as one. Your dear mother, God rest her soul, was a Christian woman. But I fear she was not always the mother she ought to have been."

"You have been a wonderful surrogate over the years."

Mrs. Weston smiled, but it was a bittersweet one. "I have certainly tried to be.

"But as for my daughter... I know that it is not my right to impose feelings upon you. But if there were anyone in the world that I should wish to be her husband, it would be you."

James nearly dropped his jaw in shock.

That was not what he had expected. Instead he had thought that Mrs. Weston would say something about him being a brother to Miss Weston. That she would ask him if he could assist her in this matter, as a brother would.

To be told that he was the favored choice... that these two people he considered family wanted for him the one thing that he also wanted in all the world...

He could not even begin to sort out all of his feelings. His stomach flipped almost painfully and his heart gave a lurch. He wished to flee but simultaneously found himself rooted to the spot.

"I do not know my daughter's thoughts on the matter," Mrs. Weston went on. She seemed oblivious to James's distress, or at least tactfully ignoring it. "If I had to hazard a guess I would say that she has not thought on any man in such a way.

"But I have faith in your ability to sway her. Of course, if you are against the idea I should understand completely. My daughter is quite the handful. A more stubborn and energetic girl I have yet to meet.

"She would be rather too much for most men to handle, I dare say. And you two have known one another for many years. If your affections for her are rather those of a brother then I should not try to persuade you to change them.

"But if you can find it in yourself to love her as a man loves a wife..." Mrs. Weston's eyes were shining. "Mr. Norwich. It would be such a joy. And such a relief. To know that a man such as you were taking care of my daughter."

James wanted to ask her how much time she had left. If that was why she was so worried for Miss Weston. Or if it was simply the fear of her beloved only child being called a spinster that drove her.

But he could not dare to ask such things. It was not his place.

"I cannot impose myself onto Miss Weston," he told her. "Not when she sees me as someone she can trust."

"She sees nothing," Mrs. Weston said firmly.

"I will not," he replied, just as firm. "Not unless the lady herself wishes it."

"How can she realize that she wishes it if you will not present yourself as a suitor? She knows you as her father's former pupil. She will know you as a man if you come to her as one."

"I cannot take that risk. I will not place our friendship in danger."

Mrs. Weston shook her head. "Julia is too generous a soul to allow that to happen. If you were to try and woo her, she would either come to realize that is the best thing or she would accept your feelings and let you down as gently as she could. She would not scorn you for it or put distance between you.

"I implore you, if there is any possibility that you would see her as a wife: pursue her. Consider it the request of a senile and stubborn old lady."

"And I have told you many times that you are neither senile nor old."

"Hmmph. Then consider it the suggestion of an eminently wise and logical woman."

James placed his hand over Mrs. Weston's, where she was still gripping his arm. "I shall give it full consideration. I promise."

Mrs. Wetson gave his arm a fond squeeze, nodding her head. "That is all I can ask for."

He bowed to her, and then said his brief farewell to Miss Weston who had just walked up to them.

Mrs. Weston moved away with a significant look on her face.

"Tonight was a disappointment all around," Miss Weston declared. "Let us hope that the future is less so. For the sake of my parents' peace of mind, anyhow. Did you enjoy yourself?"

Not at all, he thought. Out loud he said, "More so than you did, evidently."

"Evidently." Miss Weston gave him a curtsy. "Have a lovely evening, Mr. Norwich."

"And you as well, Miss Weston. I'm sure I shall see you at the ball tomorrow."

"Indeed you shall. Until then."

James's thoughts were whirling like a giddy dancer as he walked home. It was not too long a walk in Bath between houses and he appreciated the fresh, cool night air.

It was a complete shock to him—Mrs. Weston and Mr. Weston, both of them people he highly regarded, wished for him to be their son-in-law? They wanted him to try for Miss Weston's hand?

Of course, they could not force their daughter to marry anyone. Miss Weston had a right to refuse him or any other man.

To know, however, that such people thought of him as worthy... thought of him as a son... it was a boost of confidence that he had not looked for or dared to expect.

Perhaps that meant that Miss Weston might respond to him unexpectedly as well? Could it be that perhaps she simply needed to be told how he felt for her to respond?

He did not wish to be presumptuous. He did not wish to make Miss Weston uncomfortable.

But he would never have even thought that the Westons would think of him with such regard until tonight.

If he could be so blind, but so welcoming, it was possible that perhaps Miss Weston was that way with him.

After all, he had heard the story of many a girl who had longed for the slightly richer, slightly older man but despaired of having him. And he had not read such things in books but had heard them from ladies themselves.

He might just be indulging himself. He might be giving himself hope where there was none. But it was possible, was it not?

How could he know until he tried?

Mrs. Weston had a point in that. He was only going off of what he could guess about Miss Weston. He did not know for certain. Nobody knew anything of what someone was thinking for certain unless they asked.

And he had never dared to ask.

James gazed around him at the darkened streets, the few stragglers walking home from dinners and balls. He was not the sort of man who could say his feelings out loud.

Not when he was so unsure of himself.

And if Miss Weston would be uncomfortable with his declaration then he did not want it to be in person. Certainly not. He wouldn't want to have her be forced to swallow down her distress.

If things were to become awkward for the both of them then it was better that it were not done in person.

A letter would do nicely. He had always been good with words but best at emotions when those words were written down. His relationship with his brother had actually improved once his brother was in the navy. For then they had communicated by letters, and then James had been able to talk about things such as his frustrations with Mother that he hadn't been able to say aloud.

It was considered bad form for an unmarried man and an unmarried lady to exchange letters.

Such exceptions were made for close family members, such as a brother to his sister or if a man desperately needed to get information to his cousin.

But surely, just a single letter of intent, disclosing his feelings, that would be understandable?

And then Miss Weston could reply to him in person as she so wished. She did not even have to reply to him at all, if she did not want to.

Her lack of response would be answer enough.

If she did wish to respond to him, she could do so in person. But she would have time to craft a response and think of what to say.

Whether she wanted him to court her or wished to gently turn him down, she would now have the time she needed. She wouldn't be blindsided.

Yes, that would be the right thing to do. Send her a letter.

When he reached home, he went straight up to his desk and sat down. He barely even bothered to deal with his coat and hat. His valet must be despairing silently right now.

How to begin? He knew that he had to do it now before he lost his nerve or all would be lost.

He was filled with an odd kind of reckless courage. It was satisfying, almost, to know that he would have an answer. That he would know quite soon beyond a shadow of a doubt.

He knew that he had to write it all down now. Not that the words themselves would escape him. He had thought many times over the years what he might say to Miss Weston if he gave himself leave.

The problem was that if he waited until morning, he knew that his courage would fail him. He would toss and turn all night and come up with a multitude of reasons why he should not do it.

He had talked himself out of telling her many a time before. Why should this time be any different?

He could not hesitate, or his courage would fail him.

James took a deep breath and set up his paper and pen.

It took several drafts. At first, he was too terse, the words difficult. It was not enough to simply write, I love you and leave it at that.

She would want to understand why and how. She was worth more than simply a few short lines.

But then, once the words flowed, he found that he was rambling. He repeated himself, he was waxing far too poetic in his prose, he dragged it all on for too long.

A lady deserved romance, but ten pages was a great deal too far. Even Shakespeare didn't have his characters recite ten pages of a love monologue.

Then there came the problem of having to always start over with a fresh piece of paper. For once he got it all written, the pages were covered in additions and crossed-out words and scribbled lines in the margins.

That wouldn't do either. And so he had to go and copy it all neatly on a new page.

His candle had burned quite low and it was nearly morning by the time that he finished it to his satisfaction. He could see the sky out his window turning that dark, bruised purple it took on shortly before the sun emerged.

James stared down at it. He had gone over every line—no, every word—more times than he could count. It was not perfect, but then, nothing was truly perfect, was it?

And he must let it lie. If he did not he would continue to edit it until the world ended. He must do it now before his nerve was gone.

He folded up the letter, addressed it, and then sealed it for good measure.

Only then did he finally go to bed. Purged of his emotions, having strung them all out all night, his nerves frayed, he fell asleep quickly.

He'd have an answer soon enough.

It was only after he had dropped it off at the post office. After he had walked back home for breakfast. After he had been halfway through said breakfast, that he realized.

He had, in his obsessing over the contents of the letter, his own exhaustion, and his nerves—

He had neglected to add his name.

CHAPTER 53

JULIA WAS SURPRISED to find that she had a letter the next morning.

"Were you expecting anything?" Mrs. Weston asked.

Julia shook her head. "No. Most peculiar, is it not? But it must be from some friend or other in London."

She opened it and could have sworn that the handwriting was one that she recognized. But she had a great many friends with whom she corresponded. There was no one who jumped to mind immediately.

Julia quickly scanned the letter looking for the name.

But there was none.

That was odd. Who would send her a letter without a name attached?

Perhaps they had forgotten it? Ah, well, that was easily remedied. She would read the contents. The talk about local gossip and families and all would quickly narrow down the search.

When she began to read, however, she quickly saw that it was not an ordinary sort of letter at all.

Julia quickly set the letter down. Her heart was racing. She had only read the first couple of sentences but that was enough to tell her what sort of letter this was.

She knew that she ought to simply burn the letter. For a lady to receive something filled with such clear devotion as this was not proper. Only a husband or perhaps a fiancé could send this. Certainly not a stranger.

Perhaps, then, the name being left off was on purpose? In case the person's letter was ill received?

Julia could not imagine who it could possibly be. That of course only made her want to read the letter more.

She glanced over at Mother, who was reading.

"I am going to go and do my hair," Julia told her, hiding the letter in the folds of her dress. She kissed her mother's cheek and she walked by and did her best to be sedate.

Once she got out of the sitting room, however, she hurried up to her bedroom. She locked the door behind her, just in case.

She would take no chances with anyone finding out about this.

Julia sat on her bed and carefully opened the letter.

She wished that she could remember where she knew the handwriting from. For she had seen it before. Somewhere.

The letter started out innocently enough. But it quickly changed course from there.

Dear Miss Weston,

You must forgive me in writing you. I know that it is not proper. But I knew that if I were to try and say my words aloud to you in person that I would never find the courage.

I wonder if you realize quite what an intimidating woman you are. It does not surprise me that no man has yet found the courage to court you.

Not that you are an unkind person. You are generous of spirit. Indeed, I find you to be the most loyal friend that I have ever encountered.

But such intelligence and quick wit can leave a man wondering what his reception will be. I cannot be the first man to wonder. No. You are far too shining of a star for others to not have craved to stand in your light.

Julia's heart was hammering, her breath shallow in surprise and delight. She was fairly blushing. The line about being a star—it was like something out of a novel or perhaps even a poem.

Who could it possibly be from? And dared she read more? The writer was already complimenting her far beyond the bounds of propriety and they had not even gotten to their proper confession yet.

She suspected it to be a confession of love but one could never be certain. It might be some other sort of dire secret.

She did have a responsibility to read until she found out, didn't she? Just in case? She would go wild with curiosity if she did not. Always wondering what it might have been about.

And nobody had to know that she had received and read this letter, did they? She could easily burn it in the fireplace. That would erase the evidence.

Mother wouldn't think to ask about the letter she'd received and even if she did, Julia could think of a hundred excuses.

Set on her course, she read on.

And so it is like a coward that I must tell you such things in a letter. I beg your pardon in possibly compromising your propriety, an unwed man writing to an unwed woman.

So it was a man! And a single one. Julia could feel herself blushing. Oh, this was simply too marvelous. She could hardly stand it. Could this really be happening to her? Was it not a flight of fancy or some dream?

She pinched herself, just to be certain. No, she was awake.

I hope, however, that you will excuse me just this once. Now that you will know my thoughts, there will be no need to continue correspondence.

But... she must continue correspondence. She must know who this person was. Did they think to give her such a lovely letter and then disappear into the ether?

You must know—although sometimes I fear that you have guessed it. That I have been too obvious. Too attentive to you and too neglectful towards other women. Too intimate with you and too curt with men who try to take your time.

It seems, however, that you have not. Or if you have, you have been so courteous in ignoring it to spare my dignity.

Either way, circumstances are such that I cannot remain silent any longer:

My affection for you is the deepest that a man can hold for a woman. I do not know when it is that I started to feel this way. All I know is that one day I looked at you and it stole over me, like warmth from a fire, that you were no longer merely a friend in my eyes.

You were the woman I wanted to marry.

I cannot begin to express the depth of my regard for you. To say 'I love you' feels like a gross understatement. That it does not do justice to the way that I feel when I look at you.

I now perfectly understand why poets must go on for ages and in such language. They were trying to grasp at something that would flit out of their hands. They were trying to define and describe an emotion that refused to be so categorized.

You are chief in my heart. When I picture my future, it is with the hope that you might be standing at my side.

Hope is not something that I had come to associate with my feelings for you. I had long ago become aware that you did not and would not return my affections.

But a wise person told me today that of course there was no chance with you. How could there be if I had not told you of how I felt?

It made sense to me, at any rate. You could not become aware of there even being a possibility in me if I did not tell you of it.

Now that you know, I hope that you will consider the idea. I hope you will know that I do not judge you if you turn me away. I understand if your affections lie elsewhere, or if they simply cannot find a home with me.

But I also hope that you know that I would do anything to make you happy. I would let you host as many dinners and balls as you pleased. I would spend hours walking and talking with you, about any subject under the sun.

I would take you to the theatre and show you off. I would sit through hours of opera, even those annoying French operas that you seem to love so well. I would make sure that your parents were taken care of, for I know how much they mean to you.

Even when you complain about them.

I would bestow as many kisses upon you as you could stand. I would proudly introduce you to everyone as 'my wife', for I could think of no greater sweeter words in my mouth. Except, perhaps, for those three little ones.

You must forgive me for the frank nature of my writing. When emotions have been ignored and suppressed for so long there must needs be some overflow in the telling of them.

I do not hope that you will turn around upon reading this letter and accept an immediate proposal. It would take time, I should think, for someone to adjust from thinking of a person as a friend to thinking of them as a husband.

But if you would let me, I would happily court you. Show you the ways in which I would endeavor to make you happy as my wife. I would do everything in my power to ensure that you would want for nothing.

You may take your time in your answer. I know that you must have many thoughts on the matter. You always do. Your wit and thoughtfulness are two things that highly endear you to me.

I do hope that I will not remain in the pain of indecision for too long, however.

Whichever answer you give, know that I will respect it.

Should you choose to refuse me, I will not press you further. You need not provide any explanation to accompany your answer.

But if you do choose to allow me to show you the depth of my admiration and love for you, I would not fail you. I would stake my life upon that.

And there was where the letter ended.

Surely this was where the name was supposed to be signed. There was even some space for it at the bottom. Just enough room for someone to write I remain, or yours ever, or sincerely, or something of that nature. Followed, of course, by their name.

But there was nothing.

It couldn't possibly be on purpose. The person said that they were awaiting her answer. That meant that they must have intended to put their name down.

Julia had to laugh a little. This man had been so carried away with the idea of writing to her that he had forgotten to put down his name at the end!

It was rather sweet, when she thought about it.

The idea that she made someone's heart flutter. That they reacted to her in such a way. It was intoxicating.

She had not been aware that she could stir such an emotion in someone. She had wished that she could. Hoped that she would find someone who could stir such passion in herself.

And here it was, like an answer to a prayer.

It felt like some kind of sign. Like fate, even. Why, just last night she had been telling Mother that she wanted a romance.

And here it was!

Her own personal letter writer. Her mysterious admirer. Perhaps even the leaving off of the name was a wonderful intervention by fate. A little mystery on top of the lovely words she read.

The idea struck her that it might in fact be her mother. That it was some kind of awful prank.

But Mother wouldn't do such a thing. Mother had a sharp tongue but she wouldn't go out of her way to pull such a trick. Not when she had just been so calm but serious about the whole courting matter.

And the words didn't sound like Mother, either. Mother didn't have a romantic bone in her body. And Julia could not see Father writing such a thing, even in jest, to his daughter of all people.

Nor could she see either parent putting up someone else to do it for them. It was simply not in their nature. It stung a little too deeply if it was not a real letter.

Her parents would not wish to hurt her like that. Not in order to 'teach her a lesson' or anything of that nature. And besides, how could they have gotten a letter to her so quickly after her conversation with Mother late last night?

No, it must be a real letter.

But if so, then from whom?

It was clearly someone who knew her well. Someone that she was comfortable with, or else they would not have dared to call themselves a friend to her.

That, unfortunately, did not truly narrow down the list. Julia knew a great many men. She was friendly with everybody and made her interests known.

For example, she would wax poetic about French opera to anyone who would listen. She knew that the Italian opera was technically considered the 'better' choice but there was just something about the French language that she preferred.

Her care for her parents was also well known. Her mother's illness was an acknowledged fact among society. Although everyone was polite and rarely spoke of it other than to inquire after Mother's health to Julia at balls.

There was no mention of anything that could place this person specifically in her life. How could that be? Was it coincidence? Or was it in order to further obscure their identity?

No, that could not be it. The person wanted an answer. She could not answer them if she did not know who they were.

This person was not looking to marry her right away. They were not proposing. They were merely asking for her to consider their love and to let them court her.

It was a very respectful letter, overall. Julia was quite impressed with it. And there was a kind of casualness to it, in the sense that this person seemed to know her well.

Who could it possibly be?

Well, she would just have to find out.

There was no way that she was burning this letter. It would have been much more prudent to do so. But she could not bear it. She had to hold onto it and onto those lovely words.

The things said in it were enough to make her heart flutter like a bird in a cage.

She must find out who this person was. But how?

Julia turned the letter over in her hands—and saw that there was a return address on it.

Well, at least the person had remembered that much.

It was for one of those little post office boxes, and not for a house. Many people had them nowadays.

It was not a home address, but it would do. At least she could write to him and ask for the gentleman to reveal himself.

After all, how could she give the man an answer if she did not know who he was?

Julia hurried over to the desk. She would write to the gentleman and explain that she was quite fond of his letter. She would tell him how much he had moved her.

And then she would inform him that she could not give him an answer for he had neglected to include his name. Would he perhaps be so kind as to tell her who he was?

It all sounded very practical in her head. But she found that she sounded quite carried away when she tried to write the letter.

She was simply astounded at this turn of events. That this

person should be so carried away with her. It felt almost as though she had stepped into an entirely new world.

Oh, if only she could share it with someone. She could write to Georgiana, of course. And she would. She had no secrets from her oldest and dearest friend.

But it was not the same as if Georgiana was right there in front of her to tell her in person.

Julia thought she might tell Mr. Norwich—but then she dismissed the idea.

What would he want with such a fanciful romantic notion?

She had seen his face last night when she had suggested that he ought to find a wife while she looked for a husband.

The poor man had looked as though she had dumped a bucket of ice water on his head.

Clearly, he was not inclined to think about romance. She had observed him closely, as she observed everyone, over the years. She had seen how he seemed to show nothing but the barest of interest in a lady.

He clearly admired them. And he had spoken at times, with a fond tone of voice, of when he would have a wife and children of his own.

But she had never heard him talk of the more tender side of courtship. When they discussed books he had often teased her for her romantic inclinations.

What on earth would he care that she had received such a letter?

If anything, he would probably demand to find out who had written it so that he could fight them over sending her a letter. Mr. Norwich was a good man and she had long suspected that he thought of her as a little sister.

He had no sisters of his own. Just a younger brother. And they had known one another since they were practically children.

Why should he not think of her that way? She had shown him many times that she trusted him.

No, he would not care for the fine words and the soft sentiments. Except in the way that they skirted the bounds of propriety. And then he'd go and challenge the man to a duel or something dramatic like that.

Well, that left him out.

That meant that there was no one she could tell. No one she could consult. Mother would insist that she burn the letter and make no reply. Father would probably be even worse than Mr. Norwich.

She was not going to wait for a return letter from Georgiana to tell her what ought to be done. She would have to keep her excitement to herself for now.

She could manage that, surely?

Nobody would have to know. She would simply go on as before. And when her letter was received and her mystery gentleman revealed himself, she would let him court her.

Then Mother would be so pleased.

Unless...

Was this man below her station? Was he someone undesirable for her?

Was that why he had written it all out in a letter?

The man had said that telling her in person would be too intimidating for him. But could part of why it was intimidating be that he knew she would have to reject him if she knew his identity and social status?

Julia could feel her stomach twisting and her heart sinking. She had no wish to start a Romeo and Juliet sort of courtship. What would she do if this person who so ardently cared for her was not someone that she could marry?

Mother and Father would never allow it. They were practical. They had come to love one another but their marriage had been one of common sense and mutual respect.

And could she handle going down in social status? She wanted a romantic courtship but she was not the sort of person to sacrifice everything for love. She was not going to marry, say, a servant or some such.

But of course this person had called her a friend and she was not friends with anyone who was too high above or below her in status. Was she?

Could the person perhaps be quite horrid-looking? Or have some kind of other issue that meant he feared to be laughed at if he were to try and court her in person first?

Julia could not think of anyone she knew who was like that.

It was all very puzzling.

Well, she'd never know until she wrote him and asked.

Julia hurried over to the desk and sat down. Her hands were shaking with excitement and she had to take a moment to breathe and steady them.

This was just like being in a play. She thought her heart might beat right out of her chest. It felt as though she was doing something clandestine, like being a spy.

She wrote a letter that she felt was not overlong. She did not want to seem like a giddy young girl.

Judging by the tone of the letter, this person thought her to be a woman of wit and sophistication. She could hardly ruin that impression by being overenthusiastic and giddy in her response.

She double-checked everything after she had written it. It sounded quite all right to her. Nothing untoward.

It was passionate. She could not deny that she was full of excitement. But it was not too full of ardor, she thought, and it did not make her sound overeager.

She addressed it to the post office box that was listed as the return address. The original letter sent to her she hid in her desk underneath some old papers. She could not bear to burn it. Not quite yet.

When she went back downstairs she made sure to look composed and calm. She placed her letter nonchalantly on the silver tray along with the other letters that would be sent out to the post in a short bit.

"Your hair looks the same as before," her mother noted when Julia reappeared in the sitting room.

"I have changed my mind and decided to keep it in a more relaxed style today," she replied. Her voice was calm but her heart picked up speed. How could she have forgotten her excuse for disappearing upstairs? "There is no need to make it look so fine until the ball tonight."

Mother made a noncommittal humming noise and then went back to her book. Julia had to hold in her heaving sigh of relief.

Soon, she would have the identity of her letter writer.

She could hardly wait.

CHAPTER 54

JAMES CHASTISED himself all morning for his stupidity.

He had forgotten to sign his name! He had been in such a state over the contents of the letter itself that once that had satisfied him he had not even thought of the final part.

He had simply folded up the letter and sent it off in order to be rid of it before he changed his mind.

That was, he supposed, understandable. He had been in quite a state.

But still!

To forget such a thing—now Miss Weston could have no idea who sent the letter. He had made sure not to put too many incriminating details in it. He did not want her to know immediately that it was him.

Rather, he had wanted her to see just how much this person cared for her. How deep their esteem for her ran. And then, only once she understood that, would she get to the bottom and see that it was him.

If she knew that it was him right away then she might dismiss the entire thing right out before giving it a fair chance. Or even before reading it through all the way.

Now, he cursed himself for it. There were a hundred little details that he might have slipped into the body of the letter that would have told her who he was.

Instead, he kept it all as general as possible. And now he was paying for that folly.

When people talked about love making fools of us all, he had rather thought it meant compelling a person to challenge a rival to a duel or to go on a great quest. Like one of King Arthur's knights of the Round Table.

Instead it apparently made one do horrifically stupid and mundane things like forget to sign one's name on a letter.

James sat down with a groan on his armchair. He had been pacing up and down the parlor for goodness knew how long.

Ever since he'd been halfway through breakfast and realized what he'd done, most likely.

What was he supposed to do now?

Miss Weston would surely be confused as to who had sent her such a letter without a name attached. And it was not as though he had simply sent it for the sake of disclosing his feelings.

To tell someone one's feelings was to do a service for one's self. Not for them. It was to relieve his feelings, and to burden her with them in turn.

It was only in the hope that she might return his affections and thereby be made happy—that he could be allowed to try and make her happy—that was the saving grace of it.

Besides, he could hope that she would prefer to marry him over others she did not know so well. They were friends. They had known one another for years and were comfortable with one another.

Surely, that was a pleasing alternative to trying to find affection for men who were otherwise boring to her?

In any case, he had not meant to simply dump his feelings upon her and have that be the end of it.

He had asked her in the letter for an answer. If she would be able to find in herself the generosity to let him court her. To let him try and prove to her how happy he could make her.

She must be exceedingly puzzled, then, to find no name. And therefore no way of giving the answer that he sought.

He was such a fool.

Now he must see her tonight at one of the public balls for which

Bath was so known. She would have no idea that he was the man who had written to her with such passion.

Before it had been bad enough. When he had been pining for her and she was oblivious.

But now that she knew that someone cared for her in that way...

And now that he had actually told her, only she did not know it...

How on earth was he to keep his composure tonight?

It was beyond the patience of man.

Perhaps he ought to stay indoors tonight. Withdraw from the ball and say that he had pressing business matters to attend to. He was the heir to a county, surely people would understand.

No... no that would not do. Enough people knew him to know that he would not allow business to make him skip out on a social occasion.

It would raise suspicions. And he could not have that.

He would simply have to find some way to appear normal in his behavior. To act as though nothing of monumental importance had occurred.

James wondered if this was what losing one's mind felt like.

The day was nothing short of torture. He could scarcely concentrate on business. During the few house calls he had to make he was so distracted that his hosts would ask if he was feeling quite all right.

It was an utter mess.

Had Miss Weston figured it out anyway, he wondered?

She was an intelligent woman. And she had known him for quite some time.

Why, she even knew his handwriting. She had seen it often, both in his letters to her father and when he was learning his penmanship as a younger man. She had read his essays that he wrote for her father, even.

Could she have recognized him from that? Could she even now be preparing her answer?

She would not give it in the middle of a ball. At least he did not think that she would. It would be unfortunate to discuss such a private matter in a public place.

In some ways, it was a clever thing to do. There was little chance of being observed in a crowd if one knew how to do it properly.

But if her answer would cause him elation or distress—and it must be one or the other—that would be unfair to subject him to such emotions in front of others.

Then she would call upon him today? Before the ball?

But as the hours dragged on, there was no sign of Miss Weston.

She must not know, then. She must have no idea.

All right then. He must soldier on as if nothing was the matter. He could manage that. He supposed.

He was used to pining helplessly after her. It could be next to nothing to keep pretending everything was fine. But now this letter had completely changed the game that he had been playing with himself. And now he was unsure of the rules.

James got ready for the ball with more care than usual. Not that there was anyone other than his valet to comment on it. As a member of the nobility he always strove to be fashion-forward. He doubted that anyone would think anything of his outfit. Nor would they know that it had taken him over an hour to pick it out.

Public balls in Bath were a bit of a mixed blessing, if you asked James.

On the one hand, it was a wonderful way to make new acquaintances and to meet old friends. They were always lively and interesting.

On the other hand, they could be noisy. And since there was no one host, one couldn't be certain that one would enjoy all the people assembled. There could be quite a lot of mixing of the classes, so to speak.

Miss Weston, James knew, loved them. She loved to meet new people. She thrived upon a little bit of chaos. The balls were an excellent opportunity for her to people watch and gossip.

James himself could enjoy them on most occasions. He could admit that a part of why he went to them was for the chance to spend some time with Miss Weston. But he did not go for her alone.

Tonight, though... he wished like anything that they were in a slightly quieter setting.

The loud music and spinning, colorful dresses of the ladies

seemed to reflect the chaos inside of him. He felt off-balance from the moment he crossed the threshold.

Miss Weston came to him at once, almost like there was a magnet inside of him that pulled her to him. If only, he thought with a trace of bitterness.

"Mr. Norwich!" she gestured at all the people assembled. "Did you know that somewhere in here is the man that I shall marry?"

He nearly choked on nothing but air.

"Of course, Mother certainly thinks so," Miss Weston went on gaily. "Do you think that I shall have a better time of it tonight than last night? I might dance with a man twice, what do you think of that?"

"I think that you must be prudent and careful in your choices," he replied.

Miss Weston laughed. "Oh, but I am nothing but prudence and care! Have you not met me?"

"I have, unfortunately, had many occasions in which to meet you and learn your character."

"You are far too cruel. One would think that you do not like me at all and only put up with me for the sake of my father."

"Miss Weston, I can assure you that I put up with you for no reason other than to delight in your company."

"And now you flatter me! Make up your mind, Mr. Norwich. You know that we ladies are simple-minded creatures and are easily startled and confused. Like wild animals."

"Indeed, I have often compared you in my mind to a wild creature. Perhaps a great cat of some kind. You have this habit of pouncing upon people like they are your prey."

"Oh dear, do you feel like prey? I should hope not. You are not enough of a meal for me when it comes to gossip. You are too fair-minded. Miss Perry, for example. She is wonderful for feeding one's need for gossip."

"For once, I am glad to have failed you in something. I hope I should never have a reputation as a gossipmonger. Unless of course I am speaking about you."

"And what horrid things have you said to others about me?"

"That you are perfectly tolerable if one has a glass of wine at hand."

FANNY FINCH

Miss Weston smacked his arm lightly with her fan. "You are a terrible, terrible man. Why on earth do I put up with you?"

"Because who else would put up with you in turn?"

Miss Weston laughed delightedly. "A fair point, sir. It is lucky for the both of us that we are so suited."

A part of him wanted to take her by the shoulders and look deep into her eyes and explain that, of course, they were so well suited for one another. That unless all of her joviality towards him was faked, there was a real chance that he could be everything that she wanted.

How could she say such things and not see it? Not realize?

He could be overestimating how much she cared for him and his company, though. He could be letting her natural teasing carry him away, farther than she meant it to.

And he dared not say anything in such a public setting in any case. So he kept quiet.

"Would you like me to find out what gentlemen are in attendance and give you an assessment?" he asked, scanning the room.

"Oh, that would be most helpful. I know a great many of them, of course." Miss Weston frowned. "And I suspect that Mother has been spurring them on.

"Not that she truly wants me to marry any particular one of them. I do not think that she has a favorite."

James could have told her that her mother did indeed have a favorite in this race. He suspected that it would have given Miss Weston quite a shock to learn.

"But I suspect that she thinks that if she encourages the men and lets it be known that I am actively looking to be wooed... that it will then in turn spur me to choose one in order to get rid of the others."

"You have to admit," James said admiringly, "it is a fair operation. Hopefully in their actions you will also see more of their true nature through their haste."

"A fair point. I only wish that I wasn't getting the impression from her that I was doing it wrong. That there is something that I am missing.

"She keeps giving me these looks... as though there is something right in front of us that she can see and I cannot. I suppose that it is only that I am more fanciful and feeling than she is.

"Mother has always been quite sensible. As has Father. I'm not at all sure where my own sense of whimsy comes from."

"I think it might have been all those fairy books they let you read as a child."

Miss Weston smiled in fond memory. "I was rather obsessed with them, wasn't I? I believe I tried to get people to read them to me because I was too lazy to bother reading them by myself."

"I think it was more that you wanted the company," James pointed out.

"True, that as well. I never do well on my own, do I?" Miss Weston sighed. "Perhaps Mother has a point. When I am married I shall never be alone."

James could see that several gentlemen were eyeing Miss Weston and he knew that the dancing would soon begin. "I think that there are some gentlemen who wish to be added to your dance card."

"Oh." Miss Weston looked around. "Well, I hope that you shall snatch me for a dance at some point, Mr. Norwich. At least then I will know that one dance will not be boring."

Then she was off, smiling and laughing with some other man.

The change in her behavior was most noticeable. She smiled coquettishly and cast her eyes downward in affected modesty.

A pleasing flush was on her cheeks, and she was altogether far more flirtatious than she was when speaking with him.

He tried not to despair. Yet he could not help but feel as though he had missed out on his chance. That he had the one opportunity to tell her his feelings and now he had lost it.

Perhaps he ought to write her another letter? No, that would be repetitive.

Miss Weston and the man that she was with went out onto the dance floor to join the others. In a public ball, there were so many people that James for once did not have to worry about dancing every round.

Usually in smaller balls, hosted by a family, there were more women than men and so the men were obliged to dance nearly every time so that all the ladies got a turn.

Here, at least, he had a chance to simply stand and observe.

Miss Weston stood out, even among all the other lovely women who were assembled. She was in white that night, as was the current fashion. The lightness of her step, the quick and easy way that she moved...

It was easy, watching her, to see that she was the best dancer of those assembled. She made it look as easy as breathing, and the delighted smile on her face revealed how much fun she was having with it.

James felt a small smile form on his face as he watched her.

He wondered if he was obvious to others who could see him. If he looked as besotted as he felt. But standing in amongst the crowd, he felt just invisible enough that he could watch unheeded.

She was such a wonder. He could see her making her partner laugh. And not the false, forced laugh of a man who is trying to be polite. But the quick, eyes-crinkled laugh of someone who is genuinely and unexpectedly amused.

And there was no doubt that her form was pleasing to watch as she moved. She showed great skill in the dance, but dancing was also a way to show off her figure. And she had quite a lovely one.

James glanced about the room. Already he could see other men who were waiting for their chance. Their eyes were on Miss Weston and they would approach her as soon as the dance ended, no doubt.

He would not stick around and torture himself in such a way. Nor would he dance with her tonight. It might disappoint her and he hated to do that. But he had to protect himself as well.

He retired into the men's room and engaged in some debates about politics instead. It was sufficiently distracting. Miss Weston could not find him in there. She might use logic and conclude that this room was where he must be, since she would not be able to find him elsewhere. But she could not follow.

After he had spent what he felt was a sufficient amount of time —long enough to be polite—he excused himself.

"Early morning tomorrow," he told his conversation companions.

He darted quickly through the ballroom so that he would not be seen and stopped by anyone. He quickly descended the stairs to the street and set off briskly down it.

When he got home, however, he found that there was a surprise awaiting him.

A letter. From Miss Weston.

He picked it up, turning it over. There was no name on it. It was addressed to his post office box, where he had his man pick up the mail every afternoon.

This must have been put in his box with the late post.

Oh, but of course. He must have provided a return address when he had addressed the letter to Miss Weston. Although he had forgotten to sign his name, his habit of addressing was so ingrained that he had done it without thought.

She certainly could not be giving him an answer as to yes or no, could she? Not when she did not know who he was. Surely it would be folly for her to say yes to allowing a man to court her if she did not know his identity.

What, then, was this letter?

He opened it, surprised to find that his hands were shaking. He paused, walking over to sit down and then resuming in reading it.

Dear Sir,

I confess that your letter stirred in me a great curiosity. I would even have been inclined to say yes to your proposal to court me.

However, I am afraid that you neglected to include a rather important part of yourself to me. Despite claiming to give me your heart, you have neglected to give me your name.

What should a lady think of this? I was pleased, no, taken aback even by your words. They fed my soul in a way that I did not even know needed feeding.

I was astounded that I could produce such passionate and tender emotions in someone. I have to confess—and I find it is so much easier to confess such things on paper.

That is why you wrote to me, is it not? That is what you said—that you could not say such things in person.

I find that it is the same for me. In writing you this letter I can tell you easily that I do not think as highly of myself as other people believe I do.

To know that I had endeared myself to you so completely was a reassurance. A great one. Even if our correspondence and relationship were to end now, I would always remember and treasure your words.

But you have left your name out. How am I to give you an answer if I do not know who you are?

I implore you to tell me your identity. I am filled with quite a burning curiosity. Partly because I am appalled at myself. With someone who calls me his friend, how could I have failed to notice his feelings for me?

You must be quite angry with me. I hope that you are not but I would understand if you were. Is that why there is no name? So that you might have me be purposefully in the dark, punishment for my lack of observation?

Or is it some kind of puzzle that you mean for me to figure out?

I hope that you will write to me again and let me know who you are. My heart has not beat at anything less than a breakneck speed since I read your letter. I am sure I will scan the crowd for you at the ball tonight. Wondering as each man approaches me—is it you? Is it you?

Please, write to me.

Sincerely,

Miss Julia Weston

James stared down at the letter in surprise.

Miss Weston had never confided to him that she thought of herself as anything less than a marvel. She always seemed to be possessed of the greatest self-confidence.

Yet, in this letter, she had found the courage to say to a stranger what she would not admit to the face of a man she had known for ten years.

Perhaps there was something to this letter writing.

Perhaps, instead of revealing his name, he ought to continue to woo her through writing. He could say to her all of the things he did not know how to speak aloud. And she would be able to do the same with him.

Would it not enable them to be more honest than if they were in person? There were many years between them. A lot of baggage, in a way. And everyone would be watching them if they were to court. They would not truly be able to fully take the measure of one another. There would always be others listening in to the conversation.

This could be the solution.

He hurried to his desk and wrote her a reply that might be sent out with the earliest post.

Dear Miss Weston,

You have no idea how many times I wish to start these letters with something more drastic than a simple 'dear' but I fear I must hold onto some tenets of propriety.

I received your letter after a full day of cursing my stupidity. To my horror, I realized only too late that I had left out my name in my letter to you.

You can easily imagine the many names that I called myself. I despaired of the matter ever being resolved.

How lucky, then, that I had instinctively added my post office box as the return address. And how fortunate that you were kind enough to respond.

Many women would have simply burnt such a letter, I am sure. I suppose I have your adventurous spirit to thank for it?

My first instinct was to write to you and tell you my name. Dispel the mystery.

However, thinking upon it, perhaps this could be a blessing to us.

You echoed my sentiment that it is often easier to be honest when one is not standing in front of the person to whom one is confessing. Perhaps that is why, in Catholicism, the parishioners confess to the priest through a wall?

I was thinking, that is if you would not object to it, that we might then continue this correspondence. That I might reveal myself to you through letters.

A man's name is after all only one small part of his character. And I have found in my time that I am not wholly myself when I am in person.

I tend to mold myself to fit what others would wish to see. I reflect their own behavior back at them. Sometimes I feel as if I do not even know myself for all that I am playing a role around others.

If you would allow me, perhaps this way we could come to know one another without pretense and without pressure. Without worry and judgment.

Of course, I ask nothing from you. You may ask me as many questions as you like. You are obliged to tell me nothing. The burden of responsibility is on my head, to prove to you that I can be the sort of man that you would desire for a husband.

I believe that in this way we can truly come to know each other. Without the burden of our pasts and our past impressions of one another.

I can assure you that I am far more eloquent regarding my feelings when I am writing them as opposed to speaking them. You can say no, of course. The choice is yours. I only wish to woo you properly, and I think that this would be the best way for me to do that.

I know that it is unconventional. I feel a great well of shame even as I suggest it. I can only say that I am a coward.

But if you would permit me, perhaps this way we could truly come to know one another. Or, rather, you could truly come to know me and my thoughts. The ones that I have kept from you for so long.

The choice is yours. Whatever you decide, I remain...

He stared down at the paper. Should he sign some kind of... alternate name? A fond sort of nickname that she could call him instead of his actual name?

No, that would be too intimate. Too close to a Christian name. Just as he would only call Miss Weston 'Julia' if they were engaged, and she would only call him 'James' under those same circumstances.

But he couldn't just leave it blank. That felt too odd. He must leave her something.

He decided to simply sign it with deepest respects, Sir.

He was tempted to replace 'respects' with 'affections' but he was already risking far too much in continuing their correspondence. And in asking her to continue it even further.

Was he mad? Had he completely lost his mind?

But men and women did write to each other, even though it was prudent not to. Miss Georgiana Reginald, soon to be Mrs. Trentworth, and her fiancé had written to one another throughout their courtship.

Of course, the only one who did not know of their courtship was her father, since his disapproval was legendary.

If one was engaged to a lady or it was presumed that one soon would be, then there were ways in which the lines of what was and was not appropriate blurred.

That did not mean that others didn't blur the lines before then. Miss Weston had always been the adventurous type. Would she be willing to skirt along the bounds of propriety?

He was willing to risk it for her, but he would not be risking as much. He was aware of that. It was always the woman who took the fall. Rarely the man.

Even when it was clearly the man's fault.

If they were to be discovered to have been passing letters, the pressure upon them to marry would be immense. Many would assume that they must secretly be engaged to be writing to one another in such a fashion.

But if they were careful—and he for his part would be exceedingly careful—they could get away with it.

They could grow to learn one another properly, this way. Without all of the history between them. Without her set idea of who and what he was. They could manage this.

They would just have to be careful.

And Miss Weston would have to say yes.

CHAPTER 55

JULIA WAITED with impatience for the arrival of another letter.

Or, perhaps, the arrival of the gentleman himself.

She was not so sure that he would come in person. He had stated in his letter that writing was much easier for him than speaking to her about this face to face. That, indeed, writing was the only way that he could declare his feelings for her.

It would most likely be another letter, to tell her of his name.

She felt like a fiend, always checking the post, paranoid. Even all through the ball last night she had been distracted.

All that she could think as she danced with the men was, Is it you?

At the end of the night, she'd had to admit to herself that she hoped her letter writer was not one of the men with whom she had danced.

Unless one of them was doing a very good job of concealing his more romantic nature, they were all far too dull. Or, they were far too inclined to dance attendance on her.

The letter writer had written to her because he could not show his feelings any other way. That meant he couldn't possibly be one of the men fawning over her. Otherwise, why not simply woo her in person?

On the other hand, the men who didn't seem to have as much of an interest in her were quite boring. And none of them had been what she would call a friend. The letter writer wouldn't have dared to say that if they were only passing acquaintances, would he?

And so who could it possibly be?

It had so distracted her that she had not even noticed until halfway through the ball that Mr. Norwich was gone. They always did a dance together. He was the most skilled dancer that she knew. Someone who could always keep up with her.

Why on earth should he have left?

Julia had shrugged it off. Perhaps he had an early morning and had seen how busy she was with other partners. Mr. Norwich was always courteous in that way.

Still. She would have liked to have danced with him. She had not realized how much she enjoyed dancing with him until he was no longer there.

Julia resolved to tell him so when she next saw him. He would be all apologies of course. She would then tease him and he would respond and he would dance with her next time.

But who was her letter writer?

She had left the ball in a state of frustration. She had thought that it would be so easy to figure out who it was. That through his glances or words, the man would reveal himself.

Even if he had not meant to show himself. That through her new knowledge of him, he would do so inadvertently.

But this man was rather good at hiding his true nature, for she could not put her finger on any one person and say definitely, That is him.

She did not think that he had gone so far as to pretend to be fawning or indifferent in order to hide himself further from her. And again, none of the men were what she would call a friend.

That meant it was all entirely up to the letter.

Mother commented a few times on her pacing. "Whatever has gotten into you?" she demanded.

Julia could not very well be honest with her and tell her. Impatience was like an itch inside of her bones that she could not reach, similar to hunger and yet so very different.

"It is nothing," she said, trying to sound dismissive. "I am waiting for the official invitation from Georgiana, that is all."

"The woman only became engaged a month or two ago, my

dear," Mother replied. "Do give her some time. They are all most likely recovering from the grand mess that was her brother's wedding."

True, the wedding of a duke—for that was what Georgiana's brother was—had to by political necessity be a grand affair.

Georgiana had ended up doing most of the planning to help out her soon-to-be sister-in-law. Julia did not blame her if she wished to take some time before planning her own wedding.

However, it was as good an excuse as any as to why she was currently pacing up and down the hall. Julia held in her sigh.

Then the mail, at last, arrived.

She had to clutch her own hands together to keep from snatching it all out of the servant's hands as the letters were placed on the tray. She waited until the tray was offered to her, and she could take whatever was addressed to her and leave the rest to Mother.

Mother was luckily not quite so sick that she had to leave all of the matters of the house to Julia. She could still read the letters of business and send on things to Father that he needed to know about. Or read the letters from Father about things that needed to be taken care of.

Julia normally did not care much one way or another about it. She was only glad that it meant that Mother was still well enough in that regard.

But now, she was most grateful. Mother had not even asked Julia if she had received any letters. She was so caught up in the business of dealing with her own letters.

Julia could feel her hands shaking slightly as she looked at the one letter that had arrived for her. She had a great many pen pals, as did most people. Everyone lived so far away and there was much gossip to catch up on.

But today, there was just the one letter.

She recognized the handwriting at once. She had read the original letter so many times that it seemed burned into her memory.

The return address in the left-hand corner confirmed it. This was her letter writer.

Julia could feel her hands shaking slightly as she tucked the letter into her dress and quietly departed from the room.

With some luck, Mother wouldn't even notice that she had left.

She expected nothing but a short apology or two, and then the name. Or perhaps an apology about how the letter writer had now lost his nerve and she should pretend that nothing had happened.

Oh, she hoped with all of her heart that it was not that. She needed to know. She needed to hear more about this person. Understand how they saw such wonderful things in her, how they could burn so brightly for her without saying anything for so long.

To her surprise, the letter was much longer.

Julia could hardly believe what she was reading. The man was suggesting that they continue writing to each other?

It was a risk, she allowed. Although she could admit to herself that her first thought was not of propriety. It ought to have been, she knew that. But she had never been one to think too much about the rules of society.

Or, rather, she had never seen one that she couldn't bend a little.

Her father would probably say it was her reckless nature and that she ought to caution herself more against such behavior. And she knew that he was probably right.

But she could not deny that the temptation was there. She wanted to know more about this person.

Part of it was, she realized, guilt.

This was someone who called her a friend. Someone who said that they knew one another. But how could she have someone who was that familiar with her, whom she did not realize had such feelings for her?

She almost wanted to write them an apology. To tell this man, I am sorry for being so blind.

She did not think that was what he wanted to hear, though. She would not wish to wound his pride. He seemed content to have been hiding his feelings from her. Glad, even.

The poor man seemed almost ashamed of how he felt. Julia wanted to clasp his hand in hers and assure him that there was no need for an apology. People could not control how they felt or with whom they fell in love, could they?

Yet, whether it was what he wanted or not, she felt that she ought to have noticed. That she should know her friends well enough to recognize their moods. How could she not have seen that someone cared for her this much?

He certainly cared for her more than she cared for him. While she could already feel in herself the potential for more tender feelings, at the moment she felt nothing in particular for any man she knew.

It was imbalanced. It was unfair. If she could she would have apologized at once and asked what she could do to improve their friendship. It made her fear that there might be other important things from her other friends that she had failed to notice.

It also made her want to get to know him better.

It made her want to take him up on his offer. To find some way to know him as he knew her. Perhaps, then, she might love him as he loved her.

She was curious to know if she could. Could she feel for him in that way? Could his love be reciprocated? It couldn't right now for she did not know him. But he was offering...

He was offering for her to get to know him. Without the bonds of their previous knowledge of one another. Without worrying about others watching them. Without concerns about him perhaps being a bit richer or poorer than she was.

There would be no bothersome input from her parents or from her peers. There would be no need to restrain her opinions and thoughts because others were around. She could ask him questions that she dare not ask normally.

This way, she could truly learn his character, and he hers. She could admit to herself that she was not so sure he truly loved her.

After all, was not the person that she was in public different from who she was in private? Did they not all put on social masks?

She was always so much more flirtatious and confident in front of others than she felt otherwise. This man must feel the same way —and he ought to know that about her.

He ought to know what he was getting into if he married her. Just as she ought to know what she was getting into with marrying him.

It was only fair, wasn't it? To spare the both of them an unhappy marriage? It had worked out for her parents but she had heard far too many horror stories about other people's unions.

Nobody would know. Nobody need find out. They would write letters and simply be discreet about sending and receiving them.

With a little intelligence and common sense, there was no reason why this should become a scandal.

And the gentleman had already shown he was capable of restraint. Julia could think of a great many other things he might have said in his letters.

Indeed, he had admitted in this one that he was tempted to address her in the letter in a manner other than 'dear' but had held back. Julia's mind ran wild with the possibilities of what it might be. Something simple and sweet such as darling? Or perhaps more of a fond pet name, such as dove or kitten?

All right, so perhaps those last two were a little fanciful.

But it showed, overall, that the man was able to restrain himself. That he did not seem to intend to use these letters as a vehicle to share any overly romantic thoughts he might have.

Many a man would have taken advantage of the situation. Would have seen this as an opportunity to woo her in a more expressive way than would be allowed. They were already setting themselves up for a potential scandal, Julia knew.

If anyone found out about the exchanging of letters, it would be assumed that she and this gentleman were engaged. She would all but have to marry him.

A daunting prospect, to be sure, when she did not even know his name.

But already she liked him more than any other prospective husband. And if they were friends, then that meant she liked him as a person a great deal.

Some men, seeing that they were already cutting along the edge of propriety, would seize the chance to speak to her in much more... open language.

But while this man had made it clear that he cared for her deeply, he had not plunged into the deep end, so to speak. He had not said anything that could be considered jaw-dropping.

Indeed, she had read more ardent declarations in her novels.

He seemed quite respectful. And she wanted to know more about him.

If she could be smart about it...

And she would be smart about it. She was not a child. She wished to tell someone about her secret. Who did not want to share such information with a close friend, after all?

But she was not inclined to tell the whole world. She would not be the reason that information about this exchange got out.

And she felt, instinctively, as though she could trust this gentleman to do the same.

She could not put her finger exactly on why she trusted him in this. Something about the words he chose. Or perhaps it was that he had called them friends. Or that she recognized the handwriting from somewhere.

Perhaps, she acknowledged, it was simply that she wanted to trust him. That she wanted this romance so badly that she would take the risk and convince herself that it was less dangerous than it was.

Well, there were worse people to whom she could get married, she reminded herself. If they were discovered and they had to get married, she would make do. That was a risk she was willing to take.

Besides, she had always been a good liar. She could pretend they had been engaged the whole time. Or make up a story about what the letters were really about. She'd find a way.

Julia carefully tucked the second letter away with the first and then sat down at her desk.

It felt, for the first time since her parents had told her to find a husband, as though she was taking her own fate into her hands. That she was in control of herself and her life again.

Dear Sir...

CHAPTER 56

JAMES WAITED with bated breath all through the next day.

She would most likely say no. That was his ongoing thought, as he tried not to count the hours.

Miss Weston was an intelligent woman. She would not, could not be unaware of the risks involved.

Why should she place herself in a precarious position for a man that she did not know? For a man who might only possibly give her happiness?

It would be madness, if you asked him. The more time passed and the longer he thought about it, the greater the folly of it seemed to him.

He buried himself in work. He had much to take care of. Father was giving him more responsibilities all the time in preparation for when James would be in charge.

On the one hand, he understood the need for him to be prepared. Father was not sickly but life was uncertain.

On the other hand, he suspected that Father was simply taking the opportunity to foist as much responsibility off onto his son as possible. That way the count himself might spend his last few years relaxing instead of running his estate.

James did not like to think such things of his father. But he had long been aware of his family's failings.

He hoped that he would be a better husband to his wife than his father had been. Especially if his wife was Miss Weston. He wanted nothing more than to make her happy.

The thought kept plaguing him all day—he ought to walk to her house. He ought to call upon her and explain himself and apologize.

He couldn't believe that he had asked for so much from her. He should have never thought to do such a thing.

Every time he was about to leave and call upon her, however, he would force himself to focus on his work instead.

He would not be hasty. He wouldn't make this an even bigger mess than it already was by barging into her home and confessing.

Whether it was the right thing to do or not, he reminded himself, he had sent off that letter. The least he could do would be to allow her to consider it and answer it as she willed.

She must turn him down, though. She must. How could she not?

Miss Weston had always been the kind of person to skirt danger. He had counseled her against it many times himself.

She had always replied that if he would not take things seriously than neither would she. And she would not suffer his rebukes.

It was a fair point. James knew himself to be more serious than he often let on. He had been most serious, recently, in regards to Miss Reginald and her struggles.

She was a fine woman and he admired her greatly. He had been willing to offer up his own hand in marriage to her. That is, if Captain Trentworth had truly abandoned her.

Miss Reginald did not and had not loved him. But he had admired her. He had been despairing of his feelings for Miss Weston, as usual. Why not marry a fine woman and save her from spinsterhood? He could do much worse.

Fortunately, Captain Trentworth had come around. It had taken some yelling from Miss Weston and some time, but he had.

But Miss Weston had not been there for his serious moments with Miss Reginald or with the captain. She could not know that within him lay a deeper ocean than she suspected.

Letters might show her that. And he might find new unexplored depths within her soul as well. If she agreed to the exchange.

He was torn between despair and hope. He wanted her to

respond and say that she would exchange letters with him. He also wanted her to refuse and to demand to see his face.

He was not sure which would bring him more relief. Showing himself would bring him an answer and put an end to both their questions. But it might also bring an end to any chance they had of truly knowing one another.

Continuing with the letters would provide him a chance to woo her. To show her who he was outside of the box that she had constructed for him in her mind. He, too, could see her in a new light. He was sure that some part of him still thought erroneously about her. As people tended to about individuals they had known for so many years.

People changed and grew. And yet it was sometimes hard to see that in someone that he had known for so long. It was simply human nature. First impressions were strong and clung to a person's perception of another even after years of acquaintance.

He would not be surprised to find new angles to his lovely Miss Weston.

But while the letters would allow them to know one another, it would also prolong the inevitable. He would have to reveal himself in time. And how would she take it?

How would she reconcile the man she knew on paper with the witty childhood friend she knew from 'real' life?

He had no answer.

Perhaps it was best that it was up to Miss Weston. Whichever answer she chose, he would go along with it. There were obviously positives and negatives to both possibilities. He would simply allow fate and the lady to select which one.

That did not stop him from checking the letter box with near-obsession all day.

When he finally could think of no more excuse for business, he retired home and proceeded to pace. He tried reading a book but was too distracted. He kept wondering what Miss Weston would say. What she would think.

Perhaps she was not responding at all? Perhaps she had decided that the entire endeavor was too ridiculous?

He knew she was a fanciful girl. Or rather that she could be fanciful when she wanted to be. But she was not an unintelligent person. She was not silly.

It could be that her common sense won out. That she had no interest in playing games of any kind and so had thrown his letter into the fire.

Or, it could be that the letter had been discovered. She could be getting into serious trouble with her mother right that moment. He could have just set her up for belittlement and punishment.

James arranged for some tea to be brought to calm his nerves. He was behaving worse than a fifteen-year-old off at her first ball in London. There was no reason for him to be so very nervous and panicked.

Miss Weston was an intelligent and capable woman and could handle herself. There was no reason for him to panic. Panicking would not help him or her no matter what the outcome was.

If Mrs. Weston had indeed seen the letter—that was the worst-case scenario that James could come up with. If she had seen the letter, then he would learn of it soon enough. Miss Weston or her mother would be sure to tell him about it.

Mrs. Weston might even employ him to find who this letter writer was. She would want to keep it from her husband, of course. Mr. Weston need not be bothered to come from London when James was available and happy to provide his services.

Besides, it would only cause Mr. Weston needless distress.

In any case, he would hear about it. He would explain and apologize and accept any consequences that came for him. He would ensure that Miss Weston did not receive any punishment for what was his due alone.

There, he told himself. You have reached a logical conclusion. There is no need for you to pace so.

He forced himself to sit down and drink his tea.

But the knot in his stomach would not dissipate.

Finally, with the last mail of the day, it was delivered.

He knew that he was probably overestimating the postal service, but they were in the same city. Surely it should not take all day for a letter to reach him if it was posted from only a block or two away?

No matter. This endeavor might actually teach him patience. And the letter was here now.

He opened it carefully, making sure that he didn't tear it in his haste.

Dear Sir,

I admit that your proposition did not fill me with the concern that it should have. My worries about discovery and condemnation were secondary to my desire for the adventure of corresponding with you.

First, you must accept my apology. Before we proceed any further.

You say that we are friends. Yet I have not an inkling as to who you might be. You must feel some relief at that. I understand. I would be embarrassed to have such passionate feelings that I was unsure would be returned.

Please understand that from my perspective, it is quite a blow. To know that someone who I call friend feels such things for me and I had no idea. I feel as though I have failed you somehow. That I ought to have seen and been considerate of your feelings.

You might say that there is nothing for which I must apologize. That your concealing of your feelings was and is on your shoulders and not on me. But I cannot help but feel this way.

Now that unpleasantness is out of the way.

Second of all, I must thank you for placing such trust in me. This is a delicate endeavor that you are suggesting we embark upon. I'm certain that many other ladies would be tempted to spread the news of such a romantic and clandestine affair.

You could have easily exposed yourself to a dangerous game in which quite a few people knew what you had done. Yet you risked that for me. I can only offer up my humble thanks in your trust.

Third and finally:

I will accept your offer.

You have warned me greatly of the risk to myself. I understand it. I appreciate the effort that you have taken to ensure that I understand what this would entail.

I am certain in my choice, however. If this is the way that you feel you can woo me, then this is the way that we shall employ. Even if we do not agree to join in marriage, I would like to know your true heart, my friend. Whoever you may be.

Perhaps you could begin by explaining to me just how you came to develop these feelings you speak on? These feelings that are simultaneously so strong you would risk yourself in putting them down in words, and yet that you are too scared to speak aloud.

I await your return letter with a breathlessness that I probably should hesitate to confess to. But I find I do not much mind confessing things to you. Letters are so permanent. And yet, it is easier to speak my thoughts in them than to voice my words.

Sincerely, I remain,

Miss Julia Weston

James let out a slow breath.

She had agreed. They would write one another letters. They would be careful and considerate. He would have to make sure that he said nothing in the letters that would condemn her too much should they be discovered. He must not be overly ardent in his affections.

They were set on this course, now. It was almost a relief to know that. It was a decision, at least. There would be no more questioning and waiting in agony for an answer.

He went up to his desk and took up his pen and paper immediately.

The mail would have to go out first thing tomorrow but there was no reason to delay in writing it. There was no reason to delay in anything anymore.

Besides, he knew what he wished to say to her. And he really ought to say it before the words flew out of his head.

Unlike the first letter he did not have to do much rewriting. It was as though now that he had been given permission he could feel the words flowing from him without impediment or second-guessing.

He could so easily answer her question.

He only hoped that she would be satisfied with the answer.

CHAPTER 57

JULIA'S HEART thumped in excitement when the letter arrived.

She had dared to ask him how he had fallen for her. How he had come to know that she held a special place of affection in his heart.

It was a bold question, she knew. But was that not the point of exchanging these letters? To ask the questions that she would not otherwise dare to?

When the letter arrived she immediately slipped up to her room to read it. Mother was wonderfully distracted. Julia had expected her mother to say something, anything. To even shoot her a look that told her that her behavior had not gone unnoticed.

But there was nothing. No word of warning. No concerned glance.

It was marvelous good luck. Julia only wished that there was some way to communicate that would not involve her mother potentially seeing her receiving these letters.

She could put in her next letter the suggestion that perhaps they leave the letters in an oak tree nearby or some such. It would be quite romantic. And she needn't wait upon the postal office to ensure that she got her letter. Indeed she would get it faster this way.

That was too much danger, she reminded herself. That was a ridiculous flight of fancy in which she should not indulge. If they were to resort to leaving messages in a tree then who was to say they would not run into one another at one point?

It would all be too ridiculous. They might as well simply meet in person if that was the case. Leaving a letter in a tree or something of that manner was for when you knew who the person was, anyway. It was for lovers who couldn't be together and therefore had to resort to clandestine means.

No, she could withhold herself from going quite that far in ridiculous romanticism. She had already been bold enough in asking him to tell her how he had come to have feelings for her.

She retreated to her room, making sure to lock the door behind her, and read. She would not be able to read them in such a manner forever. She would have to learn patience and wait to read them in bed after Mother had gone to sleep.

After all, it was only so long until Mother noticed how her daughter dashed upstairs to read her letters every time the mail came.

But she could not wait. Not this time. She had to know. There would be time for patience later.

She sat on her bed and opened up the letter. She couldn't keep the smile off her face as she realized that it was a long one. Her suitor had certainly put quite a lot of thoughts into it. She was terribly excited.

Dear Miss Weston,

I confess to both fear and elation that you have agreed to this. I hope that I will do justice to the faith that you have put in me.

As to your question... I wish that I could tell you the exact moment that I came to have these feelings for you. However, alas, I cannot.

All that I can do is tell you when I realized them. When it came to me what I had fallen into without even realizing it.

It strikes me as quite strange that one cannot identify the moment in which one fell in love. The beginning is unknown to me and seems to be unknown to everyone else. At least according to poets and novelists.

Yet, there we are. And we cannot escape it now that we are in it. It is rather unfair of love, if you were to ask my opinion.

The moment that I realized my feelings for you had changed

was at a ball. It was barely over two years ago, if I am remembering the dates correctly.

You wore the most lovely dress. I had always admired your sense of style. You were the picture of an elegant lady.

I did not think as much of it as I ought to have. I had grown used to how lovely you looked. I had taken you and your presence for granted.

Yet that evening, there was another young man who waxed poetic to me about your form and figure. He was quite enthusiastic about you and wished to know if I knew where your interests lay.

In fact, he told me that he suspected I had designs upon you.

In that moment, I realized that he was right.

This man that I had never met before saw in me what I had failed to see in myself. That I had no designs upon you but had fallen, quite deeply. So deeply in fact that there was no way for me to extricate myself.

I confess with some shame the envy and jealousy that shot through me in those moments. Envy that he might have what I only then realized I wanted. Jealousy that he might take away from me a dear friend of whom I was so fond.

You can imagine how dumbstruck I was. This man was only trying to find out if the way to you was barred. Instead he accidentally gave me a revelation that I had not expected.

It frightened me at first. The strength of my feelings was new and concerning. I had of course had youthful infatuations. Who has not?

And like all youths, men and women alike, I thought those infatuations to be love. But it felt nothing like what I realized I felt for you.

You snuck into my heart and rooted yourself there deeply, a tree instead of a mere sapling by the time I realized you were there. Years of solid friendship had given my love a strong foundation.

For the first time my romantic feelings were not built upon looks or flirtations during a dance or a ball. They were built upon many years of acquaintance.

At first, I was not sure if this was not another infatuation. That I was mistaking it for love yet again.

I started to pay careful attention to our interactions. To how I felt when I saw you. When you walked into the room. When you made one of your quips for which you are so renowned.

I found that I was drawn to you. I felt like a moth, my steps taking me towards the flame before I even realized that I had moved.

You were my dearest companion, I realized. It felt shameful to admit such a thing. That a lady who had so many friends and acquaintances was the closest person that I had in this world.

Yet, while there were a great many people in society I admired, none of them were so close to me as you were.

I am aware that it is one-sided. You have many friends and I have but few. You may be my closest and my dearest but I am not yours.

The knowledge was not something that came to me surprisingly. Rather, as my knowledge of my own feelings grew, so did my understanding of yours. I could see almost at once that you did not hold for me the same level of depth of affections in which I held you.

I did not blame you for it. It is impossible, I think, to blame someone for their inability to fall in love with someone else. It is not really something that we can help.

One's behavior can be judged, of course. I will judge those husbands who do not love their wives and proceed to visit those less savory areas of London as a result. But it is not the lack of love that I judge. It is the breaking of a promise.

I quickly resolved to never let you know of my feelings. I could see nothing in it but embarrassment for us both if you were to learn of them.

But I could not stop watching you.

The way that you dance is a delight. You are often—in fact I think that you are always—the best dancer in the room. You move as though you are not even touching the floor.

Your smile lights up the entire ball. You must wonder I am sure why you are always the center of attention. Even when there are ladies of higher birth than you in attendance. It is because you are the most vivacious and witty of creatures.

Sometimes, I wonder if you are purposefully trying to distract me with your frocks. You always show yourself off to the best advantage in them. I confess that my valet makes most of my choices for dress. I am hopeless with fashion.

Everything that I had already admired in you for so long, in short, came into clear focus. I finally understood what had been building inside of me all of these years.

But I have gone on for long enough about this. You are probably tired of hearing such things. After all, hearing how much someone cares for you will not help you to care for them in return. It is knowing them and their character that truly breeds affection.

Ask me any questions that you like. I look forward to reading your letters and to answering your questions as best I can.

With fondest wishes.

Julia was simply burning with questions—but also with a kind of resolve.

This man had clearly known her for years. He even said so himself.

That narrowed down the field of possibilities. If she could gain more knowledge about him then she could find out who he was. She could learn his true identity.

It was a delicious prospect.

She could discover who he was and then confront him. Not in an angry sort of way. She was not upset. But wouldn't it be just like the plots of those Gothic novels everyone was so fond of nowadays?

She would be unraveling the mystery. And perhaps she would not tell the gentleman immediately when she figured it out. It would give her time to sort out if the man who she knew could hold her affections the way that this letter writer could.

They were two sides of the same coin, she knew. But to like only half of your husband's personality was not enough. Not for her. And, she thought, not enough for most people.

People would say that it was enough for them. But that was not so. They were lying to themselves. They would make themselves unhappy in time.

She would not do that. She would learn through her questions who her mystery writer was. Once that was accomplished, she would decide if she wanted to cease all interaction or if she would ask him to reveal himself.

It was almost like a game. She found herself rather excited for it, in fact. To put together the clues and follow the trail of bread-crumbs. Rather like a fairy tale.

She sat down at the desk and began to make a list of what she knew and what she wished to know. Rather, what she needed to know in order to figure out the man's identity.

What she did know was not a lot, not by any stretch of the imag-ination. But there were a few key things that she had figured out.

First, she knew by the man's own admission that they had known each other for many years.

That was helpful. She could remove quite a lot of men off the list that way.

Secondly, she highly suspected that this person was one of her father's former pupils. She was close with all of them and there were at least six off the top of her head who would openly and happily call her 'friend'.

That narrowed down the list even more. She had grown up with those men. It fit in with what the gentleman had told her in his letter. His description of how he had come to realize he cared for her fit in with a man who had known her first as a sort of sister figure.

It made sense. She had known her father's pupils as pupils first, boys second. As they got older she had become aware that some of them were quite handsome. But she doubted that any of them had seen her as a proper lady for some time.

She had run into a great deal of them frequently over the years. At least two resided in Bath. There had been gaps in between when she had seen them as a younger girl of, say, fourteen and when she saw them as an adult.

It all fit.

Third, she knew that this person was in Bath. A few of them owned houses in Bath but one or more of them might be staying in a hotel or at the house of a friend. That would explain the postal box, in fact. As opposed to using a house address.

She would not go so far as to go around to all of the hotels and give them a list of names to see if one of the men was staying there. But it was a start to have that list in front of her.

However, there was the possibility that it was not one of her father's former pupils. She could account for that. But if so, she would cross that bridge when she came to it.

First she would see if it was in fact one of those men. Which brought her to her second list: questions to ask.

She made a list of books that she would ask if the man had read, and what his thoughts were on them.

It was a natural set of questions. Discussing books, philosophy, the arts—it was how many people got to know one another. It certainly made for diverting conversation.

If a man was incapable of expressing an opinion on a book or a play then he and Julia would never be compatible. She was quite certain of that.

However, it would also serve to help her to figure out if the man was one of her father's pupils. She knew all the things that her father had taught the young gentlemen. Which books her father favored. His opinions on philosophers.

The gentleman wouldn't suspect a thing from her line of questioning. But she would be learning. She would be narrowing down her list.

The second set of questions was in regards to his plans for an estate. How did he intend to run his home? How did he see her fitting into it?

A set of practical questions that would normally not be asked until after the engagement. Courting was for love and tokens of affection. Not for discussing the humdrum and minutiae of daily life.

But she figured that she might as well know. And it would help her to narrow down the search. For in telling her about his estate and what he had in mind for the household side of their marriage, she would be able to tell what sort of family he came from.

Her father had educated a few men with titles. He had also educated those without titles but with a greater level of wealth than he had. After all, if her family had been rich, her father would not have needed to take in young men to tutor.

She suspected that the gentleman would not wish for her to know that he had a title. Both to protect his identity and to prevent her from feeling uncomfortable in speaking with him.

Part of this endeavor, after all, was to avoid judging one another through the means that society had constructed.

However, there were aspects of running an estate when one had a title that were different from when one was merely wealthy.

Julia made a mental note to ask Mr. Norwich about the details of his own estate. That way she could compare them to what this gentleman said.

If he said the same things that Mr. Norwich did, then he, too, had a title. Or at least was set to inherit one.

However, if his methods were different because of his means, such as his household being smaller, then she would know that he did not have a title. Therefore, he would have a smaller estate.

Third, she would ask him what he liked to do in town. Did he like dancing? Was he good at it?

Many people seemed to think that someone who liked dancing must therefore be good at it. Julia could attest that this was not the case. She had danced with many a man who claimed to love it and yet repeatedly stepped on her toes.

She would ask if he enjoyed the theatre. If he went to art galleries. How often he had to go into London for business.

She could then ask the same questions of her father's former pupils as she ran into them. And she would run into some of them. The ones who were staying in Bath and who were, therefore, her primary suspects.

And they must needs call upon her and her mother. It would be rude of them not to. Not after knowing her and her mother for so long while staying at their house.

Julia laughed delightedly to herself as she read over her list. Oh, this was the most exciting thing to happen since Georgiana and Captain Trentworth had been reunited.

Only this was more exciting. Because this was happening to her.

She sealed up her letter of response and hid her lists underneath some blotting paper. Then she hurried down to send the letter out with the morning post.

This was going to be great fun.

CHAPTER 58

JAMES LOOKED FORWARD to tonight's dinner party the way that he imagined those poor nobles in France looked forward to the guillotine.

The one thing that the exchanging of these letters had not prepared him for was the agony, the constant fear, of being discovered.

Not merely discovered through his own slip-up in the letters. That would be bad enough. But that he would say or do something in the middle of a dinner party or a ball.

And then, to look up and see Miss Weston's shocked, possibly even horrified face as she realized...

Oh God. It hardly even bore thinking about.

He mustn't panic or appear odd in any way through his behavior, he told himself. That was what would lead to discovery.

If he behaved with confidence, however—that would keep anyone from suspecting anything.

He had heard, once, from a lawyer with whom he was conversing, that confidence was how so many criminals were able to get away with things.

"I knew of a thief," the man had said, "who was quite successful. He stole quite a lot of jewels right from under the noses of his employers. He would pose as a servant."

The reason the man had succeeded in his simple and bold schemes was the sheer confidence that he displayed.

"When a man acts as though he has a right to be doing something," the lawyer had explained animatedly, "people assume that he does, therefore, have that right. They do not question him. A plausible little falsehood, smoothly told, a quiet ease of manner, and there you are."

James had thought at the time that it was a testament to the gullibility of society. That people ought to think for themselves instead of easily believing what was told to them.

Now, however, he hoped that the lawyer had been correct. That in his confident manner lay his safety.

If he behaved as he usually did, then Miss Weston would not suspect a thing. She would have no reason to if his manner was as always.

She would be looking for a man who was suddenly nervous around her. Who had gone from friend to careful stranger. That was what would give him away. Keeping his distance might seem to offer safety but it would spell his ruin.

He would be cautious in mind only. But his manner would be usual and open.

When he arrived at the Weston residence for the dinner he was surprised to find that he was not the only former pupil of Mr. Weston's in attendance.

"Mr. Carson, good to see you," he said, shaking the other young man's hand.

Mr. Carson was a pleasant man. He had an easy manner that James had always secretly envied. It felt to James as though he must always affix a mask to himself, to his personality. That he had to force himself to be jovial.

The only time it did not feel false was when he was around Miss Weston.

Mr. Carson, however, seemed naturally to be that way. It could be a mask just as James's joviality was but if so it was an exceedingly good one.

The gentleman was only a year or so younger than James. He had a title coming to him as well once his father passed, for he was to be a marquess.

"Mr. Norwich, a pleasure as always." Mr. Carson smiled. He had one of those faces that was not handsome but quietly pleasant nonetheless. The sort of face that one could look at for the rest of one's life.

"What brings you into Bath?"

"Mother comes down here every year and has enlisted me to come along. My younger sister was in need of an escape from London but she insists upon continuing to go to balls here."

James knew a little of Mr. Carson's younger sister. He suspected that she was being taken away from London to prevent her reputation as a flirt from getting any worse.

His own brother had been just as bad before he had joined the Navy. James was sure that his brother's behavior had not changed overmuch. But at least now it was in good company with like-minded men. And he could get on with his flirtations far away from society where he might damage himself and his family.

"How old is Miss Carson now?" James asked.

"Oh, she has just turned eighteen," Mr. Carson said. "You know how girls may become at that age. She is quite intoxicated with her first season. I think that she has let it all go to her head."

"Simply because one can flirt does not mean that one should," James observed.

"Precisely. I have tried to tell her so myself but you know as well as I do that wise counsel is not always welcome."

"Wise or not, the fact that it is counsel at all grates upon a young temperament. I was rather the same, I'm afraid."

There came the sound of Miss Weston's gay laughter, and James had to work hard to suppress the fond smile that wanted to grace his lips.

"Now, there is a young lady who knows how to walk that line quite well," Mr. Carson observed. "Miss Weston has turned into a wit and a beauty when we were otherwise occupied.

"One moment she was merely the daughter of our tutor. The next she is this wonderful lady. I feel as though I have turned my head away for but a moment only to look round again and find her transformed."

James viciously shoved down the awful, hot mixture of jealousy and envy that stirred up inside of him. Mr. Carson had every right to think of Miss Weston as a fine and lovely lady. That was what she was, after all.

James certainly had no hold on her. And Mr. Carson might not even have any kind of romantic designs on Miss Weston. He could simply be complimenting a woman that he admired. Admiration and romantic endeavors did not always go hand in hand. One might have one without the other.

"Yes," James said. He forced his voice to stay pleasant. "I have found her to be an excellent dinner companion. She is learned, of course. What else could one expect from a father such as hers."

"Well, not all fathers would care to educate their daughter. Even if she was his only child."

"Ah, but you know Mr. Weston. Who could he converse with when he was in between pupils? It must needs be his daughter. And we know how he does so hate a boring conversation."

Mr. Carson laughed. "Yes. I was hoping that he would be here, but it seems he is in London."

"You will have to make do with the daughter then."

"I shall do more than simply make do. Tell me, do you know if she has a particular suitor? I know that she must have a few. But is there one that she seems to favor above the others?"

"Why, are you suggesting a duel at dawn?"

"I could never duel at dawn, my good man. First of all, it is far too early in the morning for such a thing." Mr. Carson laughed.

"But secondly, I would not wish to step upon the toes of any man who already has a place in her heart. If I am too late, then I am too late. But otherwise she seems a delightful creature. It is high time that I am to be married. Or so my father says."

"Ah, fathers. Always looking out for our best interests. Whether we want them to be or not."

Mr. Carson laughed again. "Precisely. I shall have to get to know her better, of course. But would she not make a fine wife? You know her well, or so you said?"

"I like to think that I am someone the lady may call a friend," James replied. He struggled to keep his tone light and even. "And we can agree that she is a fine woman. Very much like her mother."

"You mean that she has a sharp tongue." Mr. Carson chuckled. "That is of no never mind to me, as you know."

James nodded, trying not to look or sound as distracted as he felt. "She would make anybody a fine wife so long as her intellect is respected."

"And there is no one man that she favors? Nobody upon whose toes I would be stepping?"

"None so far as I know."

He couldn't very well tell the man that he had been corresponding secretly with Miss Weston. And he did not even know if he was favored by her. He was throwing his hat in the ring, that was all. Doing it in an unconventional way, but still.

Miss Weston's replies to his letters spoke more to her curiosity than to any form of favoritism. He would have to keep working to earn that.

And now it seemed that he would not be alone in his efforts.

James honestly did not know how he could compete with Mr. Carson. The man was set to inherit a larger estate and a better title than James was, for one thing.

Not that title and rank were all that Miss Weston cared for. But one had to be sensible in marriage. What young lady would not be somewhat captivated by the idea of becoming a marchioness?

If she had to choose between two men that she liked equally, why would she not go with the one who would bring her better fortune and a greater title?

And for another, Mr. Carson was clearly more at home in himself than James was. He had taken one look at the young lady and was set to woo. And he would not need to hide behind letters in order to do so.

James felt a great wave of shame wash over him. He was truly a coward compared to this man. He dared to think that he had a right to woo Miss Weston through letters? He could not even declare himself to her in person?

He ought to step back. To not reply to whatever letter she sent him next. To vanish as the letter writer if he could not court her as himself.

But then Miss Weston walked over to them, smiling—and smiling primarily at him.

"Mr. Norwich," she said eagerly. "You have no idea how eager I am to see you this evening. You must prepare yourself for a proper interrogation. Are you ready?"

"As ready, I imagine, as I shall ever be when it comes to you," he replied.

In that moment he knew that his weakness was not confined to his cowardice with courting. It was also in her. Her shining smile. The way that her eyes danced with mirth. How she sought him out so easily and readily.

He was a selfish man. He could not give her up.

But how could he compete with a man such as Mr. Carson?

Speaking of which...

"Mr. Carson!" Miss Weston smiled at him and curtsied. "I was quite pleased to hear from Mother that you were in town. Thank you for accepting our humble invitation."

"I should not have missed it for the world," Mr. Carson replied. "I was only just telling Mr. Norwich here how unfortunate it is that your father is not in attendance. But I hear that you are to be commended for replacing him. You are certainly easier upon the eyes than he is."

Miss Weston laughed, and James privately cursed his inability to compliment her so easily. Why was it that he could playfully insinuate insults but could not compliment her the way that he wished? The way that she deserved?

"I shall be sure to tell him so when I next see him," she informed Mr. Carson. "Won't you please come in and meet the others? I am not sure if you already know some of them."

She led Mr. Carson away and James prepared himself for another dinner party without Miss Weston's company.

It was no less than he deserved for his behavior, of course. And Miss Weston could hardly be blamed for it.

She was supposed to be looking for suitors. Her courtship with the letter writer had only barely begun. Why should she not speak with the charming and titled gentleman who seemed so eager to compliment her?

He had only just begun to give sway to such depressing thoughts, however, when Miss Weston returned.

"Another one of my father's former pupils," she said. "What an evening it shall be. He will be sad to have missed Mr. Carson. He was one of Father's favorites. Not that any of them were so dear in his affections as you, of course."

James bowed politely in acknowledgment of the compliment. "Should you not be entertaining him, then? You have the luck and pleasure of seeing me frequently. I doubt that you have seen him for some time."

"It has been a year, I should think," Miss Weston mused. "But no matter. I shall speak with him in due course. First, I must ask some advice from you."

"Do you ever speak to me for any other reason?" James replied.

"Why, of course I do. I also speak to you in order for you to compliment my choice of dress. And so that you might criticize my life choices and my past times and my thoughts on opera."

"Ah, and here I thought that you spoke to me so that you might continue to press in vain for me to change my mind on opera. And so that you might criticize my wit and choice of dress at every turn."

"You wound me so, sir. I have nothing but the highest opinion of your wit." Miss Weston gave a falsely put-upon sigh. "If only your compassion for my poor nerves was as great."

"Your nerves, I have come to believe, Miss Weston, are made of steel."

She smiled fondly at him. "I am pleased to hear you say so. I shall remember that the next time you accuse me of being too dramatic."

"But what is it that you must consult me on?"

His heart hammered in his chest as he asked the question. Could it be that she was going to confide in him about the letter writer? Would he have to deflect or find some way to lie convincingly?

Perhaps she was having second thoughts about the whole thing and wished to know if he thought she ought to back out. That was the sort of thing that you asked a man you considered to be a brother, was it not?

To his surprise, however, Miss Weston replied:

"I was hoping that I might pick your brain, a little, on what it is like to be a man inheriting a title. What is your estate like?"

"Those are rather businesslike questions for a young lady to be asking," James replied. "You are lucky that we are so close in our friendship. And that I have such a respect for your intellect."

"I knew that you would not object," Miss Weston replied knowingly. "And besides, it is only so that I will be prepared. You know that I must choose a husband. If I am to pick a titled man I should wish to know what I am getting into."

"You could very well ask your dear friend Miss Reginald. She helped her brother the duke to run his estate until his marriage."

"But she is far away and a letter would take some time. I wish to hear it from you."

Miss Weston smiled at him prettily, and James was helpless to resist her. He supposed that it was his own fault that he could not seem to say no to her on anything.

He sighed. "Very well. You may ask away."

Miss Weston immediately began to pepper him with questions. He answered them readily and as best he could.

It did not fail to escape his notice that they were still talking alone. Not that there was anything improper in that. It was only that Miss Weston ought to have been talking to all of her guests.

He could not help but hope that perhaps it meant that she did care for him a bit more than for the others?

She is literally pumping you for information, good God man, he thought to himself. There is nothing special in it.

Others would come up and speak to them from time to time. He could see Mr. Carson watching them from the sidelines.

He hoped that Mr. Carson did not think that James had been lying when he had said there was no man that Miss Weston favored.

Miss Weston was plainly speaking to him only for the information that he could provide. And of course because she trusted him. He would not underestimate that and was grateful for it.

But Mr. Carson might not see it that way. He might even think that James had lied in order to see Mr. Carson make a fool of himself.

He hoped that Mr. Carson would not think so. But to be certain, he would have to compliment the man or instruct Miss Weston to let Mr. Carson sit next to her at dinner or something of that manner.

It grated at him to give the man another shot at wooing Miss Weston. But if the man was determined, there was little that James could do to stop him. And besides, a little kindness could go a long way.

Above all, he did not want to be seen as a liar or someone who set up a cruel jest.

And besides, it was not ultimately his choice who Miss Weston married. Nor was it Mr. Carson's choice. It was nobody's choice except for Miss Weston's.

She plied him for quite some time about his business. All while they were waiting for dinner, in fact.

James could not help but worry that this was because she was looking for a titled man to marry and wanted to be prepared. He knew that it would make her father happy.

And Miss Weston, although she pretended otherwise, wanted quite a lot to make her parents happy.

Her father had taught the sons of titled men. He had been a surrogate father to many of them. It made sense that she would want to make him happy by marrying one of them. Giving her father the pride that he had to swallow when he had been tutoring them.

James was aware that not all boys were gracious about being sent away from home to live in a smaller house with fewer servants. To be taught by a man who was below them in station.

Mr. Weston had borne it all with a patient and understanding air. To give him a chance to finally stand tall among them and say that his daughter was a titled lady... James could understand Miss Weston wanting to give her father that.

Some might call it mercenary. But James thought that it was only fair. Men sought to be the most successful in business and to possibly even gain a knighthood. Why should a lady not try and be successful at her own career, such as it were?

Well, that already put Mr. Carson in the running. He had a title, and a better one than what James stood to inherit.

He was also much more at ease and better able to compliment and charm. James could tell already that he stood no chance against the other gentleman. At least, not in person.

He must do better in complimenting Miss Weston in his letters.

It was only that he did not wish to appear too flowery or to cross any boundaries.

But if he was to have competition, then he had to raise the level of his wooing.

When dinner was finally called, Miss Weston thanked him for the information.

"I would not repeat it to anyone," he told her. "Many people would think it improper that a lady is showing such an interest."

"How fortunate then, that you are not one of those people."

"Quite fortunate for you. But you must assure me that you will not go around spouting off your newfound knowledge. Especially to gentlemen. They will be insulted and think that you are being impertinent."

"I am always impertinent," Miss Weston replied. She smiled at him cheekily.

"I mean in a way that is not viewed as endearing," he replied, making his voice grave so that she might understand. "Sometimes I wonder if you truly understand all the rules that you skirt."

"I do not need to know them, do I?" Miss Weston asked. "Not when I have you here to constantly remind me."

James swallowed down the urge to beg her to trust him more. To trust him with her heart as well as her reputation. She leaned on him for everything. And she seemed completely unaware of it.

It was frustrating, to say the least. To know that she was trusting him and turning to him. Wishing that he could give her more. Knowing that he could if she asked. Wondering if she would want that.

"You are fortunate then," he replied instead. "I am a patient person, though goodness knows why. Perhaps it is that after so many years I have built up a tolerance for you."

Miss Weston laughed. She doubtless would have said more, but then they were all going in to dinner and she needed to lead the others in.

Mr. Carson had a seat near her, James saw. He was near Mrs. Weston again. The evening was pleasant enough. But he could not help but see how Mr. Carson was charming Miss Weston.

James reminded himself to keep his cool. He could not control either Miss Weston or Mr. Carson. He would simply have to court her on his own merit.

When he received her letter he would be sure to write one in return that was so full of affection she could not help but feel flattered. He would find a way to be charming. She would forget all about Mr. Carson and indeed any other possible suitor in the wake of such a letter. He would make sure of it.

James was aware that he was now resolved to do the very thing that he had recently sworn he would cease doing. But he could not find it in him, not yet, to court Miss Weston in person.

Until then he would have to do what he could. Otherwise he was certain that Mr. Carson or some other man would come along and snatch her straightaway from under his nose.

He could not bear it.

Not while he still had a chance. If he fought valiantly for her and he lost her then he supposed he could content himself with that. Knowing that he had done all that he could had to be some kind of balm, mustn't it?

But having to say that he had sat by and done nothing. That he had not even availed himself of the slight chance he had made for himself. That he had not taken advantage of the letters, as unconventional and cowardly as they might be...

He could not live with himself that way.

The dinner otherwise passed by in a blur. It was pleasant. But he felt as though all he could hear were the times that Mr. Carson made Miss Weston laugh.

All that he could see was her pleased smile. The pretty pink blush that spread through her cheeks. The way that Mr. Carson took care to be near her at all times.

Even after dinner when they were playing cards Mr. Carson made sure to be a part of Miss Weston's set of bridge.

"Be careful," Mrs. Weston said quietly as he became her bridge partner. "Green is not a good color on you, Mr. Norwich."

"Am I quite so obvious?" he asked, keeping his voice just as quiet.

"I confess that I was not certain if you held any affection for her of a romantic nature," Mrs. Weston said.

"Yet you told me that I was your favorite to win her hand."

"My favorite does not mean that the favorite sees himself as part of the race. I can place a bet upon a horse but that does not mean that horse feels like running on that day."

"Mrs. Weston. Do not tell me that you have dared to place a bet."

"I would never tell you of such a thing if I had done it." Mrs. Weston winked at him. "I am a lady, after all."

"And you wonder where your daughter gets her streak of nonchalant rebellion," James replied philosophically.

"In any case, I suppose then that I am right? And you do harbor feelings for her?"

James sighed. "You have always been far too observant for the good of anybody around you. Yes, I confess that I would... that I would be happy to make her my wife. If she would have me."

"I would be appalled if she would not."

"I have been as a brother to her, madam. I would not be surprised if that was the only light in which she was able to see me."

"You are being unfair to yourself, I feel. How long have these feelings persisted?"

He cleared this throat. "Years, madam."

"And you have done nothing about it this entire time? Said nothing?" Mrs. Weston clucked her tongue. "And here I thought you to be a man of action. A proper English gentleman."

"I thought that it was the English way to never speak of one's emotions."

"It is even more the English way to act upon them and to seize what one wants."

"You know as well as I do how stubborn your daughter is."

"And you cannot possibly be happy sitting there turning as green as an unripe tomato watching her with Mr. Carson. Follow the advice that I gave you the other night, my boy. How can you know how she feels if you do not ask her? She might not even be aware that such feelings lie within her. Or at least the capability to harbor such feelings."

"I am not certain that you are so old that you may go around calling me 'boy'."

"I am an old and sickly woman and I shall do what I please and call you what I please, Mr. Norwich. Now be so kind as to deal the hand."

He hoped that his envy was not obvious to those around him. He certainly hoped that it was not obvious to Miss Weston or Mr. Carson. Envy never looked good on anybody.

He also hoped that he was not too stiff in bidding Miss Weston goodnight at the end of the evening. It was not her fault that she was charmed by Mr. Carson. How could she help it? It was nobody's fault. Nobody was to blame for anything.

Yet he could not stop the twisting, hot snakes that resided in his stomach. The mix of envy and jealousy that surged up inside of him.

When he got home, however... there was a letter waiting for him.

His heart soared.

He knew that it was ridiculous and possibly even stupid. But he couldn't help but think...

He was not the most charming person at the dinner table. He could not flatter her and sweep her off her feet the way that someone such as Mr. Carson could.

But he had her writing letters to him. Even if it was only for the pleasure of the mystery of his identity. She was writing letters to him.

He had her in that manner, at least. She was writing to him and she would continue to do so, so long as he held her attention.

And he would write her letters—such glorious letters. The sort of letters where she would understand his heart and she would be enraptured.

He was filled with a new determination. He almost wanted, in an odd way, to thank Mr. Carson. The man had filled James with a new sense of purpose and energy about the entire affair.

Without further ado, he sat down and read the letter. He was eager to see what she said, so that he might compose a proper reply.

He wanted her to be swept off her feet. To feel as though she was in a romantic play. He wanted her to feel special and honored and respected.

He wanted her to feel loved.

Miss Weston's letter was exuberant. He could fairly feel the energy rising up off the page as she plied him with questions.

It was rather a good thing that she was constantly asking him questions in person. He was quite used to her method of bombarding a person with long lists of questions, the answers to which only led to her asking even more questions.

The questions were, he saw with a twinge of amusement, aimed at trying to find out his identity. She asked him about certain books that he specifically remembered her father tutoring him on.

In fact, all that she asked him about were from the books that he had been taught about by her father.

Clever girl, he thought to himself. It was quite a sneaky way of going about it.

She knew that the reason he had written her a letter was that he was too nervous to speak to her in person. She knew that he did not want her to know his identity just yet so that he could come to know her and she know him without the trappings of their past experiences together.

And therefore, she had realized that simply asking him who he was would not work. That he would not respond to that question.

She must have realized that if he had known her for years as he said and he had called them friends that he must be one of her father's former pupils. What other men had she known for so long and to whom she had been so close?

And so she had put together a list of the books her father had used for his curriculum and had asked for his thoughts on them.

She probably even remembered all the books and had not even needed to look them up or consult with her father about them.

To James's surprise, however, there were little details in there that he did not think she intended to let slip.

At several points she mentioned that she was certain he would think her opinions were childish and ridiculous.

I am rather given to flights of fancy, she wrote. Doubtless you will not wish to indulge me in them. However...

James frowned down at the paper before him.

He had always thought that Miss Weston was a woman of supreme self-confidence. That she had no doubts about herself. Especially in regards to her intelligence and wit.

She always behaved as one who had not a care. Who thought first about what would please her and then secondly about what would please others.

Yet, in this letter he seemed to be finding signs of the opposite. A lack of the self-confidence that he had so expected from her.

The letter was full of phrases such as:

I hope that you will excuse my thought...

Perhaps this is childish to think—however...

You will doubtless refute this in a suitably intelligent manner but...

It filled James with a kind of heavy sadness. Frustration, as well. How could she not value herself?

The whole world was eager to praise her. She was usually the most popular girl in the room. She never had to sit down at balls for want of a dance partner.

How could she not see how he or anyone else saw her? Even those who were not in love with her admired her. She had many friends.

Did she think that they laughed at her behind her back? Or that they merely put up with her?

He wanted to ask, but of course he could not—

Or, wait.

He could.

Through the letters.

She did not know who he was. He had seen for himself, felt for himself, how the anonymity of the letters bolstered him. How it made him bold. How it enabled him to say things that he could not otherwise.

Why could he not, therefore, tell her that she was too hard on herself? Why could he not praise her and tell her that she ought to think more highly of her intellect? Why could he not point out the things he had read in her letters and ask if she truly thought that about herself?

James felt conviction stirring in him, replacing the envy and jealousy and frustration that had plagued him only moments before.

These letters could not be just for him to show himself off to her. He must also use them to show her how valued she was. How loved and cared-for she was.

He would not allow the woman that he loved to go about her life thinking that she was anything less than amazing. For she was, truly. She amazed him.

He would simply have to find a way to make her see it, that was all.

It fit in nicely with his original plan of courting her through letters. But this... this felt different.

This was not showing himself to her so that she could know him and come to care for him. This was about bolstering her up. About making her see herself as he saw her.

Yes, he could admit, it would probably charm her to hear him praise her so highly. But that was secondary to him. His first priority, the one that lit a fire in him as he sat down to craft a response, was to make Miss Weston feel her worth.

He would help her to see herself as she truly was. He would help her to banish those doubts.

He cursed himself, as well, for being so blind. He had known this woman for years. How could he have not realized her own struggles with self-worth? How could he not have seen that she had moments of doubt as well?

Instead he had been so caught up in his own woes that he had not seen hers. He had been guilty of the very thing of which he had accused her. While he was alternately lamenting and rejoicing in her inability to notice his feelings, he had been failing to notice her own, towards herself.

He was twice, no, three times a fool. A coward, and a selfish coward at that.

How could he have been so blind? How could he not have seen how badly she thought of herself?

And he had called her his friend. The worst kind of presumption.

Well, he would rectify that now. He would do whatever it took to bolster her spirits. He would show her that she was everything that the other women wanted to be. That she was popular, witty, beloved.

It would serve to distract him a bit from himself. From his worries about not measuring up and being inadequate. He would instead be focused on her, as he should have been this whole time.

This shouldn't have ever been about him. It should have been about her and how she deserved to be treated. He should have made her his priority from the start rather than himself.

Well, he knew better now. He would do what he could to make up for that horrid mistake.

Pulling out his pen, James wrote hastily.

She would receive this next letter by the morning post.

CHAPTER 59

JULIA SAT IN HER BED, the letters scattered around her.

It had been weeks of corresponding and she was no closer to figuring out who her mystery letter writer was than before.

He had taken to signing his letters Sir, a tease seeing as she always addressed him as such at the beginning of her letters.

That told her nothing.

She had hoped that over time he might slip up and reveal more. Put in, if not his actual name, a nickname of sorts that might reveal something of who he was.

But this man was clever. Terribly clever.

After her first letter in which she had asked him about various books her father's pupils were sure to know, he had barely even replied to her questions.

Instead, he had focused in on things that she had not even been aware she had written.

My dear, how can you think such low things of your intellect? I have seen you best many a man in a battle of wit and in a discussion of literature alike.

He had praised her, in a way that no person, even her mother, had praised her before. He spoke of how he admired her intelligence. Her education. How it was so refreshing to be able to converse with her as an equal and to speak of things other than fashion and gossip about others.

Not, of course, that I am averse to gossip. I quite enjoyed a conversation that we had most recently. I cannot relay to you the details, of course. But I can assure you that it was very diverting and about quite a few people around us.

He was charming and clever, alluding to conversations such as that one but playing coy with details.

But it was the praise that truly struck her.

She had not been aware that she had been quite so down on herself in that letter. It had only felt natural to speak what she felt, in a way that she did not usually when she was in person with someone.

She hadn't realized that her insecurities would leak out in such a way that he would notice them. She had thought, even, that perhaps a little self-deprecation would help.

She had tried to explain that, in her next letter.

Most gentlemen do not take kindly to my seeming an authority on a subject. Therefore I have undertaken to downplaying my knowledge so as not to appear threatening.

The gentleman had taken quite a bit of offense to that. He had told her sternly in his return letter that she ought to be nothing short of proud of her intellect and her learning.

He was grateful for it, he told her. He was always pleased when he got a chance to converse with her. She ought never to apologize for being intelligent or well-read.

If a man was threatened by it, he told her, then that was not the sort of man she wanted in her life. A man should expect his wife to be intelligent. How else could he trust her to run his estate while he was not home? Or to manage the household? How could he expect to converse with her at home and be entertained if she could only prattle on about local gossip?

She would only be unhappy with a man who did not appreciate her.

It was easy to read between the lines and know that he was telling her that he would appreciate her. But she almost did not care about the bit of self-promotion. She suspected, at this point, that it might even be unconscious. That the gentleman had not noticed it.

For while he had claimed that this letter writing was in order for her to get to know him, he seemed rather determined to spend much of their correspondence building her up instead.

She had found herself telling him things that she hadn't told anyone except for Georgiana. And even then—for Georgiana was busy planning her wedding, and so Julia had not unburdened herself to her friend as of late. She hadn't wanted to add more to her dear friend's plate.

Julia had found herself telling this gentleman her fears about her parents. How she worried about her mother's health. How she feared that her father was doing more poorly than he let on as well. That she would lose both of them swiftly and without warning.

She spoke of her concerns about finding a husband. How she felt pressed into it. How she chastised herself for not looking for one sooner. How she felt like it was her own fault that she now felt confined and pressured.

To her pleasure and surprise the gentleman had not responded by telling her all the ways in which he would make her a good husband.

Instead, he had talked to her of his own fears. How he worried about his sibling, who had a reputation as a flirt. How that sibling would fare when they returned to society. How he missed them but had only started to truly understand and connect with them once they were far away, through letter writing. How that felt like a cruel irony.

He had talked about how he felt distant from his mother. How he thought that she had been a vain woman who had not cared all that much for raising her children. He spoke of how his father was foisting all of his responsibility onto his eldest son and how he felt a great deal of unwanted pressure from it.

Julia had found herself over the past few weeks opening up to this man in a way that she had never opened up to anyone else before.

She had expected when they began this to try and find out his identity. And, in the meantime, she expected she would discuss books and such with him.

Instead, she found that the both of them were divulging things that they dared not speak of to anyone else.

It was so easy to do so by letter. To say things in the privacy of her room without the person's face in front of her. There was no immediate feeling of rejection. Although she did often feel fear afterwards that she had gone too far or said too much.

But she doubted that she could have said all of this to someone's face. It was refreshing. No, more than that—like relieving herself of a burden that she hadn't even realized she'd been carrying.

The intimacy between them was not merely romantic. Although there was plenty of that.

She ran her fingers fondly over the papers around her. Over time her letter writer had gotten bolder. Although to her credit she had certainly encouraged it.

I do wish you would not call me 'dear', she had written in one letter. It is what my parents call me and so that is all I can think of when you use it.

He had responded with, if I am too forward in this, tell me so at once. But I have thought of you for quite some time in my head as my darling.

She had thrilled to read those words. Hysterical, joyful giggles had burst out of her. All that day, she had felt as though she had been walking on air.

To know that she was so beloved in his eyes—oh it was probably not proper. Not at all. But she hardly cared.

In a world where she constantly second-guessed herself, here was one person who seemed to love her wholeheartedly.

He still would not use such names with her easily or freely. She had to coax them out of him in the letters. She would tease him and prod him and at last he would indulge her with a sweet name.

The one that she liked the most was my little raven.

It had sprung up because of her dark hair and her inquisitive nature. You are far too intelligent for your own good sometimes, he had written. Rather like a raven.

And so the name had been born. She could admit that she understood the comparison, having dealt with quite a few precocious ravens herself over the years.

It had become her favorite nickname. Whenever he used it, which was rare, it was usually to playfully chastise her.

Do not think that I do not know what you are about, my little raven. I can see you trying to ferret more information out of me. But I am afraid that our mystery must continue.

His identity, which had at first been a shield to him, was now an object of play between them. It was almost a joke, in fact. Something that she tried to learn and he tried to keep from her.

So much of their letters were playful. She was certain that he must be a witty man and not at all dull. That had narrowed down her search a bit. For if a man was clever with his words, why should he choose to be dull in conversation at the dinner table?

But all that she had learned from him and of him was not enough to help her in figuring out his identity. He could still be any number of men.

Julia stared at the letters around her, trying to organize them and trying to solve the mystery.

A part of her did not want to solve it. A part of her wanted to keep this special intimacy that they had built forever.

If they were to meet in person, if she was to know his identity... would it not possibly ruin things? Would it destroy the lovely relationship that they had built together?

What if he liked her in the letters so much better than in person? Or what if she liked him in his letters, and could not stand him in person? What if they were disappointing to one another?

Julia shook such thoughts from her head. No. He would not go to such lengths as to call her a special nickname and share with her all of his woes if he was the sort of man who would not care for her in person.

Besides, he had already been in love with her before the letters. She was the one who had not known him.

Oh, she did hope that she would like him. That he was thoughtful and intelligent, she knew. But would he be charming in person? Handsome?

She felt incredibly shallow for it but she did so hope that he was handsome. Or even if not handsome, at least pleasing to look upon. Someone with the kind of face that she could gaze at for the rest of her life. Because that was, hopefully, what she would be doing.

Many times she had been tempted to simply ask him who he was. But she was not sure that he would reveal himself to her. And trying to figure it out on her own was so much more fun.

Julia shuffled the letters around a little and then checked her paper. She had written down all the things that she knew about him that helped to narrow down her list of possible men.

First, he had a younger sibling. Possibly more, but he had only ever mentioned one.

Secondly, he was not on the best of terms with his mother. Julia was actually unsure if his mother was alive or dead. He had not been clear on that point. But either way, she frustrated him.

Third, his father was giving him a great—and if you asked Julia, an unfair—deal to do with the running of the estate. She could tell by the man's descriptions that he was set to inherit a title. But what title exactly, she did not know.

Fourth, he was indeed one of her father's pupils. He had dodged those questions as best he could, but Julia had figured him out. She would slip in mentions of books here and there and he had always replied.

She would put in a reference to this philosopher or that historical event. And she had brought up what her favorite dish was as a child. The dish that her mother had only had the cook make when a new pupil first came to the house. As a sort of celebration, welcoming dish.

The gentleman had responded that it was one of his favorite dishes as well and that whenever he had it as an adult it reminded him of his childhood.

It was possible that it was simply a dish he had eaten at home. But that combined with knowing the books and opinions her father had taught... it could not be merely a coincidence.

Furthermore, she did not know of any man that she had known for as long or as well as her father's pupils.

Fifth, she knew that he was a good dancer and that he enjoyed dancing. That he especially enjoyed dancing with her.

Sixth, he always noticed her dress. While he was glad that there was more to speak with her about than fashion he had often complimented her on her style of dress.

He was careful not to be too specific. He clearly did not want her to be able to select a particular ball or dinner that he had attended in order to narrow down her search.

It helped of course that she wore dresses multiple times. Or rather, it helped him to keep his anonymity. Only the greatest of ladies could afford to get a new dress for every single ball and dinner they attended. The newly-married Lady Reginald, Georgiana's sister-in-law, would be able to do such a thing.

Most of the time, however, ladies would order a set of new dresses at the start of a season. They would then cycle through them throughout.

It had been flattering to know that her choices were not only noticed by other women but by this gentleman. That he appreciated her fashion sense and admired how she looked.

Had it been all he admired about her she would have been less pleased. But on top of everything else, it made a pleasant flutter start up in her chest.

The gentleman was very good at doing that in general. She read his letters in bed at night so that there would be no suspicion from her mother or the maids. There she would smile, widely and possibly idiotically, as she read his lines. She could feel her face heating up when he would slip up and say something like,

You are darling when you laugh.

Or,

You always know how to make me smile.

She knew that he tried not to compliment her too much. That he struggled to maintain some level of distance and propriety despite what they were doing.

But oh, when he did slip up and those little moments showed through. When he called her little raven, when he called her darling... it made her heart leap in her chest as nothing else could.

It was almost like a sip of wine when she hadn't eaten anything beforehand. It went straight to her head and to her stomach. Made her a little woozy in the best of ways.

If he had been straightforward and complimented her in a romantic manner all the time. If he had been frank and set aside decorum completely to tell her how she made his heart race, she would not have been quite so enamored of him.

But she could see how he was restraining himself. That he was trying not to show her just how much she affected him. Even in his slip-ups there was nothing untoward. He had not once mentioned touching or kissing her. He had never spoken of the marriage bed or anything of that sort.

Instead his little moments where propriety peeled away showed how esteemed she was in his heart. How high of a place he held her in his thoughts. Not only in an intellectual way or as a person to admire. But as a person to truly love.

His struggle to remain a gentleman was what so endeared him to her. He was doing his best to maintain his self-control and succeeding for the most part. That was what made it all the sweeter when he did let that bit of passion show.

Julia bit her lip, gathering the letters up into a pile.

He had to be someone who she saw often. He was in Bath. He could not have avoided seeing her while staying in town. It would have been too obvious, too awkward.

And if he was someone that she saw often in Bath... had a younger sibling who was known for being flirtatious... was a former pupil of her father's and set to inherit a title...

There were so very few men who it could be.

Julia gathered the letters up and put them back in the drawer where she had hidden them.

Could it be?

She was open to the possibility of being wrong. But there was only one man springing to mind.

Mr. Carson.

He had arrived in Bath right as the letters had started to arrive. He was charming to her now, in a way that he hadn't been when she had last seen him.

The letters must have been giving him confidence.

He had mentioned at dinner parties that he was taking on a lot more responsibility from his father. He was set to inherit a title and a large estate. His younger sister had been brought to Bath so that she might learn to not be so flirtatious, as she was in London.

He was a former pupil of her father's. He had mentioned once that he had enjoyed the cooking there. And he did not get on with his mother—everyone knew that.

Julia found herself... oddly disappointed, thinking that it was him.

He was charming to her in person, it was true. He was an excellent dancer, that as well.

He was not quite handsome, but he had a pleasant face. She

enjoyed looking at him. His face was the sort that made you relaxed to gaze upon.

Yet she could not help but find herself torn between hoping it was him in order to end the mystery and being disappointed if it did turn out to be him.

She could not place her finger on why exactly she would be disappointed.

Mr. Carson was a lovely man. She had enjoyed spending time with him at dinners and balls. He was rich and titled and young. There was no reason why she should not be happy to marry him.

Her parents would certainly be pleased. Father had always enjoyed his company as his pupil. He thought highly of the younger man. And to have their daughter marrying a man of such wealth and stature—how could any parent not rejoice?

She would have to find out for certain, of course. Test him in some way and see if he slipped up.

While the gentleman had kept his identity a secret she could not imagine that he would lie to her if she confronted him in some way on the matter. The question of his identity had become almost something for him to tease her about. Not quite, but almost.

And he had said numerous times how he respected her intelligence. He would not say so and then do her the disservice of lying to her if she queried him in person.

Besides, did he not want her to discover him? In the end? Was not his original plan for her to fall for him so that when she learned who he was she would love him no matter what?

That of course brought up the rather prickly matter of whether or not she did love him.

Julia resolved to handle that later. It was not as important as finding out who he was.

She must find a way to test Mr. Carson. She would go through the letters and select a few little facts. Innocuous but specific enough that it could only be her letter writer who answered those questions in that way.

Yes. That should do.

But through it all, she still could not put her finger on why she hoped it was not Mr. Carson.

CHAPTER 60

JAMES WAS WELL in over his head.

He could admit that, at least. He was well and truly in deep water.

The writing and correspondence had gone on for weeks now. And he was no closer to revealing his identity now than he had been at the start of this entire thing.

The worst part was how Miss Weston tried to work out his identity. He saw her little tricks and he did his best to avoid them but he knew that he had to have let a few things slip. It was only natural.

He spent half of his time panicking that she would figure out who he was and fly into a rage at him. That she would accuse him of disrespecting their years of friendship by not telling her who he was at once. That she would reject him and declare him far too much like a brother for her to ever see him in a romantic light.

The other half of the time, he had to admit, he was enraptured.

She was much gentler and much harder on herself in the letters than she ever was in person. The witty banter was there as always but there was a vulnerability that she didn't usually get to see.

He honestly doubted that anyone usually got to see it. Miss Weston, he was realizing, put on rather a mask to the world.

Given how often in her letters she spoke of her parents he suspected that it was because she felt she had to be strong for them. She was the only of their children who had not been stillborn or miscarried.

It was not something oft spoken of in polite society. But he had heard the stories when he was younger. Miss Weston's many siblings, God rest their souls, had broken her parents' hearts with their inability to live.

She was quite the miracle for them. And now they were sick and wanted nothing more than to see her wed and set up for life.

No wonder she felt she must be gay. That she must be the belle of the ball. If one is a miracle, and if all of the hopes of a parent ride upon one's shoulders... there must be a certain feeling of obligation to be popular and desired.

As if to prove that one had earned the right to all their parents' affections. Earned the right to be the only one who had lived.

He clung to her letters with all the fervor of a man at sea, far away from his homeland and his loved ones. He loved them too much to give them up. Even as he lived in dread of the day when she discovered who he was.

And every day it became more and more likely that she would discover that it was him. They were sharing too much of each other in these letters for her not to.

Sometimes, he hoped that she would figure it out. If only so that this whole thing could end and he could stop feeling caught in the middle.

But that would mean that this intimacy would have to be given up.

It was not an intimacy of romance. Or at least not of ardent, physical romance. It was an intimacy of hearts. He told her things that he could not find it in himself to tell anyone else.

He spoke of his fears about his brother. About his frustrations with his father. About how he was disappointed in his mother, still, even after she was dead. And how he felt that it was a failure on his part that he still could not forgive her.

Miss Weston had proven herself to be a remarkable and nonjudgmental listener. She would ask clarifying questions sometimes if she needed to better understand something. Occasionally she would try to present an idea from the point of view of the person he was complaining of.

But for the most part she was sympathetic. Understanding. Thoughtful. Supportive.

He had loved her for her liveliness. For her intelligence. For her beauty. Now he loved her also for her understanding heart. For how well she listened and supported him. For her surprising and sweet and vulnerable heart that lurked underneath.

If he was being honest, and he tried to be in most things even as he remained a coward in this... Miss Weston was the person to whom he was now the closest.

His brother was a close second. But with his brother being far out at sea it was difficult to converse with him as easily and as readily as he could Miss Weston.

And Miss Weston was not family. There were things he could tell her about his family that he did not dare speak of to his brother. He could be honest with her without fear of hurting anyone's feelings or stepping upon anyone's toes and it was wonderful. Freeing, even.

He would have to give all of that up if she knew who he was. Unless, of course, she decided that she could love him after all and she married him.

James was not altogether confident about that.

She seemed to hold him in great affection, that was true. At least through the letters.

But what if she was picturing someone else when she wrote? What if she imagined another man and was disappointed to learn that it was him?

And while she teased him and was thoughtful and supportive in the letters—that did not quite equal love.

It would be improper to give a love declaration by letter. He was not expecting such a thing from her. But surely she would show a bit more to him of her affection if she was in love with him, wouldn't she?

It could be that, at the end of the day, she loved the mystery of the letters more than the man. It could be that she saw him as a place to unburden herself and that was what she valued in him, rather than his personality.

He had thought when he embarked on this correspondence that it would clear things up. That it would make things easier between them. More open and honest.

Instead it had only muddied the waters.

At least before he had known where he stood and what her thoughts had been. It had been as though they were standing on opposite banks of a river. They were separated but the water was clear and the course certain.

Now they had both stepped into the river, and they were closer. But the water was dark and muddy, and he knew not what pitfalls lurked beneath as he tried to reach her.

It did not help that Mr. Carson was continuing his play.

He was not so bold about it that people were openly speculating. But James had noticed that other possible suitors had quickly faded into the background.

The other gentlemen had noticed that Mr. Carson was truly making a play for Miss Weston. He would endeavor to sit near her at dinner and to be her partner at bridge. He was always first on her dance card. Although he was not so bold as to ask for a second dance.

Seeing a rich, titled, charming gentleman going after the notoriously witty and picky Miss Weston? The other men had seen how things lay and had faded into the background.

Some of them were probably waiting for Mr. Carson to misstep and for Miss Weston to reject him summarily. But most of them had decided not to wait and were moving onto greener pastures.

And why should they not? They had only been attracted to Miss Weston. They were not in love with her.

James was unsure what to do about the matter. Miss Weston was not openly encouraging the man. But nor was she discouraging him.

She had to know what Mr. Carson was doing. She was not a stupid woman. He had seen her neatly do away with the men in the past who had tried to court her. She could do the same to Mr. Carson if she wanted to.

Yet she almost seemed to be sizing the man up. Why? What for?

Perhaps she was keeping him as a backup option should things fall through with her letter writer. James could not blame her for that.

She still did not know who he was. He could disappear, so to speak, any time that he wanted. He could stop writing her and she would have no way of knowing what had happened.

It was only sensible that in a case like that a woman would keep the charming titled man in front of her as a second option. Marriage was a woman's career, her insurance, her livelihood.

But could Mr. Carson take chief place in her affections? Despite the letters that she exchanged with James?

Mr. Carson hid nothing from her, after all. He was right in front of her eyes. He was not the one who had to struggle to speak to her plainly even through the written word.

She was not in love with him at the moment. Miss Weston had never been good at hiding her emotions and James had known her for years. If she was in love with Mr. Carson then James was sure that he would be able to tell.

But she could become so. She could fall in love with him. Things were not set yet.

James was going to see the both of them tonight. There was another dinner that Miss Weston and her mother were hosting.

Mrs. Weston had not said much to him since their initial talks about him making a play for her daughter. He could often feel her piercing gaze on him at dinners and balls.

He knew that she was still silently egging him on. Hoping that he would do something.

It was why she kept agreeing to host these dinners, he was certain. Despite her health and how much they drained her energy.

Hosting the dinner allowed her to control the guest list. Not that he seriously thought that Miss Weston would leave him off of any guest list. But he was certain that was why Mrs. Weston was still hosting parties.

James could not help but feel as though he was letting her down by not wooing her daughter. He was wooing her, of course, but not in a way that Mrs. Weston knew of. And he hardly thought that it was in the way that she would want him to woo Miss Weston.

As far as Mrs. Weston knew, he had taken her suggestion and her endorsement and had done nothing with them. He must have seemed a coward to her. Or perhaps callous. He was not sure which was worse.

Perhaps he should tell Miss Weston tonight. He could even picture in his mind's eye how he would do it.

He would linger behind the other guests after the dinner. He would approach her...

What would he say? Something that would ensure that she knew that he was the letter writer.

My little raven. He could call her that. Surely nobody else had even thought to call her by that name.

He had thought of her that way for some time. Her dark hair, her strong eyebrows, her playful incorrigible nature. Her personality and her looks together had reminded him of that inquisitive bird, too smart for its own good.

She had seemed to enjoy that nickname. She would do what she could in the letters to draw it out of him.

That would be what he would call her.

My little raven, he would say—and then he need not say anything more, surely? That must be all that it would take, wouldn't it?

She would know, then. And she could reject him and choose Mr. Carson or someone else. Or she could accept him.

James already mourned the lack of the intimacy to which he had grown so accustomed. To whom would he speak when he had troubles? Fears? When he needed encouragement?

If she did choose Mr. Carson—he could only hope that the man would be up to the task of comforting her. Supporting her. That he would see that Miss Weston needed to be bolstered as well. That there was more to her than her pretty face and pretty words.

It was in this mindset that he went to the dinner at the Weston residence.

He was greeted at the door, to his surprise, not by Miss Weston but by her mother.

"Mrs. Weston." He bowed to her. "A pleasure, as always."

He glanced about behind her and saw that Miss Weston was already in conversation. With Mr. Carson.

James did his best to swallow the bitter taste in his throat.

"Mr. Norwich." Mrs. Weston gave a put-upon sigh. "I hope that you will do something at last," she said in a stern but much quieter tone.

"Why, do you not favor Mr. Carson?"

"You know who I favor. There is nothing wrong with him but I daresay my daughter can do better."

"It is flattering that after all this time when I have done nothing to earn her you still think that I deserve her."

"I am not holding my breath, Mr. Norwich. I have learned that is a useless folly to do when you are depending upon a man. But I had hoped that as his courtship of her grew that you would see reason and make a play for her."

"Trust me, madam, I shall," he blurted out.

Now that he had said it, of course, there was no going back.

Mrs. Weston smiled proudly at him. "I am glad to hear it. I have given her only another lecture this morning about choosing a man. But she is in a queer sort of mood this evening."

James could sense it as well. Even though he could not hear her, there was something about the way that Miss Weston was holding herself as she spoke to Mr. Carson. Something in the energy around her.

He was not sure what it was. Determination? Perhaps. But what did she have to be determined about?

He accepted a glass from the servant as other dinner guests trickled in. It did not surprise him when Mr. Carson was once again placed near Miss Weston. She had to be engineering that. Her mother's look of disapproval spoke volumes.

All through dinner, he could see her and Mr. Carson exchanging glances. They seemed to be sizing one another up. What on earth was going on?

James thought that he would find out in the next letter. He hid his identity but Miss Weston did not and so she often told him how her days went.

She had even mentioned him to himself. Mr. Norwich was in fine form tonight. A wittier man I have never met. He is the best at insulting me and making me laugh at it. For I know that he does not truly mean it.

Miss Weston at least seemed to have a high opinion of him, judging by her letters. She harbored no attraction to him. Or if she did, she had never mentioned it in her letters.

But she spoke of him as an intelligent man whose counsel she depended upon. That had flattered him. Even if it was not what he had been hoping for.

Although, he supposed it would be bad form to tell your romantic correspondent that you were attracted to another man.

James watched as the dinner progressed, and Miss Weston and Mr. Carson seemed to be in their strange stalemate.

He knew what the gleam in Miss Weston's eye was. He had known her for far too long to not recognize it.

For as long as he had known her, Miss Weston had been a meddler. She would not sit idly by and do nothing while others around her needed assistance.

This could be seen in a positive light. She was always trying to help those less fortunate than she. But it also meant that she would get involved in the lives of her friends.

It was why he had not been surprised when she had burst into his house in order to give Captain Trentworth a proper dressing-down.

She had some sort of scheme up her sleeve tonight. James was sure of it. But what could it be?

She could not possibly be thinking to convince Mr. Carson to ask her to marry him. That was simply ridiculous. He had not yet been bold enough for her to have a hope of such a thing.

And James did like to think that she was not so unsatisfied with her mystery correspondent that she wished to marry another man without any warning.

Then what on earth could she have up her sleeve? What could be making the cogs turn in that clever and meddlesome mind of hers?

James realized that he had lost the thread of conversation at his end of the table and focused back in on it. It would not do to be rude no matter how curious he was.

Still, he could tell that he was not the only one noticing the strange mood that hung in the air that night.

The discussion and bridge playing and such that went on after dinner was oddly strained and subdued. People seemed to have trouble carrying on conversations.

Miss Perry endeavored to play the pianoforte to lighten up spirits. There was a bit of dancing that came about because of it but it all felt forced. As though everyone was making themselves have a good time.

It was not that the atmosphere was uncomfortable, exactly. It was that something else was going on. There was an undercurrent beneath the main flow of the conversation. A second set of energy.

James could sense a great deal of frustration from Miss Weston. She seemed easily distracted and almost absent-minded.

Could it be that he had said something in his letters that had upset her? That he had unwittingly caused her to want to run into the arms of Mr. Carson?

He could not think of what he might have said that would cause such a reaction. Their last letter had been discussing the latest novel by a new writer.

Although, he had mentioned something about himself. About how he felt as though in public he had to pretend to be different, to be more, than he truly was.

Had that put her off somehow? Had she taken offense to that?

He could hardly see how it would, seeing as she was similar. Miss Weston was in her letters a much softer and vulnerable person than she let herself be in person.

An hour or so after dinner guests started to dissipate. James was locked into a game of cards with Mrs. Weston, Miss Perry, and another gentleman.

That was his excuse as to why it took him so long to notice that Miss Weston and Mr. Carson were conversing off to the side.

It was practically a private conversation. They were not around the corner where they were unable to be seen. But they were in the dining room. It could be seen from the sitting room, since the doorways opened onto each other. But nobody could hear what was being said.

James glanced up as the card game ended and noticed that Miss Weston's eyes were gleaming. They only looked like that when she was upset and struggling to hide it.

He doubted that Mr. Carson or anyone else who did not know her well would realize that was what it meant. Miss Weston, he had learned from her letters, was very good at hiding her emotions.

Especially those self-deprecating emotions and emotions of sadness and fear.

James stood, clearing his throat. "I think that it is best that we all retire for the evening. I myself will be heading out shortly. Miss Perry, will you need an escort home?"

Miss Perry demurred and said that the other gentleman—James struggled to remember his name—would escort her.

James was not all that surprised. Miss Perry was one of those women who was lovely in personality but far too eager to attach herself to the nearest young gentleman in the hopes that he would marry her. Being married was more important to her than who she was married to.

He watched as the final guests left. He assisted Mrs. Weston in getting up and going to her room as well.

"I think you should talk to your daughter," he told her.

"Miss Weston and I have already had words this evening," Mrs. Weston replied. James was taken aback. "She can find her own way to bed. And if she is truly eager to say goodnight to me then she knows which bedchamber is mine."

James knew that Mrs. Weston had a reputation as being sharp-tongued for a reason. He dearly hoped that she had not been too hard on her daughter.

He bid her goodnight. At almost the exact same moment Mr. Carson bid Miss Weston goodnight and then left.

It was only him and Miss Weston now.

"Mr. Norwich?"

He had rarely heard her voice so small and so upset. He crossed to her at once. "Miss Weston."

She quickly wiped at her eyes. "I apologize. You must think me quite the child."

"Never. Did Mr. Carson upset you?"

"Oh, not intentionally. I managed to hold in my tears in front of him, thank the heavens for that. It is only that I feel—I feel quite stupid. And silly."

"You are neither of those things, I can assure you." He took her by the arm and guided her to sit down. "What is troubling you?"

"I cannot speak of it."

James's heart thumped painfully in his chest. The only thing he could think of was that Miss Weston had been too bold at last. That she had finally stepped over a line that she should not have crossed.

That she had made it clear to Mr. Carson that she had feelings for him. And he had rejected her.

It surprised him that Mr. Carson had rejected her. The man had explicitly stated—or as explicit as one could be as a gentleman—that he was going to do his best to court Miss Weston.

Had something changed? Had Mr. Carson decided that Miss Weston was too bold for him? Too witty? Too energetic?

Had that old saying of familiarity breeding contempt held true? Could it have been that the more Mr. Carson came to know Miss Weston the more he realized that she was not the woman for him?

James would normally have been quite happy at such a development. But not when it so distressed Miss Weston.

A part of him, to his shame, felt anger. Anger that she continued to write to this mysterious gentleman while having feelings for Mr. Carson. Anger that she could not simply tell her correspondent that she did not feel for him and that there was another man in the picture.

Yet, he could not commit himself fully to that line of feeling. He could not find it within himself to feel only that rage.

He could understand why it might have been hard for her to reject her letter companion. It was always hard to say something that you knew would hurt someone.

And perhaps she appreciated the intimacy of their letters. Her ability to confess things to him that she could not say to anyone else. Perhaps she had been hoping in time to morph that into a friendship?

He was not sure. But he knew that he could not judge her when he did not have all the facts. Especially not when he had been the one to put her into such a precarious and strange position in the first place with this letter writing.

"Well, you know that you need not ever speak of anything to me if you do not wish it. I shall not press you."

He passed her a handkerchief, which Miss Weston took gratefully. She dabbed at her eyes and then carefully blew her nose.

"I must apologize. I know that it is not proper for you to see me in such a state."

"Miss Weston, we have known one another for many years now. I should hope that if there were any woman I was comfortable seeing cry it should be you. And that if there was any man you were comfortable crying in front of, it should be me.

"Besides," he added, attempting to lighten the mood, "this is not nearly so bad as the time when you fell out of the tree you were determined to climb."

Miss Weston smiled wanly. "I remember. Mother thought that I had died but I only got the wind knocked out of me for a moment. I was quite a wild young thing, was I not? Hardly the proper lady."

"You have never been accused of being too proper and I hope that you never shall be. It is a part of your charm."

"Careful, Mr. Norwich. That was dangerously close to a compliment there."

He smiled at her, glad to see that her spirits were starting to rise again. "Well, when you are so down on yourself, I suppose that a small concession or two might be in order."

Miss Weston smiled again at him, this one a little softer and more genuine.

"You have a right to your privacy," James told her. "I would never wish to intrude. But I hope that you know if there is anything that you need to unburden yourself with, you may pass that burden onto me. I am more than happy to assist you in whatever you need. Even if it is only a shoulder to cry on."

"It is ever so kind of you to offer," Miss Weston replied. "I am glad to know that I have such a loyal friend. But thank you, I will manage on my own. It is not precisely a matter about which it is proper to speak."

James understood. If she had been turned down she must feel horribly embarrassed about it. And she would not want the information about it being spread.

Of course he could be trusted not to say anything. And he knew that she trusted him with that. But it was better to not say anything at all. Just in case.

After all, he had not told a single soul about his feelings for Miss Weston until confessing them partway to Mrs. Weston. He had not even written to his brother about them and his brother was safely across the ocean on a ship.

He nodded at her. "Of course. Would you like me to ring for some tea for you or something of that sort?"

"No, thank you. I think it is best that I retire to bed."

"You do not have to be alone if you do not wish it. I could ring for your maid?" It would not be proper for him to be alone with her for too long of a time.

Miss Weston shook her head. "No, truly, your kindness is immeasurable. But I fear the company of another would only dampen my spirits further."

"I can understand that. There are times when solitude is important."

He rose, but took her hand and bowed over it. "If you have need of me, you need only let me know. I shall leave you to your thoughts."

Miss Weston shot him a look of gratitude. "I do appreciate it. I hope that I am not putting you out with my refusal."

"Not at all. I stay or go only on your pleasure. You are the injured party and it is to your needs that I attend."

He smiled at her in what he hoped was a reassuring manner and departed from the house.

James was filled with frustration and fear. He did not want to be her second choice as the letter writer. Would she become more flirtatious and forward with the letter writer now that Mr. Carson had rejected her?

Or would she back away altogether, unsatisfied with him?

It was clear to him that he could not confess now. Not now that Miss Weston was so upset and in love with another.

What would his confession do except for upset and confuse her?

No, he would wait and see what she wrote in her next letter to him. Her reaction and her behavior would tell him how to proceed.

He could not avoid the feeling of melancholy that sank in as he headed home. He supposed that it would be impossible for any man to completely resist feeling a bit gloomy after receiving confirmation that his beloved did not love him.

Especially after he had risked much, and compelled her to risk much in turn, in order to have a chance with her.

But that feeling was secondary. He had to shove it aside, as a proper man must. He would not let it sink him entirely into despair.

Instead he would wait and he would see what Miss Weston did next. It was fortunate that it was her turn to send a letter. He did not think that he would be capable for quite a few days of writing one himself.

His impulse would be to ask how she was doing. If she was all right after what had happened. He would be too likely to slip up and say something that would reveal who he was. Or otherwise too tempted to use his position of intimacy to find out information.

No, it was fortuitous that she was the one who would have to write to him.

James retired for the night, trying to sleep but far too worried for dreams to come easily. He could only hope that Miss Weston was not too distraught. That she was not feeling too low about herself.

For she would beat herself up about this, he knew that she would. He had read far too many of her letters for it to be otherwise.

He knew how Miss Weston truly felt about herself. How she thought that she was too annoying. That she spoke too much. That she was too forceful in personality.

She would blame herself. She would think that it was a fault of her personality. Something about her that was simply not good enough.

If only he could tell her—but hopefully he would get a chance to tell her. In the letters.

Hopefully she would confide in him. She might not tell the entire truth. He would not, if he were her. He would not only be too embarrassed, but he would think it an insult to the gentleman with whom he was corresponding to mention having presented his feelings to another.

But it was possible that she would tell him at least a little of it and seek some sort of comfort from him. He would provide it for her, however he could.

He still tossed and turned a bit throughout the night. Wishing that he was with her. Wishing that he could give her what she needed. What she wanted.

But he was not what she wanted. She wanted someone else.

His only chance to support her was as her letter writer. He would have to wait for her letter, then, and see what it said.

CHAPTER 61

JULIA'S DAY was simply not going well.

The entire thing felt like one long, slow disaster. Like a shipwreck, or a battle, everything falling to pieces the more that she tried to hold it all together.

First, she was in a state of great nervousness. She wanted to figure out if Mr. Carson was the man with whom she had been corresponding.

But it would be a risk. If he was not the man then she could easily be making a fool of herself.

Or she could give him the impression that she was being too forward and he would find her distasteful. Ladies had to navigate a strange balance when it came to romance.

They had to show their interest in a gentleman so that he would know that he could advance into courtship without being offensive.

But they also could not show too much interest. Otherwise it would be construed that they were loose. That they had no morals.

It was a difficult and rather annoying balancing act, if you asked Julia.

She would have to proceed with caution. It was tying her stomach up into knots.

Secondly, Mother seemed to be in a fine mood. And by 'fine', Julia was being sarcastic with herself.

Mother was the sort of person who had a reputation for a sharp tongue. It had gotten only worse once she was married and no longer had to curb herself. Before, she might have scared off potential husbands.

Although, Father had always said that it was her cutting wit that had drawn him to her and first led him to respect her.

After her marriage, though, there was no reason for her to hold herself back anymore. It had grown even worse than that, however, once she had truly fallen ill.

Julia could understand. Truly, she could. Her mother was ill. She could not participate in society as she had been wont to do. She was often sickly and in pain. Or confined to bed. She grew tired easily.

It only made sense that she would have less patience when it came to the prattling of others. That she would feel that life was too short for the nice little lies that everyone told.

However, while Julia could understand, that did not mean that she appreciated it when it was directed at her.

It felt as though nothing she could do that day was correct. Everything was wrong. She was too slow, too lazy, too impertinent.

"Mother," she said at last, "what on earth is the matter? Would you like me to send for the doctor?"

"I am in no need for that quack," her mother replied crossly. "I am allowed to chastise and educate my daughter when she is out of line."

"What am I doing that is so out of line? It cannot be only that my pianoforte is too loud. You are not normally so cross with me. Have I offended you in any way?"

"Offended me?" her mother started out in outrage, and then sighs. "Julia. My dear. You must learn discipline."

"That is not why you are vexed with me, Mother. And I know it. If you thought I ought to learn discipline then you would have said something years ago."

"And maybe I should have!" her mother replied. "If I had, perhaps I would have a daughter who appreciated the people in front of her. And who did not take a day and an age to get married!"

It felt like a slap in the face. But at least she now was at the heart of why Mother was so upset with her.

"Have I been lax in my duties to you as a daughter?" she asked quietly. "Other than the obvious way in that I am still unwed. I am well aware of that."

"Are you?" her mother replied archly. "Are you truly? It has been nearly two months and you have not yet selected a husband. Indeed, you have only one suitor and he is what one would call... reticent. It is almost as though he is not receiving the encouragement that he needs from you."

"If you are speaking of Mr. Carson—"

"Who else would I be speaking of? It is not as though any of the other men have received any encouragement from you. There are several people around you and in your life that are far more dedicated to you than you are to them."

"Are you suggesting that you wish me to marry Mr. Carson?" Julia was full of confusion. Her mother was fond enough of Mr. Carson. But she had seemed to possess no special affection for him.

Her mother sighed. "I am not saying that I wish for you to marry any particular man. But I am saying that you take the people around you for granted and I for one am quite tired of it."

"Do I take you for granted then, Mother?" Julia could feel tears approaching and struggled to control them. Where was this coming from? It seemed to be out of nowhere.

Mrs. Weston merely sniffed, looking incredibly irritated. As if there was something right in front of Julia that she was missing and she couldn't believe that her daughter couldn't see it.

"I only fear that you are losing out on a chance at happiness," her mother said. She sounded almost sad. "I worry that you will choose a life that is less satisfying. Because the people who love you will only wait so long to see if you will return their affection."

"Perhaps if you were not being so cryptic—"

"I am not being cryptic. I am only stating a fact. I could be talking about multiple people, you know. I have seen how various men look at you.

"Any one of them could make you a good husband. But you do not see them. You see only what you want to see. You don't have a care for how they might feel or what emotions they might be harboring."

Mother's tone gentled slightly "I do not think that you are a consciously selfish person, my dear. Nor do I think that you often act out of pure self-interest.

"But you would do better to sit back. To be silent for once instead of speaking. To observe. I think that you would be surprised at what you would see in the people around you."

Julia wanted to throw her hands in the air. To stamp her foot. It was unfair for her mother to just come out like this with no warning and shame her cryptically.

"Well, then, who have I hurt? To whom must I apologize? If not to you?"

"I am not telling you to apologize to anyone. I am only doing what it is a mother's job to do: to inform their child of how they can do better."

"And this has nothing to do with how you wish to marry me off." Julia struggled to keep her voice even. "I know that I am not succeeding in obtaining a proposal yet but surely a courtship must take time?"

"But you are not even being properly courted. You are still aloof and distant. You are holding them at bay as if with a stick. Your attitude speaks volumes to the men around you.

"Therefore, I am telling you that if you would only be less intimidating, they might grow bolder. And if you would stop and look, truly look, at the men around you, you might be surprised."

"By whom? And in what way?"

Mother shrugged as if to say you will see.

Julia clenched her teeth so that she would not scream in frustration. "And who would you have me marry, Mother? If you do not have a favorite in Mr. Carson. Surely there must be someone that you favor. Someone towards whom you are pushing me."

Mother gazed out the window. "I would rather not say."

"No, Mother. You cannot start this argument and then retreat and claim that you have no horse in the race. There must be someone that you are getting at for me and you do not wish to say it. But he exists. I know that he does.

"You might have raised an impertinent and obstinate and altogether selfish daughter. But you did not raise a stupid one. I know when you are trying to drive me towards something but do not wish to say that something straight out. Although goodness knows why."

Mother frowned, as if she was the one who was being interrogated this entire time. As if she was the one who was being inconvenienced by this conversation.

"If you really do insist upon knowing who I would wish you to marry... if it were entirely up to me. I should pick Mr. Norwich for you."

Julia liked to consider herself the kind of girl who was always poised. The kind of woman who was always ready to laugh something off and prepared for any kind of occasion.

But when her mother said that, her jaw dropped open. She gaped.

"Mr. Norwich?" she asked.

Her nerves were electrified with surprise. But—why on earth—

Well, it made sense, logically. Mr. Norwich was set to inherit a title. He was wealthy and had good connections. He was educated and a friend of the family. If she were to list his attributes on a piece of paper he would make any woman the perfect husband.

But it had never even begun to occur to her that he might be someone to marry. He was not even interested in her. She was nothing but a young girl to him still. In his eyes she would probably always be that way.

If anything, the gentleman thought of her as a younger sister. He was always happy to banter with her and tease her. They freely called one another 'friend'.

But woo her? Court her?

Surely if he was interested in her that way she would have seen the signs of it long ago. He was not a stranger to her or to her family.

They had seen one another off and on over the years. She had her entire season and her coming out. Dinner parties. Balls. Nights at the theatre. She had come into the bloom of womanhood some time ago.

If he was going to view her as a marriage prospect then wouldn't he have done something about it by now? Given her some sort of sign?

"Mother, he thinks of me as nothing but a child. A little sister, if you will. You know that he has no sister of his own. Only his younger brother."

"I think that he would be a wonderful match for you, Julia. You two get on so well. You always have. And he will be able to provide for you as few men can."

"Mr. Carson and many other men can provide for me as he can."

"True, but you do not get on with any of them so well as you do with Mr. Norwich."

"Getting along well with someone in general does not mean that I should get on with him in that particularly romantic fashion."

"There is no need for you to start a marriage with romance," Mother replied. "That is not how I did it. And I came to love your father deeply with time. I know that we do not always speak of it. It is not proper to do so. But I like to believe that you have felt it."

"I have seen and felt the regard that you have for one another," Julia replied. "But I cannot be that way. I do not wish to marry someone only out of respect. I wish to marry someone that I truly love."

"You will be hard-pressed then, my child," Mrs. Weston shot back. "And I fear that you will die a spinster. And a penniless one as well. You do not have a rich and titled brother to care for you!"

"I will move in with Georgiana!" Julia said wildly. "She would never turn me away! I should be a proper aunt to her children. Captain Trentworth enjoys my company. He would not object either."

"You ridiculous girl." Her mother sniffed. "If you are so determined to wait for love then I despair of you. You will not find it!"

"Georgiana did!"

"Georgiana found it, lost it, nearly became a spinster, endured the taunts of society, and then nearly lost it again before it came to her. Forgive me for not wishing you to go through the ordeal that she did."

"I dare say she would tell you that it was worth it in the end. If she thinks that then why should I not pursue a similar course?"

"Georgiana could afford to be so fanciful. As I mentioned before —she has a rich brother who was willing to take care of her. You do not. When your father dies you shall be penniless.

"Are you truly willing to risk that, Julia? Is that something for which you are actually prepared? I know that you say that you are but are you truly? Thinking something intellectually and experiencing it are two entirely different things. Your father has pointed this out to his pupils many a time over the years.

"Goodness knows he treated you like a pupil enough times while you were growing up. One would think that lesson as well as others of common sense would have sunk in at some point."

"Well," Julia said, drawing herself up. "If I am such a disappointment to you then I apologize. I never meant to be such a thing. I have always done the best that I could to make you proud.

"If I have been selfish in my behavior towards you then I apologize as well. But I must stay true to myself. I cannot marry a man that I do not love and who does not love me.

"I certainly shall not marry him simply because you wish me to. That would make the both of us unhappy in time. And, I daresay, it would make you unhappy as well, to see me so unhappy."

"Stubborn girl," Mrs. Weston snapped.

Julia knew that there was only one way to maintain any sort of dignity at this point.

She left the room.

Her first inclination upon hurrying up to her room was, of all things, to write to her gentleman correspondent.

She did not understand that.

Why should she wish to write to him?

Yet it felt like the most natural thing in the world to do. She was upset and she wished to tell him about it. To tell him all that Mother had said. To ask him, for he said that he was her friend, if he truly thought her to be selfish and stupid in waiting for love.

Not that she had told him that was what she was waiting for. He had declared his love for her. It had felt cruel to tell him that she was waiting to marry a man she was in love with while he was doing his best to show her that he could be that man.

But oh, she realized in that moment how she had come to depend upon him for her emotional support. How she had told him all of her secrets and all of her woes.

If she did tell him, though—would that not be childish? She would no doubt sound as though she was ungrateful. Whining like a little brat, even.

Here was a man who declared his love for her and was willing to marry her. And he respected her need to know him truthfully as a person. He was writing to her faithfully for weeks in order to court her.

And when she could have had him at any moment she still would not give him what he so wanted? What could solve all her problems and make her mother happy?

Not that it wasn't all from lack of trying on her part. She was going to risk things with Mr. Carson tonight to see if he was the man she was looking for. But she felt a deep sense of shame that prevented her from writing anything.

It was all probably just her overreaction anyway. Mother was probably right.

Was she selfish? Was she unobservant? Was she callous?

Julia was terrified to find out.

She would know soon enough if she was reading her letter writer correctly. If she had figured him out.

She would feel like an utter fool if she was wrong.

Julia hid in her room, sitting on her bed. She wanted to curl up and cry.

Mother had not been so stern to her in such a long time. Julia could feel her stomach churning. She felt almost sick.

Was she being awful to people and not realizing it? Was she a horrible daughter?

Mother had not said anything about Julia failing her parents specifically. But it was right there in between the words that she said.

Julia was not marrying the man that her mother wanted her to marry. She was not yet married, which in and of itself was bad enough.

She was, apparently, not paying attention to the wants and needs of people around her.

Her mother might not have outright said you have disappointed me but she did not have to. Julia could hear it echoing in her ears all the same.

She wished fiercely, like anything, that she knew who her mysterious gentleman was. She wished that she could run to his house and fling herself into his arms. If only so that she might feel safe.

He made her feel safe. It was odd, that. She could acknowledge it. She had never met the gentleman.

Or, rather, she had met him several times but did not know who he was.

And yet she felt safe with him. She felt that if she were to tell him everything that she was feeling that he would hold her closely and allow her to be upset and he would not judge her.

He would counsel her and give her soft but wise advice and she would listen. He would soothe her. Oh, it all sounded so nice in her head.

If only that it was true.

She found herself almost wishing that it was Mr. Carson despite her earlier reservations. If it was Mr. Carson then at least the mystery would be over. She could draw comfort from him. Bring him to her mother and say look, I have found someone. Are you not happy now?

And Mr. Norwich. Where on earth had Mother gotten that idea? It had felt to Julia as if she had been struck by lightning. She felt oddly dizzy and tingly.

The poor man had to have no idea that Mother was throwing in her cap for him to marry Julia. He would most likely laugh if he knew.

He had always seen her and never would see her as anything but a young girl. He teased her constantly. And the man was certainly not serious enough.

Julia recalled telling Georgiana once that Mr. Norwich was the sort of man raised in privilege. Because he was raised in such privilege, he did not always realize how serious life was for everyone else.

And why should he know? He had everything that a man could desire. Or a woman could desire, for that matter. It was understandable.

She could simply not see Mr. Norwich as being in love with anybody. Or if he was, she knew that he would be buoyant about it as he was about everything else. Exuberant. Excitable. Cheerful.

Not at all the serious and introspective sort of man that she realized that she craved. The sort of man that her letter writer was.

It was terrible to know that she was letting down her mother. At least Mr. Norwich was not in love with her and therefore not being let down as well.

To disappoint one person that she cared about was already bad enough. But the idea of disappointing another person, a good man, one that she considered a friend—that was far too much.

She almost wanted to cancel the dinner party now. To hide away in her room. She had thought that she was doing fine. That her behavior while certainly not something she would boast about was not something to chastise.

Instead it seemed that since the time her parents had first brought it up she had only disappointed them more in the matter of marriage.

She would have to endure it, though. She would have to endure and do better. And she would see if she was right and Mr. Carson was indeed her letter writer.

If he was not, then she would simply have to ask the letter writer to reveal himself. There was nothing else for it.

After all, he might not be the man that her mother had wished for but surely he would be better than nothing. He was a good man. He was set to inherit a title. Or at least she suspected that he was.

And he was at the very least a man with whom she felt safe. A man that she could talk to.

What she wanted had to go out the window now. She had disappointed her mother. A dying woman. The one person that above all she wished to see happy. Her time was up and she had to act.

Julia wanted to cry. But she was not a child. She was a lady and a grown one at that. She must handle things.

She rose, and prepared herself for dinner that night. She did not speak to her mother again and neither did Mrs. Weston seek her out.

It was as though they were at some kind of silent stalemate. Neither of them was willing to give up her position. Yet neither was either of them willing to charge into the fray again.

Mother was probably exhausted. The fight must have cost her energy even if she did not wish to show it and would never admit it.

She was a stubborn woman. More stubborn than Julia. Stronger-willed as well. Julia could admit to that.

Part of her wished that she was stronger-willed. That she could match her mother's force of personality and declare that she didn't give two pence what Mother or anyone else thought of her.

But she did care. She cared very much. Especially for what Mother thought. Father as well but Mother was more important. Mother was the one who would not be long for this world.

Julia kept quiet and so did her mother, the two of them getting ready. Normally she helped her mother to get ready and Mrs. Weston would make suggestions for Julia's wardrobe. Not this evening.

Julia almost wanted to scream. She had always hated silence. Why else would she fill her days with wit and banter?

Even when she was writing her letters she was filling pages and overlapping herself. She would often write diagonally over her own words as was the custom to save paper.

Her letter writer had remarked on it once or twice with amusement. His was a special kind of amusement that did not feel patronizing in the slightest. It was as though his amusement sprang from a genuine delight in everything that she did.

She was torn between hoping it would be Mr. Carson so that it would be all over. And hoping oddly that it was not him.

She could not say why she still hoped that it would not be him. It was something deep inside of her that just seemed to instinctually rebel against the idea.

Not that it truly mattered what she did or did not want anymore. She would select the letter writer because she felt safe with him. Because he knew her. Because he had done so much for her already. Put his heart out there for her for weeks.

If she had to marry then it might as well be him. Even if it was not for love.

And then Mother would be happy.

Mr. Carson was one of the first to arrive which was fortunate. Julia wanted to get this entire ordeal over with.

It was probably not the attitude that she ought to have when faced with the possibility of discovering the man who had been writing to her with such care and passion.

But how else could she feel? It was as though her back was to the wall. Like she was a starving mouse and although she knew the cheese in the trap might spell her doom, she had to try and snatch it anyway.

When dinner finally arrived, she couldn't tell if she wanted to heave a sigh of relief or throw up. Her stomach seemed to be unable to decide on the matter.

Mr. Carson was one of the first to arrive. He usually was.

Julia had not been unaware of his slow attempts at courtship. She had thought it might be because he was the letter writer. That because of that he wanted to be his usual charming self but did not want to proceed too hastily. That the shyness he spoke of in his letters was manifested in his behavior.

But could it be because she was driving him away? Was her behavior quite so awful?

She smiled at him as he arrived and immediately engaged him in conversation.

"Mr. Carson. A pleasure as always. You know, it is a good coincidence that you are here. I was just speaking to someone earlier about..."

She wasted no time, asking him at once about a book that she and her letter writer had discussed.

If he had read it and had the same opinion as her letter writer, that would be a good start.

Mr. Carson had indeed read the book. But he stated that he could not venture to give his opinion on it.

Was it because he was her secret correspondent and he knew what she was doing? Or was simply afraid that in expressing his opinion that her question, innocently meant, would reveal him?

She tried another tact instead, launching into some reminiscing about when he was her father's pupil.

Julia saw Mr. Norwich arrive at one point out of the corner of her eye. Mother went over to him immediately.

Mr. Norwich seemed to be a little out of sorts. He spoke with Mother but there was a distracted air about him. Could he have gotten bad news about his brother or father?

Julia wondered what Mother was talking to him about. It couldn't be about her, surely. Mother clearly wanted her to marry Mr. Norwich but she would not be so gauche as to tell Mr. Norwich what Julia was thinking or feeling, would she?

She certainly hoped not, at any rate.

All throughout dinner she tried to get enough information from

Mr. Carson to name him as her writer. She couldn't very well accuse him and then be wrong.

He would demand to know what she meant. Then he would find out what she had been up to. He would be appalled. She wasn't supposed to be writing to a gentleman as an unmarried woman.

He might even tell her mother or father and get her into immense trouble. She could not have that. She absolutely couldn't.

Mr. Carson, unfortunately, did not seem to be taking any of her hints or obliging her in his opinion on things.

Of course this might be because he was not the letter writer. But it might also be because he was and he did not wish to reveal himself.

But he had to reveal himself if he was. He must. She had to know so that she might proceed and make Mother happy.

By the time dinner was finished she knew that she had to be bolder. She must ask him the kind of query that he could not avoid and that would give her a proper answer.

As the others went into the other room in order to play at cards, she asked him, "What do you think of pet names among couples, sir? I often find them rather overdone and tiresome, I must admit."

"What has brought about this particular question?" Mr. Carson asked. "It feels rather as though I am under interrogation this evening."

"Can a lady not ask questions of a gentleman?" Julia replied.

"I suppose she might... if she had a particular aim," Mr. Carson added. His voice was weighted, significant.

"Perhaps I do, perhaps I do not," Julia replied.

She could feel that she was on thin ice. Mr. Carson's tone of voice could not be mistaken. He was wondering if she was finally responding to his advances. If she wanted to see if he would make her a good husband.

Julia knew that she had to step carefully so that she would not give him a false impression or make him any understandings if he turned out not to be her letter writer.

"Who is to say if I have a particular aim or not?" she replied loftily. "Perhaps I am merely trying to take the measure of you. It has been some time since we saw one another, after all.

"Mr. Norwich would not object to such an interrogation," she added. She was not sure why she said it. "He would answer my questions without thought. He is rather obliging that way."

Mr. Carson gave her an odd look. "I suppose that he would not. But then he has had time to grow used to your eccentricities."

"Eccentricities! You make me sound like an old grandmother. The sort of person with whom one must put up because she is old and perhaps a bit of her mind is going."

"I can assure you that you are not old nor is your mind going. And I should hope that you are not yet a grandmother."

"Will you answer my question then, sir? Indulge a pretty young lady?"

"I am not so certain. Given your description of yourself one might consider you to have too high an opinion of yourself and to have been indulged plenty already."

That made Julia's throat close up a little as she swallowed. The letter writer, she hoped, would not say such a thing.

She had told her correspondent about her self-doubts. About how she saw herself. He would not, she hoped, be so callous as to ignore that.

Unless he thought that it would give him away. Unless that was everyone's opinion of her and he must play along with it so that he would not stand out from the crowd.

Julia hoped that most people did not think she had too high an opinion of herself. Was that how the world saw her? Was that what her mother had been talking about?

It terrified her to think that all of her fears about herself were correct. That she had been right this entire time when she had thought herself to be too loud. Too talkative. Too sharp in mind and tongue.

But the letter writer did not think so. He always encouraged her. He was supportive and kind. He was gentle in his words and when he did criticize her for a word or action he countered it with a reminder of how highly he thought of her.

Julia cleared her throat. "Surely you do not think so, Mr. Carson. You must know me well enough by now, I should think. Given how many dinners you have attended recently. You must know me well enough to know that what I say is most often in jest.

"This includes my opinion of myself. And after all, if nobody else will compliment a lady then who is left to compliment her except for herself?"

Mr. Carson smiled indulgently. "You are never lost for a retort, are you, Miss Weston? I do not think that I have ever seen you at a loss for words."

You might soon see me without anything to say, she could not help but think.

If he was the letter writer she would undoubtedly be somewhat speechless. But if he was not she might be speechless as well with confusion and frustration.

"My reputation is based upon my wit. Therefore I must do what I can to keep it up. But you have still not answered my question, sir. What do you think of those little names that couples so often give one another?"

She could almost hear his voice in her head. My little raven. He had to know that was what she was driving at, if he was the one writing the letters to her. He had to know that was her aim.

Mr. Carson frowned in thought. "Oh, I do not think much of it one way or another. Some couples are of course far too indulgent in the habit.

"If I have to hear Mr. and Mrs. Langston call one another 'darling' in every single sentence again, I shall have to excuse myself from dinner in order to bang my head against the wall."

Julia gave a small obliging laugh.

"But overall," Mr. Carson concluded, "I see no problem with them so long as they are in moderation. Some couples, I think, use them in place of true affection. Or as a sort of barb. It is all in the intention of the word, is it not?"

"What of more specific names?" she asked. "I had heard one person call their wife..."

She had to say it. She had to now.

"...my little raven. It was because of her hair. And, I believe, because of her personality. It reminded him of the bird."

There was no response from Mr. Carson. No glint of recognition in his eyes.

Julia was aware that there was such a thing as hiding one's true emotions. And that many people were good at it.

But there was no possible way in which Mr. Carson could have hidden his response to that. She knew that he would have to show something of his surprise. It would be quickly stifled but it would be there.

Instead, Mr. Carson just stared at her placidly.

He had no idea what she was talking about.

He was not her letter writer.

A strange mixture of relief and sadness swept over her. Her stomach tightened. Her eyes felt hot and itchy.

He was still interested in her. She knew that. She had known that before she had started to wonder if he was the letter writer or not.

But now he must think that she was more interested than she was.

And she was realizing—it was sweeping over her like early morning sunlight through the window—that she could not have him.

Not if he was not her letter writer.

It reminded her of the time that she was a child. She had finally understood addition. She'd been very young at the time but it was one of her earliest memories.

The sudden epiphany, the knowledge that had filled her as she had truly grasped that oh, two and two together equaled four! It had been like nothing she had ever felt before.

This felt quite similar to that. Knowledge that had always been there, waiting patiently, was suddenly before her. She knew it, felt it, could see the truth of it.

She was in love.

She was in love with the man to whom she was writing those letters.

Julia almost wanted to find him so that she might stand on a chair and clap sardonically. Bravo, bravo! He had succeeded in his aim. She was in love with him, as he had wished her to be.

But she still did not know who he was. And he had dodged all attempts for her to find out. And now she had gone out on a limb with Mr. Carson and he must think he had far more of a chance than he truly did.

Mr. Carson was speaking to her. He was answering her question.

Talking about how giving a wife a nickname after an animal sounded rather too fanciful for him.

Too fanciful. Well, they should never get on anyway. Julia was a fanciful person. Everybody knew that.

He was still speaking but she could hardly hear him. It was as though her ears had become stuffed with cotton. Or as if he was talking to her from underwater. It was all muted.

Her heartbeat pounded in her ears. She was in love.

Oh, how foolish she had been to not realize it before.

She felt safe with her letter writer? She wanted to run to him when she was in distress? She told him everything?

She had thought that she only decided to find out who he was from the thrill of the mystery. And then so that she might have the best choice of husbands out of the ones presented to her. Because at least he knew her and at least they were friends.

But no. This whole time she had been blind. Not seeing what was right in front of her. She'd had two, and two, but she hadn't thought to put them together to make four. And whose fault was that?

None but her own.

She had to find him. She had to.

Mr. Carson was still speaking and she felt as though she would say anything he wanted in order to get him to be quiet. She could not bear to hear his voice or see his face.

She wanted her correspondent.

"...I hope that I have not been too forward," Mr. Carson concluded. "But I should like to think that your line of questioning is your way of giving me hope."

Julia's breath caught in her throat. She had not truly heard a word that he had said.

"I apologize," she replied. "I have not been attempting to give either despair or hope. I only wished to learn more about you."

"But why should you wish to learn more about me if you were not leaning towards—"

"I greatly apologize, Mr. Carson. I had not meant to give offense or false hope. Not at all. I am an inquisitive woman by nature and it is simply that I wanted to learn your opinion on things.

"You may ask Mr. Norwich, if you would like. He will be sure to tell you that this is my personality. I meant no harm, I can assure you.

"It is only that you seem eager to spend time with me and to get to know me better and so I am endeavoring to get to know you better in turn. Is that not what you are after? Is that not what courtship is for?

"If you have not been courting me or if you feel you are farther along in your courtship than you actually are then I apologize. I did not mean to mislead or misunderstand you.

"I hope that we can part this evening as friends, at least. I apologize deeply if I have given offense. I am only wishing to ask questions for that is my nature. I enjoy getting to know people and you seemed eager for me to get to know you.

"But if I may be frank, sir, I do not think that we are far enough along in proceedings for you to have too much hope. After all, you have not even seen fit to ask me to dance a second time at any balls."

Julia struggled to keep her breathing calm so that she would not panic. She did not want to offend Mr. Carson or damage her reputation.

To her relief, Mr. Carson simply nodded. "That is fair. I cannot be so cautious and then expect you to read my mind and to know what is in my heart. I will be more direct in my courtship of you from now on."

It was not what she wanted. She wanted him to give up and to stop courting her at all. But to say so would draw too great a risk of insulting him. She was already skirting too close to disaster.

"I hope that I shall have the pleasure of receiving more obvious encouragement from you soon." Mr. Carson glanced over at the others in the sitting room. "But it appears that the party has disbanded."

"Ah, yes." Only her mother, Mr. Norwich, and one or two others were left. "Have a pleasant evening, sir. I apologize for any lack of understanding or for any miscommunication."

"You have a pleasant evening as well, Miss Weston."

Well. That was only halfway a disaster.

Julia wanted to burst into tears. Indeed, she could feel the tears welling up in her despite her best efforts.

It was all too much. There were far too many emotions warring inside of her like clashing clouds in a thunderstorm.

She felt a strange mix of surprise and elation at the realization that she was in love. She felt nervous, terrified, unsettled, worried that she had just insulted Mr. Carson and would suffer the consequences for it. Or that she was now engaging him in a courtship that she had no intention of continuing.

She also felt fearful for herself. Scared that she was selfish as her mother claimed. That she had just been more selfish in her actions than she thought. That her fears about herself were true. That she had been selfish just now in regards to Mr. Carson.

It was all rather overwhelming and she thought she might have to sit down.

And of course, Mr. Norwich saw her.

He was very kind to her. Offering to get her tea and find someone to sit with her. Lending her a handkerchief.

She hoped that she was not ungrateful to him. She tried to say so. She did not want to be selfish or thoughtless. And he did treat her always with respect and kindness.

Perhaps her life would be easier if he was in love with her. If he had courted her long ago. He had certainly had plenty of opportunity to do so.

Maybe then she might have fallen in love with him. But she did not know. And he certainly did not love her. He was all gentleness and care, of course.

She could see why Mother wanted her to marry him. But she could not even conceive of the idea of marrying another. Not now that she understood why she thought so much of her letter writer.

How could she have been so blind, so stupid, so unable to realize what was right in front of her?

The man with whom she was corresponding must think her the most thick and dull-witted girl on the planet.

Did he know? Could he tell that she loved him?

It was not the sort of thing that you could easily tell another person. "Oh, I know that you are in love with me," sounded like the pinnacle of arrogance. She would not have said as much if she was in the position of her letter writer.

Or could it be that he did not know? That he was holding onto nothing but hope, still, after all of this time? Willing to wait and be patient and court her slowly through letters?

He must be the most understanding man on the whole earth if that was the case.

Either way, Julia knew that she must tell him.

After she finished having her little cry.

It was stupid, she knew, to shed tears. But she was just feeling so much all at once. She was feeling ashamed of herself and scared that she had real reason to feel shame. She was anxious over Mr. Carson. And she was filled with this knowledge that was simultaneously wonderful and horrible.

Was this what love felt like? As though you were standing at the edge of the ocean and a great wave was approaching you and you could not move to avoid it?

She had to remember to be sure to commend her letter writer for his patience. She had only known that she was in love for half an hour and already she was bursting to tell him about it.

She could not imagine what waiting years must have felt like for him.

After Julia had persuaded Mr. Norwich to leave, she took a few moments to gather herself together. She must not cry all over her letter, after all. Or else if she did the ink would smudge and she would have to start again.

When she had sufficiently composed herself she went upstairs to her room.

Along the way, however, she was stopped. Or rather, she stopped in surprise, but she was sure that her mother would have stopped her had Julia kept walking.

She was sitting in the chair that rested in the hallway just outside of Julia's bedroom door. Julia almost didn't see her lingering in the shadows there.

"Mother! You ought to have gone to bed. It is late. I thought Mr. Norwich saw you up the stairs."

"He did. He is a fine gentleman."

"Mother, please. I cannot hear about how I ought to marry Mr. Norwich or any other person at the moment."

"I know." Mrs. Weston sighed, stood and walked over to her,

taking Julia's shoulders in her hands and squeezing gently. "I have been too harsh on you, I am afraid.

"It is only that I am worried for you. As we have already talked on. And I hate to see that other people around you are not being appreciated by you.

"You are a thoughtful and kindhearted young woman. It would be a shame for you to wake up and realize that you had wasted those qualities because you did not see how the people around you truly felt about you.

"I am too harsh on you. You are my only daughter. My only child. And I fear that sometimes I expect too much from you.

"It was wrong of me to chastise you as I did. Without warning and without proper explanation. I know that finding a husband can be hard."

"I have been looking," Julia replied. "I promise that I have been. And I believe that I have found the right person for myself. That I am going to be proposed to shortly."

"Do you speak of Mr. Carson?"

Her mother's tone was carefully light, as though she were trying to hold in her disappointment for Julia's sake.

Julia shook her head. "No, Mother. It is not Mr. Carson. That I can assure you."

Mrs. Weston looked pleased, but her mouth pursed and her jaw clenched as though she were doing her best to hide it.

Julia almost laughed with amusement at her mother's attempts to hide her emotions. There was little doubt in her mind where her own inability to hide her emotions came from.

She had used to envy Georgiana that ability when they were children. Nobody knew what Georgiana was thinking or feeling unless she told them.

"Parents are not perfect either, as I hope you will someday have the joyous opportunity to learn." Mrs. Weston smiled. "I am still learning, even now. And I want the best for you.

"But I fear sometimes I am too hard on you and today is one of those times. I am sorry. Will you accept my apology?"

Julia found herself crying again. "Of course, Mother."

Mrs. Weston pulled her in to hug her and Julia laid her head on her shoulder. "I was unfair to you. My sweet girl. You are a sweet girl, Julia, do not ever allow yourself to doubt that. Do you understand?"

"Yes, Mother." She was not sure that she agreed. She was still terrified of being selfish. But it felt good to hear her mother say those things.

They stood there for a moment. Julia soaked up the love and warmth of her mother's arms, her head resting on her shoulder.

Then at last they pulled back.

"Now," Mrs. Weston said. "Go to bed and get some good sleep. I shall hear about this other prospect you have mentioned in the morning."

"It might take a day or two, please have patience," Julia said, laughing a little. "I shall inform you as soon as there are solid developments."

Her mother hummed skeptically. "If you say so."

She kissed Julia on the forehead and then turned, walking into her room and obviously heading for bed.

Julia slipped into her own room and took care to lock the door behind her.

Just in case.

She crossed over to the desk. A pleasant fire was already going in the fireplace and she used it to light a candle that she might set upon the desk in order to write.

Julia supposed that she might wait until the morning. It was rather late and she was emotional.

But she was not a patient person. She was not at all like her letter writer who had waited for her patiently all of these years. And then had been even more patient in writing to her and slowly allowing her to get to know him.

She sat down at the desk and pulled a piece of paper to her.

How could she even begin?

She did not want it to seem too startling or out of the blue. She wanted the letter writer to understand that this was genuine.

She might not know his face or his form but she knew his personality. And the disappointment that she had felt when Mr. Carson was not her letter writer was keen.

Julia still could not explain why she had not wanted it to be Mr.

Carson in the first place. That odd sensation of hoping and yet not hoping that it would be him was still confusing to her.

But that aside, she could not deny that she could not feel any affection for the man once she knew that he was not the gentleman with whom she had been corresponding.

Julia thought for a moment, and at last began to write.

Dear Sir,

You must excuse me but I shall not be continuing our lively conversation from the previous letters. I am afraid that I have something of the utmost importance that I must relay to you, if you are able to hear it.

When you first wrote to me, you told me of your feelings and that you knew that I did not return them. That you indeed had little hope of my ever returning them.

These letters were therefore a way for us to get to know one another. A way for you to court me. A way that we might see if we could in fact work together as a couple.

I must congratulate you, my dear sir.

For indeed this evening I was struck with the realization that you have succeeded in your aim.

The affections that you have displayed to me and for me are returned. They are most affectionately and deeply returned.

You have most likely guessed, for you are an intelligent man, that I have been trying since the beginning to learn your true identity.

You cannot blame me for such a thing, I hope. I did ask once, quite politely, if you would share your name with me. Instead you suggested this correspondence. You cannot blame a lady for trying.

And I admit that attempting to learn through clues and process of elimination who you truly are was quite fun. I highly enjoyed the chase.

This evening I thought that I had figured out who you truly were. Or at least who you were very likely of being. I set several clues before the gentleman but I was unable to come to a strong conclusion.

The gentleman was understandably confused and I fear that I might have caused some misunderstandings from him initially. But at last I put before him a question that he could not answer. In his lack of answer I knew that he could not be you.

Until that moment I had been unsure whether I wished for you to turn out to be that gentleman or not. He is a fine man. He has everything that many women could ask for in a husband.

But the moment that I knew he was not you, I was filled with a fierce determination. I knew that I simply could not marry him.

You can well understand my confusion at this. Why should I not wish to marry a man with a title and wealth, a man of education and charm? Because he was not you?

And it was then that I realized—it was because I was in possession of the deepest feelings that a woman can hold for a man.

I hope that you will not see me as being too bold. Given what you had declared your own feelings to be I thought it not out of the question for me to respond in kind.

Having never experienced these feelings before I find myself quite at a loss as to how to express them.

All I know is that I wish that I were in your company right now. In fact, I have longed for your company all day.

I feel safe when I am with you. And I do not mean merely in the sense that my physical wellbeing will be looked after. I feel as though I can share myself entirely with you without fear of judgment.

You entertain me. You are kind and thoughtful. You are patient with me. I have been able to tell things to you that I have not dared to tell to anyone else.

Part of it I can admit, at least in the beginning, was the safety of anonymity. Something about putting one's words down on paper instead of saying them out loud is quite freeing. We have both noted this in our letters previously.

At first I confess that I was somewhat afraid to be saying all that I was to a person who knew my identity while I did not know theirs. But then my fear and apprehension turned into curiosity. And now, it is excitement. I long to know who you are.

I might be more cautious in expressing myself if it were not for your previous confession. It has given me the strength to express my own feelings towards you.

Julia paused in writing the letter.

Should she be even more explicit? No, he had to understand her meaning.

Ought she to take out the part about Mr. Carson?

No. Her mystery writer had not been at the dinner, she was sure. And if he had been, then would he not be curious as to what she and Mr. Carson had been talking about?

Her writer had to know that Mr. Carson was also making a play for her. Mr. Carson had been a bit slow in his courtship, it was true. But it was still evident to those who cared to look.

He took care to dance with her first at balls. To sit near her at dinner. To always engage her in conversation.

Mr. Carson was being slow but not subtle. Her correspondent must know what was going on. Unless he for some reason was not attending any balls or dinners and staying out of the social life in Bath.

She saw no reason why he should. And he did mention balls now and again, as well as local gossip. He must be in the loop of things.

It would only be natural therefore that she explain. He would know that she meant Mr. Carson even though she had not said the gentleman's name. That way her mystery writer would know that he need not fear Mr. Carson as competition any longer.

Well, Mr. Carson would continue to pursue her. She would simply have to rely upon her letter writer to propose to her before Mr. Carson did in order to clear the entire matter up. It would serve the double purpose of saving herself from having to turn down Mr. Carson directly.

She did so wish to avoid that. She would not like to hurt the man's feelings.

But in any case, the writer would know that he need not fear her affections turning towards Mr. Carson.

Very well. She would keep it in the letter.

Those feelings which I allude to me dare not go much further into detail over. You know as well as I do that we must still be careful about what we say in these pages.

But I'm sure that you cannot fail to guess the depth and breadth of my meaning. I hope that I am not too late.

I can admit that there is in me still a slight fear. A fear that perhaps your feelings have faded from romance into friendship. That in coming to know me better you might have wished to know me less. That growing closer meant you wished that we were farther apart once more.

You will respond that of course you do not feel this way, but bear in mind that if you had come to this particular realization you could hardly back down from writing me. After all, you were the one who persuaded me to start this correspondence in the first place.

You see what sort of circles my mind runs in.

In any case, I hope that you will reveal yourself to me now. You can be certain of a warm reception. I find that I wish for no other man to make his intentions known to me.

You may do so in person or through writing. I know that I must think of your comfort as well as mine. If you wish to reveal yourself as you originally planned all those weeks ago then you may do so.

However, if you do wish to proclaim yourself in person, you will find a warm welcome.

I wish to meet you. I wish to know your face. Your voice. Who you truly are. I feel as if I already know you and yet, at the same time, I feel as though I am only standing at the edge of a cliff. Waiting for the fog to clear. Waiting to know you.

Please do not tell me that I am too late and your feelings have cooled. Tell me that I will get to know who you are at last. Meet you in person at last.

I confess that when I first realized how I felt about you I nearly burst into tears. Actually—I did, although only after the poor confused gentleman had left. I did not wish to cry in front of him as you might well understand.

But it was just so overwhelming. I think that I gave at least two others who know me a fright. I think that they believed me to be upset.

I was upset, in that my emotions were all askew, but not in any alarming or bitter way. In a wondrous and overwhelming way.

My day I confess had not been going very well beforehand either. I was full of self-doubt and turmoil. But I can assure that those events and those emotions had nothing to do with informing my realization about how I feel towards you.

It was rather simply the understanding, almost like when one sees the sunrise, that came upon me so swiftly and naturally.

But now I am undoubtedly rambling. I am certain that you do not wish to hear all of my wayward thoughts about my day and how I came to know how I feel for you. About you.

All that you must want to know and all that you need to know is that I long to read your words not with my eyes but with my ears and my heart. For them to be spoken instead of written.

I wish to no longer imagine a blank slate where your face is when I picture speaking with you or going on walks with you or reading with you.

And yes, I do imagine all of those things. Is it not silly of me to have not realized before what it all meant? What it signified?

You stole into my affections without my even realizing it and now I find myself completely at your mercy.

It seems only fair, though. You threw yourself at my mercy initially and now it seems I am to return the favor. Please do not keep me waiting long in your answer. Do not delay in providing me with some kind of response.

You are the person who has come to represent to me the deepest form of friendship. I blush to read your letters and I am warm for hours afterwards knowing that your thoughts are with me. Just as mine are with yours.

My thoughts are with you now. My breath is bated. I hope that I am not wrong in holding it as I wait.

I eagerly await your answer.

Sincerely, as always,

Miss Julia Weston

She was terribly tempted to sign the letter in another way. To simply say 'Julia', or to say 'your darling' or even 'your raven'.

But she did not dare. Her courage failed her there. And she was still mindful of someone else possibly seeing the letter.

Julia sealed it up and then began to dress for bed. Her heart was hammering in her chest as though she had sent the letter out already.

It would not take long for her to receive an answer, she knew. It never took longer than the span of a day for a reply to reach her. She would know by tomorrow evening at the latest.

She might know even sooner if he chose to come to her in person.

Julia took his letters out of the drawer and sat on the bed to read them, one last time.

Just in case things went horribly wrong.

She did not know how they could go wrong, exactly. But she was aware that they could and she was worried that there was still some way that she could lose in this. That she would not get to have this man after all.

The letters had become even more dear to her over time than when she had first read them. They were a little worn in places from her fingers folding and unfolding them. She knew the words almost by heart now. Yet, reading them over again still quickened her breath and set her heart to fluttering like a butterfly.

She lingered longest on the letter that held the passage where he had first started to call her by her nickname.

You remind me very much of the ravens that I used to see as my companions when at home as a child.

I hope that you will not take offense to the comparison. I admit I was rather lonely growing up in my estate. I did not find cause to become more outgoing until I was older and sent away for my education.

But there were a great many ravens that lived thereabouts. I would observe them often. They proved themselves to be clever birds. Very sociable. And with very good memories.

In fact, they were rather too clever for their own good at times. I would watch them teasing bigger birds or stealing things. They would succeed just often enough that it would make them bold.

They remind me rather much of you in that way. You are a clever lady and you do like to tease. You are quite the wit. And I do sometimes fear that you will grow too bold and land yourself into trouble for it.

But I cannot help but be amused at your antics. And the darkness of your hair, the shine of it, your sharp eyes—they strike me as being very much like the wings of that particular bird.

Some say that ravens and crows are signs of bad news but I have never thought so myself. I think that they are simply troublemakers. Good-humored at that.

I often see you fluttering about on the dance floor. You move as if your feet were not even touching the ground. And I cannot help but imagine that you are truly flying just a bit, my little raven.

That had been the first time that he had called her that. She had read that phrase and at once her heart had leapt into her throat.

Now she understood why.

He had to be in love with her. Why would he come up with such a specific and endearing nickname otherwise? One that spoke both of her physical features and of her personality?

Nobody else could possibly be so specific. He must love her.

Or at least, he had loved her when he had written that letter.

Julia looked at the clock. It was late and she had a rough day behind her. That was why she was so nervous. A good night's sleep would make it all seem that much better.

Tomorrow she would meet him. Or at least read his name in the evening mail when it arrived. Tomorrow she would know who he was.

She would know the identity of the man with whom she was in love.

CHAPTER 62

JAMES STARED down at the letter.

He had to read it several times over to make sure that he correctly understood what he was reading. That this was not in fact some dream. Or that he did not accidentally, in his haste, misunderstand what was being said.

But no. There it was, in plain letters. Or as plain as it was possible to be in writing when a letter could always fall into the wrong hands.

He had to sit down, unable to properly feel his legs.

So that had been what had happened last night.

He had been so certain, so very certain that she wanted Mr. Carson. He had been ready to find some way to give her up and to bow out.

When he got her letter he had expected nothing other than an apology and an end to their correspondence. Or perhaps she would continue on as before, although it would hurt him to know that he was simply a consolation prize.

In fact, he had been bracing himself for almost anything... except for this.

A declaration of love.

He had thought that Miss Weston was so upset last night because she was dejected. Instead it had been because she was overwhelmed with emotion in realizing she loved him?

He was not so surprised at the being overwhelmed part of it all.

Miss Weston had always been an emotional girl. She was imaginative. Prone to daydreams and outbursts of passion. He had seen her give quite a few lectures in her time.

It was the fact that she was overcome because of him. Because she cared for him.

James knew that he was reading it and that it must be true but it was so difficult to reconcile what he had known for so long with the new truth that was in front of him.

He realized, for the first time, that despite his writing letters to her he had still not truly believed that he could win her. That he could actually change her mind and convince her to fall in love with him.

And yet, it had happened.

He was a bit concerned for Mr. Carson. Not only for the man's feelings but also for the situation in general. But he supposed that they would cross that bridge when they got to it.

In the meantime, though... in the meantime there was Miss Weston.

Miss Weston who had been crying because she was so overwhelmed with how she felt about him. Who had written at once to tell him about it.

She must have written at once. How else would the letter get to him so quickly? It must have been sent out with the first morning's mail in order to reach him in time for him to read it over a leisurely breakfast.

He wanted to ask if she was certain. If this was not merely the throes of the moment.

James called for a paper and pen. He had to write to her at once.

He owed it to her to tell her the truth. But he could not do so over letter. He had been a coward for long enough.

When the materials were brought to him he began to write, right there at the table. He did not trust his legs to bear him if he tried to stand up and walk to his desk.

Dear Miss Weston,

Are you certain of these feelings?

I do not mean to insult you by doubting you. It is only that I know you are prone to great bouts of emotion. I do not wish for you to declare anything that you will regret in time.

Are you positive that this is not merely the product of a moment of excitement and confusion?

I would hate to reveal myself to you and have you already have changed your mind. I do not wish to embarrass either of us.

But if you are certain, then let me know and I shall call upon you at your earliest convenience.

I remain,

James hesitated over what to put as his signature. He always hesitated, no matter how many letters they exchanged.

But this was the last letter that he would send to her. If she had changed her mind and told him not to meet her and reveal himself then he would not write to her anymore.

This must have done. Clearly this correspondence was messing with both of their heads. It had to end. Either by revealing himself or by disappearing into the ether.

She would possibly be disappointed but if she did not truly love him then that disappointment would be easily gotten over.

But if this was to be the last time...

He hovered his pen over the page and then finally signed it,

Yours.

For he was. And always would be.

Miss Weston's reply was a swift one.

It was short, and James was already getting ready for the ball that night when he saw it laid upon the tray at the front door.

His hands shook slightly and he had to calm down his breathing as he opened it.

Dear Sir,

I am in earnest. Please, tell me who you are. I feel as though I am going to burst if you do not tell me your name.

James nearly burst out laughing hysterically in relief.

She was certain. She loved him.

But then doubt came in again, swift and terrible.

She loved the writer of the letters.

Would she be able to reconcile that man with him? With James Norwich?

Or would she be far too entrenched in her opinion of him? Would she reject him? Find him wanting? Would she wish that he was more like Mr. Carson or some other man?

There was no time for him to ponder it now. He had to get to the ball.

Miss Weston would be there but he could not tell her then. Not in front of all of those people.

He would have to tell her in the morning.

James hurried to the ball, smiling at those he knew as he entered, a trifle late.

"You seem distracted," Miss Perry noted. "Are you quite all right, Mr. Norwich?"

"I am as well as anyone can be," he replied. As well as anyone can be when they are in receipt of such news as I am, he thought.

Miss Perry gave him an odd look that suggested that she did not believe him, but she left him to it.

James could see her, gazing about the room with far more openness than she should have.

Miss Weston.

She was wondering if he was there. Her letter writer. She was terrible at hiding her emotions and always had been. James almost wanted to laugh.

It was just so sweet. She thought that she was being subtle and yet everyone in the room could probably tell that she was on edge. Looking for something. Or someone.

"You're as on edge as my daughter tonight," Mrs. Weston remarked, walking sedately up to him. If he didn't know that it was because of her illness, he would have thought that she was moving with such stillness and care because she felt like it.

As it was, the crowd practically parted before her.

"She seemed rather upset last night," James admitted. "I lent her my handkerchief but she would not let me stay with her. She wished to be alone."

"I am afraid that we exchanged some harsh words earlier in the day," Mrs. Weston replied. "I said some things that I had to later take back. She is a good girl."

"That she is."

"And are you going to do anything about it?"

"I am, actually. Tomorrow. If you will permit me. I plan to call upon you at your earliest convenience."

"As early as you would like. I plan on sleeping in so do not be worried if my daughter receives you alone. She has done so often lately with morning callers. I find that if I am to go out in the evenings I must save my strength throughout the morning."

"I must say, madam, you carry your misfortune with a dignity that I have rarely seen."

"Thank you. Your kindness has not been overlooked. Your calling upon us is fortuitous in its timing. I fear that Mr. Carson will make a firm play for her shortly."

"I have it from the lady herself that she does not care for him."

"Is that so? Well, I wish that she would have told me so in order to help me with my poor nerves."

"She was not certain until last night. That was part of why she was in such tears, I believe. She would not tell me much at the time."

"Well, I am glad to hear it. There is nothing particularly wrong with the man, of course. But he is not for my Julia."

Mrs. Weston watched her daughter dancing, a look of such complete fondness on her face that James wished that he had some way to preserve it. If only so that Miss Weston might see it later and know how much she was adored by her mother.

Her letters to him had revealed her doubts about how well she was doing as a daughter. He wished to take away those doubts. Miss Weston was a beloved daughter. She had not disappointed her parents. She could not. They would love her no matter what.

"My Julia. Look at her, Mr. Norwich. Is she not a true flower?"

James looked obligingly, both to please her and because he was glad of an excuse to watch Miss Weston dancing. "Truly."

"She is my only child, sir. You would do well to remember that. Your wife she might be but she never ceases to be my daughter. If she is not made to be perfectly happy I shall have more than just words with you."

"If she deigns to marry me, I would make my mission in life nothing less than ensuring her constant pleasure."

"You know, you are lucky that I saw the awkward, serious boy you were growing up. You are far too charming nowadays. I cannot trust a word that you say when you are like that."

"If it is any consolation, madam, I am being far more forthright with you about my feelings for your daughter than I have been to any other person about her."

Well, other than to Miss Weston herself in the letters. But that was to her, and not about her. A fitting enough loophole.

Feeling that things had perhaps become a little too serious, he sought to lighten the mood. "And how do I know that you will not be listening or peeping in at the keyhole tomorrow when I call?"

Mrs. Weston chuckled. "You are a clever one. Rest assured, my daughter will tell me whatever transpires between you. She always tells me everything."

James felt another swift pang of guilt. Miss Weston had not told her mother about the letters. He had made Miss Weston keep a grave secret from both of her parents.

Well, he was going to remedy it all tomorrow. Everything would be out in the open. Perhaps Miss Weston would then be able to tell her mother about the letters as well if she so wished.

James watched Miss Weston dancing, out of his reach. But only for that evening. Tomorrow he would tell her who he was. And then it would all change. It would all be different. Hopefully, it would all be better.

CHAPTER 63

JULIA WAS TERRIFIED.

She had put on her best frock, her favorite one, and had done up her hair with care. She had eaten early and was now pacing up and down the sitting room.

Waiting.

Hoping.

Her letter had hopefully arrived by yesterday evening. It was possible that it had not arrived until this morning's post, however.

She could be waiting all morning. If the gentleman had not received the letter until this morning at breakfast then he might not be able to call upon her until later.

He might not even be able to call upon her that day at all.

In fact, he might not even call. He might simply write her a response. Then she would not know who he was until that evening with the post.

Julia could feel her heartbeat climbing and took slow, even breaths in order to calm herself. There was no use in getting all flustered. This was something that was out of her control.

She did so dearly hope that he would call upon her that morning. She could hardly stand it. She had to know who he was. This suspense was more than she could bear.

How on earth had the man endured being in love with her for so long without telling her? She had only gone two days without a proper response from him and she was already halfway to going mad.

Julia forced herself to stop pacing and sit down. Should she ring for tea? What if someone else came to see her this morning? They would be surprised to find her so nervous. She was sure to be a horrible hostess.

As if her thoughts had summoned someone, there came a knock at the front door.

Julia froze. Her breath halted in her throat.

Was this him? Could it be?

There was the sound of the servant opening the door, and then the sound of voices. Julia thought that she recognized one of them.

Then, to her surprise—Mr. Norwich strode into the room.

Julia stood up, completely unsure of what to do. "Mr. Norwich."

"Miss Weston." Mr. Norwich looked uncomfortable. She had never seen him in such a state. He always appeared to be so easygoing. So relaxed. "I hope that I have not come at an unpleasant time."

"Certainly not. Would you like some tea?"

"Ah, no, no thank you, Miss Weston."

Julia stared at him. It was so unlike him to behave in this manner. What on earth was going on?

"Is there something the matter?" she asked. "Perhaps you would like some water?"

"No, there is nothing—I apologize. My manner must seem quite strange to you. I am not often so nervous."

"No, I can easily see that." Julia attempted a smile and a small laugh, but neither seemed to work out for her very well. She feared that it came out strained, and her laugh sounded hollow and nervous.

"Was there a particular reason that you came to call?" she asked. Mr. Norwich did not usually call in the mornings. They saw one another every night between dinners and balls.

"Yes, actually." Mr. Norwich looked around, as if casting about for some kind of excuse, or hoping that someone or something would change the conversation.

After an awkward moment of silence, Mr. Norwich cleared his throat and took a few steps closer. Julia had the strange thought that he looked oddly handsome, when he was disheveled like this.

And he did appear to be quite disheveled. He looked as though he had hardly slept all night. His clothes were just the slightest bit askew and his hair was only half done.

If Julia did not know any better, she would have thought that he had received some horrible news. That his brother had died overseas or that his father had unexpectedly passed.

She hoped that was not the case. She would hate for him to have to lose another member of his family. Although she was not sure how Mr. Norwich had reacted to his mother's death.

Then he began to speak.

"Miss Weston. You must forgive me. I am not very good at this— I am not good at this at all—when I am speaking aloud. But you did ask to know who I was. You did say that you wished to see my face, to have a proper name to go with your letters."

It felt as though the bottom had dropped out of Julia's stomach.

Mr. Norwich—he was her mystery gentleman?

She never would have guessed that. Not in a hundred, no, a thousand years.

But he—he thought of her as a sister. He did not care for her in the romantic sense at all.

...didn't he?

Julia would not have been surprised if she had been told that the world was spinning in the opposite direction now.

Mr. Norwich cleared his throat again. "I apologize. I am certain —all but certain—that this is, that I am not, the person that you wanted or expected."

"I did not know who to expect," Julia told him honestly.

They sized one another up for a moment. Julia felt as though Mr. Norwich was as unsure as she was.

She had expected her mystery gentleman to be confident when he approached her. Surely he had to know by now that she was his, as her letter had said. Why did he still seem as worried and anxious as she was?

"You can see now why I did not think you would receive me well if I simply came to you in person as I am," he said quietly.

"It is merely that I am—I am so—surprised," Julia blurted out.

"I wish I could say the same," Mr. Norwich said, sadly. "That your reaction was not something that I had expected."

"You expected me to be... taken aback?"

"Why would you not be?" Mr. Norwich did not sound—not angry, no. More like... disappointed? Or sad. "You have done nothing but overlook me for years, Miss Weston.

"I have been here in front of you. Always your closest friend. Other than Miss Reginald, who else can you say is closer to you?

"We banter at parties. You always invite me over for dinner. We dance together at balls and speak about others, gossip, knowing that whatever we say to one another will be kept in complete confidence.

"You sought me out only the other day for advice. It seems that I am the person that you run to when you most need assistance.

"And yet, would you have ever considered me as a possible suitor? Did you ever once, in looking at the men who could possibly be your mysterious correspondent, think that I might be the one? Did you think of me at all, even once?"

Julia realized with a horrible, sinking feeling in her gut that she had not.

Mr. Norwich was one of her father's pupils. He had a younger sibling who was considered a flirt—his brother.

All of the things that had led her to consider Mr. Carson, she realized had also pointed at Mr. Norwich.

But had she ever really seriously thought of him as a candidate? Or had she dismissed him without a backwards glance?

It had been the latter.

Julia could feel shame coursing through her like thick, black ink. "I—I apologize. I had not realized that I was not giving you the attention and credit that was your due.

"You are right. I have completely overlooked you. For that I am terribly sorry. I never meant to offend you or to... to ignore you. I never..."

She had been selfish. She had been thoughtless and self-centered. All of the things that she had feared, she had been.

Julia did not know what to say. How she could possibly make this better. Make it right.

Mr. Norwich appeared to be at just as much of a loss as she was. After another long moment of silence he said, "I hope that you are not too disappointed with me."

He sounded—he sounded dejected. As though he already knew what her answer would be.

"I—I confess that I do not know what I am feeling," Julia replied.

It was not the swift relief and elation that she had been hoping for. But nor was it the strange anticipation of disappointment that she had when she thought that Mr. Carson might be her mystery correspondent.

Mostly, she just felt confused. And ashamed of herself.

If she had only paid more attention to Mr. Norwich. If only she had not taken him for granted. Then she would have thought of him long ago. This whole mystery would have been solved.

Not that he seemed to want the mystery solved or anything. But perhaps then she could have greeted him with a bit more of a welcome and a bit less shock and shame.

Mr. Norwich nodded. "Perhaps I should—leave you to your thoughts, then. I would not wish to make this awkward for you."

"It is only that I do not understand," Julia blurted out. "You were always—but why did you not say anything? You have had ample opportunity."

"And would you have accepted me at any point if I had told you?" Mr. Norwich replied. What hurt her the most about it was that he did not sound angry at all. Rather, he sounded resigned. As though this was something that he had thought about many a time.

"Would you have welcomed my courtship? Would you have seen me as a possible suitor to you? Or would you have simply been discomforted? Would you have turned me down gently?"

Julia opened her mouth—and then had to close it again.

For she would have simply turned him down. She would have possibly been just as shocked as she was now. But she would certainly never have thought of him romantically.

She was at a loss as to what to say. For he was right, and she had to acknowledge that. But neither could she fill him with assurances that now she was in love with him. That now she was drawn to him in the way that he wished.

Julia could not deny that Mr. Norwich was a handsome man. And that he was a good one. That his heart was in the right place, she had no doubt.

But...

Mr. Norwich sighed. "I must apologize. I see that I have brought you distress. That was never my aim. I ought to have remembered to sign my name on the first letter and this entire business would have been concluded that much sooner.

"I am sorry for taking away someone to whom you were close. For I suppose that in losing me you must lose your correspondent and I know that he was, as you stated, a safe place for you.

"It is my own fault that this folly continued on for so long. If I had not been a coward—if I had been a person possessing of an ounce of true responsibility and bravery I should have come to you at once. I would have rectified the situation once it had become such a mess.

"I will certainly not trouble you any further. If you wish to not see me at any future gatherings then you need only inform me. Please extend my deepest sincerities and apologies to your mother."

"To my mother? What for?"

"That I shall not be seeing her today," Mr. Norwich replied.

Julia could not help but feel that there was more to it than that. That in delivering that message she would be providing her mother with a second meaning lurking underneath the first.

"Yes, she does prefer to sleep in given how late the nights can run," Julia replied lamely. She felt completely wrong-footed and didn't know how to get back onto solid ground.

This was one of the few people in the world with whom she could always easily converse. And now it was as though they were strangers.

"I... suppose that I will take my leave of you, then," Mr. Norwich said at last. He bowed, and turned to go.

Julia swallowed around the sudden lump in her throat. She did not want him to leave. But she also did not know how to convince him to stay. Nor did she know what she would do or say if he did stay.

"How—how did you believe that this meeting would go?" she asked.

Mr. Norwich paused. He did not quite look at her as he spoke. Rather, he stared in the direction of the floor but seemed not to see it, nor to see anything else that was in front of him.

"I had hoped—I had allowed myself to hope—that I would be given the chance to propose to you.

"That I might officially offer you my heart and my hand. I can admit that I was not quite certain of how I would deliver such a proposal. I was rather hoping that I could rely upon... the impulse of the moment to carry me through.

"But I see that I overestimated myself and grew to hope for too much. We need not speak of this again. If you wish we may even pretend that this conversation or indeed even our entire correspondence never happened. I will follow your lead and behave in whatever manner will make you the most comfortable.

"Now, if you will excuse me, I have business to attend to this morning. You have nothing but my kindest thoughts left with you."

Before Julia could even think of what to say next, or if she even wanted to say anything next, Mr. Norwich was crossing out of the room.

He was gone.

Julia stood there for she knew not how long. It might have been only a minute or two. It might have been a full hour. She knew only that she felt rigid, fixed to the spot, even while her stomach churned and made her feel almost dizzy.

She still could not quite believe it. Mr. Norwich was her correspondent. He was her mystery gentleman.

He had been in love with her for all of this time. And she had never even begun to suspect.

Mother had known, though. Hadn't she?

Surely that was a part of why she had said that she wanted Julia to marry him. And that entire lecture the other day—Mother's whole speech about how Julia did not appreciate the people around her. How she did not see what was in front of her.

That must have been referring to Mr. Norwich.

Why else should her mother bring it up? Why else should she say all of those things to Julia? It was so out of the blue for her, but it hadn't been for her mother and wouldn't be if Mother had spent all of this time watching Mr. Norwich pine unrequitedly over her.

Julia did not wish to wake her mother up immediately but she knew that the moment she heard that Mother was awake, she would be speaking to her.

She had to sort out this mess inside of her head and her heart somehow. And who better to speak to about that than her mother?

Besides, she needed information. She needed to know what her mother knew. Because if she did know that Mr. Norwich was in love with Julia then what else did she know?

Did she know about the letters? Had the first letter been her idea? Had she been a part of this the entire time?

Or had she only observed the state that Mr. Norwich was in and felt pity for him?

Julia could feel shame rising in her, choking her. Her mother had pitied the man who was in love with her, because Julia herself could not see it.

She informed the servants that she would be taking no more calls that morning. She had a headache, and if anyone was to call, kindly tell them that she was indisposed that morning and to leave their card.

Then she went upstairs to her bedroom, locked the door, laid on her bed, and cried.

CHAPTER 64

JAMES WALKED HOME but did not notice anything on his journey.

The carriages, the other people, even the weather, were all lost to him. He could not have said whether it was raining or blessedly sunny. If he passed any acquaintances then he had no recollection of it. He did not see them.

She did not want him.

Despite growing close to him through letters. Despite declaring in those same letters that she loved him. Despite saying that she cared for him and wanted to know who he was.

She had realized who he truly was and she had found him wanting.

He ought to have known. It had been the greatest of follies to delude himself into thinking that she might ever see him and fall for him. He should have realized that she would be picturing some other man. A better man.

When he reached his home, he immediately informed the servants to begin packing up the house. "Prepare it for vacancy," he told them. "I shall be leaving as soon as everything is arranged for me to depart."

He sent a letter to his father to inform him that James would be returning to the estate in the country early. He asked that if there was any business in London that James needed to take care of for him to please inform James posthaste so that he could take care of it on his way home.

A few days should be long enough to get everything settled and to receive a letter in return from Father if he was needed in London.

He then went out, visiting business associates, letting them know that he would be concluding his business here for the time being. Most of them expressed sorrow at seeing him go but none questioned it.

He was to inherit a title, after all. It made sense that he would have to leave and go home to check up on the estate.

James made sure to send out his apologies to those who were hosting dinner parties and outings. He had been invited to some and had already accepted a few.

Now, however, he would not be in Bath to attend them.

He figured that it would take him no more than three days to take care of everything in Bath and prepare the house for a long absence. He saw no reason why he should be returning any time soon. Unless Father wanted to come and use the house for some reason. Which he did not count as likely.

Perhaps it was yet another act of cowardice. Perhaps this was running away. But he would not stay and torture himself any longer.

No more would he stand by the side of the woman that he loved and torture himself with knowing that she did not care for him as he did for her.

No longer would he pine after her and be her friend while hiding his true feelings.

He would always be her friend if she needed him. He could not exactly blame her for her lack of feelings. One could not control with whom one did and did not fall in love.

But he would need time to get over this blow. It was a crushing one and he did not think that anyone could expect him to recover from it in the span of only a day or two.

He would take his time in the country. Focus in on his work with his father. Go hunting and riding. Immerse himself in things that would hopefully distract him from Miss Weston.

James figured that if he timed it right, he would return from the country at the start of the next London season. He would undoubtedly see Miss Weston there. Most likely to be married at that point.

He was not sure if he could attend the wedding—but he knew

that he must. He was her friend. He would always be there for her if she needed him.

If she were to write to him out of the blue and ask for his aid, then he would give it. So many years of acquaintance demanded it. And besides, he would want to. He wanted to care for her and provide her with whatever peace of mind that he could.

It was only that he needed time. Hopefully he would have enough of it that he could see her during the season with a smile. That he would no longer feel that ache deep inside.

Many acquaintances expressed dismay when they received his messages informing them that he would be quitting Bath posthaste. He was a bit comforted to know that he was so valued by his social circle, but it was not enough to compel him to stay.

On the morning that he set out, he was almost tempted to ride past Miss Weston's house. He was leaving early, before most people of his station were up and about. She would most likely be asleep.

But there was no need to torture himself with that nonsense. He rode out of Bath, towards home.

Hopefully, towards the beginnings of healing his heart.

He did not look back.

CHAPTER 65

JULIA CRIED herself into a light slumber, awaking only when there was a knock at her bedroom door from the maid.

She quickly splashed her face with cold water, let the maid in, and then went to find her mother.

Mrs. Weston was sitting in the drawing room, enjoying a leisurely cup of tea, staring out one of the windows.

"I thought that I had heard you get up this morning," her mother said. "But then I saw that you were still abed. Or that you had gone back to bed. Is everything all right? Do you feel ill?"

"I am not ill. At least, I have no illness of the body." Julia sat down next to her. "Mother. When you spoke to me the other day. When you were so harsh.

"You said that there were people around me that I did not appreciate as I should. People who I had overlooked.

"Were you speaking of any person in particular? Were you speaking, perhaps, of Mr. Norwich?"

Understanding lit up Mrs. Weston's eyes and she gave a slow nod. "Ah. I see. Did he call upon you this morning?"

Julia nodded.

"And that is why you went back to bed."

She nodded again. She did not trust herself to speak without crying.

Mother reached over, taking Julia's hand in hers. "Ah, my darling. You know that he would never wish to upset you."

"It is not his feelings that upset me," Julia admitted, her voice going high as she struggled to hold in her tears. "It is the knowledge that I have been so selfish. So unobservant. I ought to have known."

"He did not wish for you to know. He hid it from you. He hides himself from everyone very well. Better than most people realize. They only see the jovial heir. But I remember the boy that he was and I think I am one of the few who knows of the depths hidden in his heart.

"But he did not wish for you to know how he felt and so he put on his mask. The mask that he has been wearing all of his life. How were you supposed to see through it when it was not his intention that you should?"

"He is my friend. And I took him for granted."

"I am not saying that you did not. And I do think that an apology of some kind might be in order."

"How did you know? Did you suspect?"

"I confess that I did not. I thought that it was always a possibility, seeing as you are a lovely young lady and he is a gentleman.

"But when I approached him and confided in him that I wished he would be the man to win your heart, I thought that this might be the first time that the idea had occurred to him."

"You—" Julia stumbled over her words. "You asked him to try and court me?"

"I thought that you two would be well suited for one another. Out of all the gentlemen of your acquaintance, he was the one that I liked best. Both for his own sake and as a partner for you."

"Did you—were you—did you suggest to him how he might win me?"

She honestly did not know if she expected her mother to say yes or no regarding the letters. On the one hand to suggest such a thing was improper. On the other hand, her mother telling Mr. Norwich at all that she was rooting for him was also improper.

And her mother was not always one to stoop to the strictest definitions of propriety. Her wit saw to that.

But her mother shook her head. "No. I only told him that you might not realize how much value he held for you until he told you of his feelings.

"He was adamant, you see, that you did not care for him in that fashion. I agreed that either you did not or that if you did you were unaware of it. I told him that it would not hurt him to try. After all, one cannot be certain of one's reception until one asks."

"And that was when he told you that he harbored affection for me?"

"He hinted as much, although he did not confess it outright until later when I pressed him as to why he was not courting you."

Mother did not know about the letters, then. Julia was unsure if she was relieved or not.

For how could she confess to her mother what she and Mr. Norwich had been doing? There was a strong likelihood that Mother would be furious and condemn both Julia and Mr. Norwich for the scheme.

But on the other hand, how could she disclose to her mother all that had happened, how could she seek her mother's full advice, if she did not tell her the entire truth?

"Did he propose?" Mrs. Weston asked gently. More gently than Julia had expected.

"I believe that he meant to. But he did not get much farther than disclosing his feelings."

"Did you tell him that you did not return them?"

"I was not sure what to think. It was quite a shock to me. I tried to inquire further so that I could understand. But I honestly do not know what to feel, or what to think."

Julia looked up at her mother. "Tell me what you think I should do."

Her mother thought for a moment.

"I think that you are welcome to all the time that you need in order to process what you have just been told. There is nothing wrong with needing a bit of time to adjust to some new information.

"But I would assure him, in person or through writing, that you have not fully rejected him. That is most likely what he believes to be the case and I think it would be unfair of you to keep him in despair for too long."

"Would it not be more cruel to give him some kind of hope only to take it away again if I decide that I do not care for him in that manner?"

"I suppose that is one way to look at it. But you can also consider that at least this way he will know that whatever your answer may turn out to be, you gave him the thought and consideration that he deserves.

"This way he will know that you did not dismiss him out of hand. That you do care for him, enough to think about his potential as your husband."

Julia thought that was a fair point. "You want me to marry him."

"I want you to be happy. And I believe that he will make you happy. I know that we are past the age of purely arranged marriages. And I do think that a lady should be allowed her choice in a husband.

"But there is also something to be said for how well a parent does—or should—know their child. I believe that I do know you rather well. And that all parents should understand what sort of person their child is. The kind of person their child would be good with, the sort of person who would be able to give their child what they needed in a marriage.

"I believe that out of all the young men that I know, Mr. Norwich will be best able to take care of you. That he will be able to provide you with what you need. That he will safeguard your heart.

"I know that you do not love him as of this moment. But you do respect him. You know him well, and you two have spent many years as acquaintances. You have respect for him. And he is in love with you.

"You could do far worse for a husband, if you should ask me. And I think that his temperament is perfectly suited for yours.

"Mr. Carson, for example—he would never indulge your imaginative nature, your sense of romance, the way that Mr. Norwich would. If you but gave him the chance I think he could be capable of quite a bit of romance."

Oh, Mother, you have no idea, Julia thought. He was a romantic man. He had written her letters. Made up a special pet name for her. Poured his heart and soul into his correspondence with her.

"He respects you greatly and appreciates your intelligence. And you two are equals in wit. He makes you laugh. I do not know of any other man who makes you laugh or stands up to your wit as he does.

"Most other men would be irritated at such an intelligent and headstrong wife. But he appreciates it and indulges it when you are getting to be a bit too much for most others. I think that is something that you cannot afford to overlook.

"I could simply be your overprotective mother. I know that I worry about you and your father too much. Especially you. But if you do want my honest opinion, dear, and if I were to pick out any man for you to marry... it would be him.

"And he is a darling boy. He always has been. He was your father's favorite, you know. Or perhaps you don't. But the poor man was never close to his mother. Flighty, vain thing she was. I never could stand her.

"I know it's wrong of me to speak ill of the dead so I shan't go on about it but in any case. Your father and I always viewed him as a son to us. We would like for him to be happy as well.

"Because when you are looking at a potential couple—you aren't simply looking at one half of it, are you?" Mrs. Weston smiled softly at her. "You're looking at both parts. He might be good for you but you might not be good for him, or the other way 'round.

"I fear that too many people find someone who will be good for their child and then never stop to think about if their child will be good for that person.

"After all, it takes two people to make a marriage happy. If one person's needs are fulfilled but the other's are not then we have an unhappy union on our hands. And nobody wants that.

"I believe that you would be just as good for him as he would be for you. You would help him to be genuinely lighthearted instead of pretending to be. You would be a safe place for his heart, I think, my dear."

Julia almost wanted to tell her mother that she already had been that for him, through their letters. But now she was no longer certain if that was true.

She had been so focused on what her mysterious gentleman was to her. How important he was to her happiness. She had never stopped to think about just what she was contributing to the relationship. If she was being all for him that he was being for her.

He had told her that he had feelings for her. And so she had taken it for granted that she was fulfilling his emotional needs. But had she been? Truly?

She didn't know anymore. It terrified her to think that perhaps she had been failing to hold him up and support him as he had been supporting and holding her.

"It is your choice in the end," her mother concluded. "But now you know my thoughts on the matter. I actively encouraged him to pursue you. I thought only that it might help."

"When did you know that you were in love with Father?" Julia asked.

Mother thought about that for a moment. Then she said, "You know, it was in the middle of the most mundane of days.

"I know that I have spoken to you before about how true romance is to be found in the little things. This was one such time.

"You see, I had just learned that I was pregnant with our first child." A sad light came into her mother's eyes. "He was named after your father, although he died without having once breathed. But that was later. At the time I was just so happy.

"For while I had respected your father and been well acquainted with him, the true reason for my excitement over marriage was that I wanted to have a child. Several children."

"I am sorry," Julia blurted out, "if I have not been enough. I know I cannot make up for the loss of so many."

"You are more than enough," her mother said sternly. She patted Julia's cheek. "You are the apple of my eye, my darling. You have no responsibility to make up for the losses we received. That is not your burden."

Julia nodded, and Mrs. Weston smiled, squeezing her hand and then sitting back.

"In any case, I was quite excited. It was also my first time dealing with such a thing, and as you can imagine I had quite a lot to learn.

"One of the things that I had not thought about was that I would develop such unusual food cravings. I did not think that your father noticed since he was so busy all the time. And I was the person who spoke with the cook and handled such matters.

"But I had developed the deepest love of apple pie while I was pregnant. I struggled not to ask for it from the cook too much, for I knew that they would soon be out of season and I did not wish to bother her. Nor did I wish to waste our funds on such a frivolous matter.

"Furthermore, your father did not—and he still does not—like apple pies. I did not wish to impose them too much upon him.

"Yet I noticed that even on the nights when I did not ask for them, there would be an apple pie for me. And not a large one, either, but a small one that was the perfect size for just one person.

"I asked the cook about it, and she told me that your father had come to speak to her about the matter. He had noticed how unhappy I was when there was not an apple pie after supper and had asked the cook to always make one for me, only a smaller one so that we would make the apples last longer and I would not feel ashamed of making him eat any.

"It was such a simple little thing. But it showed how well he noticed what I liked and what I wanted. And he went out of his way to make sure that I knew I could have what made me happy.

"And the smaller pies just for myself meant that we could stretch the crop of apples longer and I was able to have the pie for longer than I should have otherwise.

"It was rather sweet of him. It was him giving me permission to eat what I wanted and never to mind him. And for a gentleman to go into the kitchen and avail himself of the domestic side of things, so that his wife could be happy!

"In that moment, I realized that I was in love with your father. This sweet man who had done such a gesture for me and who had not expected praise or recognition for it.

"To be sure, it was not a new dress, or a fine piece of jewelry, or a trip to the seaside. But it was a sign of how much he paid attention to me. How he was willing to go out of his way for me. That he truly cared."

Julia could not help but smile. It was a sweet story, and one that she had not ever heard before about her parents.

It made her think about Mr. Norwich. Or, rather, him and her mystery correspondent.

Her correspondent had taken great care to pay attention to her. He had given her a specific pet name, one based upon both her looks and her personality. He had responded to her fears and had supported her.

Mr. Norwich had though as well, had he not?

He was always the person that she knew she could trust. If she had told him about the letters she knew he would have kept the secret. It had only been her fear of laughing about it that had prevented her from saying anything.

She had not thought that he had a romantic bone in his body. Yet his letters had been filled with such sweet things.

He was a loyal friend to her. He always bantered with her and sat with her at dinner. He never seemed to grow tired of her. He helped her out when she felt that she was in trouble. When her parents had told her that she must marry, he had been the person to whom she had run for support.

True, he had not given her what some would consider to be proper romantic gestures. But what were flowers or ribbons when he poured his heart out to her in a letter? When he trusted her not to spoil the whole exchange of letters by gossiping? When he validated her and told her not to settle for anyone refusing to accept who she was, including her intelligence?

Not to mention the whole mysterious letter business was fairly romantic in and of itself.

She had a romance in front of her the entire time. Waiting for her. She had simply failed to notice it.

And then when it had found her in spite of herself, she had bungled it.

Julia wondered if she would be able to know if she loved Mr. Norwich the way that her mother had known that she loved her father.

"Oh, my love, don't be upset," her mother said, sensing her distress. "You will find it in time. I think that you will find it with Mr. Norwich but you are a very loveable person. If not him, then someone else."

"Am I not running out of time, though?" Julia asked. "You and Father have said..."

"Well I do wish that you would hurry up with finding it," Mother laughed. "And that you would take the entire thing more seriously. But there is no reason to panic."

"I fear that I have lost not only a potential husband, as you say, but a friend."

"Whether you harbor romantic feelings for him or not, I know that Mr. Norwich will not abandon your friendship. He is too decent of a man for that. He might need some time to recover from the blow, but he will not turn his back on you."

Julia nodded. She had quite a lot to think about.

"Is there anything else that you wish to ask me?" Mrs. Weston asked, an amused twinkle in her eye.

"How you can be so lighthearted about this, Mother, I have no idea. You do know that the poor man's heart is at stake. And possibly mine."

"Trust me, my dear, I am very much aware. But somebody must play the part of laughing at heartache and sorrow. Otherwise we should all be far too serious for our own good."

Julia smiled wanly. "I hope that it will be all right if I do not go to the ball tonight. I would prefer to stay at home."

That was the benefit of the public balls at Bath. She would not even have to bother sending a regretful letter informing her hostess that she could not attend. For there was no official host.

"We will make an evening of it together," her mother replied. "I can read to you as I did when you were a child. We can play cards. Perhaps I shall even have the strength for singing while you play the pianoforte, hmm?"

Julia's smile grew. "I would like that." She had not had an evening with just herself and her mother in far too long.

"Good. Now, off with you. I have to nap in the sun and you I am sure have household business to which you must attend."

Julia rose, kissing her mother on the cheek. This, at least, was a love that she did not doubt.

CHAPTER 66

WHILE SHE WHILED AWAY the afternoon, for once not getting ready for a ball, Julia decided to write to Georgiana.

She had been writing to Georgiana faithfully, but she had not told her about the mystery gentleman with whom she was corresponding.

First of all, she had not wanted to bother Georgiana with such news while her dearest friend was busy planning her wedding.

Second of all, she simply had not been able to risk the letter falling into the wrong hands.

The more people who knew about the secret, the more likely it was to get out. A moment of carelessness on Georgiana's part and her maid might read the letter. Then the maid would tell another, and another, and one of them was sure to tell her mistress, whoever that might be.

And then it would have been all over.

Not to mention, she could not have asked Georgiana to keep such a secret from her fiancé Captain Trentworth. Those two told one another everything.

But now she simply had to write to her. She needed the advice of her best friend. And she knew that Georgiana would not judge her for her actions.

She spent nearly all afternoon on the letter. She had to get rid of several first drafts. They were far too rambling, too detailed, and too emotional.

There was no reason to make Georgiana read words that were smudged with tears. Nor did she need to know every single detail about each letter they exchanged.

And if she was to write to her, then it must have some sort of cohesion and follow the timeline of events. Rather than skipping around and stumbling and interjecting all over the place.

Honestly. It was as if she'd never written a letter before.

At least it was Georgiana and so Julia could be more candid than she could with anyone else.

Well, anyone else besides her mystery correspondent.

She had not realized until now just how much she had told him until he was taken away from her. Normally if she was upset, she would write him a letter.

It had not been something that she had intended. It had simply... happened. It had become a habit to share with him not only her dreams and aspirations but her fears and her woes.

Now that she had lost him, she was able to understand how important he had been to her. How unfair was that? How could life dare to be so ironic?

Or, rather, how could she dare to be so very stupid.

She felt like a hopeless little girl, a silly little girl, all over again. She told Georgiana as such in her letter.

I am at a complete loss as to what to do. I fear that I have wounded him irreversibly.

And I deeply mourn the loss of my companion. Both my friend Mr. Norwich and my mysterious gentleman. I had not realized how much I relied upon them both until they were taken from me.

Although that is an unfair way to put it. Mr. Norwich did not take my leave for any reason other than my own selfish behavior. I pushed him away in both of his forms.

I wish that I knew what I wanted. It feels as though all of my feelings and thoughts are a jumble and I don't know which way is up.

Part of me wishes that I had not pressed so hard to find out who my letter writer was. That I could have continued to have him in my life. For I did love him.

I do love him.

But I am unsure as to my feelings for Mr. Norwich.

I am terribly sad to have potentially lost his friendship. He has always been a man upon whom I could rely. I know that he was most kind to you when you were going through that unfortunate business with Captain Trentworth. Before things were all sorted out, I mean.

He has been a loyal man and most thoughtful with me. I always knew that he was someone I could talk to in a crowd. I most enjoyed dancing with him at balls and now I suppose that I shall have to avoid him. Or that he will avoid me.

Mother says that he will not go so far as to end our friendship. He is a generous man, far more generous than I deserve, but I cannot help but wonder if he would be quite that generous.

I have, after all, dashed his hopes. And this was after I led him on for so long—but I did not mean to. I am in love and yet I am struggling to reconcile the man that I know from the letters with the man that I have known as my friend all this time.

She hoped that she was not rambling too much, or that if she was, Georgiana would forgive her. Georgiana was used to her explosions of emotion and rambling by now.

Julia concluded the letter with the sincere hope that Georgiana was doing well and to please inform her all about her wedding plans. Julia did genuinely look forward to the wedding and she wanted to hear all about how it was all going.

Once she sent out the letter, she retired to spend the rest of the day with her mother.

It was a surprisingly relaxing day. She did not quite manage to forget her woes but her mother did an admirable job of distracting Julia as best she could.

And it had been far too long since she had spent time only with her mother. It was important that she focus on that relationship. She didn't know how much time with her mother she had left.

She could not hide forever, however. She had her obligations to society. The next day she had to go out to a dinner party.

Julia could not deny that she dreaded it. The last that she had heard, the dinner would be attended not only by her but also by Mr. Norwich.

They had discussed it, in fact, only a week or so ago. They had both been looking forward to it.

She was not at all prepared to face him again. She felt so ashamed. And they would have to act as normal. Nobody knew that he had even been trying to court her.

When it came to a man proposing to a woman and being turned down, normally everyone knew that man had been courting her. It was a small mercy, because it meant that hostesses around the area could take care to not invite both parties to one place.

Or, if they did, it was to a much larger ball or dinner party where they need not interact with one another. It was a concession to the embarrassment that both parties must be feeling at that time.

But nobody knew. As far as anyone could tell, she and Mr. Norwich were still quite good friends.

Julia tried to brace herself all day for the inevitable. She would be courteous. No, more than that. She would be kind. Attentive.

She could not speak plainly but she could show him through her attitude and actions that she still respected him. She would not approach him, of course, unless he approached her.

She would not jump at him like a yippy sort of lap dog. She usually did, she had come to realize. The moment he walked in the door she would pounce on him, asking questions, throwing information at his head, yammering on.

How had he ever put up with her? She must have been horrid.

Well, she would have to find some way to apologize to him for it. For everything. All of the mistakes she had made over the years.

But when she got to the dinner party that evening...

The very first thing that her hostess did was hurry up to her. Mrs. Longsome was a chatterbox but well-meaning.

"Ah, Miss Weston! How is your mother? Is she doing better? Have you heard from your father? We do so miss his company at the dinner table. Quite a wit he is."

Mrs. Longsome could and would go on for quite some time if she was allowed to. Julia allowed it to simply wash over her, not really worried. The longer she spoke to Mrs. Longsome, the less chance she'd have of running into Mr. Norwich and being forced to speak with him.

Yes, she was aware that it was a cowardly thing to do. But with so much still left unsaid between them, as well as too much that had been said already and could not be taken back... She did not think that the two of them speaking with one another was the best idea.

"...it is rather sad that Mr. Norwich had to send his regrets and not come after all..."

"What?" Julia blurted out. "Mrs. Longsome, what did you say? Mr. Norwich will not be attending tonight?"

"Oh, but I thought that you must know! Your families are such great friends, after all. You two are always talking together at parties and such. Why, there was even a time where..."

"Mrs. Longsome, please, did he say why he would not be attending?"

"Did you hear nothing at all?" Mrs. Longsome looked torn between concern over this and eagerness to be the one to share such news with her. "Well, it appears that he has been called back to his home estate by his father. He has quit Bath entirely."

"Entirely?"

"Oh, yes. If he has not left already I expect that he will be gone by tomorrow. Or perhaps the day after. But it should not take him long to set his affairs in order so that he can depart."

It felt as though all of the air had gone out of the room.

Mr. Norwich had left. He had gone. And but for what reason other than because of her?

Julia did not buy that excuse about his father sending for him. She did not buy it for a single moment.

Others might believe it. And why should they not? They knew nothing about what had only just gone on between her and Mr. Norwich.

But she knew. And this astounded her.

She had not realized that she had hurt him so deeply that he must flee. For it had to be in order to avoid her that he had gone.

Oh, she must be the most awful and ungrateful of people. To drive away a good man in such a fashion!

It was a good thing that nobody knew about their almost-courtship. She would never hear the end of it through the gossip chain.

Nobody would have dared to say anything to her face. That was not proper. But she would have managed to hear all the same. Just as Georgiana had unfortunately heard all those barbs about becoming an old maid, before Captain Trentworth had shown up on the scene again.

She was glad that she had taken the risk along with Mr. Norwich in the writing of the letters. It meant that at least now that things had gone sour, nobody knew about it.

Yet, Julia could not suppress the ache in her chest at the thought of him leaving. Not only was it because of her and her own awful behavior, but it was also because she was going to miss him.

She did miss him. Who was she going to speak with at parties now? Who could she rely on as a wonderful dance partner at balls?

She had thought that having to see him at these social events and enduring the awkwardness would be awful. And it would be. She knew that it would be, she could tell. But it would be a different kind of awful from this and she wanted that other kind of awful.

This was miserable. She felt his absence like someone had taken something out of her chest and left it nothing but an echoing and empty cavern.

The dinner party felt dull to her. As though the lights had been dimmed. She could hardly remember any conversation afterwards on her way home.

When she got home she slept roughly, lightly, waking up several times, discomforted.

"How was everything?" her mother asked when Julia came down to breakfast the next morning.

"Everything was quite up to standard. Mrs. Longsome gives her regards and says that they miss Father at their parties."

"And how was Mr. Norwich? Were you two able to remain civil to one another?"

"He was not there," Julia admitted.

Mrs. Weston frowned, setting down her knife and fork. "Not there?"

"He has gone out of town. Back home to his country estate. They said it was because his father summoned him but I know that it is because of me."

"Oh, my dear." Mrs. Weston's face was sympathetic. "It will all blow over with time, I can assure you. At the least, you do not have your own broken heart to worry about."

But I do, Julia wanted to scream. I loved the man I was writing to. I do still love him.

She knew it was cruel of her to think in this way. But it felt as though Mr. Norwich had snatched that man from her. That the man she was in love with had melted away like snow in spring.

Now she was left with a double image. A man that was both the person she knew and loved and a friend that she was realizing she did not know nearly so well as she thought she had.

In fact, she did not know her friend at all.

He was a stranger to her. He had long harbored thoughts of love for her that she had not even guessed at. And she had always considered him to be the sort of man who had not a care in the world. Yet it turned out, through his letters, that he was a very thoughtful and serious person who was private, hiding himself from others.

She could vividly recall when she had spoken of Mr. Norwich to Georgiana, who had not yet met him. She had called him the sort of person who had everything in the world and so did not always consider why others would take things so seriously.

How foolish she had been! How she had underestimated him! It made her stomach clench in embarrassment to think on it now.

Georgiana had told her of Mr. Norwich's kindness towards her during the trying time of her courtship with Captain Trentworth. There had been much frustration and mistakes made by the captain and Georgiana during that time. Although, if you asked Julia, the majority of the blame still lay on the captain's shoulders. Though she had forgiven him, for he adored Georgiana, and Georgiana loved him dearly.

When Julia had heard about it all from Georgiana she had been uncommonly impressed with Mr. Norwich. She had taken it to be because Mr. Norwich had felt some measure of attraction towards Georgiana.

She could not blame him for that. Georgiana was a remarkable woman. And if he was in love with Julia all that time and knew she did not love him back, why shouldn't he consider another woman instead?

In any case, she had thought it was all because of his attraction to Georgiana. And because Captain Trentworth had known Mr. Norwich's brother and was staying at his house as a result.

But now she could easily guess that Mr. Norwich would have been so kind and supportive no matter who the lady in question was.

How badly she had misjudged him.

How could she say that she was in love with someone when she did not, in truth, know who they were? When they were a stranger to her? Someone that she had written off and misjudged all of these years?

If only she had seen him for who he truly was. If only she had not been so narrow-minded in her judgment, so self-centered.

At the very least, she supposed, she could learn not to make the same mistake with others in her life. If it was not already too late with some of them.

Mrs. Weston seemed to sense her continued dark mood, for she said little and allowed Julia to eat her breakfast in silence.

The next two weeks felt empty, drained of color. She had not realized until he was gone how much she had relied upon Mr. Norwich for companionship at balls and dinner parties.

He would even accompany her and her friends, or her and her mother, when they went shopping. He would carry their parcels for them. And when she wanted to go out on an excursion, he was the male chaperone who would go with her and the ladies so that they would be safe from any misadventure.

Now that he was gone, she found herself without one of the pillars of her social life. She would have to find a new male chaperone for some things, and she did not look forward to it. Why on earth would she want to pick another man when they were all so dull-witted and boring and full of themselves?

Julia had always struggled to find a man who could hold her attention. A man who appreciated her wit. This was not new. But it was only now that she realized that Mr. Norwich had been fulfilling those roles for her, those needs, and she had not even realized it.

Every time she had to talk to a man at a dinner party or dance with one at a ball, she found herself wishing that she was speaking with Mr. Norwich instead.

How she had relied upon him. She had gone to him in between each set of dancing in order to speak with him. Now she could not.

When she got a new bit of gossip she would instinctively turn to find him and share it with him—but now he was not there.

She was tempted to write to him. To share through letters all that was going on. To tell him that she missed him.

But how could she do such a thing? It would be selfish of her to focus only on the ways in which she missed him. She had to think about what she had been to him and not only on what he had been to her.

He was her dear friend. But she had been his source of unhappiness. The woman who had taken him for granted.

She could not write to him now talking about how she missed him. He was not a servant who had the job of entertaining her. She had no hold over him, could make no demands.

It was as she was trying to balance herself in this new, strange equilibrium that Georgiana's response arrived in the mail.

Julia opened it eagerly, hardly breathing as she tried to read her friend's words.

Georgiana had always been the more level-headed out of the two of them. Georgiana, surely, would know what to do. How to sort this out and make things right again.

My dear Julia,

It feels as though it has been an age since I saw you last. I confess that I deeply miss your cheerful and energetic company...

The letter detailed how the wedding plans were going. How wonderful Captain Trentworth was. How Georgiana's brother and sister-in-law were faring. And so on.

Julia read through that part happily but with a bit of annoyance. She was desperate to know what Georgiana thought about the entire Mr. Norwich situation.

But she did acknowledge that it was clever of Georgiana to put all the other news first. If she had put it after the Mr. Norwich part, Julia should never have read it.

Clearly, her friend knew her all too well.

At last, Georgiana got to the part that Julia was dying to read.

...as for your situation with Mr. Norwich.

I must say that I am a bit surprised. I had never guessed, not even once, that he harbored such feelings for you. Which I can assume was his aim.

He was, as you know, perfectly thoughtful and kind to me when I stayed with you in Bath. He even insinuated that he would be happy to marry me if I had no other options.

I thought it strange that he should suggest such a thing. His admiration for me was genuine, I could sense, but it did seem premature.

Now that I know he was in love with you, it makes much more sense. If a man cannot be with the lady that he loves, then saving another woman from the ruin of spinsterhood is a perfectly acceptable option. Especially if one does truly respect the lady in question.

The one facing spinsterhood, I mean. I should hope that if a man is in love with a woman that he would of course respect her as well. I do not see how it is possible to love someone that you do not also respect.

But in any case.

While it was astonishing to me in the moment to read, as I reflected upon it, it made quite a lot of sense that he should be in love with you. I think that a great number of men have been in love with you at one time or another, my dear.

If you truly do not love him in return then I think perhaps some distance would be wise. This will give the both of you time to reflect and to calm yourselves after what has happened. You can both begin to heal.

However, I must be frank with you.

The way that you spoke about Mr. Norwich in your letters revealed a tenderness towards him and a reliance on him that I do not think even you have realized. I do not think that you know how deep your affection for him goes.

You were aware that you had feelings for the man to whom you were writing those letters. How is that man any different from Mr. Norwich?

And unless I recall him inaccurately, he is a handsome man. Rather your type of handsome, I believe. The sort of look that you find most attractive.

The man that you know as Mr. Norwich is still the man that you know from the letters. They are not two different or separate people. Therefore, if you love one then you must love the other.

But even if that were not enough to persuade you, my dear Julia, I must again point out how you spoke about Mr. Norwich himself.

Even I had not grasped until your letter just how important he was in your life. The depth of regard that you hold for him is immense. He is a fixture in your life already. I would not be surprised if many people believe you two to already have been courting.

You speak of him as your friend. As your confidant. As someone who is entertaining and witty. Your favorite person to dance with. Someone who is so a part of your life that you cannot imagine your life without him in it.

Julia, darling. Do you not see what has happened?

You are indeed in love with Mr. Norwich as well as your friend from your letters. It is fortunate that they are one and the same. If they were not, then I suspect you would have gone through your entire life without realizing how and what you felt for Mr. Norwich.

But since they are the same person, now the truth may hit you full in the face, as it really ought to. My dear, silly girl.

I think that perhaps that was even part of the reason why you fell in love with this letter writer. You told me that when you thought it might be Mr. Carson you felt an odd sense of disappointment.

I believe that is because, whether you realized it or not, you wanted it to be Mr. Norwich.

Love is not always something that strikes us suddenly. It is something that can creep up upon us without looking. It is found in the small things.

You are not in love with one version of a man and confused about the other side of him. Rather, you are in love with one person, and have simply allowed yourself to overthink yourself into a tizzy.

Please forgive my forward language. But it is my duty as a best friend to inform you when you are making a mistake, is it not? And this is far from the first time you have done such a thing, my dear. Your imagination and emotion are wonderful but they can also allow you to become carried away or to overthink things.

Now, I cannot tell you how to proceed. This is your affair and indeed your life. Not mine. But if I were you, I should inform him of my thoughts.

I should tell him that I was in love with him and returned his affections to their fullest depth and extent. I should apologize for any confusion and for taking so long to come to the realization.

I would tell them that all the things I said in my letter to him when he was simply my mystery correspondent were true.

Now, I know that must be a frightening prospect for you. I am certain that it would be frightening for me as well.

Telling Captain Trentworth about the truth of my feelings for him the second time was quite terrifying. Standing up to him was terrifying as well. But both things were necessary and we are better off for them.

It might be difficult for you to find the words. Personally, that is why I think a letter should be best. You have a tendency to rather... well, there was the time you rather lost your temper with Captain Trentworth.

Not that he did not deserve it. He wishes to have me inform you that he does understand the... what he calls a 'tongue lashing' was richly deserved.

In any case, I do think that to avoid saying anything you would later wish to take back, or to avoid any embarrassing moments such as bursting into tears... it might be for the best if you write him a letter.

But I really would consider doing such a thing, Julia. I do not know if you can hear yourself when you speak of him. Or if you truly read what you have written about him when you go back over your letters to check for spelling errors.

The regard in which you hold him is so painfully obvious to me. I'm certain that I cannot be the only one who has noticed such a thing. Has nobody ever asked you about your relationship with him? Am I going mad here or is everyone else blind? Or perhaps too scared of the retribution to say anything?

I would not be surprised if that were the case. You really are too witty for your own good at times.

Which reminds me of that lovely little pet name he gave you. Julia, most people only dream of finding a love like that. Most people consider themselves lucky to continue to respect their spouse after the initial blush of infatuation has faded.

I know of far too many couples where one spouse has come to despise the other. Or where they both barely tolerate one another. Or, as seems to most often be the case, they are simply used to one another and treat each other like furniture. There is no warmth or true regard in their interactions.

But you have been lucky enough to find a man who truly loves you and understands you. Please, do not be so foolish as to throw that away. Not when you also understand and love him.

As someone who once practically threw away her own chance at love, I know of what I speak. I was lucky enough that the captain came back into my life and gave me a second chance.

Not everyone is so fortunate.

And finally, my dear, I must say that I think that you have done yourself a disservice.

You say that you do not know the man. That you do not appreciate him and that you have overlooked him. Now, this all may be true to an extent. I think it is important that we admit our faults and confess when we have done something wrong.

But you do understand him. You do know who he truly is. You have seen it through the letters.

Who Mr. Norwich is in public is not a complete lie. It is merely another side of himself. You have spent enough time with him over the years that I daresay you knew him better than you thought you did, even before the letters.

You are inclined to be far more tough upon yourself than is your due. You are not so selfish as you fear.

We are all guilty of being short-sighted at times. Of making mistakes. Of not appreciating those around us or not even seeing them clearly. Not appreciating how much they mean to us.

I cannot say that I was blameless in my courtship with Captain Trentworth. Nor can he. When my brother was courting his wife, they both made grave errors in judgment. I remember that there was one point where they were both convinced that the other hated them.

Shakespeare can be rather overdone but he had a point when he wrote that the course of true love never did run smooth. There are going to be times when you make mistakes. The point is to acknowledge them, apologize, and do better. Without destroying yourself inside because of it.

To err is human, my dear.

I do hope that you will take a look at your own words and actions and realize what I have seen. That you will come to understand that you had fallen in love with Mr. Norwich without realizing it. That he is the same man that you fell for through letters and that he would make you happy.

I truly think that you two will be happy together.

This is all simply my opinion, of course. But you did ask for my opinion. And so now you have it.

Please be sure to write to me and tell me how you fare and what your decision is. I admit that I am full of excitement over the developments. And it will give me something to think about other than this wedding.

I am quite looking forward to being married. The wedding itself, however, is much more work than I think is due.

In any case. Please do let me know how it gets on. I wish for nothing but happiness for you. It is in your grasp, I am certain, if you only will have the courage to see what is right in front of you and seize it.

With all of my love and support I remain, as ever,

Georgiana

Julia stared down at the letter.

Already in love with Mr. Norwich?

She was in a chair before she even realized that she had made to sit down.

In love with Mr. Norwich... and not even having realized it?

It sounded ridiculous. Like something only a heroine in a particularly stupid play would do.

Yet... Mother had talked about how she hadn't realized she was in love with Father until that gesture with the apple pie.

Could it be that she had fallen for him and had not seen it because it was all in the little things, as Mother and Georgiana had said?

Was it possible that part of why she had realized she fell for the letter writer was that he was obviously romantic in the way that she

was looking for? He wrote to her in secret, risking his and her reputation. He gave her pet names. Spoke ardently about himself and
about his thoughts for her.

He had been clear in his romantic intent from the moment that
they had begun their correspondence. In his day-to-day self,
however, he had not been.

Instead he had shown her his love through subtleties. Through
being trustworthy. Through always carrying her shopping, always
chaperoning her. By listening to her and being patient with her. By
making her laugh and indulging her sense of humor and wit.

In all of those little ways, he had shown her that he loved her.
And she had accepted them and fallen for him without even realizing that was what she was doing.

It stole over her softly, like realizing that she had taken one glass
of wine too many and was now beginning to feel fuzzy in her head,
that whooshing feeling in her stomach.

She—she was in love with Mr. Norwich.

She had been for some time.

All this while she had seen him only as a friend, consciously,
while in her heart she had been harboring for him the feelings that
he had been holding for her.

How could she have been so thoughtless towards the workings
of her own heart?

She was suddenly, immeasurably grateful that Mr. Norwich had
written to her. Had he not, she would never have considered him.
She would have gone on as she had been and never would have
realized the depth of her feelings for him.

It explained why she was not happy when she thought Mr.
Carson was her mystery correspondent. And why she was so
wretched and distraught when Mr. Norwich left. Why she thought
of him so often.

She had not only overlooked his place in her life and his feelings for her. She had overlooked her own feelings for him.

Truly, was there any woman quite as stupid as she? Could any
other person on Earth claim to have been so unaware of
themselves?

She wanted to find a carriage and go right to his estate and run to him. If he had still been in town she would have been tempted to quite literally run, through the streets, to bang on his door.

It felt as though there was something inside of her, far too big for her body to hold. It swelled up, overpowering and gentle all at once. A great wave of feeling.

Yet at the same time, it felt as though she was simply coming home.

But could she dare to say all of this to him?

How could she possibly admit that she had not known not only how he felt but how she herself felt? How could she say such things to him?

He would think that she was lying. Making fun of him. Or else he would think that she was the most witless girl on the planet.

Either way, he could not possibly want her, could he?

Not after the way that she had treated him. Not after her own ignorance had chased him away. Not after she had been selfish and unthinking.

Julia remembered what else Georgiana had said—to be kinder to herself. To not be so hard upon herself when she made a mistake.

She was worried that Mr. Norwich would not be able to forgive her. But perhaps the better question was whether or not she would be able to forgive herself.

She didn't know.

If he forgave her—then she might. But she was not sure. What could she do that could possibly make up for the way that she had behaved?

"What does Georgiana say?" Mrs. Weston asked.

"She says that in my writing to her, it sounds as though I am in love with Mr. Norwich and have been for some time without knowing it."

Her mother hummed thoughtfully.

"She also says that I must forgive myself for my mistakes and not to be too hard upon myself. And that I ought to write to him and tell him of how I am feeling."

"Wise words."

"I do not know if I can follow them."

"What, you will not write to him?"

"I am still considering that matter. I meant more that... I am not certain if I can forgive myself."

"It might take time. We must allow for that. But, do you love him? Has Georgiana got it right?"

Julia took a deep breath, then nodded. "I believe that she is right, Mother. That I have been... oh such a wretched fool."

"Ah, none of that. We have all been fools for love in our time."

"Yes, but usually we are fools for love in the sense that we do stupid things in order to win over the people that we love. Not in the sense that we are not even aware that we are in love!"

"You raise a fair point. But everyone is different. You have learned greatly from this experience, have you not?"

"Well... yes. I hope that I have."

"That is all that life is about, my dear. We are all of us constantly learning and growing. There is no need to hurt yourself too much over it.

"For it is not truly the mistakes that matter. We are all going to make them at one time or another. What matters is what you do about them once you make them.

"Do you sit there and cry about the matter? Do you rail against yourself but take no steps to actually remedy the situation? Or do you step up and admit to your misstep and clean up whatever mess you have made?

"That is what matters. That is what people will remember. Not whether you made the mistake in the first place but what you did to fix it once the deed was done.

"Your ability to move forward. Your ability to forgive yourself. Your ability to be humble and to admit to your wrongdoings. Those are what matter in the end.

"Nobody wants to hear anyone go on and on about all the things that they did wrong. You will remember your own mistakes and failings for far longer than anyone else will.

"Just as there will be people who will accidentally or purposefully wrong you. You will forget about what they have done far sooner than they will. Your own guilt eats at you more than your condemnation of others eats at your opinion of them."

Julia nodded. She did not suddenly feel as though she was worthy of forgiveness. But her mother's words were wise. She supposed that she would just have to let time take care of her opinion of herself.

"Please do write to him, dear," Mrs. Weston said softly. "It is what will make you both happy. No matter what apologies must be made. No matter what matters must be sorted out. Even if it will take you two some time to come together.

"If you love him, and he does still love you for love cannot simply be banished by rejection, then you must find a way to make it together. Because it is unfair to let your guilt and fear deprive you both of a happy relationship."

Julia could feel herself trembling with fear and anticipation. "Very well then," she whispered.

She would write to him. She did not know what would come of it. Or even if anything would come of it at all. But she would write him, and she would see.

Mrs. Weston smiled, clearly pleased. Her eyes were soft. "Oh, my dear. I do so hope that the both of you will be happy. You are both good children."

"We are neither of us children, Mother, and have not been for some years."

"Ah, but once a child in the eyes of a parent, always a child," her mother replied.

Julia could not help but smile at that. "Very well, I will allow the comparison."

"You both deserve happiness," Mrs. Weston repeated. "And I believe that you will be able to give it to each other."

Julia could only hope that her mother would prove to be right.

CHAPTER 67

SHE RESOLVED to write to Mr. Norwich the next morning. She needed the rest of the day to gather her thoughts and settle her mind.

But when she sat down to write the letter the next morning, she had scarcely pulled up her chair when she heard the sound of someone downstairs.

She had a caller.

Julia sighed and double-checked that she was presentable. It was most likely Miss Perry. She supposed that she ought to go down and receive the young lady or whoever else it might turn out to be. It was not her caller's fault that she was impatient to begin this letter.

She could start writing it once the person left. Who knew? Perhaps the call would distract her from her nerves.

Mr. Norwich was not even in front of her and she found herself trembling with the anticipation. She both wanted to know immediately what he looked like when he read the letter and what he was thinking. And she also did not want to know at all.

She both knew and did not know what to say. She thought she had an idea but she kept second-guessing herself.

Was this how he had felt when he had written that first letter to her? When he had not realized that he had forgotten to put down his name? When he had no idea what her response would be?

She had not given him enough credit for his courage. Now she knew his particular fear in this situation, for she was feeling it herself. She had of course known intellectually that it must be quite frustrating upon the poor nerves to do such a thing.

But knowing intellectually and feeling it, truly experiencing it, were two very different things. As she was now realizing.

Yes, perhaps some diverting discussion with Miss Perry or someone would do her some good.

Julia came down the stairs to enter the drawing room and receive her visitor—and paused.

It was not Miss Perry. Or any other woman, for that matter.

It was Mr. Carson.

Julia almost wanted to smack herself. She had completely forgotten about him in the midst of all of her other emotional turmoil.

Now it looked as though her time was up.

She almost wished to shake him. Almost. Letting out her frustration in that way, she knew, would not do her or anyone else any good. But it was quite tempting.

She knew that it was her own folly that one night that had led him to be hopeful. But since then she had given him no sign of favor. She had taken care to stay away from him. To be too busy to dance with him at balls.

Julia could not, of course, outright deny him. Not when he had not directly asked her for any promises. And not when propriety dictated that she do him the courtesy of responding to his company.

But she had done her best to make it clear, since that night, that she was not interested. Or that she was at least not going to encourage him in any way.

It was a delicate balance that ladies had to play. They could not be outright impolite to a gentleman. That would not be proper. It was important that everyone interacted at parties and that everyone was polite and understanding towards everyone else.

However, neither should ladies encourage a man or be too friendly with him. Both for the sake of propriety and to prevent the man from retaining any false hope.

Julia had thought that her lack of interest would be enough. A lack of response, surely, would show him that she was not prepared to continue their courtship. Such as it was. Mr. Carson had been rather slow in his courtship.

Perhaps he had sensed something about her relationship with Mr. Norwich that she herself had not perceived? Julia was full of questions and thoughts and possibilities. Perhaps that was why no other man had truly approached her or tried to court her.

But in any case, Mr. Carson had not been nearly so forward as suitors generally were. Julia had seen other men courting other women many a time and Mr. Carson had been practically meek about it.

It did not suit the man, if she was being honest with herself. But it might be her saving grace if he was about to do what she suspected he had come here to do.

"Miss Weston." Mr. Carson smiled at her. "It is a pleasure, as always, to see you. I was glad to hear that you were home. I worried that you might be out and about, making other calls."

"No, sir," Julia replied. "You have caught me at a fine moment. I was only writing some letters to friends. What can I do for you today? To what do I owe the pleasure of your company?"

Mr. Carson smiled at her. "Perhaps you might wish to sit down?"

"I thank you, sir, but I am fine just as I am, standing."

He nodded, as if to himself. Then he squared his shoulders and cleared his throat. "I hope that I am not about to be too forward. But I am hopeful. I cannot deny it.

"You are a wonderful lady. I remember you as a brilliant girl when you were a child. I was your father's pupil and I admired you as a person. However, I did not see you as a woman.

"Now I do. Having seen you again these past few months I have been struck with your grace and beauty. Almost instantly I was captivated by you."

Julia tried to keep her face neutral yet polite. Inside, however, she was cringing.

Mr. Norwich had never loved her simply for her looks. He had always seen and appreciated her personality, her intelligence, her wit. He had always truly seen her.

How could she have not appreciated him until he was gone? She must find a way to get him back as soon as possible.

When Mr. Norwich praised her in his letters and spoke of why he loved her, he mentioned first her wit. Her knowledge. Her energy. He spoke of who she was. He loved her quirks and her sharp tongue and her flights of fancy and her overwhelming nature.

Mr. Carson was droning on about her looks. Mr. Norwich had praised her fashion sense, her hairstyle, her dancing—parts of herself over which she had control.

She could not control whether she was pretty or not. It was nice to be told that she was but truly, she did not want a husband who only cared about what she looked like on his arm as they entered a ballroom.

"You are truly the shining star of any ballroom that you enter. It is little wonder that you are so popular. I am surprised, I confess, that more men have not asked for your hand. I thought for certain that you would have turned down at least one other proposal by now."

His words were charming but altogether too much for her. Ridiculously flattering, to the point of making her wish that she could roll her eyes and dismiss him with a wave of her hand.

"But I suppose that it shall give me the happy opportunity of being the first. I am ashamed that the men around me have not given you the proper notice that you deserve.

"But I am simultaneously grateful for it, since it means that I have a chance to ask for something. Something that, when I first saw you, I thought that I could not dare ask, for surely you must be untouchable. Out of reach.

"I confess that I am a practically minded sort of man. I have always believed that a marriage should be made up of opposites. Of two people who are different in nature so that they might balance one another out.

"You are a lively and vivacious girl. You have wit and charm in abundance. You are wonderfully romantically inclined. I believe that we would be able to make one another a marvelous match."

At last he seemed to be wrapping up.

Julia did not wish to have to tell him her own thoughts on marriage, although she would do so if the need arose.

A balance of personalities was needed, yes. She could agree on that. But total opposites? Surely a couple also needed common interests. Points of personality upon which they could find common ground.

If there was no way in which their personalities or interests converged then what on earth should they talk about? Would they not always be at odds? Arguments were sure to result.

They had to find a way to agree on some things. To laugh about similar things. To come to an accord on important decisions.

And was he only asking her to marry him because she matched his idea of who his wife should be? Because she matched a list of criteria and not for her own sake?

It was frustrating, perhaps even angering. But mostly Julia just wanted it to be over. She was already weary of him being in her house.

He was a fine man and there was nothing wrong with him. But now that she knew where her heart lay she could not find it within herself to have patience for any other man.

She knew who it was that she wanted. Who it was that her heart longed for. Why should she waste her time with anyone else?

"Miss Weston," Mr. Carson at last began. It was the official proposal portion, thank goodness. "Would you do me the honor of accepting my hand in marriage and becoming my wife?"

Julia's stomach twisted with nervousness.

This was the part where she had to refuse him, without offending him.

If he chose to complain about her behavior then most people would see her as being in the wrong. Society and the law were so rarely on the side of the woman. The last thing that she wanted was a scandal.

And goodness forbid that Mr. Norwich find out about this through gossip if things went south. Julia did not know exactly what his response would be but it could not possibly be anything pleasant.

Would he be angry with her if he heard? Upset? Would he think that she accepted? Would he think that she had purposefully led Mr. Carson on and condemn her? Set her aside in his heart for good?

She could not bear the thought. No, she must do this correctly, gently. That way Mr. Carson would have no need to condemn her to others and the news would never reach Mr. Norwich. Not unless it was through her own disclosure.

"Sir," Julia began. "Sir, I am most flattered by your offer. I admit that it is rather startling and out of the blue for me to hear such a declaration. I was not aware that your feelings had become so deep and so vast."

"I am surprised at your being surprised," Mr. Carson replied. "I had thought that my feelings were perfectly plain."

"They were the sort of feelings that might give a lady cause to be hopeful or speculative," Julia replied. "But not enough to give her the solid ground of certainty.

"I do not mean to criticize you. I only wish for you to under-stand. I did not realize that you were quite so far gone down the path of courtship. If I had known, I should have taken greater pains to prevent any further progress.

"That is my own fault and my own folly and I do own it fully. I know that I am often harsh in my words. My wit, I fear, can be too cutting. And so I have striven to be more gentle as of late.

"This includes in regards to any particular suitors. I thought that I ought not to dash your hopes in too extreme of a manner. Instead I had hoped that my shown lack of interest would be enough to tell you of how I was feeling."

"Yet, the other day—at dinner—"

"I told you then that I had not meant to encourage you. That I was only curious. That I enjoy searching the minds and hearts of others.

"I have been called by a dear friend a 'little raven'. It is not because of any particular look of mine, nor because I love birds. It is because I have been noted to be too inquisitive for my own good.

"I allow my curiosity to get in the way of my sense of decorum. I will bother people, as a raven bothers other larger birds and even humans.

"That is all that I meant in my querying. I was curious about you as a person and I pushed too far. I can see that now.

"You will have to forgive me for the improper behavior which led you to believe that you had hope where there was none. I received your attentions with grace because I did not think that they

were altogether as serious as they are. I thought you to be only at
the beginning of considering a courtship with me."

"I apologize, then, for not being more obvious in my affections,"
Mr. Carson said, interrupting her.

Julia wanted to tell him that he ought to do her the honor of
waiting for her to finish. Just as she had done for him. It was a
courtesy.

But she could also understand that he was distressed. She
ignored the irritation and kept her thoughts to herself. For now.

"I see now that I was a little too delicate in my approach," Mr.
Carson said. "And that in attempting to be gentle in my courtship
with you I went too far in the other direction. I was timid. I can
assure you that I shall not make that mistake again."

"Sir, even if you had been not quite so timid, you would not have
succeeded in your aim," Julia replied. "All that it would have done
would be to ensure that you got a more direct answer sooner for
your troubles.

"I do apologize that you have now wasted some weeks on me
when you might yet have found another lady who would better
receive your attention. It was never my intention to lead you astray.

"I beg of you to think on me kindly and not to think too harshly
of my behavior. It would have suited us both better had I paid more
attention to your subtle clues. But alas, we cannot undo what has
been done. You will simply have to accept my most sincere apologies instead."

Mr. Carson looked as though he had been struck by lightning.
The surprise on his face was almost comical. Had Julia not been so
worried that he would give way to an outburst then she might even
have been tempted to laugh.

There was a moment of silence. It was odd, how like and yet
unlike it was to the silence between herself and Mr. Norwich only a
couple of weeks ago. How they had stared at one another.

The both of them had been so afraid to speak. So unsure. It was
both sad and amusing how two people who had known one another
almost their entire lives could still become awkward and speechless
around one another. If the circumstances were right.

Yet that silence was nothing compared to this. That silence had
been confusion. Uncertainty.

This was as though she was standing at the executioner's block. Waiting to see if the axe would fall or if she would be pardoned.

A bit melodramatic of her, she knew. Mr. Norwich would have laughed if he'd been there and she'd told him. And she would have told him. Because she trusted him completely, irrevocably.

Mr. Carson, however, would not be nearly so amused. And only partly because he was serving as the role of the executioner in her little metaphor. She did not think that he would have found it amusing even if she was talking about another man entirely.

She could not possibly marry a man who could not indulge or at the very least put up with her moods. Especially her little flights of fancy.

"Please do not think of me too harshly," she begged. "I have the highest opinion of you, sir. Truly, I do. You might not believe it of me right now but I can assure you that it is so.

"It is not for any reason in particular that I must turn away your generous proposal. Other than the truth that I do not think that we would truly make one another happy.

"If I thought that we could be joined in a union that would benefit us both then I should say yes at once. But I believe that in the end, we would only end up tolerating one another. And I cannot abide that prospect. It is fair to neither you nor to me to subject ourselves to such a fate."

Mr. Carson's eyes narrowed. "And it is not because there is any other man in your heart?"

"My decision, and any lady's decision, should not be because of her feelings in regards to infatuation. Affection that steals in at once because of a handsome face does not tend to last.

"A woman ought to look for a man who will take care of her. A man who has strong moral character. A man who will respect her and listen to her. It is not a decision that should be taken lightly."

She did not take lightly her decision to write to Mr. Norwich. It was not an infatuation that she held for him. It was because of his thoughtfulness and his respect for her that she loved him. It was because he thought well of her parents and took care of her mother when he came to their house.

It was common sense and affection both, mingled, and making something stronger as a result of their combined forces.

"And so no, sir. It is not because of any other man that I have to decline your offer. It is because I know that I must seek for some sort of civil happiness with my husband. And we would not be able to provide that for one another."

"You and Mr. Norwich are extraordinarily close," Mr. Carson replied. "I asked him if he had been courting you and he said that he had not. Have circumstances changed?"

"No, sir. It is not because of my relationship with any other man that I turn you away."

Even if she had not been in love with Mr. Norwich, she would have turned him down. She had told her mother that she would not marry except for love. She had meant it then and she meant it now.

"If I may be frank as well, I rather resent the implication that I should lie to you as to my reasons why I must turn down your proposal.

"Were I seeing another man I would have told you so at once. I would have taken care to be seen with him by others so that this sort of misunderstanding could be avoided.

"This is not a decision made because my heart is elsewhere. It is a conclusion that I had already come to some time ago. I can only apologize that I did not do a better job of conveying that choice to you in my actions."

Mr. Carson, at least, seemed satisfied. He nodded, then bowed.

"I cannot say that I am not disappointed. But I will not do you the discourtesy of going on for some time about what state my heart is in. I wish you all the best, Miss Weston. Give my regards to your mother."

Julia curtsied, and stood aside for him as he exited.

The moment that the door closed behind him, Mrs. Weston entered the room. "Well!"

Julia jumped, startled. "Mother! Do not tell me that you were listening in."

"I might have paused partway down the stairs when I realized that I was hearing voices," her mother replied innocently.

"Mother!"

"Can I not take a vested interest in my daughter's social life? My dear, you certainly know how to catch them. The poor man."

Julia sighed, all but collapsing into a chair. "Do not act as though you feel sorry for him now. You never wished for me to marry him."

"That does not mean that I cannot be sympathetic to his feelings, Julia."

"He is not truly in love with me. He shall get over it soon enough."

"Mmm. I must say that I believe you are correct. You handled it well, my dear."

"I hope so. I do not wish to be the reason that I break a man's heart. Nor do I wish for people to gossip about me."

"You will always break a few hearts along the way," her mother replied. "It is how life works."

"Well I find that to be completely unacceptable."

Her mother hummed noncommittally.

"He did not seem inclined to be too angry with me," Julia went on. "I do not think that I shall become the subject of ridicule."

She paused, considering. "You overheard what we were saying. Was I right to tell him that he ought to have been more obvious in his courtship?"

"I believe so," her mother said, sitting down as well in her favorite chair by the window. "The only reason that you knew he was thinking of you in such a manner was that no other man was doing anything at all.

"It was only the absence of other men's interest that made his interest prominent. That is not the proper way to court a woman. It must be plain to her so that she can properly refuse or accept him.

"But in any case, my dear, why are you wasting time worrying about him? He is inconsequential to your happiness."

"I think that it is my right to worry about whether a man is about to damage my reputation."

"He will not. Otherwise he is not a man of honor. A lady has a right to a refusal. Now, have you decided on writing to Mr. Norwich?"

Julia sighed. When her mother seized upon a subject there really was no turning her away from it.

"I was about to write to him when Mr. Carson interrupted me."

"Then by all means, go." Mrs. Weston smiled. "Julia, I did not start out in love. I married a man that I knew would respect me and provide for me. I married a good man.

"But I did not marry a man with whom I was in love. I was fortunate that I fell for him later on in the marriage. And if Mr. Norwich was not in love with you and you not in love with him I should advocate doing the same as I did. Finding a husband who is a good man, a man who will respect and provide.

"However, you are fortunate enough to be in love. And to be loved in return. That is no small thing. Now that you have found it, I beg of you to seize it. Not everyone is so lucky to fall in love with their spouse later on as I was. And even fewer are so lucky as to be in love with one another before the marriage even starts."

Julia could not help but smile. Her mother spoke in such a loving and sweet tone, quite unlike her usual manner. She sounded so very earnest. But also happy—as though she could already envision the joy that her daughter would experience in such a marriage. If she would only seize her chance.

If Julia had not already determined that she would write to Mr. Norwich, she would have come to that conclusion right then. For she could not deny what her mother was saying. Especially not when her mother looked so happy and hopeful for her.

She rose. "I suppose that... that I had rather get started on that, then, mustn't I?"

Mother smiled proudly at her. "Do not spend too much time apologizing. It will not become you. Rather, focus on the way that you feel about him. That will convince him."

Julia could already feel nervousness bubbling up inside of her again, but she nodded and went upstairs to begin writing.

How could she even start the letter? She felt as though she ought to write I'm sorry over and over again. Until the entire page was filled with it. That even then, it still might not be enough.

How could she begin to explain her own folly? Or even, on top of that, the mental paths through which her mind had run to come to her new conclusion? Dare she mention speaking of this matter to her mother and Georgiana? Or would he consider that to be a breach of trust?

At last, she realized that if she did not begin writing this letter she would not write it at all. There was no way for her to determine what the perfect thing to say to him would be. And the longer she pondered over it, the more she delayed in receiving a possible reply from him.

An imperfect letter was better than no letter at all. His hearing of her realizations and emotions in a clumsy or frustrating manner would be better than his never knowing of them.

If she erred, at least he would know. And that would be better than all else.

She sat down and carefully began to write. She must not be hasty. She could not afford to let her words become smudged.

Dear Sir...

Julia ended up having to go through a few drafts before she was satisfied. She found herself wondering how many drafts Mr. Norwich had gone through when he was writing that first letter of his to her.

Had he been so nervous? Had he crossed out whole lines, and written in new ones? Had he crumpled his paper in disgust and thrown it into the wastepaper basket?

In the end, she simply had to write what was in her heart. And what was in her heart was him. His absence was like an aching hunger only in her chest, her soul, instead of her stomach.

She wrote for him to come to her. To try again. To step into her drawing room and say the words that he had realized would be improper to say the other day.

Let him say them, and he would find the warmest of welcomes. The words were already on her lips. She was only waiting for him to say his so that she might then reply.

Let her folly not have made her too late in being able to accept his affections. Let him understand that she was only confused and lost. That she never meant to hurt him or reject him outright.

Please, let him understand that she had meant everything that she had said to him when he was only her mysterious correspondent. She had meant them, from the bottom of her heart, and she meant them now.

When it felt as though she had exhausted herself, when it felt as though she had said everything she needed to say twice over, she folded up the letter.

She was tempted to copy it all out neatly onto a new set of pages so that it would look nice for him. But she felt that honesty, in all of its forms, was the best way to go about this.

The crossed-out lines, the cramped writing, the additions in the margins, those were all honesty. Those were her feelings, scribbled and scratched into the paper.

Hopefully he would see the mess and through it would understand what it had cost her to write this all out to him. Hopefully, it would help to convince him of the truth and depth of her feelings.

Hopefully. Hope. That was all that she had.

But, she supposed, he had taken a leap of faith on her. It was only fair that it became her turn to take a leap of faith for him.

Julia sent the letter off, her breath bated even as she handed it over. She knew his estate and so could fortunately send the letter there. She could only hope that he had not quit the estate and gone to London or somewhere without her knowing of it.

"Good girl," Mrs. Weston said when she saw that it was sent off. "It will all turn out as it should, you will see."

Now there was nothing to do but wait.

EPILOGUE

JAMES WAS SITTING at the breakfast table as he went over the morning's mail.

There was, as always, much to be done at the estate. Father was shirking his duties yet again. Much to James's everlasting frustration.

He could understand the desire for retirement. To live out the last few years of one's life in peace.

But Father was far from sickly or old. He was hale and hearty and all the other lords of his age were managing just fine in their duties to the estates. Father was simply being lazy.

There was nothing in the mail from his brother, alas. There were some letters of business. He would see to those in a moment. One letter from a friend in London. And...

He nearly dropped his fork.

Even before he read the return address he knew who it was from. The handwriting was too familiar and beloved for him not to realize.

Miss Weston.

She had written to him—but why? What for? So that she might apologize in an official manner for not returning his affections, he supposed. Or perhaps she wished to inquire about how he was faring. She had to know that she was the reason for his quitting Bath. She was not a stupid woman and never had been.

James glanced up in order to make sure that his father had not come into the room while he was distracted. Father tended to sleep in far later than he should as the lord of the estate.

Now that James was around, however, Father seemed to think that James would take care of it all.

And he had been, because if he did not, who would ensure that the tenants were being looked after?

James gritted his teeth at the thought of the impossible position Father had put him in. If nothing else, Miss Weston's letter would give him something else to think about.

He opened the letter.

The first thing that he noticed was how messy it was. He was surprised, in fact. Miss Weston's penmanship was lovely and she had always sent him quite neat and organized letters when they were corresponding.

Yet here, there were added words and sentences scribbled in the margins. She had crossed out bits here and there. Some of the handwriting was smudged.

It was, quite honestly, adorable. Worrying as well, however—was she in such an emotional state that she had not even had time to write out a fresh, proper draft before sending the letter?

He could not imagine what would have her in such a state. Not unless...

Oh, no. Had her mother taken a turn for the worst?

Feeling his heart climb into his throat, James began to read.

Dear Sir,

You must excuse my writing to you like this. You must not want to hear from me ever again. If that is the case and you simply throw this letter into the fire without reading another word, I shall forgive you. I shall understand.

I treated you most poorly. I behaved as though you were two separate people: Mr. Norwich and my correspondent.

When of course you were the same person the entire time. If I loved one, then I must love the other, for there is no difference between you two.

I was confused and surprised. That is the only excuse that I can offer, and it is a flimsy one at best. I know that I have treated you poorly as a result of my own lack of observation. I know that I have not given you the understanding and attention that was your due.

The only thing I can say to that is I am terribly, truly sorry. I hope that you can feel it through the pages. I hope that you can sense, despite the distance and my lack of presence, the turmoil inside of me at knowing the pain I have caused you.

I meant every word that I sent in my last letter to you. The feelings that I expressed in there, I still harbor. I still feel them.

To be perfectly honest... I wrote to Miss Reginald. I told her everything. My mother knows some of the story but not about the letters. I fear that her wrath would be beyond what either you or I could handle.

Miss Reginald replied to me with the most astounding revelation.

She told me that I was already in love with you. As Mr. Norwich.

She pointed out to me the way that I spoke about you. How much I had missed you since you quit Bath. And I have missed you, terribly. I had not realized how important you were in my life until you were gone.

When I thought that you might be Mr. Carson, I felt a strange sense of disappointment. I see now that it was because, without even realizing it, I wanted it to be you. I hoped that it would be you.

You have been my dearest friend all of these years. Aside from Miss Reginald, you are the person that I trust the most. You are the person whose company I most enjoy.

Please, forgive me. Forgive me for being a selfish and thoughtless girl. Forgive me for not seeing. Forgive me for toying with your emotions in such an awful manner.

If you will still have me, I am yours. I understand if you do not wish for that any longer. If I have poisoned your heart against me with my actions then it is no less than what I deserve.

But if your feelings are still the ones that you expressed to me so eloquently in your letters... then you need not doubt your reception were you to call on me.

I await your answer. If you do wish to take that final step in our courtship, then I implore you not to do it through writing. Please. I miss you terribly. All of you, both as my years' long friend and as my correspondent.

Forgive a little raven for pulling on your tail. For cawing a little too loudly. For getting too audacious for her own good.

I will wait for you, as you have been so kind as to wait for me.

I remain,

Miss Julia Weston and, if you still wish it, your little raven.

If he still wished it, she was his.

If he still wished it? As if his heart could have changed course so thoroughly and easily? As if he could have found a way to so quickly drop the sails that had powered the ship of his heart, the winds that had dictated his course, after years of carrying on?

She had clearly been in great emotional distress when writing the letter. He could see it in her scribbled words, her lack of poise with her lettering. As if the content of the letter was not enough, the manner in which it was written spoke volumes.

She loved him. She was in love with him. Not only her letter writer but him, James, all of him.

She even said that she had, possibly, been in love with him without realizing it, all of this time.

He stood up without feeling his legs. His heart was pounding. He must write—but she wanted him to come in person. If he did so then he would arrive before any letter that he sent her. She would have no warning of his coming.

No matter. She said that she would wait for him. He had to trust in that.

James hurried to the study where he dashed off a letter to London, for Mr. Weston. Her father.

Dear Sir,

I hope that this letter finds you in good health, and that your business is going satisfactorily. I miss your conversation at dinners and my father sends his regards.

I apologize that this letter must be brief. If you reply, please do so to my address in Bath. I shall include it at the bottom in case you are not in possession of it already.

To be short and frank in my manner, sir, I wish to put forth to you a question that might seem rather out of the blue to you. I doubt that either your wife or your daughter has apprised you of the situation.

In short, I wish to ask your permission to marry your daughter.

For quite some time I have harbored the tenderest of emotions for her. But I had long given up hope of her returning them. It is to my great surprise that I learn that she does return them, and that I have reason to be tentatively optimistic about the question I am about to pose to her.

This letter will most likely reach you as I am proposing to her. I hope that I shall receive a favorable answer from both of you. I have always held nothing but the deepest of respect for you and will honor whatever answer you give me.

But know this, sir: I would do anything and everything under the sun to make your daughter happy. She is the dearest creature in the world to me.

I hope that you will find me worthy of her. I know that she is dear to you. Know that I address you in the humblest of tones, knowing that she is your beloved child. I will care for the woman as you have cared for the girl.

With esteem and affection,

James Norwich

He folded the letter up and sent it off, and then immediately ordered his servants to begin packing.

"Something light, only for a few days," he told them. "We can send the rest of my clothes after. I must travel light in order to take an express carriage."

He could have ridden on horseback had he felt truly desperate. But Bath was just far away enough that it would have been too much hard riding, and it would have taken him more than a day at that. He did not fancy turning up to see Miss Weston in stinking, muddied clothes, exhausted and disheveled.

As soon as he was prepared to go, he departed. After so many false starts, after so much waiting, after so long in between despair and hope... he was not going to waste another moment.

The journey was arduous, but that was mostly because of his own feelings. His heart would not stop racing. His hands clenched and unclenched where they rested on his thighs as he looked out the carriage window, watching the English countryside roll by.

When he arrived in Bath he resented every moment that he had to spend returning to his home and taking care of things. He wanted to rush straight to Miss Weston but of course he could not forget himself.

If she said yes—and she had said that she would say yes—he

would be staying in Bath indefinitely. After the proposal there would not be time for him to open up his house again. He would be too busy swept up in the congratulations and planning and informing everyone.

He hurriedly deposited his things, let the servants know that he was back, that yes it was only himself, and to keep the staff minimal as a result. His valet and others would be arriving shortly. They had taken another carriage.

After everything was dealt with it was already late into the night. He could not possibly call on her then.

Instead he slept. Fitfully, of course. But he did manage to get some amount of rest. In the morning he outfitted himself. It was not ideal but that was what he must endure for racing ahead of his valet.

One of the other servants helped him to tidy himself up and ensure that he had not missed anything in his appearance.

Then, at last—he could go to her.

He tried not to leave too early in the morning. Rather, he attempted to arrive just early enough so that she would have had no other callers yet, but not so early that she was still abed.

His heart pulsed in his throat as he knocked on the door. The servant let him in and announced him.

It was time.

He entered into the drawing room and saw her.

Mrs. Weston was not there. Either she was still asleep or she had heard who it was and had wisely quitted the room. Whatever the case may be, he was glad of it.

Miss Weston stood upon his entering. Her dark eyes were wide but dark. Nervous. She looked paler than usual.

He wanted nothing more than to cross the room to her and take her into his arms. But not yet. Not quite yet.

"Miss Weston."

"Mr. Norwich." Her voice was almost breathless, as though she could not believe that he was truly there in front of her.

Had she thought that her letter would be ill-received? That he would throw it into the fire as she had said?

No, never. He couldn't—he couldn't have stopped loving her if he'd tried. If he'd even wanted to.

"Would you like something?" she asked, her voice soft and hesitant in a way it so rarely was. "I can call for some tea, or..."

"No, thank you," he replied automatically. "Perhaps. Ah. That is."

He gave a rueful chuckle. He was all but certain of what her answer would be and he was still fumbling like a schoolboy. "Forgive me. You have always had the power to render me incapable of the speech and manners that I normally find quite manageable."

Miss Weston smiled at him, sweet and soft. "I find that it is rather the same with me. My wit has quite abandoned me. And at a time when I perhaps need it most. I do so love to be witty for you. I enjoy that I can entertain you. That I can make you laugh."

"It is the same for me," James confessed, rapidly, on an exhalation of breath. He could feel some of the tension going out of him, knowing that she was as nervous as he was.

"Can you forgive me?" Miss Weston whispered. "For how I have behaved?

"I confess that I... I have not been able to sleep much these past few days. I knew that it would take some time for the letter to reach you. Yet I kept checking the mail in the morning, to see if you had written me a response. To see if you had rejected my apology."

"I couldn't," James blurted out. "I could never—I should have known that you would need some time to reflect. To reconcile who you thought I was with who you now knew me to be."

"But I was so awful..."

"And I was a coward who should have told you who I was from the first instead of putting you in a position of confusion."

"And I could have insisted that you tell me who you were instead of playing along. We can blame ourselves all that we like."

"Then stop blaming yourself. I do not blame you. I hold no anger towards you. Only..." James took a deep breath. "Only love."

Miss Weston's eyes went a little wide and started to shine. "Oh," she said, the sound small, almost a gasp.

He dared to take a small step towards her. "Would you—I am torn between hope and the despair with which I am so familiar when it comes to my feelings for you. Even now, with all of your assurances, I still find it hard to speak the words. Forgive me."

"There is nothing to forgive," Miss Weston said quickly. "Would it help if I—if I were to say how dear you are to me? How I have missed you all of these long days? How the time seems to drag so unbearably slowly now that you are not around to distract me?

"I had never taken the time to peer into my own heart. And when I did it was with great surprise that I found you were already there. You were rooted like a tree and I could not get you out. Nor do I want to get you out.

"If you are in even the slightest doubt about my thoughts towards you, I beg of you to look at me now. I have no stipulations. No hesitations. I only want to be yours."

James reminded himself to breathe. "In that case, Miss Weston, I...

"You have heard me say so many times in my letters to you just what you mean to me. Some days it feels as though you are every-thing to me. That you own my whole heart.

"Even on the days when I remember that I have a duty to other people, that I must run an estate, you are still more important to me than anything. Sometimes I wonder if I would not run to Gretna Green with you if you asked. Although I know that it would be folly and that furthermore you would never ask such a thing.

"You make me feel a fool with how deeply I feel for you. You brighten up every room that you are in. Without you, social gather-ings feel lifeless. As though the color has been leeched out from them.

"You are my first thought in the mornings and my last thought at night. Writing these letters to you has been a way to share my burdens and myself with another person. It's been a joy that I sorely miss. I wish to keep sharing my life with you in that manner. For always."

Miss Weston was looking at him with a face so full of emotion that it nearly took his breath away. She looked as though she wanted to laugh and burst into tears and fling herself at him all at once.

It was rather how he felt inside, as well. The idea that all he was feeling towards her was being reflected back at him—that she felt about him as he felt about her—

"Miss Weston," he said. "Would you do me the honor of becoming my wife?"

Miss Weston let out an odd sound, almost a sob, and nodded frantically. "Yes, yes, a thousand times—"

He was across the room and in front of her before he even realized that he had started to move. Finally, after years of waiting and despairing and hoping, he wrapped his arms around her, pulling her into him.

Miss Weston was crying in earnest now, and he allowed her to bury her face into his chest so that she might wring herself dry.

"Oh, my little raven," he mused. He gently petted her hair. "This has been quite a trial for you, hasn't it?"

"You are not allowed to give a lady such lovely letters and think that she will not fall for you," Miss Weston said accusingly, her voice muffled from her face being pressed to his chest. "It is most unfair of you."

"And you are not allowed to be so charming and lovely, and then think that a man will not fall for you. It seems that we have both been rather unfair."

Miss Weston pulled back enough so that he might see her face. "I am rather too much for my own good, aren't I? It is fortunate that I shall have you to rein me in from here on out."

He pulled out a handkerchief for her. She laughed, taking it and dabbing at her eyes. "And you are always there whenever I am reduced to tears. What must you think of me?"

"I think that you are allowed some tears now and again and that I shall always have a handkerchief available for you to use."

She laughed again, then looked up at him, her eyes shining. "Well, Mr. Norwich. You have caught me at last. What do you intend to do with me?"

"Well, I did write to your father, so hopefully the first thing I shall do is secure his permission."

"You need not worry about that. Father will be delighted. Mother has been telling me to marry you for weeks now. She thinks it is rather ridiculous of me that I have waited for so long."

"And she is listening in right now, I have no doubt."

"Oh, no, you are lucky that she is still in bed. Give it another half an hour and she will indeed be listening at the door."

He laughed. "Well then, if you will permit it, I believe my first order of business is to kiss you."

"That does seem to be an acceptable first step. We are engaged, after all. I shall allow it."

"Already speaking like a true titled lady. I fear you will become more spoiled than you already are."

"That is impossible. And it is too late to take your proposal back. I have accepted. You will have to deal with the consequences of that as they come."

"I'm certain that I shall delight in every consequence," he assured her.

She was perfect, smiling up at him, her dark eyes shining. She should always look this happy. He would do everything in his power to ensure that she was.

He leaned in, slowly, because even though she had given him permission he did not wish to startle her.

Miss Weston raised herself up onto her tiptoes, and he kissed her softly.

Of course she was not content merely with that, and brought her hands up to catch his face so that she might kiss him with a little more passion. When he pulled away she was smiling at him, mischievous and impertinent and lovely.

"I suppose we ought to tell your mother," James remembered, stepping back. He reluctantly let go of Miss Weston.

Julia. He could call her Julia now.

Not in front of others, of course. Even married couples would generally call one another by their last names when in front of company. He certainly could not dare call her by her Christian name around others until they were married.

But he could think of her that way in his mind. Julia. His Julia.

He waited patiently while Julia went upstairs to awaken her mother. He couldn't stop thinking her name in his mind. Julia, Julia, Julia.

Mrs. Weston came down a short while later. She was wearing a simple dress and was not quite done up as she usually was. Most likely in her haste she had not bothered with the trimmings.

"Mr. Norwich." She crossed to him, smiling warmly. He took her hands and bowed over them when she offered them to him. "You know what a pleasure this is for me. I know that you will both make each other very happy."

"It is all that I could have hoped for," he assured her.

"Mr. Carson is going to have a fit of some kind when he hears of this," Julia said suddenly. The thought seemed to have only just occurred to her. "He proposed to me, you know. When I turned him down he asked if it was because I had feelings for you.

"I should have turned him down no matter what my relationship with you might have been. But he is going to be quite put out when he hears."

"Let him be put out," Mrs. Weston replied. "What does his opinion matter? You two are to be married and you are happy about it. That is what matters.

"And I daresay the news will not be a complete surprise for most of us who know you. I have not spoken to anyone directly on the matter but it would not surprise me if many people have been expecting this for some time."

"Are you telling me that I was the only one who did not know of my own feelings?" Julia asked. "Or of his?"

"Well, my dear, you are so smart in other fields. There had to be one in which you were not quite so well versed."

Julia looked simultaneously put upon and fond of her mother. "Well. I suppose we ought to put the banns up then and get it over with. Let the hordes of well-wishers descend! I shall meet them as if in battle."

James laughed. "And there is that humor that so won me over, my darling."

He could call her that now as well. All of the things that he had been keeping stopped up inside of his heart, he could now freely express. It was liberating and rejuvenating.

Julia smiled up at him. "I am glad to hear it, for you will be experiencing quite a bit of it in the years to come."

James looked forward to it. In fact, he couldn't wait.

THE EXTENDED EPILOGUE

I am humbled you read my novel *"Love Letters to A Lady"* till the end!

Are you aching to know what happens to our lovebirds?

Visit a search engine and enter the link you see below the picture to connect to a more personal level and as a BONUS, I will send you the Extended Epilogue of this Book!

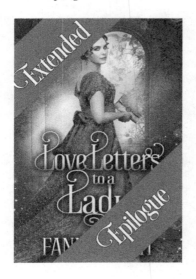

https://fannyfinch.com/ff-003-exep/

If you enjoyed the Collection, just send me your feedback by leaving a review on Amazon!

BE A PART OF FANNY FINCH'S FAMILY

I write for you, the readers, and I love hearing from you! Thank you for your on going support as we journey through the most romantic era together.

If you're not a member of my family yet, it's never too late. Stay up to date on upcoming releases and check out the website for all information on romance.

I hope my stories touch you as deeply as you have impacted me. Enjoy the happily ever after!

Let's connect and download your Free Exclusive Story here!

(Available only to my subscribers)

http://BookHip.com/MMLGXA

ABOUT STARFALL PUBLICATIONS

Starfall Publications has helped me and so many others extend my passion from writing to you.

The prime focus of this company has been – and always will be – *quality* and I am honored to be able to publish my books under their name.

Having said that, I would like to officially thank Starfall Publications for offering me the opportunity to be part of such a wonderful, hard-working team!

Thanks to them, my dreams – and your dreams — have come true!

ABOUT FANNY FINCH

Fanny Finch was born in United Kingdom but moved to Denver, Colorado when she was very young. She attended Washington University where she studied for several years and she now lives with her husband and their bulldog.

Upon leaving university, Fanny found a job as a proof reader for a small press. There, she honed her skills and also met and worked with author Abby Ayles, who helped her polish her books to perfection.

But she is also an author in her own right and is working hard to become recognized as such as she starts to publish her own novels through her website. Her genre is in the Historical Regency Romance category and if you like your reading material to be emotionally clean then you will be undoubtedly thrilled by the characters and scenarios Fanny develops.

When she has time to relax, Fanny enjoys listening to opera music and taking long walks in the outdoors. She writes almost every day as well and hopes to produce many more great books in the future. You can contact Fanny Finch through her website, or download a free copy of her books at: fannyfinch.com

You can contact the author at:
fannyfinchauthor@gmail.com

ALSO BY FANNY FINCH

- The Transformation of the Bashful Lady
- The Marquess' Reluctant Bride
- A Tricky Courtship for the Heartbroken Duke
- A Love Worth Pursuing
- For the Love of a Broken Marquess
- The Curse of Lady Clarabelle
- A Christmas Miracle for the Marquess
- The Earl, the Lady and the Song of Love
- Regency Confessions
- For the Heart of a Rebellious Governess
- Taming the Thorn of Blackwell
- Braving the Outbreak with the Duke
- Training Lord Somerset
- Tales of Secrecy and Enduring Love
- An Unexpected Love (The Heart of Dorset Series: Book 2)
- What the Gentleman is Hiding
- Their Childhood Promise -The Heart of Dorset Series: Book 3
- In Love with her Childhood
- Light to the Marquesses' Hearts
- The Marquess's Forbidden Love
- A Second Chance to a Widow's Heart
- Finding her Duke
- Dukes' Burning Hearts (The Heart of Dorset Series)
- Letters to the Marquess

Made in United States
North Haven, CT
27 April 2024

51837122R00383